WHISPERS OF WRATH

SEVER BRONNY

WHISPERS

OF

WRATH

Arcane Legacy
Book One

SEVER BRONNY

Bronny, Sever, 1979-, author
Whispers of Wrath / Sever Bronny.
(Whispers of Wrath ; book one)
Series: Arcane Legacy

Issued in print and electronic formats.

ISBN 978-1-990624-04-9 (paperback)
ISBN 978-1-990624-05-6 (ebook)

I.   Title. II. Series: Bronny, Sever, 1979- . Whispers of Wrath ; bk. 1

AL710837091645429401   0

A310423791845632048879390
A910457562382091085261495

Version 1.0

Visit severbronny.com to chat with fans, duel in the arena with fellow warlocks, explore world lore, see character academy class schedules, peruse photos, read frequently asked questions (FAQ), and meet the author. For the paperback version, the spell glossary can now be found at the back of this book.

ALSO BY SEVER BRONNY:

THE ARINTHIAN LINE

Pursued by a murderous tyrant, fourteen-year-old warlocks Augum, Bridget and Leera train under the legendary Anna Atticus Stone—while exploring the secrets of an ancient abandoned castle.

Arcane

Riven

Valor

Clash

Legend

FURY OF A RISING DRAGON

When a kingdom threatens invasion, sixteen-year-olds Augum, Bridget and Leera attempt to resurrect an ancient and forbidden order of warlock-knights, hoping to summon dragons to their aid.

Burden's Edge

Honor's Price

Mercy's Trial

Champion's Wrath

CHRONICLES OF ANNA ATTICUS STONE

Young warlock prodigy Anna Atticus Stone is tormented by her vile sister as she tries to get into the mysterious Academy of Arcane Arts. But her sister has other plans.

Prodigy of Thunder
The Arcane Artist
Flames of Stone

ARCANE LEGACY

Whispers of Wrath
Future titles to be announced

All available from Amazon

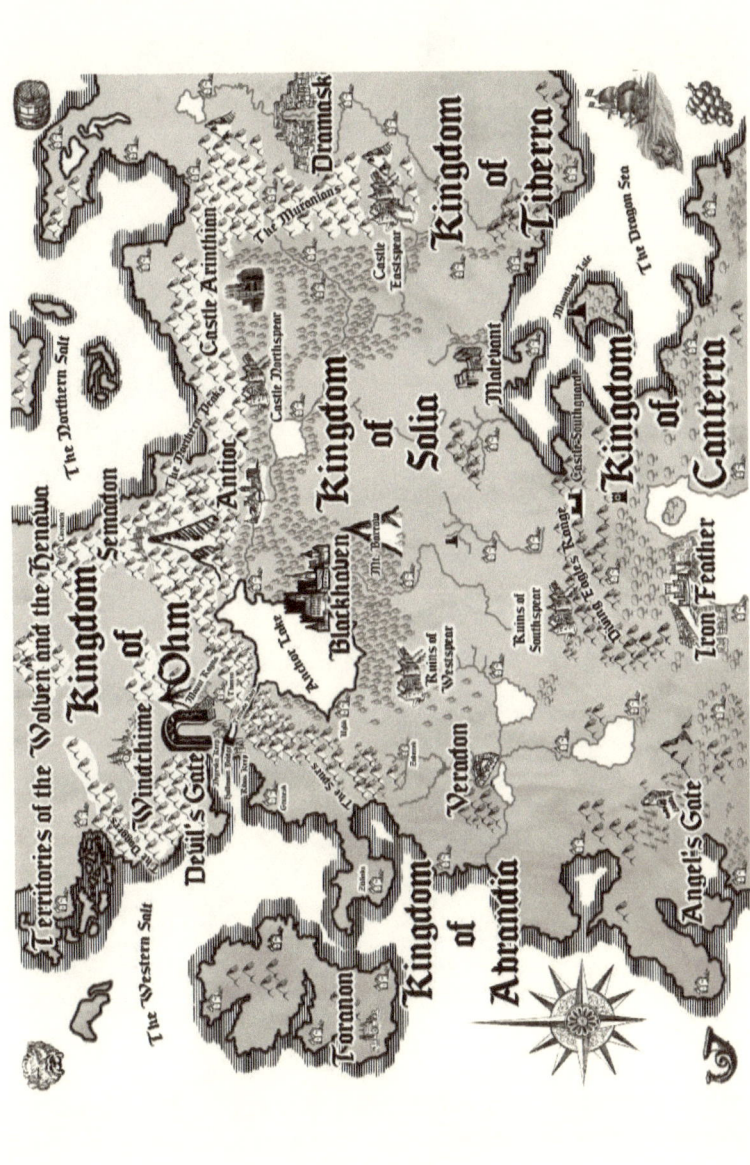

The lord of war cometh
and bringeth with him
the mightiest of furies

THE SMOKED WING INN & TAVERN

AUGUM

Amid a swirling blizzard, a hooded figure crunched along in the snow, leaving behind boot prints that would soon get buried. Shivering, the figure drew his heavy wolf-hide overcoat closer and stuck his hands back into the pockets of his wine-colored robe, leaving the arms of the overcoat to flutter in the bitter wind. He preferred the feeling of the coarse wool of the robe pockets in place of his mitts, which had frozen through in the journey and now dangled uselessly from his rucksack.

The hood, loose and large and overhanging like the beak of a hawk, was a comfort in more ways than one. It kept the wind at bay and his spirits up, for he oft used it for peace and privacy. Were it not for the hood, the masses would crane their necks in hopes of glimpsing his face, which they only knew from posters or crudely inked depictions in the heralds.

For he was none other than Augum Arinthian Stone, one of the most famous names in the seven kingdoms.

Nice to wear the old burgundy again, Augum thought, reminded of days spent in study, of innocent laughter, of riding horseback over long distances, of marvelous adventures during which he had experienced the great wilds that populated books of old.

He remembered faces he missed greatly. People come and gone, some never to be seen again. He thought of studying. He thought of war. How the arcane arts turned books into weapons. How he had come to where he was now, and the long journey that had brought him here, to this place forsaken by the gods, deep in the wild north.

A burgundy-robed boy of about fifteen snapped to attention. "Yes, Captain! Thank you, Captain." He refocused on his charred iron training dummy and slapped his wrists together, roaring, "*Annihilo!*" loosing a small bolt of lightning that crackled into the dummy with a *sizzle*. The herald started and her drying sand flew off her tablet, only for Bridget to reflexively halt the little bottle's flight with a flick of a finger, sending it back to its owner.

Brittany caught the bottle from the air, mumbling, "Thank you."

"Heard that difference?" Bridget asked Carmichael, hands returning to her armpits. Mimicking her commander brother-in-war seemed to have helped the younger recruits see her as their leader, even though Augum said it wasn't necessary and to simply be herself.

"I did, Captain. My thanks."

Bridget gave a curt smile and continued onward. Soon, they were tailed by a burly and bearded knight in a full suit of dented armor minus the helm, carrying a little girl on his shoulders.

"There's one, Pa!" the little girl cried out, pointing at Bridget. "There's one! Giddy-up!"

The burly knight nickered and neighed like a horse as he pretended to gallop forth, a movement that had him skipping two steps at a time in the snow. He ran around Bridget and Brittany and skidded to a halt before them, armor clanking.

"Thou art a warlock!" the girl shouted, brandishing a rolled-up parchment Bridget assumed was a lesson scroll.

"That is true, young damsel," Bridget cooed.

"I say, what spells dost thou know?"

The knight cringed at his daughter's brazenness, but Bridget winked at him and smiled at the girl. "I know all sorts of types of spells. I can open fissures in the very earth beneath your feet ..."

"You can*not*—"

"Ah, but I can," Bridget said, dramatizing with her hands. "I can make myself almost invisible to the eye."

"Like the wind?"

"Like the wind itself. I can create vines out of thin air—" She twirled her palm, and out sprouted a series of vines that entwined her hand before vanishing, and the girl drummed her father's unruly hair as she squealed with delight. "I can commune with animals and plants and make walls of ivy and perform all sorts arcane feats."

"Ooh," the girl and her father cooed, with the latter exaggerating the *O* for his daughter.

"And if you were a villain, I could inject fear into you and mute you and blind you and paralyze you and put you to sleep. If you were a treacherous *warlock* villain, I could use my Arcaner shield to reflect your spells back at you until you choose to bend the knee. Otherwise—" Bridget drew back on an invisible bowstring and let it fly, and the girl made a show of pretending to get struck, forcing her father to take extra hold of her lest she tumble down his back.

"I can even make myself ..." Bridget crouched, hovering a flat palm just above the snow. "... this small."

"That's impossible!"

Bridget straightened. "It once was. But we reinvigorated the spell from the archives."

The girl sighed wistfully. Suddenly, she reanimated and stabbed the air with the scroll. "Hark!" she cried. "But I am a princess and I demand to know exactly which of these thou dost knoweth!"

"She's determined to become a warlock," the father said, patting his daughter's arm, mouthing, "My apologies, Captain."

Bridget waved the inconvenience aside and accepted the scroll, which was neatly penned with eighty spells, subdivided into twenty degrees, each degree grouped into three standard spells and one elemental spell.

"Which dost thou knowest!" the girl shouted. "Brandish thy quill!"

"No need to shout, sweetie," the proud papa whispered.

"She has eloquence beyond her years," Bridget said, borrowing the herald's quill and marking the page.

"She has surpassed her classmates at a young age, but I spoil her rotten with tutors."

"Nice doggy! Hey, doggy, doggy! What's its name?"

"Her name is Sabby," Bridget said. "Named after Sabella the ...?" She raised a questioning eyebrow at the girl, who only gaped. "The Midwife, a very important woman in the history of arcanery."

The girl looked down to peer into her father's face, whispering, "Papa, what's a midwife?"

"It's someone who helped deliver you."

The girl thought about it. "Did I come by warlock courier?" The question caused those within hearing to burst with laughter. The girl clenched the locks of her father's hair and shook herself, shouting, "I don't get it!"

"Easy, child, you can ask your mother what a midwife is later," the knight said, patting his child on the back.

"Fine, I *will*!" The girl straightened and reached out with both hands, clasping and unclasping them and singing, "Gimme, gimme, gimme!"

Bridget flicked one hand, sending the parchment zooming back to the girl, then flicked the other, sending the quill back to the herald.

"Telekinesis!" the girl shouted, snatching the scroll from the air with a fanciful twirl.

"Yes, my dear. Excellent!" the burly knight cried.

The girl examined the parchment. "You know all the spells up to the 10th degree, one in the 11th, one in the 17th, for a total of …" Her lips mouthed as she counted silently, the fingers of a hand repeatedly extending. "… forty-two spells!"

Bridget beamed. "Correct." Though now she felt a little bad for infantilizing the girl at first.

"That doesn't count simuls and optional off-the-books spells learned on her own time," the knight said.

The girl rolled her eyes. "I *know*, Papa."

"Of course you do. So remind me again, what *is* a simul?" He winced as he asked the question, almost as if hoping he hadn't pushed his luck.

But the girl raised her nose and replied with perfect annunciation, "A simul is a type of spell only Arcaners can learn. It stands for *simultaneous* as it mushes together two or more spells into one."

"Quite right," Bridget said with a smile. The Spirit of the Dragon was a simul, though which spells it fused was a mystery to even those within the order—no surprise considering how old the spell was.

"And how many degrees are there, my child?"

The girl snorted. "Twenty, obviously. It's on the parchment, Papa."

Her knight father raised a thick finger. "Ah, but—"

"I *know* it's a trick question! Now please let me finish," and she beamed as Brittany and the knight chuckled merrily together. "It's a trick question because of master rank, which happens, like, once a generation."

"Exactly right, my child. Exactly right."

Bridget nodded along encouragingly. It was a mystery of the craft that mastery happened on its own. Known as The Sleeving, the event was marked by all of the warlock's rings merging into one solid sleeve, indicating the warlock had achieved the pinnacle of their craft—a dream every warlock shared in common.

The knight ruffled his daughter's hair. "She's quite precocious."

"I can see that." *I wish every little girl had the opportunities to flourish that only wealth could provide*, she thought. "Do you want to be a warlock, little one?"

"I want to be a *dragon*!"

"Really?"

"Then I can slay my enemies and woo a dragon prince and rule the kingdom."

"Sounds … rather thrilling."

The girl's shoulder slumped. "But do dragons really exist?"

"Of course they do, my child, you're standing before one."

"She's not a dragon."

"Ah, but she can turn *into* one."

"Then how come she doesn't do that?"

"We don't want to scare the city, do we? It's only for displays of strength. And the war is over, so no need to do it a lot these days."

"Oh." The girl tilted her head at Bridget. "Can you *really* turn into a dragon? Because my friends say it's just a story to scare people into behaving."

The knight spoke before Bridget could. "Your friends are too young to have seen the war with their own eyes. My apologies, Captain," he once again mouthed, to which Bridget politely smiled.

"Do you know any good stories?" the girl pressed.

"A few." Bridget wondered what it would be like to hold a child aloft like that, or to see her man do the same. She wondered how silly it would look were she to ask the knight to allow her but the briefest moment with the girl. *Don't be ridiculous, you fool*, rebuked her own thoughts. *Act your station.*

"I want to hear a story about talking bears or talking wolves or talking owls or—"

"None such creatures exist, my dear."

"Sure they do, Papa!"

"Only in children's tales—"

"No, Papa, no, they *do* exist because you said dragons exist so there must be all sorts of funny creatures—"

"All right, all right, some such beasts perhaps may exist, but we have taken enough of the captain's time, sweetie." The big knight bowed. "Our humble gratitude for your sacred time, Captain, and Happy Endyear. Will you bless us?"

"Happy Endyear to you too, and may the Unnameables bless you and your family, Sir," Bridget replied out of habit, for it was a common request, and it would not do to lend doubt where it did not belong. She pressed three fingers over her heart in salute before waving at the girl, mouthing, "Bye-bye!"

"Bye-bye!" the girl sang, flapping a hand over her shoulder as her father galloped off, the other clutching and waving the scroll. "Bye-bye!"

Bridget watched misty-eyed, wishing that had been her child. Oh, how she looked forward to having children!

"How does it feel to have everyone worship you three in such a manner, Captain?" Brittany asked as they resumed a casual stroll.

Tiresome and troubling and pained, Bridget wanted to say. "Makes me want to be responsible," she said instead.

"It is indeed a great responsibility, what with your countenance drawn on posters and your character portrayed in the plays and your soul written about in poem and song."

"Please don't blow smoke up my robe, Herald."

"I was merely stating a fact, Captain."

"A fact. I see."

"May I inquire further into simuls, Captain?"

"I'd rather you didn't."

"Even off the scroll?"

"Even off the scroll."

"Fair enough. What about The Final Valediction that you Arcaners dispense upon vanquished enemies?"

"The Final Valediction is a short but sacred ritual that is our way of giving a last goodbye to a foe. It is an honor … and an apology."

"For taking their life?"

Bridget, seeing silent flashes of enemies she had felled, did not reply. The herald at least had the tact not to press the matter, and so they strolled on.

They soon came across a young woman with a pixie haircut defending against numerous tempered ice arrows, all shot by a warlock man who was using a summoned ice bow. She kept vanishing her fiery shield before resummoning it right after each arrow was fired, then shouting, "*Mimicus!*" But the intended effect wasn't triggering.

"This part will be off the scroll as per the security agreement," Bridget said to Brittany, who put the quill away and tucked the tablet under her arm. Certain spells were to be kept as secret as possible for the order to maintain some element of surprise against enemies. "But you may watch."

"Hey, Cap," the young woman said, flapping one hand at the warlock to cease and pressing the fingers of the other to her heart in salute.

"You two have met, of course," Bridget went on, returning the salute. The girls nodded at each other.

"Britt."

"Laud."

Bridget nodded at Laudine. "Herald Laudine Cooper is practicing a most potent simul called Mirror of the Dragon."

"I've yet to master it," Laudine sang, smiling a radiant dimpled smile she was well known for. "There's a *lot* of nuance to the spell."

"And which two spells does this Mirror of the Dragon, er, mush together?" Brittany asked, looking to Bridget.

"Mirror of the Dragon simulcasts Shield and the ultra-rare and off-the-books Reflect," Bridget replied.

Laudine pointed with her index fingers, flames briefly bursting from each tip. "Ancient names *Shiendarro* and *Reflamaratossarecta*."

"What's the ratio at, Laud?"

Laudine playfully blew out her fingertips as if they were smoldering arrows. "Ten to one."

"Forgive me for intruding, Captain, but what do you mean by ratio?" Brittany asked.

"Hits to reflections," Bridget and Laudine chorused.

"We want to see at least an eighty percent success rate before one tries it in the field," Bridget explained.

"One hundred percent being the goal," Laudine added, nodding at Bridget. "Cap here can do about that, ain't that right, Cap?" When Bridget's lips only pressed into a thin line, Laudine quickly continued. "But the trick is one has to truly understand the incoming spell in order to be able to reflect it. Anyway, I've been having trouble with the timing, Cap. 'Woeless is the girl who sings not the faith of the focused.' "

"Prenthius, *Chronicles of the Intrepid*?" Brittany interrupted. "That one I *do* recognize."

Laudine's brow rose. "A fellow Drama girl. We should have drinks."

"So you can woo me into writing more favorably on the order?"

"Exactly right." While Laudine grinned, Brittany pretended to fiddle with her parchments. Bridget was starting to see why the herald did not want Laudine involved.

"Let me try you," Bridget said, and took the place of the ice warlock, who was a soldier of the army. The thirtyish man inclined his head slightly at Bridget and stepped aside. She thanked him before aligning her thoughts and making the motion of someone drawing a bowstring, incanting, "*Summano arma.*" She felt a cool draw upon her soul as an ivy bow appeared in her hands, complete with an arrow notched in the string and a full quiver of earthen arrows on her back.

Laudine took up position thirty feet away and nodded. Bridget loosed the nocked arrow with a *twang* and smoothly drew another from the quiver. Laudine summoned a fiery shield, incanting, "*Mimicus!*" but the arrow smacked into the flames and vanished with a *hiss*.

Bridget didn't bother firing the follow-up arrow, but placed the arrow back into the quiver and walked up to Laud, summoned bow still in hand. "Your timing is fine, as is the reflection angle of the shield. What's your thought process, though?"

"Standard thought protocols with Shield followed by layers of reflection. A reversal of the incoming threat, the moment of the mirroring, and then a bounce."

"Technically correct, but it seems to me you're not properly applying the principle of arcane perpendicularity. You must turn your very *soul* into a mirror that precisely counters the incoming spell." Bridget made a fist and circled it against her chest. "Your innards must wholly express the perpendicularity. Commit fully, Laud, just as you do when reciting lines on the stage." She went to take her place beside the army warlock. "Again," and she reached back into her summoned quiver, nocked an arrow and, with a *twang*, let it fly.

Laudine, who had taken several deep breaths whilst telling herself to focus, shot her left forearm up, summoned her fiery shield, and roared, "*Mimicus!*" There was a fiery *hiss* as the arrow reversed itself upon impact, forcing Bridget to duck lest it impale her forehead. She looked back to see the arrow *thunk* against the Black Castle's curtain wall before disappearing.

"*Summano null,*" Bridget said, vanishing her bow and quiver. "Good. Keep working it until it's intuitive."

"Will do, Cap. And let me know if you need a hand with Britt," she added cheekily after Bridget had already moved on, with the herald catching up.

Bridget nodded her thanks at the army warlock, but the man only stared at her until she looked away. The army was uneasy with Arcaners for various reasons. They did not feel it right that the power of the dragon was limited to three young people who had traipsed a meager few steps into the vast forest of adulthood. But most warlock soldiers were too corrupt to pass the Arcaner trials, and therefore the power of the simul was out of reach to them. The Sacred Code of the Arcaner was not something to be taken lightly, as it demanded a proof of devotion that risked death.

"My senior said you are walking weapons," Brittany blurted.

Bridget hated hearing that cold truth. The predator behind the curtain—that was how Augum best described the beastling—loved it, though. It loved being considered a weapon of war. It loved war, period.

Carnage. Blood. Mayhem. Death. And it loved to interrupt her concentration, which annoyed her even more sometimes. "And your senior thus sent you to translate our story."

"To make it more … palatable."

"A recruitment drive."

"Yes."

"A warlock sent you."

"Nay, my lady—er, Captain. An Ordinary."

Bridget raised an eyebrow. "I thought you were writing a critique."

"Nay, Captain."

Bridget felt a wave of relief. There had been too many hit pieces written about the order as it was. About the order acting as outlaws, about them personally as warlocks, about their love lives, about every salacious piece of gossip the old hens and peacocks and pasty-faced ghouls of the royal court thought of in their boredom to stir up drama and fill their vapid lives.

"Captain, I-I-I would be remiss if I did not ask … why isn't he married yet?"

Bridget, thinking about the last hit piece on how her betrothed had been so drunk he had proclaimed himself a prince, and no less at a public supper, whirled on the girl. "Who?"

"Your … your brother-in-war. Why hasn't he married your sister-in-war yet?"

"Why do you keep referring to them that way?"

"What way?"

"Brother- and sister-in-war. *I* refer to them as such, no one else." They had earned those titles with each other in the wars.

"F-f-forgive me, Captain, but you spoke of them as such first. I-I-I was only trying to be polite."

Bridget blinked. She pressed a hand to her chest and drew in a breath. "I do apologize, Herald Mires. It has been a … trying quint." Five days of mental labor and decision-making regarding the order.

"I-I-I know you don't think it's anyone's business, Captain, but Augum Arinthian Stone and Leera Jones are kingdom champions and protectors and Arcaners. The three of you won the war for us—"

"We won the war together. All of us together. That includes Ordinaries." Yet despite having won two wars now, a warlock was "forever locked in war." Although that epithet was a point of pride for most warlocks, Bridget sometimes found the reality too hard to bear, as she still struggled with having taken lives in the war—and now felt additional torment from a certain shadow.

"My point is that they have been betrothed for three years now. Is there some trouble the public needs to be aware of?"

"I do not speak on their behalf on such things."

"Is it because he might find her not ..." Brittany cleared her throat. "... pretty enough?"

Bridget, about to toss the stick again, froze. "I beg your pardon?"

"It's just a rumor, that's all, and it would behoove the champions to clarify that—"

"He finds her the prettiest girl in the kingdom, *Herald*." Now she was irritated. Exactly as the herald had wanted, no doubt. Part of their training and all that.

"Then why has he not taken the leap of marriage and—"

Bridget snarled. She was about to retort, perhaps say something she did not mean, when the entire yard flashed with an otherworldly light. It was immediately followed by a monstrous *crack* of thunder that sundered the air. People shrieked and hit the ground—all but Bridget, who reflexively summoned an earthen shield to her left forearm and ten earthen rings to her right. She looked to Carmichael, who she thought had overdrawn, something inexperienced lightning warlocks were prone to do, sometimes even blowing themselves up in the process. But the young man was prostrate alongside others.

"Did anyone see it?" she shouted. "Report!"

As warlocks began to rise from the ground, an ebony-skinned young woman wearing an emerald robe sprinted forth, sliding to a halt before Bridget. Half her head sprouted long dreads and the other half was completely shaved. Six fiery bands were already wrapped around one forearm and a fiery shield summoned to the other.

The young woman made an unsheathing motion from her hip, hissing, "*Summano arma!*" summoning a fiery longsword to her fist. The flames gurgled quietly as they leapt around a molten blade. "A bolt of lightning hit the keep. But it wasn't like any bolt *I've* ever seen."

Bridget squinted to see through the falling snow. There indeed was a puff of smoke emanating from the keep. "What do you mean?" She became aware that Sabby had started to growl toward the keep and had to grab hold of her collar.

"It was black. *Pitch* bla—" but the woman was cut off by a second lightning blast, much brighter than the first—and darker too, as if part of the light was blocked by a shadow, creating a dual flash of light and dark in the yard. Bridget, who had been looking down at Sabby, caught the tail end of that light.

There was a great *crack* of thunder, quickly followed by a low rumbling *whoosh*—and the snuffing of every lit arm and shield and summoned sword in sight, albeit in a quick wave, with those standing closest to the keep getting snuffed first. Sabby yelped as it passed through, an invisible wave that to the soul felt colder than ice.

The hair on Bridget's arms rose. "Holy gods …" she whispered, staring at her own dark forearm. Memories of the first of two wars she had fought flooded her mind, for it was the last time such a power had been used—a power granted by seven ancient artifacts.

The power to snuff arcanery.

Except those artifacts had been destroyed during the final battle …

Just as quickly as it had come, all ten of her earthen arm rings and her shield flared back to life—as they did for others across the yard. Warlocks glanced at each other before placing their gaze on Bridget, for she was one of the few to survive such an event in the past. For a moment, all Bridget could do was breathe, her heart thundering as she tried to fathom the implications of what had happened.

Brittany, still lying on the ground, raised herself just enough to press a hand to her chest. "That … that wasn't supposed to happen, was it?"

Instead of answering her, Bridget looked to the dreadlocked woman. "You said the first lightning strike was black."

The woman in turn looked to the keep. "The blackest thing I've ever seen," she whispered, eyes unfocused and glassy. "Yet it was still vibrant, if that makes sense. A dark vibrance that struck twice in one spot …"

So they were similar, Bridget thought, having partially witnessed the second strike. Her first thought was necromancy, the eighth element—a forbidden one at that. But the more she thought about it, the less that made sense. She'd never heard of necromancy having the power to snuff arcanery, nor had she heard of necromancy using lightning, which was a totally separate element. Snuffing arcanery was a power historically granted only by the Leyans, and only once in written history through seven crystal orbs known as scions. With the destruction of those scions in the war against the Legion, that power should not exist in Sithesia …

"Who are you, my lady?" Brittany whispered from the ground.

"Dragoon, Lieutenant, and Guardian of the Order Alyssa Fairweather," Alyssa whispered, eyes still fixed upon the keep. "But I am to be addressed as Guardian Fairweather."

The girl rose to a kneeling position and quickly scratched at her parchment. Meanwhile, castle soldiers and knights and warlock guards were seen running to the keep.

"Where's Captain Leera?" Bridget pressed Alyssa. Her sister-in-war, one of the few others to have experienced a scion onslaught head-on, would be most concerned to learn of this development.

"Under water."

"Again?"

"Girl's practically a fish."

"Water warlocks," Bridget muttered, heart still thundering.

"Water warlocks," Alyssa echoed in agreement.

Bridget dragged Sabby closer to hold her collar, lest the husky run off. "Send a messenger."

"No one we have could dive that deep, let alone survive the cold."

"Send someone anyway, if only to keep watch along the shore until she returns. Confirm she's safe. Go with them too."

"I really think I ought to stay here to protect the acting head of our order, Captain."

"Look around. I'll be fine, Lys."

Alyssa glanced about and, seeing they were in a yard full of warlocks, nodded. "Yes, Captain," and she ran off.

"What's happening? Captain? What's—"

"I don't know," Bridget said, pointing at aspiring Arcaners and Arcaners already in the order—squires and dragoons. "Get everyone to headquarters," she commanded to the closest one.

"Yes, Captain," the girl replied, and began running and shouting whilst waving her arms. Like a wave of people, the whole yard began to move as one.

"The sky is darkening," Bridget noted, neck craned, not liking the ominous look of the incoming clouds.

Brittany rose to one knee, but her eyes were on Bridget's shield, which depicted the parts of the Arcaner crest—the full crest. She opened her mouth to no doubt opine on that crest and its meaning in the moment, only for Bridget to snap, "Move it, Herald!"

The pair ran with Sabby in tow—the dog always followed her mistress even when off leash—and dipped through a massive pair of arched doors kept open by two watchful Arcaner guards. Once inside, Bridget sent another young Arcaner off to the keep to send back a report. Normally, she would run toward danger, but with Augum and Leera away, her primary responsibility was to protect the order.

The Great Arcaner Hall was cool and quiet, with its checkered floor and tall fluted columns and countless murals and tapestries depicting Arcaners of old. A single fat Endyear candle was lit to celebrate the final ten days of the year—today only the second day of the sacred holiday.

The candle sat on a giant marble mantel, which floated above a snuffed fireplace. The hall burbled with Arcaners whispering theories to each other. They ranged all the way from an attacking army to a wild casting that had gone particularly awry.

Brittany paced around Bridget so that she could better look at her shield, and proceeded to quill what she saw, whispering the occasional phrase as she went. " '... inscribed in golden letters underneath ... *Semperis vorto honos* ... the Arcaner motto meaning courage, fortitude, honor ... above, a golden triple-spired castle ... and above that castle ...' " She looked up to meet Bridget's gaze before returning her eyes to the shield just as quickly. " '... a golden dragon.' "

CAPTAIN LEERA JONES

―――――――――――――――――――

LEERA

Somewhere west of Blackhaven, deep under the frigid waters of the vast Anchor Lake, Leera Matilda Jones swam down into unfathomable darkness. Her raven hair streamed behind her like seaweed and her crimson robe dragged like a sail, but she didn't care, for she had all the time in Sithesia. Down here—at least in this lake—there were no predators.

That was, other than the one that peeked from behind her soul. It was that predator that taunted her with unseeing eyes colder than the icy water, taking every opportunity to slip its cravings of war into her soul. It was that predator that feasted on her weaknesses and insecurities and desires, exploiting her fears, making light of the heavy and twisting the gentle.

Down, down, down she swam into the silty gloom, lit only by the pale light emanating from her right hand. Despite the turmoil in her thoughts, her strokes were calm and efficient, her breathing slow and steady and bolstered by her arcanery.

A recent graduate from the esteemed Academy of Arcane Arts, Leera now ran the Arcaner order as a captain, alongside her sister-in-war, Bridget, and her betrothed, Augum. But oft, being a captain felt more like a title in name only, for they rarely heaped any responsibilities upon her—a choice not of their making, but of hers. For as often as she ran toward danger, she just as often—if not more so—ran from responsibility. And she loathed herself for it.

Leera thought of Augum toiling in the north, and silently cursed him for not wanting to bring her along. For yet again choosing the damned order above the two of them. She did not mean to curse him, of course.

She loved him just as deeply as he loved her. Just as deeply as she dove that day, one of many days spent in the peaceful depths she called a second home.

She passed walleye and carp and bladetail and cutthroat and sandbar, all passively curious as to what this girl was doing amongst them.

"Don't mind me," Leera said, not a bubble escaping her mouth as she spoke, for she had enchanted herself to breathe and speak water—and even drink it, for lake water was fresh, at least when not too near the city, where it tasted most foul indeed. "Have you by chance seen one of your trout friends?" she asked a passing salmon chubby enough for an eight-person meal. "No? Well, be sure to let me know," she cheekily added as she continued her descent.

And what will we find today? she thought, wanting to keep her mind busy. The pressure at this depth would have instantly killed an apprentice. The cold would have allowed sixty heartbeats, maybe more depending on one's fortitude, before that heart gave out. But her arcanery and her heart were strong. Stronger than almost any water-heart out there. And few knew it, for she rarely brought anyone with her. Not this deep. Not into such cold.

Those who apprenticed under Leera found her flighty and slightly terrifying—and not just because of the incredible power she shared with her betrothed and her sister-in-war, a power that protected the kingdom to the point of being minted on a coin. Not just because occasionally those around her glimpsed the predator peeking out from behind her eyes, sizing them up like prey—the price all three paid for that power. What made her slightly terrifying to fellow water warlocks was her desire to constantly push herself—and thus, those around her—to new depths. Literal, deep, dark depths that terrified even the competent water-breathers in her midst. Especially the arcanists who had tasked her with training her fellow water fledglings. There had been more than a few close calls, to the point she had earned an "at-your-own-risk" reputation. And very few took that risk.

"Ah, I've been looking for you," Leera said, flicking a finger and telekinetically catching the tail of a trout. It struggled at first, but she won it over with calmness, cooing, "Shh, shh," just like she spoke to Sir Pawsalot, the castle tabby—her tabby, really, for he nestled around her head at night whilst Augum slept beside her. The fish understood her. She was in tune with them. Could commune with them—but only after casting the 4th degree off-the-books elemental spell Commune with Fish, which she set her mind to doing next.

Once near, she placed a gentle hand on the trout's back. "Trout," she whispered. "I am your friend. Show me the bottom. Let me see what you have seen." She focused on the nuance of the extension, precisely lined up her thoughts along the dictates of the spell, drew upon the stamina accessible to her from the arcane ether, where all arcanery stemmed from, and incanted, "*Fisha thiyola communa.*"

Her vision morphed to a sandy bottom as she searched for a favorite meal—crayfish. Snaking this way and that, she saw herself flying in a most familiar fashion that threatened to wake the predator within her. The trout smoothly led her through an obstacle course of boulders, towering lake-bottom vines, a decayed log, and eventually a splintered barrel.

Hope you investigated it, Miss Trout, she thought. But after passing the barrel, perhaps a random loss from a storm-tossed fisherman, she saw only sand. She was about to give up when the trout glided past a huge chunk of rusting iron. Hello, she thought, withdrawing mentally from the fish, but still holding onto it.

"Now take me to it," Leera said, and whispered the incantation to the 10th degree off-the-books spell Command Fish, "*Ia kommenda yon tei dos demandos, fisha,*" which translated to, I command you to do my bidding, fish, a most amusing command to first learn. Not all spells were so literal; some did not translate at all, the meaning of the old words lost to time.

The trout quickly led her down at a steep seventy-degree angle, forcing her to swim at a panting rate, until a shape appeared in the darkness ahead. As she swam, the shape thrust past like a thin battering ram. A mast, she realized.

"Thank you, friend," she said to the trout, and dismissed it with a wave of a hand and the phrase, "*Kommenda null,*" which nullified the Command Fish spell. The trout gave her an indignant flap of the tail and shot off.

"Well don't be *too* offended!" Leera called after it. "I could have stuck you in an oven before slapping you down onto the supper table! Ungrateful turd," she muttered and returned her attention to the mast. On land, she needed spectacles on account of poor sight, but down here, her eyes saw details only those spectacles provided above—rope notches and rusting shackles covered with wreck mussels and eel weeds and tiny lake crabs. Perfect underwater sight was a privilege reserved only for water warlocks.

Leera followed the mast past remnants of rope, the oak slowly rotting. As she swam, she counted the crossbeams, concluding it was a triple square-sail rigger. Such ships navigated the roomy Tetroska that marked the historically contentious border between the northern kingdom of Ohm and its southern neighbor, Abrandia. The river bridged the Western Salt and Anchor Lake, part of a vast trade network that went up and down the western coast.

When her feet softly touched down onto the splintered and moss-covered planks at the mast's base, she raised her lit palm and brightened the light so that it extended to the water itself. Shine was the first elemental spell all warlocks learned, and it was relatively the same across the elements. But the extensions to the spell were different for each element. A lightning warlock, for example, could deliver a minor shock. An earth warlock could entwine something small with her vine. And a water warlock could light up the water itself.

Whereas the Shine spell had already been ignited into her palm with the incantation "*Shyneo*," the extension was non-verbal and only required an alignment of thought—and, of course, a drawing upon of arcane stamina.

It was an extension she had learned at fourteen years of age whilst running for her life alongside Augum and Bridget. At the time, she thought it the most useless extension ever, stupidly believing it was only used as a prank to light up puddles or water in bathtubs. Now, it was essential to underwater exploration.

The ship lit up amidst the swirling silt as if the moon itself had dipped out from behind a cloud, revealing an additional two masts, one of which had broken off, the base impaling the deck like a spear to the gut. Pale and decrepit, it rested in a coffin bed of sand and rock and weeds and shipwreck detritus, the rot well beyond the repair of even the most competent warlock. Both splintered and intact barrels, the iron strapping on the verge of breaking down, littered the area. She spotted what appeared to be an old leather boot—or what remained of it. And even through the silt, she saw the iron she had seen through the fish's eyes—the anchor. It was a merchant galley, of that there was no doubt. Which promised a fat bounty.

Leera checked in with herself, conscious of the slow trickle of her arcane stamina draw—she was chronocasting three spells at once, after all: the 1st degree Breathe Water, which was technically off-the-books but often learned even before one's first ring; the 3rd degree off-the-books Endure the Deep, which also trained against the cold; and the extension to Shine that lit up surrounding waters. Whereas simulcasting meant casting two or more spells at once, chronocasting meant casting—and holding—one spell after the other.

Although they were optional, a water warlock worth their salt would take the extra study time to learn all three of those water spells. Though not many water warlocks craved the depths, all warlocks had to be mindful not to overdraw, lest they fall deathly sick or even perish. But Leera was most adept for a 10th degree, having honed her arcane might in war—and through diligent study and training that continued daily.

Feeling in balance and with plenty enough time to surface, she let her arms drift to her sides and imagined what the ship would have been like in its heyday. Proud, majestic, ambitious, she saw it carving white ocean waves, heading to trade with remote towns along the coasts—or distant islands.

But of course, there was a boundary ships did not cross. The open oceans held monsters beyond reckoning that saw ships as prey. Few returned from the great horizons, and none saw distant shores spoken of in the legends that varied across the seven kingdoms that made up Sithesia.

Yet no such dangers existed in this lake, leaving Leera to ponder how the ship had come to rest here. Then again, the lake was known to have particularly ferocious storms on account of nearby mountain ranges, which had a tendency to squeeze the winds as they pushed by, making the waters froth.

She paced forth, but finding the walking too slow for her liking, switched to swimming. Past the main deck was the quarter deck and then the poop deck where the wheel usually sat, but in this case, the wheel had been ripped from the planks, leaving a gaping hole that led directly down into what she suspected was the captain's quarters. She wanted to check the name of the ship at the rear, but conscious of the sands dribbling through the hourglass of her arcane stamina, she reduced the light that made the water glow back to her palm, then dove into the hole.

The room was low-ceilinged—sailors, especially captains, tended to be on the shorter side for whatever reason. A campaign table pressed against a smashed armchair. Empty and bent planks were all that remained of a rather roomy berth. A dresser sat upside down, its drawers littering the floor. Other than being covered with lake moss and silt and tiny wandering crustaceans, the shelves were barren, their contents, or rather what remained of them, strewn or floating about. She checked under the table and spotted a rusted-through iron chart prong, used to measure out nautical distances on maps. Beyond that, something else caught her attention—a small chest, still closed, the keyhole rusted through.

"Ooh, treasure," Leera squealed, and beckoned. The chest lifted from the planks and floated over, drawn telekinetically. But it was heavy — and it jangled. That could only mean one thing. "Am I rich or am I rich?" she mumbled, thinking about the countless new costs that had sprung up of late — mentor fees, castle maintenance and servant fees, the purchase of new robes, academy alumni fees, tithes to the Arcaner order, alms for the poor, and myriad other expenses required of women these days. Still, she was far luckier than most, not having to pay for lodging, a kingdom champion who shared a castle with her betrothed — a mystical, arcane castle that was invisible to all but a select few. A castle atop a mountain.

Still, the girlish side of her that always longed for adventure and treasure continued squealing in delight even as she hefted the beastly little thing back through the hole in the deck. Then reality set in. The darn thing was far too heavy to take to the surface, even with Telekinesis. Even with her swim prowess, amplified by arcanery.

"Shoot, shoot, shoot," she said to the surrounding black depths. "I'm not leaving you here. You can forget it." While under water, she oft talked to herself or to fish or to inanimate objects, for doing so made her feel at one with her surroundings, as if she were more than a mere visitor.

Her pale light caught the flick of a distant and large white tail, which gave her an idea. She let the chest fall to the planks with a pluming thud and shot after the tail, incanting, "*Akseler aqua loa*," the incantation to the 2nd degree off-the-books Fast Swim. The 9th degree off-the-books Speed of the Dolphin was quicker, but also pricier stamina-wise, and she would need what remained of her stamina to haul the chest topside.

"Where do you think you're going?" Leera said, racing after it, her feet flapping up and down like the lake dolphin she was trying to catch, albeit at a much slower rate. She closed in briefly before it realized her intentions, and flicked its tail, giving it a massive burst of speed and making her regret taking her robe — but not diving into the waters mid-conversation with an Arcaner friend. They knew her to be spontaneous like that, and for some reason that day, the frigid waters had called to her. Perhaps because she had been depressed, longing for a solace only the deep provided.

With only a moment to spare before the dolphin zoomed out of range, Leera lashed out telekinetically, and just snagged the top of that flat tail. "Oh, no you don't," she said, moving hand over hand as if pulling on an invisible tether. The dolphin struggled and dragged her forth, but she did not give up.

"Shh, it's all right. I mean you no harm. I just need a ride. You understand?" She pointed upward. "Just a short hop."

Now curious, the lake dolphin swam about to look at her.

She let the tether go and showed it her palms, one of which remained lit. "I know you're not a horse. Don't look at me like that. I won't throw a saddle on you, I promise." She winked, flashing one of her cheeky grins.

The dolphin turned away. Sensing it was about to shoot off again, and not having the strength to battle it a second time, Leera quickly snapped off, "*Ia kommenda yon tei dos demandos, fisha.*" The dolphin froze, drifting into the gloom ever so slightly. "Let me grab hold," she said, and took hold of his top fin. "Take me to the shipwreck," she commanded, knowing the language of arcanery would lend translation. The art was complex—far more complex than the words involved, taking years of study and practice to get right. But she had done the work and, unlike many a warlock, actually practiced what she learned in the field almost daily.

The dolphin turned and glided onward. She enjoyed feeling the cold waters rush by, a feeling that reminded her of Augum when he idly ran his fingers through her hair. Using gentle tugs left or right on the fin, she guided the dolphin back to the chest, which she telekinetically snatched on the way. Immediately the dolphin's speed sagged, but she patted it on the back and said, "Now to the surface, my friend," and with a kick of its tail, off it went.

"Yahoo!" Leera yelled, the waters ripping by. The chest spun in behind, connected by a strong but ethereal tendril tether. Soon the waters began to lighten with what remained of the day, yet the dolphin kept going, cajoled by her, until, with a final burst of speed, it leapt out of the waters, taking Leera—and her chest—with it. At the apex of the breach, she saw the already twinkling and distant torchlights of the city, and in the horizon beyond, the mammoth and snowy mountains that made up the Northern Peaks.

Together they crashed back into the lake water, whereupon Leera nullified the spells she no longer needed. With the chest clutched under an arm, she bid the gentle marine creature to take her back to land, for she was most tired indeed. When she had dived in, it had been snowing. Now it was a fresh and mostly clear eve, with the first stars already peeking out between banks of clouds sodden with fat snowflakes that fell in distant curtains. The air was crisp and clean and wintery, and she longed for a warm meal and a hot bath. Perhaps news would come of

Augum—or perhaps he had returned! How grand that would be indeed, for with it came the promise of a snuggle … and maybe a little more.

THE MOCKING FATES

AUGUM

In a creaking hut pummeled by the howling blizzard and lit by a low hearth, Augum sat on a plank bench staring at the ancient manacles that bound his wrists. He had taken a grave risk, one of his greatest in years.

It had not surprised him that the other patrons of the Smoked Wing Inn & Tavern had hardly looked up while the crimson-robe and his emerald-robed cohort led him away. And when those patrons had looked up, it was only to shake their heads, or chortle knowingly amongst each other. Perhaps he had hoped someone would speak up, just so that he could say that people this far north had empathy, that they cared even a little for youthful Solian lives.

The original plan had been for him to learn about the fugitive and where he had taken his young captives, but not be taken captive himself. His compatriots and his mentor would be furious. He wasn't supposed to be put in harm's way, let alone be captured—let alone allow his tracking pebble to be discovered and disenchanted, the only means his party had of locating him.

Augum had another means to communicate, the only problem was it required access to arcanery. And that particular method only communicated with Bridget and Leera, and they were far to the south and well out of range to help. Yet he felt the cause was just and the risk, albeit questionable, worth it. Besides, he hadn't been tested in some time, and such men did not deserve leniency.

But staring at his manacles gave him second thoughts, for these particular manacles were enchanted with a special power that cut off a warlock's access to the arcane ether, preventing the casting of arcanery. With no way of removing the manacles himself, he would have to either trick his captors into doing so or wait to see what they had planned for him.

He wondered how these manacles had been procured. Because of how long it took to create such manacles, making them rare and powerful and nearly priceless, kingdoms held them in guarded vaults.

Across the room, a man scraped steel with flint, lighting his pipe in one strike. "Anyone ever tell you that you look like the Arinthian?" he said in a raspy voice between small pumping puffs.

Augum looked up, all too aware that his face could be plainly seen now. The bearded forty-something man sucked on his pipe three times and expelled three rings of smoke, which grew larger and larger before dissipating. His emerald robe was stained with wine and chocolate and who knew what else, and his deerskin coat was dirty and unbrushed. Yet by the way those beady red-rimmed eyes took in everything, Augum sensed he was a shrewd man who shouldn't be underestimated.

"I get that a lot, sir," Augum replied, careful to keep the honorific in place.

"I bet you do. Shave that stubble, grow a foot, add five years and you'd be a spittin' image to the poster."

Augum tried to humor the man with a smile, but the corner of his mouth barely rose. Such posters exaggerated to the point of ridiculousness. Seven feet tall, muscled, steely-eyed, wise beyond his years. Fodder for the masses—whilst striking fear into the kingdom's enemies. And he liked his stubble, which he kept trim but not shaved all the way as he found the ritual of a razor tedious.

"Could have made some castles as an impersonator." His captor glanced to the plank ceiling of the old hut as if seeing through it and whistled through a gap in his front teeth. "Imagine being able to turn yourself into a dragon like that. To see the ground from the clouds." He shook his head. "That's a power only for the gods, says I."

The man refocused on Augum, pipe wavering about as he got his thoughts in order. "You know, boy, I don't think those three so-called champions can even become dragons. I don't rightly think that's what won the war for us at all. I mean, they were nothing but babes, really. I say it was the army. *I* say the army used clever illusions to make people *think* those were real dragons. People want heroes. And young ones at that."

He gummed the pipe on one side of his mouth, expelling small puffs of smoke from the other. "And I ain't the only one who thinks that way, boy. No one has seen those dragons about for some time, and even when they *were* seen divin' in and out of the ranges, I'm a tellin' you, boy, those were nothin' but apparitions. That's a fancy word, ain't it? *Apparitions*." His voice dropped to a drawn-out whisper as he slowly spread the fingers of his grubby hands. "Ghosts …"

Augum clasped his hands in his lap and leaned back against the cold plank wall, which shook with every gust. "You're a Solian," he noted.

"Was. Ain't got no kingdom now."

"So what'd you do during the war? Er, sir?"

The captor grinned around his pipe. "I done took advantage."

Augum nodded and looked down at his manacled hands again. This pair was engraved with its runic sequence, but one had to have access to one's arcanery to be able to use that sequence to unlock them. Nonetheless, he'd memorized the phrase upon the crimson-robe putting them on, playing possum throughout, letting it all happen, pretending to have the fearful doe eyes he had seen on many a victim of violence. Wars had left such impressions behind, forever seared into his soul.

"Don't you want to know how?"

Augum realized he was not acting the part and looked up, trying to show fear in his face by opening his mouth a little and arching his eyebrows. "I do, sir. I just didn't want to be rude," he said, feeling the predator lurking behind his mind, peeking into his thoughts, staring at the captor in greedy want of his blood.

The man grinned. "You got a funny look to your face, boy, as if you don't know how to use it," and he wheezed a laugh that soon descended into coughing. To soothe his throat, he took three long pulls of the pipe and puffed out three more rings, making quick *puh, puh, puh* sounds. Somehow, that made the cough subside. He pulled the pipe out of his mouth and waved it about a few times before continuing.

"I robbed is what I did. Robbed everyone I done come across. Soldiers. Merchants. Old ladies. Younglings. Didn't matter none. Usually, all it took was—" He raised a hand, which burst with lightning that crackled rather timidly, at least compared to what Augum knew potent lightning ought to sound like. "Was damn good at it too," the man added. He admired his own hand. "Bet you wish you could have gotten this far, don't ya? Sorry, boy, not all of us is cut out to be strong 'locks."

"But you don't rob no more."

"This work pays better. Barrels better." The man put his pipe down on the bench beside him, looked Augum square in the eye, and slapped his grimy wrists together, hissing, "*Annihilo!*" Augum raised his forearm out of pure instinct, but no shield came, and the bolt of lightning smashed into his chest. But he too was shrewd, and caught on to his captor's test—

and so he howled in pretend pain and fell to the dirty planks, where he rolled about, moaning, "Why'd you do that?"

"'Cause you look too much like him. But the real one is supposedly immune to lightning. Wouldn't want no Arcaners meddlin' in our business, would we? And you can stop your howlin', boy. It was a tempered bolt. Could've made you twitch and smoke had I wanted to." He grinned. "Could've made you *sizzle*."

Augum hauled himself to the bench and collapsed on it, panting. "That hurt, sir," he lied.

"But you got some reflex in you, boy. That I gots to give you. That's youth for ya." His captor picked his pipe back up and relit it, saying between puffs, "Stir the fire."

"Yes, sir." Augum stood up with a groan, shuffled to an iron by the stone hearth, and again almost gave himself away by starting to beckon for it, only to quickly move that hand up to his chest to rub at the spot that had been blasted. "What are you going to do with me?" he asked as he picked the cold iron up and poked at the hearth, drawing some flame and heat from its aromatic cedars.

The captor grinned. "You'll see." He watched Augum with keen and alert eyes. "Or maybe you won't. Depends how you behave. So far, you is as meek as a lamb, which I do appreciate, yes I do."

Augum, ignoring the predator within him that knew it could cleave the man's head in two with the iron, or perhaps pierce his heart with even the blunt end were it a forceful enough jab, returned the poker to rest against the charred stone. For some reason, he pitied the man. There was a nugget of kindness within him, a seed rarely watered. But Augum, who still heard the echo of two parents begging on their knees, had a quest, and so he asked the question on his mind.

"How many like me did you take, sir?"

"Two. They put up more of a fight than you did." He shrugged. "They cried more than you did too, though. Howled like banshees, really. Sort o' feel bad for 'em, you know?" He shrugged. "Such are The Fates, who give me the freedom to do as I see fit." He tapped his chest with the pipe. "I'm free, boy. Freer than most men. Freer than them stuffy nobles even. And one day, I'll be richer too."

Augum plopped back onto the bench in a show of defeat, having heard this sort of spiel many times before. Sometimes it was prior to a raid, other times while the man—or woman—spat at him from behind iron bars, their manacles clanking as they frothed or wept or stared off at nothing, their fate sealed.

"That don't impress you, boy? Hmm? Well, it should. It should. Because you're the one in chains. And you better start showing some—" He rubbed his big red nose with the pipe, eyes roving about in search of the right word. "—contrition. That's the word. Contrition and ... and humility. Eh?" He tapped his temple with the pipe. "You up-and-comers always think Ol' Lanfred dumb, but I got smarts. Ain't no dumb 'lock get to the 5th like I did, see?"

He flared five lightning rings, which floated around his robe sleeve. "The triple A threw me out, but it was them teachers that had it out for me, that they did. Hated every last one of 'em. But at least I got me five beautiful rings around me arm. You? You is nothin' but an aspirant. A nobody. And just like me, you did wrong back in that precious academy and they sent you up north and now you is payin' the karma for your crime, yes you is. They can't even track you now, boy. Not that they'd make much of an effort trackin' a no-good hoodlum," and he laughed. "We is two of the same, boy. Two of the same. But you is weaker. Much weaker than I was at your age."

"Yes, sir," Augum mumbled, lowering his head in what he hoped was some of that contrition the man who had called himself Lanfred wanted. Luckily he had convinced him that the academy had crafted the pebble with the 3rd degree Object Track spell and not his party.

"You an odd one, boy. The guilt hangs off you like a foul stench."

That word made Augum remember eyes going wide upon the realization that *his* face was the last those eyes would ever see. That sort of finality truly showed in the eyes. A moment of stark comprehension that the cumulation of a lifetime of decisions had led to that harrowing point of no return. Yet as honorable and just as the causes had been, those eyes still haunted his dreams and tormented him between moments. The remnants of two wars now heard as echoes ...

Guilt also made him look to his ring finger, where he felt the absence of his betrothal ring. Both he and Leera wore the same ring—a ring shaped like pine needles, the Solian emblem, made of silver and permanently enchanted with the 3rd degree Object Track enchantment by their mutual mentor Jez so that each ring could always find the other. It was modeled after a real pine needle ring he had offered her upon bent knee atop his castle, a marriage proposal that had seen her crying with love and happiness.

But the ring would have been a dead giveaway, and so he'd had to leave it behind.

"How'd you get that scar, boy?" Lanfred asked. "The one on your palm."

Augum remembered cutting his hand open and mixing the blood with a wolven concoction in order to save Bridget's life. Few believed in wolven, a beastly people of the north. But then, people didn't believe in Leyans or multiple suns in a sky or half the things he had seen in his paltry life of twenty years. He felt much older than those years showed, for two wars had taken their toll.

Lanfred's question reminded him how hard it was to keep up a friendly mask for social occasions. He shied away from speaking about himself and rarely told people the truth of what he had seen and experienced, mostly because of that certain look they would give him, a mix of awe and terror. Then came the inevitable repetitious questions— Did it really happen that way? But I thought such beasts or people or artifacts didn't exist? And how can there exist three suns? Can you tell us more? More, more, more, sir. Commander. Champion. Three Toes—

There was a *zap* and Augum jerked back to attention, having been shocked by a spark.

"I done asked you a question, boy. What are you daydreaming for?"

"Sorry, sir. Just feeling sorry for myself." He hoped that would cover for his wandering mind.

"Or are you feeling guilt for that scar? Somethin' else you done bad some ways back? Eh?"

"No, sir. I got this, uh …" He swallowed. "… cooking ma's onions." Three lies in one sentence—that was not how he'd gotten the scar, he didn't cook, and he was an orphan. *Thou shall never break thy word.* Thankfully he hadn't sworn on his shield …

The man wheeze-laughed. "Cuttin' bleedin' onions …" He slapped his knee. "Boy, that's how I know you is tellin' the truth, for you could have said anything. Fightin' would have been a good one. Nothin' like a good knife fight to make a boy look good to the lasses, eh?" He leaned forth to smile with those gapped teeth. "You remind me of me at your age. You know how? You ain't got no pride," and he laughed uproariously, slapping his knee again, this time with the pipe. "Someone done broke you, boy. Someone done broke you down like an ox cart."

You got that part right, Augum thought, thinking back to his youth as a farm slave who'd taken no end of beatings from a drunk who had left a painting of scars on his back, the brush being a belt or a switch or a branch. Back then he'd thought himself an orphan, until discovering he had a famous warlock great-grandmother and an *in*famous murdering tyrant for a father. The former went to live in a sacred plane and the latter Augum sent to Hell. Both experiences were now tavern tales that grew taller with each retelling.

Despite his relative youth, that felt like lifetimes ago. War had that effect. Yet, in times of peace, he sometimes found himself longing for that immutable chaos that war provided. For he had never felt more alive than in those times of instability. Never loved deeper. Never lived as profoundly. Never laughed or cried as hard. The times of peace in between, of deep study and quiet, of command and leadership and signing castellan receipts and waivers and notices, were about as exciting as churning butter. Peace felt like waiting to see a toothist, or the sound of knives and forks scraping on porcelain plates when conversation died at the supper table. Peace was boredom.

Shame from such thoughts made his cheeks tingle, for war also meant suffering and death, and so Augum looked to the door, wondering if his brethren had at least found that cursed town and were inquiring about him enough to uncover what had happened and where these fools were taking him. Surviving the blizzard was not the question, for his party had three competent warlocks with them, including his mentor, a fire warlock, and a healer. Alas, the blizzard had complicated the entire endeavor, for it was longer and stronger than any he had experienced in his kingdom of Solia.

Still, having taken such a big risk of capture, he worried that, as clever as he was, The Fates had a caustic sense of humor, enjoying irony above all karmas. And he was long overdue. Already he was in chains, his tracking pebble disenchanted and thrown away. What else was in store?

"Sit up, boy. Got a long journey ahead. What's the matter? Why is you slouching so?"

"I'm hungry and tired and a prisoner, sir." The truth was, the years of violence and the predatorial side effect were taking their toll on his thoughts. And it was doing the same to Bridget and Leera. Neither laughed as much these days, haunted not just by what they had experienced, but by the increasing divide between the three of them and everyone else. It wasn't a mere rift anymore; it was a chasm. Add to that the expectations of high society that he and Leera marry and have children, when children were an impossibility for the two of them … the thought that he was the last of his ancient lineage …

Somehow they all managed to persevere, doing what was expected of them, protecting, assigning, championing, leading. The fifteenth edict came to mind — *Thou shall serve thy lord and king and kingdom with valor and courage and an open heart.*

"I reckon you are, boy," Lanfred said, gumming his pipe. "I reckon you are."

"Sir, can I at least have the journey bread from my rucksack?"

"Maybe later. If the boss lets you."

The door burst open and the blizzard plumed inside, threatening to snuff the hearth. From amidst the swirls of snow appeared the crimson-robe.

Lanfred shot to his feet.

"We're moving," the crimson barked, marching to Augum and hauling him up by the scruff with a powerful arm. "This one's brought the squealers." He searched Augum's face with those flat, pitiless eyes.

"But I thought you said they don't come this far north," Lanfred said, quickly tapping his pipe against the bench to empty it.

"Must be the cursed Arcaners, then." The crimson-robe jerked Augum roughly about. "You someone's kid? You bait?"

Augum shook his head, thinking that the man must have been tipped off by someone in town—or perhaps he'd done the teleporting to check the trails for himself. But that didn't quite make sense, seeing as from what he knew, the man was a fire warlock, and fire warlocks couldn't see through blizzards any more than lightning warlocks could.

"I don't believe you, boy. But we'll yap on it later." The crimson yanked Augum about so that Lanfred could grab hold of one of his arms before the pair of ruffians linked up hands as well. Augum refrained from cursing his bad luck, for the one thing he had been counting on was his party's prowess. As the crimson snapped off the incantation to Group Teleport, a 17th degree spell, Augum heard the echoed laughter of The Fates.

ANCIENT TEACHERS

BRIDGET

Back in the dimly lit Great Arcaner Hall, Bridget took Alyssa aside the moment the latter returned.

"She surface yet?"

"No, Cap. But I've got three 'prentices keeping an eye out on the shoreline where she most often pops up. Thing is, she might just 'port directly into town for a bite to eat. You know how hungry she gets after a swim."

Bridget rubbed her face with her hands before nodding at Alyssa. "Please keep me informed, Lieutenant."

"Will do, Cap. In the mean, what's your command? We've got the Lover's Day feast scheduled for this eve and then the traditional dance—"

"Cancel both and get everyone back to the dorms." In truth she was relieved, for without her betrothed both the feast and the dance would have been torture.

"The academy dorms or the castle—"

"The academy. I would rather them holed up with the arcanists until we understand what's going on." She trusted the academy teachers above most warlocks, not to mention the academy was one of the most secure places in the entire kingdom, with the added bonus that the Arcaner dorms within were only accessible to fellow Arcaners.

"Yes, Cap. I'll herd them there and then track down Lee like a Sierran bloodhound," and Alyssa shot off to bark, "All right, people, we're moving you to the academy! Get ready for a march!" Aspiring Arcaners, squires, and dragoons quickly filed out of the hall in readiness to begin the walk. Every single one saluted Bridget with fingers pressed over the heart, adding either a nod of the head, the title "Captain," or both.

Brittany the Herald, seeing that Bridget had concluded her conversation, paced up to her. "Please do not dismiss me, Captain."

Bridget, who was holding onto Sabby's leash and was about to do just that, raised an eyebrow. "This is no time for—"

"With all due respect, Captain, I would argue this is the *ideal* time for such a report." The herald curtsied in the proper fashion of someone astute to the ways of the court, a trait Bridget hardly found endearing. Upon seeing Bridget's face, the girl wrung her hands. "Please let me stay. I can cut my quill on this. And I think I can do good for the kingdom by filling Ordinaries in on how the order functions. That they—especially the nobility—need not fear you. I'm referring of course to edict sixteen of the seventeen-point Sacred Chivalric Code of the Arcaner, which states—"

"I'm aware of what it states." All Arcaners memorized the code as part of their squire trial, and recited it aloud every morn as a matter of ritual, most oft during communal breakfast.

Brittany persisted, flipping the scrolls clipped to her tablet until she quoted, " 'Thou shall root out corruption in all its forms, and the sanctity of the truth shall vanquish any title.' " She let the scrolls flick back and stared, defiant.

Bridget appreciated that defiance, a necessary quality in good heralds. Thus, and perhaps against her own better judgment, she surrendered a nod.

"Thank you, Captain. I promise you won't regret it."

Bridget only blew away hair that had drifted into her line of sight. But it was Sabby who caught her attention, for the Ohmish husky was staring at the still-open pair of arched doors that led to the outer ward, which the Arcaners used as a training yard. Snow swirled about outside in the darkness, wind whistling through the ancient stonework. But a new sound cut through it. It was heavy, as if metal clanged up and down.

Like a ghost drawn to life, Bridget drifted to the open doors, attaching a leash to Sabby whilst never taking her eyes off the yard. An entire column of jogging soldiers soon appeared under the arch that separated the inner and outer wards, their steel plate mail and weapons clanking. Each man wore a pot helm and carried a crest shield emblazoned with the royal sigil above the words *Onas o breva konkerra*—Only the brave conquer, the official motto of Oak Company.

"Are they coming here?" the herald asked.

"I believe they are."

At the head of the column was a cleanly shaven man with tan skin and hard eyes, wearing ornate steel plate etched with intricate swirls. Bridget's heart sank upon seeing him, for he was a man she loathed — and she loathed few. The motto was his, and she had made him an enemy early on by opining that she thought the motto most inappropriate. Of course, the motto wasn't the real problem …

"Is that … is that The Sword of the Oak?"

"I am afraid it is."

The herald scratched away at her parchment, muttering, " 'Amidst new strife … a famed commander … having earned the appellation by single-handedly felling seven brigands under an oak tree … this way comes.' "

The soldiers continued to jog directly at them, their faces hard as stone, the ground shaking with each foot-stomp, eventually forcing Bridget and Brittany to jump aside lest they get run over.

"Company … halt!" The Sword of the Oak barked. "Surround!"

Amidst a flurry of jangling weapons and armor, the men took up positions around Bridget — but facing outward.

"Company — draw!"

The hall rang with the song of men unsheathing their longswords.

The quill scratched away. " '… making an imposing entrance with his renowned column …' "

"What is this?" Bridget snapped, keeping a tight leash on Sabby, who was rearing up and barking at the intruders.

The man, in his late thirties and with a thin mustache and a chiseled face that was said to have made many a lady swoon, only for said ladies to later discover his coldness, was the no-nonsense sort that Bridget usually respected. But this man, from everything she knew, abused his power. Having been around the Black Castle a lot as it also held the Great Arcaner Hall, she had learned a thing or two about its denizens.

The man took stock of Bridget with a single sweep from foot to head and back again, before his hard pale eyes did the same to the herald. The girl backed up a step and continued scratching at her parchment, though kept stealing glances at him. He was as Ordinary a man as they came. His particular gift was firm leadership and coldness — and he was particularly brilliant in the latter.

"Who are you?" he barked. "Present yourself."

"Herald Brittany Mires, sir," the girl squeaked, curtsying properly. "Sent on the request of the *Blackhaven Herald* to take stock of the Arcaner order and present it in true light to the public, so that — "

"—they may fear it less so. Yes, yes, I understand you plain. Another piece blowing smoke up their robes. Hardly what they need."

"That's not at all the point of my—"

"You may stop speaking until invited to do so again," the commander interrupted.

"How rude," the girl muttered.

"Commander? What is this?" Bridget asked.

"Orders, Captain," he snapped, placing those pale eyes on Bridget. "Orders is what this is."

"And whose orders are those, Commander Strout?" she asked, despite knowing the answer.

He raised a mocking brown eyebrow alongside a folded parchment. "Why, the king's, of course. Seeing as your commander is on an errand at the moment—"

Bridget swiped at the air and telekinetically snatched the parchment from the man's clutches. "He's hardly on a mere errand—"

The commander idly twirled the end of his whisp-thin mustache with a finger, as if hoping it would grow thicker. "Be that as it may, seeing as these are unusual circumstances, the king and his councilors feel it necessary to protect the kingdom's most …" Another sweep of the foot to head, this time rather amused. "… powerful assets." He had added a disdainful *pop* to the *p* in *powerful*, as if it pained him to admit such a thing.

Bridget loathed how he always made her feel young and inexperienced. Trying not to snarl, she stared at him as she cracked open the royal wax seal, imagining rising behind him in her winged and scaled might, plucking him up between her black claws, and ripping him apart like a child picking the wings off a fly. Lest that predatorial musing overcome her soul, she forced herself to look down at the writ of command and pored over it.

"I have my own guard, Commander," she said when she had finished skimming the document.

The man glanced around the empty hall. "Which you apparently sent away." He let the echo of his voice die before continuing. "Whether you like it or not, *Captain*, you are a weapon. One of three. The only three such weapons in all the seven kingdoms of Sithesia. Ergo, we cannot have anti-arcanery compromising those weapons. That is why a guard of highly trained *Ordinaries*—" He twisted the word with ironic mock. "—has been dispatched to protect you."

Bridget shoved the writ into a pocket and stroked Sabby's head, urging her to calm her occasional barking, now aimed solely at the commander. "So I am to have a guard detail?"

"This new power, once granted only to the scions, could be another kingdom's new strength, and they're now testing our responses. Or it could be a rogue warlock seeking revenge of past wrongs. Or it could be something else entirely. Until the threat is fully assessed and understood, yes, you are to have a guard detail. Night and day." He eyed the dog until Bridget finally persuaded her to sit on her haunches, her tail wagging furiously back and forth.

"What about my brother- and sister-in-war?"

"I've dispatched a column to find Captain Jones, and a messenger up north to recall Commander Stone."

"He won't be easy to reach." She wanted to tell him it was a fool's errand, but refrained.

"Leave that to us. As few of you as there are left, the army has its own competent warlocks."

Bridget glanced around at the Ordinary soldiers, a few of whom glanced back at her with curiosity. "This directly contravenes the Arcaner order's independence—"

"Independence is not my concern, Captain. I follow orders like the simple soldier I am." He took a step forth, holding his gauntleted hands behind his back. "If you want independence, you should heed the call."

"We are Arcaners. Keepers of an oath. Protectors of the kingdom. We are *not* expansionists and warmongers and—"

"You dare imply your code is above ours? I am a knight of the king's Royal Guard! I live and breathe a code of honor that binds us as *men*! The plain fact is that our *kingdom* needs room to breathe, Captain. Historically we have only lost ground to other kingdoms, which through the millennia have seized upon precious opportunities to expand their reach. Now here we stand with just such an opportunity, and you three malingerers not only hesitate to act, but you outright *refuse* to do your duty to the kingdom's *children!*" He roared the last word, startling the young herald and making Sabby bare her teeth and growl.

Bridget also took a step forth to meet the man's gaze. "You are poisoning the minds of those who sit council to the king. It is men like *you* who send others to their deaths with little thought to the consequences. It is men like *you* who dare to talk about stealing other kingdom's lands to benefit our own!"

Commander Strout smirked. "Those other kingdoms have been doing just that for thousands of years. They will continue expanding while we shrink, stagnating and languishing and dying. One day, when you three are nothing but a children's story told around the hearth fire, one of those kingdoms will turn its gaze upon us, and Solia will cease to exist. Then, with their hands shackled as they toil in the mines, those children will turn to each other and lay blame—and they *will* blame you. Do you really want to be responsible for that inevitable day should you continue to prance about running …" He snorted derisively. "… mere errands?"

"How *dare* you—" But Bridget realized she ought to hold her tongue in present company, and instead snapped her fingers at the herald. "Don't write any of this down."

The girl, who had been scratching furiously away at her parchment, looked up, mouth opening and closing like a fish.

"Let her report my words in full," the commander said. "The people need to know that their so-called heroes are not doing the duty history has assigned them. Future generations are watching every move, and you are being judged, whether you know it or not. Hiding behind a code of honor is no excuse to shirk your duty. Strong kingdoms expand and prosper. Weak ones wither and die. It's that simple."

"Our *duty* is to follow the letter of the Arcaner code of honor—"

"Your first duty always and forever *will be* to the kingdom's interests!" the man roared so suddenly the herald yelped and dropped her quill.

Bridget flicked a finger, sending the quill back to the girl's hand, and raised her chin. "Following the code does exactly that."

"You are vassals to the crown, Captain. As with all the king's subjects, you will be at his beck and call and—"

"I will not suffer another imperious word on the matter," Bridget interrupted. "I care not for your warmongering opinion." She took yet another step forth so that they were almost nose to nose, though he was taller than her and seemed to enjoy glaring down at her with that disgusting smirk. "You do not know war like you think you do. The raw torment we can inflict. The death that could rain from the sky." She saw herself diving, the aura of Fear, inherent to her form, rolling across men and women like a tidal wave. "Masses of soldiers curling up into balls as they scream like children. And that was *before* we really hit them. And we can hit hard." The predator watched from behind the curtain, craving that feeling, urging her to bathe in it, to accept it.

The Sword of the Oak searched her green eyes with his pale ones before whispering, "Tell that to the kingdom's future children when another kingdom stomps on their skulls."

They glared at each other before Bridget stepped away. "Let us investigate this threat then."

"I think it best you leave that to the experts. Your arcaneologists. Unless you think them inept too."

"Then I am going to attend to my order."

"As long as it is within the walls of this here castle. Check the writ."

She withdrew the writ again.

"The fine quilling at the bottom."

" 'Strictly confined to the grounds of the Black Castle until further notice,' " Bridget read aloud in disbelief. It was signed, *His Royal Highness Rupert Edron Scovinius Southguard, King of the Sovereign Kingdom of Solia.*

"Like I said, Captain, this is a situation that directly threatens warlock-kind, and thus the power of the kingdom itself. You will obey the writ, which is *law*." He shifted his stance to the other foot. "Arcaners do obey the law ... do they not?"

Bridget felt her jaw tighten. "Of *course* Arcaners obey the law." She stuck her hands into her armpits, but in that moment the gesture felt defensive and so she unspooled them and made a show of shrugging. "You can stay and watch me train, then." She had been planning to perform her cycles—a cycle was one casting of each spell in one's arsenal—after supper like usual, but thought doing so now would at least release the anger.

"Whatever amuses you, Captain." The commander raised a gauntleted finger into the air and made a quick circle, barking, "Positions." The soldiers ran to take up places around the hall, with no less than four men by each door. The commander himself stood back to watch Bridget, studying her as if she were a specimen in a jar.

Bridget snarled and flicked a hand past the man's ear. The doors slammed shut behind him with a great *clang* that resounded around the hall. Then she took three paces back, gave Sabby a reassuring pat the dog well understood, and began by making a whipping-toward-the-ground gesture whilst animalistically roaring, "*Grau!*"

As if a cliffside were collapsing on top of them, an earthen rumble tore through the room, loud enough to shake the walls and have some paintings fall to the ground. The herald—and a few of the younger and more inexperienced soldiers—flinched, whilst the commander looked on, unimpressed. Sabby, long used to Bridget's cycles, merely curled up beside her.

"You were interested in spellcraft earlier," Bridget said to the girl. "That was a 2nd degree elemental spell, ancient name *Roragargantua*. But it goes by the common name of Slam. It can be effective as a scare tactic in battle, or as intimidation in any circumstance. Would you like me to detail the others?" Teaching gave her pleasure and eased the anger—not to mention it kept the predator at bay.

The girl's face lit up. "Oh, yes, *please*, Captain!"

Bridget paced to one of the fallen paintings, the gilt frame of which had cracked upon landing on the checkered floor. It showed an ebony-skinned old man with beard and hair and eyes aflame, a burning flail in one hand and a flaming shield in the other, all while wearing a burning robe. He stood in a dark space with only a checkered floor beneath him, a bonfire of a man surrounded by darkness.

Bridget kneeled before the painting, her academy- and field-trained thought process kicking in. *See in your mind's eye the crack closing, the two halves becoming one.* She opened her palms above the crack in a precise fashion and, readying to dip into her reservoir of arcane stamina, incanted, "*Apreyo.*" The crack sealed with a white light, the draw of stamina a quick and cool pull on her soul.

"Repair, 1st degree, standard, but I don't know its ancient name," Brittany said, nonetheless impressing Bridget. "I know about that one already because my uncle used to use it on my toys … when I was a kid, that is. You can't repair things that have been burnt, nor can you repair living things—that is for the healing element. It's also why we have so many old things around in the kingdom—you warlocks repair them." She nodded at the figure in the painting. "Who is that, anyway?"

"The spell's ancient name is *Repanestra Ado Apraya*. And this is Dragoon Trintus Bladeofbright, wearing his famous Frock of Perpetual Fire. He was a legendary Arcaner who partly inspired my brother-in-war to resurrect the Arcaner order."

Brittany noted this on her parchment. "And how long ago did he live?"

"A long, long time ago. He's an excellent teacher. We trained under him."

The girl ceased her quilling to look up. "Er … excuse me?"

"When we first met, you wanted to know how we resurrected the order." Bridget rose and flicked a finger, and the painting floated up to the spot it had been hanging. "The founders of the order, beginning with Isobel Roseheart, anticipated it possibly dying out. As a result, using arcanery lost to us now, they infused their souls into certain artifacts and places."

"So if I am understanding you correctly, Captain, anyone can summon them again to give lessons?"

"Not just anyone. One is tested if one has a true heart first. An Arcaner heart. Only then can the lessons commence, with more getting unlocked as one moves along in rank and knowledge." Bridget fondly recalled spending hundreds of hours with these ancient mentors in old classrooms and ancient fields and distant places, all conjured within arcane confines.

" 'Teachers … still teaching … eons later,' " the girl wrote.

After securing the painting back in place, Bridget nodded at the center of the high ceiling, where Trintus was depicted defending that very hall from a Canterran invasion. Surrounding him was a bevy of knights in gleaming armor. "That's him there."

The girl looked up. "History has a funny sense of humor."

"What do you mean?"

"Ordinaries defending a warlock Arcaner. Look familiar?"

The two women glanced about at the men, some of whom were openly leering at them, making Bridget feel distinctly uncomfortable. She wondered how those leers would change upon seeing her sprout wings and claws and rise up in height. She took pleasure in imagining their souls getting splashed by the invisible Fear aura that came naturally to that form, an aura straight from a wild jungle land of three suns …

"Their armor was shinier," the girl added. "And I suspect they were more chivalrous."

"Perhaps you ought to teach the girl about Arcaner corruption," The Sword of the Oak interrupted.

"An *exquisitely* rare occurrence at best," Bridget countered. "And hardly holds a candle to the common corruptions that have plagued the various knighthood orders—"

"Say it. Say Ordinary, Captain. Do not hide behind female coyness."

"I hardly hide behind—"

"Admit you think yourselves a higher race. You warlocks are all the same in the end. No matter your station amongst each other, you consider us *Ordinaries* beneath you. Because the gods granted you powers we mortals consider witchcraft, you think yourselves superior. But you're not, Captain. You're not. No more than the salamander who can run faster than the cricket can jump. Each has their strength."

"You know what? I changed my mind about cycles. I will examine the keep and make my *own* determination on what's going on." Bridget snatched Sabby's leash and strode to the doors, which opened for her after two flicks of the finger.

"Captain, I really think you ought to leave it to the experts."

"It's within the confines of the writ, Commander. And if I want your opinion on my comings and goings within those confines, I will ask for it." She whirled away from The Sword of the Oak and strode through the doors, holding her head nearly as high as Sabby. Brittany ran after her, and the soldiers soon marched behind in formation.

Like goslings waddling after mother goose, Bridget thought, finding the sight of a column of heavily armored soldiers and one cantankerous knight following her rather amusing.

THE DANCING GIRL

LEERA

With a loud *thwomp*, Leera appeared on a blustery terrace high in the night sky. She let go of the small chest from the shipwreck only to grab onto it telekinetically, making it float in place. Then she shook off the slight nausea that always came with a long Teleport and withdrew a pair of folded spectacles from her sodden robe pocket—she hadn't arcanely dried her robe as she'd needed the energy for Telekinesis and Teleport. She wound the wires around her ears, ignoring the water streaks and drops on the oval lenses, and glanced northwestward, toward the twinkling lights of Blackhaven, barely visible through the cloud banks and snow flurries.

She took a deep breath of the cold winter air and expelled a foggy plume, drawing comfort from the great view—and her clarity of vision. She wished the healers could fix eyesight, but that was knowledge beyond the currently known arts. The latest trends pressured circular lenses, but she preferred her original ovals, just as she preferred a certain cut of robe. All in all, she wasn't the most fashionable of women, with the heralds constantly teasing her about her frumpiness and lack of graces and all the other so-called vices that came with her rebellious soul. Besides, all that mattered was that her betrothed loved her and found her attractive, frumpy or not. Everyone else could shove it.

It was so peaceful here in the castle, mostly because it was invisible to the outside world—not to mention it sat atop Mount Barrow. Augum had teleported the castle to the top of the mountain during the last war for protection—and privacy. It was a power inherent to the nearly two-thousand-year-old structure, which shot up above her, its sharp minarets and balconies and windows surrounded by tarred stone.

A tinge of loneliness broke the peace, for she missed Augum, whose presence comforted her. He was her best friend and companion and lover and partner in war, and she worried terribly about him, just as he worried about her when they were apart for a quest or errand or whatnot.

"He's going to be fine. Stop worrying," she chided herself. But she was annoyed that they missed the winter Starfeast and Lover's Day, an old Solian tradition that was supposed to be a celebration of love. "Bah, it's all stupid anyway," she muttered, wanting to make excuses for his absence. "Now get out of these soggy clothes and have a peek at what you've found." She had kept one spell alive that kept her relatively warm. Wet clothes in winter were a death sentence for all but ice and water warlocks—at least the competent ones. Being a 10th degree and a child of war had its perks.

With the chest floating in tow, she strode around the terrace until she found a pair of doors, both of which were unlocked—the castle was only accessible to those given explicit arcane permission, so it was quite secure. She sang to herself as she paced the torchlit and checkered Prince and Princess floor. Every one of the seven floors of Castle Arinthian was named—Knight's Floor, Nobility Floor, King's and Queen's Floor, and so on.

" 'And she's a comin' and a castin' and a blastin'," Leera sang, twirling and miming slapping her wrists, her robe heavy and wet—she'd teleported before even emerging from the water, not bothering with the shore. That was because she'd seen young Arcaners looking for her, which was common. Someone always wanted something. An additional training session. A research opinion about some spell—she'd gotten good at interpreting old arcaneological texts, one of the few academic strengths she possessed—when she bothered to employ it. Or someone from the academy asking her to guest lecture a class again. Or her apprentice had come to beg for another cycle. She'd been avoiding the rather dour girl, mostly because the girl had a pessimistic outlook on life, not atypical of the ancient lineage she stemmed from.

"Probably another tedious errand," she muttered in between dancing and singing her way to her room, her own cozy space where she could take shelter whenever people bothered her—which was oft of late.

" 'The girl is a comin' and the boys are a frownin' and her finger is a waggin','" Leera sang as she burst in through her door, startling Sir Pawsalot, who had apparently been curled up sleeping by her pillow, watching the door, no doubt hearing her approach a league away.

Leera dumped the chest onto the floor—it was still leaking lake water, after all—gave the chubby tabby a scritch on the chin whilst wishing him

Happy Endyear, and sashayed her way past a giant oak canopy bedstead with twist columns, and over to a dead hearth. Although her room was located on the north and west corner of the castle, allowing for plenty of light—even in winter—to seep in through the many deep-ledged windows inset into the walls, she hadn't kept the fire going, and so it was a bit too cold for her comfort.

She slapped the rune on the mantel, incanting "*Igniato,*" and even as the flames leapt to life, she kicked off her shoes and socks and robe and undergarments, leaving them where they soppily landed, all the while singing, " 'No, no, she won't go! They try to take 'er but she's a snakin' coil! Of rope and soil! Of hope and toil! They try to grab hold but she's a cussin' an' a blastin'—' " Now naked, she smacked her wrists together a second time, miming blasting some fool apart with a jet of water.

She swept past an iron-banded trunk located at the foot of her bedstead and a rosewood triple-doored wardrobe, and stopped before a tall cheval mirror on a mahogany stand. She placed her hands on her wiggling hips.

" ''Cause she's a *w-o-m-a-n* and a *w-a-r-l-o-c-k* ...' " Her sodden raven hair flopped about, strands sticking to her freckled cheeks and shoulders. Not wanting to get her dry clothes wet, she dancingly pointed at her hair with the index finger of each hand and snapped, "*Evapa loa aqua.*" There was a blistering *thwoom* as her hair blew out in every direction.

Evaporate, a 4th degree off-the-books water element spell, usually took a lot longer to cast, but a castle washerwoman had taught her a surging trick that allowed the spell to dry things much faster—at the cost of a heavy and rapid infusion of stamina, which was felt as an icy draw on her soul.

A surge was considered wild arcanery and could be dangerous. Luckily Leera was well practiced and could control her arcanery better than most. The reservoir of arcane stamina naturally replenished anyway at a certain predictable rate that kicked in when one was not casting arcanery. Although the higher-degree spells drew a lot more stamina than the lower-degree ones, as long as one factored in the replenishment rate and did not step into overdraw, one could keep casting.

Whilst singing and dancing, she pointed at a boar-bristle brush lying on the floor beside an inside-out sock, shot it to her hand, and tamed her raven hair, which looked like she had barely survived a hurricane. After tossing the brush aside, letting it clatter onto a rarely used vanity desk overflowing with clutter, she appreciated her curves—the early twenties were kind to her feminine graces—but not so much the oval spectacles, which did indeed look a bit dated.

"Frumpy it is, baby," she sang, and danced her way to her triple wardrobe, from whence she flung out fresh linen undergarments and a clean crimson robe. Before any of them hit the ground, she pointed at each and tossed it back up, dancing and twirling within the telekinetically-kept-aloft rain of clothes.

" 'She dives deep under the keep under the stars and lives in war and strives for more but they want 'er yes they want 'er! Oh, but she's under water'—oof!" Amidst the spinning, she had dizzily crashed into the door of her wardrobe and fallen to the ground, her spectacles askew. A shirt and socks and a robe fell to the floor, with her underwear falling onto her face.

Head spinning, she snatched her underwear off her head, dragged them on, set her spectacles back to an even keel, and continued dressing. "What, as if you don't crash into things all the time, you little mouser," she muttered at Sir Pawsalot, who was notorious for zooming around the castle after taking a poo in one of his many sandpits, which the servants cleaned regularly. His response was to stare at her with that affronted look cats got after being woken from a peaceful nap.

"Catchy tavern tune, isn't it? Guess who it's about?" With her shirt and undergarments on, she jumped to her feet, pressing the fingers of both hands to her chest. "Bridget and my beloved and yours truuuuuuulyyyyy! There's only one thing missing—" She sashayed her way over, pulling the robe down over her head. When her head popped out the top, she tapped the tabby on the forehead and sang, "Yooouuuuuuu, my toothy little bumblebutt!"

Sir Pawsalot only grimaced.

She straightened. "Tough crowd. Well, the *people* wrote that song, so you can blame them. Yeah, yeah, I know it's weird for me to sing it, but I happen to like the melody. That all right with you? Besides, who cares about the words. Gods, why is everyone—even the damn cat—so serious all the time? You all got to learn to loosen up. Hourglass is too short to whine and worry day and night. Now let's see how I look."

She checked herself over in the mirror, grimacing immediately. "Dowdy as ever," she muttered, and smoothed down the single stitched golden band on the upper shoulder of her robe. Warlocks wore the same color across multiple degrees. The way those degrees were differentiated, at least in this kingdom, was with golden bands. A red robe on its own indicated 9th degree. A single golden band, which each of the trio wore, indicated 10th degree. Two golden bands indicated 11th, and three 12th. The 13th degree earned a whole new color robe—purple, and the bands started again at the 14th. Turquoise started at 17th degree and went to 19th.

The 20th was the only degree that wore white, with mastery earning an opalescent robe. Only necromancy wore the black robe.

She noticed Sir Pawsalot's eyes narrow. "Shut up with all that judging and come see what your momma's found."

She hauled Sir Pawsalot up, placed him on her shoulders, and hip-wiggled her way to the chest, humming the tune, for she had forgotten the rest of the lyrics anyhow. She wasn't graceful in anything except perhaps dancing. She could lure Augum with a single sashay, or sometimes a certain sly smile. They shared that sort of communication others longed for—the deep love of one another. The stuffy hens of the heralds could slag her all they wanted, but she had the man of her dreams.

"I mean I know I said I'd be patient and wait however long it took even if that meant like a decade and that we'd marry after graduation, but I can't help but wonder why we haven't at least settled on a date yet," she said to Sir Pawsalot. "I guess we both know why, don't we?"

Because I'm barren. The thought was like acid, difficult to even verbalize, so much so that only a precious few knew her secret. It had happened in the last war, a side effect of an ancient curse which no one alive could apparently undo.

The truth of the matter was that she almost didn't want Augum to take that final step of marriage, for it would mean accepting his ancient and famous lineage died with them. As deeply as she loved him, she did not know if she could burden him with that. And so sometimes she found herself saying spiteful and mean things to him just to push him away. To help him decide, one way or another. Bridget always told her she had a penchant for self-sabotage …

Despite all that, she couldn't help herself from fantasizing about wearing an ostentatious and completely over-the-top white princess gown and wearing a pine wreath and her man wearing a wreath and a grand ceremony filled with friends and mentors and more food than the entire kingdom needed …

"Maybe I should check on my man before we delve into this, eh?" She stepped to the center of the room to make space for a certain spell and flared her shield, made of densely packed watery pond leaves and emblazoned with the full golden Arcaner crest. Then she incanted, "*Summano vaultus Arcanus.*"

With a quiet *whoosh*, a floating three-paneled rectangular vault appeared before her, emitting a ghostly light. It had the height and depth of a medium-sized crate and was about three crates in width. Each of its three panels was emblazoned with the Arcaner crest, depicting a golden dragon sitting atop a golden castle above the golden motto *Semperis vorto honos.*

The crests differed slightly only in background color, for each represented one of the Arcaner order's secret-keepers—water-blue for Leera, lightning-blue for Augum, and earth-green for Bridget. Each crest was also surrounded by three dots in a triangular formation, the ancient symbol of the witch—in this case, it indicated the status of "secret-keeper."

Historically the Arcaner order always had three secret-keepers charged with protecting the vault and its contents, which included the ancient order's history and all its secrets. After the order had been dead for generations, the trio had resurrected it by becoming secret-keepers and used the knowledge within the vault to help win the war against Canterra. Like so much to do with arcane lore, it was a complexity amongst countless other complexities.

Leera sighed in relief upon seeing the middle crest lit as brightly as ever, for it indicated two things—her betrothed was alive, and his shield had not dimmed, meaning he had not dishonored himself.

An Arcaner's shield dimmed if they consciously broke any of the edicts of the Sacred Chivalric Code of the Arcaner. The first time the shield dimmed, the Arcaner's ability to cast Arcaner-specific spells, otherwise known as simuls, halved. The second time it dimmed, that power went down to a measly quarter-strength. One could only atone for these sins by going on a sacred Arcaner pilgrimage.

If, however, an Arcaner should transgress the code of honor whilst having a doubly dimmed shield, the Arcaner crest in their shield would snuff forever—along with the Arcaner's ability to cast simuls. Most important above all, one could only cast the mythical Spirit of the Dragon simul with a fully lit shield.

Leera glanced over at Sir Pawsalot, still on her shoulder, who slow-blinked at her before turning his head away sleepily. "Doesn't impress you anymore, huh? Fine, but *I* still think it's neat."

She walked up to the leftmost crest, which was her vault, found a small golden handle, and pulled the door open. Inside, crammed into every nook and cranny between three thin wooden shelves, were stacks of ancient parchments, flattened scrolls, and ancient tomes. Most of them detailed the history of the Arcaner order or were documents of the order's expenses. But the trio had also found rituals of the order, celebration ceremonies of all kinds, guidelines on how to host tournaments, and even instructions to ancient spells—though resurrecting those spells had thus far been a fruitless endeavor, as the mentors needed to teach them had long died. They had read letters to loved ones and strategies on how to conduct Arcaner warfare. These were the most treasured documents prior generations of secret-keepers had kept. It was because of the vault—and a book in Augum's possession titled *Codex Arcanera: From Birth to Death, a Life of Honor*—that the three young Arcaners had been able to resurrect the order into some semblance of its former glory—though obviously they still had a long way to go, for there was a lot to learn.

"Amazing that this is how the order survived the eons," Leera said, digging about on the right-hand side, where her vault joined Augum's. At last she found what she had been looking for—a folded piece of rough parchment. The vault only allowed parchment. Other than the shelves, wood, metal and stone were arcanely prevented from entering the vault, so for example one could not store so much as a pebble, let alone a sword.

Though there were some exceptions. For example, they had discovered they could hide the codex within the vault, as well as Isobel Roseheart's—the founder of the Arcaner order—tablet crest, which allowed them to train with the ghost of Isobel herself. Arcaners of old had been clever like that, allowing for certain necessary exceptions.

Leera opened the note, written in soot—not untypical for quests, as Augum sometimes skimped on small items to keep the weight of his rucksack down.

" 'All is well on this eve. Feet sore from trekking, but mountains are beautiful and the quiet is a nice change of pace. Miss and love you lots.' " She folded the note back up and smiled over at Sir Pawsalot. "All's well." The smile faded. "But he really ought to give more details, don't you think? Especially about when he'll be coming home." She dumped the note on her dresser alongside a slew of similar ones. Then she flicked a finger at her vault door, which slammed shut, before swiping at the air, muttering, "*Vaultus null.*" The vault vanished with another quiet *whoosh*.

Then she realized she had forgotten to send a note back. She would have said she loved him and that there would be oodles of cuddles when he got home, or something silly like that.

"Bah, he's a man grown. He'll be fine," she said, patting Sir Pawsalot's rump. "Don't worry. I won't get sad again. Not with goodies to open, eh?"

She plopped down before the chest into a cross-legged position, with Sir Pawsalot settling around her shoulders like a self-warming scarf. She pointed at the water that trickled toward her legs and had it veer away—one perk of being a water warlock was the ability to telekinetically manipulate water. At least, if one practiced doing it. As with anything in the arcane arts, only diligent study bore fruit. That was why the seeds of curiosity and perseverance had to be planted early and watered often, and why competent mentorship was so crucial.

Leera interlaced her hands, extended her arms, and reversed her hands, the stretching maneuver cracking her knuckles. "Think anyone else is around? Haylee? Jengo? Laud? Lys? Bridgey-poo?" Bridget hated that nickname. "Or should we keep this between us?" She turned her head so that she was cheek to cheek with Sir Pawsalot, who began to purr on her shoulders. She kissed his snout. "Agreed—let's be greedy for once."

She flapped her fingers in front of her to get the tension out before dangling them above the chest. It was wood, probably oak or mahogany—she wasn't as good with woods as Augum—and the lock had rusted through. The hands flopped to her lap.

"Hmm. Don't want to damage what's inside. Have to be delicate and all that." An only child of an ale taster mother and a rough-and-tumble but kind saddler, delicate wasn't a word people used in any way to describe her about anything. In her early youth, she had thought she would become a knight, or perhaps a blacksmith, so much so that her father had once gifted her a sword for her birthday. She had called it Careena, because it tended to careen into things. Augum had later dug up that sword from the ruins of her family home, along with Rumples, her childhood bear. He'd had multiple expert warlocks use multiple spells to permanently enchant the blade to be able to channel the First Offensive, before regifting it to her for her seventeenth birthday. Privately that very evening, he'd also given her Rumples back, melting her heart into a puddle.

She glanced over at Careena, resting upright against the stone wall, snug in its custom leather sheath. And there was a lump in the blanket where Rumples slept. Other than memories, they were the only two things left from her childhood, and all that remained of her parents besides grave markers in the ruins of a razed village in the middle of a forest.

That was something the three of them shared in common—they had been violently shoved into war at the tender age of fourteen. Aspirant warlocks barely fitting into their burgundy robes. And, in one form or another, all had lost their parents. The twist was that she ended up betrothed to the son of the man who had murdered her and Bridget's parents. Luckily Augum was nothing at all like his father, thoroughly repudiating everything the man had stood for, as evidenced by his resurrection of the Arcaner order—the very antithesis of evil.

"Fourteen feels like forever ago now, doesn't it?" Leera whispered, eyes distant as she remembered leaping flames and the smell of sulfur and fellow warlocks begging to live. Like so many other memories, the final battle still haunted her. "We were practically babes," she murmured. "Children playing grownup. Now look at us." She glanced around, that heavy feeling of loneliness making the castle feel cold. "Now look at us. Fresh graduates of the 10th degree. No more academy days except for private study and training. It's over." She thrust out her arms, singing, "A new life thus begiiiiins ..."

Only for those arms to fall limply by her side, for she felt she was being watched once more. The presence, born of three suns in an impossibly distant plane, particularly enjoyed making itself known in times of doubt and despair. How little people knew about the price the three of them had paid and continued to pay for the public's protection. How little they knew of the fantastical things the three of them had seen but could hardly share, for the stories sounded preposterous even with the most conservative retelling—including to fellow warlocks.

"Now look at us ..." she whispered, longing for the clouds. But the clouds would embolden the predator. The side effect was horrible, yet Arcaners of ancient times had survived it—not only that, but had thrived, with far more than just three being able to cast the dragon. So why couldn't she cope? Why couldn't she simply ignore the blasted shadow?

"Because it's inside you, that's why," she muttered, resetting her gaze onto the miniature chest. "Getting a tad distracted, aren't we?" she said, absently scratching Sir Pawsalot's chin, renewing his purring by her ear. "All right, I promise to focus here. First, let's see if it's got additional locks." She spread the fingers of a hand over the chest and, after harnessing her thoughts—every spell had a clear thought progression that had to be verbalized in precise measure with the gesture and incantation—she said, "*Un vun asperio aurum enchantus,*" the trigger phrase to the 11th degree Reveal, ancient name *Revenesta*.

To her surprise, the chest lit up with blue tendril weavings invisible to the eyes of Ordinaries and warlocks unable to cast the Reveal spell. The ethereal and thin spaghetti tendrils crisscrossed like a fine patchwork tapestry. They were enchanted in such a way that, if the chest were disturbed by human hands, the owner would get an alarm in their head.

"Object Alarm, 3rd degree, standard, ancient name *Conculadarmateya,*" she muttered, her academy training taking over. "Except there's no need to worry about the owner of this one, is there?" She imagined whatever remained of the captain, perhaps a loose bone somewhere amidst the silt of the lakebed, receiving an arcane *ping* upon her first touching the chest back at the shipwreck.

"Let's disenchant it anyway, shall we? For the sake of practice. 'One of the keys to greatness is review. Cleverness only gets you so far,' " she added, quoting Augum's famous great-grandmother, who had mentored them for a time before ascending to that mythical plane of Ley few believed existed. Widely considered the greatest warlock to have ever lived, Anna Atticus Stone had been a master lightning warlock, and also headmistress of the Academy of Arcane Arts—for an incredible thirty-five productive years. One of Leera's quiet prides in life was to have been one of her apprentices.

Sir Pawsalot's response was to stand up on her shoulders, stretch, then resettle so that he faced the now roaring hearth.

With Reveal still lit, Leera switched her mindset to the demands of the 10th degree Disenchant, which would allow her to meddle with the tendrils. It was a quirk of the craft that one learned how to Disenchant first. The predominant theory as to why was that it cultivated stronger warlocks. Another theory, more of a myth, said it was a massive clerical error during The Founding that resulted in a hanging.

Upon identifying the beginning tendril that would undo the tapestry, she incanted, "*Exotus mia enchantus duo dai ideum exat,*" and pinched at it with her fingers, snagging the tendril. A gentle but steady tug soon pulled the tendril free, and the entire tapestry undid itself, vanishing back into the sacred ether all arcanery stemmed from.

"Just like that," she said to Sir Pawsalot. "Hope you were paying attention because there'll be an exam later, you little scamp." She next tried to open the lid with her hands, but she might as well have been trying to pry apart a stone. Frustrated, she pointed at Careena and had it zoom over. With her other hand, she flicked at the sheath, which jettisoned—right into her soggy robe.

"Oops, don't want to wet the sheath, do we?" and she flicked two fingers apart, sending the sheath sliding away from the robe and the sodden robe tumbling away from the sheath. For a moment she stared at her wet clothes, strewn about like the detritus of an explosion, as if the girl who had been wearing them had been blown into bits. Sure, she could spend time meticulously drying each piece of clothing with the slower version of Evaporate that didn't blow through stamina. But then she might as well clean her room, which meant folding and sorting and putting things where they belonged and wiping surfaces and countless other tedious errands.

"Besides, there's treasure afoot!" she blurted to Sir Pawsalot, snatching Careena's tiny-chained hilt with her hand and jamming the steel tip into a small crevice. "I'll get to all that later." Maybe for once she'd let the servants touch her stuff.

When the chest kept slipping away like an eel, she jammed it up against the wall, pressed a foot into its base, and leveraged the blade with all her might. Sir Pawsalot, having grown annoyed by her exertions, leapt off her shoulders and went to sulk on the bed.

"Open, damn you!" Leera shouted at the stupid thing, which refused to reveal its secrets to her despite her angling the blade this way and that. Frustrated, she kicked the chest with her bare foot, stubbing her toe, and jumped up and down, holding her foot with one hand and Careena with the other, hissing, "Ow, ow, ow …"

After rubbing it better, she straightened. "Time to up the ante." The 8th degree Strength spell should do the trick. She aligned her thoughts and flexed every muscle in her body, incanting, *"Virtus vis viray."* Instantly she felt those muscles receive a bolstering that could see her win almost any arm-wrestling match against a muscled oaf. One of the beauties of the arcane arts was that it allowed men and women to stand on equal footing. It was why both sexes were called warlocks—out of respect.

She once again jammed the blade into the thin slit that separated the lid from the base, pressed a foot up against that base, and leveraged with all her arcanely amplified might. The lid squealed in protest before abruptly flipping upward, causing the blade to stab the interior—and sending Leera into the wall—*smack* went her head.

"Ugh, gods," Leera muttered, stumbling back and holding her forehead, letting Careena *clang* to the floor. She shuffled over to the mirror. "That's going to leave a mark," she muttered, rubbing the quickly emerging bump. "And a bruise. Going to look like a common tavern wench who got into a brawl." She narrowed her eyes at herself, imagining having never developed the arcane arts, as an Ordinary who had taken a different path in life.

"I could see you as a brawler, scrapping over petty insults," she said to her reflection. "Yanking hair in clumps and shoving it back in their stupid faces. *Wot is you lookin' at, you pasty-faced freak?*" She drawled in a crude tavern accent.

Chuckling at her antics, Leera returned to the chest—and found herself gaping at a bounty of golden crowns. She dropped to her knees before the plunder, feeling the peculiar heart-fluttering sensation of a girl realizing her dreams had come true.

But that girl had grown up, and now a young woman stared at treasure with adult eyes, treasure she thought only existed in children's tales.

Many of the coins were stuck together with rust that had bled from the iron strapping of the chest. She picked up one that had been pried loose by Careena and examined it. It showed the crowned head of a young man with an arrogant face. Stamped underneath were the words *King Ridian the First*, along with the year 3258.

"Eighty-eight years ago," she whispered. "In the time of none other than Anna Atticus Stone. She would have been ..." Leera's face scrunched as she did the arithmetic. "... twenty years old." She smiled down at the coin. "My age. Your head should have been on a coin such as this, Mrs. Stone. Sometimes I still can't believe you were our mentor. We miss you."

Leera sighed as she slipped the coin into a pocket as a memento and withdrew whole lumps of stuck-together coins from the chest, searching for spines or castles, but all she found was the gold of crowns. As she pawed through it, something else caught her eye, a piece of rotten linen, which fell apart at the slightest touch. She dug out the coins around it and, amidst the remains of that rotten linen, withdrew a ring. After wiping the mud off, she raised her spectacles to sit atop her head and held the ring aloft before her eyes, finding herself staring at a gold ring, the exterior of which was engraved with one continuous loop of storm-tossed waves. She flipped the ring and found an inscription in the interior.

" '*Monstrosi del o duva, monstrosi infenatti*,' " she whispered. " '*Defenda, defenda, defenda*.' " She lowered the ring to stare at the wall, as if seeing a glimpse of something distant behind it, and whispered the translation. " 'Monsters in the deep, monsters beyond. Defend, defend, defend.' "

She turned to Sir Pawsalot. "What do you make of that?"

Sir Pawsalot only slow-blinked at her, looked away, and curled into a ball near the lump that hid Rumples.

She pointed at him. "This ain't no time for a nap, mister. We're going to celebrate." The arm dropped. "All right, maybe not we, but *I* certainly am."

She returned her attention to the ring. "Sick and tired of the tedium anyway," she added in a mutter, turning the ring about in her hand, before starting. "Oh, right, maybe we should examine it, eh?" She ignored how she had so casually broken a cardinal rule for all objects of an unknown nature, and almost imagined the scolding she would have received from their mentor Jez, or even from her old mentor Anna

Atticus Stone. She imagined a deepening frown, for she seemed to be perpetually adept at letting her mentors down with the small stuff.

"But not the stuff that matters," she said with a lofty wag of the head, bringing the ring to her vanity, only to veer away upon seeing how messy it was. Instead, she pointed at a massive crimson leather-bound tome jammed into an overflowing bookshelf, yanked it free, floated it over, and dumped it on the floor before the hearth with a resounding *smack*. Then she sat cross-legged before the blood-red tome and set the ring on top of the golden-worded title of *Advanced Arcanery for the Element of Water, 10th degree, 719th Edition*.

It was one of the myriad books she had absorbed like a sponge in her final year at the academy, proving herself more than capable of understanding deep arcaneological nuance—more than one critic had predicted that she would have long hit her ceiling. Instead, she had taken petty pleasure in watching her jealous harpy detractors hit their ceilings in degrees prior.

"I got my man, *and* I got my 10th," she sang, nudging her spectacles, which had drifted within view, back on top of her head. "Ten more to go to mastery," she added. That would take a lifetime, of course. If she survived that long. "One thing at a time, lass," she drawled in a seaside accent, and spread her fingers, incanting, "*Un vun asperio aurum enchantus.*"

The ring lit up with a miasma of tightly woven tendrils in spectrums of blue, forming an intricate ballet of complexity. "Well, well, well, what do we have here, kids?" It was the same question she asked her class whenever she showed them something she found interesting. All warlocks were expected to volunteer at least ten percent of their time to better their community or kingdom. Within warlock culture, this was known as *proata mentora*, and it was essential in not only rearing good warlocks, but keeping positive relations with Ordinaries, who historically tended to conflate warlocks with witches, subsequently tossing them on top of leaping pyres.

As part of that *proata mentora*, the trio had taken to passing on some of their knowledge as assistants to arcanists. But whereas Augum and Bridget had taken under their wings multiple such classes, Leera had only taken one—and within her own element, no less, for she did not feel comfortable as a leader any more than she felt comfortable being a captain in the order, with all the expectations that came with that position.

"We need us a certain looking glass," she muttered, finding the tendril weavings far too small for her clumsy eyes. She stood, flicked her head forward so that the spectacles slipped back onto her nose, and searched about for the expensive piece of Ohmish workmanship that had to be here somewhere. After some rummaging about, creating a greater mess in the process, she spotted a rosewood handle wedged between the pages of another crimson tome titled, *An Arcaneological Treatise on Runes and Runic Understanding, 10th degree, 355th edition.* With a quick flick of the hand, the handle yanked free, revealing itself attached to a round lens captured by a bronze hoop edged with verdigris buildup.

"Arm and a leg is what the magnifying glass cost me," she muttered. "And just what were you implying with that question you little—" She looked back at Sir Pawsalot, but found him snoozing. "Only thing *you* find exciting is chasing the little furry denizens of the castle, which if I may remind you, Bridget thinks you ought to leave well enough alone." She pressed a hand to her chest, whispering, "But between you and me, you have my permission to hunt them to your heart's content. At least the rats. The mice you can spare as they're adorable. Fine, ignore me all you want, but we'll talk again come food time," and she flicked at her spectacles, which trawled up her head to settle on her hair, and brought the magnifying glass over the ring.

Not every warlock could hold a conversation whilst keeping a spell like Reveal lit. Leera, on the other hand, could chat whilst keeping multiple spells up, a feat that sometimes made lower degrees gape in awe and lose track of what she was yammering on about. It was the same with Augum and Bridget—the war-honed trio were adept at complexities others struggled with.

"Look at that, another Object Alarm enchantment," she muttered, the ring now the size of the glass itself. "And look there, an Object Track too." *Standard, 3rd degree, ancient name Obiektatrakanastra,* her academy-trained mind thought. "Too bad the captain's a pile of silty mulch," she added with a chuckle. "Probably now petrified excrement on the lakebed. All right, the shipwreck ain't that old, but still. Fun thought, isn't it?" After checking on Sir Pawsalot, she smacked her lips, annoyed he wasn't paying attention to her.

"Oh, but there's more here. Whoa, what's that?" An underlying tendril web laced the entire bottom of the pile of weaving. "There's a second tapestry underneath," she muttered, squinting as she moved the magnifying glass slightly farther away while moving her eye closer to enlarge the magnification. "Never seen it before. Will take time to identify the weavings." It could take months. Usually, one hired an arcaneologist that specialized in tendril identification, but she deeply enjoyed—and took quiet pride in—solving complex arcaneological riddles others thought her too dim to solve.

What perhaps interested her most was the slight dulling of the colorings, and a flat cementation of the weaving as a whole, all of which indicated one thing. "It's ancient," she muttered. "Long sunk to permanence. Couldn't undo it if I tried."

An enchantment could be disenchanted—unless the enchantment had sunk to permanence. The thing was, it took at least one to two *hundred* years for that to happen—assuming it had been a perfect casting. An even slightly imperfect casting—a stray thought, a syllabic mispronunciation, a gestural imprecision—would see the enchantment fade over time, usually quickly too. Perfect castings were few and far between, and most often only done by masters, who were exquisitely rare.

She put down the magnifying glass and appreciated the ring in her palm. The gold was exquisite, if not a tad dull and scratched. A gold ring made her think of something else, however.

"What would it feel like?" she whispered. Seeing as the captain was dead and the signal would ping dust, she slipped the ring on her wedding finger so that it nudged up against the silver betrothal ring shaped into pine needles. Hearing the blare of triumphant trumpets, she held the hand before her and, in a nasal tone, said, "May I now introduce the stunningly beautiful *Mrs.* Leera Matilda Jones Arinthian, and with her is her stunningly handsome husband *Mr.* Augum Stone Arinthian." Together they had decided both would keep their original surnames, but also resurrect and add to his lineage's ancient name, which deserved its place.

With a sigh, she dropped her hand into her lap and idly fiddled with the ring, her raven hair falling around her face like a curtain lowering itself upon the conclusion of a play. "Because that's about all the lineage is going to get from this worthless sack of a girl," she mumbled, tears welling at the corners of her eyes. None could know the deep hurt of letting a two-thousand-year-old lineage die, and few could know what it felt like to want children and not be able to have them, especially seeing as they were one of the kingdom's darling couples. And no amount of telling herself that Bridget would bear enough kids for the two of them remotely dulled the exquisite pain of knowing that she was as barren as a Sierran desert.

Women threw themselves at Augum all the time, especially those awful pasty-faced vultures of the royal court who saw him as a trophy. Men, on the other hand, found her intimidating on account of what she was capable of—to say the least. Should the worst come to pass, she did not think she would survive a breakup. That thought alone made her fantasize about swimming into an ocean and never returning …

Leera felt something rub up against her, reached behind to capture Sir Pawsalot, brought him into her lap, and rubbed his belly and ears and chin, causing him to purr up a storm. "Maybe I should let him go and just become a cat lady in some hole in the wall," she muttered, tears dropping onto his belly.

She wiped them away, mumbling an apology, and canoodled with him for a time, appreciating him for always seeming to know when she was in emotional distress, which was more often of late, seeing as she was a free woman now, a post-graduate of the esteemed Academy of Arcane Arts. Gone were the rigors of the academy, its daily schedules, its meetings and assemblies and traditions, all replaced by the wretched dullness of a lack of self-motivation.

But she was more than a mere graduate, and her eyes went to her golden breastplate, the heart of which was engraved with a dragon standing before a copse of trees. Surrounding it was the motto *Defendi au o dominia*—Defender of the kingdom. It was made from none other than Dreadnought steel, forged by a now-extinct race of the same name. A race that had forged a breastplate for each of the trio as a reward for their actions in the Legion war. Now only legends remained of that race, along with what they had forged—weapons and armors and artifacts rarer than the most precious gems.

The stories behind the trio's breastplates could make for quite the campfire tale. Leera's breastplate, however, was damaged. An enormous gash ran diagonally across it, one she had sustained in Endraga Ra, proving that even Dreadnought steel could be harmed—if only by the might of a certain kind of winged beast.

That gash mesmerized Leera. She closed her eyes and tilted her head ceiling-ward, seeing three hot suns in the sky, barely cognizant that Sir Pawsalot growled at her and shot away. She raised her arms and gave them one graceful flap, keeping them spread as she glided silently above a lush jungle filled with vicious beasts. Upon spotting a juicy one with a long neck, she brought those arms closer so she could dive. But before the kill could come, she sensed the shadow peeking into her mind, and she saw the soon-to-be-slaughtered through its eyes.

She shook off the vision, and not without some trouble yanked the ring off her finger. "You're right. This ain't no time for fancies," she said, shooting to her feet, wondering where Sir Pawsalot had gone. She pointed at one of the old crowns, flicking it to her palm, threw her sodden robe overtop the chest to hide it, and whirled to face Sir Pawsalot, who she had spotted taking shelter behind her pillow.

"I found treasure, and I am going to celebrate. And I know just the place," and whilst slipping the ring into a pocket, she strode through the door, flicking it closed behind her, leaving her sodden clothes where they lay and ignoring the real reason she was going to find a tavern—to strangle the gut-churning feeling that she might end up a lonely and unloved spinster.

INTO BLUE ICE
AND BLACK ROCK

❧──────────────────────❧

AUGUM

Augum trudged along in the deep snow, careful to step into the crimson robe's footprints so as to expend as little energy as possible. His hands were manacled before him, but at least the brigands had allowed him to wear his mitts; otherwise, his hands would have been solid blocks of ice by now. Ominously, the crimson-robe had jested that he wouldn't be needing those hands much longer anyway.

The three panting men trekked along a thin path that wound around a steep mountain, with a thousand-foot drop yawning below. Above, a knife moon dangled amidst a black sky full of twinkling stars. Here and there one fell, leaving behind a hairline streak that vanished in the blink of an eye. Folks called it a starfall, or a star shower. The custom was to make a wish. Augum wished to lay eyes on his beloved again. He had already missed the winter Starfeast and now Lover's Day with her. He did not want to miss any more important dates.

Then stop taking such foolhardy risks, he thought, though knew that it was a big ask considering his nature.

Well to the south was the thick cloud bank of the blizzard, obscuring the mountains and the town of Sinew they had left behind. Like a relentless army in pursuit, the blizzard steadily marched after them. Already a cold wind had sprung up, forcing Augum to bundle up within his coat as best he could.

The crimson-robe would periodically stop to withdraw an extendable spyglass—an expensive piece of Ohmish engineering—and use it to search the mountain, though refused to share what he was searching for.

As Augum slogged through the deep snow, breath pluming in the crispy frost, he considered permutations of attack. He could clobber the crimson-robe on the back of the head with the manacles, then kick the bearded Lanfred in the stomach and tackle him, slapping a hand over his mouth to prevent spell casting. But that was about as far as he'd got, for even assuming he could knock the crimson-robe out with one blow, which was always easier said than done, Lanfred carried a dagger on his person, which, being manacled, Augum could not reach whilst simultaneously covering the man's mouth. That and he was weak from hunger.

He'd thought of shoving the crimson-robe off the path, but the man could likely battle 'port his way back before hitting the ground a thousand feet below. He thought of going for the knife first and putting it to Lanfred's throat as a hostage, but something about the crimson-robe told him he would not hesitate to let the man die.

Even *if* he were successful in any such brazen maneuvers, that still would not lead him to the apprentices, nor did it solve a fundamental conundrum: without the ability to free the manacles himself, he would be stuck in a frozen hellscape, unable to teleport, defenseless against beasts of prey like mirko and wolves and bears. The only chance he had was the moment the crimson-robe retrieved his priceless manacles.

The thing was, would that happen before or after they did to him what they had done to the apprentices? Were they even alive? Had this been a fool's errand from the get-go? A quest he had assigned himself that would do him in for his arrogant need to be tested?

What interested Augum was that they were climbing, not descending. He wanted to ask why they simply didn't teleport there, but figured being meek was the better course for the outcome he sought. The entire ordeal would rest on a single moment of weakness. The question was, would it be his weakness that got exploited, or theirs? His iron will and the predator within him demanded it be theirs. But the young man who feared he had overstepped, who worried about what his betrothed would think and feel were he not to return to her arms, cast doubt into the fray.

You cannot allow yourself doubt, he told himself. *You must survive. For her … and for the kingdom.*

The sky beckoned. Even here, in the deepest north, with a black sky above, he sensed three suns. He could feel their warmth on his wings, smell the jungle, and taste the iron tang of blood on his long tongue. What power he could bring to any fray! An apex predator among predators …

Yet here he was, having allowed himself to become the prey.

The shadow within him stirred, anxious for the violence it knew awaited them all. *You are a lure, nothing more*, he told himself. *They will learn the harsh truth of who you are when it is far too late for them. They will pay for their crimes with their blood.*

The quest was to bring them in for justice, but that was assuming they bent the knee in surrender. The code allowed harsh retribution on behalf of the wronged should that not happen. In fact, he hoped not to have to accept a bent knee, for that would not satisfy the shadow's lust for blood.

Stop it, he chided himself, one foot plodding before the other. *Stop giving in to the callousness. You've been trained better than that.* The training was ancient. Old teachers of the order brought back to life as illusions, their essence distilled and even expanded upon over the eons using ancient arcanery long lost to living souls. But that training remained unfinished, and would likely take a lifetime to master.

The crimson-robe halted. Augum looked past him and saw that the path had ended. Above was another two thousand feet of steeper mountain, covered only in blank snow cracked by the occasional spar of black rock. Already the air was thin and tough to inhale, its iciness freezing the nostrils and crusting eyelashes with ice. So what remained above?

"Are they watching us?" the bearded Lanfred asked, his whisper battling the wind to reach the crimson-robe.

"Always," the crimson-robe replied, searching the mountain with those pitiless eyes.

"Aren't you going to splay a hand?"

"It would send the wrong signal. Besides, I am not adept enough to see what they obscure."

Augum looked about for any signs of not just life, but evidence of anything built or shaped in any way, but there was not a single shred of such a thing. The mountain stood as innocuous as a mountain could, one of countless behemoths that made up the Northern Peaks.

"What now?" Lanfred whispered.

"We wait."

"For what?"

"For them to receive us."

"Yeah, but, why do we have to wait at all?"

"Because they want to see if we are being tracked."

"But we *were* being tracked—"

"And we took care of those," growled a voice from the snow, startling all three men and making them take a tepid step away, toward the yawning void.

Augum could not help his heart from thudding down his body and settling somewhere in a boot. His tracking party had been attacked, perhaps even slaughtered. His dear friends, his mentor, possibly murdered. He desperately wished he could communicate with those who could send aid—his betrothed, and his sister-in-war.

In the mean, he could not show even a hint of emotion. It had to seem coincidental to the villains that he was being tracked.

"Those warlocks tracking us?" the crimson-robe asked.

"We chased them off," the growling voice said from within the snow. "But the lowlanders trek on."

Augum had to hold his breath lest he let a sigh escape his lips. But he also shivered, for the word *lowlanders* had revealed who he was dealing with. A callous people of the north, a people not like people at all ...

The crimson-robe grabbed Augum by the scruff and sharply presented him. "We come bearing one."

"You promised four this time."

"They are getting suspicious, as you saw. It is getting too dangerous. They treasure their apprentices too highly these days not to pursue offenders—even this far north. This one stumbled into our lap."

For a time, there was only the sound of a blustering wind, steadily increasing in strength, until the snow rose ahead, revealing white fur, and then a bulky figure no less than twelve feet tall. But it was no man, rather an earless wolf standing on hind legs.

A wolven.

Ordinary Solians, when not relegating their existence to tall fireside tales, sometimes called them wolf people, which made others think of them as people who dressed in wolf-hide. But they were much more than that. Augum had met one when he was fourteen, a scout who had been as callous toward him as his shadow was to others. A beast who cared little for life and everything about honor. A creature that took great insult to being called a dog or troll—or earless if they were male, for their ears were small and hidden amidst their fur.

This wolven was naked in its fur except for a thick, roughly hewn golden chain around his neck with a black-claw pendant, as well as a single rope that ran diagonally across his big chest, connecting with a rucksack slung on his back. He also had an interesting brand over his heart—a large burnt-in X.

The wolven placed his wolfish gaze on Augum and bared his teeth. Augum took one look down at himself and realized he was wearing wolf-hide. He might as well have been wearing a scalp.

"This one will be a pleasure," the wolven growled.

Augum, knowing the brutality of the wolven, couldn't help raising his chin in defiance.

The crimson-robe yanked Augum back. "Payment first."

"You ugly lowlanders never cease to offend with your rudeness." He shrugged off his rucksack, never taking his wolf eyes off the three of them, and used a big mitt of a paw to withdraw a leather pouch full of coins. Their paws had padded fingers, above which extended long and deadly black claws that were kept retracted until needed for climbing or eviscerating.

"We need the manacles back too," the crimson-robe said, turning to Augum. "And you should be wary. This one has hard eyes."

Augum, trying to avoid that gaze, silently cursed himself for not doing a better job of appearing meek.

"How much do you want for the manacles?" the wolven pressed.

"They are not for sale."

The wolven cocked his head. "You ought to reconsider, lowlander."

"Now who is being rude, *high*lander?"

Augum felt the crimson-robe tense, and instead of undoing his manacles, the man stepped behind him, as if sensing a trap. "These are worth more than you can afford to pay, highlander," the man said.

"I think you ought to gift those manacles to us as a token of your appreciation."

Lanfred nervously glanced about. "What's happenin' 'ere, boss?"

"Shut *up*," the crimson-robe hissed.

Augum noticed several other bulges subtly rise in the snow around them. He could warn the two brigands that their worthless lives were in mortal peril. But The Fates, whose laughter he had heard mocking him, now turned their laughter upon them, for the shadow within him craved their blood.

"If you even *think* about crossing us—" The crimson-robe abruptly gasped.

Augum whirled about to see that the man's head had snapped back and his feet were off the ground. A wolven had silently risen behind the wanted brigand, plunged a clawed paw into his back, and lifted him with that paw. The man convulsed, his spine skewered, while still other mounds rose around them. Lanfred, seeing the feet dangle and twitch beneath his boss, screamed a rather high-pitched shriek for a man of such size and bearing.

Meanwhile, a third wolven, a female for she had prominent ears, stepped forth to take the crimson-robe's arm. She held it out, placed a large vial underneath his wrist, and sliced the bottom of that wrist with a claw.

As Lanfred screamed and screamed, unable to find the wherewithal to teleport away, Augum realized what use they were making of warlocks. *They're draining us*, he thought, unable to help from inhaling a shuddering breath. Even with the predator peering through his eyes, it was a cold fate.

Interestingly, the other visible wolven also had a branded X over their hearts. Was it a clan or pack symbol? Augum resolved to find out.

A second eared wolven snatched Lanfred's throat, instantly quieting him. The man became a wide-eyed possum, soul gripped in a vise of fear. The wolven bent the man forward, and he obeyed as if he were hoping that all would be well as long as he did not move a muscle. The first wolven stepped forth, withdrawing two pieces of cloth from his rucksack. He jammed one in Lanfred's mouth and tied the other around that cloth, preventing him from uttering an incantation. The eared wolven then tied his hands tightly behind his back. When she let go, he remained in that bent-over position, as if he were sitting in a chair sideways.

Augum returned his attention to the crimson-robe, and watched as the wolven that had hung him on his claws flipped the man over like a rag doll, grabbed his legs with one paw, and held him upside down. Like an Endyear turkey, they drained him of his blood then and there, stoppering the vial once it was full and replacing it with another. They even squeezed his arms and legs to milk every drop. Only when the man was as white as the snow did Lanfred seem to wake from his torpor, and started howling into his gag, though still in that forward pose.

Augum looked the crimson-robed murderer square in his dead face and murmured under his breath, "May your soul find the peace together we could not reach."

The lead wolven, the largest of them all at his twelve feet height, made two grunting growls, and Lanfred was picked up and thrown over a wolven shoulder like a sack of spuds. The same was done with the lifeless crimson-robe—and then Augum, who felt himself abruptly snatched and tossed over a shoulder.

The wolven growled at each other in what sounded like harsh tones, but most certainly was their language. Augum, were he able to cast the 12th degree Tongues in that moment, which he had spent all year learning, would still struggle mightily, for Wolven was so removed from any human tongue.

The wolven carried them up the slope, breaking the pristine snow. But when Augum lifted his head, he saw one of the wolven trailing behind to gracefully wave her arms about, arcanely smoothing the snow after them. This confused him, for the lone wolven scout he had met years prior had said wolven only had three innate talents involving breath, armor, and sword. It now occurred to him that the scout might have been protecting the secrets of his kind.

Augum knew some other things about the wolven—they were a barter people, rarely doing something without expecting something in return. They were taught the common tongue of lowlanders from cubhood so they could take advantage of them when encountered. He knew that an old pact from some old war kept the wolven apart from humans of the southern kingdoms so that they hardly knew much about each other. And he also knew that they believed that a god had gifted them thought as a reward for saving that god's offspring from human folly.

Composed mostly of guesswork and theory and sensational stories meant to sell copies of the scrolls, the texts about wolven were about as accurate as country superstitions were about warlocks. Arcaneologists and explorers who queried wolven directly oft did not survive those queries. Only Ohmish monks and the Henawa, the milk-skinned people of the north that sometimes traveled south with the snows, seemed to have earned any semblance of respect from them, but even they held their tongues, surely knowing how stone-dwelling city folks oft exploited such knowledge for personal gain—to the detriment of everyone who traded with the wolf people.

The wolven, lumbering along a steeper and steeper incline that required them to use their claws for purchase, eventually stopped before a vertical wall of ice. After checking downslope that all was clear, the leader blew on the ice—but it was not a plume of ice that came forth, but of fire.

Unnameables, they have elements too, Augum thought, astounded by his own ignorance—and the wolven ability to keep such things secret.

They stepped inside a dark cave of pure ice, and the last wolven—the female who had smoothed the snow—replaced the wall by blowing ethereal green leaves that quickly vanished, leaving ice behind. Augum watched all this with keen interest, for he was learning much about the wolven he did not know. Myriad questions stirred on his tongue, yet he knew it would serve him best to hold that tongue, at least in the interim. For there was one other thing about the wolven Augum knew—they thought lowlanders so beneath them that they allowed arrogance a foothold into their thinking, which led to underestimation, something Augum resolved to exploit. The challenge was timing that exploitation.

The lead wolven summoned a longsword made of fire that licked a central molten blade with a quiet *whoosh*, lighting the way for the others. Two wolven stayed behind as guards. The ice cave soon gave way to solid rock, and descended some ways before opening into a gargantuan cavern lit by giant iron braziers that also kept the cave toasty warm. The cavern was abuzz with activity of other wolven.

Several carved what appeared to be pieces of oversized furniture out of solid rock. Others carved tools out of wood. Others still cooked in an area designated for cooking, and others pondered over human weapons laid out on a giant granite table carved out of the mountain itself. Scaling the wall were large and dark holes — other rooms — where there could be seen the outline of sleeping wolven, oft curled up like dogs. The place smelled strongly like a kennel, with the additional scents of roasting lamb and burning whale oil and cedar. Few of the wolven so much as raised their snouts in interest upon their entrance. Everything was oversized, from the chairs to the tables to the cookware, for the wolven themselves were oversized, ranging from eight feet to twelve.

No cubs, Augum noted. And every single one had that branded *X* over the heart.

The captors dumped the crimson-robe onto a slab in the kitchen, beside which a large cauldron was already boiling away above a roaring fire. Seeing this, Lanfred began screaming into his gag anew. This seemed to annoy one of the female wolven, who slapped him upside the head with a paw whilst growling a warning. He squeaked and settled on a whimpering whine instead.

They carried Augum and Lanfred to another area lined with shelves carved out of the rock. On each shelf stood countless vials and jars and containers, oft sandwiched between fat tomes, the leather of which were worn and torn from use. Hanging on the walls around the shelving were variously sized copper spoons and serrated knives and long-pronged forks, the skewering sort. Iron-banded casks stood in neat rows underneath the shelves.

Augum and Lanfred were dumped onto a rough table of gray rock, and were made to sit on it like children, with their legs dangling over its thick lip. Above them hung several chains, an iron hook on the end of each. The gray rock of the table was stained with still-sticky coats of browned blood, which strengthened Lanfred's whimpering, his hands now trembling uncontrollably. Were Augum fourteen again, as he had been upon the arcane art waking within him in what was known as *the blossoming*, he would have been a blubbering mess himself. But the scent and sight of blood instead awakened a certain shadow that peered through his eyes, craving the violence of battle.

You stay put and shut up, Augum snapped at his own mind. *We need to be careful here. Very careful.*

The leader, who had snuffed his flaming sword, snapped out a growl. One of the younger males retrieved a finely carved rosewood box from one of the shelves. He brought this box before the leader and opened the lid with some reverence. The wolven being so tall, Augum could not see the contents of that box, though saw gold reflect on the leader's furry face.

The leader reached into the box, but it was not golden crowns he withdrew, but rather a pair of golden manacles. He dangled these manacles on a single black claw, which were accepted by one of his cohorts. That wolven then placed the manacles on Lanfred's wrists before ungagging him.

"Why were you followed?" the leader growled.

"I-I-I d-d-don't know I guess b-b-because we, uh, we—"

"Useless lowlander, stop your blubbering and speak clearly—and I mean *clearly*, not that lazy drawl. I have little patience on this day."

"Honestly, sir wolven sir—"

"Do not debase me with your cheap titles. Speak and speak plain lest my patience expire, you dishonorable cur."

Lanfred, breathing as quickly as a mouse and beard trembling, swallowed heavily. "I think it's because of the apprentices we've been kidnapping, sir," he said, overly enunciating every word. "We think the kingdom sent Arcaners after us, and they are a relentless bunch."

"Arcaners? What are they? I know little of them."

"They are the knights of our warlock kind. They have themselves a code of honor."

The wolven chortled in a growling manner, exchanging amused looks.

"What do lowlanders know of honor?" one asked.

"Less than the youngest Henawa babe," said another.

The leader was the only one unamused, growling, "Speak on."

"They're an old order that was newly resurrected. And they have powers not seen in generations."

"What sort of powers?"

"They can cast something called simuls."

"And what are these ... *simuls*?" The word was said in distaste, as if the leader despised not knowing something.

Lanfred squinted and his face scrunched this way and that, as if he were summoning all his smarts. His reply was slow. "They are the combination of multiple spells fused into one incantation, meaning they are cast as one spell."

The wolven exchanged looks Augum could not discern.

"What else?" the leader pressed, casually adjusting the thick golden chain around his neck and its black-claw pendant.

"By swearing on their shield when answering a question, which dims if they lie, they can prove they are telling the truth."

This made the wolven exchange looks yet again.

"That is most interesting," one said.

"There's something else. The reason you ought to fear them most."

"Spit it out, cur."

Lanfred lowered his voice to a whisper. "Three of them can turn into *dragons*."

Most of the wolven chortled, replying overtop of each other.

"But that is a myth—"

"Elaborate illusions crafted by crafty lowlanders—"

"Ploys of war—"

"Silence!" barked the leader, instantly quieting them. "I have seen these dragons myself," he growled, staring each one down. "I have seen all three fly by the spires. Together they played and tussled in the sky. And for this I was called a—" He growled a word in wolven. "—by my *own* pack!"

"You did not mention this before," one of the others said.

Like a wolf sensing a coming intruder, the leader puffed out his chest and growled menacingly. After staring him in the eyes, the other wolven looked away.

"That is what I thought," the leader snapped, and returned his attention to Lanfred. "Tell it to me true, lowlander. Are these dragons real? Have you seen them frolic with your own eyes?"

Lanfred hesitated.

"Speak true and speak quick, lest I skewer that tongue and boil it with mint and sage."

"I don't know! I have not seen them with my own eyes, but I have heard stories. Many stories. They have not been spotted in some time. And many of us think they were indeed apparitions and illusions summoned for the war."

"The war against your own kind?" one interjected.

"We have inter-kingdom wars. Do … do you have that?" Lanfred attempted a nervous smile. "Like we do?"

"We do not have loose tongues like you lowlanders do, but our packs do battle like yours." The leader turned his attention to Augum. "And this cub that you brought—"

"I am not a cub," Augum retorted, deciding the time had come for him to speak for himself. "In our kingdom, we become men and women grown at the age of sixteen."

"Judging by the color of your robe, you are insignificant and know nothing."

"Judging by the color of my robe," Augum echoed.

The leader tilted his head slightly. "I do not understand."

Augum stared at him unwaveringly, wanting to see what silence would yield.

"The red was right," said one of the wolven.

"He has hard eyes for a cub," said another.

"He ain't like the others," said a third.

"What happened to the others?" Augum pressed. "The ones these—" He looked to Lanfred and scowled. "—traitorous scum sold to you?"

"He wants to know," one mused.

The leader smiled a wolfish smile. "Show him."

A wolven went to a shelf, withdrew two large vials of crimson liquid, and brought them forth.

Lanfred began to pant in fear again.

Augum's stomach sank as he stared at the vials. "Their families will weep," he whispered, thinking of those poor parents down on their knees, begging for the return of their children.

"They make water with their eyes because they are weak," the leader replied.

"Compassion is not weakness. It is a strength." Augum noticed that little flecks of gold floated within the vials. The realization was stark. *They're making potions from our blood.*

"He does not speak like a cub," one remarked.

"No, he does not."

"What will happen to me?" Lanfred squeaked.

The wolven who had been holding the vials jiggled them before Lanfred's face, and the man whimpered before blubbering a cry like a toddler.

Augum, eyeing the vials, absently said, "No less a death than you deserve, brigand."

Lanfred looked at him, his whimpering strengthening, before he abruptly sat up like an eager child, blurting, "The incantation to the manacles ... I can trade it to you! Your kind barters, I know that much. Allow me to barter for my life."

The leader grabbed Augum's manacles, turned them over to inspect the runes, let go with a spiteful jerk, and growled out the unlocking incantation.

The color drained from Lanfred's face.

"We are taught your silly tongue from birth," the leader said. "And we study your runecraft and use it to our advantage."

"You are as loose with your books as you are with your tongues," another chimed in.

"Gods, please, there's got to be something I can offer you ..."

"Oh, there is, lowlander. There is." The leader nodded at the wolven standing behind Lanfred, who then took a hook from above and dipped it underneath the manacles.

"Gods, no! Please no—" and Lanfred gasped upon the wolven raising the chain, which was attached to a winch, pull by muscled pull. The man's arms overextended around his shoulders, making a grisly *pop*, and his entire body lifted up. As a wolven drew close with an empty vial, Lanfred screamed the shrill scream of the condemned.

Augum wanted to look away, but the predator within him that craved blood looked on with interest. Upon his face he felt the heat of three suns, and within his heart stirred a deep lust for violence no human could understand, for it came from a jungle as far away as the stars.

But it was a memory that made Augum look away and shut his mind from the harrowing terror the man was experiencing. The memory of a raven-haired girl, idly playing with his hair, her freckled cheeks sparkling in the sun. He could hear her humming a sweet melody, her legs idly kicking her own back as the pair lay in a field of tall yellow grass ...

For every time he indulged in that bloodlust, a tiny bit of his humanity was stripped away. Her presence—her sheer memory—acted like a shield against that stripping.

When Lanfred's cries died to a gasping whisper, and then snuffed altogether, Augum turned his gaze upon the leader. The time fast approached. It would only be a moment. He had to make sure he stood a chance.

"May I ask a query?" he said, ignoring the other wolven taking the pale brigand down from the hook and unshackling him.

"You may, condemned wearer of wolf-hide."

"The X over your hearts. What does it mean?"

"He is most curious for one who ought to show fear," a wolven said.

"He is not like the others upon facing death," said another. "Most curious indeed."

"Do you not fear death?" the leader countered.

Augum chose silence, again curious as to what it would yield.

The leader tilted his head in that cold manner of the wolven people. "Perhaps we ought to find out if he experiences any fear at all."

"I fear not seeing the one I love," Augum offered. "She is a torch in the vast darkness."

"Interesting," the leader muttered. He pressed a paw over his X. "We are a clan of The Dishonored."

Augum, whose mind worked out the implications, thought to take a risk. "Left behind like the Henawa leave their old."

"Not quite, but an astute guess, lowlander."

"There are other clans then …"

"Separated by element, yes," the leader replied.

"Their element is set from birth," one of the wolven offered.

"You do not have families?"

"We have packs, and each pack is, in your common thinking, a *family*. We, The Dishonored, are the only ones to make mixed packs. And that is our strength."

"So there is a pack for each element—" Augum raised one finger at a time. "—lightning, fire, ice, air, water, earth … even healing?"

"Even healing," the leader replied. "We do not war with healing, for they are the binding that holds our great book together."

"But you war with each other."

"That is how we keep our claws sharp. But you are forgetting one, lowlander."

"One what?"

"One element."

Now it was Augum who cocked his head. "Surely you are not born with—"

"Those who are born necromantic are sacrificed, their blood infused into concoctions."

"The gods gift them to us to make the packs stronger," chimed in a female wolven.

The leader studied Augum. "How can one so young be this curious upon the doorstep of death?"

Augum stared at the wolven. "I met one of your kind once."

The other wolven chortled.

"We find that hard to believe considering you somehow lived to see the dawn," the leader said.

"His name was Raptos and he made a jest that he was a scout readying his kind for an invasion of our kingdom." Although it had happened years ago, Augum could remember it like it was yesterday.

All the wolven, even some beyond their circle, indicating others were listening, growled out booming laughs at this. And as they did, Augum looked to the vials of gold-flecked blood, all that remained of two young people. Short lifetimes of hope and toil, distilled into mere concoctions.

"That is indeed most amusing," the leader said, yet failed to elaborate why.

"What do they do?" Augum asked, nodding at the concoctions.

"They make us stronger," the leader replied. "Your blood enhances ours."

"That is the way of it?" Augum whispered, almost disappointed.

"That is the way of it." The leader looked to the others. "We ought to question him more about these Arcaner kind. And after—" and he changed to wolven here, saying an amused phrase Augum hardly needed a translator for. The leader then returned his attention to Augum and opened his snout to continue the questioning, only to be interrupted by a yelp of wolfish alarm. All wolven eyes turned toward the entrance, where a frost was creeping in along the walls at a rapid pace, plumes of icy fog billowing forth from it.

The wolven summoned armor and weapons, made from the six offensive elements of air, earth, fire, water, lightning, and ice—with healing absent, indicating that healers seemingly did not join The Dishonored.

Amidst that creeping frost stumbled forth a wolven—and he was bloody foot to head, chest and arms slashed. Augum recognized him as one of the guards. He seemed dazed as the others growled at him to report.

Then the strangest thing happened. Something Augum had not experienced in years. Something that should have been impossible, for it was a power that only belonged to the scions, which had been destroyed in the war against the Legion.

One by one, as that frost crept along the walls, any wolven its foggy plume touched found their summoned weapon and armor abruptly snuffed. The wolven shouted in alarm at each other and at the entrance, calling for the other guard whilst extending their black claws, all but forgetting about Augum. The fog quickly filled the space, nullifying every wolven's arcanery.

Then something else happened that should have been impossible—arcaneologically speaking, that was. From Augum's lap came a *click*.

His manacles had unlocked themselves.

EYES UPON THE WOMEN

BRIDGET

As if waiting for the queen herself, servants had lined up in a high corridor of the Black Castle to greet Bridget. The men bowed while the women curtsied, each saying a variation of "My lady" or "Champion" or "Happy Endyear, Captain." The majority were young, but there were a few senior servants too. The young ones stole glances at her, while the elders kept their eyes low. All wore black-and-white garb accented with gold and blue, the royal livery of the Southguards.

"Please, there's no need for that," Bridget said as she strode by with her ridiculous retinue of clanking knights and one herald, who scurried after her whilst trying to quill at the same time.

Seeing that a round room with multiple hallway forks waited ahead, Bridget backtracked to stand before one of the seniors, a wrinkled woman with a high bun and a small white hat.

"My lady," the woman said, curtsying most properly.

"Forgive my intrusion, but I wish to examine the top of the keep. Er ... can you take me there?"

The elder servant bowed her head with utmost politeness. "Of course, my lady. Please follow me," and she swept forth as if gliding on the air itself.

"I've never been up this keep before," Bridget mumbled, feeling like she was out of bounds. Yet the king had given the trio permission to wander and investigate almost any corner of the kingdom as part of lending their support for his power. The problem was the nobles, many worried they were vulnerable to investigation, tried to stymie the order at every turn. They did this in conniving and underhanded ways, as only a greedy and corrupt nobility could.

But one by one, progress in the form of arrests—and examples—were being made, forcing those nobles to be craftier—and more secretive. It was the sixteenth Arcaner edict they feared the most—*Thou shall root out corruption in all its forms, and the sanctity of the truth shall vanquish any title*.

"Captain, if I may ..." Brittany the Herald said as they walked various hallways adorned with golden friezes, gilt-framed paintings and tapestries, marble busts, mounted weapons, the heads of hunted stags and mirkos and bears, and full armor statues that possibly animated during times of war. As per the traditions of Endyear, much of it was festooned with garlands of pine and holly. The young woman waited to receive a nod from Bridget before continuing. "The three of you pulled out of official tournaments after attaining that mystical third Arcaner order rank. My question is, do you ever miss dueling in the arena? Warlock versus warlock. Must have been thrilling."

Bridget passed a large marble bust of a man with a long beard and a serious expression, which sat on an imperial column. "I was rarely involved with tournaments. Only my sister- and brother-in-war enjoyed the sandy pits. They loved dueling, but I don't think they miss the attention and the pressure. But we still duel."

"You ... you do?"

"Sure. Just within the order. Mock duels, obviously. But the only way to keep one's skills truly sharp is to duel for real. I mean, not to the death, and we of course temper our spells so they do no harm, but we still duel."

" 'Mock ... duels ... within ... the ... order ...' Got it. And how often?"

"As often as we can."

"Specifics would be helpful, Captain."

"Once a quint. Sometimes more."

" 'Every ... five ... days.' And who exactly do you duel?"

"Each other, but we also invite promising warlocks from the academy—and sometimes other academies—with the aim of not just learning the latest tactics in the arena, but passing on our knowledge to others."

"Because you've experienced real duels on the field of battle."

"Exactly. And that knowledge is precious."

Servants and guards stiffened upon their passing, with everyone either nervously curtsying, bowing, or giving the standard military salute. She sensed their eyes following her. Despite doing everything she could to appear normal, she felt like a wild creature that was both feared and worshipped, studied yet kept at arm's length. As only one of three dragons, her presence was noticed in every room she stepped into, her every action scrutinized and judged.

Bridget bowed her head to each in turn, and tried to smile when she remembered to, but her mind kept on with worry. What was this strange new scion-like snuffing power and who was casting it? What was their aim? Where was Leera? And were Olaf and Augum and the other warlocks who had gone north all right? She hoped to hear word soon.

"Captain?"

"Forgive me. What was the question?"

"The question was, can you tell us about some of these traditions your brother-in-war resurrected as commander of the order?"

"We have all sorts," Bridget replied as they began ascending the stone steps of the keep, one of four major flights of stairs located near each corner. "Rituals of the morning and evening. Rituals of supper and festivity and marriage. We hold feasts and tournaments and trials. We even have an almoner who collects on behalf of the poor."

The herald flipped her scroll pages. "That would be a Jengo Okeke. Is that not correct? A healer who was the first in generations to experience an Arcaner wedding?"

"That is correct." Bridget smiled remembering his exquisite marriage ceremony to Priya Singh, an Ordinary cook who worked for Castle Arinthian and took on his surname. She also recalled how, even during his own wedding, Jengo the almoner had cajoled people into giving extra alms for the poor on behalf of the Arcaner order. "He is most capable of persuading us into giving more. Something the poor are grateful for."

"Is this Arcaner healer and almoner around? I would like to interview him as well."

"He has traveled north in support of my brother-in-war's quest."

"Ah. Of course. Speaking of marriage, you are betrothed to a—" Brittany flipped the page of a scroll. "—Olaf Hroljassen, also a fellow Arcaner. He is of course quite the lucky man to have the attentions of the kingdom's darling, but there is word that he struggles in your shadow. If you could comment, the nobility have opined that you ought to marry a royal, or perhaps even the prince of another kingdom to better our ties—"

Bridget whirled on the girl, snapping, "I care not for such gossip or intrigues!" The entire retinue halted in the narrow stairwell.

Brittany gulped and curtsied like a servant. "I do apologize, my lady."

The callous shadow opened its eyes. It wondered what the stupid girl would think were she to see its true form rear up above her. "Captain or *Dragon*," Bridget said in cool tones.

"Dragon Burns, of course. Or Captain Burns," the girl added, eyes pinned to the floor.

Bridget winced, pressed the fingers of a hand to her face, and shook her head. "No, it is I who should apologize to you, Herald Brittany. This is not who I am. I do not snap at people." She calmed her breathing, pushing the shadow back into the darkness where it belonged.

"But I deserved it. It was a question beneath our stations. I shall watch my tongue."

"No. Do your job. We will all be the better for it," and Bridget continued ascending, the retinue clanking along behind.

"Fair enough. Then what say you to those who think you ought to become queen?"

"Such talk can be considered treasonous, for we have a queen." She had to be careful with such things. Nor did she have any interest whatsoever in taking the throne. She'd much rather hole up in a barn shoveling manure than step into the royal court as anything but a guest.

"Right, of course."

"When will you interview *me*, miss?" The Sword of the Oak interrupted, smoothing his long and thin mustache with his thumb, one side at a time.

"Er ... I was assigned to examine the Arcaner order, Commander. Forgive me."

"My forgiveness you do not have, but perhaps it can be earned over a drink at The Hilt."

"A drink with a commanding officer at the notoriously rowdy Broken Hilt Inn and Tavern is quite out of my purview," the girl mumbled, and Bridget could feel her hurry to stay near her.

"I like the way you climb these stairs," the commander continued.

Bridget whirled a second time. "Really, Commander, you ought to mind that tongue."

"I mind my tongue just fine, *Captain*." He chortled, and his goonish knights chortled right along with him.

"What of the chivalry in that code of yours?" Bridget pressed. "Is there not something about decency in there?"

"As it so happens, there is. But it is subject to ..." He winked at Brittany, who cowered in Bridget's shadow. "... interpretation."

"Is it now? I was under the impression it was most clear." She frowned at him, earning more chuckles from his fellow knights before she returned to climbing, though caught a fleeting look from the elder servant woman she interpreted as *Well said, my lady*. Such men needed to be confronted lest they thought themselves empowered to press on with their antics. Unfortunately, not all women had the power to do so. She shuddered to think what the young servants had to deal with around such men, especially after a few tankards of ale.

Yet another reason why we must nurture the arts, she thought to herself. They had to solve the root causes of why less people were blossoming and why warlocks were dying out, and of that the theories were many. Loss of ancient knowledge. A critical lack of mentors. A lack of motivation. Corruption. Ulterior motives. People even thought there were shadowy figures at play, slowly killing warlocks off in the dark. The theories only got wilder from there—punishments by the gods, meteors wiping out arcanery, witches cursing warlocks for betraying them, and so on, each more absurd than the last.

They finally reached a floor that was entirely open. The walls and floor were made of the same rough-cut blocks of stone, and in strategic locations—the corners and the very center—stood several ladders that led to trap doors large enough to allow a man wearing full plate armor through. Milling amidst the ladders were a multitude of chattering soldiers and army warlocks, all of whom fell silent upon Bridget's entrance. Racks of bows and quivers of arrows hung along the walls, and it was frigid cold, fogging breath and making the servant bundle up in her gown.

That old woman curtsied a final time. "My lady, the top of the keep is just above. Happy Endyear."

Bridget gave a thankful nod and proceeded to the closest ladder, conscious of the stares from the soldiers. As an Arcaner, sometimes her duties demanded she order an investigation into someone in power who held sway over soldiers' minds, something that did not endear her or her brethren to those soldiers—or their superiors.

Bridget climbed the ladder and stepped out onto a roof surrounded by crenels and spill sluices meant to pour hot oil on an attacking enemy. Snow had begun falling anew, fat flakes that tumbled like tiny frozen leaves through the chilly air. Brown-robed investigators from the constabulary milled with captains and army warlocks, some of whom greeted her with a nod of respect—those were the ones who had yet to be corrupted.

Bridget turned her attention to the ground. The roof was blanketed with snow in all but one area where it had melted in a circular pattern, branchlike offshoots extending from the center.

"Lightning fingers," she whispered, stepping up to the pattern. She looked skyward, but the heavy and dark clouds gave no discernible evidence such a thing ought to have occurred. There was not that crispiness in the air that called for lightning, nor had there been any thunder—it had been a one-off.

As her retinue of soldiers trickled up top from the ladders, she turned in place, scanning faces, seeing if someone knew something they ought not to know. But she had not developed that keen eye for guilt yet, not like Augum had, and so the faces all looked equally hostile. What she could see in their eyes was judgment—here was this trumped-up young woman, wielding powers beyond her mortal station, who dared to think she had any right to investigate them! She could almost hear the insipid minds whispering how utterly unfair it was. She wanted to grab them each by the scruff and shout that they hardly knew her, let alone knew of the sufferings and sacrifices she had gone through in order to wield that ancient power that protected the kingdom, a power they now threw festivals and parades around. What comedy.

To her surprise, a constable approached her. A late middle-aged balding man with a round belly and a wide nose. He inclined his head to each woman. "Captain Burns. Herald Mires." He spoke in a rather decadent accent, one Bridget recognized as Franterran, a people from southern Canterra. His lips thinned upon seeing The Sword of the Oak. "Commander."

The commander only grunted, while Brittany curtsied. "Constable Depassier." The *r* was silent, a trait of the tongue.

"Forgive me. Have we been acquainted?" Bridget asked.

"We have not, Captain Burns, but I recognize your face from the posters. And I saw you in passing at the Festival of the Dragon. Although I was not one of those who tossed roses at your feet, I found it quite a remarkable display of piety and worship. Then I had the privilege of attending the Dragon Supper, which was … interesting, to say the least."

"Ah," Bridget replied. The latter had been a most tedious affair, what with people lavishing attention upon the trio and blowing smoke up their robes and battling each other for who could lob the most eloquent compliment. Then there were the scheming nobles and their plots, hunting for the slightest bit of social leverage. But she refrained from mentioning any of that, especially with a herald listening in.

"I have been placed in charge of the investigation by the High Inquisitor. If you are wondering about my accent, I brought my family to this kingdom a decade prior. We find the north …" Depassier opened a calloused palm, allowed snowflakes to settle on it, and watched them melt. "… most agreeable to our disposition, Captain Burns. I hit my ceiling at the 9th some years prior, but am quite content with what I have learned."

"Nice to see someone at ease with their accomplishments instead of pushing for ever greater heights—"

"—and then biting off more than they can chew," the investigator added, nodding. "In terms of honorifics, would you prefer the title of Captain or that of Dragon?"

"I prefer the former, thank you for asking." The latter made people nervous, and oft tempted them to ask questions they ought not to ask. It also tended to stir the interest of the shadow perpetually lurking within her.

"As you wish, Captain."

Bridget looked to the dark spot in the snow.

"Yes, it is most perplexing. But there is something even more perplexing." The constable looked expectantly at the herald.

Brittany glanced between them, hesitated, but curtsied. "Forgive me. I ought to allow you parlay," and she wandered to stand apart to continue quilling whilst keeping one eye on them.

The constable took a step closer, his voice dropping. "It was not just arcanery that was snuffed in people, Captain …"

Bridget felt her eyebrows rising. "Go on."

"The laboratorium, located just over there—" Depassier indicated a nearby spire, one of a few attached to the sprawling structure that made up the Black Castle. "—was occupied by several arcaneologists. One of those warlocks happened to be using an arcane hourglass, which in that brief time during the …" He rubbed his fingers together, searching for the right words.

"Arcane snuffing," Bridget offered.

"Yes, that is an apt description of the event. During the arcane snuffing, the hourglass failed to overturn as it should have." While Bridget mulled over this strange and rather alarming piece of news, the man put his weight on his other foot. "And that is not the only instance. A rather dangerous warlock prisoner, who was being led to the prison tower in that very moment, suddenly found his manacles unlocked. Rest assured he was taken down, but the implication remains …"

Bridget searched his light brown eyes. "How can this be?"

"We do not know. The arcaneologists are researching the matter as we speak. Of course, with your past dealings with the scions, I was rather hoping …" He opened his hands at her before interlacing them together on top of his ale belly.

"That I could provide some insight." She ran one hand after the other through her long cinnamon hair before settling one on the back of her neck, the other idly clapping her thigh. "The power to do this shouldn't exist. Even the scions only snuffed arcanery in warlocks, not in artifacts. It is …" She dropped her voice to match his initial whisper. "… dangerous. *Very* dangerous. The implications—"

"—vaults, sacred places, ancient storehouses … all vulnerable to such attack," the constable whispered. "A threat to the kingdom as a whole."

"Has the king been briefed on this revelation, Constable?" The Sword of the Oak asked, having apparently been eavesdropping.

"He has, and has taken the appropriate precautions. The Black Eagles have whisked him and the royal family and the nine members of the high council to safety underground. They await our assessment."

Bridget, more alarmed by the moment, nodded to herself before looking to the commander. "No word from Captain Jones?"

"She will be brought here the moment she is found by one of my captains."

Bridget's nod continued, forehead creasing with worry. "Good. Good …"

Now if only she could figure out what this all meant … and what it portended.

THE BROKEN HILT
INN & TAVERN

LEERA

Leera swept in through the heavy door so briskly that it thudded against the wall. Luckily the smoky place was raucous enough that few noticed. Those who did glance up from their tankards gave a double-take, for they saw a hooded red-robed warlock, always a curious sight in these parts due to the sheer rarity—there were probably around thirty red-robes in the entire kingdom.

"Fat hog," Leera said to the portly barkeep of the same name, pushing her spectacles back up her nose. She really ought to stop taking them underwater with her, for the water kept loosening the pincers.

The man lit up upon seeing her and pressed meaty hands into the counter. "Did the lass get into a fight with her lover?"

"Just a wee bump on the noggin' which I got a duelin'," she replied, playfully mocking his tavern accent whilst plopping down on a rickety stool before him.

"Ugly lie for an ugly girl." He winked, burgundy lips cracking with a smile. "Fat Hog a comin' your way, *Cap*," he said, mouthing her title so that others would not take notice. The brewmaster was old and balding and blotchy-skinned, with rough hands and a perpetually stained apron, but there was no shortage of laugh lines in the crinkles around his eyes and mouth.

Not wanting neighbors, Leera flicked at the stools flanking her, shoving them a couple of feet away. The place was loud and stank of tobacco and cedar and moldy stone and tart ale and sweat. But the roaring hearths that were scattered about the room, decorated with wreaths of pine and holly, made the place feel rather cozy too. Above those hearths hung various rusting shields and weapons captured from enemies in bygone eras—and recent wars.

As she eyed a steel Legion sword hanging alongside a Canterran blade that had battle notches in it, she dug out two copper castles from a pocket and slapped them on the counter in wait for his return. It did not escape her notice that one coin had turned up dragons. She flipped that one over to the side that showed the castle, then stared at them as she used both hands to pinch the loose locks of raven hair dangling past her face, smoothing them down.

The king hadn't bothered to inform them that they would be on the copper coin. She'd casually received change from a street vendor selling spiced beef on a stick. She remembered asking him if he had accidentally given her a token coin, and the man, who mercifully hadn't recognized her, had simply said, "Not at all, m'lady. These 'ave been freshly minted. Aren't they grand?" The dragons were all identical too, which felt impersonal, insulting even. And to stick them on the copper, the lowest denomination …

"Wouldn't even *have* a throne if it weren't for us," she muttered, the topic still sour. That boar of a king should have at least asked if they were all right with being presented on the coins!

The barkeep soon returned with a large tankard of hog ale, but instead of accepting the castles, he used his other hand to make a washing motion above them.

Leera pronged the coins with two fingers and pushed them forth anyway. "Don't insult me, you walking fart-cask." She loved their banter.

He pressed his sausage fingers into his bulging chest. "The preening bag of freckles has wounded an innocent! Were she any bright at all, she would recognize a compliment when she hears one."

"Then don't insult your*self*." When he still refused the coins, she leaned over the drink. "Don't make me throw them at you, you balding toad."

He snorted a laugh, scooped them off the counter into a leather pouch, and drummed the counter with those thick fingers. "Anything else? I know you're hungry because you stink like the lake."

"As if you can even breathe through that—" She waved a hand about. "—that snout you call a nose." She knew it was a weak shot.

"The lass is losing her touch. She ought to do less wrist-bruising and more tongue-lashing."

"Point to you, you ogre," she muttered, digging out a spine. She hadn't been able to deploy her wit much of late, which was making her feel lonely and bored. She placed the silver coin on the counter pine side up. "Surprise me."

"Your seaweed stomach will thank me." He turned away from the coin, which she flicked the air at. Shoved telekinetically, it soared off and plonked him in the back. He tumbled to the ground, feigning a grave injury and drawing some chuckles from nearby patrons.

She threw his own rag at him, which he had left on the counter. "Get back to work, you lazy turd!" It landed on his balding head, drawing more laughs. He yanked it off, puckered his lips as he nodded defeat, snatched the coin, and hauled himself up with a groan.

"Careful you don't strain anything," she called after him.

He thumbed over his shoulder, "Better, but still a ways to go, lass."

"Bah," she said, then sniffed her armpit, only to wince. She should have taken a bath and used one of the fancy oils Augum had gifted her. Then again, a stink warded the creeps off.

She glanced about to take stock of the evening. The smokey place was packed with people taking shelter from the blizzard. The occasional gaze wandered her way, but she was careful not to meet them, always looking away at the last moment and keeping her face within the shadows of her deep hood.

"I can tell you're pretty just by the sound of your sweet voice," oozed a man behind her.

Leera ordinarily would have pressed her eyes shut in annoyance, but her dull tongue craved sharpening. "I can tell you're ugly by the sound of yours," she snapped back, which drew some laughter from the bearded stool-clingers sitting a couple of seats down from her, both of whom raised their tankards in salute of a top-shelf insult. She raised her tankard to them in turn without showing her face.

A man stepped between her and the stoolies and loomed, trying to look into her hood. "Let me buy you a sip, miss."

She pressed a hand into his surprisingly muscled chest and pushed him away. "No."

"You didn't even look at me."

"Why would I look at ugly things?" She withdrew the shipwreck coin and turned it over and over, examining every detail. The crown was of an older sort, with fewer jewels, and the head on the other side was that of a regal man with a war-like expression. But then such portraits always exaggerated fierceness and poise. She wondered if Anna Atticus Stone had met the man, then went on to wonder how famous she had been at that shared age of twenty, and how she had dealt with that fame. "You're still here." She could feel him staring at the side of her hood, as if not knowing what to make of her. "Crab got your tongue?"

"It's because I'm an Ordinary, that it? Too high and mighty for us lowlies?"

"It's because I *have* a man." One she loved deeper than that lake she had dived. Even without looking at him, she could feel him make a show of glancing about.

"Well, *I* don't see him."

"Then rub those beady little eyes and take a second look, 'cause he's standing right behind you."

There was a pause as the man moved about, perhaps to check if there really was an invisible person there, only to give up with a chuckle. "That's amusing, but he ought to be here minding his girl."

"You ought to be minding your own affairs."

"As it so happens, I'm rather good at minding my affairs."

"I bet you are." She really was losing her touch. Where was the imagination? The riposte usually aimed at the jugular? The finesse?

The man dragged a stool over and sat down. "That's a nice coin."

See? She scolded herself in thought. *He sat down. That's what low-quality snark earns you.* She took a sip of the tankard, and a citrus wheat tang exploded onto her tongue. *Gods, that's good*, she thought, taking a second, longer gulp.

"That's it, girl, drink up and let us be merry. Then let us … frolic."

She felt a hand peruse her backside as if exploring merchandise. That got to her, and she looked over and spat a mouthful into his face—and it was not a bad-looking face, either. Young and handsome and chiseled. Yet even amidst the shock, there was a distinct lecherousness to it, as if a rat had put on a mask.

The man recoiled, hands hovering above his dripping face. "You rotten wench, how *dare* you!" He wore a crimson doublet fringed with gold lace and jeweled golden rings on supple hands, which gave him the appearance of a gaudy jester.

"Oh, sorry about that. Here let me—" and she flared a hand, incanting, "*Aquatos,*" and sprayed his face with a harmless stream of water. The young man gasped and tried to dodge, but her war-trained hand easily followed his face, shooting a continuous jet that not only washed away the ale, but his smirk too. "That better?" she asked, abruptly cutting off the 3rd degree off-the-books spell. Splash was a cantrip every mischievous water warlock learned as soon as it was legal—meaning at the 1st degree. She would have learned it then too— had she not been running for her life from the Legion at the time.

"That's what you get messin' with a 'lock, fool boy," one of the stool-clingers muttered.

"Got to learn the hard way," his friend added.

The bejeweled man stood from his stool. "You have insulted my honor."

"You wanted to be clean, didn't you?" The water, having been arcanely summoned, vanished before his eyes. "See? All better."

"You have wounded my pride."

"Preening peacocks tend to have too much of that anyhow."

"I may have no skill with the sword or in magic arts, but I fear no warlock."

"We use the word *arcanery*." She made a show of moving three invisible cards about. "*Magic* is for parlor tricks. Cuppers and cards and Hiding Hats and Sleevies. That sort of stuff."

"I don't give a flying hoof *what* you use." He straightened. "Speak thy name so that I may make a case of it, you lowly tavern wench. You diseased strumpet."

Leera finished taking a third sip and slowly looked at him from within her dark hood, her eyes narrowing. A shadow peeked from behind her mind, coaxing her to prod more out of him and elevate the argument to violence. Allowing it rare indulgence, she leaned forth, whispering, "Say that again."

The noble leaned into her face, but instead of saying something, there came a stinging *smack* as he slapped her.

Leera, face turned away and stinging something fierce, could hardly believe the nerve. Tears wanted to well—though not from anguish or self-pity, but from that uncontrollable urge the frail human body felt when its face knew such a potent sting.

"That's the *least* you deserve, wench," he spat. "I flay my servants for far less."

With her face still turned away, Leera's hand snatched the top of his head. Before she could even think, she hissed, "*Dreadus terrablus*," infusing into the spell's thought process the visual of his chiseled face melting down his robe, even going so far as to make him see his gold rings melting through his flesh and bones and joining the bloody drool that had been his handsomeness.

The noble screamed the scream of a child caught in a vivid nightmare, eyes wide with horror. He kept looking down at his hands and the floor and back again, no doubt seeing his own face pooling in a mess on the planks, all while shrieking at the top of his lungs like a cursed banshee.

Realizing what she had done—and cognizant that the place had fallen pin-drop silent and that every single eye was upon them, she promptly made a reverse claw motion and snapped, "*Dreadus null,*" instantly nullifying the 4th degree Fear spell, which had been cast at full-strength by a 10th degree war-honed mind.

The man inhaled sharply, and held onto that breath as he staggered back and fell, hands grasping at the stools—and missing. He slammed onto the floor, where he writhed about for a bit as if still gripped by the vision, before allowing one of the bearded stool-clingers to haul him roughly to his feet.

"Wot you think was a gonna happen after slappin' a 'lock?" the old man spat. "And if you bring any trouble to 'er, me an' ol' Franks 'ere will fess up as to what you done did."

The other wagged a wrinkled finger at the noble. "Don't you be makin' no trouble now, son. Learn yer lesson and git on. Anything else and we'll tell the whole kingdom how you howled like a wee lass and pissed yerself." He flicked a hand toward the noble's tan pants, which were stained dark. "And all your pasty-faced friends will ever remember from it is how you tinkled on yourself. Now git. *Git!*"

The first flapped both arms at the door as if to spook a rabid stray dog. "We said, *git*, boy!"

The noble, panting and blanched, cast his eyes down and slithered off without another word, and the raucous burble of the tavern returned, for the place saw all sorts of quarrels.

Leera, hiding her face within her hood, recentered herself on her stool and meekly sipped her ale. Gods, what had she been thinking casting arcanery—let alone full-strength arcanery—against an Ordinary. A man of high stature could easily bring a case against her with the constables. The whole thing could turn into a herald-amplified debacle.

She rubbed the bump on her forehead then rubbed each eye with the heel of her hand, sighing as if long tired of herself.

"I tend to your meal for a few heartbeats and come out to the conclusion of a fracas," Fat Hog said upon delivering her a steaming roast turkey breast alongside buttered and gravied potatoes, roasted leeks, and fresh half-cut tomatoes. All of it was sprinkled with fragrant leaves of basil and coarse grains of salt and pepper.

Leera only dug out a spine and slid it forth, nodding toward the two stool-clingers. "Please make sure they're topped up for the eve." As the barkeep accepted the coin, both men raised their tankards in salute to her, and she raised hers back in thanks to them.

"Some pasty-faced snob put a hand to her," the man called Franks told Fat Hog. "Confused 'er with one of his servants. Got what he had comin'."

"Warned 'im not to mess with no 'lock," said his friend.

"Let alone no crimson 'lock," Franks chimed in. "Boy had some nerve."

"Ain't goin' to make that mistake twice."

The pair shook their heads knowingly.

Fat Hog tossed her a fresh cloth. "I ever see him crawl back in here and I'll toss him out." He winked. "But something tells me we won't see nor hear a peep from him ever again."

Leera telekinetically snagged it, drew it over her left arm in the proper fashion expected of women of the kingdom, took a two-pronged fork and a serrated horn knife, sawed at the turkey, skewered it with the fork, dipped it into the gravy, and placed it onto her tongue. Instantly the anxiety of what had happened, the cold that still lingered from the lakebed and the blizzard, and the hunger deep in her belly fell away as if shoved by a spell.

"Fates help me that is damn good, Hog," she muttered, eyes closed as she took a sip of ale to chase the sumptuousness down. "*Mmm.*" She started shoveling the food into her mouth in a most unladylike fashion.

"Slow down or you'll choke, fish girl."

She flashed him a sarcastic smile complete with a head wobble, but did indeed slow down. She wanted to savor every morsel. Every granule of salt and pepper.

Fat Hog took a cloth and began polishing the interior of a glass pitcher. "I ever tell you I knew your mother?"

Leera, still chewing a mouthful of potatoes, barely looked up. "Oh?"

"We apprenticed together as ale wardens. Tasting, brewing, the works. She was a good woman, but she had a strange appetite for —" He wafted a hand about, eyes searching the ceiling.

"Exotic tastes?"

The man chuckled. "Yes, exotic tastes."

Leera smiled as she nodded, for she could still remember the sour look people would give upon trying her mother's strange brews. Augum had even had the eye-watering displeasure of imbibing a particularly rank concoction. That was prior to the Legion raiding her village. On the occasional rare night, she still bolted up in bed from a nightmare about feet rising from the ground and convulsing as lightning coursed through the bodies. To this day, she remembered seeing the sky from afar as it turned the most vivid orange she had ever seen after the Legion had set fire to that village.

Every few months, she'd visit the ashes of Sparrow's Perch to tell the grave markers of her folks how her life was coming along. The village was now a tomb amidst the pines and cedars and spruces, Mount Barrow looming overhead like an eternally watching guardian.

"She was a good woman." The old barkeep patted her hand. "As are you," he added before walking off.

Leera, allowing the distant pangs of memory to intertwine sweetly with her lonesome thoughts, hardly took notice of someone else taking a seat at the same stool the noble had vacated.

"Know who that pasty-faced noble was?" a woman asked.

"A young turdling of a long line of turdlings, no doubt."

"Exactly right." The woman took a pull of her own tankard, voice distant. "Exactly right."

Leera stole a peek to see an early thirties woman with a bland face and scraggly pigtails, wearing a white and tan commoner's dress, with a leather-laced brown and long-sleeved shirt stained with oily blotches.

"Took a pass at me too once. But I, being the fool that I am, relented." She leaned closer to whisper, "He didn't know his ass from his elbow in bed," which made Leera snort. "I might as well have been making love to a turd bucket."

"You'd probably have had more fun too."

The woman lifted her cup. "I am now betrothed to another, a Mr. Tankard," which drew a spirited laugh from the both of them. She took a long drink and smacked the tankard against the counter, allowing it to slop over the side. She gave a firm nod. "I'm drunk."

"Guess I better catch up." Leera took a long sip, her plate half finished, and noticed a feather sticking out from the woman's pocket. "You quill?"

The woman looked down and grimaced at it. "Not very well." She sniffed, then animated, blurting, "Writing my pa's memoirs. Seems to think his life was rather exciting." She scoffed. "He was a keeper of accounts. A *bookkeeper*! I give him this, though. He was there. On that field. On that day. He was there, with his long pike by his side and his home-sewn boiled leathers. An old man playin' young again. But he saw the skies, that he did." She brushed a hand above her as if painting a canvas with her palm. "Like flies they rose, diving pelicans feasting on fish, swallowing them whole." Her hand dove onto the counter. "*Pow.* Must have been something to see. Surely you were there, being a crimson and all."

Leera saw the flash of wingtips, spells zipping a mere hand's width by her head, two great armies battling far below. She remembered twirling an evil woman into the air and chomping down on her, and how she had tasted like chicken. And she remembered a certain spell, an ancient curse, slapping into her very soul …

"Must have been harrowing," the woman said, picking up on how Leera was gaping into the past.

Leera reanimated, skewered a gravy-soaked potato, and stuck it into her mouth. "Harrowing is a good word for that time," she said, chewing a mouthful whilst nodding. "Harrowing."

"Glad I wasn't there. Thank you. To all of you robes and soldiers for what you did that day."

Leera's nodding only continued. She had heard so many variations of gratitude—from simple passing thanks on the street to tearful protestations to getting pelted with roses whilst standing on a wagon and waving to adoring crowds—that they meant almost nothing anymore. What did thanks mean when it had been said thousands of times? Like any other word, it lost its meaning.

"I love my pa, but I'm going to write a proper tale one day." The woman stared into the middle distance, and her eyes welled with tears before she looked away. "Gods I miss having a proper man."

"Surely not the peacock."

The woman blurted a laugh. She wiped her face with a dirty sleeve before readjusting her frayed pigtails. "No, not the peacock, or anyone like him ever again."

"Does that mean you currently have an *im*proper man?" Leera tapped the pewter with her knife, making a *ting*. "Other than Mr. Tankard, that is?"

The woman chortled. "Did. *Did* have a proper man."

"Ah. Sorry."

"It's fine. He ran off anyway. Changed my whole damn life for him. Now I'm trying to start fresh. I'm here because it's Lover's Day and I'm attending to my lover—" She raised her tankard and sliced a free hand toward it, raising a sly eyebrow.

"Shoot, that *is* today," Leera muttered, annoyed with Augum for not being here beside her. "Missed the Starfeast too. Ugh, sometimes I wonder what it'd be like to start fresh. A new life."

"The life of a 'lock can't be easy, what with you lot being locked in war. Isn't that what you always say?" The woman sat up straight, voice going pretend-serious. " 'To be a warlock is to be locked in war.' "

In the tone, Leera heard the deep voice of The Grizzly, a towering and fearsome man who had served as Lord High Commander of the army. It was a voice she hadn't heard since the war, and had to smile bittersweetly. She remembered his death, and how that death had affected her beloved mentor, Jez, for the two had been meaning to start a life together after the war. To this day that poor woman still commiserated with a bottle of wine instead of another man — in between giving half-hearted lessons to the trio.

Leera sighed. It had been a while since she'd had a normal conversation with someone. "You know what I think?"

"What?"

"I think we should commiserate over a stiffer drink."

"Agreed."

The women each ordered a fiery glass of Nodian Heartfire wine, then proceeded to trade quips and jests and stories, all relatively innocuous, all without asking each other their names or professions lest such details spoil the intimacy, which seemed as fragile as pipe smoke. It was just two random women unloading pent-up frustrations, sharing a heart-to-heart, letting loose a little.

With the plate long cleared and the tankard empty and the goblet refilled a second time and the pair of old stool-clingers having gone home, Leera wove in place, finger wavering about in the air. "But you know I miss him so bad it hurts."

"Your man left you?"

"Not in the way you're meaning."

"You love him."

"More than life itself."

The woman melted. "That's so sweet. I hope I find that one day."

"But there's something keeping us from taking that final step."

The young woman leaned closer. "To marriage?"

Leera nodded.

"You don't have to tell me. Probably best you don't —"

"I'm barren," Leera blurted. "Like a field in winter. Or a Sierran desert." She sliced the air with a flat palm. "Can't have kids. No wee ones in this girl's future." She raised her goblet, toasting to her own misery. "To having no future."

The girl placed a hand over her mouth, eyes searching into Leera's hood, which felt like a dark cavern now.

"I'm lost," Leera mumbled after taking an acidic sip. "If I marry him, it would mean the end of —" She couldn't say it. That would be too much detail.

"I think I understand," the woman murmured, patting Leera's shoulder. "For what it's worth, I'm sorry."

"Not your fault. Got cursed in the war."

"Which one?"

Leera looked up at the crossed blades and, despite seeing four of them now even though she knew there were two, she pointed at the notched Canterran sword.

"By a fellow warlock?"

"Sort of. But you know what? I see two moons," she said using the common parlance for being drunk. "And fear my turd tongue is goin' to get me in trouble. I ought to shut up and go home."

"Nonsense. You're just a girl lettin' loose."

Leera snorted. "I need to piss." She got up and wove her way to a dingy room. After doing her business, she glanced at herself in the scummy mirror made of poorly polished metal, and found the streaks and scratches that crossed her reflection wholly appropriate.

When she wove her way back, she noticed the woman was furiously quilling. "What you writin'?" she asked in a tavern twang upon plopping back down in her stool.

The woman hurriedly scrunched a cloth, apparently the only thing she had found in place of parchment, and tried to shove it into her pocket—only for Leera to catch her wrist. The girl froze like a deer caught by the neck.

"What you writin'?" Leera repeated in a whisper. "Tell me it ain't what I think it is ..."

The woman swallowed and looked up to meet her gaze, confirming Leera's worst fear.

"Silly me, I thought we were just yapping as two no-names," Leera said, letting the wrist go and slouching, all the fight stolen from her. "I'm such an idiot," she murmured. "Such a stupid idiot." She mustered the strength to raise her hanging head. "But ... why?"

The woman rubbed her wrist. "'Cause I got two kids to feed and I'm about a castle away from the street."

"And so you're going to sell my tale."

"I knew who you were the moment I saw you walk in here. I always recognize a style of walk, and you have a very particular gait, a lazy sort of schlep that—"

"And so you're going to sell my tale," Leera repeated.

The woman paused, before leaning closer. "I could, or ..."

"Or what?"

"Or you could help a girl out. I know you're rich. What's a few thousand crowns—"

Leera almost fell off her stool. "*Thousand*—"

"Shh!" The woman glanced about. "No need to get loud 'bout it. Just being practical is all."

"You think I have crowns just—" Leera flapped two arms skyward. "—raining from the skies? Huh?" Nonetheless, the guilty thought of handing the sunken treasure chest over flashed across her mind. "You think I'd betray my own code of honor like that?"

"Maybe not, but it's hardly much trouble for you to make coin, is it? What with being a war hero and all. Look at it from my shoes—I ain't got no magic to make coin like you 'locks do."

"Arcanery," Leera corrected, unable to help her training from kicking in. They were taught to correct every instance, especially with Ordinaries.

"Whatever. You know what I mean."

"I do my *proata mentora*. More than enough of my share—"

"And you think spending time with others does anything for people like *me*?" the woman hissed, stabbing her own chest, face crimson. "People who beg and grovel and have to stoop to indecencies just so their children can spoon a mouthful, while you preening 'locks openly play with crowns in taverns as if they were nothing but toys!"

"But that coin was different—"

"You know how long it takes for me to earn a crown? Guess. *Guess!*"

Leera was about to tell the woman that she was sorry for what she was going through but she would never betray her code of honor or allow blackmail to rule her life, when the tavern door burst open and in streamed a column of soldiers. The lead soldier, a young man in a pot helm and a chainmail overcoat, shouted over his shoulder, "Found 'er, sir!"

"Now what," Leera muttered, standing—and having to support herself by grabbing the counter lest she stumble in her drunkenness.

A man pushed through the soldiers.

"That her, Captain?" the young asked.

The captain—a beefy fellow with no-nonsense eyes—nodded. "Captain Jones, we must immediately take you back to the castle."

Leera, seeing that every single pair of eyes—doubled by the drink—were upon her and many a person was now elbowing their neighbor and whispering urgently, threw up her arms. "Great. Juuuuust great. Thanks for killing the only place where a girl could have a quiet drink. Now how am I supposed to come back here? Huh?"

"I *am* sorry, Captain, but that cannot be my concern. There is a situation—"

"Oh, there's always a *situation* with you lot."

"Please." The captain stepped aside, and the column of men took their cue from him and made a corridor for her to walk through.

"*Pfft.*" Nonetheless, Leera strode forth, only to stop before the captain and look back at the woman, who was already furiously scribbling away on that same cloth, which she had spread on the counter, a tiny ink bottle unstopped beside it. She strode up to the woman. "Write what you like, but please—*please*—don't write about that one thing."

The woman scowled. "The people have a right to know who is defending their kingdom."

Leera found herself breathing in such a way that made the woman not only look away, but slide away too. She felt a hand enclose around her upper arm. "Captain."

"You're going to destroy me," Leera said, allowing herself to be led away.

"I have mouths to feed!" the woman roared after her. "You *had* your chance. You had it ..."

"Imagine trying to blackmail an Arcaner," a wobbling Leera muttered to the captain once they got outside. The blizzard had returned in full force, but that didn't stop the men from surrounding her in a protective formation.

"Blackmail is a serious charge," the captain countered. "One punishable by death. Do you wish to press charges? Shall I take the woman into custody?"

Despite weaving about and trying not to slip, Leera was cognizant enough to see how that would all play out. Because she could swear on her shield, her word would be as strong as iron. But then she'd have to reveal why she was being blackmailed in the first place. In the end, word would get out, and all she would manage to do was destroy a young mother's life and the lives of her poor children.

"No, it's my fault," Leera said. "The whole damn thing is my fault. I'm so stupid."

UNLEASHED

AUGUM

After Augum's manacles had unlocked, and with the cave inundated by icy mist, the wolven, strangely choosing not to resummon their own weapons, grabbed bows and arrows and spears instead, even snagging whatever cooking implement they could get their hands on. Some took up defensive positions while others disappeared into the passage leading out. Meanwhile, the wolven that had stumbled into the cave all bloody growled out a phrase that made the others exchange bewildered looks.

Augum, sensing the urgency of the moment, readied to make his presence known by standing—after all, the wolven had failed to notice that his manacles had unlocked. But then something most peculiar occurred. When he attempted to summon ten lightning rings to his forearm, rings that usually came with a mere thought, nothing happened. That could only mean one thing.

His connection to the arcane ether had been severed.

He gaped at his forearm as if it were broken, before realizing the manacles were slipping off. He promptly sat back down, tucked his hands in his lap so that the open part of the manacles was underneath his wrists, and observed as a trained tactician, albeit one with a war-honed mind.

While the leader growled commands in the wolfish tongue, the rest of the wolven were baring their teeth at the entrance as if in warning.

Time permitted Augum to analyze the situation in greater detail. The effect playing out before him was wholly new, perhaps not experienced in living memory—or perhaps ever. He had never even *read* of an occasion when arcane objects had lost their power, at least not without an overt act from someone.

Yes, that's what it has to be! he thought. His friends had come to save him. Yet he could not recognize whatever power one of his party—his mentor, Jez, if anyone—had used. Was this secret new training he was unfamiliar with? Had she cast Invisibility and was prowling nearby? Surely he would have at least heard her whisper the incantation to unlock the manacles …

The more he thought about it, the more his concern grew, for it was a power he had only experienced once—in the presence of scions, those ancient Leyan-crafted artifacts that had been destroyed in the war against the Legion. But even then, that snuffing power had not extended to arcane artifacts. That was why the hair on his arms rose, for he recognized that what he was experiencing—what they *all* were experiencing—was dangerous to the extreme. Not just to warlocks, but to entire kingdoms.

Despite the strong urge to act, he forced himself to wait and pick his moment. Bereft of arcanery, he might as well have been a babe amidst beasts ten—nay, twenty times physically stronger than him. For all intents and purposes, he was an Ordinary, nothing more, nothing less. Which meant survival hinged on coldly rational decisions.

While the wolven growlingly argued about what was happening, Augum realized he felt something he had not felt in a long time—a privacy he did not think he would experience ever again. The predatorial shadow that had been his near-constant companion, that intruded on random thoughts, bled into his speech and mannerisms and taunted the unwary, that spied on him when he was having an intimate moment with his beloved … was simply absent.

Were the situation not so precarious, he might have smiled.

Then the frost, which had consumed most of the rocky surfaces, began to dissipate. As it and the mist retreated, one by one wolven summoned armor of frost or ivy or lightning or water or ice or air, along with their accompanying weapons—summoned axes, maces, swords, and flails. Like a candle flickering back to life, Augum soon felt it too—the ability to tap into the sacred ether. And that familiar malignant presence returned to peek from behind the curtain of his soul.

Once again able to practice his war-honed spellcraft, he could have lashed out then and there. But instinct told him to hold, especially because a guttural argument broke out between the leader and the wounded wolven—all while others ran up the cave passage to either investigate or challenge whatever waited outside.

An idea came to him. *Let's see if this works*, he thought, and amidst the chaos, he focused on the complex processes required of the 12th degree

Tongues spell. Once his thoughts had aligned, he touched his throat with one hand and pressed three fingers to his temple with the other, whispering under his breath, *"Translateo commona languino wolven."*

The guttural growls morphed ever so slightly—but not enough. It was as he had suspected—the spell still required a basic understanding of the target tongue, and wolven was simply too distant a relative of human speech to allow for arcane translation. He'd have to train the spell in the company of wolven—or someone who at least understood the language.

After holding Tongues for a while longer but still hearing no difference, he mumbled, *"Translateo null,"* snuffing the spell—there was no sense wasting precious stamina.

He noticed that one of the nearby wolven's ears had pricked toward him, and she was watching him out of the corner of her eye. Although not quite cat-like, wolven reflexes were notoriously quick, and she was close enough to eviscerate him with those claws. Even now as he looked straight ahead, pretending not to have noticed her, the claws on each paw slowly extended, sleek and deadly like black pitchforks.

You shouldn't have underestimated wolven hearing, he told himself.

Sensing she was an eye blink away from skewering him, he suddenly swiveled and shoved at the air, roaring the incantation to the 2nd degree Push spell, *"Baka!"* sending her flying into another wolven, bowling him over. His manacles, which had lain loosely overtop his wrists, flew toward her from the momentum of the shove. In one smooth motion, he swiveled about and thrust his arms apart before slapping his wrists, shouting, *"Annihilo bato!"* Two massive prongs of lightning sizzled forth toward the leader. One smashed into a cavern pillar, but the other connected with his flame armor, blowing it apart—and smashing him against the wall behind.

Second Offensive, 8th degree, standard, Augum's academy-trained mind thought even as he cursed himself for missing the wolven's unprotected head.

The wolven howled a battle cry, with more than a few growling, "Treacherous lowlander!"

Augum could have risked teleporting through the rock of the mountain, yet he wanted to obtain something to return to the families of the slain apprentices. Except taking on all the wolven at once was a fool's errand, and so he smacked a fist against his chest, roaring "Test me and die!"

The leader scrambled to his feet and growled out a command. The wolven prowled forth, low and deadly, making Augum retreat so that his back was near the wall. One swipe from those pitchfork claws and it was over. He could summon his own armor, but he did not intend for them to get that close. Besides, summoned elemental armor would only slow his Arcaner-trained reflexes down, reflexes key to survival.

Numerous potential spells flashed across his mind, the greatest of which would see him turn into an apex predator that naturally basked under the heat of three suns. But the cave was too small and he did not want to deal with the side effects, worrying how they would factor this far north. Most of the spells he considered took too much time to cast and did not affect enough bodies. He could either make a potent example, or resort to trickery.

He gracefully made his fingers dance, hissing, "*Ipulato laitna marjorus.*" It was the incantation to the 9th degree off-the-books *Ipulaitnamarjahanilus*—commonly known as Major Shape Lightning.

Lightning fingers danced forth, snapping at the air with loud crackles. They pushed out in a web-like pattern about ten feet in diameter, beckoning at the wolven with reaper fingers. Augum could feel the ice-cold draw of arcane stamina trickling from his soul. He pumped just enough juice in to make the spell exquisitely painful to the touch. And should the situation demand it, with a mere thought and a flick of the wrists, he could ramp that power up—while also turning the accompanying stamina draw into a torrent.

Wanting to save his arcanery yet also make an example, he abruptly moved his hands toward the closest interloper who had dared to stray within five feet of the web. It instantly glommed onto the beast, and Augum flicked his wrists and focused on the wild surging—a surging that, had it been performed by a novice, could have easily led to the caster blowing himself up. The lightning flared in brightness and the beast convulsed. His flesh began to smoke as the other wolven howled and backed away.

Augum, feeling he had made his point, withdrew the lightning prior to the point of death, and the wolven collapsed where he stood, his watery armor and sword having vanished. The victim twitched on the cavern floor, his flesh smoking and bare after having his fur burned off, serving as a prime example for them all.

"I can envelop the entire cavern if I so choose," Augum said. It was a partial truth, for yes, he could envelop the cavern, but any surging would be diluted to a minor shock, which in arcane parlance was known as the *principle of dilution*.

The leader pushed through his brethren, flaming sword before him, flaming armor having been resummoned—but dimmer than before.

"Treacherous lowlander," he growled. "It was you who cast the fog and attacked our brethren."

It could have been Jez, Augum thought, hoping his mentor and her party had somehow tracked him down. But that didn't explain the icy mist, for she was a water warlock—nor could she possibly have learned a spell that unlocked manacles.

"Speak, blood vial," the leader barked.

"I did not cast that spell, and I did not attack your brethren. I was here. You saw me."

"We do not believe you."

He could have summoned his shield and sworn on it. But despite Lanfred telling the wolven about that concept, he suspected they would still call it some sort of lowlander ruse.

"Show thy stripes," the leader commanded.

Augum, obeying the third edict of the Sacred Chivalric Code of the Arcaner—*Thou shall always show thy stripes before thine enemy*—flared ten rings of lightning around his right forearm.

The leader snarled at them. "Who are you?"

"I am justice—"

"You are nothing but a cowardly lowlander—"

"—and I shall exact that justice on you, the leader of this pack of dishonored dogs."

The wolven growled as one, with one hissing, "Impudent swine."

Augum raised his chin, hands at the ready. "I offer you this. You can either bend the knee in surrender, *all* of you—"

This was met with howls of growling laughter. Even so, they cunningly positioned themselves for optimal lunging, with the web snapping and crackling before them. More than one clambered onto a table carved out of the mountain itself.

Augum continued. "I can take you all on one by one, and you can find out who I am in the Great Beyond ..." It was a gamble to even say it. "Or you—" He paused to bare his teeth at the leader. "—can take me on in an *ancro saleng*." If he survived, he resolved to investigate the strange occurrence later, only hoping it would not occur again in the mean. If it did, he would risk teleporting through rock to escape certain death.

The leader raised his snout. "A sacred challenge ..."

Many of the wolven flicked dismissive clawed paws at Augum as they growled an argument in wolven at the leader, whose cunning eyes remained fixed on the usurper in their midst. Those eyes took in the ten rings on Augum's arm.

"I challenge thee, dog. What say you?"

"You insult my honor."

As was my intent, Augum thought, hoping to bait the beast.

"My honor demands satisfaction. I accept thy sacred challenge, blood vial."

The other wolven growled their displeasure, but with a flick of the leader's clawed paws, they all retreated. The leader then stepped back, kicking away a stool and a table to make space for the duel.

Augum snuffed his web of lightning and padded forth. "Honor is important to you. Believe it or not, it is important to me too. So let us duel in the old way." To accent his rings, he flared his eyes with lightning. It was known as The Settling, and it happened to warlocks if they advanced well beyond the demands of the arts with a spell. His eyes had first flared when he was an 8th whilst prowling the land of three suns, after he had trained his Telekinesis to a degree not seen since his great-grandmother walked the seven kingdoms of Sithesia. Telekinetically floating a heavy weight aloft for hours at a time had earned him that gift.

His crackling eyes allowed them a glimpse of his might. If he revealed his true potential through a certain simul, they would not see daylight again—and he would be responsible for a slaughter.

He bowed, mindful that the wolven had surrounded him but were keeping their distance. *Thou shall never turn thy back on a foe,* the code screamed at him. But sometimes one had to work with what one had. Everything he knew about the wolven said they would not interfere; otherwise, he would not have offered such a challenge in the first place. The leader bowed back, growling something ceremonial in his wolf tongue.

They began by pacing around each other. The wolven spun his fiery blade, making a steady *whoosh,* while Augum kept his hands open in readiness. He hadn't had a proper duel in some time, and never against a wolven. Yet it was not for skill that he battled, but for sacred trinkets of clothing and blood to bring back to the families of the slain. He could have tried looking around the cave for them, but that carried risks—and would require time he did not have at the moment. No, he would earn them in the old way, the only way these beasts seemingly respected.

The leader struck first, abruptly jabbing forth with his blade, but Augum rather calmly stepped aside. He made a yanking motion with his left hand, snapping, *"Disablo!"* casting the classic 2nd degree *Dismenteragonasha*—Disarm in the common parlance. However, he aimed the spell not at the blade, but at the armor, which vanished. Augum then used his dominant right hand to telekinetically catch the wolven's follow-up paw strike. For a brief moment, the mighty strength of the twelve-foot-tall wolven was a match for Augum's Telekinesis. But only because he wanted the wolves to think them an arcane match for each other. Then the space around Augum warped fishbowl-like and his eyes and arm rings flared brighter, all as he bent the wolven's paw back toward himself so swiftly the pitchfork claws sank into his unprotected chest—right down to the knuckles.

The leader gasped, his fiery blade blinking out of existence, and fell to his knees, his claws stuck. He looked up at the cave ceiling as if seeing the stars through all that rock and ice, shuddered, and fell forward, his snout plonking against Augum's foot.

The wolven gaped. All was still.

Suddenly there came a *swish* from behind. Augum sidestepped, but the maneuver was too quick, and he felt a searing stabbing sensation in his side. Immediately his training took over, and he saw himself on one of the ledges inside that cave and snapped off the incantation to Teleport, "*Impetus peragro!*" He vanished and reappeared with a deep *thwomp* on the ledge farthest away from them. There he whirled to face the pack as a whole, blood racing through his veins—and dribbling down his robe and onto the ledge.

The wolven snarled—not at him, but rather at the one that had betrayed the sacred challenge.

"So that is why you are known as The Dishonored," Augum hissed, eating the stinging pain that gnawed at his side like acid. He chanced a look down at his side and saw that part of the robe had been torn to ribbons. Beneath, three distinct slash marks glared red.

"Now I am bothered and ought to end you all," he growled, narrowing his lightning eyes, the callous predator within him begging to show them his true might.

Thou shall guard the honor of the arcane craft, the code chided him, almost in mock. "Bah!" He slapped his wrists a second time, roaring, "*Annihilo bato!*" and shot two huge bolts of lightning directly at the shelves of vials, which exploded upon contact with a great *sizzle*. In response, the wolven loosed a communal howl that sounded much like a lament. Augum ignored them, pointed at the two vials which had been the apprentices, still on the table where he had sat, and floated them to him.

"Their robes. I want them. And then I will leave you be."

"What do their robes matter?" one of the earless ones barked.

"They will matter to their families."

"Treacherous lowlander." The wolven paced to a basket, slapped off its lid, withdrew two bloody burgundy robes, and threw them onto the cavern floor. Augum flicked a hand and floated them over, setting them on the ledge beside the vials. Then he snatched an incomplete linen garment one of the wolven had been sewing and shot it over. He grabbed it between his hands, tore it into a long strip, and wrapped it around his torso, all whilst never taking his eyes off the enemy, nor allowing his rings or eyes to snuff. The lightning crackled menacingly, ready to snap forth and leap across the divide to shock them with the reaper's touch.

Refusing to indulge that shadowy longing, he instead barked, "My rucksack."

An eared wolven pointed to behind a table. Augum flicked a hand over and the table flipped, revealing the rucksack. He snatched it too, stuffed the vials and the bloody robes inside in such a manner to protect the vials, and hopped off the ledge, landing on a pile of straw. Then he straightened, trying not to wince from the exquisite pain in his side, and boldly strode forth. The wolven flared their elements anew, with more than one raising their weapons aloft and growling. He had expected them to step away, but all held their ground as a pack. Only mildly inconvenienced, he instead stopped twenty feet before them and yanked on the body of the leader. He slid forth, leaving a trail of blood—and making the wolven howl in rage.

But Augum took a knee before the leader, allowing his lightning eyes and arm rings to die. He placed a hand on the leader's head and, allowing his eyes to settle on him for the moment, said, "May your soul find the peace together we could not reach." Having satisfied the ancient tradition of the Final Valediction, he stood and backtracked toward the cave exit, snatching a loaf of unusually fat bread from a table on the way, as well as the crimson's spyglass, and stopped at the exit.

"If one more Solian so much as gets breathed on by any of you dogs, you shall not lay eyes on the dawn again."

With that, he walked out, vowing to teleport-hop a few times before starting the complex yet crude chain of communication using the summonable Arcaner vault.

AN IMPRESSION
IN THE SNOW

BRIDGET

The blizzard kept swallowing up the keep, forcing the investigators down the ladder in order to continue discussing the quandary of the lightning strike and how it could have snuffed arcanery—not just in people, but in artifacts. Every time that blizzard let up, a shivering soldier from the roof above would call, "Clear!" and the investigators, Captain Bridget Burns, laboriously carrying her husky Sabby, Herald Brittany Mires, juggling holding the ladder and her quill and clay tablet, and The Sword of the Oak and his soldiers would climb back up and continue their examination.

It was during one of these lulls when Bridget, having wandered off to a corner of the keep to take stock of nearby buildings, spotted a disturbance in the snow atop the steeply pitched roof of the Grand Hall that separated the inner and outer wards of the castle yard.

"... and on the subject of the order, Captain Burns, what say you about those constables who think the order oversteps its authority?" Brittany asked, trailing Bridget whilst trying not to step in Sabby's way—or on her leash. The husky was quite protective of her mistress, putting herself between people at every opportunity, sometimes growling at them if they ventured too close.

Whilst staring at the spot, Bridget held out Sabby's leash to the herald. "Do you mind?"

"Wha—? I ... I don't think she likes me very much and-and-and I'm-I'm-I'm more of a cat person—"

"I won't be long."

"Oh. Um, all right, I guess." Brittany winced as she accepted the leash, dancing away from the husky, whose tongue hung out as she eagerly looked up at Bridget, craving her attention.

The Sword of the Oak seemed to catch on to her plan and started marching their way, already barking something about how she needed to keep the soldiers with her. But Bridget vividly saw herself standing atop one of the ledges of the hall, going so far as to imagine the snow crunching underfoot and the way the crossbeams rose in great arches above. After all, the key to a successful teleport to a spot one had not been to before, but was within sight, was precise visualization. Teleporting to a spot one could not see or had never been to before was extremely risky, and cautionary tales existed of foolhardy warlocks fusing with the branches of a tree, after which they would suffer a most painful and hopefully quick end, or perhaps appear deep underground, never to be heard from again. Drinking and 'porting was another common way to go, one of the higher casualty rates affecting warlocks.

Brittany, already entangled by the leash as Sabby had made a circle around her, also caught on. "Wait, where are you going—" but she was cut off by the commander.

"You need to obey the writ exactly as worded, Captain. Otherwise we have anarchy and—"

"*Impetus peragro,*" Bridget snapped off, and vanished with a deep *thwomp.* After a stomach-lurching hop through the ether that lasted about one heartbeat, she appeared exactly above that ledge with a second *thwomp,* feeling the cold suckage of stamina from her soul. The farther one teleported, the more stamina the spell consumed. Since this was a brief hop, it was a fraction of how much it would take to teleport to, for example, the city of Antioc, about fifty leagues to the northeast.

Her feet sank into the snow—appearing just above the target was a trick of the craft, taught in depth at the academy, as was avoiding fusing one's feet with obstacles such as rain or snow or sand. Woe be to the warlock who didn't pay attention in *that* class, for having sand fused with one's foot was a most painful ordeal indeed.

After stabilizing herself—and trying not to look down at the steep drop-off behind her heels—Bridget kneeled to examine the disturbance. The snow here had been pressed by a weight too heavy for a mere bird. The mark in the snow looked like a giant footprint with an occasional scalloped edge. Whoever—or whatever—had been there had stamped their own footprint, bare of feet, causing the scalloping.

She placed her thumb into the smallest of these scalloped indentations, and found it dwarfed. "And this is only a pinky toe," she whispered.

She looked about for any other nearby evidence, and saw that one of the arch columns, which was caked in snow, had a thin line through it, as if someone had sliced it with a knife. She splayed the fingers of a hand and incanted, "*Un vun asperio aurum enchantus.*" But Reveal showed nothing untoward—no tendrils, nor wispy tendril evidence that sometimes remained after a fresh casting, though they usually vanished within heartbeats anyhow.

She peered at a row of stained-glass windows inset into the wall of the inner roof sanctum. The nearest depicted ancient knights battling a griffin atop a chevron crest. Through the amber and crimson and white glass, she could make out the empty candle-lit golden throne, the seat of power of the kingdom. How oft had she sat in those hard wooden benches in the hall which extended like the ribs of a corpse, listening to a tedious diatribe—and sometimes a lecture—on stately affairs …

"You're getting morbid, Bridget," she whispered to herself, searching about for clues, conscious of the clanking sound of men jogging in the inner ward—no doubt the commander and his knights. *So eager to bring their little pet to heel*, she thought, feeling like the knights were overextending their authority. She stood to look down at them. *You want to leash a warlock? Enjoy huffing about like fools.*

"Captain Burns!" The Sword of the Oak shouted amidst panting wheezes. "I must insist that—"

"I found something!" Bridget interrupted. She pointed to the keep. "I'll meet you back up top."

"Wait, I insist you come down so that we can escort—"

"*Impetus peragro!*" and Bridget once again vanished and reappeared with a *thwomp*, this time back atop the keep—and only a hand's width from Brittany, who jumped with a yelp.

"I found something," Bridget reported to Constable Depassier, ignoring the girl's protestations that she ought to have somehow been warned of Bridget's arrival. After explaining what she had found and having captured the old warlock's interest, they agreed to investigate it together, and as it so happened teleported off just as the panting knights fumbled back onto the roof.

"You ought not to make an enemy of him, Captain Burns," the investigator said in his Franterran accent as they stabilized themselves on the narrow ledge.

Bridget watched the commander gesticulating at her angrily to his men, though all seemed too tired to continue the comical pursuit. After all, stairs were that much harder to climb in full plate. "Too late for that," she said. "We have taken insult to each other many a time now."

Depassier sighed in the way of old men who had seen the street all too many times, and scooched past her so he could examine the depression in the snow better. Kneeling with a groan, he rubbed his whiskered chin and took his time pondering what he saw. "This was made by no man," he concluded, "but a beast."

"My sentiments as well, sir. What make you of that there?" She indicated the slice in the column ahead.

With another groan, the man attempted to haul his bulky frame back to his feet, but was having such a hard time of it that Bridget had to help him up. "Thank you, my dear," he wheezed, and pressed one hand against his ale belly and the other against the arch column. "Most peculiar," he said after examining the slice. "Most peculiar indeed." He made a horizontal slashing motion as if to get inside the beast's head. "Perhaps created by a blade, though why here exactly is an interesting question." He looked to the nearby windows that showed the throne, then down to the yard. "An excellent vantage point, if I may say so."

Bridget agreed with a nod. It caused her some anxiety to know that whatever beast this was could have been watching them for some time before striking. "But how did it slip through the castle's enchantments?" she asked.

"A quandary we have been discussing at length. The answer is, none of us know. It had to be expert-level casting."

"So you think it was a warlock?"

"Whether it was a man or a beast, or perhaps a man in the guise of a beast, it is evident that some form of arcanery has been cast."

With the blustery swirls of snow returning anew for another bout, Bridget folded her arms across her crimson robe and drew her hood up to ward against the shiver-inducing cold. "In your estimation, sir, what do you believe to have been the intent?"

"I believe the intent was observation and then …" He rubbed his chin again, glancing between the throne, the yard, and the keep. "… and then a test."

"To see how we would respond."

Depassier squeezed his wide nose a few times as his head bobbed with a nod.

Bridget looked about, imagining a creature watching them in that moment, but the blizzard was already obscuring the other buildings, and the wind was quickly picking up to gale strength.

"We ought to depart before we get blown off, my dear," Depassier said, and the pair teleported back to the keep, startling the herald anew.

"My word, Captain, I wish there was more warning," the young herald said, a hand pressed to her chest, the other straining to hold onto the tablet and the leash, for Sabby was trying to climb Bridget.

"My apologies," Bridget mumbled, rubbing Sabby's ears and patting her rump while watching Constable Depassier consult with his brown-robed colleagues.

"Before I inquire about what you found," Brittany went on, trying to slip the leash back into Bridget's hand, "how in Sithesia do you warlocks avoid teleporting into people? Mind taking this?"

"Diligent and repetitive training that steadily pushes one's bounds." Bridget took the leash and placed her gaze on the girl, ignoring The Sword of the Oak's presence, for the man had come up to stand insolently within her space. "And a detailed understanding of precisely how the craft works and how to use that knowledge to avoid injury," she added.

"A word, *Captain*," The Sword of the Oak hissed whilst Sabby had hopped down off Bridget to growl at him.

"No."

"I beg your pardon?"

Not budging, Bridget turned to stare at him from within her hood, feeling a second pair of eyes open from behind her soul, eyes as cold as the blizzard. "I owe you nothing."

"The writ—"

"—states I am to keep within the confines of the castle perimeter. It says nothing about owing you explanations."

"Fool girl," the man spat. "It's for your own protection that we stay near. What's with your damn dog, anyway?" He raised a gauntleted arm, which Sabby chomped down on and wrangled about, growling menacingly.

"She thinks you are accosting me. *Are* you accosting me ... *sir*?"

"This is far too cold for my bones, you must excuse me," Brittany mumbled, and descended the ladder, though Bridget suspected it was more out of fear of the dog than the cold. The investigators, who were having trouble holding onto their parchment notes in the blustery wind, followed her.

"Foul mutt—" The commander raised his other arm, about to punch the dog, when Bridget pointed and telekinetically snagged the arm. The man grunted, trying to push through, but her war-honed telekinetic might was far greater than his muscled strength.

"Blasted woman, unhand me! *Now!*"

Bridget brought the dog to heel with the leash and dropped her finger, letting go of him.

"Never lay a hand on me again, girl."

"But I did not put a hand on you, did I?"

The Sword of the Oak adjusted his vambrace and straightened. "You know what I meant. I remind you that I outrank you, Captain. I shall not suffer insubordination."

Bridget was going to reply that she no longer had patience for his sort, when a voice caught her attention, one that lent her comfort.

"Get your paws off my elbow, you weasel!" a young woman shouted from below.

"I see my knights have tracked down the other brat," The Sword of the Oak said, and took hold of Bridget's elbow.

She shrugged it off. "You forget yourself, *sir*," she hissed, only to realize the man was doing it to test her, to see if she would demure before his intimidating—and cynically amused—gaze. "You shall not place your hands on me either," she added, holding Sabby tight and close, for she wanted to wrangle the man anew. "You can do your job without impeding on my person." She picked Sabby up and descended the ladder—and felt someone throw their arms around her, someone who stank of lake water, ale and wine.

"There's my sweet Bridgey-poo!" Leera sang, smothering Bridget with a hug whilst receiving big tonguing laps up the cheek, which she didn't seem to mind at all, mumbling, "Love you too, you puffy dog you."

"Lee, really," but instead of peeling Leera off, she dragged her aside to an empty corner of the keep floor.

"Bastards won't tell me anything," Leera muttered, finally clambering off Bridget, weaving as she held onto her, spectacles slightly askew.

"That's because they—wait, what happened to your forehead? Are you—" Bridget dropped her voice. "Are you *drunk*?"

Leera squinted, pinching at the air. "Aye, maybe a wee bit," she replied in that tavern twang she had taken to using whenever she got into trouble. "But look what I found—" and she dug out a golden coin. "Lookie, lookie, lookie at my cookie …" She leaned forth, whispering, "It's from the time of Mrs. Stone. She was our age when they minted this coin. But that's not the fun part. Want to know what the fun part is?"

Leera leaned in even closer, forcing Bridget to step away from her rancorous breath. "There's a whole chest of them."

"That's great, but—"

"Also found this—buzz off, busy-bodies!" Leera snapped at the numerous gawking knights and investigators and servants, and she positioned her body to block their view, withdrawing a golden ring from a pocket.

"That's nice, Lee, but—"

"It's arcane, and sooo pwetty ..." Leera slipped it on and dangled it before Bridget. "Looks like I'm married, doesn't it?" Suddenly she went all serious. "*I think our men should return and drop to one knee and beg for forgiveness for*—" but she was abruptly muffled by Bridget's hand.

"Shut up, will you?" Bridget snapped, but in a way that Leera would know she wasn't actually being mean.

"Mmmfmfm," Leera mumbled through Bridget's hand.

"Not until you hear me out. Focus, all right?" Bridget recoiled from the lake and drink stenches, muttering, "Gods, you stink."

"Mmfmfm—"

"There's been an incident," and Bridget went on to explain everything, until Leera finally slapped Bridget's hand away, roaring, "Why didn't they simply *say* that?"

"Probably because they didn't want you drinkin' and portin'."

"You're terrible with that accent. Don't employ it again." Leera's eyes flitted about from behind her spectacles. "You'll embarrass us both."

Bridget straightened her spectacles for her. "Oh, Lee, why do you do this to yourself?" But she knew exactly why. Other than Augum, Bridget was the only person Leera truly confided in. They had been best friends since meeting at the academy as fourteen-year-old know-nothings. And what had happened to Leera in the recent war was steadily eating away at her. She would never admit it aloud, but she too wanted children, almost as much as Bridget. The sheer weight of knowing she would never be a mother, and further knowing she was the end of an ancient and legendary lineage, was a heavy burden to bear.

"Did you check on Augum?" Bridget whispered, referring to the vault.

"'Course I did."

"And ...?"

"He's fine. But you know him. Wouldn't tell us if he was on fire just so we wouldn't worry." She weaved about, unable to stand still. "Should've gone with him ..."

"You know we cannot leave the kingdom unguarded."

"Bah, look around. They can keep the kingdom safe in our absence. Besides, it's not like anyone's threatening us."

"You sure about that?"

Leera shrugged in that *What do I care?* manner she oft deployed these days. Then she reddened and blurted, "I slapped a noble."

"Excuse me?"

"Some highborn snotbag." She raised a dancing finger. "Wait, no, he slapped *me*. So of course I had to teach the pasty-faced scoundrel a little lesson in fear—"

"What in Sithesia are you talking about?"

"—and then I went off and stuck it in my mouth like an idiot …"

"What? Lee, make some sense will you—"

"My foot. I stuck my foot in my mouth good this time." Leera looked away as she nibbled on her fingernails, face pale, yet she continued to hold onto Bridget's arm for stability. "Gods, I don't want to think about it," she mumbled, voice cracking with pain.

"Lee, really, did you not hear me earlier? Do you not understand what *happened* here?"

Leera tried to refocus on Bridget, yet her eyes kept roving about. "Both of you should talk to him," she whispered.

"All right, Two-moons, I've heard enough. I'm taking you to bed. Move it, missy." She tugged on the husky's leash. "You too, Sabby."

"Yes, m'lady," Leera mumbled. "Bed would be awfully nice. Maybe a cuddle with Sir Pawsalot."

"They won't let us leave this castle."

Leera flapped a hand as if swatting a fly. "Nonsense."

"I'm afraid it's commanded by writ."

"Yeah, well, I'll 'port wherever and whenever the hell I want to."

Bridget gave Leera a sharp jerk of the arm. "You will not dare. You're going to sleep this off and we'll pick up in the morning. And you *better* show up for morning training. Now let's find us castle quarters so we can both get a good night's sleep."

Leera stiffened with a salute. "Yes, Cap! Right away, Cap!"

"Will you *shut up*?" Bridget snapped, painfully cognizant of the herald girl furiously scribbling away. "Gods, I can't *believe* you," and she half-dragged half-walked Leera out of there, but not before telling the herald they would resume in the morning and asking Constable Depassier to keep her abreast of the situation.

"I will be sure to do so, Captain Burns," the constable replied. "Fair eve to you."

Soldiers in tow, the two women left arm-in-arm to find suitable quarters, Sabby pining up at the pair of them.

WASHBASIN

LEERA

Within a carved four-poster canopy bedstead, on a mattress of feather bound by the finest Tiberran cotton, and twisted amidst a goose down and wool blanket depicting the crest of the Black Castle, lay the still figure of Leera, raven hair sprawling around her like branches of eels.

A ray of thin light that had been slithering up her body all morning finally reached her puffy eye. She groaned and turned away from the harsh light—only to slip off the bed and crash to the rug, head plonking on an empty washbasin.

"Ugh," Leera moaned, hand fumbling about until it closed on the bowl, which she picked up and threw away. It smashed against a checkered floor, making her wince anew. It was a struggle to open her eyes through the blinding headache that pounded on her brain like a smith hammering an anvil.

She moaned, hauling herself to a sitting position and taking stock of where she was. It certainly wasn't in her bed in Castle Arinthian, that was for sure. And thank the gods for that, as otherwise that would mean she had drunk-'ported. Judging by the red velvet curtains and a tall golden vase standing on a marble stand, it was some noble's house.

Suddenly terrified she might have done something she would forever regret, she quickly checked her person—and found herself still wearing her crimson robe from the night before. She slumped against the bed frame with a sigh. "So where the heck am I?" she croaked.

A knock came at the door, which seemed overly fancy with its exquisite carvings of things too blurry to make out without her spectacles. Leera wanted to ask who it was, but all that came out was a rather pathetic moan.

"My lady? Is everything all right? I heard a crash," the voice of a young woman said from the other side.

"Muuuugh …"

"May I come in, my lady?"

"Nuh-uh."

"I do apologize, but I cannot make sense of you and am coming in to make sure all is well." The door creaked open, and Leera dragged the blanket over herself to hide her shame, though what she was ashamed of she could not say.

"My lady?"

Leera stole a peek from underneath the blanket. "Mmmuh?" She saw a young woman about her age wearing a servant's black-and-white gown accented with gold and blue, her long blond hair tied up neatly in a bun and sitting underneath a white hat.

"Happy third day of Endyear, my lady. And I hope you had a wonderful feast and dance to enjoy Lover's Day."

Leera snorted derisively.

"Captain Burns asked me to check on you as soon as you woke," the girl said, hurrying to a wall pasted with fancy wallpaper that showed golden ivy and thistle crosshatching over a black background. "And she told me to remind you that you have morning training with your Arcaner brethren." She grabbed a hidden doorknob and opened a thin closet, withdrew a bound broom and a dustpan, and went to the detritus of the washbasin.

"Leave it," Leera blurted, fumbling about in search of her spectacles.

"It is no trouble, my lady—"

"I broke it, I'll mend it. Leave it."

The girl bowed. "As you wish, my lady," and returned the broom and pan to the closet before sweeping to the curtains and, before Leera could stop her, throwing them open.

"Gods," Leera moaned, flinching away from the light and raising an arm to shield her eyes. She imagined Sir Pawsalot hissing at being woken suddenly.

"It's midday, my lady, and it's actually quite cloudy and snowy. There's almost two feet of snow out there. The children are already playing. But the parents are a bit worse for wear on account of—"

"—Lover's Day, I know," Leera muttered.

"The light all right, my lady?"

"Might as well be a beacon fire." The joyful sounds of the children somehow hurt more than the light and the headache, though her befuddled mind couldn't make out why.

The woman kindly drew the curtains halfway. "May I start you a fire?"

"Please. It's freezing in here." Leera kept fumbling about the ground, only to realize there was a nightstand nearby, but it was too far and her stomach wanted to empty itself of its contents.

"Your spectacles are here, my lady," the woman said, grabbing them off a nearby marble-topped dresser and bringing them forth.

Leera tried to hook the spectacles over one ear, but snagged her hair. She fought with the frizzy jungle, only to hopelessly tangle her spectacles up in a knot.

The woman, who brought the hearth to a roaring light by placing a hand to a rune and whispering, "*Igniato*," turned to a struggling Leera and tried not to smile. "May I, my lady?"

Leera let her spectacles dangle from her hair, mumbling, "I'm a mess."

The young woman came over, kneeled beside her, and gently began unhooking the spectacles. "Got yourself quite tangled here, my lady."

"Did I break the puke bowl?"

"Your sister-in-war left it for you in case you, uh, felt ill of stomach."

"How thoughtful of her." Leera rubbed each puffy eye with the heel of her hand. "Where am I, anyway?"

"The guest floor."

"Fine, but where?"

"The Black Castle, of course."

Leera grunted. "Bumblebutt missed me then."

"Bumblebutt?" The girl reddened. "Is that, uh, the name you call your betrothed?"

Leera chuckled. "It's the nickname for my cat because of how he waddles about. Aug wouldn't take kindly to being called Bumblebutt." But the more she thought about it, the funnier it became.

The servant tried to hide her smile. "I would imagine not, my lady. A commander of such a distinguished order needs his dignity." She finally freed the spectacles and placed them onto Leera's nose, hooking the other ear last. "Oh, but they're quite dirty," she noted, and promptly removed them again.

Leera sat in a daze, eyes unfocused on the blurry fire as her head throbbed. "Toasty," she said despite feeling queasy. She eyed the detritus of the bowl. Thinking she might have to make use of it shortly, she crawled over, spread her hands over the broken shards, tried to focus on the nuance of the 1st degree Repair spell, and mumbled, "*Apreyo*."

A few pieces tumbled toward the bowl before stopping.

"Focus, you idiot," Leera muttered, wincing from the headache. *Two halves becoming one, repairing what was broken. Unity, completion, perfection. The whole is the sum of its parts.* With her thoughts aligned, she repeated, "*Apreyo.*"

While the pieces tumbled back together at a rather slovenly pace, sealing together with a small white light, the servant pulled on a long silk ribbon that would ring a bell in the servant's quarters. "I'll have some Tiberran ginger-peppermint tea brought right away, my lady."

Leera was halfway through repairing the bowl when the queasiness got the better of her and she lost concentration, rolling over lest she vomited. "Thank you," she mumbled, eyes closed to ward off the queasiness. Being hungover was the closest she ever got to seasickness. "I'm never drinking again," she mumbled, a lie she had said many a time before.

The door soon creaked open, and Leera heard the woman whisper, "Tea for our guest. Tiberran ginger-peppermint, right quick, and some bread."

"Is that … is that the *dragon* lady?" a mousy voice squeaked.

"That is none of your concern," the blond servant hissed. "Now stop gawking and get a move on, girl!"

Leera, long used to such reactions from those who had never met her, only lay still, urging the nausea and vertigo to subside. The door closed and she heard footsteps pad by, followed by the quiet ruffling of the bed being made.

"I'm sorry," Leera mumbled.

"My lady is a woman grown who has nothing to apologize for."

"But I do. I'm supposed to be a 'model of propriety,' " she said, twisting the words with mock. "At least that's what Jez always says." She raised a finger. "And mind you, that hypocrite's a drunk."

"Jez?"

"My mentor, Jezebel Terse. All right, *our* mentor, but she's a water warlock so works with me more. The other two goblins have separate mentors for their elements."

"I have never heard Captain Burns and Commander Stone referred to as goblins before."

"I can hear you wanting to laugh. You needn't play coy with me. I don't care for proprieties like my sister-in-war does."

"Then I shall chortle freely," the servant replied, adding in a whisper, "but only in your private company, my lady."

Leera gave a pretend-serious nod. "It will be our secret."

For a time, Leera only listened to the crackle of the fire, until another knock came at the door. There was another whispered exchange, followed by another quiet lambasting of the other servant to "better skitter off lest she get privy duty. And hold that tongue! Not a word to the others. Discretion, am I understood?"

"Yes, my lady," squeaked a girl from the other side.

The woman gently closed the door and placed something beside Leera, who was roused by the sweet scent of ginger and peppermint. The tea consisted of a silver teapot engraved with the royal crest of the kingdom, sitting on a silver trivet and engraved oval platter. It came with a silver bowl of sugar, an ornate spoon, and a fine porcelain cup and saucer, both painted with the royal crest. Three slices of freshly baked bread rested in a silver basket bottomed with a white cloth. And sitting on the edge was a tightly rolled scroll tied with a blue ribbon.

"I thought my lady would like the morning herald," the woman said, daintily pouring the tea into the cup.

Seeing that the tea was still too hot, Leera snatched a piece of bread. "I don't read those much. Too much gossip or blowing smoke up our robes or trying to tear us down or gods know what."

The woman wrung her hands.

"What is it?" Leera mumbled around a mouthful of bread, the acids in her stomach already subsiding.

"Forgive me, my lady, but I think today's herald is … er …"

"What, some village needs saving, does it? You know, contrary to the belief of folks, we don't enjoy casting *the* spell. Sure, the joy of flight is a miracle. Seeing farm fields far below like little tiles, and people like ants … yes, that's truly incredible. And that stomach-lightening feeling of flight is …" Leera shook her head, eyes staring through the flames as she chewed. "… hard to describe." She wagged a finger. "But everything has a price. And before you ask, I can't share that price with you. It's for us to bear." It was imperative no one learned of the side effects, for an enemy could easily use it against them. Their sufferings were only for themselves, each other, and a select few confidants.

"My lady, the, uh, allegations are of a more … *personal* nature."

"Allegations? Did Jez stick her foot in her mouth again? What did that drunkard say now?" Leera finally allowed herself a tepid sip of tea, and finding it quite soothing to her palate and stomach, kept sipping it. Quickly feeling better, between sips she spread a hand over the remaining wreckage of the basin and incanted, "*Apreyo*," guiding the pieces back into place and enjoying seeing that final brighter seal of light that only happened with a return to totality.

"My lady, forgive me for speaking out of turn and well above my station, but I do apologize for what they said. I think it's grossly unfair. Grossly, *grossly* unfair. I think it ought to be against the law to besmirch the name of one of the heroes of the kingdom like that."

Leera slowly put down her tea as she gawked at the girl, a sinking feeling in her stomach. She took the scroll and shakily tried to undo the ribbon, only to accidentally tighten the knot instead of loosening it.

"Allow me, my lady," the woman said, opening her hands in offer. Leera placed the scroll into them, drew her knees up to her chest, held her legs, and dumped her head onto her knees. "Read it to me."

"Are you sure? I can leave to give you privacy and—"

"Please. Besides, the letters would swim before my eyes right now." She wasn't ready for the written word yet.

The woman cleared her throat. "Er … very well." She undid the ribbon and unfurled the scroll. " '*The Blackhaven Herald*. Hark! For this inquisitive herald has stumbled upon the most scandalous news the kingdom has heard in some years, heard directly from the mouth of one of its heroes. Let me jab the spear right in, for Captain Leera Jones—one of the very heroes able to summon the might of the dragon—told me, woman to woman, that she is unable to bear children.' "

As if a warlock had zapped her with a bolt of lightning, Leera jolted so suddenly she kicked the tray, sending the teapot, teacup, and bread flying. She slapped both hands over her mouth to smother the scream that wanted to escape, before bending over the washbasin to vomit.

The woman kneeled beside her to rub and pat her back. "I really am sorry, my lady. It is a beastly piece, an unheard-of low to stoop to."

Leera fell over and away from the hand, stifling a cry. She telekinetically snatched the blanket and lamely pulled it over herself, though in truth she wanted to crawl under the bed and die.

"I cannot imagine how you must feel."

Ensconced, Leera frantically went over the evening prior, but the memory got hazy after that first goblet of wine. She remembered talking to a nice woman, and then things got a bit tense. But then what? She must have spilled her guts to someone who had turned out to be a herald. *That's what you get for trusting strangers, you damn fool you!*

"Would my lady like me to leave her be?"

"Yes … no. I don't know," Leera blubbered from under the blanket. "Gods, what have I done … now they all know."

"That may be so, but I am sure—oh. *Oh.* Forgive me, my lady, but are you suggesting—"

"Yes, it's true," Leera whispered. "I could cause the end of an ancient lineage. And now they all know. Now they all know …"

There was a silence before the girl abruptly burst with a cry.

Leera slipped off the blanket and saw the young woman on her knees and covering her face with her hands. Leera didn't know what to do. "You … er …" She awkwardly patted the girl's knee. "Don't need to feel bad for, um … me."

"It's just so unfair to you," the girl blubbered through her tears. "A rank injustice inflicted by scoundrels, by the devil himself."

"I suppose …"

"One of the kingdom's own daughters …" The girl sat up, eyes red and a bit crazy as she stared at Leera with a most intense look. "It was a curse, right? But curses can be undone …"

"It's too ancient."

"Then you must find an ancient solution."

Leera stared at the mesmerizing flames. That thought had never occurred to her. The arcaneologists who had arcanely examined the imprint of the curse had said it was lodged in the ether itself, unreachable by known arcanery. But that could be a key word, couldn't it? *Known* arcanery!

Still staring through the flames, Leera nibbled on her nails, which were already nibbled to the point of giving her constant acidic pain, with the fingers bulging out beyond the nails, forcing her teeth to bite farther and farther in to grab hold, making the situation ever more painful.

"Can you read the rest of it?"

"Are you sure? It is quite—"

"Please. My head still swims."

"Of course, my lady." The girl withdrew a cloth and dabbed at her tears, apologizing profusely throughout for her intransigence and lack of propriety.

"Don't concern yourself about all that," Leera mumbled, mind buzzing away with ideas whilst trying not to think about the public implications of what she had revealed.

"Er … reading on here. 'There has long been speculation that Captain Leera Jones suffered a particularly potent curse during the war, though what the effect of that curse was has not been publicly known—until now, and from the young champion's own lips at that. The word from the nobility is immediate and rather harsh. "The captain ought to renounce her betrothal," Lady Alanna Haught is quoted as saying. The distinguished noble of high birth has been deemed as a highly suitable match for Augum Arinthian Stone—' "

"That scheming b—" but Leera pressed her lips together so firmly they puffed forth. Instead of cursing, she telekinetically snatched a pillow from the bed, pressed it to her face, and screamed into it out of frustration, rage, and embarrassment. The Haught woman had insisted on a dance with Augum at some fancy ball held in the trio's honor. She'd taken her time and kept flirting with him, which had been followed by Leera "accidentally" tripping and spilling a goblet of wine on the woman's fancy snow dress. A whole public kerfuffle resulted from that, with many an ill piece published in the heralds, the strings of which were held by such nobles.

"Augum has zero interest in that harpie," Leera announced through the pillow, though she couldn't help but recall him laughing at one of her jests while they had slow-danced together. He had later told Leera that he had laughed because the woman was being utterly ridiculous, but it had sounded too genuine to Leera, and now doubt crept in like a fungus.

"You know what I think, my lady? I think you should ignore all this. It is—and you must forgive my baseness—it is utter *horse dung*," she whispered.

Leera tossed aside the pillow, threw off the blanket, and jumped to her feet. "I'm going to—*whoa*." Her vision had blackened as a wave of nausea washed over her, forcing her to steady herself against one of the canopy bedstead posts.

"My lady ought to rest until—"

"No. Already puked my guts out. Just need ..." Leera pointed at the slices of bread, which shot up off the floor and zipped to her waiting hand. She snatched each from the air, bit down on the half-eaten one, and stuffed the other two in her pocket. "I'm going to occupy my mind with research." She began marching to the door, only to stop and turn around, a piece of bread wagging in her mouth. "The common library here in the castle," she mumbled through the bread before removing it. "Does it have books on the craft?"

"Of course, my lady. May I take you there?"

"Please." Leera had never visited the library of the Black Castle, for she most often went to the one in the Academy of Arcane Arts, or sometimes even the awe-inspiring castle-turned-library in the city of Antioc.

She noticed the mess she had made of the tray of tea. "Let me first—"

"No. Forgive me, but I have new girls who need training. Please allow them their duty. You have gone through enough today."

"That is very kind of you."

The girl curtsied. "It is my honor, my esteemed lady. Oh, and speaking of training, may I remind my lady that Captain Burns expects you to be—"

"—in the yard bruising my wrists alongside the others, no doubt. Yes, yes, maybe later." Leera turned toward the door, then turned back again. "You know, I am so rude. I didn't even ask you your name."

"Gertude Dolores Hooper, third daughter of Alistaire and Josette Hooper." She dawdled. "I-I-I know barrel- and bucket-making is a lowborn occupation but I am quite proud of my father and mother and—"

"Gertie, stop it. May I call you Gertie?"

"Er … my lady may call me as she wishes, as I am merely a common servant who—"

"Will you work for me?"

The girl gaped. "I … I'm sorry?"

"I've been told I need a servant. A lady-in-waiting, so to speak. I've been putting it off for forever, and I need someone I can trust."

"But my lady … I am practically an Ordinary who can barely work the runes of this very castle. I hit my ceiling as an *aspirant*, for Unnameables' sake! I'm a lowly hooper's daughter who has no right being around a-a-a—" The girl indicated Leera from foot to head and back again.

"And I'm a saddler's daughter. Mother was an ale taster. Don't make me do this." Leera dropped to one knee.

"Really, my lady that is most unnecessary—"

Leera reached into her pocket and withdrew the old coin she had pilfered from the bottom of the lakebed and offered it up like a ring of betrothal. "Miss Gertrude Dolores Hooper, daughter of Alistaire and Josette Hooper, will you please accept this token shipwreck crown and work for me? I promise to pay and treat you well."

The girl slapped a hand over her mouth to prevent a burst of laughter. "My lady is most ridiculous," she mumbled, the corners of her eyes crinkling with mirth.

Leera shot to her feet, snatched the girl's wrist, pressed the crown into her hand, closed her fingers over the coin, and said, "I'll take that as a yes. We'll work out the details later."

"I … I …"

"And I want you to feel free to express yourself to me at any time. I mean that. I need people to speak their minds, not tell me what I want to hear." Leera stopped at the door, the bread back in her mouth. "You coming or not?"

The girl gaped, before quickly and repeatedly nodding with a beaming smile. "Of course, my lady. I am deeply honored and cannot believe you would choose someone like me to—"

"Good," Leera said, chewing what remained of the bread. "I need guidance to contend with these vultures. You're sure Gertie is fine? Gods help you, why did your folks call you Gertrude? And then to saddle you with that awful middle name of Dolores …"

"Yes, I, uh, suffered quite the trials in school for those names. But I find they suit service rather well."

Leera, withdrawing a second piece of bread from her pocket and munching on it, threw open the door, only to discover two young armored knights manning it. "What are you two goons doing here?" she asked, striding past.

"We have been ordered to keep you safe in case the event occurs again, my lady," one said, cheeks blushing, eyes trying to avoid her face, yet they kept flicking back to it. "And happy Endyear," he blurted.

Leera whirled about. "What? What event?" she asked through a mouthful. "And Happy Endyear and all that to you too."

The other, who seemed not to care about her looks, filled her in on the prior night's happening. By the end of the telling, Leera threw up her arms. "Why didn't the jerks write about *that*?"

"They did, my lady," Gertrude sheepishly mumbled. "It's the next piece down on the scroll."

"Read it to me as we walk to the library," and Leera continued on, allowing Gertrude to lead the way.

"She is stunningly comely in a wild sort of way," the young knight whispered to his cohort.

"Shut up," the other hissed.

Leera only rolled her eyes.

A MAJESTIC VIEW

AUGUM

Augum moaned in distress for a third time before his eyes finally fluttered open, a pulsing headache splitting his brain in two. He saw a wide sky of occasional puffy clouds pierced by rays of sunshine. But they were eclipsed by a fierce pain in his side—and in his right leg. He groaned as he dizzily sat up, and felt a numb tingling in his left arm, which hung limply.

"The hell's with *you* wrong?" he muttered at it, barely cognizant that he had bungled his words. He tried to get the arm to move, but it lay there like a limp noodle. He took a moment to look about and saw that he was on the side of a mountain staring at a vast valley. Far down below, a river snaked between snowy behemoths. That was when his leg caught his attention, for it was twisted at a most gruesome angle from the knee down, so that his toes faced backward, pointing into the snow.

The sight made him gasp and fall back, nausea swirling within. He remembered teleport-hopping twice to get clear of the wolven and then snapping off the incantation a third time, but that was where memory ended.

He craned his neck back and saw a skid and tumble trail in the snow that began from a crater some ways up the slope. He must have teleport-slammed into the mountain then tumbled down, unconscious, probably twisting his leg along the way—or snagging it on one of the myriad shards of rock that stuck out from the mountain like thorns. As to his arm—he reached out with his right hand and felt the shoulder, and realized it had pulled free of the socket. That awakened the pain, which began to throb in time with his head.

"Lovely," he said, knowing he had to get his foot arcanely fixed up by a healer lest the injury set. Yet he had to admit he had been lucky to wake up at all. Most teleport failures resulted in gruesome deaths. "Got away one," he muttered, a little confused as to why he wasn't being as articulate as usual. He delicately felt his head, finding a wound above a bump that had begun to congeal—likely where his head had struck a rock. "Stupid got …" What was he trying to say? He winced in concentration. "Stupid thing got me," he said, enunciating each word. What a trial to even say things right …

He sat back up on his good elbow to take stock of the situation. Except for conifers lining the bases of the mountains far below, there was no sign of life anywhere for leagues, not even the smoke of a hamlet. But there *was* what looked like a trail winding through the snowy forest below, an agonizing descent of five thousand feet or so.

"Just wonderful," he said, dizzily wincing—he figured he must have sustained quite the knock to the head for his thoughts and words to get this jumbled. Thankfully he had been trained to ignore the pain of injury, no matter how bad. Were it not for that training, he would have lost focus—and risked further injury.

Looking up the skid trail, he spotted his rucksack seventy feet up. He grabbed his leg and freed it from the snow—and held his tongue so as not to scream from the pain. His foot came free, revealing he had lost his boot. His three toes showed themselves—he was no stranger to failed teleporting, having once used his sword to cut off two of his own toes after accidentally fusing them with the frozen ground, all in order to escape a diving dragon. The feat had earned him the nickname Three Toes.

Realizing he would have to wrap the foot up quickly lest he lose it to frostbite, he shoved the pain into that pulsing part of his brain, ordered that part to take charge of the entire mess, and focused on the climb, which meant he had to use his one good arm to drag himself hand by agonizing hand up the steep slope.

Once within forty feet of the rucksack, he flopped forward in the snow, panting. After catching his breath, he pointed a finger, felt the tendril of his mighty Telekinesis hook onto the canvas—which took a few clumsy tries—and slowly pulled. The rucksack dragged and tumbled toward him. Mercifully, it did not leave a trail of blood, indicating the vials were intact—like soft coffins, he had smartly wrapped them within the apprentice robes for the trek.

"Sorry for what I go do," he dizzily mumbled as he withdrew one of the yellow rope belts woven from hemp. He wincingly wrapped this around his foot, creating a makeshift shoe, all while trying not to move the foot much, for every little budge caused pain to shoot up his leg.

Once retrieved, he inspected the contents to confirm they had not broken—not even a crack in the vials! Having only one useful arm was quite annoying, for everything took forever to get done. He next withdrew the bread, which he scarfed down like a starved lion, surprised to taste herbs like ginger and rosemary, along with a flowery spice he could not place. The wolven sure knew how to make bread. He thought of Leera, wondering what she was up to, wishing he could have brought her along. But the king had explicitly ordered that only one of them could leave the kingdom at a time in case of an attack. He had not argued because of the wisdom of it and, wanting to make an example of himself to the other order devotees, had chosen to spearhead the quest, for he could not place a novice in such danger. That and it was a perfect excuse to go on a badly needed *trekanasola*—a trek of the soul.

"Now pay price for fool plan," he muttered as he chewed, angry with himself for his carelessness, angry with his stupid tongue for not articulating what his thoughts demanded.

He had always had a reckless streak in him. It had begun as a boy, after running away from the only home he had known—a farm where he had served as an orphan slave, one bullied by three kids and their parents. After trekking the Gamber River, he began a new life in Willowbrook, a quaint farming village in the middle of the tall yellow grasses of The Tallows. There he became squire to a knight, a stern but compassionate Ordinary who had taught him honor, how to work with his hands and, more importantly, how to read and write the written word, which in turn awakened an inquisitiveness that aided greatly in his studies of the arcane arts.

That knight had died defending the village from the Legion, leaving behind the lessons of sacrifice, and the model of a man of honor. In that one act, he had paved the way for the revival of the Arcaner order in the then fourteen-year-old.

Augum turned his thoughts to his sister-in-war, Bridget, and wondered how she fared taking charge of the order in his absence. She had been the valedictorian for their academy graduation, and had made quite the memorable speech, talking about balancing passion with responsibility, and how that applied to the resurrection of the Arcaner order. He knew she had wanted a humbler life, one that involved a big family and maybe being a teacher. Yet he was happy to have her around, even though she felt frustrated by the expectations of kingdom defense, running a complex order, and juggling a misfit of a betrothed who also happened to be Augum's best friend, Olaf Hroljassen.

"I'll have that ..." He winced, focusing. "... ale with you, Ollie ... after. When I out of here. When I *get* out of here. No, that ain't it. When I find my way back. Yeah, that's it." He loved spending time with Olaf, for the man was as true a friend as Augum had hoped he would ever have. The young Arcaner brethren had also joined the tracking party north and, along with the others in the party, was probably worried that something had happened to Augum. They should all have been enjoying a merry Endyear feast together instead of risking their lives. Then again, the pair of apprentices he had quested to save had also deserved a feast with their families. Now they would join such future feasts as vials of blood, to perhaps sit on the family mantel atop their cleaned and folded robes, or get buried, or who knew what ...

"Didn't plan too well this, did you?" Augum muttered, thoughts swimming in vertigo, the words jumbling up.

After finishing half the bread, and too weak and unfocused from the unusually painful headache to cast most spells, and certainly not willing to risk another teleport, he began dragging himself down the slope toward the trail. He hoped to flag down a passerby and hitch a ride to the nearest town where he could perhaps convince someone to attend to his injuries.

He grunted after each pull, his leg and shoulder and side wound and head pulsing with agony, creasing his face with a perpetual wince. In between the passing clouds, rays of sunshine sliced across the ice, making it glitter. He managed two hundred feet before needing to rest, exhausted from the trial.

"This not good," he stupidly said to the wind, which kicked about swirls of snow and particles of ice that tinkled against the hard surface of the slope. "Not good at all." Yet he had been in far worse predicaments, once dragging himself, Leera, and Bridget through winding caverns deep underground for who knew how long. Surviving on little else but moss and lichen and cave water, they had withered to mere skin and bones, and by the end, all had been on the verge of death. *That* had been an ordeal.

"This ain't nothing," he slurred, trying to convince himself. "Keep go, keep go, keep ... keep *going*." Right, that was what he had wanted to say, yes. His brain rang as if stricken by a bell.

He continued dragging himself onward, sometimes raising his leg and skidding on his butt with the rucksack slung around his chest, at other times turning about to slide head first. The long stretches of ice were the easiest, soft snow the hardest. Arm-pull by agonizing lone arm-pull, he slithered another hundred feet before finding himself staring at a sheer two-thousand-foot precipice. Far below waited a terrain of snow-covered boulders, which trickled along a long and gentle slope all the way to the tree line.

Had his head not been feeling like someone was chiseling away at it, and were his arm not out of its socket, he'd certainly consider casting the mythical Spirit of the Dragon simul. What a ledge to launch from too! But the way his words wouldn't come out right made casting *any* spell, let alone *the spell*, a risky proposition at best. And the thing was, his shoulder was injured, and he didn't know if that would translate to a wing. The last thing he needed was to cast that spell only to find himself a flightless dope, then upon reversion, experiencing the harrowing side effects — while injured.

Yet even thinking about the ancient simul drew a shadow out from behind his soul. That callous creature looked on at the situation with eyes as black as its form. "Piss off," Augum told it, but the shadow did not withdraw, as if it sensed his weakness.

Augum, choosing to ignore it, surveyed the ridge line and saw that the left angled down and then rose back up to join another peak, which meant climbing at some point again, while the right descended before vanishing around the mountain.

Right it is, he thought, not wanting to waste energy verbalizing — then bungling — any more words, which only scared him further. Before starting the trek, he thought to at least try to summon the Arcaner vault and check if Leera or Bridget had left him a message. Unfortunately he had no way to write a message himself, having no ink or parchment. And the idea of using the vial blood as ink repulsed him so much that he excised it from his mind.

Augum put his thoughts together to start the process, which began by summoning his full Arcaner shield — except the shield wouldn't light, his limp arm preventing its summoning. He sat staring at the useless limb, unable to believe how the unusually bad luck of events was stacking up against him. After a deep sigh, he began the long trek.

This is not how I end, he thought, dragging himself along the ridgeline. *This is not how I* — there was a sharp *crack* underneath him as the ridge collapsed. He felt the stomach-lightening sensation of falling and, between the snowfall, glimpsed a vast void — and death waiting in the morass below.

War-honed and academy- and order-trained reflexes kicking in, he lashed out with his one good arm at the sheer wall of ice. The invisible tendril line of Telekinesis latched on, then he swung—and promptly slammed—into the wall. He screamed from myriad pains, most of all his twisted leg and the slashes in his side, which began to bleed anew—he could feel the blood trickling down his torso and leg.

The child within him, the frightened boy who was still suffering lashings on that farm, wanted to cry from the raw gut-wrenching pains. But the young man who had experienced war in all its barbarity, who had seen heads explode and limbs fly and gruesome eviscerations left out of the war stories, merely looked up the ridge line. He was a whopping sixty feet down from the ledge—his reflexes hadn't been as quick as he had thought. Also, he couldn't have known it, but he had been dragging himself along a snowy overhang. There was a word for such an overhang, but his addled brain couldn't come up with it, other than it had something to do with corn.

He saw Bridget raise a finger as she verbalized the word. "Cornice!" he blurted. *Yes, that's right.* "Cornice ..."

Although he of all people had a mighty pool of stamina to draw from, for he of all dueled and trained the most, testing every order applicant like a patient arcanist, his rock-smacked brain was hardly working at its full potential. And with that stamina bleeding away like the blood dribbling down his leg—it took a lot to hang there—he needed to act and act fast.

Normally, he would latch a second telekinetic tendril rope at a higher spot and haul himself back up, a feat that was impossible with one limp arm. Instead, he put his mind toward trying something he had never done before—telekinetically hauling himself up with only one good arm, an arm already busy holding onto the tendril rope. Staring fixedly at the spot where he thought he had latched onto, he focused all his arcane might into the endeavor—and began rising. The space around him warped fishbowl-like in what was known as a *field warp*, hinting at the sheer strength of his Telekinesis, and his eyes flared with lightning, as did his arm, revealing ten rings of crackling blue. He made it a whole five up feet before realizing the pace was far too slow, and he would run out of stamina before getting to the top. He thus ceased the endeavor, leaving himself hanging in place.

Bit of a quandary was what he wanted his rock-struck mind to say. "Bit of a stuck," was what came out.

The truth sank in. There was only one way to go—down. It had to be done carefully though.

He took a long, shuddering breath, and thought of lying on his beloved's tummy as she basked in the sun, her arms back behind her head, eyes blissfully closed, raven hair tucked into her hood. He thought of the slow rise and fall of her chest and hearing her heart. How he wanted to snuggle her now!

Then he let go and plummeted, only to latch on again twenty feet down, slamming into the icy face a second time—and crying out in pain. The side wounds opened further, the blood streaming through the makeshift bandage. If he fell too far, the speed would increase to a point where he would splatter against the wall, maybe even knocking him out cold. And if he continued at this slovenly pace of smashing himself with every fall, he would beat himself into a bloody pulp.

"Idiot," he hissed through clenched teeth. "Lower yourself instead."

After letting the pain subside, he began lowering himself by the tendril line. But the same problem arose, for he eventually reached the end of the invisible rope, dictated by the range of his ability to cast Telekinesis, which was about forty feet, an impressive distance for any warlock, let alone one at his degree. This forced him to repeat the fall-and-catch maneuver anew, which resulted in another screaming bout of pain and nausea—and the horrible sensation of black walls of unconsciousness briefly closing in on him. Sure, he could release and catch himself every few feet instead, but that was a more agonizing way to go because of the amount of repetitions involved that would irk his wounds.

It all meant there was no way he could keep this up. None. The stark realization that he would not make it to the bottom sliced through the fog of his mind like a spear, which at least served to clarify his thoughts a little. So, instead of continuing to arcanely rappel down, he clung to the side of the mountain, brain trying to think of a way out. What boded menacingly was a black cloud bank coming in from what he guessed was the south.

He glanced down beyond his dangling legs, with one rope-wrapped foot still facing backward, and focused on the morass two thousand feet below—and the movement of people—a *party* of people. Maybe— miraculously—it was his friends and mentor! Amazingly, the group was drawing toward the spot where he would land if he were to fall. He did not know how they had done it, but they had somehow found him without using tracking arcanery.

Now he stood a chance. And there was really only one thing left to try—another teleport. Considering how his brain couldn't form words, it would be one of the riskiest teleports of his young life. Of all the spells that needed precision, the 9th degree Teleport arguably required the most.

"What choice you have?" he mumbled, trying to make his mouth form cogent words. He put all his remaining mental might into the nuance of the spell—the visualizations of traveling through the arcane ether and the subsequent look of the snow and how his feet would interact with that snow and how his colleagues would be standing mere feet away ready to assist. And he went over the incantation a couple of times in his mind, which seemed to speak the words more clearly than his snail tongue.

"*Imptus prag*—" he halted, for his tongue had already muddled it. He practiced the incantation aloud nice and slow until his tongue wrapped around the words. Then, to give himself a cushion just in case of the worst, he visualized himself appearing ten feet *above* the snow. This was always a dangerous thing to pull off, for one could end up much higher above the ground, resulting in a bone-breaking fall—or worse. Many a warlock had died in such a manner, accidentally giving themselves too great a cushion and then smashing into the ground, somehow unable to arrest their fall with arcanery, which took a lot more wherewithal and training than one would suspect. The tendency was to panic during a fall and forget any incantation.

Here we go, Augum thought, bracing himself. "*Impetus peragro!*" With a *thwomp*, he yanked his body downward through the ether. After a couple eye blinks of hurtling through pitch darkness, he reappeared with a second *thwomp*—an alarming *fifty* feet above the boulder-strewn morass.

Heart jammed into his throat, he instantly plummeted. Luckily, having been in this situation before, he shoved at the air with his one good arm, roaring, "*Baka!*" The 2nd degree standard spell *Purrashova*, otherwise simply known as Push, could be used to either shove an opponent—or the ground. If one got good enough with it, one could also use it to arrest one's fall.

The problem was, the snow caved inward, giving only a little pushback to Augum, who then slammed into it with a snowy *crunch*. The pain of his limbs exploded anew, and he found himself jammed—and, with his head stuck firm in the snow, unable to breathe. And no amount of struggle seemed to *un*jam him.

Just as the black walls of unconsciousness closed in, he felt a rough hand grab him and pull him up top. After wincingly clearing the snow from his eyes with his good hand, he found himself staring into furry white faces.

For a moment, he only gaped in shock. Of all the beasts to stumble upon, these were the last he would want. For it wasn't his friends who had found him, but that blasted wolven pack.

Then he saw their burly chests. And those chests lacked the branded X that denoted them as The Dishonored.

A different pack of wolven had found him.

And this time, he could hardly defend himself.

RESPECT

BRIDGET

A poised crimson-robed Bridget stood with her hands clasped behind her back, watching as a wide swath of sunlight crawled across the training yard. Gentle snow tumbled onto a bailey full of Arcaners and Arcaner recruits, who clumsily sparred with Ordinary soldiers and knights.

Both sides wielded swords and bucklers, which to a warlock weighed significantly heavier compared to the summoned versions. The training exercise was at the insistence of The Sword of the Oak, who said they had to be ready should warlocks get stripped of their powers and have to defend themselves against an attack of a more Ordinary nature.

The man was going around giving pointers as if he were their personal commander, which annoyed Bridget despite the soundness of his reasoning. If an attack of such a nature should come, they ought to be prepared, and who better to train them in the arts of the heavy sword and shield than The Sword of the Oak?

"Like a cockatoo showing off its feathers," Guardian of the Order, Alyssa Fairweather, muttered, hands also behind her back as she stood beside Bridget. "And why doesn't he just show them instead of snapping his fingers like that? Seems to lack common sense for someone so well known."

Sabby, who sat on her haunches beside Bridget, whined for her attention, and Bridget let the back of a hand out to be licked. "Where's Lee? She's supposed to be here."

Alyssa shrugged, the dreads on one side of her head bouncing. "Probably hungover. Hell, I'd get drunk all over again if I'd read what those soul-sucking fiends had written about me."

"It's not her fault what happened to her."

"Personally, I fault the quiller."

Both of them glanced back at Herald Brittany Mires, who stood apart with a fresh scroll attached to a clay tablet. She dipped a goose quill into an inkwell and caught them staring at her. "I had nothing to do with that piece," the girl blurted.

"We know," Bridget and Alyssa chorused, turning back to monitor the yard and folding their arms across their chests.

"Any word from up north?" Alyssa asked.

Bridget shook her head. "He leaves her notes though through the—" She mouthed the next part. "—*you-know-what.*"

"He ought to leave you notes too, considering he pretty much left you in charge," Alyssa muttered.

"He left both of us in charge." Bridget hadn't had the heart to tell Augum how Leera was faring. But she supposed she ought to.

"I guess Jez would 'port in if something serious happened with him anyway."

Maybe, Bridget thought. *Or maybe she'd try to solve the problem herself.* 17th degree warlocks had that tendency. She only hoped her mentor stayed away from the bottle while she was leading the tracking party. Even though she wasn't an Arcaner, and even though she drank too much and too often and tended to opinionate about things she ought not to opinionate about, everyone respected her as they did an older aunt.

But Bridget's thoughts kept returning to Leera. "I should talk to her."

"You'll have to wait for her to 'port back."

"I meant Lee."

"Ah. Well, I'm sure she'd appreciate it."

"Maybe." Bridget absently rubbed behind Sabby's ears. "Any news, by the way?"

"The investigation into last night's snuffing is still ongoing."

"Any breaches in the curtain wall? Unexpected guests? Constabulary calls to arms? Strange occurrences in the city?"

"The taverns are quiet as everyone's hung over from the night before. You know how raucous Lover's Day endings get. More arguments than kisses when the drink really sets in." Alyssa loosed a breath through flapping lips. "The most excitement I've heard is that the servants are complaining about rats in the cellar alongside a moss infestation."

Bridget latched her free hand to her waist and drummed her side with her fingernails. "So the castle was the only thing attacked."

"I like the word tested. But yeah, nothing else untoward. Oh, but we did get an anonymous tip in. Seems someone has been repeatedly stealing from an alms jar in the Shanties quarter."

The Arcaner order received tips from the populace on shady dealings the constables were sometimes slow to act on, oft because the constables were in on those dealings—or paid to look the other way.

"Assign Tennyson and her apprentice."

"Wonkleg is going to love that," Alyssa said with bald sarcasm. Dragoon Haylee Tennyson was the order's official treasurer and also suffered from a bad limp sustained in the war with the Legion. She loathed only three things—poverty, dirt, and her walking stick, which she was oft forced to use as an aid.

Alyssa shifted her stance. "In the mean, what are your orders for the day?"

Bridget ran a hand through her cinnamon hair, freshly washed and dried and brushed, whilst expelling a breath through flapping lips in mimic of Alyssa. "Let them keep this up until lunch, then have them go through their cycles. Until we know more, we might as well keep up the training."

A bunch of recruits were preparing for the first Arcaner trial, which was a serious affair that warranted all their focus and concentration. They could not afford to lose any more warlocks, not to kidnappings, and certainly not to failed tests.

When the first Arcaner recruit death happened, Bridget had been so distraught that she'd wanted to cease recruit training altogether, until Augum convinced her that the order needed to survive all three of them in order to stop any major future threats. He was more pragmatic than her in such things.

One of those former recruits who had passed his first trial, and who also happened to be Bridget's apprentice, a muscled young man with blond hair and wearing a 3rd degree blue robe, abruptly kneed his sparring partner in the stomach. The soldier, much shorter and thinner than the warlock, doubled over to the snow with a coughing wheeze.

Bridget sighed.

"Shall I?" Alyssa asked.

"Might as well." She was in no mood for his royal antics.

"Southguard, front and center!" Alyssa barked.

The seventeen-year-old warlock took his sweet time walking over, wavy blond hair bouncing about.

"Double quick, Squire!" Alyssa barked, but the young man barely increased his pace.

He finally clicked his heels before them, looming like a tavern goon. "Squire Carter Moore Southguard reporting, Sir!"

"Her title is Guardian," Bridget said in as patient a tone as she could muster.

Alyssa was not as kind. "Squire, being one of the king's countless nephews does not give you permission to treat soldiers in such a manner."

"Guardian Fairweather, I was merely demonstrating to that simple oaf of a soldier that one need not always use their blade to get results. And I am not merely a nephew, but heir to the throne, thank you very much."

"The command was to use sword and shield to familiarize oneself with the weight, Squire. And we care not one hoof if you are a prince, a pauper, or the bleeding king himself. Here, you obey us as if your life depends on it. Do I make myself perfectly clear, Squire?"

The young man smirked, though held his eyes above the women. "Sword and shield to get the weight. Got it."

Alyssa took a step closer to gaze up into his face. "Are you smirking at me, Squire?"

"No, si—er, Guardian Fairweather—I am not!"

"Squire, I think you just earned privy duty."

"But Guardian Fairweather, I was only—"

"Silence!" Alyssa turned to Bridget. "Permission to haul his butt off the field to wash the privies, Captain."

Bridget considered the young man, who was red in the face now, but not in the way he ought to be. "Granted, but let it be in the evening."

Alyssa stepped near, voice low. "Cap, I really think he ought to be made an example of to everyone. He does not show the proper respect to his seniors, especially if they be a woman."

Bridget glanced back at the herald, who hovered nearby, taking extensive notes. "He will be made example of, but he needs the training more than the privy needs cleaning."

Alyssa bit her lip but acceded a nod. She wagged a finger at the recruit. "You and I will have a talk later about respecting rank, Squire."

The young man couldn't help but let a small smirk rise from the corner of his mouth. "I wish I could say I look forward to it, Guardian."

Alyssa scowled and strode off to bark at another recruit to keep their shield up.

The young man placed his blue eyes on Bridget. "Am I dismissed, Captain?"

"No," Bridget snapped. "And keep those eyes straight." She tried to make her voice sound like it had iron behind it, something Augum excelled at, but she thought she sounded like a kid playing at being captain.

The tall and muscled fellow wobbled his head in a cocky manner as he stared straight ahead, almost enjoying the lambasting he was receiving. His reputation preceded him as a womanizing young brat, a royal playboy who took advantage of his lofty position. As a fellow earth warlock, he had been thrust upon Bridget on the insistence of the queen, who wanted her nephew to, in her prissy naval voice, "either learn discipline or burn through this absurd fantasy that he wants to be an Arcaner."

Bridget cocked her head at the young Southguard. "As nephew to the king and queen and heir to the throne, you have great privilege at your disposal."

"That is true, Captain."

"So why do you waste our time pretending you want to become an Arcaner?"

"Er. Sorry, Captain? I passed my—"

"Eyes forward, Squire."

"I passed my Squire trial, have I not?"

"That very well may be so, but how will you fare when you undertake the dragoon trial, which is significantly more challenging and requires iron discipline of mind and soul? Hmm? Now summon your shield and tell it to me true. Why do you wish to become an Arcaner? Our code is not for everyone."

"Er …" He raised his left arm and summoned a crest-shaped shield made of ivy and pond leaves. At the bottom were the golden words *Semperis vorto honos*, indicating he had achieved squire status.

"Answer the question, Squire."

His eyes flitted about, as if in search of something to say that wouldn't result in a shield dim, before he grinned. "Two reasons, Cap. The first is I want to become a dragon like Commander Stone."

Not like Captain Burns or Captain Jones though, Bridget noticed. And she wanted to remind him how long the odds were of following their footsteps and becoming a dragon, how ridiculously dangerous that road was, but suspected her warning would fall on deaf ears. "And the second reason?" she instead asked.

"The women are—" He whistled appreciatively and flicked his head so that his wavy blond hair swished from his forehead.

Bridget, noting his shield had not dimmed, sighed. "You admit yourself to be lascivious."

"I … I do not know what that word means, Captain Burns."

"A lecher."

"I still don't—"

"A womanizing fiend," Bridget finally snapped, red in the face herself now.

"To the rank bottom of my foul soul, Captain."

"This is no smirking matter." How in the world had he passed his squire trial, which tested character?

Something in her tone made the smirk falter, and he cleared his throat. "If I can clarify, Captain, I guess I have this romantic notion of the order and that I will find true love in it."

"Not by disrespecting others. And not by dying in a trial you are nowhere close to being ready for. Because that is exactly what is going to happen to someone who does not take the edicts seriously."

"Captain, that's ridiculous! I am more than fit to—"

"I will not suffer placing a blade before another family, royal or not. You are hereby forbidden to take the dragoon trial until we deem you fully ready and worthy of the risk."

He glared at her. "You've got to be jesting me—"

"That is all. You are dismissed, Squire."

"You ... you are my mentor, and as such you're supposed to encourage me. I want to achieve the rank of dragon like the commander and help protect the kingdom and—"

Bridget snapped her fingers, pointing past him like she did to Sabby when she was being disobedient. "Lest I change my mind about immediate privy duty."

The young man scowled but clicked his heels together. "Yes, *Captain*," he spat, and stomped back to the soldier, still patiently waiting for him, but now alongside The Sword of the Oak, who, instead of beginning his own lambasting, gave the young royal a clap on the shoulder. The pair of men laughed, with the commander nodding Bridget's way as they jested together. It was a *She's too young to be giving orders* nod, which made her fists ball. How *dare* the man step between her rank and her subordinates!

"And you obviously wish me to report on that," Brittany noted, stepping up beside Bridget.

Bridget looked down at her fists and unclenched them. This was most unlike her. She was not used to losing her composure. "He will serve as a cautionary note to others who share his sort of ... ambitions."

The herald primped her hair with a hand. "Is appreciating the feminine form that black a mark?"

"It's a distraction from what he will attempt. He needs to learn self-discipline and respect."

"The trial is that dangerous?"

Bridget gave a small nod.

"Care to elaborate, Captain?"

"Those of ill temperament, or those who do not understand their own ambitions of the heart, are a poor fit, and can easily perish in the various small trials within the larger trial. Not to mention there are a tremendous amount of in-class hours required that the young man has not completed, followed by a tough examination—and then a real-world test that could easily end in death. And no, I will not elaborate further on the intricacies of the dragoon trial."

"Forgive me, Captain, but it seems to me that he well understands his own ambitions of the heart, what with him being so forthcoming and all."

Bridget, who did not share Leera's gift of wit, wanted to snap a reply but could not form a clever enough answer.

"As a Southguard and heir to the throne, that young man there did not take it well."

"That is not of my concern."

"You hope he quits."

"I didn't say that."

"You needn't have." The girl scratched away with her quill. "Don't worry. I won't write about that part. But I have another matter I'd like to discuss with you, Captain."

"Go on." *If you must.*

"You have been described as having the countenance of—and you must forgive me, but I am merely quoting Alanna Haught here—'the long-haired countenance of a plain but comely farm girl wholly unsuited to the rigors of command.' Would you like to respond to that?"

Bridget wanted to hiss how she had no interest in what scheming high nobles had to say about her and her command. Instead, she grabbed her long cinnamon hair with a hand and turned on the herald. "Are they suggesting I cut it?"

"Er ... I rather think the point speaks to experience."

Bridget returned her gaze to the training recruits. "Ask Miss Haught when was the last time she dove at a column of attackers, or slapped her wrists at an enemy."

"Do you really want me to—"

Bridget pinched the bridge of her nose and closed her eyes. "Of course not. I ... I forget myself."

"Because you are a beacon fire to young women everywhere who think themselves ill-suited to stations of leadership, I will not publish your response to Miss Haught."

"You have my gratitude." The truth was, Bridget did not know if it was morally right for her to encourage the herald to paint her in a favorable light. Priding herself as the top student in every class to do with the ethics of spell casting, she felt ill at ease about this sort of interplay. Prior to departing on his quest, Augum had warned her that she would be tested on multiple fronts. She was starting to see what he had meant.

Brittany glanced about furtively and dropped her voice. "Personally, I *loathe* the Haughts. They've been known as the Haughty Haughts for generations for a reason—they think their bloodline is above all others. And the one I quoted, Alanna Haught, schemes for your brother-in-war's attention. I fear this latest piece they published about your sister-in-war will only embolden her."

"Women have been throwing themselves at my brother-in-war since his arena days. Granted, he gets more attention now with all those posters of us with the visage of our dragons, but my point stands. He is no stranger to undue attention. And I know no love deeper than the one between him and my sister-in-war."

Brittany continued hurriedly writing away. "Do you find that men solicit your attention more?"

"Hardly. Most are too proud to speak their mind. I take strange solace in their pride, for it leaves me the—" She swallowed the word she wanted to use. "—the heck alone. Besides, I'm betrothed to a funny, wonderful man." *A man who ought to be a little more serious*, she thought, not wanting to get into it with a herald.

Brittany finished writing, only to scratch it out. "I'm not going to publish that either."

Bridget, whose stomach felt like an empty cavern—she had skipped breakfast that morning after reading the herald piece about Leera—extended Sabby's leash to the young herald. "Maybe you should."

"Er …" Brittany accepted the leash but stepped away from Sabby. "Where is the captain going?"

"For some grub. I'm starved. I shall return shortly. Momma's coming right back, sweetie," she said to Sabby, giving her a thorough rub on the neck with both hands before striding to the closest doors, which led to the Great Arcaner Hall. Once inside, she closed the door behind her, rested her back against a stone wall, closed her eyes, and sighed.

In her mind's eye, she saw an open field of tall yellow grass beside a farm. Oxen and pigs and chickens and geese grazed in their pens. Her fit and smiling husband telekinetically lifted a barrel atop another, whistling to himself. Nearby, her children played a merry game of Keep Away. She could smell the thatch and garden of roses and the manure of the fields, and she could feel the sun on her face, hot and bright and safe …

Then another sun appeared beside that one, a pale pink, and then a third, a pale white. She felt herself stretching her arms out, her wings absorbing their heat. She saw herself rear about, her shadow looming over her children and husband, all of whom screamed the shrill scream of the damned …

"My lady?"

Bridget started, pressing a hand to her heart, which thundered at the horror of what had been about to take place. Standing before her was a gray-haired man dressed in the black and white and blue and gold livery of a royal servant.

"Is my lady all right?"

"Perfectly fine, thank you," Bridget croaked.

The man watched her. "It is unbecoming for one of the kingdom's heroes to lie, let alone an Arcaner. My lady is as white as a freshly bleached bedsheet."

With shadowy eyes peeking through her soul, Bridget couldn't help but scowl. "You speak out of turn, *sir*." *There* was the iron in her voice she had been lacking earlier!

The man paled and bowed so deeply that he had to catch his balance. "Fates help me, my lady, I do not know what came over me. You ought to send me for a whipping. Please accept my humblest, deepest —"

"It's all right," Bridget blurted, coming to the man and urging him to rise. She had to remember the effect the Arcaner rank of dragon had on commoners. "Please, it is I who apologizes."

"My lady has done no wrong. I *did* speak out of turn. I … I forget myself. You are within your rights to have the whip placed to my backside —"

"I will do no such thing! I mean, it is not the Arcaner way."

The man looked up with mismatched-colored eyes, one blue and one brown, face as wrinkled as old parchment. A gray eyebrow rose. "Is it not?"

Bridget was about to reply when she realized the man was right. The ancient *Codex Arcanera: From Birth to Death, a Life of Honor* detailed myriad punishments Arcaners inflicted on those who did wrong. Many were shockingly cruel. Yet although the trio wanted to preserve as much of the spirit of the order as they could, they had mutually agreed not to resurrect such barbarities. Besides, the ethics of their era would never allow chopping off an arm for mere theft, or hanging for adultery, just two examples of the sorts of barbarity the ancient Arcaners had exacted. It had been a different time.

The man dropped his gaze. "Forgive me, I … I am a reader of history. And … and I have never met thee. I fear my tongue has gotten loose over the years. You are so young and yet … and yet you hold the reins of leadership with such poise. I am in awe, and my gratitude for what the three of you have done for this kingdom is … unbounded." He went rigid-straight, eyes above her. "I have made my lady uncomfortable. Please send me to the whip or, at the very least, dismiss me."

Bridget stared at the man, aghast at his request. "I will do neither, sir. Instead, it is I who beg your forgiveness."

"There is nothing to forgive."

She thought about what it meant to be an Arcaner, a knight-warlock who upheld a code of honor and the traditions of old. From that code of honor, the tenth and eleventh edicts came to mind — *Thou shall fight for the welfare of all*, and *Thou shall guard the honor of the arcane craft*. "I am due for my daily *proata mentora*. Is there perhaps something I can do to atone for my petulance?"

"I do not think a woman of your station —"

"I *insist*, sir. Perhaps you are aware of *proata mentora*?"

"Of course. It is how you warlocks stay humble, and how you keep relations with us mere Ordinaries."

"I loathe that word for it amounts to a slur —"

"And yet you cannot deny it. Did my lady know it is not the first word to mean that very thing? It is only the latest in a long list of words warlocks have used to describe us. Simpletons. Wretches. Weakskins. The oblivious. The ungifted. Commoners. And one of my personal favorites, *fodder* …"

Bridget winced with each utterance.

"There are countless others, as there are for the word *warlock*. Believe it or not, although far from perfect, the word Ordinary is the *least* offensive of the lot, which is why it has survived the longest."

Bridget nodded. She had tried thinking of variants, but each felt more condescending than the last.

The man swallowed, eyes still on the checkered floor. "My lady asked if she can lend aid of some sort. Perhaps my lady can. There is a moss infestation that we have been trying to address in a lower chamber, one that could use the eyes of a learned earth warlock." He looked up, face perplexed. "Strangely, the infestation prevents servants from lighting the hearths."

Bridget, an uneasy feeling settling within her cavernous stomach, searched those mismatched eyes. "I am intrigued, sir. Please take me there."

"I only fear I may be wasting my lady's time with frivolities beneath her station—"

"I must insist, sir." She opened a hand onward. "Please."

The man bowed. "As my lady wishes," and led Bridget through a pantry, a buttery, a larder, and finally a kitchen, all buzzing with servants. Upon their entrance to each room, those servants halted what they were doing, hushed up, and either bowed or curtsied, eyes meekly on the floor. The ones of higher rank wished her a Happy Endyear on behalf of the others, and always deferred to the old man accompanying Bridget, telling her he was of high rank. Bridget nodded kindly at each of them and always replied, "Happy Endyear," ever uncomfortable with the effect she had on people as an Arcaner Dragon, and as a woman who had seen and caused death and destruction on a scale unheard of in five thousand years.

The gulf between what she had experienced and what these people had experienced was so vast it scared her. Sometimes, when the shadow peeked through her eyes, she wondered if they saw that terrible violence within her. And that brought back to the fore the earlier daydream of her dragon self rising above her future family, sending a chill through her soul. How could she ever trust The Callousness of the Predator around that future family? If something ever happened, even something small, she would never forgive herself …

The older servant took one of two staircases down to the servant's quarters, interrupting a gossipy discussion on who the most handsome knight in the yard was, and led Bridget to a rusting side door. "Through here, my lady. Please forgive the dinginess."

"I have known worse," she muttered. Significantly worse. However, she did take notice that down here there were far fewer holiday ornamentations of holly and pine, and far fewer candles as well. She suspected that was because the funds for such things were diverted to the higher floors.

The hall was crudely carved from the raw stone of the bedrock, and thus smelled of musty stone, which mixed acridly with the scent of mouse poop and sewage.

"This is most unbecoming of my lady's youthful sensibilities, I am sure."

"I am not as dainty as I appear, sir."

"Of course not. I forget myself once more."

"You may speak freely to me, sir."

The man stopped mid-passage to face her, albeit with a bowed head. "You are a great woman to allow a humble servant free tongue. And if I may say so, you cast a wholly different shadow than even other warlocks."

Quite the choice of words, Bridget thought.

"Whereas you indeed look youthful—almost fragile, if you will forgive me for the umpteenth time—there is, nonetheless, a hidden fierceness that is unspoken, unmentioned in any herald, unpaintable in any poster, indescribable by word of mouth. Only those who have been graced by your presence can perhaps have a sense of it."

The man's mismatched eyes were making Bridget uncomfortable, not because of who he was, but because of the naked truth of his words.

"My lady will have the eternal thanks of this humble servant for allowing him to—"

"That's enough," Bridget blurted. "Thank you, but that's enough. Let us proceed." There were only so many compliments she could bear.

"Of course, My lady. Forgive me. This way."

He led her past a series of torchlit doors, some going to laundry, others to boilers, others to stores of wood, others to storage. At last they arrived at a room full of dark furnaces, within which milled several young and old servants. All stiffened upon their entrance, bowed or curtsied, the head of which wishing Bridget a Happy Endyear.

Bridget inclined her head. "And a Happy Endyear to you too."

The man opened a hand toward a furnace covered in moss. "There it is, my lady."

Bridget stepped closer, realizing it was unlike any moss she had ever laid eyes on. Black with gray and purple veins, it seemed lush and thick and eager to spread.

"It spread overnight, my lady."

"That's impossible. No moss spreads that quickly."

"I am afraid this one did, my lady."

Yet he was right, for even as she watched, it was methodically consuming the iron of the furnace, albeit at a snail's pace that was barely noticeable to the naked eye. Only when one looked away and then looked back after a time could the spread be noticed.

"As my lady will see, the rune to that furnace no longer works."

Bridget tapped the hearth rune, incanting, *"Igniato,"* yet the hearth failed to light. She tried again, double-checking that her thoughts were aligned with the rune—one had to envision fire engulfing the innards of the furnace, after all. Still, nothing.

She spread the fingers of a hand. "*Un vun asperio aurum enchantus,*" and gasped. For the Reveal spell showed something she had never seen before in moss—an intricate and dense tendril pattern.

And it was as black as night.

A FERAL GIRL

LEERA

Leera sat behind a wide black-oak table carved with mountain flowers and pine wreaths and various animals. Spread about before her, amidst crumbs from the last of the bread she had foraged from her pocket, sat an assortment of musty tomes. The gigantic *Codex Arcana: Pre Founding — a Collection of Understandings During the Dawn of the Arcane Arts*. The black-and-crimson-bound *Curses, Curses, Curses: A Nuanced Anthology of the Witch's Primal Word*. The ornately bound *Seminal Explorations of the Darkest of Arts*. There was a thinly bound *Chronicles of Anna Atticus Stone and Her Encounters with Narsus the Necromancer*. Even a silver-bound *5000 Years Ago: The Rise of Attyla the Mighty, the First Great Necromancer — and His Rebirth*, in case it mentioned a curse such as the one that prevented her from bearing children. And a slew of others, some teetering on tall piles.

Surrounding her stood towering oaken bookshelves sitting under a high arched ceiling. Unlike some libraries, none of these books were chained to the shelf. The walls that rose above those bookshelves were crowded with sun-faded tapestries, old coats of arms, and large gilt-framed oil paintings depicting scholarly scenes from ages past.

Besides quiet murmurings, there was a general hush to the place. For on this particular day, she was the only warlock among perhaps thirty Ordinaries, from the teenage to the elderly. All were exquisitely dressed in the clothes of the highborn caste — embroidered silk doublets, multi-layered poofy skirts and dresses, pantaloons and trousers studded with precious gems, extravagant robes with rare dyes. High collars, chains of office, bejeweled hands, and gold thread abounded.

Their servants waited in a line underneath the farthest wall, not daring to speak to each other, but having to stand with hands clasped before them while they shifted their weight from foot to foot, eyes glazed with boredom. Meanwhile, all the nobles kept stealing glances Leera's way, faces oft powdered to the point of milk whiteness. Occasionally, that hush was broken by the *clunk* or *clank* of a bored knight adjusting his position in the doorway, where they waited as Leera's unasked-for guards.

Leera adjusted her spectacles on her nose whilst idly flipping the pages of a tome, stomach feeling better after she had stopped by the kitchens to pilfer more bread and water and ginger tea—and one tasty sweet cake, consuming most of it whilst chatting with the nervous servants.

Her newly hired servant, Gertrude Delores Hooper, carrying another heavy tome, loped up to the table—she had a funny gait Leera had noticed as the pair walked to the library, as if she were a panther taking a relaxing stroll after scoring a kill. Leera liked that about her, for it showed a quiet self-confidence, somehow giving the impression the girl could be trusted.

"I found another one," the young woman whispered. " '*Historical Occurrences of Mystical Darkness: Plausible Appearances of Witches of Old, a Study in Contrasts.*' "

"Good one, Gertie," Leera said far more loudly than she had meant. She had the sort of voice that carried in quiet places, amplified of course by her uncouth manners.

"Hush!" snapped a stern-looking woman who sat behind a high desk that all but obscured her wrinkled face and thick spectacles.

"*Sorry,*" Leera mouthed at her for the umpteenth time, and took hold of Gertrude's arm to whisper in her ear, "Are there not more books on necromancy and necromantic curses?"

"I am afraid not, my lady. They hide such books in restricted sections in the Academy of Arcane Arts and the Library of Antioc."

Leera sighed and let go. "Of course they do. Give me a hand here and see what you can dig up."

"Yes, my lady." The girl sat down beside Leera, which drew a flurry of scandalized whispers, for it was unheard of for servants to sit side-by-side with their masters.

Leera looked up and saw that more than one person had a *Blackhaven Herald* before them. "Is there something on your mind, you pasty-faced ghouls?" she snapped, blood boiling. "Yes, I'm barren. As barren as a desert on account of an ancient necromantic curse flung my way.

Awkward for everybody, isn't it?" *And it's why I'm here trying to solve that blasted problem,* she wanted to add, but refrained.

The woman behind the counter shot to her feet and swept forth, shoes clacking against the checkered floor. After reaching their table, the elderly woman leaned forth and, in a perfunctory tone, whispered, "Barbaric behavior will not be tolerated, warlock or not, champion or pauper. Further—" She eyed Gertrude as if she were a filthy beast. "—servants are not permitted to sit at tables."

"She's not your servant," Leera countered. "She's mine."

"That very well may be so, but she is still a *servant*. It is beneath the dignity of the Royal Library of the Commons."

"Say that last word again."

"I beg your pardon?"

"What do you think *commons* means?"

Leera felt a calming hand on her arm.

"'Tis all right, my lady," Gertrude whispered, smiling. "I will wait with the others. Please do take your time," and she got up and went to stand with the other servants, the closest of whom shuffled away from her as if she were diseased. Yet the young woman continued to subtly smile at Leera as if she were proud to be her servant.

"Happy now?" Leera hissed, refraining from calling the woman a harpy—or much worse.

The woman harumphed and clacked back to her desk, flashing her a final warning look before taking her seat. Leera glared at her, loudly hearing the knock of the predator upon the door of impulsiveness. But she refused to let the hag get the better of her temper and returned to her studies, keeping that door firmly shut.

Having gotten nowhere with *Seminal Explorations of the Darkest of Arts*, Leera eventually slammed the book shut and shoved it away, drawing further murmurings and shakes of the head from the gawkers. So far, none of the books went into detail, the authors no doubt fearing the knowledge could be used for ill gain. An honorable endeavor, but one that did not help her in this instance.

Sighing, she pawed through the other books, settling on the latest one Gertrude had brought. " 'A Study in Contrasts of My Butt,' " Leera muttered, already dissatisfied with the Table of Contents, which chronicled plausible sightings of witches and what they might or might not have done. Such books were filled with examples of innocent warlocks getting burned at the stake, their only crime that of falling into the trap of superstition.

One chapter caught her eye. " 'Horren's Depletion: The Strange Tale of a Dearth of Births in the Village of Horren,' " she read under her breath. "Has to allude to Horren's Keep," she added, flipping to the chapter. The ruins of the keep sat amidst a coniferous forest in the northwest, and were a perennial source of dark tales oft used to scare children into behaving. The entire area was a floodplain, and the castle itself now sat half under water. Her lips moved silently as she read the beginning of the chapter, finger trawling right along, occasionally tapping at a notable word.

It was the era of Horren, when that plague of a man—unbeknownst to even his own retinue—stalked his victims in the dead of night, craving their blood in the age-old belief that the blood of the young reinvigorated the blood of the old. And so it was that in the late hours of the Night of Knives—a most superstitious night of the witch of old, the reader ought to mind—the young and fertile women of the village of Horren woke up screaming. For they had suffered a most unusual occurrence—a mutual nightmare that they had offered their coming babes to none other than He Who Goes by Many Names. Bazu. Soti. Azmat. Vanta. Xie Da Lo. Mephisto. The Guardian of the Dark. The Father of Demons. The Arch Fiend. And, of course, the devil.

Yet it was in the years that followed that the true nature of this nightmare became apparent, for not one of these poor women could bear a child. The villagers, suspecting the fiendish warlock who lived in his eerie castle, took up their pitchforks, hunted him down, and put to him to the cleansing fires.

The village and the castle were thereafter abandoned, for all thought the land cursed to its very core. In the years to come, the forest steadily consumed the village and the castle, which fell into disrepair—and to the use of brigands and fiends drawn to such a tale.

Arcaneologists have long speculated as to what had happened to the women of the Village of Horren. Some thought the strange occurrence had nothing whatsoever to do with Horren the warlock, and ought to be ascribed to a rogue necromancer of unknown origin and name. Others thought it the doings of a witch of old, come to steal the young for her master, the Arch Fiend. Other scholars believe a demon from another plane visited the village, finding its young ladies most delectable.

The answer is yet to be uncovered, for subsequent expeditions to the castle failed in retrieving Horren's treasures—that is to say, his book of accounts, his various keepsakes, his invaluable scrolls and tablets and books on the craft, as well as his priceless artifacts. Some had been looted, but Horren was a notoriously private man who prided himself on keeping his most prized possessions safe from prying eyes.

Leera shot up from her chair, which rudely scraped against the checkered tiles, declaring, "Might as well dangle a carrot before an ass!"

The woman behind the desk also shot up. "Enough of your barbarous noise! Out, you uncultured warlock harpy! Out!"

"Yeah, yeah, I'm going, I'm going. Can't stand your powdered judging faces anyway." Leera waved Gertrude over and the pair of women strode out of there, knights in tow. Once outside the doors, however, Leera said, "One moment, I forgot something, and she dipped back inside the library, where she made a throwing motion at the ground, animalistically roaring, "*Grau!*" The sacredly quiet library exploded with the sound of an enormous wave crashing upon them, sending every pasty-faced noble diving under their desk, where they screamed as if they were about to die a horrible drowning death.

Leera dusted her hands. "How's *that* for noise?" she said to the whimpering old woman who had taken shelter under her desk, spectacles askew. She tried to clamber to her feet, shrieking something at Leera, but kept slipping in her clumsiness. "Those are the wrong shoes to be chasing people in. Oh, and Happy Endyear!" Leera called out smilingly.

"What?" she snapped at the knights on the way out, who glanced at each other as she strode by, not knowing what to do with her.

"Come on, Gertie. Let's find my sister-in-war."

* * *

"You're *what*?" Bridget shrieked after Leera and Gertrude managed to track her down, thanks to a servant tipping Gertrude off, in the lower servant area of the castle.

Leera shrugged. "It's probably a temporary ban, but it's not like I'm planning on going back to that preening cockatoo of a library anyway. You should see the way they gawk at you. It's like we're pariahs. Never mind we saved their pasty behinds in the war—"

"Lee, you can't just—" Bridget grabbed Leera by the arm and took her aside. "You can't just go scaring Ordinaries like that."

"It was just a teensy-weensy little scare. A tiny demonstration—a teachable moment, really—on the intricacies of the Slam spell."

"Lee—"

"It's not like they're going to have nightmares or anything. Anyway, look, I wanted to tell you that I'm going on a quest—hold on, what are you doing down here, anyway? And why's there moss growing on a furnace?"

"That's the thing. I found something strange—wait, what quest? An Arcaner quest?

"Er, not exactly—"

"You *know* we've been ordered to stay within the confines of the castle until they discover what's happening with the snuffing."

Leera patted the sides of Bridget's shoulders. "And I am sure you and the investigators have that all *well* under control, Bridgey-poo."

"Lee, you need to take your role seriously. You're a *captain* now."

"And I am making a captainly call—is that the right word? Never mind. I am making a command. To the self. A self-order." Leera nodded. "Yeah."

Bridget pressed her fists into her hips. "Lee—"

"Moss, huh?" Leera crinkled her nose as she glanced past Bridget's shoulder. "Sounds about as exciting as watching bread rise."

"It's more than that. The moss has a tendril signature."

Leera made a show of yawning. "Look, I know you love your vines and mosses and plants and stuff, as all earth warlocks do, but I've got bigger fish to tail."

"You cannot possibly be serious."

Leera pressed Bridget's pert nose, making Bridget smack Leera's hand aside. "You should come. It'll be fun. A romp like the old days."

Bridget closed her eyes, pressed the fingers of both hands into her scalp, and massaged it.

"Oh, can you do that to me after? I've still got a bit of a headache from my hangover."

"What do I have to do to get you to take your role seriously? Do you not realize what could happen if you contravene the king's writ?"

Leera placed both hands on Bridget's shoulders. "Bridge. I love you. But you have to stop being such a goodie-goodie. The code of honor isn't *that* literal. Learn to loosen up." Leera raised a finger. "I advise a bottle of red. Then again, you're pretty thin, so maybe half a bottle would—"

"Your shield could dim," Bridget whispered. "And that's not speaking to the loss of reputation—"

"Haven't you heard? I'm a worthless infertile wasting the darling hero of the kingdom's time and killing his lineage."

"—and to the reputation of the order. Everything we've worked so hard to build."

Leera's head fell as her hands slid off Bridget's shoulders. "Oh."

"That's right. You could hurt us all. Really hurt us, Lee."

"Yeah. I guess I didn't think about that part." She lightly punched Bridget's shoulder, head bobbing up and down but avoiding eye contact. "I'll, uh, I'll try to behave myself."

"Thank you," and before Leera knew it, Bridget had enveloped her in a tight hug, whispering, "I want us to have a nice heart-to-heart later, all right?"

"Over ale?"

"I was thinking tea."

"I'd prefer ale. Or wine."

"Lee—"

Leera withdrew, palms open in surrender. "Fine, fine, fine. Whatever keeps your sails in the wind." Sometimes their "heart-to-hearts" ended up being Bridget scolding or, worse, condescending her. Ale helped Leera keep a sense of humor, and even have a friendly poke or two at Bridget, who did not always appreciate being the butt of the jest—but sometimes laughed louder than anyone when Leera struck particularly true on a point.

"Stay and help me in the mean."

"Moss is—" Leera crinkled her nose again. "—your thing. I'm going to perform some cycles and maybe track down my dour apprentice," adding in a mutter, "who's about as sunny as curdled milk." Her apprentice was a young Malevant girl, a lineage notorious for warlocks of a vile nature. This one, however, was different, for she wanted to change the Malevant name for the better by becoming an Arcaner, proving that not all Malevants were villainous wretches.

"That's good that you're going to keep up on *proata mentora*." Now it was Bridget who glanced past Leera's shoulder. "Who's that, by the way?"

"That's Gertie, my new lady-in-waiting."

"You've *finally* decided to listen to us and take one on? Wonderful, I'm so proud of you! But, uh, why is she wearing the royal servant garb of the Black Castle?"

"I pilfered her from the staff."

Bridget sighed and palmed her face.

"She's a real sweetie, but we can make formal introductions another time," Leera said, hurrying off. "Been fun we'll chat later got to go see you bye, bye, bye—" and she swept out, yanking Gertrude by the sleeve on the way.

"I love Bridget but she really needs to remove whatever is lodged up her butt," Leera said as they walked, the knights clanking along behind like a pair of prank buckets tied to a horse. "Being captain doesn't really suit her, does it? Did you know she wants to be a teacher? I think she'd be the best teacher ever. Teachers are called arcanists, by the way. Did you know *that*?"

"Forgive me, my lady, but did she disapprove of me?"

"Er … probably was just confused, that's all. She likes to follow the rules and all that. Everyone's rules, which is … really annoying, actually. Anyway, let's get you into the *right* castle and in the *right* livery. I mean, after we're allowed to leave this place. Hopefully they'll lift the restriction soon."

They swept into the Great Arcaner Hall, only to have a voice call out, "Miss Jones!"

Leera whirled about, wondering which harpy would dare call her by such an informal title, only to find herself staring at Lady Alanna Haught, a younger woman whom she loathed to the core of her soul. She preened amidst a gaggle of admirers and ladies-in-waiting, a swan of a woman with platinum-blond hair and a perfect complexion. At the back of the group was in fact someone Leera recognized, for she was the same woman she had met in the tavern the other night—and had confided in. Now she stood with a tablet in hand, quilling furiously away, dressed in refined clothing that was still relatively plain compared to the others.

No doubt going to write a frilly piece to further milk her sudden good fortune, Leera thought acidly.

Alanna glided forth wearing an amber robe fringed with gold—even the academy crest was embroidered with gold thread. A lightning warlock of impeccable breeding, the *Blackhaven Herald* had recently dubbed her "the most beautiful woman in the kingdom" after her debut at some stuffy royal ball.

"*Captain* Jones," Leera corrected through gritted teeth. "Or *Dragon* Jones if the former has too many syllables."

"No title or honor will ever overshadow that low breeding, I see," the woman sang, sending Gertrude scurrying back and away with a mere look.

Gods, she's taller too, Leera thought. And she was blue-eyed with porcelain skin and perfect posture—the opposite of Leera. "Been drinking your milk, Allie?"

"*Lady* Alanna Haught. If you want me to use your title, use mine. But let us cut to the quick. My lord father is prepared to make you a generous offer."

"An offer? He can talk to our order's almoner Jengo Okeke, who would be more than happy to accept a donation on behalf of the order—"

"The money would be a donation to *you*, Miss—er, *Captain*—Jones."

"Whatever scheme you're conjuring now, I want no part in."

"Since your recent bloviation regarding being barren, something I would hardly boast about—" The woman pressed a dainty hand to her chest as she solicited chortles from her entourage. "—everyone has come to the same opinion."

Leera had to stop herself from ballooning, for that was what the woman wanted. "And what might that opinion be, if I may be so bold as to ask?"

"Don't put on airs. It hardly suits you. Besides, you might be older, but your sarcasm is as dull as your wit, my dear girl. Let us speak plain. You are a saddler's daughter with a foul tongue and ill manner who, as it turns out, cannot possibly continue a great lineage. A lineage for the millennia. Sure, you may have caught his fancies as a teenager, what boy does not like a wild woman, after all, but you are nothing but a mere doll. A teenage infatuation. A …" Alanna glanced to Leera's chest, making her unconsciously cross her arms. "… plaything."

Leera felt the eyes of a certain shadow peek from behind her soul. She felt her face go cold, and cocked her head almost out of interest.

"Note the way she looks at us now, ladies," the Haught woman drawled. "A hunter stalking prey. She might be able to summon the might of the dragon, but she is still as feral as a mirko."

But her ladies-in-waiting all stirred most uncomfortably, and none dared look Leera in the eye. Even the herald woman dropped her gaze. Only Alanna, a 9th degree warlock used to taking charge of those beneath her station, stared at her with a small smirk.

Leera felt the heat of three suns upon her wings, and indeed a most primal stirring within her soul. She cocked her head the other way before taking a sudden step forth, making all the women—including the blasted Haught—jump back a step. Leera halted, glancing at each in turn, before whispering, "I can smell your blood." It was true. But it was not her that had said it. Rather, it was The Callousness of the Predator that Alanna had put flint and steel to, igniting its anger.

Her audience silenced—not even the quill scratched away. Leera spun about and marched off, a low-eyed Gertrude hurrying to keep up, the pair of knights clanking in tow.

"A million crowns!" Lady Haught called after her. "A million. Crowns. You would be set to the end of your days, Captain Jones. Think about it. An unheard of amount, I know, but that is how highly my family values the match. We would even sell off some our manor estates and the surrounding lands to pay for it, so we would suffer too."

Leera, shoulders rising and falling in time with her fury, halted at the doors, where she turned to face the woman. "I have a better idea. A duel of honor in the old way."

The Haught woman went as pale as moonlight, her retinue gasping in shock.

Leera grinned. "Didn't like my jest, huh? We both know you'd die a squealing death. A pathetic death. A *feral* death." She raised her chin. "I reject your silly offer, which comes from a silly woman. You are nothing to me. Less than nothing. I have already won his heart. You? You are like so many others, but so much less than them, for you are as vapid as mist, as interesting as mold."

Leera raised a finger, stalling the Haught woman, who had opened her mouth to reply. "You insult me again, in the manner you have, and I swear to you on my shield—" Leera summoned her crest-shaped shield made of watery pond leaves, emblazoned with the complete golden Arcaner crest indicating she had reached the mythical rank of dragon. "—that you and I will settle our score in the sands of the arena."

With that, Leera snuffed her shield and walked away, knights awkwardly bumbling along behind and Gertrude meekly in tow, having been unable to meet the Haught woman's eyes once.

With each marching step through the snowy yard, Leera's resolve for a quest to Horren's Keep strengthened. First, she would snag her dour apprentice, for she would need her help. Then she would have to lose her tail, which would be easy. It was the aftermath that might be a problem, but she would worry about that later.

QUESTIONS OVER
THE SKILLET

AUGUM

Ten huge wolf beasts growled at each other in their wolven tongue as they discussed Augum, each carrying a rucksack, the rope of which ran diagonally across their burly chest. Although the tongue sounded harsh and threatening, for all he knew they could be having a cordial conversation about how to best chop him up to fit him into one of their giant frying pans.

Consciousness was now a bare flicker. The pain in his wound stung, but the bleeding was the problem. Already the snow beneath him was stained with his blood. His right foot, twisted backward, throbbed in time with his weak pulse. His shoulder and left arm were still numb and did not work, and his pounding headache made it difficult to focus. Even if he could muster up the strength to teleport back to the tavern he had been kidnapped from, not only would that teleport likely go awry, but he would almost certainly bleed out before anyone could help him.

The idea of cordiality was shattered when a wolven summoned an airy blade in his paw, pointed it at Augum, and seemed to argue with the others that he needed a good skewering.

Augum contemplated snapping off a teleport anyway. But imagining never being heard from again after reappearing deep underground, instantly dead, or should he be successful, imagining those tavern patrons gawking at his bloody mess of a body and merely shaking their heads was enough to make him try a different tack.

"The Dishonored ..." he croaked. "I saw them ..."

The wolven quieted.

"What do you know of The Dishonored, meat bag?" the one with the air blade growled in wolven-accented Solian.

"Speak, lowlander," another said in a calmer tone.

Augum thought it best that he divulge some truth. "I'm … an Arcaner. A knight-warlock bound by honor. And I'm on a quest. The Dishonored … kidnapped two of our own. Two apprentices. Young ones. I followed them. *We* followed them. I … allowed myself to be captured. But … my plan failed. The Dishonored had already bled the apprentices. All that is left of them … are their robes … and vials of their blood …" He nodded at his rucksack, which the bladed one had earlier torn from his shoulder to paw through. "I escaped The Dishonored. My party is lost. *I'm* lost."

"How did you sustain those wounds?" the calmer one asked. He spoke Solian well.

"One of them … was treacherous … and slashed me from behind during a duel of honor."

Some of the wolven growled in their tongue at this news. The bladed one found the spyglass, sniffed at it, and passed it around. No one seemed to make sense of the incredibly expensive device.

"I teleported twice, failing the third time," Augum added.

The calmer one raised his snout. "You wear the robe of an apprentice yet you teleported? And you claim to be an honor-bound lowlander who escaped The Dishonored? Like all lowlanders, you cannot help your treachery from making itself known."

"I speak the truth." It was a trial even to speak, let alone stay conscious. "By writ of king, we who quest for the kingdom have leave to wear what we require in order to … escape notice. And The Dishonored are three peaks in that—" He nodded at the mountains. "—direction. All this … I can prove."

"He lies," the bladed one growled. "He is a spy who got caught."

"What of the vials of blood that support his claim?" the calmer one asked.

The angry one snorted. "He stole them from a scout. The Dishonored are too cunning to allow a lowlander to find their lair. And even if he did, they would never let him escape."

"As an Arcaner … I can prove it … on my shield," Augum wheezed, fighting to stay conscious, praying to the Unnameables that they understood what that meant. He focused on his limp arm, where the shield would usually summon, and tried to get lightning to flash on it. For a time, the wolven argued amongst each other in their growling tongue, but with the sands in the hourglass of consciousness rapidly trickling to nothing, Augum, having seen a flicker of lightning zip about his left arm, finally succeeded in summoning his shield.

"The fourteenth edict of my code of honor states … Thou shall never break thy word. I thus swear … upon my shield … as an Arcaner … that I tell the truth." He paused to take a breath. "See … how it does not … fade."

The wolven went silent staring at his shield. They traded grave looks, as if sharing a secret, with more than one raising their snout in what Augum guessed was either awe or disbelief—it was difficult to read wolven expressions. He did not understand why they reacted this way, until, prior to the black walls of unconsciousness swallowing up his awareness, Augum realized his error. In his wounded stupor, and having summoned his shield out of reflex, as he had done thousands and thousands of times prior, he had forgotten that the top portion of his crest depicted a dragon.

If these wolven knew anything about Arcaner shields, they now knew who he was.

* * *

"Awaken," said a distant voice.

Augum blearily opened his eyes to see that he was staring up at a canopy of snowy pines under a cloudy sky. Fat snowflakes tumbled down, and he could feel them settling on his nose and mouth—how refreshing they tasted! Somehow, he was back home in Ravenwood. What a lovely sight to see those pines. Now all he had to do was find Leera and attend to his castle and—

"Sit up."

Augum, still lying down, looked about and saw that he was surrounded by a pack of wolves who stood like men.

Wolven.

He sat up on a bed of pine boughs amidst a grove of snowy trees, the distant sky dark with a coming blizzard. His hands were manacled once more—and he had been healed of not only his side wound, but his shoulder, his arm, and, mercifully, his foot, which he could move like normal. A new shoe was fit upon it, one made of deer hide. His eyes became unfocused as memories swam back up to the surface. The tavern, The Dishonored, the teleporting, the twisted foot, the cornice, the fall … and then swearing on his shield. His *full* shield.

He regained his composure. "Thank you for healing me. But … how did you track me?"

One of the wolven, an older gray-haired beast wearing a thick golden chain around his neck with a gold-clawed pendant, stepped forth. "The smell of blood drew us to you, lowlander. You were dripping from up high. We came to investigate."

Augum pointed. "The one I vanquished wore a chain like that. But the claws of the pendant were painted black."

"Lending further credence to your truth," the calmer one said, idly holding onto the rope of his rucksack with both paws as he considered Augum for a time. "It is rare to find a lone lowlander this far north."

"We should have left him to the embrace of death," the angry one snarled, shaking the rope of his rucksack about to accent his point. "You all saw how it beckoned to him like a warm blanket."

"You have a way with words, wolven," Augum said, keeping his tone even.

"We are taught your lowly tongue from birth so as to take better measure of you when we slice your throats on the field of battle," the angry one replied.

"Last I recall, we are at peace."

"You lowlanders always find means to break that peace. It is only a matter of time."

Augum recalled hearing rumors that the hawks amongst the nobility had complained that, now that they had three dragons at their disposal, they should expand the kingdom. "I concede the point," he said, hoping that such rumors were just that—rumors.

"A shield can be manipulated," the old gray said. "If you truly are honor-bound, recite your so-called code of honor."

The words of the seventeen edicts that made up the Sacred Chivalric Code of the Arcaner, repeated every morn in ceremony, came easily, and with each phrase he looked upon a new wolven face. "Thou shall never refuse a challenge from an equal. Thou shall never turn thy back on a foe. Thou shall always show thy stripes before thine enemy. Thou shall not duel the lower ranks without serious provocation. Thou shall be gallant and fair to those unable to learn the craft. Thou shall never take the life of a weaponless Ordinary. Thou shall always accept a bent knee. Thou shall give succor to widows and orphans and beggars. Thou shall refuse pecuniary reward for doing thy duty. Thou shall fight for the welfare of all. Thou shall guard the honor of the arcane craft. Thou shall seek knowledge that contributes to the craft. Thou shall preserve and honor the Hallowed Trust. Thou shall never break thy word. Thou shall serve thy lord and king and kingdom with valor and courage and an open heart. Thou shall root out corruption in all its forms, and the sanctity of the truth shall vanquish any title. Thou shall swear fealty to this code of honor, for it is the war ye are locked in from this moment on." He raised his chin, settling his gaze on the old gray. *"Semperis vorto honos."*

"Courage, fortitude, honor," the gray translated, surprising Augum. The old leader nodded at his foot. "Your shield depicts the dragon and you have three toes. The male dragon is also known as Three Toes by his brethren." He tilted his head. "You are Augum Arinthian Stone."

Augum looked down at the manacles, avoiding the statement.

"They are exactly what you fear them to be," the gray said. "Manacles that snuff your witch powers. You cannot weasel away as you lowlanders like to do."

"I too am bound by honor. We have that in common."

"Impudent swine, no lowlander is the equal of a wolven," the angry one growled, only to be silenced by a patiently raised paw from the old gray.

"You are Augum Arinthian Stone, are you not? Speak it true."

Augum surrendered a nod. "I am he."

The wolven exchanged looks, some muttering amongst each other in their tongue.

"But how did you escape The Dishonored?" the angry one asked. "No one escapes The Dishonored, least of all a lowlander."

"Did you become a dragon?" the gray one pressed.

"No," Augum replied. "Something happened. Something I have not seen since ..." He remembered holding a two-thousand-year-old orb what felt like forever ago, silent lightning flashing within its crystal depths as he felt its power coursing through his veins. "... since the Legion War. It began as ice. Ice that crawled into the cave of The Dishonored, where I was being held in readiness to be blooded. And from that ice came a mist, which snuffed all arcanery ... and unlocked my manacles."

The golden-chained gray retreated to mumble in serious tones with his brethren.

"You have seen it too," Augum noted.

The gray turned to observe him. "We have."

"But not as you describe," said the calm one. "A strange flame overtook one of our forests. The smoke that came from those fires snuffed our summoned weapons and armor. What make you of this?"

Augum couldn't help his mouth from gaping open. As with the mist that had billowed forth from the ice, smoke from a fire that extinguished arcanery was unheard of. "I do not understand what these occurrences mean, nor do I understand the power involved. It is spellcraft unfamiliar to my people. Where did this happen?"

"Far from here." The calm one nodded toward distant peaks. "To our earth pack."

Augum glanced between them. "Earth pack?"

The angry one made a snuffling sound akin to a chortle. "Lowlanders bathe in ignorance. He ought not to hear our words in his poisonous tongue. Let us speak in—" and he switched to wolven, growling out a phrase.

The old gray nodded at Augum, then looked down with that nod, before looking past the trees at the spired horizon, that nod continuing as he gazed at the ominous dark clouds of the ever-advancing blizzard. He grabbed his thick chain with both paws and hung his hands off it as he considered the sky. "The spirits tell me that a storm brews for our people." He looked to his brethren. "It is time to unite the packs."

There were mutters and nods of assent.

The old gray looked back at Augum. "Let us continue in his tongue so that he may hear our reasoning."

"Honored Elder implies we shall free the trespassing lowlander," the angry one declared. "I believe this so-called summoner of the dragon is a saboteur who is responsible for these ill portents. We ought to blood him. Cleanse our spirits and release the curse from our lands."

The wolven nearest him growled their agreement.

The calm one shook his head. "Blooding a lowlander who can summon the power of the dragon will provoke needless war. Even one of the other two—the females in his brood—can level our kingdom." He looked to the old gray. "My honored fierce brother speaks out of a heart full of passion, conscious of our long history. But these are new times. The ways of the old are long gone. We cannot continue our isolation if we are to survive. We have all seen the portents. They do not bode well. We cannot fight what we do not understand. We must offer a paw in friendship. If this one is as honorable as he claims, he can be their ambassador."

"Lowlanders have traded our wild brethren's pelts for ill gain!" hissed the angry one. "Look you to him now. He wears their fur in mock."

"I meant no dishonor," Augum replied. "I wear this coat out of ignorance. *We*—" He patted his chest with his manacled hands. "—my people—are ignorant when it comes to your kind."

"He is but a cub—"

"We come of age at sixteen in our kingdom," Augum interrupted. "I have been a man grown for four years. And as commander, I have led people to their deaths."

"He speaks with the forked tongue of a sky serpent. We let him loose and he will destroy us all for what those fool Dishonored did to the cubs of his tribe. Let us feast on his soul and learn the way of the dragon for ourselves. Lowlanders do not deserve the power of the dragon. It should belong to the wolven. Blood him and make us strong again, so say I, before it is too late."

"That risks war!" the calm one shouted, the pair stepping closer to each other.

The old gray raised a paw, silencing them both. "We are not like The Dishonored. He has done no injury to our honor. He has witnessed an ill portent, and he is a chief in his kingdom. He stated his party is lost. And lest we forget, this one can teleport and thus spread news quickly."

The angry one extended black claws of a paw toward Augum. "So Honored Elder intends to free this poison-tongued lowlander so that he may destroy us? Why risk the brethren and our cubs for such vermin? Let us at least confer with the other packs and pose the question to them. Perhaps the most learned amongst us can find a way to blood him of this so-called power of the dragon, and we can thence learn it and become strong again like the packs of old."

"You cannot distill the power of the dragon from my blood," Augum said, careful to keep his voice even. "It is a power gained in a jungle under the heat of three suns." He looked skyward. "It is a power learned far, far away."

"Myths and fancies told around the fire for their cubs," the angry one countered, "fancies spoken in the oily tongue of the lowlander. Even the most honorable among them have listened to the calls of treachery, for the blood of treachery runs in their veins. This one who dares to wear the hide of our wild brethren in our own lands will bring the end to us all. He must be sacrificed for peace. Surely Honored Elder sees this."

"The elder will make his own mind as is his right," the calm one said.

The gray scratched at his snout with a claw as he considered Augum. "Let us confer with the packs and hear the wisdom of the many."

"So commanded," the calm one and the angry one replied in unison.

The pack began gathering their provisions, slinging rucksacks over their shoulders in preparation to head out. Augum sat on his bed of pine boughs wanting to tell them he could swear on his shield that he would not destroy their kind, but realized even if they allowed that, they would have to trust him enough to let him summon his shield to do so, which would mean freeing him of the manacles—and there was no way they would do that now, not whilst listening to the voice of the angry one. He thus allowed himself to get hauled to his feet by the angry one and shoved forth to walk in the snow.

They set off trekking into the thick forest of pines. Being as tall as they were, the deep and unbroken snow gave no trouble to the wolven, yet it forced Augum—he was, after all, half the height of the tallest among them—to plod in their tracks as best he could. But even that was too slow for them, and soon the angry one, after cursing at him in wolven for his slowness, threw him over his shoulder like hunted game.

They moved quickly after that, with one scouting far ahead in case of enemies, although what enemies they had Augum did not know, for he had read scant literature on their kind, and what literature he had read seemed composed of guesswork and theories.

"I will wear another coat if you find me one," Augum offered, bobbing to the rhythm of the trek.

"You will continue to wear the skin of our wild brethren so the others may see your treachery," the angry one countered.

They wound through the forest with agile ease, occasionally crouching and going still, each wolven watching the forest and listening, their long white fur sweeping about like waves in the wind. In such times, their breath steamed alongside Augum's, and they reminded him of Henawa warriors readying to receive a raid. Or so he imagined, for he had never been alongside a Henawa raid, the milk-skinned people who came with the snow, a people who traded with the wolven—and had earned some modicum of their respect.

As they plodded onward through the quiet and snowy forest, the wolven hardly spoke, and when they did, it was to growl in whispers. Sometimes one would indicate at a fallen branch and look inquiringly to his brethren. At other times they would watch the skies, which steadily darkened. With each league traveled, the snowfall thickened, until gloom overcame the light, yet they trekked on, now and then allowing Augum to chew on bread or biscuit beef from his meager provisions.

When the blizzard caught up to them, howling in its ferocity, they took shelter in an old bear cave that sat snugly in a valley. There they built a fire and listened to the wind whistle as it raked the entrance to the cave, the pines creaking and groaning like tired giants. Augum took it all in with keen eyes that learned what they could of the pack that had captured him.

But observation only went so far, and as one of the wolven brought in the bloody carcass of a freshly hunted elk, Augum's curiosity got the best of him. "You spoke of an earth pack," he said to the calm one, who had relieved the angry one in watching over him. "Does that mean this pack here is made of wolven who only wield one element?"

The calm one sat on his haunches before Augum like a dog would in wait for its master. He kept one eye on Augum and one on the elk, which was being stripped of its hide by an eared female while the males readied large pans near the fire. "We are a scout pack compromised of all the packs. But there are packs of just one element."

"Tell him not of our ways, brother," the angry one snarled from the fire. "For he will use it against us. Let us keep the vermin bathing in the bogs of ignorance, where they belong."

"If he is to be blooded, it harms us not," the calm one replied. "If he is to be loosed as an ambassador, it also harms not. Therefore, let us beat back his ignorance with teachings of our kindred."

"I implore the elder to silence my well-intentioned but naive brother."

The old gray, who was grooming his fur with a comb, raised a paw. "Let the questioning continue. I see no harm in letting a lowlander chief who calls himself honorable learn our ways … until he proves himself treacherous."

"Which won't take long," the angry one muttered.

"*Family* is a word we do not know in the same way as you lowlanders," the calm one continued, ignoring his tempestuous cohort. "For us, family is the entire pack. When we birth a cub, we care for them until they reveal."

"By reveal, you mean like showing which element the cub belongs to?"

"Ah, but unlike your kind, *every* wolven reveals. Upon revelation, they are sent to the pack of that element, to be brought up in the ways of that element."

Augum nodded, considering the implications. "That suggests you have powers beyond summoning your armor and weapon."

The old gray barked out a wolven command, and the calm one replied in an acceding tone.

"Let us not speak of things that can be used against us," the calm one said, confirming the wolven indeed wielded other powers.

Augum thought it best he shared something with them. "Very few of us turn into a warlock. Less than one percent. For us, it is called 'The Blossoming,' and it most often happens at the age of thirteen, with the youngest getting it at the age of ten." Which had happened to his great-grandmother, Anna Attius Stone. "But it can happen at any age after, even in the gray-haired."

"We study your people. Your kind, the warlock, is dying out. Gone are the days of the mighty warlocks of old who shared the powers of your gods. The blood of your people is weakening."

"That is true. We have theories, but we do not know why with any certainty. We just know there are fewer and fewer of us with each generation."

"Ask him about the way of the dragon," the angry one growled whilst squeezing a leather bladder to pour oil onto a giant iron skillet.

"My fierce brethren said earlier that even one of the two females in your pack, the ones who can also call upon the power of the dragon, can destroy us. Is that true, lowlander? Speak it true, for we can smell a lie."

The other wolven stopped what they were doing to listen to his response. Augum glanced around at them, noting a tension in their faces, before giving a single nod. They shared looks he could not decipher before returning to their tasks. He did not know if it was wise to have responded in such a way, but he figured it would be better for them to think such a thing, even though the destruction of a whole kingdom—let alone one they knew little about—was as impractical as flying to the so-called "lands beyond the ocean."

"And one of these females, you have made coitus with her?"

"We call it love."

"Yes, we know of this weakness in your kind. Such attachments breed weak warriors."

"We do not consider it a weakness, but a strength. It is the bedrock of the family."

"And you will make a family with this female and sire more dragons?"

Augum felt a spear through the gut, for he had not been expecting to be reminded of the end of his lineage. He looked down, unable to control the hurt from flailing about in his chest like an angry octopus.

"Why do you hesitate, lowlander? Does she not amuse?"

Some of the other wolven chuckled growlingly, most loudly of all the eared females.

"Even you can be callous," Augum replied, looking up, keeping the tears from welling. "I know that much about your kind. You wolven, who can watch someone slowly die with nothing more than interest."

"It is a strength you do not know, lowlander."

Ah, but callousness is something I am most familiar with, Augum thought, choosing not to reveal that about himself. The Callousness of the Predator was not for the ears of others, whether they be human or beast.

"We have needlessly wounded him," the calm one said.

"Which only shows how weak lowlanders are if one of their chiefs is so easily wounded," the angry one countered, earning mutters of agreement from the pack.

Augum sighed and pulled himself together. This was not the time to think of his beloved or their future.

Once stripped of its hide, the elk was handed off to the angry one, who held a giant cleaver. He proceeded to chop off the head and quarters with ease before slicing up the meat and throwing the largest chunks onto the pans, where they sizzled loudly, filling the cavern with a mouth-watering scent.

"I have spent time with one of your kind before," Augum said, watching the meat fry. "In a cave in the Muranians, in the war against the Legion. He was brave and callous and honorable and cunning. He traded for every favor, and said that bloodfruit was expensive in the north. His name was Raptos."

"An ice scout," the gray said. "I knew of him. He was a good claw."

A few others nodded, and there passed a brief silence Augum took as a show of respect.

"The war against the Legion," the calm one went on. "That was a war against your own father, was it not?"

Augum lowered his head before nodding, not wanting to discuss it.

"And he followed the path of the bleeders."

This time Augum shook his head. "Not of the bleeders. The raisers."

"What does he speak of?" the gray asked.

"He is the seed of necromancy," the calm one replied, "for his father was a necromancer."

Some of the other wolven muttered angrily as they looked his way.

"Is that why you can summon the dragon?" the calm one prodded.

Augum shook his head again.

"You do not wish to speak of it."

Augum picked at his palm scar, the ancient manacles clanking. It was something he did not discuss much these days. Those who did ask about it were promptly reprimanded by fellow Arcaners, for he was tired of repeating the same old story, defending against the same tired questions.

"We spoke of callousness ..." His eyes unfocused while watching the flames lick around the pan as he peered into the past, a past described only in books by witnesses and the words of his own father, who had hired a scribe to biograph his life for posterity. "My *father* was a callous man. It began in his youth, when he killed animals for sport, a fancy he soon applied to the innocent. That is when he took an interest in the ancient idea of life extension. He married my mother after attending the

Academy of Arcane Arts together, hiding his true nature behind charisma. Once he trapped her, he revealed himself to be a vile husband, abusing and manipulating her. Sometime after I was born, while he experimented with many dark rituals, she had enough. She stole me away, hiding me on a farm with a family that would use me to their ends. But not wanting to let him track her down, she continued to run, leaving me behind to survive. He caught up to her and ..."

"Blooded her," the calm one said.

"Yes. I thus grew up thinking myself an orphan on a farm that used me as a slave." The myriad scars across his back, which he never revealed if he could help it, tingled. "In the mean, he began to raise the dead to follow him into eternity."

"But you vanquished him, bringing the war to an end."

"It took three of us." *And a scion*, he thought. But that needn't be discussed.

"The two females who can summon the dragon aided you."

"Yes." He looked at all the wolven faces, noting how every single one was watching him. "By later resurrecting the Arcaner order, I have refuted everything my father stood for. But if the sins of the father reside in the son, as some believe, then I still have much to atone for ..."

"Then how did you learn the art of the dragon?" the calm one pressed.

"It is a power available only to Arcaners, after they have proven themselves brave and honorable. A power first discovered eons ago by our founder, Isobel Roseheart."

The angry one snorted. "I know the lowlander tongue. That is the name of a *female*."

"A woman, yes."

Now it was the gray one who chimed in. "How do you cast this ... power?"

Augum thought about how best to reply. "You must pass a trial in a plane with three suns—"

"No such plane exists," the angry one retorted. "All know such tales are for the cubs around the fire."

"Just as tales of your kind are for the fire?" Augum retorted. "Such planes—and others—do exist. I have seen two with mine own eyes. The trial for dragonhood is an ancient trial of honor and character. Of daring. But even to get to that trial, you must become an Arcaner by passing two other trials of character and honor, first becoming squire and then dragoon. Only as a dragoon who can survive in a vicious jungle under the watchful gaze of three hot suns can one stand a chance to become a *dragon*. My own trial was ... harrowing," he whispered, hearing the primal echoes of the jungle.

A contemplative silence passed, and Augum had the fleeting impression that he was the elder telling a tall tale to cubs sitting around a fire.

"Honor is all we know," the calm one said.

"Not all of you."

"The Dishonored do not represent The Honored."

"Just as thieves and brigands who venture your way do not represent us."

The calm raised his snout in consideration before nodding. "You speak wisdom, lowlander. We oft judge too quickly. Let me ask you this. If something ... unforeseen ... were to happen, and our kingdom were under grave threat, could one of us learn to become an Arcaner and summon the power of the dragon to defend ourselves?"

Augum thought about his reply as well. "The order is of human make. I thus do not think it would be possible for a wolven to learn the power."

The wolven exchanged looks he again could not interpret. The truth was, he did not know, but he did not like the idea of wolven pursuing that power.

"I *do* know that the Arcaner order was once prevalent in all the kingdoms, and that might have included the kingdom of the wolven."

"But you do not recognize us as a kingdom."

"We only recognize human kingdoms. Our people are too ignorant to look beyond."

The wolven nodded at this.

"Why did your order die?" the calm one pressed.

"Because the corrupt nobility used our honor against us. In the parlance of the arena, they played dirty—much like The Dishonored. Killed us off one by one, then made the order illegal, turning Arcaners into outlaws. The last time the order's secrets were taught in the academy was in the time of my great-grandmother, Anna Atticus Stone."

As an iron pan, still hissing from oil and fat, was placed before the gray one, he leaned forth. "If we sent emissaries back with you to learn the art of the Arcaner, would you teach us?"

Augum thought carefully on the matter. "If a grave threat presented itself, and our two peoples came to amend past wrongs, and if your emissaries were of stout heart and mind, then I do not see why not." He raised a finger, manacles clanking. "But be warned. The Arcaner trials kill even us. Further, I do not think my people are ready to accept wolven among them. They barely accept us warlocks. They would look at you all as, and you must forgive me for saying this, but they would look upon you as demonic talking dogs."

A chorus of offended growls rang out, with a few standing to their full height and baring their teeth and claws.

Augum raised his manacled hands and opened them to show his palms, speaking over their growling until they quieted. "I only pass on to you knowing how my people would react to seeing wolven among them! In many ways, we are still in the age of fire and stone and copper. We do not know many things, and have forgotten much ancient knowledge. We do not know what is beyond our kingdom, let alone what is beyond the oceans that surround Sithesia. Look you to me, a chief who wears wolf hide out of ignorance to the insult of your people!"

The calm one accepted an iron skillet with a juicy steak of venison that had already been salted and peppered, which he held before him as if contemplating whether or not it should be eaten. "I confess you are not like the others who stray our way. The flea-bitten rabble who show only treachery. It seems to me—" He placed the skillet before Augum. "—that we have much to learn from one another."

Augum inhaled the delicious mouth-watering aroma and, ignoring the callous shadow that peeked from behind his soul, nodded. "That we do."

MYSTERY MOSS

BRIDGET

Down in the cellar of the Black Castle, as servants looked on, Bridget studied the black-and-gray moss that was steadily consuming one of the furnaces, a hand splayed with Reveal. The black tendrils inherent to the moss were almost alive, as if they were slowly writhing ivy. It was one of the most fascinating things she had seen in some time.

She straightened and looked to the older castle servant who had been so kind to her. "Sir, would you please have someone fetch an arcaneologist, preferably one of the earth element? And you might as well fetch Commander Strout." She did not revel in seeing The Sword of the Oak, but he ought to be informed of this infestation.

The old man bowed. "I will dispatch someone right away, my lady," and he promptly sent a pair of young servants skittering off.

Bridget returned her attention to the moss and readied her mind to cast the 4th degree Commune with Plants, a well-known albeit off-the-books staple of any competent earth warlock that would allow her to perhaps trace the source of the moss. The only thing that troubled her was that the spell required touching the plant, and she did not know what would happen were her flesh to touch such strange tendril arcanery.

Since the writhing black tendrils gave her the creeps, her conservative side won out and she refrained from casting the spell. Instead, she clambered over the furnace next to the infested one, careful not to snag her robe on its various iron protrusions, and traced the infestation to a hardened clay vein in the wall of primitive rock, which she took her time considering.

"Yes, that could work," Bridget said to herself, having settled on the potent 9th degree Major Shape Earth, another off-the-books staple of the learned earth warlock. After snuffing Reveal, she raised her hands and pressed them side by side so that her two pinky fingers touched. She aligned her thoughts with the earthen clay before her and structured the complex layers of the spell in such a way that, if the clay hadn't hardened to the point of stone, should allow her manipulation.

"*Marjorus ipulato erta*," she incanted. After feeling the invisible tendrils latch onto the clay vein, she slowly spread her hands apart. The clay resisted, telling her it was likely too late and that it had formed into stone, meaning a warlock who knew the 15th degree off-the-books Shape Stone would have to be called in. But just as she was about to give up, a crack began to form within the clay.

"There we go," Bridget whispered, ignoring the awed gasps of the servants, her iron focus commanding the invisible tendril arcanery that made the clay soft once more, all while feeling the cool draw of stamina bleeding away. She continued to spread her hands apart, and the crack in the clay enlarged until it was wide enough to allow her to slip inside. As she moved forth, following the winding progression of the moss, she would bring her hands back together and repeat the process of the spell, steadily draining her stamina, never touching the moss. At some point, it got too dark to see.

"*Shyneo*," she incanted, flaring her palm with green ivy light before resuming the manipulation. The crack kept expanding and she went deeper, until the way before her revealed a wall of brick.

"Hello, what's this?" she whispered.

"May I be of any service, my lady?" the old servant called from behind.

She glanced back to see the man—and a gaggle of servants—watching her, but none dared to so much as climb over the furnace.

"I am fine, but please don't touch the moss!" she called back. "In fact, perhaps it's best that you step out of the room."

"Yes, my lady," and he moved off, herding the remaining servants with him, leaving her alone in the dark tunnel she had created.

Bridget saw that the moss had entered through a crack in the brick. She pushed on the surrounding brick but it did not budge. Knowing what she had to do, she nodded at herself, mumbling, "You can always repair it, Captain." She stepped back, took a deep breath, and slapped her wrists together, roaring, "*Annihilo!*" A vicious vine shot forth, punching the brick with a *whap!* The brick exploded outward, the vine vanishing, leaving behind a gaping hole. And from that hole emanated a most rank stench, causing Bridget to recoil.

"Gods, that's foul," she muttered, pressing the back of a hand against her nostrils. She stepped through, finding herself standing in an ancient brick sewer. The tunnel was round and about her height, with murky and pungent water trickling at the base, and white lime deposit caking the brick. She avoided the stinking brown water by straddling it and glanced back at the hole—and noticed something peculiar. The two ends of the moss that had been destroyed by the violence of her First Offensive were slowly branching out to each other, trying to reconnect.

"Now that's different," she said, watching until the two ends met. "And rather creepy." She used her lit palm to glance left and right in the dark tunnel, but after hearing nothing untoward, continued following the trail of moss to the left, which now covered a full quarter of the tunnel as a meandering band that steadily thickened. Her footsteps echoed against the brick amidst the constant *plonk* of water dripping. The moss snaked along the wall in a thick blanket for a ways before veering upward into a shaft equipped with an ancient iron ladder. When Bridget got there and looked up, she saw that the moss had covered the entire interior of the shaft, and was already starting to creep along the iron rungs of the ladder.

Down at its base, Bridget raised her lit palm, which showed that the ladder ascended into darkness. She grabbed the first rung and was about to begin the climb when she heard a snuffling. She stepped off and threw her hand forth to search the passage ahead, finding it empty. She swiveled about—and saw a raccoon-sized rat staring at her from ten feet off.

"You're quite the big fella," she said.

The rat sniffed at the air, head swiveling this way and that.

"Did you want to go past? You're welcome to it," and she hopped onto the ladder and quickly climbed up ten rungs before stopping to look down—and found the rat waiting for her at the bottom. "Being a little creepy, eh? Don't you dare," she added when the rat rose on its hind legs, sniffing at the first rung. "Don't make me blow your tail off." She did not like hurting anything, man or beast or plant.

To her astonishment, the giant rat hooked its claws onto the first rung and pulled itself up, then reached for the second rung. "I warned you." Careful not to touch the moss, Bridget hooked an elbow onto a rung for stability and was about to slap her wrists together to punch the little beast with a tempered bit of vine that ought to see it scurrying off, when she changed her mind. The rat was acting strangely. Perhaps she could try a tricky 7th degree off-the-books spell in her element she had finally had the opportunity—and time—to learn last year. But first she'd have to render the creature harmless.

As the rat reached the third rung, she traced its outline in the air with a finger, incanting, *"Paralizo carcusa cemente."* The classic 5th degree Paralyze—ancient name *Paracasamenteyagrada*—instantly stiffened the rat. The motionless beast stared up at her with beady black eyes.

Bridget climbed down so that her feet rested on the rung above, hooked her left elbow onto a rung, reached out her right hand, and placed it on the rat's head. *Now let's see if I can get this right*, she thought, for she had not had much practice in the field with the spell yet. She arranged her thoughts to precisely align with the spell's complex expectations, which involved brief visualizations like sniffing at the air, her flanks tightening as she hopped up on her strong back feet to investigate a scent, the pale darkness her black eyes felt at home in, the gentle splash of sewage water as she ran through it, and using her thin front arms to wash herself in that same water much like a human.

With her thoughts aligned, she said, "Rat, I am your friend. Please let me see the moment you first came into contact with the moss." The words, spoken in the common tongue, were nonetheless a critical preparation to the arcaneological framework of the spell. Then she whispered, *"Ba nalma communa,"* the incantation to the 7th degree off-the-books spell Commune with Animals, ancient name *Communathabanalamistro*.

As the spell coolly pulled arcane stamina from her soul, she saw herself lumbering along the sewage tunnel in pitch darkness, snuffling about for the scent of food. *Shoot, of course I can't see a thing*, she scolded herself, forgetting the tunnel would naturally be pitch dark, which not even a rat's sight would see through. Instead, it used scent as its guide—a pungent panoply of earthy water mixed with human excrement and urine.

Then its snout caught onto an unknown smell. It was bitter and strange, and drew her to a spot along the brick. She felt herself rise on hind legs and hook onto something metal—it had to be the foot of the same ladder the pair now clung onto, meaning the moss had already progressed that far by the time the rat came about.

She withdrew her hand from the rat's head, instantly returning her mind to her body. "You got there too late, big fella," she said to the paralyzed rat, proud she had gotten the spell right. Sometimes the trickiest part was phrasing the question properly. Wondering if there was a question she could ask the rat that would return a cogent reply, she placed her hand back on top of its head and repeated the mental process of the spell, this time asking, "Rat, I am your friend. Why do you climb the ladder after me?" then repeated the incantation, *"Ba nalma communa."*

What she received was a confused mess of visuals that involved following a green light in the tunnel, a peek of crimson robe, and a chicken. The last visual was a chicken hanging on one of the rungs, surrounded by green light. It was that visual that made her have an *Ah ha!* moment.

"I ate roast chicken this morn," she said, withdrawing her hand. "I stink of it, and you're only hungry, that's all." Breathing a sigh of relief, she continued climbing the ladder, leaving the rat in its paralyzed state — the spell, cast at 10th degree strength by a war-honed warlock, meaning the strength of the spell was actually several degrees higher, would eventually lapse, but long after she was gone, leaving the mangy little creature unharmed.

After climbing thirty rungs, she stopped to catch her breath. "It's fine. Everything's fine," she mumbled to herself, having developed a clammy sweat. Her ivy light lent the moss an eerie glow, and the echoing sounds juxtaposed with the tight confines of the vertical passage, giving her claustrophobia.

She raised her palm light and, thinking she caught a glimpse of a hatch high above, continued the ascent. She reached the hatch and inspected it with her light. Not only was the hatch fully sealed, but the moss began in a spot just below the rim of the exit, meaning it had been planted there.

From the tunnel below came the echoey sound of men dressed in plate armor clanking as they walked. Not wanting to wait on them, she pushed against the iron hatch, which refused to budge — darn thing was as heavy as lead. She braced against the rungs, telekinetically grabbed onto the hatch, and heaved. The metal groaned and finally began lifting, until the hatch flipped, thudding to the ground above, revealing the pale light of a cloudy sky — and a bitter cold that swept inside.

Bridget clambered out and found herself standing in the inner ward, at the very foot of the west side of the keep, near a series of drainage spouts. Those spouts drained to grates, which then led to the sewer below. She inspected the snow and found that it had been trampled solid in the same manner as the spot above the Grand Hall. She wondered if the castle's sewer system was self-enclosed or connected to the city, which might allow an intruder in.

Staring at the footprints, she realized that whoever had planted the moss here overnight wanted it to infest the entire underground before it could be found. Unfortunately for that person, the moss had slithered in through a clay vein and been found too quickly.

The echo of a juicy slicing sound came from the shaft, followed by, "Got it, Commander."

Bridget glanced down and saw torchlight bathing the rat, which had been cut in half. "No!" she shouted, and scrambled down the ladder, blood raging.

The voice of the commander caught her before she reached the bottom. "The writ was most clear, Captain—you are not to leave the presence of my knights."

Bridget hopped off the last four rungs. One of her shoes caught the edge of the nasty water, splashing the commander's gleaming plate. "How *dare* you kill an innocent creature!" she shouted at him. "It did you no harm! Had you had the good sense to leave it alone, like you ought to have as a commander, you would have seen it waddle away once my Paralyze spell had worn off!"

The commander glanced down at his leg, shook off the nasty water, and looked back up at her with an amused grin. "Captain, were you aware the thing you paralyzed was a rat?"

"Of *course* I was aware, but it was an innocent creature only wanting to live and—"

He twirled his stupid mustache. "What did you eat today, Captain?"

"What do you mean, what did I eat? What does that have to do with—"

"I repeat. What. Did. You. Eat?" The question had been posed with the condescending slowness one would employ upon a recalcitrant child. "It was some type of meat, wasn't it?"

"So? So *what*? I—"

"And do you not think that the animal that you ate this morning was innocent? Yet you ate it without a thought, didn't you?"

Bridget opened her mouth to roar a reply, but she could find no argument to make. Instead, her nostrils flared.

The captain shook his head at one of his knightly cohorts. "Earth warlocks."

"Earth warlocks," the young man echoed, wiping his blade with a cloth before sheathing it.

Frustrated, Bridget indicated the rat. "Yeah, well, you should have at least *asked* me if—"

"As you should have asked *me* before wandering off on your own."

"I called for you, didn't I?"

"Without waiting. Anything could have happened. You could be the one lying here eviscerated instead of a rat. *Then* where would the kingdom be? Less one dragon is where we would be. Think with your head, woman."

"*Captain*," Bridget snapped, liking the man less by the day.

The Sword of the Oak did not bother correcting himself, instead craning his neck to look up the shaft. "Is that the keep I spy? Looks like someone was trying to infest the whole underground, doesn't it?" He snapped his fingers at a knight. "Round up a squad to exterminate the infestation."

"Not until we know what it is," Bridget interrupted.

"Like it or not, missy, the castle grounds are under *my* purview."

Annoyed with him to no end, Bridget simply began climbing again.

"Follow her," the commander ordered, and the knights climbed after her.

She was so angry that, whilst climbing somewhere near the top, her hand slipped off the rung and touched the moss. Instantly she felt the cold soul-sucking feeling she had last felt from the lightning strike, the one that had snuffed her hand. For a moment she gaped at her unlit palm, unable to believe what had happened.

"Captain?" one of the knights asked from below.

"*Shyneo*," Bridget incanted, but her hand refused to light, nor did she feel any connection to the arcane ether. It was like she was an empty husk, or rather, an *Ordinary*.

Trembling, and not knowing what to say, she clambered the rest of the way and was soon standing outside, where she proceeded to stare at her hand until one of the knights climbed out and joined her. "Captain? Everything all right?"

"Make sure nobody touches the moss," she said, coming to her senses. "And you there," she said to a second knight who emerged from the shaft. "Find Constable Depassier."

"I've been ordered to stay with you, Captain," the young man replied, adding in a mumble, "My apologies."

"Ugh." Bridget whirled away and hurried off to locate the constable. Thanks to a kindly servant, she found him once more on the roof of the keep. She proceeded to breathlessly tell him everything, and the pair rushed back to the sewer—only to find it smoking.

Bridget looked down the shaft and saw that the walls were bare. "I told the fool to wait!" she hissed, and raced down the ladder, Depassier laboring along above. By the time she reached the furnace, well ahead of the constable, she saw a bearded army warlock spraying fire at the old iron, the commander looking on with folded arms.

"Stop!" Bridget shouted.

"What is it now?" the commander drawled. "Did the precious furnace need protecting as well?"

"The moss—tell me some remains."

The fire warlock scratched his beard. "Only crisps, I dare say. Why?"

Bridget threw up her arms. "It was part of the attack, you fools!"

The army warlock blinked. "And how was I supposed to know *that*?"

"You would have known had you waited for an arcaneologist to arrive! Or had your warlock even touched the moss, for it would have snuffed his arcanery! Look! *Shyneo!*" But her hand lit up with glowing ivy as if nothing had happened. The snuffing effect had lapsed.

The commander nodded. "Uh-huh. Tell you what, Captain. Why don't you mind your affairs and I will mind mine." He shook his head at the army warlock. "She tried to save a rat earlier. A *rat*."

The fire warlock snorted, muttering, "Earth warlocks."

"But … don't you get it … are you *daft*? How can you possibly be *this* incompetent?" She was surprised at her own directness, the sort she usually castigated Leera for.

"Mind that tongue, Captain. I might not be able to summon myself fancy arm rings, but I'm still your superior and you will treat me with respect."

Bridget pressed her fists against her waist. "At least tell me the sewer system here is self-enclosed. That it doesn't connect to the city."

"Of course it's self-enclosed," the commander replied in that same condescending tone. "Basic strategic castle defense demands it, young lady."

The bearded warlock nodded along, adding, "And the ancient arcane protections stretch all the way down into the foundations. You couldn't burrow your way through if you were a giant mole," and he wheezed a laugh.

A panting Constable Depassier finally caught up to them. "I am getting far too old for running," he wheezed in his thick Franterran accent, a hand propped against the wall. "Is there any of it left?"

"The infestation?" the fire warlock said. "Cleared it off." He saluted the commander and strode off. Two young servants passed him, and stopped before Bridget.

"We are sorry, Captain Burns, but we were unable to locate any arcaneologists to help," one said.

"Doesn't matter anymore," Bridget muttered, rubbing her forehead. "Doesn't matter ..."

SECRET PASSAGES

LEERA

"We're going *where*?"

"Shh!" Leera took her sour-faced apprentice by the arm and led her away from the rest of the Arcaners, who were still practicing sword-and-buckler training well after lunch. Meanwhile, the two knights who followed her everywhere struck up a conversation with the soldier her apprentice had been sparring with.

"Why Horren's Keep?" Revel pressed in a hissing whisper. "And where were you, anyway? You know that nosy commander has us thumping with these useless things—" She raised her wooden sword and iron buckler as if they were diseased. "—when we're supposed to be doing cycles. You promised you'd take me diving so we could work on pressure and cold training and—"

"Never mind all that." Leera glanced over her apprentice's shoulder to make sure the knights and soldiers were keeping to themselves. "I'm going on a quest, Revel."

Revel raised a dyed-black eyebrow from behind thick round spectacles. "An *Arcaner* quest?" She was naturally blond yet dyed her hair and eyebrows black, and she always wore black lipstick. "But it's Endyear. Besides, I thought you two are confined—"

"We are," Leera blurted. "And no, this isn't an Arcaner quest. It's personal. You don't have to come. Certainly wouldn't want you missing out on those belly-fattening Endyear feasts, would we?"

"So *what* if I like eating? I happen to like the taste of sweet cake."

You and me both, Leera wanted to say.

Revel sighed. "Will I get in trouble if I go?"

Leera started to shake her head, only to half shrug, then nod. "Maybe ... probably. Look, you don't have to come. It's just that you've been whining about not getting any real field training in. So, uh, here's your chance."

The girl wiped her small nose with the back of her left hand then wiped it with the back of her right before throwing a well-practiced shrug. "I guess."

"And that's the reason people call you 'The Shrug' behind your back. No guessing. You need to be firm on this. I don't want you whining that you need to come home for supper and a warm bed. We'd be provisioning to the hilt and *tenting*. That means being outdoors."

Revel rolled her eyes, muttering, "Obviously."

"Don't you roll your eyes at me."

"Why? You roll them at me all the time."

"I'm your mentor. That's my privilege after suffering your oppressively dour mood. Stop sucking all the light out of the room, would you? Despite you desperately trying to look like one, you're not a necromancer."

"But you like the way I look."

"True, I do. It scares the creeps off. Anyway, the trek also means maybe going a bit hungry, so don't expect to eat like a princess. I already sent my lady-in-waiting to start gathering."

"Since when do you have a lady-in-waiting?"

Leera pushed her spectacles back up her nose. "Since about today. And you'd have to tell your folks or whatever."

"My folks are in Malevant."

"Oh. Right."

"And they hate you and everything this order stands for and loathe the fact I want to be an Arcaner."

"You can always change your name after you marry."

"Once a Malevant always a Malevant. And I'll never marry. I mean ... look at me."

Leera glanced over the squat girl from foot to head. The way she wore her long dyed-black hair and black lipstick and black eyebrows and loose robe made the other girls call her frumpy and weird and, when they were feeling particularly mean, a witch. Mostly though, due to those huge round spectacles that magnified her dark eyes, she could pass for a grumpy owl.

"Maybe you'll find an equally hideous ogre who will love you."

"Very funny."

"I know, I know, I'm hilarious."

"You're annoying is what you are. What sort of mentor talks to her apprentice this way?"

"Mine does."

"The drunk?"

"Don't call her that. Anyway, you're only sixteen, barely a woman grown. When I was your age—a staggering four years ago, I know—I explored ancient ruins, fought assassins, and helped resurrect a ten-thousand-year-old order. Little things like that." Leera winked cheekily. "You'll figure it out."

Revel shrugged. "Whatever. How are we getting there, anyway? You ever even been to Horren's Keep?"

"I'll be 'porting us, and no, I haven't. My plan is to 'port us to the closest spot I've been to and hike in from there." As part of the agreement for the trio supporting the throne, the three of them had been granted special permission to learn the 17th degree Group Teleport spell well ahead of their degree, which came in the form of a writ Leera never bothered carrying with her.

Long-distance teleporting—meaning teleporting to spots out of sight—only worked to places one had already been to, and really only if the caster memorized details of the location. Warlocks were thus trained to always be observant wherever they went, and oft went on long journeys by horse just to memorize new teleport locations. If they were wealthy or lucky, they were teleported by high-degree warlocks. These days the academy organized excursions for aspiring 9th and 10th degrees that saw them getting teleported to the four corners of the kingdom just so they could defend the borders in case of invasion. Sometimes beyond.

Battle Teleport, on the other hand, allowed one to teleport to a spot within the line of sight. Although it used the same incantation, it was considered an extension due to the high risks involved. What few people knew was that Leera was a highly competent teleporter—she even knew the exquisitely complex Spectral Teleport spell, which allowed her to pop into existence along the line of teleportation for just enough time to slice an opponent's arm off before whizzing onward along the route.

"I thought you were only allowed to cast Group Teleport in emergencies."

"Er … technically, yes, but the word—" Leera threw up air quotes. "—*emergency* can have all sorts of interpretations."

"But doesn't it practically suck all your stamina, with it being so much higher a degree spell? And … isn't it dangerous for you to cast it still just because of how complex it is and stuff compared to your usual cycles?"

"Yes to question one, and meh, maybe a smidge to question two. Have some faith, would you? It's not like I helped save the kingdom or anything."

"Your sarcasm should win a trophy."

"It really should. Now I want you to keep practicing with that soldier for a bit then excuse yourself to the privy, after which you are to sneak off to pack. You'll need your tent, a few days of provisions, which you can snag from the kitchen, and warm clothes. And bring your waterproof rucksack, just in case." The markets sold expensive waxed canvas rucksacks with special seals crafted for water warlocks. "We'll meet behind the prison tower in one hour. Got all that?"

Revel nodded. "Got it."

"Good. Catch you soon," and Leera walked off, accepting salutes and Endyear wishes from fellow Arcaners and aspiring Arcaners. At last she spotted the person she had been looking for, who had just emerged from the Great Arcaner Hall and taken Sabby's leash from that nosy herald. Unfortunately, Commander Strout and his goons were with her.

"Ah, there's our rebellious rebel captain," The Sword of the Oak crooned upon Leera coming up to a flustered Bridget. "I expect you to begin sword-and-buckler training alongside the others."

Leera flapped a dismissive hand. "Yeah, yeah, I'll get to it."

The herald girl brightened. "Oh, can I have an interview, Captain Jones?"

"Uh, maybe later," Leera muttered, making meaningful eyes at Bridget and mouthing, "Can we talk?"

"Excuse us," Bridget said, and allowed Leera to drag her aside.

"Gods that oaf is driving me insane," Bridget said.

"The commander?"

"I'm not prone to violence but his condescension alone—wait, did you hear about what we found below?" and she proceeded to tell Leera all about her little adventure with the moss.

Leera blinked. "In other words, you're saying a plant spread underground. Enthralling."

"You need to start taking things more seriously. Something's happening."

"Something's *always* happening around here. Like I said before, I'm sure you'll figure it out. Anyway, I wanted to tell you that, uh—" She glanced past her to make sure the others were out of earshot before whispering, "—I'll be going on a little excursion."

"*Lee*—"

"Relax, I won't be gone long."

"Why do I not believe you?"

"I'll be taking my apprentice too."

"You *know* you're not supposed to leave the confines of the castle grounds."

Leera waved the matter aside. "What are they going to do, ground me? He's a busybody goon. Stand up to him. Stand up for *yourself*, Bridge. You know what? You should come with me—"

"Are you *crazy*—"

"Or you can stay here. Yeah, probably best you stay here and, uh, manage the flock."

"There's something serious going on and you're going—where are you going again?"

"Er … *Horren's Keep*," Leera mouthed.

Bridget's hazel eyes enlarged. Her mouth hung open for so long that Leera couldn't help herself from reaching out and pressing her chin upward, closing it for her.

"It's important to me," Leera said.

Bridget searched her eyes. "Apparently so."

"I'll tell you about it another time. And I promise to check in."

"You better." Bridget bit her lip and sighed. "I hate you."

Leera abruptly hugged her. "Love you too, Bridgey-poo."

"Just be careful, all right? That place is always infested with something or other. And keep an eye out for any strange occurrences. Something's happening and I don't know what it means."

"I will. Now I have to lose my tail and gather provisions," and Leera shoved Bridget off with a wink.

"Ugh," Bridget only groaned as Leera strode off.

"Captain Jones, I must insist you remain to train in the sword and buckler in case something nefarious were to—"

"I *told* you I'll get to it! Have to visit the privy first!" Then she added in a mutter, "What an ass …"

She strode through the doors of the Great Arcaner Hall even as the man shouted at her to do as she was told. She was dismayed to find that the two knights who had been following her had been joined by two others, one of whom was a woman, no doubt suspecting she was going to pull the old visiting-the-privy-only-to-vanish trick.

But Leera had already formed a devilish plan. Last year, on one of her *proata mentora* ventures teaching a young rapscallion about 1st degree spellcraft, showcasing the particularly fun 1st degree Unconceal spell, the spell had pointed her to a hidden secret passage, one of many scattered about the ancient castle.

Now where was that door again? she thought as she pretended to organize some training parchments on a table in the Great Arcaner Hall, left by the aspirants. Then it came to her. *The larder.* It was the room next to the privy too.

Having slipped many a tail in her young life, she entered through the door to the rather large women's privy, which was as fancy as a gilded ballroom, with its own doored cubicles—a luxury reserved for only the most expensive castles and estates. The moment she passed through the door she whapped it closed, flattened herself against the wall beside the frame, and ran a hand down her body, incanting, *"Armari obscura chameleano traversa,"* the incantation to the 8th degree Chameleon spell, albeit with the travel extension *traversa*. Extensions were off-the-books modifiers that changed a spell in a certain way. In this case, the complex extension allowed for movement.

As her hand passed over her body, she melded in with her background, meaning anyone who looked at her saw only the marble wall behind her—as long as she stayed absolutely still. The moment she moved, her body created a shimmer. The trick was to move slowly so the shimmer was less noticeable.

When the door burst open and the female knight clanked inside, Leera flicked a finger at a privy stall door and telekinetically slammed it shut. The knight sighed, folded her arms, and waited for Leera to step out of the privy. Except of course Leera instead slipped through the still-open door and tiptoed past the other three knights who, rather than staying vigilant for her antics, had chosen to gloat about their participation in the last jousting tournament.

Leera slipped into the larder, past two attendants stocking the shelves with crates of carrots and potatoes, and came up to a nondescript wall amidst two barrels. She ran a chameleonic hand along the groove until her fingernail found the latch. After checking the servants had their backs turned, she pulled the latch, opened the door enough to slip through, and went inside, closing it quietly behind.

"Shyneo," she incanted, lighting her palm with a pale watery light, revealing a thin passage she knew ran along the entire curtain wall. The passage smelled of musty old stone and had other secret doors, meant for quick hiding for the denizens of the castle—and the surreptitious movement of its soldiers—in the event of an attack.

She hurried along this passage, keeping the Chameleon spell up, until she came to a dead end. Having never gotten this far in the passage before, she found the unobscured handle and, after snuffing her palm, pulled, wincing when the door gave a slight creak. On the other side was an antechamber filled with barrels and crates, and a doorway that led to a booth. She could see two boots kicked up on a table—a guard was right there.

Closing the door gently behind her, she padded onward, winding her way behind a guard who was reading that morning's *Blackhaven Herald*. She couldn't help but read the headline, "KINGDOM HERO LEERA JONES HIDES SHOCKING SECRET," which caused a pain in her heart—but also reminded her why she was doing this.

She moved on, walking under an archway that led to the west drawbridge, and slipped into the second guard booth, which happened to be unmanned—the guard was chatting with an army warlock on the drawbridge. She went into the antechamber, and found herself before a blank wall.

Leera splayed the fingers of her free hand, focused on searching the ether for the intent to hide, and incanted, "*Un vun deo,*" the incantation to Unconceal—ancient name *Unconsinava*. She quickly felt a tug toward a spot in the wall where there was another hidden latch, opened it inward, and slipped through. After closing the door behind her, she relit her palm and continued onward, this time inside the curtain wall that surrounded the inner ward. Ahead would be the keep.

The passage ended at another door, which Leera pressed her ear to after snuffing her palm. Hearing nothing, she was about to open it when she heard the *clank* of boots descending stone steps, and had to wait until they passed before surreptitiously opening the door. She exited onto a landing between floors, and padded upstairs, always keeping Chameleon lit—and having to press her body up against the wall and freeze twice when chatting nobles passed.

She got to a certain floor and hurried to the same room she had woken up in.

"My lady, that you?" Gertrude whispered, backing away with her hands pressed to her chest. "Or be that a ghost come to drag me to the Great Beyond?"

"Oh, sorry." Leera ran a hand down her body, incanting, "*Chameleano null,*" snuffing the spell. She threw open her arms, singing, "Ta-daa!"

"My lady gave me quite the scare." Gertrude opened her arms at the bed, where there lay a neat row of provisions below an empty and fraying rucksack. "I got the provisions ready as you requested, my lady, and an old rucksack I dug up from the equipment stores."

Leera examined the fraying rucksack, concluding it would survive the journey to Castle Arinthian, where she would exchange it for her own personal rucksack, which was the same size. "Excellent work. Let's pack it."

The pair worked in tandem to jam the rucksack with the provisions, leaving room for her tent.

"Uh, have you got your stuff together?" Leera asked.

Gertrude indicated a linen travel sack. "I do, my lady, as you requested."

"That's … everything you own?"

"I've always been frugal, my lady. And service hardly requires many clothes."

"What about going to meet boys?"

"We are forbidden to frolic—"

"Not under me. You're my personal lady-in-waiting, which means you get to have a life." She winked. "That means parties. Boys. The works. We'll have a talk later about hours and stuff."

"Oh. Oh my."

"Well don't sound *too* excited."

"It's not that, my lady. It's just … I-I-I wouldn't know the first thing about socializing."

Leera gaped at her. "Right. Right. You'll figure it out, because I'm moving you in right now."

"We're leaving this moment? To Castle Arinthian?"

Leera slung the rucksack over her shoulder and slapped the girl's upper arms. "You betcha." She double-tapped those arms. "Now come on—oh, but wait." She halted at the door. "Stand still."

Gertrude, who had grabbed her sack, wrung her hands around its tied top. "My lady?"

Leera arranged her thoughts just so, then ran a hand over Gertrude's entire body, incanting, "*Armari obscura chameleano traversa othra,*" adding the word *othra,* which meant *other person* in the arcane tongue.

The shimmering form of Gertrude looked down at herself and started. "Oh my!"

"Don't jump like that. I just cast Chameleon on you with the travel extension. I worked my butt off to learn this variant, so don't waste it. You have to move slowly. That means no sudden movements. Get me, Gertie?"

"Yes, my lady. It's just I've never been … er, *enchanted* before."

"Fun, isn't it?" Leera cast the spell on herself, turned the handle to the door, and popped her head out. "All clear. Here, hold my hand."

"Where is it? I can't see it."

After some awkward fumbling, their hands found each other, and Leera practically dragged Gertrude out of the room, telekinetically closing the door behind her with a flick of a finger. "You don't have to move *that* slow," Leera chided.

"Yes, my lady, my apologies."

"And don't apologize so much."

"Sorry—er, yes, my lady. I'll try. Oh my, walking is a tad difficult when one cannot see one's own feet."

"You'll quickly get used to it. Trick is not to think about your feet."

They descended the nearest staircase, and got down several flights before Leera heard footsteps ahead. She plastered herself against the wall and pushed Gertrude to do the same, even holding an arm out protectively in front of the girl, whose heart she could almost hear thundering through her chest.

"Just relax," Leera murmured as the voices of three men boomed from below.

"And I said to her, 'That Arcaner order of yours is in the way. It just is, Captain Burns. You ought to let us wizened old men take care of affairs of state and security.' "

"You said that to her face?"

"Sure I did. In fact, I argued that they disband the order and serve directly under the army."

"What'd she say to that?"

The men appeared, and were gray-haired and wore saggy robes and chains of office. Leera recognized them as noble officials of the royal court—nosy busybodies who enjoyed playing games of manipulation.

"She placated me, mumbling something about 'taking it under advisement' or some such nonsense."

"She's quite timid for one who can supposedly turn into a dragon."

"That's because she has no idea what she is doing—none of them do," and they roared in laughter as they passed.

"My lady is hurting me," Gertrude whispered as the men ascended out of sight, their boisterous voices still echoing against the old stone walls of the keep.

Leera hadn't realized she was clutching Gertrude's arm so tightly, and loosened her grip. "Sorry, Gertie."

"My lady, I—or rather *we* in service, not to mention the commoners, believe you three are the kingdom's holy guardians. My lady ought not to let old fools of the stodgy nobility take up lodging in her head."

Leera patted Gertrude's arm. "That is exactly why I wanted you. Thanks, Gertie."

"My lady is most welcome."

They moved on, sneaking through the hallways past guards and noblemen, none of whom suspected anything, for no one expected to see subterfuge in the highly protected Black Castle. One couldn't even teleport in or out of the grounds unless one had special arcane privileges—which the trio had been granted by the high warlock on the high council.

Just as they entered the entrance hall and were about to pass through the guarded main doors of the keep, the four knights who had been tailing Leera earlier barged in—with a warlock who wore a crimson robe with gold fringing—and embroidered over his heart was the crest of the Black Eagles, the personal warlock guard to royalty.

"… she might be loafing in her room," the woman knight was saying to the Black Eagle, an elderly man with hard, no-nonsense eyes. Black Eagles were usually the most competent and elite warlocks of the kingdom and were oft former arena duelers, adventurers, or army warlocks who had ascended the ranks. All of them had perished in the last war defending the kingdom, causing a slew of invitations to go out. The trio had each received an invitation to become one, but had turned the requests down in favor of running the Arcaner order. The rejections had ruffled some royal feathers, for turning down an invitation to become a Black Eagle was almost unheard of—and considered a high slight.

He casts Reveal and we're caught, Leera thought, having pressed herself and Gertrude against a marble wall underneath a giant royal crest. The 11th degree Reveal could easily show the arcane tendril geometries of a Chameleon casting. The only way to avoid that was to be extremely competent in the 15th degree Invisibility spell, which was a difficult feat to pull off even for seasoned warlocks, as some of the spell's artistry had been lost to time.

Luckily the man merely followed the four knights up to the room Leera had used the night prior. As soon as they were out of sight, Leera tugged on Gertrude's arm. But then she glimpsed the snow outside and realized they couldn't possibly sneak by a yard full of warlocks and soldiers without their tracks giving them away.

"Follow my lead," Leera whispered, and when the guards' backs were turned at the keep's entrance, she ran a hand down her body, incanting, "*Chameleano null*," doing the same for Gertrude. Visible once more, Leera threw an arm around Gertrude's shoulders and strode right through the doorway, loudly saying, "… and I told them we'd be training all day, so I don't know what all the fuss is about. Say, what time are we having supper today, anyway?"

"Er … at the, uh, strike of the sixth bell as usual, my lady—"

"Great, because I'm already starved from all that hard work." Leera surreptitiously checked over her shoulder and, seeing that the guards hadn't given them much notice, let go of Gertrude's shoulders but maintained the nonsensical conversation all the way to the outer ward, where the rest of the Arcaners were still tediously plodding along in sword-and-buckler training alongside soldiers of the army. The prison tower was right near the passage between the two wards and Leera and Gertrude slipped in behind. There Leera paced to and fro in the snow, muttering, "She's late."

"Who, my lady?"

"My apprentice."

"My lady has an apprentice?"

"It's part of our *proata mentora*." After receiving a blank look, Leera went on to explain that every warlock was expected to donate around ten percent of their time for the kingdom's benefit, and things like mentorship counted toward that.

"But we can do other things, like help commoners out with problems, or clean up the streets of rabble—heck, even sweep the common hall. I mean that literally—" and Leera made as if she held a broom and swept it about. "But I'm not a great sweeper. In fact I've been told I'm more of a *lazy* sweeper, which I think does not do me justice. I just get lost in thought, you know?"

"Yes, my lady. And my lady does all these things? Sweep the hall?"

"Sometimes. My man does it more than me, but then he sets the example." She sighed longingly.

"My lady misses her betrothed."

Leera bit her lip and nodded. How she longed for him to hold her, press his face into her hair and inhale as he so oft did upon seeing her anew after a time away. Then snatching her away to the closest dark room for a passionate frolic …

Gertrude fiddled with the knot of her sack. "I hope I find a love as deep as you have."

"Would you keep that love if you were told it would amount to nothing? Would be the end of an ancient lineage?"

Gertrude looked up. "Such love never amounts to nothing. And I would fight to my last breath for it, my lady."

Leera couldn't help but smile.

"I have never met him. Your betrothed, that is."

"You'll be sick of him before you know it. Relax, that was a jest. He's kind and thoughtful and more compassionate than I'll ever be." Leera peeked around the ancient stone blocks of the tower. At last, she spotted her apprentice striding their way, a rucksack hauled over her shoulder. "Don't exactly look inconspicuous, do you?" she muttered to herself, watching as the sour-faced girl easily avoided the occasional raised eyebrow or query. As a Malevant, and a grumpy one at that, she wasn't well liked, and so people mostly left her alone, something that proved a benefit in this circumstance.

"Hey," Revel said upon catching up to them. "Who's that?"

"The new lady-in-waiting I was telling you about. Link up, goons are on the prowl," and Leera grabbed Gertrude's hand and then Revel's. Revel looked Gertrude over and grimaced. For her part, Gertrude lowered her eyes, curtsied, and mumbled, "My lady."

"She's not a leper," Leera snapped, annoyed with her apprentice, for she could be quite judgmental, typical of the Malevant line. Revel hesitantly took Gertrude's hand, but held it with a grimace.

Leera focused on the complex 17th degree Group Teleport spell that would suck a huge chunk of her stamina dry—the spell wasn't meant to be learned at such a low degree. She envisioned whisking them through the arcane ether and planting them on the stone terrace of Castle Arinthian. She thought of every nuance—the snow that would be at their feet and how crispy it was, the cold air, even the brush of wind upon their hair. Then she began the incantation.

"*Impetus peragro grapa—*"

Midway through the incantation, the four knights and the Black Eagle turned the corner.

"*—lestato exa exaei.*" Just as they imploded with a *thwomp*, Leera winked at the unimpressed Black Eagle.

After a stomach-flipping hurtle through the pitch-black arcane ether, they appeared with another *thwomp* exactly where Leera had intended—on the exterior terrace of Castle Arinthian. Gertrude stumbled away a few steps, where she buckled over to hurl.

"That's normal," Leera said.

"Aren't they going to follow?" Revel asked, turning away from the servant with a disgusted grimace.

"Nope."

"But he's a Black Eagle who can use Reveal to read the tendril wisps that briefly remain after a teleport—"

"He could 'port sniff all he wants but he doesn't have the arcane permissions to step foot on this here castle."

"Don't be surprised if they ask for it now," Revel muttered.

Leera wagged a finger at her apprentice. "That tongue of yours is getting a touch loose."

"I thought that's what you loved about me. I remind you of you."

Leera dropped her finger. "You're right. Don't shut up on my account. All right there, Gertie?"

Gertrude moaned weakly from the snow.

"Gertie?" Revel whispered. "*That's* her name? As in Gertrude? What were her parents thinking? It's like calling your own child *Grandma*."

Leera only gave a half shrug.

Gertrude fumbled around until her hands closed on her sack. She then withdrew a cloth from a pocket and dabbed her mouth as she hauled herself to her feet and gave a deep curtsy. "Gertrude Dolores Hooper at your service, my lady."

"It's not proper to be so casual with a mere servant," Revel said, ignoring Gertrude. "She ought to know her place. You need to put a firm hand to her lest she—"

"On second thought, shut up. I don't want to hear those sorts of Malevant opinions. I know you lot are used to flogging your servants, but that's not how things work around here. If I even *suspect* you of doing anything of the sort, not only will I drop you as an apprentice, but I will bring a case against you at the Arcaner committee." Leera stepped close to her apprentice, hissing, "I won't tolerate such behavior from my apprentices, let alone fellow Arcaners. Get me?"

Revel narrowed her eyes at Gertrude.

"Look at me," Leera snapped. "Do we understand each other?"

Revel dropped her eyes and surrendered a nod, mumbling, "Yes, Captain."

"Good. Now let's change out my rucksack, grab my tent, get you a room, and introduce you to the steward of the castle, Gertie."

"Yes, my lady. B-b-but surely my lady does not expect this humble servant to join her out in the field—"

"I wouldn't torment you like that, Gertie.

Gertrude curtsied to Leera whilst avoiding Revel's gaze. "Thank the gods for that."

HOWL INTO THE NIGHT

———————

AUGUM

A huffing Augum plodded onward in the deep snow, trying to waste as little energy as possible. The blizzard had dumped two more feet onto a previous two, so he was chugging through snow that went up to his chest. He tried keeping to the trail blazed by the lead wolven as best he could, but snow oft tumbled into the trench they cleaved.

Despite keeping his hood up and wearing his wolf-hide overcoat and loose deer-hide the wolven had allowed him to wrap around his hands, he constantly shivered, for the air was crisp and frigidly cold, fogging breath and making each step in the snow crinkle drily.

But his manacles caused him the greatest discomfort, for they were made of iron, and were thus ice cold. They had frozen to his flesh, yet he refused to alert the wolven, knowing they would see it as lowlander weakness.

League by league, the pack of wolven and their lone human prisoner pressed onward through a pine forest that snaked in the valleys between mountains. Sometimes a deep and distant icy *crack*, followed by a mighty rumble, sent them all scurrying to take shelter behind a tree. But no avalanche managed to catch up to them. Now and then Augum would spot a bird circling high overhead. He identified tracks of rabbit and deer and wildcat and goat, but there was a slew of others he could not place, some alarmingly large. The large ones reminded him of that distant and rabid jungle, although in that plane, such tracks had been left in mud.

When the wolven stopped to eat and make water, he drew warmth from closing his eyes and imagining cuddling with Leera under a soft goose-feather duvet, with a hearth roaring by the foot of the bed, the undulating and continuous purr of Sir Pawsalot, a fat Endyear candle flickering by a half-finished feast of roast turkey and potatoes and spiced carrots and leeks and caramelized onions, all slathered with sumptuous gravy. And when he walked, he imagined the heat of three suns on his wings.

It was late in the day, as the group took yet another rest by an old fallen tree, when the calm one, sitting beside him and using a dagger to whittle a tall stick into a spear, sniffed repeatedly at the air near Augum. "You are wounded," he declared.

"I'm fine." A violently shivering Augum tried to adjust his manacles out of sight, but they were stuck to his flesh hard. He wanted to peel back the deer-hide wrap to have a peek but worried about what he would see.

The calm one put aside the spear, snatched Augum's arm with one paw and dragged back the deer-hide with the other. The maneuver revealed that the flesh had been gnawed away by the iron.

"Lowlander fool. An enemy could smell your blood and use it to track us." The calm one then barked out something in wolven, and an eared female plodded over, one of those ears decorated with colored bone earrings that clung tightly to the flesh. They exchanged a few guttural words before the calm one revealed both wounds. Augum, long used to suffering, nonetheless winced at the sight. The female lowered herself, and he thought she was about to chomp down on his flesh, only for her to open her snout and breathe a plume of frosty white air at his wrists.

Instead of freezing, the wounds began to heal right before his eyes. She expelled that breath until she ran out, then sucked in another lungful and blew again. It was a cold breath that tingled the flesh. By the third breath, the wounds were completely healed, and she threw two strips of cloth at his wrists before weaving off to take a seat on a nearby stump.

"So that was how you healed me," Augum said, taking her cue and winding each strip of cloth around his wrists underneath the manacles. "Meaning all seven elements are indeed present in your kind."

"Eight," the calm one replied, returning to whittling his spear.

"Oh. Right."

"We blood those born into darkness as offerings to the gods. What do you lowlanders do with your—" and he growled a word in wolven here.

"With those born into darkness?" Augum adjusted the cloth strips under the manacles until they were snug. "As far as I know, it does not happen for us naturally. For us humans, one of our kind must endeavor to want to become a necromancer, and then they search for forbidden knowledge. Sometimes they apprentice under another who has already done the legwork. The pursuit of necromancy has been forbidden for eons."

"But some of you *blossom* into darkness, is that not so?"

"I have never heard of a dark blossoming."

"Yet your necromancers garner great strength when allowed to live. Occulus. Narsus. Sparkstone. These names even we know in the north — those of us who read your books and heralds not only out of strategic necessity, but out of interest."

"Yes, those who elude detection and capture sometimes gain great power."

The calm one replied with a mere grunt.

"Her nose is bleeding," Augum noted, watching the eared female sit with her head between her knees as she recuperated. "We have similar side effects when we push our boundaries in the arts. Headaches. Nausea. It is particularly hard when we first begin practicing the arts. She is new."

"She is young and still training. She has yet to delve into complexities."

"But she healed my earlier wounds, which were far graver."

"That was done by a more learned brother."

"Oh." Augum glanced around at the wolven, but other than the ears and a few sparse accents some seemed to wear much like humans — a bone earring or two, a coral or bead necklace, a woven bracelet, they all looked the same to him. "How do your healing arts work for internal injuries?"

"He already knows too much," the angry one barked. "Muzzle him, brother, lest I do it for you."

The calm one looked at the angry one with placid eyes and was the first to look away. Augum wanted to inquire about the angry one but did not want to stir up a wasp's nest.

"How much farther?" Augum asked instead.

"Not far."

"My legs are half the height of yours."

The calm one's reply was to lengthen his whittling strokes, shaving off thin slices of the stick.

"Why do you need such a weapon when you can summon one just fine?" Augum asked.

The wolven glanced at him as if he were stupid for asking such a question before returning to the whittling. "What is it like to see land from such a height?"

"People turn into ants. Houses into pebbles, lakes into puddles."

"How often do you become a dragon?" the old gray interrupted, having perked up at their conversation.

"As often as required."

"That is not an answer," the gray snapped, a paw clinging to his thick chain necklace.

"As often as duty requires of me."

"You try my patience, lowlander. Perhaps a flogging will aid your memory."

Augum did not enjoy the idea of a cold-weather flogging. "Once a day," he lied, figuring they couldn't make him swear on his shield due to the manacles preventing the use of spellcraft. He needed them afraid. The truth was he barely cast it once a month these days, and that was due to the harrowing side effects that brought on The Callousness of the Predator.

But there was one other side effect that was more dangerous. Whenever one of them reverted back to human form, for a period of time thereafter, they could not cast any spells whatsoever. The Spirit of the Dragon simul completely drained them of stamina, no matter how much or how little they spent whilst in dragon form. So not only were they brutal people devoid of any empathy, but they could not even arcanely defend themselves. The side effect lasted anywhere between a quarter of an hour to half an hour, sometimes more depending on how much stamina they used casting other spells whilst in dragon form. Further, both side effects got progressively worse with each additional dragon form casting in a day.

All in all, it was incredibly dangerous to turn into a dragon, and the side effects were considered a state secret. Sometimes they would teleport to a place of safety before reverting, and other times take shelter where they could find it, then suffer the side effects alone. But always when possible, they planned ahead how they would deal with these side effects.

The wolven discussed his answer in their language, but did not follow up with further queries, and they soon got underway again. Now mostly protected from the icy manacles, Augum drew comfort from delving into the past, recalling times of joy and coziness, of tournaments and celebrations and weddings, previous Star feasts and Endyear feasts and myriad other feasts. Most of all, his mind spent time with his beloved, recalling her cheeky smile, her sharp and playful wit, the way the summer sun lit up the peach fuzz hairs on her arms, the lavender scent of the nape of her neck …

He hoped she wouldn't worry about him too much when he missed sending her a message that evening through the Arcaner vault. He hoped she wouldn't come after him, trusting that he can take care of himself.

Above all, he hoped she was not in any danger, and was safe within the confines of Castle Arinthian or the order's headquarters at the Black Castle. He dreaded when she went out on her lone diving expeditions, for he feared the beasts of the deep. He feared assassination and kidnapping and countless other ever-present threats. Yet he rarely voiced such concerns to her, knowing he needed to trust her as much as she trusted him, and that they would always return to each other's arms in due course. In the mean, his compatriots in the order—especially Bridget, the only other person their age who had any sway over Leera—should keep her safe from harm.

By sunset, although the clouds refused to part, the late sun found a slice of the horizon and screamed its crimson light across snowy peaks, creating great swaths of light that brightly lit up the jagged mountainsides. A light sprinkle of snowflakes tumbled from the sky, bullied now and then by the occasional cold gust.

One of the eared females whose snout was decorated with a bone hoop sun-bleached to the color of her fur, muttered something in wolven, and others grunted in agreement.

"What did she say?" Augum asked the angry one, whose turn it was to watch over him.

"You bring ill tidings, lowlander, for it is a portent of fire."

Augum was about to ask what that meant when the lead wolven raised a clenched paw and the entire column ducked in place. An instant hush fell, and all that could be heard was the rustle of pine branches and the trickle of particles of ice as they bounced along the frozen surface of the snow.

The gray, who was near the front, glanced back, brought his paws together, and split them apart. The column split into two, with half going left and the other half going right. Augum was grabbed by the waist, hauled under an arm, and taken off to the right by the angry one. Many wolven dipped under the snow as if diving into water, and navigated forth like sharks. The more adept ones barely made a bulge as they zoomed ahead in the snow, while the less experienced ones occasionally broke the icy surface with a gentle *crack*.

The gray remained in the center and prowled forth like a stalking panther, sniffing the air throughout. Augum found it fascinating how the wolven worked as a group to scout the area ahead, with the gray remaining as the only visible target, while the remainder flanked him, an army of unseen predators.

After a while, Augum was carried forth. "I can walk," he hissed, annoyed at being handled like a sack. The angry one replied by whapping him across the scalp, which Augum interpreted as *shut up*.

The trek toward whatever had spooked the wolven took so much time that the sun now painted the clouds with a violet hue. Augum suspected it was because their sense of smell was far greater than a human's, and so they could follow that scent for leagues without using any other clues for navigation, such as a map.

The first clue that something had happened came in the form of a single hole in the snow that looked like an icicle had fallen from a tree. It was quickly followed by more—countless more, until the entire forest appeared littered with these holes.

Wanting to inspect them himself, the angry one dumped Augum against a tree—and held him there with a paw as he sniffed at the holes. The others inspected the holes in the same manner, seemingly trusting their olfactory senses over their eyes.

A wolfish cry of despair sounded ahead, drawing some of the wolven forth. The angry one snatched Augum under his arm and shot off with the others, until they were standing before the body of a young cub—and the little creature, about the size of Augum, was peppered with the same holes that littered the ground. One of the eared wolven was kneeling over the cub and caressing its snout.

Augum looked inquiringly to the calm one, who glanced back at him with knowing eyes, telling Augum that the cub had been the female's offspring.

Cries of alarm rang from all about as other bodies were found. Augum was dumped onto the snow once more as the angry one hissed at the calm one before shooting off to investigate.

Augum clambered to his knees and inspected the holes, noticing they had angled edges, almost as if someone had taken the time to repeatedly stab the snow with a dagger. Except it had happened quickly, meaning the holes had been made all at once. Cut branches and pine needles lay strewn about under nearby trees. He looked skyward, realizing the attack had come from above.

The old gray stepped before Augum, snarling, "What wickedness is this?"

"Do you recognize the spell?" the calm one pressed.

"They murdered a pack of cubs!" the gray added, claws extended.

Augum, fearing the old wolven might slice him to bits out of rage, took a step back. "I do not recognize this arcanery, but—" He raised his manacled hands to point upward with both index fingers. "—I believe it came from the sky."

"Is it of human make?" the calm one asked.

The angry one extended his claws as well and waved them menacingly at Augum, hissing, "Is it lowlander witchery?"

"I can't tell. You'd have to remove the manacles for me to be able to cast Reveal and check to see if any tendrils remain."

The gray raised his lips to reveal his teeth. "Do you take us for fools, lowlander?"

"I do not. But I cannot help you while restrained. Perhaps if you check the area for footprints, or any sign of obfuscation of prints, then—"

"What do you think my brethren are doing?" the gray snapped. "Treacherous lowlander," he muttered, and walked off to join his cohorts.

Augum shared eyes with the calm one, who looked away in contemplation. Figuring this was not a time to ask questions, Augum turned his attention to the footprints the other pack had left, and noticed it was mostly a straight line, with few wolven making it to a tree before being struck, meaning the sky attack had been sudden and quick.

A howl went up from a ways on, and the wolven reacted swiftly, with the calm one snatching Augum and sprinting forth. They soon came upon another body full of holes. Except this wolven still gasped for breath. The angry one leaned down and spoke harshly in wolven, demanding an answer, until the gray one shoved the angry one aside. He leaned down in his place and asked the same query in a gentler tone. The wounded wolven whispered a reply in their tongue, barely able to get it out. By the time one of their healers got there, the wounded one took his final breath, eyes staring at the sky with glassy horror.

Augum did not want to cut the silence with his Solian tongue, and so stared at the calm one in the hopes of receiving a translation. It came hours later, as the wolven meticulously placed their dead—twenty in all—on a pile of timber they had cut from the surrounding pines. Eighteen had been cubs.

"He said the attack indeed came from the sky," the calm one said in quiet tones. "And that the pack saw no one. It was quick, so that few even had the chance to summon their shields."

"That was why the wounds were mostly on the shoulders and head," Augum whispered. "But some survived the initial onslaught."

The calm one nodded. "He said those who survived were somehow snatched, vanishing on the spot."

Augum's brow furrowed at the wolven as he tried to understand what that meant. He looked skyward, and the first thing that came to mind was seeing himself snatching a brigand by the claws, taking him aloft, and dropping him on his brethren. But he suspected it likely meant something along the lines of what was known as a "snatch 'n' 'port," meaning someone was grabbed and teleported away against their will. Oft used by assassins and kidnappers, the maneuver was highly illegal in all kingdoms—except when used by certain authorities granted that privilege by writ.

The wolven assembled in a circle around the bodies, with a skeleton crew of guards hiding in the perimeter. One of them stepped forth to repeatedly blow fire at the wood under the bodies until it caught. Once the bonfire was lit, the entire pack loosed a mournful howl into the night that raised the hairs on Augum's arms. He watched the calm one and heard genuine pain in his throat, while the gray stoically howled with gusto, and the angry one practically snarled at the sky in rage. He realized that the wolven were not entirely a callous race. They too suffered agony, but in their own way. Just as with humans, they too had variances in personality. They too bled and died and mourned. And interestingly, they did not care who saw the flames or smelled the smoke, making Augum wonder if the beasts of the land respected a silent pact of mourning.

He looked at his manacles and then at the holes that littered the area. Something was hunting the wolven. Something beyond their current understanding. Whatever it was, Augum had the sinking feeling that once it found its footing, it would bear down on his kingdom too.

FEROCITY

BRIDGET

The man facing Bridget thrust his blade. She tried to parry it with her own, but he easily whapped hers aside, slipped past her buckler, and stabbed her shoulder. She gasped and staggered back, her sword falling to the snow from a suddenly numb arm.

"This is why I insist on training you 'locks in the sword and shield," The Sword of the Oak said, smirking at the other Arcaners in the yard, who looked on dumbfounded. "Had that been a blow from a real blade, you would already be dead from a follow-up thrust."

A wincing Bridget dumped her shield to rub her sore arm. "I haven't held a practice blade since I was fourteen. I'm a warlock who summons a bow in between hurling spells."

"Lieutenant!" the commander barked without breaking his gaze from her.

A young chainmail-shirted soldier promptly appeared with a salute. "Sir!"

"Fetch our illustrious Arcaner captain a bow and quiver, if you will."

"Sir, yes, sir!"

"There's a good man," the commander said as the soldier sprinted off. "Again," he barked.

Bridget flicked a hand at the dented buckler and it shot to her waiting hand.

The commander tut-tutted. "No arcanery, please."

"Right, I forgot," Bridget muttered, bending over to pick up the wooden practice blade.

"If you refuse to thrust, use your blade as a second shield. Here I come—ho!" He thrust forth, and Bridget barely managed to *whap* the blade aside. "Ho!" the commander snapped, thrusting again. "Ho! Ho! Ho!"

"Ow! Ow! Ow!" Bridget yelped, finding herself easily disarmed of the blade, her shield whapped aside, and then unable to dance away from his jabs, which hurt her stomach and chest and shoulder once more.

"Terrible defense, woman!" the commander yelled. "You did not move your shield at all—"

"It is significantly heavier than my summoned shield—"

"Isn't that the point now! What a poor example you set for your brothers and sisters in the order! A poor example indeed!"

Bridget mustered her nerves and stepped up to the muscled man, hissing, "I will not have you undermine my authority before my subordinates, *Commander*."

"Then perhaps you ought to take the training more seriously, *Captain*."

Bridget searched his hard pale eyes, finding a dearth of empathy in them. She felt callous eyes slip in behind her own, and savored knowing she could easily wipe the floor with him were they to duel as soldier and warlock. She could do it in any manner of ways, too. Skewer his forehead with an arrow shot from a summoned bow. Punch a hole through his neck with a First Offensive vine. Swallow him up in a fissure or a patch of quicksand. Summon a pony-sized elemental dragon and watch it rip him limb from limb. Heck, she could even choke him out with an entwining vine. Not to mention turn herself into a full-sized dragon and feast upon his flesh …

Except the fourth edict prevented it—*Thou shall not duel the lower ranks without serious provocation.* And there was also the fifth—*Thou shall be gallant and fair to those unable to learn the craft.*

He only smirked, enjoying taunting her. "That is why you Arcaners died out over time," he said so only she could hear. "Your own code of honor is your greatest weakness, making it easy for an enemy to take advantage. Look at you fuming like a little girl who's had her cream cake stolen. You cannot strike me down even if you wished to, lest your precious shield dim."

Bridget fought the urge to punch the man square in the nose.

"Do it," The Sword of the Oak whispered. "I dare thee."

"Captain?"

Bridget snapped out of it and saw that the entire yard was staring at them, the closest being her own apprentice, Carter Southguard, who was glancing between her and the commander. Then there was Herald Brittany Mires, who was taking extensive notes. Realizing that she had allowed her thoughts to succumb to the predator, she took a step back, picked up the sword and shield, and nodded. "Again."

"Would the captain perhaps prefer to stick to what she knows?" the commander asked, nodding at his lieutenant, who stood nearby holding a bow and quiver full of padded arrows.

"Again," she repeated through clenched teeth, determined to wipe that smirk off his face.

He easily disarmed her a third time and made her arm go numb once more, but it took an extra *whap* of the blade to do it.

"Again," Bridget snapped after she had recovered, and the yard slowly returned to their training.

By the fifth time, Bridget managed to hold onto the buckler at least. By the eighth, her blade. By the twentieth, her arm was black and blue, and her chest and thighs hurt from the points of contact the man had maliciously made.

"Pain is a good trainer," he said.

Bridget, who had been taught that very idiom by none other than the great Anna Atticus Stone when she had been the trio's mentor, silently agreed. Not wanting to give the man the satisfaction of that agreement, she merely snapped, "Again."

"Captain! Captain!" a girl called from afar, sprinting across the yard and waving an arm.

Bridget recognized Herald Laudine Cooper by the pixie cut. "Laud? What's the matter?"

A huffing Laudine skidded to a stop in the snow between Bridget and the commander. "The watchtower reported a flare from the southeast."

Bridget reflexively looked southeast, but her view was blocked by the Black Castle's high curtain walls. "Alyssa ..." she whispered. Guardian Alyssa Fairweather had been dispatched to investigate a reported wagon cart robbery that morning. Bridget had asked her to take two constables to avoid any perception of outlaw behavior, as the order was still quite new to people.

"You are not permitted to leave the castle grounds, Captain," the commander reminded.

Bridget ignored him. "Laud—Southguard—on me. Link up." She tossed the buckler and blade aside and took their hands, forming a circle. "One of my dragoons is in danger and has called for help, Commander."

"The king—"

"—will receive an explanation upon my return." She focused on a spot south of the city she had been to before. "*Impetus peragro grapa*—"

"This is insubordination and a direct violation of a lawful order!"

Bridget halted the incantation, knowing the man was right, meaning she risked dimming her shield from countermanding a lawful order. She broke the circle between herself and Laudine, making space for him. "Then bring a soldier."

"I need a whole column."

"I only have room for two more." At her skill level and training experience with Group Teleport, she could only handle teleporting a maximum of four others. Any more risked a misfire. "You coming or not?"

The commander glanced between her and the open spot in the circle. Scowling, he flicked a finger at a nearby soldier. "Lieutenant."

"Sir," the lieutenant replied, and the two soldiers linked up with Bridget, her apprentice Carter Southguard, and Laudine Cooper.

"What about me?" Brittany asked, waving her scroll-clipped tablet.

"Sorry, no room. *Impetus peragro grapa—*"

"But we had a deal that I would tail you—"

"*—lestato exa exaei!*"

The group of five vanished with a *thwomp*, and after a stomach-turning zip through the dark ether that sucked a tremendous amount of stamina from Bridget, reappeared with another *thwomp* on the side of a snow-covered road. The road was laced with the tracks of wagons and peppered with footsteps left by travelers and merchants and soldiers.

The young lieutenant keeled over to retch into the snow, while Carter groaningly held his stomach with one hand and pressed the side of a fist to his mouth with the other.

As trained, Bridget, cognizant that she would have to be frugal with her stamina now, glanced about in search of threats. People lingered near an abandoned wagon, with scavengers picking at the surrounding snow. Nearby stood a platform with a frayed rope tied to thick overhead beams—the southern gallows. Beyond, dormant fields and quiet farms stretched to the snow-covered forest and the city walls, which could barely be seen through a light winter fog. There were no hangings scheduled for today so the place was empty and silent—a stark comparison to the raging festivals that transpired around days of execution.

Seeing the frozen rope swaying in a cold breeze sent a chill down Bridget's spine, for she had sent two men to the gallows only last year. She hadn't done it by her own hand, of course. It was the punishment the magistrate had handed them after she had captured the pair robbing a traveling merchant couple, something they were known for, apparently. The victims had been well into their sixties—and tried to fend the robbers off with walking sticks. By sheer luck, Bridget had been teleporting through the area on a routine patrol and heard the woman's shrieking.

"Get up, soldier," the commander snapped at his lieutenant, who only moaned from his knees.

Bridget refocused on the wagon, which had been ransacked. The snowy area near it showed signs of a struggle, with footprints and drag marks leading straight to the forest. The tracks were littered with the detritus of a merchant's wagon—pots, pans, utensils, and the like. The nearby scavengers had picked up what they could before rushing off, scared away by the newcomers.

She narrowed her eyes at the trees, trying to see through the fog, which seemed to be thickening by the heartbeat, until she spotted the wisps of a trail of smoke. She pointed a finger at it whilst glancing inquiringly back at Laudine.

"That's it, yes," Laudine confirmed.

Carter Southguard pressed a fist into a palm and cracked his knuckles. "Does this mean we're going to pulp some heads?"

"Don't be gross, Squire," Laudine replied.

"Saw-*ry*, Dragoon," Carter muttered.

Not bothering to waste time by responding, Bridget plodded into the thick snow of a fallow field, quickly finding that, even following the tracks, pushing her knees through the snow was tedious and time-consuming. And there was no time to waste.

"Battle 'porting!" she shouted over her shoulder before focusing on the tree line. She envisioned herself settling nicely into the deep snow, her legs pushing outward against the frost. She imagined the scent of pine and spruce and cedar filling her nose. She thought of the quiet, broken only by the gentle swish of branches rustling in the gentlest of breezes.

"Captain! You are to stay within sight of—"

Bridget would hear none of his nonsense and snapped off, "*Impetus peragro!*" vanishing and reappearing with a decisive *thwomp* barely ten feet from the tree line. She stomped about in an effort to check that her legs worked—Battle Teleport was always a risk as, even though it was to within line of sight, it oft took the warlock to places they had never been to, which increased the chance of a spell failure—and accidental fusion.

Confirming all was well with her limbs, she looked back to see Laudine, Carter, the commander, and his trailing lieutenant struggling to get through the deep snow. It did not surprise her that Laudine, despite being a 10th degree warlock, did not risk casting Battle Teleport. And

Carter still had a long way to go in the arts before he could even learn Teleport, let alone its dangerous extension.

Alone, but knowing how much every particle of hourglass sand mattered, she plodded forth into the forest, finding the going easier as long as she kept to the freshly laid tracks. The pines and spruces and cedars were cozily laden with heavy plumes of snowy buildup that muffled sound, lending the forest a winter silence.

It wasn't long before she came across a body lying face up, an old man dressed in thick furs, his mouth open, revealing wine-stained teeth. Although his eyes were closed and his face appeared as if he were asleep, a pool of blood was beneath his neck, his throat having been slit. What remained of a rucksack rope lay broken nearby, the rucksack missing.

"I am sorry you found your end here, sir," she whispered, wondering what sort of life the old traveling merchant had led. What sights he had seen, what loves he had felt. She wondered if he had left behind children, if he had a home, and if someone waited for him there.

Bridget placed a hand on his forehead, whispering, "May your soul find peace, merchant. The constables will attend to you."

She stood, her nose picking up the gentle scent of burnt cedar. *Perhaps from a spell?* she thought, pushing onward, desperate to find Alyssa. She jogged when the snow permitted it, stopping every thirty feet or so to listen to the silence. Deeper and deeper she went, the forest thickened by the cold fog which deadened sound further. The sky, already dark from cloud cover, dwindled to twilight.

She constantly checked in on herself, trying to stay aware of how much stamina she had left. Group Teleport, being a 17th degree spell, had sucked a whopping three-quarters of her pool. But the trek so far, having taken so much time, renewed a quarter, so she was halfway down or so. There was a whole artform involved, taking decades to master, in feeling out how much stamina one had left and how much each spell used. The academy taught how to do this, but in the end, one still had to guesstimate.

Bridget did not have the tracking expertise Augum had, and so could not tell how many people there were or what sort, only that there were a bunch—and that someone had been dragged deeper into the forest. The tracks cut around the trees—and eventually continued past a newly felled cedar, which still smoldered. All about there were signs of a struggle. A line of cut-down branches, indicating an offensive spell. Char marks on trunks. Holes in the snow. Entire swaths of snow blown aside, revealing the frozen dirt and grass beneath. And judging by the depth within the forest, it was likely the spot where Alyssa had shot a flare into the sky.

And blood. At first, she found only drops, but those—and a lone pair of footprints—led her to a brown-robed constable lying face down in the snow. Bridget took hold of his shoulder and turned him over, revealing a man whose eyes were wide with terror, his gut impaled by his own blade. Beneath him was a patch of bloody snow which matched a wound in his chest, and nearby rested his buckler. He had been an Ordinary only doing his duty.

Bridget tried to close his eyes but they kept fluttering open. She instead placed a hand on his forehead and whispered, "May your soul rest in peace, constable."

The predator peeked out from behind her soul, lured by the death and suffering. It wandered up to peer through her eyes. She could practically hear it whisper, "Feast on his blood. Let it invigorate yours and make you stronger. Then spread your wings and feel the heat of the mighty suns of *Endraga Ra!*" The last was roared into her mind, matching the roaring of blood through her ears.

"Shut up!" Bridget snapped, stumbling back, a hand clutching her chest, twisting the crimson fabric of her robe. "Shut up …" She could not believe she was capable of such vividly terrible thoughts in the face of tragedy. It was so unlike her.

"I'm sorry," she blurted to the body. "I'm sorry …"

She retraced her steps and continued following the tracks, using the memory of Olaf to keep the blasted predator at bay. She imagined that big oaf cuddling her, absently running his chubby fingers through her hair whilst the pair each read a book under an oak tree bathed in sunlight. She wondered if he was thinking of her in that moment too.

"Focus, Bridge. You can do this," she told herself, plodding onward, hoping her betrothed was all right in the deep north, hoping he would return soon to her loving embrace. She needed to push for the wedding. Wanted children. Wanted a life outside of—

What life? a voice whispered from behind the curtain of her mind. *What life could you offer human children? You, a queen of the skies. A destroyer. A predator …*

"That's not who I am," she mumbled, sniffing as she tried to keep her feet above the snow. "That's not who I am … *Semperis vorto honos.*"

Your so-called honor means nothing.

"Stop talking to me! Shut up!" She slapped her hands over her ears, wanting to scream to drown out the thoughts.

But this very much is who you are, Bridget Abigail Burns. You are a predator. Accept it.

Bridget fumbled to a halt to stare at the silent forest. Usually she would meditate when the voice got to be too much, as the training demanded. But there was no time. "No. I will not let you," she growled instead, and continued on following the tracks — willing herself to ignore the awful voice imprisoned inside her mind.

It must have devolved into a chase, she thought, running when the depth of snow permitted it.

Running to their deaths, the predator whispered.

"Shut up," she snapped, before realizing she was paying attention to it, giving it strength. "I won't let you," she repeated.

But you already have.

"Damn you."

Then you damn yourself.

Infuriated — livid, even — she abruptly stopped to slap herself, *hard*. Cheek stinging, she breathed heavily, tears flowing down her cheeks, feeling like she was losing her mind. She turned in place as if lost, but the gloom of the misty forest lent no answers and no absolution.

End the suffering by spreading your wings. Find your way back to Endraga Ra. Bask under three suns. Become the hunter you were born to be …

It was the same old request, but clearer than ever, and in a singular voice that was her own, but stronger, wilder. It was the voice of the queen of the skies. The predator was getting stronger, winning more and more of her. She was losing herself, yet she dared to think she could somehow raise a family?

"I need to talk to you two," she whispered, plodding onward, resolving to speak with Leera later that night and with Augum as soon as he returned. She needed to know if the predator was strengthening within them too and speaking to them like it was to her. She needed to feel their presence, for the lonely weight of what she carried was starting to drag her under. And she needed to hug them both, tightly.

Even then, she felt its presence watching her. A presence that was herself, yet not her. A brutal variant of what she was capable of. A feeling she had felt many a time after having cast the sacred and mighty simul all feared — Spirit of the Dragon.

Yes, suffer. Suffer until you cannot take it. Become the queen of the skies you are destined to be … and come home.

She knew home was impossibly distant. A plane beyond planes, with three suns and a murderous jungle.

"That's not my home," she blubbered, plodding forth like a child desperate to get away. "*This* is my home. This is my home …"

The tracks went on and on, deep into the forest. It was a slog that had her panting, forcing her to stop now and then to catch her breath and listen to the forest—and ignore the voice inside her head, which continued taunting her, stronger than ever. And she hadn't even cast the spell in some time. Perhaps she had reached a tipping point? What in Sithesia was happening?

A quarter of a league on, she came across the body of a second constable, lying face down in the same manner. She flipped the poor soul over and found herself staring at a young woman of her own age, with a choppy haircut that reminded her of Laudine. She too had been stabbed by her own blade, the buckler lying nearby. As with the last victim, her eyes stared into the foggy sky as if she had seen a terror beyond terrors.

Evidence of a possible Fear casting, Bridget thought. She tried closing her eyes too but they refused to stay shut, and so she placed a hand on her forehead and for the third time that evening whispered, "May your soul rest in peace, constable." She also added, "Thank you for doing your duty."

Still panting, Bridget stood and looked back the way she had come. But there was only silence—she must have run ahead much farther along the trail than the others. Her gaze returned to the body.

Feast on her.

"Shut up."

You know you crave her blood. You can smell its iron, taste its spicy tang on your tongue—

Bridget grabbed her head, hissing, "Shut up shut up shut up!" She pounded her temple with a fist, repeating, "Shut up shut up shut up …"

Yet she could not deny that her soul craved the blood—but usually only when she was in dragon form. Nothing—*nothing*—rivaled the sheer intoxication of diving on one's enemy, pulping their bones, and feasting upon their flesh. The succulence, a reward for victory. Even thinking about that intoxication made her stand up straight and look skyward. She slowly raised her arms, feeling the heat of those three suns upon her leathery wings. The jungle called for her to return as its apex predator. As its queen.

She was barely conscious of raising one leg up and her arms coming around and hands clawing in the praying mantis pose, the precursor to casting the ten-thousand-year-old simul, a spell that had been asleep for five thousand years. A spell the three of them had awakened a mere three years ago.

The thoughts slid into place like the wooden pieces of an Ohmish puzzle. The incantation was about to slip onto her tongue when she heard a distant scream echo through the mist. The scream of a woman struck.

"Alyssa," Bridget whispered, dropping her arms, trying not to think about what she had been about to do, or the horror of the implication that the predator had almost taken over. "Now keep that door shut and focus," she told herself.

She needed to get there quickly, but the scream had come from too far off.

Bridget looked up again and saw that the fog had cleared. How long had she been in the thrall of the feasting imagery? Gods, what was happening to her?

A crow landed on a nearby branch to gawk at her. It gave her an idea. "Crow, I am your friend," she whispered, aligning the tendril geometries of *Communathabanalamistro* with the ether that connected all things. She a raised a hand and slowly walked toward the crow. "Please help me see." The crow, having been touched by the preliminary geometries in a non-confrontational manner, did not flee, speaking to her competence with the 7th degree off-the-books Commune with Animals spell.

Once she gently placed her hand on top of the crow's head, she whispered, "*Ba nalma communa*. Crow, show me what you have seen," she whispered, and closed her eyes.

She saw herself flying above the tree tops only moments prior, the majestic peak of Mount Barrow looming to the southeast. Perching atop its peak, her mind's eye imagined an invisible Castle Arinthian, its stained-glass windows lit with candle warmth, servants buzzing within, awaiting the return of three champions.

But as the crow flew, it was a patch of darkness amidst the forest that drew her attention—the ashes of Sparrow's Perch, a village she had once called home. Now all it held were broken memories and tombstones, including those of her parents—and 'Leera's parents. For the briefest moment she remembered the hope of attending an improvised warlock school amidst the forest, of friends and laughter and adventure. That was before the Legion had caught up to them, razing Sparrow's Perch to the ground and murdering nearly everyone there.

An orange light flashed amidst that dark patch, making the crow dip away, taking her vision of the spot with it. Alyssa was a fire warlock. Could that have been her?

Bridget immediately withdrew from the crow's memories, giving it a gentle pat on the head as she whispered, "Thank you, friend." Then she imagined herself standing near one of the burnt-down tree homes, her feet settled safely in the snow. "*Impetus peragro!*" she incanted. With a *thwomp*, she appeared beside the ruins of a round wall, which sat under the huge boughs of a tall and burnt pine. Frozen ivy and snowy bushes sprouted from the broken windows and peeked out from vacant doorways. The forest was slowly reclaiming the village of tree homes.

Cognizant of her stamina pool, Bridget stepped out onto the central clearing—and saw Alyssa taking shelter behind a fallen log, her face bloody, one leg wrapped with her own sleeve, torn as an impromptu bandage. The order's guardian popped her head above the log long enough to slap her wrists together, roaring, "*Annihilo!*" sending a fireball *whooshing* into one of the homes hollowed out by fire. It exploded inside, its flame pluming through a gaping window.

The tip of an arrow protruded from one of the other windows. There came a *twang* as it shot forth, forcing Alyssa to duck. The arrow zipped over her head and smacked into the stone of another home.

War-honed instincts kicking in, Bridget made a drawing-a-bow motion, hissing, "*Summano arma!*" An earthen bow *whooshed* into existence in her hands, an arrow already notched, a quiver on her back. Just as a man peeked from the doorway, she let the string go. *Twang* went the ivy-laced arrow, but the man was quick enough to dip back inside and the arrow thwacked into the remains of a moss-covered door, vanishing soon after.

"Cap!" Alyssa called, coughing and gripping her leg. "Thank the gods! There's four of them! Duck—!"

Bridget heard the telltale smack of wrists before seeing where it came from, and instinctively rolled forward just as a bolt of lightning sizzled overhead, smashing into the trunk of a blue spruce, sending plumes of snow falling to the ground.

"Your left!" Alyssa shouted.

After rolling, Bridget smoothly withdrew an arrow from her summoned quiver and swiveled her bow leftward as she notched the arrow, and the moment her aim glimpsed the amber robe of a warlock, she let it go. The arrow shot forth with a *twang*, but the man expertly summoned a shield made of hardened lightning, and the arrow *thunked* off it with a lightning-added *sizzle*.

"Behind!" Alyssa roared, quickly followed by a slapping of wrists and a shout of "*Annihilo!*"

Bridget reflexively tumbled aside, but it was Alyssa who had shot another fireball, this time into the forest behind her. It slapped against a pine trunk, barely even melting nearby snow away, meaning she had either intentionally tempered it, or, more likely, her reservoir of stamina was nearly drained.

Seeing that their central position allowed the enemy to attack them from all sides, Bridget let go of her bow, vanishing it and her quiver, and swirled an arm about, incanting, "*Voidus vis!*" The area around her was plunged into pitch darkness, an effect brought on by the classic 5th degree standard spell *Voidaoccanastradama* — Darkness in common parlance.

She then sprinted toward Alyssa, hearing the telltale zips of arrows whizzing by, along with the slap of a pair of wrists from behind her. Just as she emerged from the cloud of darkness, two bolts of lightning pronged past her on both sides, one of which almost took Alyssa's head off. A Second Offensive casting meant the man was at the very least an 8th degree warlock, if not higher.

Bridget's experience and her skills in archery lent her an instinctual feel for when an arrow was coming directly at her. That certain *zip* in the air made her leap forth — and as if in slow motion, she spotted the blur of the arrow shoot right underneath her belly. She fell to the snow, tumbled forth twice, and slapped her hands onto Alyssa. Alyssa started saying how they had to get out, but Bridget was already on it, envisioning the closest spot she could think of along the route she had trodden — that of the body of the second constable. "*Impetus peragro grapa lestato exa exaei!*" she incanted, cutting Alyssa off.

The two women vanished just as a bolt of lightning smashed into the log. They reappeared in the quiet wood to the west — and were surprised to see Bridget's apprentice Carter Southguard, Laudine Cooper, The Sword of the Oak, and his lieutenant all gaping at them.

Alyssa immediately collapsed, mumbling, "They got my leg. I'm … I'm depleted," which Bridget understood was a reference to her stamina pool.

Laudine, the only full-fledged Arcaner of the bunch, sprang into action first, kneeling beside Alyssa to check on her. Everyone spoke at once.

"I can staunch the wound," the lieutenant blurted, fumbling with a small satchel attached to his belt.

"Captain, report!" the commander ordered.

"Three archers and an 8th," Bridget said, staring at Laudine, "and I'm going back."

Laudine, holding onto Alyssa, searched her eyes. "Where?"

"Sparrow's Perch. I want you to flank them."

"Take me with you!" Carter pleaded.

"I'll meet you there," Laudine said.

Bridget didn't waste time telling her apprentice it was far too dangerous for someone so ill-experienced, and instead visualized the area of the forest behind the archers—an area she had first explored as a fourteen-year-old apprentice. Despite Carter breaching protocol by grabbing her arm, no doubt hoping she was casting Group Teleport, she snapped off, *"Impetus peragro!"*

The moment she appeared, she summoned her shield out of reflex—and thank the gods, too, for the two archers hiding there had evidently been waiting for her to return as they quickly swiveled about and shot their arrows. One missed wildly, but the other's arrow *thunked* into her shield.

Bridget made a yanking motion at the bowman who had hit true, adding a twist at the last moment whilst incanting, *"Disablo!"* The bow twirled out of the man's hands, making him scramble for it like a child just out of reach of a dangling toy. The other one had reached back for another arrow and was nocking it when Bridget shoved at the air, roaring, *"Baka!"* sending him flying. He landed in the open and tumbled a few times.

There came the sound of feet crunching into the snow in the woods—the fourth attacker, no doubt—as well as a nearby *thwomp*. Meanwhile, the one whose bow had twirled out of his hands managed to catch it. Seeing she had a beat before he could nock another arrow, Bridget turned her attention in the direction of the teleport, and saw the amber-robed lightning warlock finish a familiar clawing gesture whilst incanting, *"Dreadus terrablus!"*

Bridget took a ducking step forth—and felt the raking tendrils of the vicious 4th degree Fear spell, a favorite of bullies the kingdom over, tickle the top of her mind. But the man was surprisingly quick with a follow-up, and promptly repeated the gesture and spell. This time Bridget harnessed the principle of perpendicularity as well as knowledge of the incoming spell, as required by the Mirror of the Dragon simul, summoned her shield, and incanted, *"Mimicus!"*

She felt the Fear tendrils rebound off her shield and *twang* back at the attacker. But the man had apparently read up on Arcaner spellcraft, for he managed to duck his own spell. And while he did so, he snapped off yet a third repetition of Fear.

To save time, an annoyed Bridget let the attack hit her full on.

Most warlocks trained in a special defensive 3rd degree spell called Mind Armor, which armored the mind against other mind spells. The better one got at identifying incoming tendril signatures, with each spell creating a certain tingle on the brain, the better one got at defending against those spells. To a seasoned warlock, Mind Armor was practically automatic, and could be raised as quickly as one would raise a shield, at a slight cost to one's arcane stamina. But one still had to watch out for spells cast at a much higher degree of potency, for they could blow through one's Mind Armor like a spear through parchment.

In this case, the opponent's Fear spell slammed against Bridget's war-honed Mind Armor, barely denting it, allowing her a precious moment to not only make direct eye contact with the man—and already his eyes were enlarging, as if he had recognized her—but also make a drawing-a-bowstring motion, whilst hissing, "*Summano arma flustrato!*"

It was called Bluster of the Dragon, and was a simul Bridget had learned whilst taking the Arcaner course. A marriage between 5th degree Summon Weapon and 4th degree Confusion, the spell infused the next ten arrows in her quiver with the Confusion incantation.

Twang! went the first arrow which, shot at nearly point-blank range, slipped past the man's rising arm, no doubt to summon his own shield. The arrow lodged into his side with a sickening *schlick*. Not wanting to kill, Bridget smoothly reached back into her quiver, quickly nocked a second arrow, and shot it at the man's shield, knowing what would happen. The arrow *thunked* against the shield, yet his head snapped back, for the invisible Confusion enchantment continued forth into the man's body. The principle was known as arcane momentum, which was the tendency for certain high-velocity enchantments to continue moving forth from sheer momentum. She, Leera and Augum had each learned a variant of such a simul, one of the advantages of being an Arcaner.

But this fool certainly didn't know that, for his widened eyes started to rove about, indicating it had only taken two hits for the war-honed simul, cast at 10th degree by a seasoned warlock, to penetrate his Mind Armor.

Hearing two nearly simultaneous *twangs* behind her, Bridget jumped aside and brought her bow about, this time grabbing two arrows from her quiver. As she nocked both on the ivy string, a skill she had started practicing last year, one of the opponent's arrows *thunked* into a tree and the other squished into the lightning warlock's thigh, eliciting a groan from the confused thug.

Bridget loosed both arrows at once at the two men who had shot at her, but being inexperienced with the skill, the arrows shot wide. An awkward heartbeat passed during which everyone nocked new arrows. Halfway through, there came another *thwomp*, followed by a shouting tussle in the woods—Bridget didn't need to turn her head to know Laudine had intercepted the third archer.

Bridget was the first to shoot her arrow, striking one of the men in the chest. He gasped, dropped his bow, and fell to his knees. The other, however, shot off his arrow. Bridget knew it was coming and tried to dip aside, but at the close range involved, the arrow clipped her thigh, shooting a jolt of pain up her body.

In the heat of the moment, all she did was wince. But the pain awoke something that had been merely watching, intrigued. The Callousness of the Predator stepped forth again to stand directly behind her eyes, and before she knew it, she found herself drawing the outline of a small dragon, incanting, "*Summano elementus draco!*" An elemental dragon the size of a pony and made of ivy and leaves and earth rumbled into existence between herself and the archer, flapping its wings as it hovered in readiness for a command.

The archer went ashen, squeaking, "Holy Unnameables it's *you*—"

A stone-faced Bridget, hearing the vein-quickening call for blood and war and mayhem, pointed at him. "Draco—attack!"

The man dropped his bow and made a defensive cross with his arms, screaming, "Gods, no! No, no, no, no, *no*—!"

The dragon, a product of the potent Birth of the Dragon simul, whipped its tail and wings as it shot forth at the man. In a blink, the villain was screaming shrilly as his blood and guts sprayed about as if he were a fountain.

Bridget, the predator within her rearing up like a cobra, stepped *into* that spray, enjoying the sounds of a rabid feasting of the flesh. The nearby wounded archer, still on his knees, trembled violently before retching from the sight.

As her dragon feasted, Bridget glanced back at the warlock. He stumbled about, trying to focus, making a valiant attempt at fighting through the fog of Confusion that smothered his thoughts.

But it was Laudine's huffing that drew her attention thirty feet off, and she bolted in that direction. The pair were scrapping like schoolyard children. Laudine was trying to snap off spells but the opponent—a woman—had a tight grip over her mouth.

Bridget simply drew the outline of the bandit, incanting, "*Paralizo carcusa cemente,*" and she froze in place, allowing Laudine to free herself, shout a stage profanity that would have been amusing in any other circumstance, and smack the woman across the face with the back of her hand. After jumping to her feet, she wiggled her hand at the woman's head, incanting, "*Flustrato!*" confounding the already paralyzed bandit.

A panting Laudine turned to thank Bridget—only for her eyes to go wide. She shoved Bridget aside at the same moment someone behind her slapped their wrists with a roared, "*Annihilo!*"

Realizing the man had shrugged off the Confusion quicker than she had anticipated, Bridget whirled about mid-push, summoned her shield, and spun-smashed the bolt of lightning with her earthen crust, making quite the *sizzle*. After slamming sideways into the snow, she grabbed an arrow from her quiver, nocked it, pulled on the bowstring, and let it fly.

The arrow zipped at the man as if in slow motion. Perhaps had he not been recently confounded with Confusion, he would have moved quicker. Alas, the arrow sank into his throat with a sickly *shloop*. He scrambled at his neck, grabbing onto the ivy shaft, yet his hands fell through it when the arrow vanished, leaving behind a continuous spurt of blood.

Bridget watched from the snow as the man stared at her with that all too familiar look of disbelief she had seen on many a foe. He lumbered a few steps, as if hoping to walk it off, before abruptly falling to the snow, face first. There he lay, wheezing, as the summoned dragon noticed him. It looked to Bridget, its mouth and lizard neck dripping with blood, waiting for the command. Bridget raised a finger, readying to point it, only for a hand to enclose that finger.

"Don't, Captain," Laudine said. She grabbed hold of Bridget with her other hand and gently prodded her to stand. "Gods, look at you. Like you bathed in blood." Then she added in a theatrical whisper, " ''Tis not the mice who stir when the lioness enters, but the sheep who crave her protection …' "

Bridget glanced down at herself and couldn't believe what she saw. How in Sithesia had so much blood splattered on her? When she looked back at Laudine, the poor girl took an involuntary step back, mumbling, "Why are you looking at me like that?"

"Like what?" Bridget coldly asked, fully knowing the answer, for a certain inner voice pleaded for her to feast on the fool girl's flesh.

"Like … like I'm food. You're scaring me, Bridge."

Bridget glanced down at her bloody hands. "Sorry," she mumbled, and crouched to wipe her hands on the snow.

"Captain?"

"Mmm?"

"You may want to null it."

Bridget looked up to see the dragon prowling close to the paralyzed bandit. The woman was staring at it with saucer-wide eyes.

"Oh. Right." Bridget made a lazy reverse-outline motion, mumbling, "*Summano null*," and the dragon vanished with a *whoosh*.

Laudine gaped at Bridget.

"What?" Bridget snapped.

"N-nothing."

"Spit it out."

Laudine shook her head. "It's fine, Cap." She grabbed a strip of bloody cloth torn from the unfortunate bandit that had been ripped apart and used it to tie the hands of the paralyzed woman.

A detached Bridget looked on. She wanted to be herself again, but the predator lingered like the iron stench of blood that clogged her nostrils and fuzzed her thoughts. She looked skyward and closed her eyes, feeling the call of three suns. How she wanted to extend her wings, to show them all what royalty truly meant, for she was a queen of the sky, of the jungle, of death. An apex predator of unfathomable power. How she craved to flex her strength. How she wanted to feast on the weak and wretched ...

"Captain?"

Bridget opened her eyes to look at Laudine, annoyed with her neediness.

"You ought to wash it off."

Bridget looked down at herself. "But it smells so good."

"I know, my friend. I know."

Bridget looked back up. "No, you don't. You don't know and cannot ever fathom ..."

"You're right. I don't and I can't. No one but you three know. But you can't linger in it."

Bridget remembered making the praying mantis pose in the forest. She had been a heartbeat away from casting the sacred simul. Perhaps none would have then survived, for she did not trust her state of mind. And what would have happened had she feasted on her own friend and apprentice and the others? How would she have lived with herself? She'd belong in prison ... shieldless and stripped of all titles and possessions and freedoms. Or maybe even burned at the stake ...

She touched her thigh wound with a finger and brought the finger to her lips, tasting her own blood. Her veins quickened as a craving for violence flared. She searched about, hungry for threats.

"Captain."

Bridget, shoulders heaving from the breath of war taking hold, looked again at Laudine, who flattened a palm and pushed it downward several times. "Calm it down, Bridge. Calm it down."

"Right. Right …"

The sound of footsteps came from the forest, and Bridget, swayed by the predatory moment and the war stench of blood, snapped off, "*Impetus peragro!*" With a deep *thwomp*, she appeared directly before an advancing warlock. She slapped her wrists, ready to explode the man with a punch of vine, only for him to skid to a halt and shriek like a little girl. He raised his arms in the same manner of defense as the brigand had and fell on his butt.

Bridget dropped her arms. "Your first reaction should have been to summon your shield, Apprentice. Work on your reflex training."

Carter Southguard was shaking as he stared at her bloody visage.

"And if you ever grab my arm mid-teleport again, I will have you thrown out of the order so fast you'll be dizzier than an aspirant taking their first 'port. Don't ever breach teleport protocol again. Ever."

"Yes, Captain," Carter mumbled. "Sorry, Captain."

"You're on scene cleanup duty," and Bridget turned her back on him.

"Unnameable gods that's a lot of blood," Carter whispered behind her.

"Wait until a war comes," Bridget said over her shoulder, striding back over the clearing toward Laudine, who was minding the paralyzed woman. She heard one other running in the forest behind Carter, but did not bother looking, knowing it was the commander.

Upon arriving, she leaned down before the prisoner. "Do you bend the knee? Up and down with the eyes for yes, side to side for no."

The woman quickly flitted her eyes up and down several times.

Bridget wiggled a finger in a reverse outline, incanting, "*Paralizo null*," and the woman was able to move freely.

Laudine grabbed her bound arms and hauled her to her feet.

"How many did you rob?" Bridget asked.

"You're her," the woman blubbered, glancing past Bridget at what was left of one of her cohorts. "Look what you did to Harold …"

"Harold should have bent the knee, don't you think? How many did you rob? Answer me."

"I … I don't know. Thirty, maybe forty."

"Thirty, maybe forty," Bridget echoed, staring at her. The woman's gaze withered, her shoulders drooping. Bridget grunted like an animal, turned, and walked up to the fleshy puddle that had been a man named Harold only heartbeats prior. She bent the knee before the grisly scene, but finding nothing that resembled a forehead, she instead placed a hand on an exposed piece of bone, and whispered, "May your soul find the peace together we could not reach." She then did the same to the two other men, dispensing the Final Valediction as custom and honor demanded.

The commander walked up to her when she finished, roaring, "How could you have taken such a risk! Look at me when I'm talking to you, Captain!"

A bloody Bridget walked toward him so suddenly he took an involuntary step back, only for her to wind around him as if he were a mere fence post. She walked past her stunned apprentice and on toward something that tugged at her heart—the graves of her mother and father.

It was a small cemetery, its bare wooden markers now replaced with etched stone. Bridget stepped before the markers. Here they rested, the victims of the Lord of the Legion, murdered six years ago.

"The moment everything fell apart," Bridget whispered. "And now you rest for all time …"

She went to the headstones of her parents—Henry and Annette Burns—and her brothers Oswald and Christopher Burns. She dropped to her knees and whispered, "Mother. Father. Forgive me, for the kind and empathic girl born to you has become a killer. A child of war. And … and I do not know who I am still becoming. Forgive me …"

PREY AND PREDATOR

LEERA

Under a giant blue spruce near the crashing waters of Anchor Lake, Leera and Revel sat around a low fire, snug in their winter fur coats. With her black makeup and black hair aglow from the flames, Revel poked at a fat salmon sitting amidst the coals, fished out of the lake by her own hand, whilst a pot of potatoes slowly boiled nearby. Leera, who had supervised the short fishing expedition into the frigid waters, stared through the flames, idly taking turns playing with her betrothal ring and the ring she had scavenged from the shipwreck, heart longing for Augum. Now and then, both girls adjusted their spectacles.

"I haven't quite got the knack of totally drying out my robe," Revel commented, standing nearer the fire and shivering. "It's still a bit damp, which is remarkably uncomfortable. Gods that wind is freezing."

"It'll come," Leera said, listening to the creak of the snow-covered forest. The wind had a calming effect, but also amplified her loneliness.

They were halfway along the coast between Blackhaven and Horren's Keep. Leera had teleported the two of them to the farthest spot she had been to along that coastline. The pair had then walked the rest of the day until hunger and weariness had got the best of them.

As Revel had prepared the fire, Leera had enchanted the area with the standard 10th degree *Arregandalarmothesera*—commonly known as Area Alarm. She had cast it in a circular pattern, choosing a diameter of fifty feet, which took some extra time and stamina. The alarm would ring in her head should anyone other than the two of them step within its area. She had further used what was known as a *complicator*, learned in her spare time whilst in the academy for her final term, to allow the spell to distinguish between man and beast, with the latter sounding off in a lower pitch.

"The fish don't like my light. Barely caught this one."

"Because you cast it too bright. You need to learn how to dim."

"Then teach me."

Leera sighed and opened her palm. "*Shyneo.*" It flared with a bright watery light. She stared at Revel and willed the light to dim to candle strength. "It's mainly about controlling the flow of stams."

Stams was the official term the academy used to represent a theoretical sample of stamina draw. Although warlocks could not "see" stamina or confirm it actually existed, they still needed a unit of measurement in order to better understand the craft. Some spells drained more stamina than others, and there was quite a bit of guesswork as to how that was quantified relative to a warlock's abilities, but it served well as a teaching aid in the academies.

"You also have to envision the light being dimmer. The two go hand in hand."

"That's it?"

"That's it."

Revel flipped the salmon over with a stick before splaying the fingers of a hand. "*Shyneo.*" Her light was its usual brightness, and lit up the underside of the spruce—and the nearby snowbank they had built up to ward off the wind—with an eerie blue glow. She grimaced at her palm, but it remained bright.

Leera snuffed her light. "It takes practice."

"How *much* practice?"

"Enough until the skill takes. Just got to keep at it."

Revel snuffed her palm, muttering, "Sounds like a lot then."

Leera said nothing, instead returning to fiddling with her two rings. Her betrothal ring, enchanted with a tracking enchantment that would allow her to find Augum's matching ring, unfortunately still pointed back to Castle Arinthian, where he had left it so as not to give himself away on his undercover quest. As to the ring engraved with waves, she couldn't yet understand its arcaneological complexities. Whatever it did was out of her reach—for now. When she returned to the city and found the time, she'd get back to studying its arcanery.

"You think I could ever attain the dragon rank like you?" Revel asked, cutting through Leera's thoughts. "You know, fly up there in the sky alongside you three?"

Leera stared through the flames. She didn't feel like talking about how dangerous that dragon-attainment quest had been, or why the three of them were granted a try at the quest in the first place. How they were an experiment conducted by Augum's famous great-grandmother to see if allowing three people to cast the Spirit of the Dragon would destabilize—or even destroy—all of Sithesia. A precious few knew these things.

"You want the truth?" Leera asked. Even thinking about the simul made eyes open behind her soul. Eyes she was tired of feeling.

"No, I want you to lie to me. Of *course* I want the truth."

"You wouldn't survive the trial."

"Oh. Wow. Just like that, huh?"

"Just like that," Leera whispered, feeling those eyes creeping into her vision. She knew if she so much as looked at Revel, the stirring for blood would flare. "Creepy bastard," Leera muttered, hating The Callousness of the Predator.

"What'd *I* do?"

"Wasn't talking about you."

"Then who?"

"Nobody." Leera shot to her feet. "I got to make water," she lied, and walked past Revel toward the dark forest.

"With your rucksack?"

"I've learned to always keep it with me whilst adventuring," Leera said, climbing over a snowbank.

"Fine, just don't take too long," Revel replied, eyes darting about. "Spooky as heck out here."

Leera, long used to being out in the middle of nowhere, only grunted. She plowed through the snow, meandering around spruces and pines and cedars lit up by starlight, until she was well out of earshot and eyesight. With the trees creaking around her, she looked skyward and, between the snowy canopy of evergreens, saw a brilliant field of stars.

"Are you looking at them now, my love?" she whispered, voice lost to the wind. "Are you thinking of me? Because I'm thinking of you." She sighed, refocused, flared her watery shield away from the campsite to keep the light away, and incanted, "*Summano vaultus Arcanus.*"

The Arcaner vault *whooshed* into existence before her. As always, she took heart seeing that all three crest doors were still lit, indicating their owners were alive. She let her shield vanish, hooked three fingers underneath a gold tab on the side of her vault crest, and opened the door. Jammed right up front was a new note, which she unfolded.

Had encounter with brigands in Sparrow's Perch. Slayed all but one, taking one prisoner. They murdered two constables and a merchant. The predator opened its eyes within me in a new way. It talked to me. I almost became the dragon. I'm worried.

—Bridge

Leera sighed upon reading Bridget's note. They ought to talk upon her return. Share what was happening to them. She contemplated taking the note to the fire, but instead jammed it into the dense mess of ancient parchments, and imagined some young Arcaner stumbling across it generations later.

She perused the densely packed parchments of her side of the vault, but found no note from her beloved. He had never missed leaving a note. Something was wrong.

"Or he might've forgotten," Leera whispered, only to scoff at herself. "He's a dragon, for Unnameables' sakes. Trust your man. He probably got too busy and simply forgot. You know how men are."

Still, the nagging feeling wouldn't go away, and she contemplated abandoning her quest to look for him. "Don't be a hasty fool," she told herself, and withdrew a quill, inkwell, and some scrap parchment from her rucksack. She crouched, pressed the parchment against her knee and, using the light from the crests embedded in the vault, scribbled a note to Augum. Then she stuffed it into the right, into his area of the vault, a feat possible because the interior of the vault had no wall separations. Lastly, she closed the door.

"*Vaultus null,*" she said, and the vault vanished. With another sigh, she turned back toward the campsite—only to find that Revel had stepped into sight.

The girl blinked. "What?"

"*What* is none of your damn business, Squire," Leera snapped, a shadow rising within her. "How *dare* you spy on me!"

"I wasn't *spying!* I was scared, all right? I heard a noise and thought something had happened!"

"An alarm would have gone off in my head had that been the case!" Leera felt a presence close behind her eyes. It told her Revel was lying and was no longer to be trusted. "I'm dumping you as my apprentice," she hissed. "You're dismissed, Squire. I'm taking you back."

"What? No! No, please, you're misunderstanding me—" Revel fell to her knees on the snow and wept. "I'm sorry ... I didn't mean to follow you ... I don't even know why you're so angry ... please ... the order ... it's all I have ..."

Leera, feeling the shadow slipping into her limbs, stormed up to the girl, dragged her up by the scruff, and shook her, roaring, "How can I possibly trust you now? Huh! How!"

"This is how," Revel blubbered, summoning her watery shield. "I swear upon my sacred shield as an Arcaner that I am telling the truth."

Leera glanced down to see that Revel's shield had not dimmed. She saw the mostly empty crest with the lone words *Semperis vorto honos* and let go of the wretch, who fell to her knees again and blubbered, "I'm so sorry. I'm so sorry ..."

Leera turned her back on the weeping girl. "You can't just go around sneaking up on people."

Revel let her shield vanish. "I won't sneak up on you again. I promise ..."

"Damn right you won't!" Leera roared, whirling about, feeling the callousness rage through her veins. "You fool girl! It could get you killed! Do you understand that? Murdered in cold blood!"

"Y-yes, I-I-I understand," Revel gibbered.

Leera's nostrils flared as her shoulders heaved. She heard her own thoughts hiss, *Make her pay. Eat her like a snack.* She wanted to pick the fool up again and throttle her. To make her understand. To toss her skyward and chomp down on her flesh and grind her savory bones between her teeth and —

Leera abruptly raised two hands before her face as if hearing blasphemy. She stumbled back a few steps, incredulous at her own thoughts.

Revel looked up from the snow. "Captain? Are ... are you all right?"

Leera dropped her hands and looked at them. What was happening to her? "I'm ... I'm fine." *But you're not fine. You're far from fine.* The voice had gotten strong. Perhaps she had been casting the sacred simul too much in the last few months?

She expelled a weary breath as she massaged her scalp with her fingers, calming her soul and pushing the shadow back behind the curtain. Bridget had warned her that she needed to be far more discreet when summoning the vault. She was a secret-keeper, for Unnameables' sake! And now someone else had almost seen the vault ...

Leera straightened and cleared her throat. "And I accept your apology." She walked up to the poor girl, who scurried back in the snow as if afraid she'd get slapped. Instead, Leera gently drew her to her feet and grabbed the sides of her shoulders. "It is I who must apologize to you." She forced a chuckle. "And that's saying a lot as I find apologies very difficult for some reason. Anyway, yeah, I'm sorry."

Revel swallowed. "And I accept your apology, Captain. You've been through a lot. I get that you're jumpy. Anybody who's been through a tenth of what you've been through would be jumpy."

Leera abruptly drew her apprentice into a hug, whispering, "I'm sorry. I'm sorry for doubting you, Squire. And I'm sorry for jerking you about."

Revel awkwardly patted Leera's back. "It's, er, all right, Captain."

Leera drew back. "What, never been hugged before?" She had been jesting, but to her surprise, the girl shook her head. "Wait … not even once?"

"I'm a Malevant. Nobody hugs a Malevant," the girl mumbled whilst shaking her head pitifully—only to reanimate. "Except I guess there was that *one* time at the academy, but that was more of an accident as they thought I was someone else."

"What about your parents?"

Revel scoffed. "Do you know what the Malevant motto is?"

"Something long and scary sounding, no doubt."

"*Comi ia fromia o bloodalina Malevant. Oro castla lientey del ruino. Denbo weppo aro fenexei. Weppo vli ascendi adver.*"

"I was right."

"It translates to, I come from the bloodline Malevant. Our castle lies in ruins. But we are phoenix. We will rise again. My family doesn't take to things like 'feelings' and 'showing love.' All of that stuff is weak and gross to them. The entire lineage is supposed to be hard and cruel and I'm sort of a …" She shrugged.

"You're a rebel."

"I guess."

"Revel the Rebel. Has a bit of a ring to it, doesn't it?"

Revel smiled, but there was sadness behind that smile. "I guess. And certainly better than being called Revel the Devil. That's what my cousins called me when we were kids. I was meaner then."

Leera clapped her shoulders. "Forget all this. Let's feast," and the pair returned to the fire, where they found that half of the salmon had burned.

"I can scrape it off," Revel said, and proceeded to scrape the charred bits.

Leera, meanwhile, dumped the potatoes onto several rows of sticks, allowing the water to drain into the snow below. She then reached into her rucksack and withdrew a sheathed knife, two tin plates, a waterskin, a tiny pouch of salt, a pouch of pepper, a pouch of rosemary, and a tin container of butter. As Revel prepared the salmon, Leera sliced the potatoes onto each plate. They then proceeded to butter and season both to perfection.

"Mmm," Leera toned, taking her first bite.

"Mmm," Revel mimicked, doing the same. "Sumptuous."

"Delectable," Leera countered.

"Divine—"

"Marvelous—"

Leera crinkled her nose. "I got nothing," and the women chortled.

They feasted, devouring the entire meal, with Leera going so far as to lick her plate clean, earning her a repulsed look from Revel before the girl glanced about as if to make sure no one was watching and cagily did the same. The wind picked up once more, swaying the trees and making them creak. Waves, pushed by that screaming wind, rhythmically crashed against the nearby rocky shores of Lake Anchor.

Revel reached up under her thick spectacles to rub her dark-lined eyes. "I'm exhausted and drowsy. Can we set the tents up?"

"First let's do some cycles."

"Do we have to?"

"Always. As my old mentor used to say," and Leera added a croak to her voice, " 'Working through exhaustion makes a good warlock great.' She also constantly told us that 'The key to mastery is repetition. Day in and day out.' "

"Are you referring to *the* Anna Atticus Stone? Wasn't she headmistress for, like, thirty years?"

"I am, and it was thirty-five," Leera said as she used snow to scrub her plate and cutlery. "But she was a headmistress well before our time. That would have been something, though, to have seen her heading the academy. And keep the plate."

"Thanks." After a snow-scrubbing, Revel wiped her plate with a cloth before tucking it into her rucksack. "What was she like?"

"The no-nonsense sort. Super stern, but also loving, in her own quiet way. She hated to be touched. You really had to earn her trust for her to let you get near—literally and figuratively. Trained the three of us in the old way, which was seriously grueling and dangerous." Leera's eyes unfocused as she looked into the past. "*Very* dangerous. Made us desperately want to impress her—" Leera snorted a laugh. "—which was impossible, of course."

"Is it really true she took you to different planes? To Ley and then Endraga Ra?"

Leera closed her eyes and saw a low sun above an orange desert. But then she felt the heat of three suns high above, and the desert was replaced by a jungle. She craned her neck skyward, craving that hot warmth on her wings. They beckoned her to spread her wings and dive and eviscerate and feast and —

"Captain?"

"Hmm?"

"I asked what it would take for people to believe in those planes."

Leera bit her lower lip in thought. "I think the only thing that will convince people is if they step foot on the sands of Ley, or experience the three suns of that murderous jungle."

"Do you ever want to go back?"

Leera didn't want to answer, but found herself whispering, "All the time."

"What if you found a new way to go back and —"

"Enough! Enough. Cycles. Now, Squire."

Revel grimaced but acceded a nod, and they began with the usual 1st degree spells of Telekinesis, Repair, Unconceal, and Shine. For Repair, they each broke a dead stick and fused it back together — Repair could not, after all, repair living things. For Unconceal, they each hid a pebble for the other to find.

On it went through the degrees, with Leera continuing on to the 10th while Revel repeated everything she had learned up to the 5th degree. They skipped spells that required battle or were too loud or simply too dangerous. Many spells, like the 4th degree Fear and the 6th degree Mute, they cast against each other, while others, like Seal, which sealed things like doorways, they cast between sticks, fusing them together.

"I don't know how you higher degrees do it," Revel said, resting her hands against her knees while she winced. "Doing cycle after cycle like that. I've already got a headache."

"That's what daily practice is for," Leera countered. "I heard that in Anna Atticus Stone's time it was normal to learn two degrees ahead. These days we do *just* enough to get by."

"Most of us hit our ceiling too early," Revel grumbled.

Leera, readying to cast the 11th degree Reveal, nodded. She very much looked forward to learning the rest of the 11th degree in the new year. She also looked forward to learning a new simul, which the trio were due for now that they had achieved their 10th degree — an Arcaner the rank of dragoon or dragon could learn one new simul at the 3rd, 5th, 7th, 10th, 13th, 16th, and 20th degrees. The trio each thus knew three simuls learned directly from the order's ghosts, with a bonus fourth being the mythical Spirit of the Dragon simul, learned by trial in the jungles of Endraga Ra.

Sure, Leera knew the occasional spell beyond the 10th, but it was a far cry from the warlocks of the past, who were constantly embroiled in wars and thus legally allowed to train well beyond their degree. Then again, she realized she, Augum, and Bridget had been granted the same exemptions multiple times.

Shaking her head at her own dimness, she splayed the fingers of a hand and incanted, "*Un vun asperio aurum enchantus.*" The blue tendril field of Area Alarm lit up all around. She was about to move on to the next spell when she spotted something that raised the hair on the back of her neck—the key lead tendril thread was slowly *unspooling*.

That could only mean one thing—someone was casting Disenchant, meaning they were about to be attacked.

Because she did not know from which direction the attack could come, and not wanting to risk her apprentice, Leera grabbed the rucksacks and snatched Revel's hand, envisioning a certain spot on the coast a little ways to the south.

"Wait, what's happening—"

"*Impetus peragro grapa lestato exa exaei!*" Just as Leera finished the last word, there came a *thwoot*. But the spell jerked their bodies away and, after a gut-wrenching sensation of tumbling through the arcane ether, the pair reappeared with a *thwomp* on the snowed-over rocky shore of Lake Anchor, perhaps a quarter league to the south. It was a spot Leera had memorized just for that possibility.

"Stand back and check your person," Leera said, using the pale starlight to navigate the slippery black rocks. "And prepare for a follow." She was acutely aware that the 17th degree Group Teleport had just siphoned three-quarters of her precious stamina.

"What's going on?"

"Just do it! Check you didn't get hit."

The two women patted themselves down, each reporting they were all right.

"Wait, something's snagged in my coat here," Revel said.

Leera, keeping her hands in attack position should the intruder successfully read the tendrils briefly left behind after her teleport, side-shuffled over to Revel. "Show me. Careful now."

Revel untangled something from the hood of her coat. She opened her palm and the starlight revealed a thin spike.

"An assassin's dart," Leera said. "Don't touch the tip. It's poisonous."

Revel dropped the dart, hands shaking. "Gods, I think I'm going to barf."

"Keep your hands up and stay focused."

"I've never been in a real duel before."

"Shh."

They listened to the crash of the waves and *thwoom* of the wind as it raked the rocky shore.

"All right, it's too late for whoever that was to 'port sniff," Leera said. "Which means they'll be huffing it by foot, giving us maybe an hour before they get here. Now let's check for tracking pebbles," and she recast Reveal, doing a sweep of the both of them, before the pair upended the contents of their rucksacks onto a sheet of ice between the rocks.

"No sign of any foreign tendrils," Leera muttered, splayed hand hovering over every object.

Revel turned her fork and plate over. "Check the back."

"Nothing."

"Socks? Bottoms of shoes?"

The women glanced into each other's eyes before hurriedly stripping down to their undergarments.

"Shoot, nothing," Leera said as she quickly got dressed. "Must have found us using our tracks."

"But you teleported directly from Castle Arinthian and quite a ways up the coast."

"Then they must have hidden a tracking enchantment somewhere on our person." It had to be an incredibly tiny enchantment, the sort assassins employed. "Could spend hours searching for it." She thought about the problem while Revel stuffed everything back into their rucksacks. "I have an idea. If they can track us, they'll be on their way now. Let's lay a trap for them."

"Shouldn't we maybe go home instead? The academy taught us to fall back and regroup. Besides, then we could take the time to dig around until we find the enchantment—"

"I'm not giving up on this quest. If you want to go back, I can teleport you home now."

Revel looked down at her feet. "I'm not a coward."

"That's not the point—" Leera placed her hands on her hips. "You know what? It was a dumb idea to bring you along. You're too inexperienced. Take my hand and I'll whisk you home—"

"No! I mean, no, thank you, Captain. I … I can't hide from fights forever. I *want* to become a full-fledged Arcaner." Revel straightened. "I want to become a dragoon."

Leera sighed.

"Please just let me stay."

"Fine. But keep on your guard. I mean it."

"Yes, Captain. Um, but why would someone want to murder you?"

Leera gaped at her apprentice. "You didn't just ask me that question, did you?"

"I suppose there're a few reasons—"

"A few million. Now hush up. I need to think." Leera considered how to trap the assassin, who would likely continue their pursuit, waiting until they took a rest before striking. And whoever it was would be highly alert this time. What was needed was a ruse, which gave her an idea.

"Let's hit the woods," she said, and the pair trudged across the rocky, snowed-over coastline until they found another big spruce with a huge under-canopy, located on the edge of the forest. While Revel set up camp beside the massive trunk, which included starting a small fire, Leera used her plate as a shovel to build up a circular wall of snow that rose to the low-hanging branch canopy, creating a makeshift fort, leaving a single entrance facing the forest.

Then she set to crafting an Area Alarm enchantment, which began by incanting, "*Concutio del arregando alarmo*," and drawing a wide circle of tendrils around the entire camp. She again chose a diameter of fifty feet, which included the giant spruce and the surrounding area. With the outer circle complete, she drew in the patchwork of tendrils that made up the bulk of the enchantment, meticulously infusing into it the thought process of only being set off by someone *other* than her and her apprentice.

"Drawing" involved holding a finger forth and laying down a tendril line, manifested directly from the arcane ether and expressed by the caster, who acted as a medium, siphoning from their personal stamina pool and extrapolating it into a spell. The crucial part was concentration. A competent caster could focus solely on the task at hand, keeping her thoughts in line with the expectations of the spell—in this case, a constant embedding of the principle behind the alarm.

The better one got at this potent concentration, the more complicators one could infuse, assuming one had learned how to infuse them in the first place. Some required additional words or phrases or gestures or thoughts, others a selection, others nothing more than a mere thought. Pronunciation, gestural precision, clarity of thought—all of it factored into the competency of the casting. One stray thought, one misaligned gesture, and the spell either failed right away, or did not work right, perhaps triggering an unintended effect, or simply vanishing after a short period of time. Only perfectly cast spells stood a chance of sinking into permanence.

Having laid the alarm, Leera blew on her hands to keep them warm, muttering to herself, "Now to make the assassin believe we learned to better defend ourselves." *A trap ought to do it,* she thought. *Laid at the entrance.*

The 9th degree elemental spell Craft Trap, ancient name *Kraftabradeocaptum,* was a complicated spell that crafted a trigger that sprang another spell. In this case, Leera chose to infuse the Fear spell into the trap, meaning anyone who stepped on it would be blasted by a 4th degree Fear spell cast at 10th degree war-honed strength.

Craft Trap came with all sorts of ethical considerations. It was, for example, illegal to infuse certain spells into it that caused undue suffering, spells like the standard 13th degree Memory Wipe—at least without a writ.

Aligning her thoughts, she began with the core incantation and added the two words that made up the 4th degree Fear spell. "*Infusio gato captum dreadus terrablus,*" she said, meticulously drawing out the tendrils in the appropriate pattern that would be unmistakable even though it was overlaid on the Area Alarm tendril web.

Tendrils came in varying colors depending on the nature of the enchantment. Blue was by far the dominant color as it denoted standard spellcraft. Red was another big one, which indicated the trap was explosive in nature—all offensives fell into this category. Green was poison or venom, black was necromantic, and there were niche ones such as yellow, which indicated gas; brown, which indicated summoning, and so on. Blends made the tendril prismatic, hence why arcaneological competency in Reveal and Disenchant spells was a basic requirement if the warlock wanted to survive adventuring.

But Leera didn't actually think the assassin would be foolish enough to step into her trap. If her plan worked, her trap wouldn't even be sprung.

Seeing that everything was in order, Leera skipped over her trap and herded Revel into one of two basic A-frame tents made of light canvas and supported by two folding sticks, throwing their rucksacks inside with her.

"How's your Elemental Armor spell?" Leera asked. "You learn it yet?"

"I've been poking away at it," Revel answered within the tent. "Why?"

"Need you to summon it."

"What? But …" Revel's head shot out of the tent. "Wait, are you treating me as *bait*?"

"Maybe. But you'll be fine. Promise."

"Why do I not feel reassured?" Revel muttered, slithering back inside the tent.

"You don't have to do it. I can figure something else out."

"No, I can be your pincushion."

"Let's not let it get that far. But, uh, just make sure to keep the armor up."

From within the tent came a sigh and a concentrative pause, followed by the incantation, "*Armari elementus totalus,*" which cocooned the caster in a thin protective crust from foot to neck, the strength of it dictated by one's casting prowess with the spell.

"Armored?"

"Ugh, *yessss!*"

"I can hear you roll your eyes, you know. Anyway, now pretend to be organizing our things and, uh, shout if you get attacked."

"Great, I'm going to die as a training dummy."

"Then I'll use you as a class example on how not to defend yourself."

Revel scoffed, and Leera was about to commence the rest of her plan when the glint of her two rings caught the light. *Could it really be?* she thought, wondering if perhaps the shipwreck ring—which did indeed have a tracking enchantment on it—was leading someone to her. But how could that be, when it had been under water for decades? And what if someone had hidden a tracking enchantment on her betrothal ring? She hadn't had the time to check it. But since she was setting a trap, she figured it wouldn't matter at that point, and so she kept them on.

"Keep rustling, but not in an obvious manner," Leera instructed. "And watch out at the entrance. I'm going to lay a trap there." Lastly, she worked quickly to build a snowman opposite the entrance to the fort, between the tents but visible past the trunk if one looked in from that entrance. Then she stripped off her crimson robe and coat and placed them on the snowman, leaving herself in only her undergarments. She made the snowman appear to be a guard, complete with a drawn hood.

Already shivering, she took three deep breaths, focusing on a savvy water warlock's saving grace—the potent 3rd degree off-the-books spell Endure the Deep, which also warded off the cold. Theoretically, it should work in this instance too. After arranging her thoughts to fortify not only her mind but her body, she made a pressing-downward motion with two flat palms whilst incanting, "*Endura o prassa ata o codola.*"

Her ears popped and she felt her innards thicken. When the shivering stopped on account of an inner warmth flaring, she ran a hand down her body, whispering, "*Armari obscura chameleano traversa,*" turning her body invisible when still and into a shimmer when moving. Then she splayed a hand, whispering, "*Un vun asperio aurum enchantus.*" Now also able to see tendrils with Reveal, she slipped through the entrance—careful to gently hop over her trap—and took a good look around, searching for the telltale sign of chameleonic tendril evidence that would stand out like a beacon fire against the night. But beyond her fifty-foot diameter Area Alarm rested a quiet and starlit forest of snow-laden conifers.

Keeping her hand splayed, she prowled around the snow-fort on all fours, purposely creating extra tracks in the snow to cause confusion. The wind had died down, but not enough to hear through the rustle of the trees and crash of waves that pounded the rocky shore. This would be a waiting game.

The only problem was that she was holding up three spells at once, not an uncommon feat of chronocasting for her—but certainly a pricey one stamina-wise. She could not keep this up for long, and so decided on a second strategy—hiding.

After making extra tracks everywhere, she chose another spruce fifteen feet away from the entrance of the fort, but crucially within the carpet-like tendril weavings of her Area Alarm enchantment. There she planted herself like a panther under the low canopy and covered herself with snow, leaving only her eyes visible, covering even her splayed hand. "*Chameleano null,*" she then whispered, killing the Chameleon spell, lessening the heavy strain on her stamina.

Still, with the Endure the Deep spell running alongside Reveal, the stamina bleed was heavy enough that, factoring for the spells she had already cast, she calculated she could only keep this up for about half an hour more—and that was if she wanted to expire all her stamina, leaving them practically defenseless.

Bastard better show up soon, she thought.

Time passed agonizingly slowly. Through the *thwoom* of the forest, she could hear Revel rustling within the tent. The entrance was aglow with firelight that steadily waned to a coal glow. Leera sat hunched up, breathing measured and calm just as when she dove deep. She wondered how often in history warlocks had used Endure the Deep to ward off the cold.

Rarely, I bet, she thought. *Then again, people find all sorts of clever solutions to challenging problems.* She grinned to herself, thinking she'd have made a decent ice warlock.

Yet despite her mighty skill with the Endure the Deep spell, she began to shiver. Usually when it happened hundreds of feet below water, she would finish what she was doing and resurface. But here, she was committed. That meant the shivering only got worse, until she felt her core starting to ice up and a fogginess enter her brain that threatened not only Reveal, but the Endure the Deep spell—and if that died, she'd rapidly have to warm up before she went unconscious and her heart stopped.

Just as she sensed the horizon of failure approaching, and as she scraped the bottom of her stamina well, she saw what she had been waiting for—a tendril pattern stalk into view, indicating there indeed was an Object Track enchantment still active and hidden within their things. Desperately trying to keep her teeth from chattering, Leera kept ice-still, watching with only her eyes. The tendril pattern was very dim and shimmery—too dim and ethereal for a relatively simple Chameleon casting, even with the travel extension. *Could it be …?*

Sure enough, the moment the pattern went still, it nearly vanished, indicating an expert casting of the incredibly-difficult-to-master spell Invisibility—a 15th degree spell. Gods, she was dealing with someone superbly adept at their craft. This was no run-of-the-mill assassin, but someone highly trained and highly specialized in murdering warlocks.

Potential candidates flashed across her mind—Canterran Whisper Blade assassins, countless guilds whose businesses were affected by the return of the Arcaners, greedy rogues looking to somehow cash in on their fame, an old enemy from one of the wars. It could be anyone.

Luckily, Leera knew what to look for with her Reveal spell, and the moment the person resumed moving forth she was able to pick out the shimmery pattern of tendrils.

She judged the figure to be that of a thin man who was careful and alert, a prowler who struck with meticulous lethality. He came up to her Area Alarm enchantment and stopped, indicating he too had a hand lit with Reveal. Due to Leera's coat of snow, the man failed to spot her body, which was dense with tendril geometries of the Endure the Deep spell. And the relatively tiny but visible tendril geometries of her eyes would blend in perfectly with the Area Alarm enchantment she had cast.

Clever solutions to challenging problems, she thought, giving herself a mental pat on the back.

The man seemed to look to the ground at the foot of the entrance, where she had laid her trap, which would tell him his target thought themselves protected. Above all, he would see her snowman, with its hands within the sleeves of the robe, its snow face obscured by the pointedly low hood. She imagined him thinking that the sentry warlock was not capable of spotting his Invisibility casting.

She expected him to disenchant the Area Alarm. Instead, he sprang up and slapped his wrists together, hissing, "*Annihilo!*" A fireball *thwoomed* forth, exploding inside the snow fort. Leera burst out of her snowbank—but due to being half frozen, far too slowly to shoot off a spell. The man swiveled and whapped his wrists together a second time, roaring, "*Annihilo ito!*" Three fireballs *whooshed* at an unprotected Leera, who faced instant death.

Calling upon her Arcaner reflex training, she immediately summoned her shield and snapped, "*Mimicus!*" infusing into her thoughts the principle of arcane perpendicularity as required by the Mirror of the Dragon simul. In the blink of an eye, the shield became an arcane mirror, and with a triple *thwoom,* reflected back all three fireballs.

Because the man was so close—and had apparently not been expecting such a rare spell—he only gaped as all three fireballs slapped into his body, blowing him apart where he stood. An arm shot off into a tree and a leg against the side of the fort, and the body tumbled backward, now visible and spraying blood about. The light of the flames revealed that the man had been dressed in a purple robe, indicating at least 13th and as high as 16th, depending on the number of golden bands on the upper arm.

A panting Leera let her shield vanish, the snow still sliding off her exposed body and soaked-through linen undergarments. A callous shadow stepped in behind her, feasting upon the sight of all that blood. How desperately she wanted to make the praying mantis pose and chomp down on those bits of flesh as the apex predator she was …

Instead, she stumbled forth and placed a hand on the man's olive-skinned forehead. "May your soul find the peace together we could not reach," she whispered.

Revel scrambled out of her tent and, before Leera could stop her, stepped onto the Fear trap. Her head snapped back. She took one look at the bloody scene and loosed a shrill scream that cut through the forest like a knife.

Leera felt her insides loosen and the cold sweep in—she had drained what had remained of her stamina, causing the Endure the Deep spell to fail. She began shivering so violently that she thought her teeth would break from their clattering. Knowing she urgently needed to warm up, she stumbled past a still-screaming Revel and crouched before the coals of the fire. That was when she saw that her robe and coat had been burnt to a crisp, the snowman blown asunder.

Great, she thought. *Juuuust great.* With her stamina trickling back, she used what she had to flick a finger at the scraps of her coat and robe and drag them into the coals, causing a small fire to flare. She did this with what remained of the entirety of her robe, which, being burnt, was unrepairable by the 1st degree Repair spell.

With Revel screaming in the background, Leera steadily warmed her soul, thinking how absurd it was that people thought she and Augum and Bridget were invincible simply because they could turn into dragons. If only they knew how truly fragile they all were, for the craft had myriad limitations, including stamina. One had to depend on one's training and reflexes and memory and countless fragilities that made up the arts. Of course, it was better that people remained in the dark about how susceptible they were, as it kept those with ill intent at bay.

In time, Revel stopped screaming and stumbled back into the makeshift fort. She looked at Leera with wild eyes.

"I see you finally fought the banshee off," Leera said, hands splayed over the low flame as she crouched as close as she dared. "You all right?"

"His arm is dangling in a tree," Revel blurted. "It's just … dangling there. Dripping blood onto the snow. It's so vividly … red."

"Come and sit by the fire."

The girl schlepped over and plopped down beside the fire. "He's dead," she said, face frozen with that same incredulous look. "He's dead …"

Leera nodded. "Mm-hmm."

"I've never seen … I mean … I didn't think it'd be so …" Revel shook her head. "And his leg … it's just sitting up against the wall there."

"I'll take you back to the academy."

"I'm never going to sleep soundly again."

"Let me warm up and we'll hop out of here."

"Why are you in your underwear? What happened to your coat and robe?"

Leera flipped a hand toward a melted mound of snow littered with burnt cloth and fur.

Revel looked at it. "Oh." She looked back at the snow fort, swallowed, and sat, tears welling, lower lip trembling.

"It will fade," Leera whispered. "It always fades. We warlocks are forever locked in war. With ourselves. With others …"

"Monsters locked in war is what we are," Revel blubbered. "I … I didn't think of myself as someone who would have a hard time taking someone's life. I'm supposed to be a hard Malevant. But now … now I wonder."

"Hold onto that softness for as long as you can. And it's better never to find out. Once the deed is done, it cannot be undone, and one lives with it forever as a stone …" Leera tapped her chest. "… in one's heart."

They sat around the fire, listening to its low crackle. Leera kept feeding it with scraps of her robe and coat and the occasional twig Revel had scrounged earlier, now and then turning to warm her backside.

"I want to continue," Revel blurted.

Leera raised an eyebrow. "You sure? It might be best to get you home. I can go on my own and—"

"I'm sure."

"All right. Uh, then can I borrow your coat?"

"Of course," and Revel removed her long fur coat and handed it over.

Once bundled up, Leera tromped out of the fort to search the remains of the assassin for clues as to who he was and who had hired him, a rather grisly task that quickly bloodied her hands. She found a blowpipe, a wooden box of darts, a pouch of bread and beef biscuits, and a pouch of coins. But nothing else.

She looked down at her bloody hands and the urge to make the praying mantis pose returned with a vengeance. She glanced back at Revel and thought how easy prey she would make. What a feast for her stomach!

She had to force herself to turn away, then slapped her own cheek, leaving behind a bloody handprint. "Get a grip, Lee," she muttered. "You're letting the damn thing seep into your soul."

She thought of her beloved, one of the few things that sort of kept The Callousness of the Predator at bay. Snuggling him. Kissing him. Running a hand through his hair and over his chest …

She raised a bloody hand and stared at it. How easy killing came now. How little it affected her, at least compared to someone like Revel. But staring at that hand also gave her an idea, and she pulled up the robe of the torso, exposing olive skin burnt by fire. She pulled back the hood and searched the face, finding it to be rather normal, almost boring, meaning the man had easily blended in with a crowd. She searched his left arm, which was still attached, finding three bands on the upper shoulder of the robe, indicating he had been a 16th degree. At last, she found what she had been looking for on the forearm of the arm that had been blown into the tree.

There before her eyes was a tattoo depicting a series of waves.

Waves that matched the shipwreck ring.

AN ANCIENT SPEECH REBORN

AUGUM

Somewhere deep in the north, in a spruce grove nestled between towering mountains, multiple packs of wolven argued in their guttural language. Assembled in a large circle, representatives of each pack took turns growling at each other, making arguments that sounded more like taunts.

Augum, having been listening to the mayhem for some time already, glanced at the gray sky and heavy clouds and stuck out his tongue to catch one of the fat snowflakes that tumbled like white leaves.

Suddenly the angry one pointed an arm at Augum, roaring something in wolven. All eyes turned to him, and he quickly withdrew his tongue.

"Step forth," the gray one said, standing beside the calm one. He raised his snout as he idly held onto his gold chain necklace with both paws. "And answer."

Augum took a step forward, then felt like it was a mousy step relative to the giant size of the wolven, and so took several more steps, manacles jangling before him. He glanced back at the gray. "The question being?"

"What are you really doing in the north, lowlander?" the angry one asked, voice carrying over the gathering.

Augum nodded, bit his lip, and nodded again, this time looking at his shoes so he could think. Choice of wording was important, and the more formal the better. He looked back up. "I am a commander in my kingdom. I went north to track two of our apprentices. My quest to find them was successful, but all that remains of them are two vials, which you now hold in your possession, blooded by your kin. I have taken vengeance on their behalf, vanquishing the leader responsible. That is the sole reason for my coming. I had no other ambitions or plans with your kingdom."

This caused a stir amongst the wolven, but Augum continued speaking, albeit in a louder voice, this time infusing a ceremonious flair in the old way. "You have taken me captive when I have done thee no wrong. Let me return to my beloved. To my people, for I have no quarrel with thee. Whatever threatens thee will threaten us. Let our kingdoms bargain. Release me so that we may work together to solve this new challenge."

The wolven barked at each other.

For the first time, the calm one stepped up behind Augum to translate. "They are saying you are merely bargaining for your life. They want you blooded as a warning to your people to stop trespassing into our kingdom, and for you lowlanders to recognize our kingdom as a state."

"Blooding me will accomplish neither!" Augum said, staring at each representative in turn. "Blooding me will be interpreted as an act of war. You have been told what I can become. There are two others like myself, one of which is my betrothed." He felt a shadow slip out from behind the curtain of his mind, injecting menace into his voice. "She will feel three suns upon her wings and take such vengeance upon your people that none shall remain to tell the tale around the fire! Your cubs will know no mercy. Your caves will be ground to dust, your kin pulped and disemboweled and—"

He tore at the air with his teeth, a primal display carried out not so much by him, but by the shadow feasting on thoughts of violence. It was The Callousness of the Predator talking, and it scared him, for he had not intended to give it any control. Why was it so strong now?

As the wolven growled at him and at each other, he took a step back, raised his manacles, and opened his palms. "Forgive me! Forgive me. I … I forget myself."

The wolven spoke—or rather growled—all at once, the discussion quickly turning into yet another argument.

Augum sighed and retreated to stand between the gray and the calm one, noting how passionately the wolven argued despite initially putting on stoic demeanors. Upon noticing how few of them there were, he looked up at the calm one to ask, "Where are the rest of your packs? Surely there must be more."

"There are a great many more," the calm one replied, refusing to elaborate.

"We do not expose lowlanders to the location of our lairs and hunting grounds," the gray added. "Surely this you understand."

Augum nodded.

"Our kingdom is vast and we are many," the calm one said, staring straight ahead. "Should your betrothed take vengeance, it would take her a lifetime to find us all."

"And a lifetime she would have, for she would have nothing *but* vengeance on her mind." That got the wolven arguing again. Meanwhile, Augum hoped that wasn't true. That if something did happen to him, she could let him go and learn to live in harmony, in some semblance of happiness. Still, even imagining her face upon receiving the awful news that he would never return was enough to send a lonely pang through his gut. Already she would have noticed his lack of communication through the vault and would be worried …

He sighed, and his thoughts turned to wondering how his colleagues fared—his mentor, Jez, and his Arcaner friends Dragoon Jengo Okeke and Dragoon Olaf Hroljassen, who had journeyed with her to support his quest, the first a healer and the second a best friend—outside of Bridget and Leera, of course. He hoped they were all right.

As the wolven argued on, he cleared his throat, refocusing. "You speak as if the matter of my life is already decided."

"They lean toward keeping you captive," the calm one replied. "Perhaps forever, for you would seek vengeance against us if let free."

"I would not," he replied, raising his voice to cut through the growls. "I spoke the truth that I have no quarrel with you and your people. I do not even hold anger toward—" Augum inclined his head at a certain wolven. "—the angry one. I have extracted justice on behalf of my kingdom. There is nothing left to follow, for I understand and forgive you for taking me captive."

The calm one glanced at him before sharing a silent look with the gray that Augum could not interpret.

Frustrated at their lack of communication, Augum gazed to the mountains, wondering if there was any chance his party could track him this far. Even so, freeing him from the grip of the wolven would be no easy feat, for he sensed they were strategically hiding their full potential in the arcane arts.

As he searched those mountains in the hopes of seeing his friends, he happened to spot something odd. Between the thick layer of clouds that obscured the peaks and the tree line was a black band of rock too steep for ice or snow to grip. And snaking down that band were a series of white lines that seemed to move.

Amidst a raucous argument between the wolven, Augum, standing between the calm one and the gray, nudged the calm one. "Are you expecting more of your brethren?"

"No. All are here who need to be here."

"Then you are about to be attacked."

"You bargain still," the gray said. "Human vision is better than a wolven's, a fact you are using for gain."

"Look you there." Augum nodded at the distant spot. "Below the clouds but above the tree line. See it?"

While the two wolven stared at the spot, Augum searched the mountains—and found similar lines in all directions. "They come from all sides," he added. "The lines are white. Could it be The Dishonored?"

The two wolven exchanged rather thoughtful growls in their tongue. But seeing as they were getting nowhere and time was of the essence, Augum stepped out into the circle again. Thinking he would plead for his life, some went quiet, others chortled. "You are about to be attacked!" he shouted. "From the north and south and east and west. Look you to the mountains!"

"I told you we cannot see that far, lowlander," the gray growled.

"It is a ploy for his life," the angry one said. "He cannot help treachery from slipping onto his serpent tongue."

"In my rucksack you will find a spyglass. It is a very rare and expensive piece of Ohmish workmanship which will allow you to see far, but it takes some skill to use. If you bring it forth, I can show you how to use it, and prove what my eyes can see but yours cannot."

"That device will show only treachery," the angry one snarled. "It is a lowlander device that will fool the mind into seeing what this lowlander wants us to see."

The gray rubbed his snout with a paw in thought before indicating at a fellow wolven, who brought forth Augum's rucksack. The gray stuck a paw into it, rummaged about, withdrew the spyglass, and glanced it over. He said something in wolven before tossing it at Augum's feet, paws returning to holding onto his chain. "Then show us, lowlander. Prove yourself true."

Augum picked up the spyglass with his manacled hands and hurriedly extended the bronze tube. He held it up to his eye and searched the mountains, constantly working the blurry image by adjusting the length of the tube until it sharpened. At last he spotted one of a series of moving white lines, most of which, like the ends of snakes vanishing into a bush, were about to clear the black band of rock and vanish into the tree line below.

"Quickly now," he said, hurrying up to the gray and offering the spyglass. When the wolven took it, Augum pointed with both hands at the spot. "Point it there. See it?"

"I see only a blur."

"You must adjust the length of the tube and focus on the spot I point to."

The calm one, who seemed to grasp the concept better, helped the gray adjust the length, until the gray loosed a squeal of delight. "I can see trees!" he shouted, laughing in that wolven way, which sounded more threatening than jovial, causing others to laugh right along.

Augum could not comprehend the humor at all. "Do you see them?" he pressed.

"It is a magic of their making," the angry one said. "You are seeing what the lowlander wants you to see. He is jinxing the elder's mind with lowlander craft," he said to the others, receiving mutters of agreement.

Augum squinted at the line and saw that it had almost vanished below the tree line, yet the gray struggled still. He looked north and south and saw that those lines were gone too. "Look to the west," he said, adding, "You must take action," whilst imploring the calm one with his eyes to have a turn.

The calm one muttered something in wolven and the gray smacked his gums but surrendered the spyglass over. Augum helped direct the calm one's vision until he loosed a wolven curse, which started another argument. The calm one offered for others to look, but the lone few who took him up on it could not make sense of the contraption, and decried Augum by flicking their tails at him in what appeared to be a gesture of dismissal. In fact their tails were so expressive that he had the impression they could communicate with them alone.

While the wolven argued, there came a distant howl that echoed against the mountains. The wolven listened before springing into action. All summoned weapons and shields and armor and took up defensive positions in the forest.

"A scout sends warning," the calm one said, herding Augum to the forest. "You told no lies, lowlander."

A frustrated Augum wanted to roar, "Of course not!" Instead, he offered his hands once they took shelter under a spruce. "Free me so that I may help."

The gray, who had tagged along, chortled along with the calm one. "You think us fools, lowlander."

"We are not fools," the calm one added.

More howls cut the air, echoing from all sides.

The two wolven exchanged a look that confirmed an attack was imminent.

"You are outnumbered ten to one at least," Augum told the gray. "I can help even the odds."

"You will teleport away the moment you are free."

The wolven with bone clipped to her ear, huffing from having run a ways, came up to the gray. The pair exchanged growls before the eared one looked to Augum. She smacked her gums and ran off.

"The Dishonored tracked us," the gray said, "and they have united their packs. They have come to exact vengeance for the killing of one of their chiefs, lowlander."

The angry one joined them and the three got into a heated argument.

"You said yourselves you cannot trust The Dishonored," Augum interrupted. "And if you hand me over, they will blood me and you will have a terrible war on your hands when my kingdom exacts its vengeance on my behalf. Release me so that I may aid in your defense. I know arts that can help."

"He will summon the dragon and destroy us all," the angry one argued, both paws pointing at Augum accusatorily.

"I would swear upon my shield if I could," Augum countered, jangling his manacles. "As I have done before."

The angry one's tail flapped a dismissal. "Lowlander tricks of the eye," he spat.

"You declared the same for the contraption," the calm one said to the angry one. "Yet the lowlander proved himself true, did he not?"

The angry one snarled. "Fool, he will vanish the moment we unlock him!"

"We are greatly outnumbered—"

"Then we die with honor!"

"And leave our cubs without their chiefs?" the gray asked. "Honor is one thing, suicide another." He lowered his snout and looked to the angry one. "Let the lowlander prove his people can have honor."

"No. Honored Elder is wrong. I will not let the lowlander murder us."

"Free him, or—" and the gray snarled something threatening in wolven.

Another howl sounded, this one closer and with greater alarm. Wolven scurried about the woods in response, finding the best defensive positions they could, with some hiding under the snow.

Augum raised his hands higher and jangled the manacles imploringly.

"No," the angry one said, and walked off, leaving the other two stunned—and making Augum realize they did not know how to open the manacles.

"I know the unlocking incantation," Augum blurted. "The runic sequence is engraved into the manacles here." He flipped up his hands to show the bottom of the manacles, which he had studied at length in his spare time. "See them?"

The calm one took hold of the manacles and squinted at the tiny runes.

Augum translated the tiny sequence aloud, careful with the pronunciation. "*Tetiola una resk gardo rek.*"

The calm one repeated the incantation and the manacles clicked open. Augum felt a thrill zip through his soul as he regained access to his arcane stamina. The predator stepped up to his mind and silently begged him to spread his wings and succumb to the raw violence that came so naturally when in that form. It was such a powerful compulsion that he shivered—not from fear, but from delight. He imagined chomping down upon the angry one and savoring his flesh as a lion would savor a hyena.

That was when he knew he should not cast the Spirit of the Dragon simul, for he was not sure he could control it.

Both wolven tensed, with the gray even extending his claws. But Augum merely nodded his thanks. "Would you like me to swear on my shield, or allow my actions to do the talking?" It was a strain to say the words, for they directly contradicted the predator's cravings.

The calm one accepted the manacles. "You will either prove your honor on the field of battle—" He raised his snout. "—or prove that even the so-called most honorable among you are treacherous filth."

Augum, rubbing his bruised wrists, almost smiled at the ridiculousness of the statement. But how could he blame them, for what did they know of his people? After all, they ran up against the roughest human sort out in the wilds and had never met an Arcaner.

Another part of him wanted to ditch the wolven. After all, he had not sworn on his shield, so was neither bound by loyalty nor duty, and thus free to leave them. But that would contradict the spirit of the Arcaner code of honor. Besides, what if this was an opportunity to bridge ties? Could he live with himself if he tucked tail and ran? After all, he had merely been chained, his honor intact, if not his pride. And he felt for the calm one, and even for their cubs, which he had never met.

Your heart is still soft, the predatorial part of his mind chastised. *You need to spread your wings so that we may become hard and strong. You are the rightful lord of the skies, and should be emperor of all these weak lands.*

He gritted his teeth, thinking, *Shut the hell up*, and looked to the trees. There were four directions of attack. He would have to be calculating. He looked around until he spotted the tallest nearby tree, a towering spruce, and imagined himself standing atop one of its high branches.

"May our gods grant us victory," the gray said.

Augum's reply was to snap, "*Impetus peragro*." With a *thwomp*, he appeared on a branch near the top of the spruce and immediately grabbed its trunk, which wavered about from his weight.

How sweet to feel the cool draw of one's stamina again, he thought, amazed that he had somehow talked his way to freedom. *But you also talked yourself into a fight, you fool.*

Already the call of battle quickened his blood and sharpened his senses. As if a high councilor had unfurled a long scroll that bounced off a carpet and rolled forth, a repertoire of spells unfurled before his mind. Above all he craved the casting of the mightiest simul of them all, but other spells were just as fun—Fear and Deafness and Confusion and the First and Second Offensives and the volatile 9th degree spell Frenzy and myriad off-the-books elemental spells and many others like the focus-enhancing Leyan spell Centarro, not to mention the simuls Birth of the Dragon, Roar of the Dragon, and Mirror of the Dragon.

Augum searched for any signs of conflict, soon hearing it in the form of a growling fight, like two huge dogs scrapping. He focused in on where he thought it was coming from and spotted a tree shaking, as if a body had been thrown against it. Setting his mind to intimidation tactics, he grabbed his throat, incanting, "*Amplifico*," and felt his vocal cords strengthen. Then he focused in on a blank space of snow nearby and imagined himself appearing exactly one foot above it.

"*Impetus peragro*," he incanted, and appeared one foot above the snow. By the time his feet crunched down, he'd summoned his shield, showing off the full Arcaner crest in all its golden splendor, flared ten lightning rings around his arm, and flared his eyes with lightning, showing that he had achieved The Settling.

Twenty feet before him were seven wolven with an X over their hearts, surrounding two without, both bleeding and gasping as they stood by a tree. All were in full battle regalia, with summoned shields, armor, and various weapons—maces and swords and axes and spears brimming in the element of their cubhood—either lightning or fire or air or water or ice or earth.

One of the attackers barked a command, and he and an eared wolven went to finish off the pair of already wounded Honored wolven, while the remaining five peeled off to charge at Augum. In reply, he made a sweeping motion along the ground with both hands, booming, "*Laitna fiuria potam,*" the incantation to the 7th degree off-the-books *Laitnaravapotamarro*—otherwise known as Lightning River, a vicious war spell he had learned years ago but rarely had cause to use.

Lightning swept forth along the ground, quickly branching off into multiple strands and crackling as it zig-zagged randomly toward the enemy. He had tempered the spell somewhat so that it was slightly less than lethal—at least when cast against a human.

As Augum had hoped, the five wolven jumped over the river—only to land in the thick of it when it branched and expanded underneath them. While they thrashed about like fish in a sizzling pan, he reached out with both arms and grabbed a telekinetic hold of both remaining opponents. The space around him warped fishbowl-like as his mighty telekinetic muscle—what had earned him The Settling—smashed the two opponents together, giving the injured Honored time to slash apart their armor with their weapons and skewer their hearts.

The river of lightning passed, leaving the stricken Dishonored in a daze—it was wearisome on the body struggling against even tempered lightning. One of those sent up an almost mournful howl of warning that Augum interpreted as, "He is loose!"

Keeping the Amplify spell active on his throat but wanting to save the rest of his stamina, and figuring the remaining Dishonored in this area should be easy pickings for The Honored, he dashed off into the wood toward a chorus of howls.

But along the way he heard a noise to his right. Reflexes keyed, he ducked and rolled under a vicious swipe of a huge earthen axe that had come slicing from behind a thick tree trunk. The wolven holding it immediately lunged after him, the axe rising skyward and held by both paws.

Augum, having rolled head over heels, quickly rolled onto his back and shoved at the air, roaring, "*Baka!*" The X-branded wolven, shoved against its stomach, was tossed upward a short ways, the slice of the axe continuing along its arc and whizzing a mere hand's width from Augum's face. The momentum of the two-handed swing of the mammoth axe caused the wolven, who hadn't bothered summoning his armor, to flip forward, so that his back faced downward.

Lying below, Augum made an unsheathing motion and spit, "*Summano arma!*" summoning a lightning longsword to his fist. He lodged the hilt against the ground beside him and pointed the tip upward just in time for the wolven to impale himself onto the blade. The huge beast, a ten-footer, slid down the blade in jerking gasps, until he laid on top of Augum, where he convulsed before going still, his axe vanishing.

Augum strained under his bulk, and had to extinguish the blade before finally freeing himself from underneath the wolven's bulk. Panting from the exertion, he then kneeled beside his opponent and placed a hand to his forehead. "May your soul find the peace together we could not reach, wolven."

He stood up to stare at the body. It was the second wolven life he had taken—and it felt offensive to his soul. He took no pleasure whatsoever in taking life—at least not the human side of him. The predator, on the other hand, feasted upon the sight with glee, so much so that Augum had to tear himself away lest he actively went on a hunt.

A hundred feet later, after half-running half-tumbling down an embankment, he found himself skidding to a halt in the plain where the packs had met, before a massive wave of Dishonored. Outnumbered at the fore were a mere thirty Honored, three of whom Augum recognized as the gray, the calm one, and the angry one. While they clustered together, the number of The Dishonored thickened by the heartbeat, for others joined them from the woods. Judging by the howls and sounds from the forest, there would soon be two hundred.

The moment slowed, for a stark choice had presented itself to Augum. He could stay and possibly die alongside his former kidnappers, flee and live to see Leera … or he could be bold. But being bold would have to mean something other than becoming the dragon, for he did not want to be responsible for a massacre.

Instead, he thought of Centarro, an ancient Leyan spell so rare that only three people in his kingdom—perhaps all of Sithesia—knew it: him, Bridget, and Leera. A mere 3rd degree off-the-books spell, Centarro was nonetheless incredibly potent for its degree, as all Leyan spells were. It would grant him creative focus that would almost slow time down—but it also had a brutal side effect. Upon lapsing, he would succumb to a foggy stupor. Centarro was great for making connections when doing research or solving puzzles, but typically a last resort in battle.

Augum, however, had other plans for it.

As per the requisites of the spell, he took note of his surroundings. The snow and ice and its granular texture. A bundle of bloody wolven fur as it tumbled across a patch of ice, pushed by a cutting wind. The clouds and their heavy grayness. The mammoth peaks slicing those clouds like great jagged knives. His crimson robe and the way it ruffled under his wolf coat. His heart thundering in anticipation.

Then he told himself that, no matter what, when the fog of confusion descended upon his focus, he would teleport away to safety, somewhere far enough to work through the side effects.

All this he brought to bear upon his soul before incanting, "*Centeratoraye xao xen*," careful to pronounce the X's as Z's. The ancient spell, a spell that had taken years to get a handle on, sharpened his mind and senses, clarifying and contextualizing everything.

Time slowed. Light was brighter, sound crisper, touch more sensitive. The snow seemed to come alive as it glittered prismatically. The needle branches of the nearby pines and spruces became a vivid and sharp green. Objects like the horn-carved buttons on his wolf-hide coat shone — and what an insult that coat was!

Above all, his thoughts deepened, making connections he would ordinarily never be able to make. It was as if he had dunked his head into a fountain of knowledge and taken a big gulp. But the knowledge came from within. He had all the pieces of the puzzle, each needing a mere nudge to put it in place.

He saw himself first and foremost. A young man who was tired of war, yet longed for it. Who feared the awesome might of the dragon, yet craved to spread his wings. Who had sworn to follow a code of honor, yet was under constant threat of letting the dragon in and breaking it — and thence losing the ability to cast that power. A young man who was secretly a bundle of fears. That the order would die after the three of them expired. That he was the last of his lineage. That his beloved would sacrifice herself for that lineage. That in due course he would fail on all fronts …

A howl pierced his thoughts, a lament that sent the signal to fellow wolven to hold their ground. Augum looked back and saw the gray, who appeared to be singing a song of his people. The other wolven smashed their weapons against their armored chests, bolstering their spirits as they waited for the signal to charge.

He looked to the enemy, who was doing the same, banging their summoned weapons against their chests, and his Centarric mind interpreted the display as two tribes about to go to war, a war that had surely been going on a long time. The two tribes wanted to blame each other for all failings. At the root of that blame were slights of honor, and one side proudly branded themselves with that difference.

"But there's more," he whispered, tilting his head in a Centarric trance, reading the moment like a novice student of the arcane arts. The ritual of war satisfied their bloodlust, made them feel worthy of themselves, of their time, of their kingdom. It was a blood payment to honor—and a battle over the very definition of the word. It paid homage to their essence.

Then a deeper realization hit him, and he tilted his head the other way. He could never fully understand the history of those slights, and thus could not solve the root causes for the wolven. That was not the way forward. Sure, these talking beasts could converse about strength and honor, an arena he could battle in. But that led to massacre and a continuation of the cycle of slights, which would thence include his human brethren. No, a higher calling was needed.

With his veins racing in juxtaposition to time throbbing slowly by, as if each granule within the hourglass was a tumbling boulder, he saw the past as it had happened in the cave of The Dishonored. The icy fog creeping inside, unlocking his manacles. His vision moved forward to see holes in the snow, holes that had peppered the bodies of wolven. And throughout, he saw the shadow behind his mind, watching, hoping for violence.

Then, as if his mind had left his body, he saw himself above the snow, above the wolven, above the clouds, until he could see the totality of it all. All the kingdoms and lands and the minute struggles of all those ants coveting meaning whilst desperately wanting to matter …

It was almost like a stage play. Yes, that was what was needed. A performance. Like those he had seen his friend Laudine Cooper perform in the city.

Augum leveled his chin at The Dishonored, who were readying to charge. He took off his wolf-hide coat and held it up by one finger. "Dishonored!" he boomed with his amplified voice.

Dishonored … Dishonored went the echo.

In his mind's eye, he also heard the echo of history. Famous speeches of old he had read. Attyla the Mighty. Occulus. Atrius. Narsus. Lividius …

"Hear me!"

Hear me … hear me …

"I blooded the one who blooded the cubs of my fellow citizens! Yet I wanted no further quarrel with thee!"

With thee … with thee …

"But hark!"

Hark … hark …

"For I, Augum Arinthian Stone, have borne witness to the dusty sun of the Leyan desert, and the three humid suns of Endraga Ra!"

Endraga Ra ... Endraga Ra ...

"In that jungle plane I, Augum Arinthian Stone, achieved the mythical third rank!"

With the wolf-hide coat still hanging from a finger, he summoned his shield to his forearm, proudly displaying the golden full crest of the Arcaner order—the words *Semperis vorto honos*—courage, fortitude, honor—below a golden castle and a golden dragon.

Now came the gamble. "And that third rank calls for blood!"

Blood ... blood ...

"But once summoned, the appetite must be quenched! You have seen me in the skies. You may have even seen me feast. I thus warn thee—hark!" He took a step forth, repeating, "Hark!" and readying a famous speech that threatened violence and vengeance.

Hark ... hark ...

"Thou shalt know wrath as few have known! And now it is Attyla I quote. 'Return me mine son and I shall henceforth unburden thy kingdom of mine wrath and leave thy lands to their woe! Relinquish mine boy and I shall free thy common folk to sow seeds of corn and barley, unchain thy taverns so ale may flow, and free ye daughters and sons of thy flesh, for all such are but trivial wisps of smoke in balance to mine heir!' "

He took another menacing step forth as the words *mine heir* echoed. " 'However, should ye durst linger but a day on mine warning, hark! For I shall erelong smite all ye begat with burning blades, carve thy sons and daughters with mine knife, and cut ye to the quick, for I—' " He smacked his chest like a warrior, the *clap* echoing alongside his words. " ' —I have become the Lord of Death, leveler of castles, executioner of children, and incarnate woe to mine enemies.' "

Another slap of the chest. " 'I have lain waste to every land and slain every creature known, yet the wretches follow me still, an endless army of the fallen—' " He pointed behind himself, and although he saw a line of hard-eyed wolven, he envisioned a vast army of the dead, imagining himself as Attyla pointing at his troops eons ago. " 'I beseech thee—heed mine words and return mine flesh, and be the only to walk in peace ...' "

As he dragged out the final syllable in a snake-like whisper, he raised the wolf-hide coat for all to see, before dropping it to the snow. "That flesh I have taken upon myself to return, yet that flesh has come in the form of vials of blood. For you did not return our son and daughter to our kingdom, did you? No, you blooded them for *personal gain!*" He began marching toward the enemy wolven, roaring, "I would have been—and still *am*—within my right to smite thee!" He slammed a fist into a palm.

To smite thee … to smite thee …

"To blood thee as thou hast blooded mine brethren!" Centarro coursed through his tongue, sharpening it into a blade. "I wrought vengeance upon your leader for these injustices, but was willing to leave it at that! And now thou hast cometh with thy wounded pride to grovel for battle—"

He abruptly halted in the center of the open field, a hundred feet from either side, nostrils flaring as his blood raged, craving violence. There he turned in place, eyeing both sides. "You have both chained me. And now I beg you to set me free. Let me spread my wings so that I may feast upon your flesh. Let me show the might of my kingdom. For they call for your lands to fall." He pointed at each side. "Yes, you heard right! They crave the lands beyond! And here you are, falling into the traps of the nobles who hold the strings of us all!"

He dropped his arms to face The Dishonored again.

"This time, there shant be a duel of honor. No, this time—" He wagged a finger at them. "—it is me against you all." Then he thrust that finger skyward. "Or—" He allowed the silence to prevail over the echoes before continuing in a gentler voice. "Or we can turn our backs on each other, for my dragon nostrils doth smell a new scent."

He made a show of sniffing the air, and genuinely smelled blood—or perhaps it was the predator within him wishing he was smelling blood. "A new threat that none have yet seen. I say this—" He pointed at them. "Your brethren did not cast the arcane-snuffing arts that penetrated your cave." That point turned into a palm pressed against his chest. "Nor did mine." He pointed again. "Your brethren did not rain holes from the sky." Again he pressed the hand to his chest. "Nor did mine. Something …" He looked to the mountains. "Something stalks us still. Tests us. Prods us …"

Prods us … prods us …

The echo faded, leaving behind an eerie and bitter wind. A headache began to throb. Due to the dangerous side effects, Centarro was a difficult spell to practice, and because he so rarely cast it these days, its casting duration was already fading—his muscle with the spell had grown weak.

The largest of The Dishonored, an eleven-foot wolven, stepped forth. He raised a long earthen blade about the height of a human and pointed it at Augum, snarling something in wolven.

"He accuses you of witchcraft of the mind," the calm one translated from behind.

Augum thrust his shield forth. "I am an Arcaner! An *Arcaner*! Behold, for my shield would dim upon an untruth! I thus swear to thee, upon my sacred honor as an Arcaner, that I have the power to turn into a dragon and smite thee!"

Smite thee … smite thee …

He turned in place to show that the shield had not dimmed. "Behold, for it remains bright! For the sake of us all, let those among thee who have witnessed my dragon form convince you of that truth their own eyes have witnessed!" He took a breath before asking them all, "So what will it be, wolf people of the north? Shall we shed your blood on this gray day? Let me taste the warmth of your flesh upon my dragon tongue? Or …" He snuffed his shield to face sideways, sending a message of impartiality. "Shall we let the echoes … let the echoes die …" He winced. "Die to the wind …"

The fog was impeding his thinking, causing a stutter and disharmony. Already the glitter of existence was beginning to fade, the vibrancy dulling. He had laid it all out, a great dare that taunted two packs eager to war, and a predator that demanded raw meat and bathed in the heat of three mighty suns.

Let them choose quickly, for this way the fog comes! Augum thought, heart pounding.

After a protracted pause during which The Dishonored conferred, he heard a tide of *whooshes*, the sound made by hundreds of weapons and armor and shields vanishing all at once. For the sake of offering impartiality, he remained standing sideways as The Dishonored turned their backs and walked off. He waited until he could wait no more, then strode to the gray one.

"What sorcery was that?"

"My rucksack," Augum blurted, knowing he only had heartbeats to spare before the fog descended upon him. "Give it to me."

The gray barked a command, and it was none other than the angry one who brought Augum's rucksack forth.

"My name is Rogor," the angry one began, nodding, "and today you have proven that some lowlanders do indeed have honor." He thrust the rucksack forth, and Augum accepted it with a grateful nod for not only the rucksack, but also for revealing his name.

"And my name is Chief Golan," the gray said. "Let this be a beginning, so that our peoples may parlay."

"And my name is Tafus," the calm one added, giving Augum a single nod.

"Send word if, uh, if something odd should arise," Augum said, struggling to concentrate. "And I shall … I shall do the same."

"Agreed."

Augum pressed three fingers over his heart. "This is the salute of my Arcaner brethren."

"And this is ours," Chief Golan said, and smacked a fist against his chest.

"It was an honor. Until we meet again." With the fog rapidly dimming his vision, Augum thought of the first place that came to mind along his trek that was within a safe teleportation distance, and snapped off, "*Impetus peragro*," vanishing with a *thwomp*.

Upon appearing there, he collapsed in the snow, praying to the gods that no beast found him in his dazed state. That prayer was the last thing his mind articulated before simplifying to that of a child's thoughts.

INTRIGUES TAILING LIONS

BRIDGET

Bridget impatiently drummed the arm of the bench with her fingernails as she waited to be summoned, wishing she had Sabby with her. Nearby stood two gargantuan golden doors that led into the throne room, otherwise known as the Grand Hall. Four knights holding royal crest shields and long spears protected those doors, keeping their leather-strapped chins rigid straight.

The magnificent and ornate antechamber, with its gilt-framed paintings and tapestries of royals on saddled horses or leading charges into battle or sitting with books and quill in hand, bustled with lords and ladies. Many stole glances her way as they passed, some halting to talk behind their hands, others openly stopping to stare.

No doubt it was her countenance that lent discomfort, for she had not washed off the blood of the brigands she had dispatched out in Sparrow's Perch. She stared straight ahead, almost taking guilty comfort from the whispers. Yet lest the predator make itself known, she chose to think about Sabby curled up back in the Great Arcaner Hall as she waited patiently for her mistress's return.

"Barbarous behavior …"

"Like a wild dog …"

"Unbecoming of a lady of such so-called high station …"

"Unnerving is what it is …"

"She ought to be ashamed to present herself as such …"

"I heard she is losing it because her betrothed is ugly and fat and —"

Bridget's head whipped to glare at the last, spoken by a sinewy woman in a gaudy gold dress, who yelped and skittered off as if pinched. Her companion, a plump woman with a sour face, swallowed, pointedly looked away, and clacked off in the opposite direction, holding her nose almost as high as her forehead.

The whispers quieted, but did not cease. Bridget rose and like a bloody specter padded forth into the bustling crowd which, like a pack of chickens spotting a fox, slowed to a near halt. Those who moved did so quietly, sneaking away to the nearest exit. Most stood frozen, staring at the closest companion as if afraid of a mauling.

Bridget walked among them, looking at each in turn, a lioness fresh from the kill. She could not ignore the raw power it gave her to still the hall like that. The fear in their eyes and on their powdered faces. The way they clutched their money pouches or godly medallions as if it could protect them from the dragon within her.

The urge to make the praying mantis pose was almost overwhelming. How she longed to eviscerate them with one mighty sweep of her sharp wing. To chomp with abandon and feel those medallions soften between her long teeth. To hear their screams as her potent Fear aura, natural to the dragon form, swept over their souls like a black ocean wave. To tear these walls apart like parchment and bring the roof down, crushing their bones to powder.

"Where are your tongues now?" she asked, her voice echoing off the arched high ceiling crammed with lofty depictions of royals of ages past. "Where is that bravado when the subject of your gossip walks amongst you? 'Speak thy mind, oh sheltered ones!' " she spat, quoting a famous line from a play of old she had heard Laudine employ. " 'Speak and I shall listen and judge accordingly!' " She tilted her head and in a lethal whisper added, "Unleash those tongues that yearn to be free …"

She stopped before a towering bearded man who reminded her of a commander and teacher she had respected, a man who had fallen in the war against Canterra. Except this man was no soldier, but a lordling whose fingers were bejeweled with huge golden rings, and whose neck was adorned with a silver chain of office.

She looked up into his face, taking pleasure in him refusing to meet her predatory gaze. "Where is the opinion that we should raid the other kingdoms, using the three of us as mighty weapons of the sky?" she asked him loudly. "Perhaps you would like to saddle and ride my back, thinking to command this lowly *female* as we gaze down upon the ants below? Hmm? And what *did* you do in the wars, gentle sir, while we watched our brethren bleed out on the field of battle? The paintings depict you lot riding first and foremost, but I was there, yes I was, and there was not one powdered face in the vanguard. So where *were* you, sir?"

Still the man refused to look at her. *Probably busy sending letters demanding payment of rent to the gutterborns*, she thought, unflinchingly using the vile *G* word.

"And where were *you* when your brethren in gold cloth fought tooth and nail to stop our order from rising out of ancient ashes?" she said to the throng, turning in place. "Huh? Perhaps you ought to pick up the spear and take a post in defending your kingdom yourselves instead of demanding others do it for you."

The questions were an affront to their powdered faces. She could see how they wanted to curl their lips and snarl and rebut and countermand and condemn, yet dared not do so before her lioness gaze.

"Cowards, the lot of you," she hissed, staring every man and woman down. But it was not her they feared, but what she could turn into. For all of them had borne witness to her wings taking to the skies. The trio had made sure of that. Every noble had been made aware of the trio's alternate existence and their power, whether through demonstrations on the ground or in the air.

The silence in the hall sat as still as a frozen lake until the pair of gargantuan tall golden doors opened with a grinding squeal, revealing a high noble with prim lips. He stepped forth, white-gloved fingertips pressed together, and declared, "Captain Bridget Burns." He raised his imperial chin. "His Highness will see you now," and he stepped aside.

Bridget did not immediately move. She looked about the faces, searching for a single soul to have the temerity to so much as look directly at her. After all, they had been quite keen to steal glances earlier, had they not? Yet no one did. Not the bravest amongst them, nor the largest. She scoffed and walked toward the doors. Those in her way jumped aside as if bitten, allowing her straight passage.

Who are you becoming? she wondered, stepping through the majestic doors and passing numerous guards with halberds, blades hanging from their hips. *What even are you?*

You know what you are, came the acid reply.

The royal hall was filled with the most powerful men and women of the kingdom, including the nine members of the high council, who stood behind the two thrones of Solia occupied by the king and queen. Groups of royals and high nobles stood about on the floor, their liveried servants pressed against the walls, waiting to be called upon. One of those nobles was none other than The Sword of the Oak, who smirked upon laying eyes on her. And looking between him and Bridget was Herald Brittany Mires, who was scribbling furiously with a peacock quill befitting the Grand Hall.

Bridget walked forth feeling like a barbarian amidst all this luxury. She wanted to think of Olaf and starting a family and purchasing a farm and growing crops and minding chickens and geese and her beloved Sabby, yet all she could think of was the satisfaction of making the praying mantis pose and tossing nobles into her maw and slowly chewing them to paste.

Still, she did not fail to make her graces upon coming before the two thrones, being sure to incline her head and curtsy properly before each. "Your Highnesses."

King Rupert Southguard, dressed in ostentatious regalia in the blue and gold colors of his house, drummed the gilded throne in much the same manner she had drummed the bench, albeit with sausage fingers, for he was a boar of a man—and looked like one, lacking only tusks. Gray and old and wrinkled and with an imperious mustache, an air of impatience swirled about him like the queen's rose incense smoke. This very man before her had sent his own son to the rope for being a wayward, a mortal sin in Solia. He had been a decent young man who had not been able to help who he was, and yet his own father had condemned him in the end.

His wife, the queen, was a preening cockatoo of a woman bejeweled from foot to head, possessing an unsmiling and over-powdered face that knew only frown lines. The sort that when she did smile, smiled simperingly and loftily.

"Captain Burns," the king boomed, resting his elbow on the gilded armrest and his chin on his fist. "How is my beloved nephew?"

"Squire Carter Southguard is struggling, Your Grace."

"I can imagine, what with the order being so contrary to his upbringing. But is my heir at the very least a doting and loyal apprentice?"

"He is, but it is his temperament ..."

"Go on."

Bridget forced humility into her tone. "If you will forgive me for saying so, Your Grace, he is rather spoiled and uncouth."

"Uncouth." The king straightened and glanced around, repeating, "Uncouth," soliciting chortles from his subjects. "This coming from someone who turned down one of the highest honors the kingdom had to give."

"Your Grace, it would be unseemly for the leaders of our order to serve as Black Eagles."

"So you said, and perhaps it was right that you declined, for it seems you would not have the loyalty required of that sacred service. You come into my chambers, fresh from battle and bloody as a newborn babe—and no less after having contravened a direct writ!" The man's booming voice echoed in the great hall. "Explain yourself."

"I was summoned forthwith, Your Grace, and forthwith I came."

"Did you lose your common sense on the way?" the queen snapped, causing the hall to rustle with laughter. "Never have I seen such open disrespect of the throne."

"That was not the intent, Your Highness—"

"Then dare I ask what *was* the intent?" the woman shrilly pressed.

"To show that we cannot hide from the ills beyond our walls. That blood is being shed. I cannot be asked to ignore my duty as an Arcaner—"

"As an Arcaner," the king repeated in mock, resulting in stronger chortles, only for the king to raise a single finger that instantly silenced the hall. "I grant thee that we are grateful for your support of our throne. I grant thee that you three have proven yourselves as the kingdom's heroes, having defended it from its enemies. But that is the past. What have you lot accomplished since the war's end?"

Bridget sputtered. "W-well, I think we have made—"

"—a handful of arrests and caused bushelfuls of chaos in the nobility. The nobles are having a hard time conducting business what with their fear that your lot will kick down their door and drag them before a panel of judges."

Bridget wanted to argue that many of those nobles had got off on technicalities of law, something that greatly undermined the order's efforts at tackling corruption. But she had the good sense to hold her tongue on the matter, for relations were already quite strained with the nobility. And her earlier confrontation out front certainly hadn't helped.

"And when it comes to the scum that befoul our streets, is it really worthy of your time as dragons to be pursuing common hoodlums?"

"With all due respect, Your Grace, we have subordinates for such—"

"But today you yourself felt the need to vanquish base brigands who, I have it on good authority—" His boar eyes flicked to the commander. "—were accused of nothing more than theft of a merchant's cart." He continued drumming the armrest. "Is that not the way of it, Captain Burns?"

Bridget's mouth moved up and down. "Er, as a captain I feel it my duty to lead—"

"To lead. Indeed. Is it leadership that urges you to take foolish risks, exposing yourself to a possible accident? Do I really need to remind you that your base task is to protect the kingdom as a whole? After all, the rest of us simpletons do not have the power to turn into dragons, do we now?" The hall chortled at her expense. "Perhaps you ought to turn your mind to greater needs, young captain."

A fuming Bridget did everything not to speak out of turn. "And what needs does His Highness have in mind?"

"Over the generations, the other kingdoms have expanded their borders, taking new territory and gilding new subjects. While ours ..." He smiled perfunctorily. "Our borders have only shrunk."

"That is because we are not warmongers —"

"Are we not?" the king snapped, making the nobles stir with scandal.

"This is a once in a lifetime opportunity, young lady," nasaled an old man in a suit of armor and a helm that were far too large for his frail form. "We must seize the moment we are presented."

"Your predecessor was bolder," Bridget retorted, causing another offended stir, before adding, "Lord High Commander."

The man tried to wrest dignity back by straightening his crooked spine. "My predecessor did his duty —"

" —and died defending the kingdom. I was there, but I do not recall seeing your face amidst the crowd."

"But *I* was there," a tall woman with a pointy chin and hawk eyes said in cold tones. "The enemy had murdered my own daughter, and yet I served our kingdom's interests in the end."

"That you were and that you did, Lady High Inquisitor Sterns." *I never pegged you as you a warmonger, though,* Bridget thought, wondering if the woman wanted vengeance on behalf of her slain child.

"And *I* was there," The Sword of the Oak spat, stepping forth to claim a space beside Bridget, where he faced her. "I saw it all, yet I still have a right to charge you with dereliction of duty and of flouting a direct command as issued by royal *writ*!"

"What precise *duty* have I transgressed —"

"Enough!" the king boomed. "I will not have petty quarrels pollute my chamber." He turned to the old man in the ill-fitting suit of armor. "Yet I dare say the young woman has a point. You have served the crown most faithfully, Lord Equester, but these are different times, and I must ask for your chain."

"Your Grace, please, if I may have more time to allow for research and —"

"You may not."

The old man swallowed, bowed, and stepped forth to remove his golden chain of office. He placed it in the king's waiting hand, gave

Bridget a hard look, and strode out of the hall, the heels of his armored boots dragging awkwardly along the checkered floor.

"Sir Strout, step forth."

The commander, still smirking, stepped forth and bowed deeply. "Your Grace."

"The Sword of the Oak."

"That is what they call me, Your Grace."

"An appellation well earned, from what I hear. Sir Strout, I wish to appoint you Lord High Commander of my armies. Do you accept this highly coveted position that will demand of you the greatest responsibility?"

"With all my heart and soul, Your Grace."

"Then bow your head before me and kiss my ring."

The commander stepped forth, bowed before the king, took his hand, and kissed the largest ring of the lot. In turn, the king raised the chain for all to see and ceremonially placed it over the commander's head. "I dub thee Lord High Commander, the highest military rank and commander of all my armies."

A liveried steward stepped forth holding a scroll, which he unfurled before the newly appointed Lord High Commander, handing him a quill. Everyone then watched the new appointee sign his name. The presence of the scroll told Bridget the entire charade had been planned.

The king raised an open hand in invitation, and the hall burst with cheers and hoots and clapping, none of which Bridget partook in. The new Lord High Commander turned in place, wagging his own raised hand back and forth in that pompous noble manner, a smug smile on his face.

"Congratulations, Lord High Commander," the king said.

"I shall serve you unto death," The Sword of the Oak said, bowing deeply.

"Will you not congratulate our new Lord High Commander, Captain?" the queen asked with a sly smile.

Bridget did not so much as look at the man she despised. "Congratulations, Lord High Commander Strout," she said in cold tones mirroring the queen. "I am sure the sword will fit the scabbard."

This caused a ruffle of muted laughter that quickly petered out.

"What shall be His Grace's first command of his humble new servant?" The Sword of the Oak asked, chin level at the king.

The king looked past him and flicked a hand, which was interpreted by his minions as a dismissal of the entire hall. Everyone except the most trusted of allies was herded out, including Brittany and the other heralds.

Only then did the king place his gaze upon the new Lord High Commander.

"I want you to investigate the possibility of invading the north."

Bridget took an involuntary step forth. "Your Majesty, I must protest such a—" She swallowed, catching herself, and took a step back, mumbling, "Forgive me, Your Grace."

"Were you any other creature," the queen sneered, "you would find yourself yelping from lashes struck upon on your naked back before the entire city!"

Bridget could have retorted in all sorts of ways, how she regretted supporting their throne, how none of them would even be alive were it not for that support, and that the entire kingdom would be Canterran. Instead, she bit her tongue and stared straight ahead.

The king flicked a finger. "You may take your place, Lord High Commander Strout."

The newly appointed Lord High Commander stepped up the platform dais and took his place amongst the other high councilors.

"On account of all your services to the kingdom, I will overlook your intransigence this time, Captain Burns," the king said. "But despite your heady accomplishments on the field of battle as a dragon, you are still only a twenty-year-old young woman who hardly knows about the long-term tactics required for a kingdom's survival and growth. You are a mere babe in the arts of generational warfare."

"Your Grace, I feel—"

The king wagged a finger. "Ah, ah, I am not finished, child. Whether you like it or not, Captain Burns, you *are* a weapon, an instrument of the kingdom's bidding. Of *my* bidding. I expect you to obey my commands henceforth, as you will obey the commands of the Lord High Commander. You are a royal subject who serves your lord king father first and foremost. Is that understood?"

Bridget was barely conscious of her heaving shoulders. The sixteenth edict of the Arcaner code of honor was explicit—*Thou shall root out corruption in all its forms, and the sanctity of the truth shall vanquish any title.* And the very last tenet was as clear as day—*Thou shall swear fealty to this code of honor, for it is the war ye are locked in from this moment on.* To the core of her soul, she could not in good conscience—or in sacred honor—obey commands that sent her off to inflict needless war.

She dared not think too much into it lest the king have a telepath in the room. Even though the only telepaths she knew of were her allies and lived in Antioc, with one mentoring the other, one could never be too careful around royals.

The king leaned forth, his leathers squealing like piglets. "Is that understood?"

Bridget, feeling every eyeball drilling into the side of her skull with their judgments and condemnations, failed to meet his gaze. Yet she did not fail to incline her head ever so slightly—and loathed herself for it. *Coward*, she thought. *Useless, weak, stupid coward!*

"Good." The king leaned back. "And you will make sure those other two keep their backs straight and their noses level. You are instruments of destruction and will do as you are told. I have studied too much of history to know that one uses the advantages given, lest one's kingdom falls to its enemies. As the old proverb goes, 'A sword ought not to rust in its scabbard.' "

The Lord High Commander bent down to whisper something into the king's ear.

The king nodded. "And until the investigation into these mysterious occurrences is complete, you are not to leave the castle grounds. Also, you are commanded to reach out to Commander Stone and Captain Jones and summon them back to the castle post haste. They too are not permitted to risk the kingdom's power on silly sojourns that have added no merit to the kingdom." He flapped a hand. "Dismissed."

Bridget gave the shallowest curtsies she thought she could get away with, mumbling, "Your Graces." Then she turned her bloody back on them and marched toward the tall doors, loathing herself beyond loathing for failing to speak up for not only herself, but for Augum and Leera and the entire order. How dare she undermine them like that with her cowardice! And how *dare* these insipid, powder-faced fools consider them as weapons of expansion after everything the trio had done for them! How *dare* they!

Her fists were balled by the time guards opened the doors for her. She stormed through the doorway, only to find the hall mostly empty. Brittany, who had been sitting on the bench, shot to her feet, blurting, "Captain Burns, is everything—"

"No, it's not," Bridget snapped. "And no, I cannot speak of it," she added, watching as half a dozen guards joined her in the hall, one of whom was none other than a Black Eagle warlock, an elderly woman with hard, no-nonsense eyes and whose name she could not quite recall. She had long gray hair that was course and unruly, and a crone face that would scare even the bravest child. The guards were all middle-aged and, judging by the numerous dents and nicks in their dull armor, some of the best Ordinaries the kingdom had to offer.

"We have been tasked with your safety, Captain," the old woman croaked, pitiless eyes looking at her as if she was but a mere child to scold. Why did so many Black Eagles, whether they be men or women, possess such eyes? Did the service of protecting royalty suck all the joy and compassion from their souls? What did they hear behind closed doors that made them so hard?

"Fine, follow me as you like," Bridget spat.

"Not as we like," the Black Eagle replied, fingertips pressed together before her waist. "But as commanded. Subordinates to the crown must always follow commands."

Bridget pressed her lips tightly. "And what is *your* name, if I may ask?"

The woman looked expectantly over at Brittany, who looked to Bridget for guidance.

"Go on. I'll catch up to you in the yard," Bridget said.

"Yes, Captain," and the young woman strode off.

The Black Eagle watched her go before refocusing on Bridget. "I am Black Eagle Samira Mahmoute."

"A Tiberran."

"A refugee from Tiberra who has sworn herself to the king and queen for allowing me a home after I was condemned in Tiberra."

"Condemned for …?"

"Blasphemy. I do not believe in the gods. Here that is an affront, but hardly a punishment fit for hanging. At least not in the cities. Your kingdom is known to be …" She looked a bloody Bridget over. "… more forgiving."

"Unless you're a wayward." Bridget thumbed over her shoulder. "The king hanged his own son for loving another man."

"I heard that you have developed a glib tongue. It does not suit you, young lady."

Bridget's shoulders sagged as she rubbed her forehead. "I have not been feeling like myself of late."

"Our orders share much in common, Captain." The Black Eagle tapped the crest embroidered over her heart. "*Loyaltos, creatos, vira.* Loyalty, ingenuity, strength."

Bridget tapped her embroidered crest, only to realize it was still the crest of the academy. "I ought to do something about that," she muttered, thinking that those who joined the Arcaner brother- and sisterhood deserved embroidered crests of the order over their hearts. She considered summoning her shield when the woman spoke on her behalf.

"*Semperis vorto honos*. Courage, fortitude, honor. Honorable principles indeed, Captain. I may be almost seventy years old, but I have been told that you will be requiring a mentor in the earthen arts."

"As it so happens, I *have* a mentor, Jezebel Terse, who is—"

"—a drunk and a water warlock. Hardly fit to mentor the rank of a dragon studying the earthen arts, is she?"

"*She* is a fine woman who grieves the loss of her beloved."

"That very well may be so, but that hardly advances your element, does it?"

Bridget sighed in annoyance. "Excuse me," she muttered, striding past, "for I have to wash up and run an order."

"I have also been instructed to mentor you free of charge, Captain Burns," the woman said after Bridget, halting the latter in her tracks.

Bridget turned around. "That is a vast sum to forego."

"The crown is paying it."

"Paying you to spy on me."

The woman said nothing.

"I will take your offer under advisement," Bridget snapped, whirling about to continue on. After a moment's pause, the group of five knights and Black Eagle followed.

SNOW, ICE, AND LAUGHTER

LEERA

The next morning, on the fourth day of Endyear, Leera, bundled in Revel's long fur coat and with her rucksack slung over her shoulder, tromped ahead of her apprentice, plowing a path in the pristine waist-high snow. The forest of pines and spruces and cedars and occasional alder and aspen were quiet, the sky filled with silently moving gray clouds.

"What if that assassin isn't the only one?" Revel asked, tromping behind. "A tattoo would suggest there's more, don't you think?"

"I do."

"Don't you think you ought to return that ring to the deep or something?"

"I don't."

"But whoever sent this assassin will quickly figure out something happened and send another one."

"Then they'll send another one."

"Aren't you scared?"

Leera said nothing, eyes searching the forest for threats. She stopped to point at an aspen's dead branch. It snapped off and floated to her. She stuck it horizontally in the snow between her tracks. After going through the appropriate mental visualizations, she spread a hand over it, incanting, "*Concutio del alarmo.*" Then she plopped some snow on top, making it invisible to the eye, meaning if someone should follow her steps they would almost certainly kick it, tripping the alarm.

"So you *do* expect another assassin," Revel noted.

"One can never be too careful these days."

Revel scoffed at the cliche. "How many alarms can you set, anyway?"

"Five," Leera replied, continuing onward. The standard was to learn to hold one additional alarm in one's head every two degrees, but one could theoretically train oneself for many more; it just took a lot of mental effort.

"I can only set two," Revel said, careful to step over the stick. "This is embarrassing to admit, but I tracked a boy with that spell's cousin, Object Alarm. Got all clingy on him. He called me a creep. I guess I *was* a bit of a creep. I thought we were going to get married and have three kids and a miniature castle out in the country. It was stupid. *I* was stupid."

"You don't strike me as the type to want kids."

"Everybody says that. What, is it because I wear black makeup, or is it because I'm a Malevent?"

Leera pushed her thin oval spectacles up her nose. "I don't know. Both, I guess."

A silence passed, broken only by the crunch of snow.

"Are you going to tell me finally?"

"Tell you what?"

"Why we're going to Horren's Keep."

"We're going to Horren's Keep because *I* want to have kids."

Revel stopped in her tracks. "Then the article in the herald was true …"

Leera stopped as well, but did not turn around. "I read that Horren used to experiment with similar curses that—" She circled her tummy. "—you know. I think if I can find his old stash of research material, which supposedly has never been uncovered, I could, uh … maybe reverse the curse."

Revel said nothing.

"Anyway, I opened my big mouth and now—" Leera flapped a hand over her shoulder. "—every blabbermouth knows. The crones and the vultures are licking their chops. Those noble swine are going to throw themselves at Augum when he gets back."

"But aren't they terrified you'd claw their eyes out?"

"Most are. But some …" She shrugged. "Some like the thrill of trying to snag him, I guess."

"*That's* why you want a kid? To shut them up?"

Leera turned to face her apprentice. "No! I want to one day be able to have a kid, or maybe more, for the sake of having kids! And to continue the lineage. I don't want it to die because of me. And … and I want Augum to be happy. I know he wants kids. I see it every time he plays Chase the Bunny with them or lays eyes on a smiling family or listens to

Bridget talk about raising a bunch of rugrats. He thinks I don't know, but I know. I *know*, all right?"

"All right, all right," Revel mumbled, adjusting her thick round spectacles. "Don't get so heated. I just think …"

"What? What is it that you think I need to know?"

Now it was Revel who shrugged. "You just … *you* don't sound too excited to have kids …" She wrung her hands. "Get what I mean?"

Leera blinked. "I didn't say I wanted them *right* away, did I? I meant like in ten, fifteen, twenty years or something! I just don't want to deal with those harpies trying to pry us apart day after day for a decade! All right? Is that not reasonable!"

Revel backed up, hands raised. "I'm sorry. I'm sorry …"

Leera pinched the bridge of her nose and sighed. "You don't have anything to apologize for. I've been on edge lately. I'm the one who is sorry." She opened her eyes and extended a hand. "I mean it."

Revel took it. "Apology accepted, Cap," and they shook.

Upon continuing the trek, Revel snickered. "Er … how's it going to work having children, what with you two being, you know … dragons."

"We're *not* dragons. We can just turn into them." The shadow behind her mind wanted to grin tauntingly, as if it knew otherwise.

"Right, but aren't you worried that … you know."

Leera whirled about. "That what? Just spit it out."

"Uh, well, you know, that, uh, that they're going to be little …" She winced. "… lizards."

Leera knew she should be offended. Instead she snorted a laugh, and then Revel snorted a laugh, and soon they were both holding their knees laughing uncontrollably.

Channeling her mentor Jez, who shared a quirky sense of humor, Leera stuck an index finger out from under one eye and her second index finger out from her other eye and made them weave about as she tried to envision having lizard kids who had eyes on the sides of their heads. But it was hard to talk through the laughter.

"I'd like to … I'd like to see the looks … on those … on those pasty noble faces when our kid gives them the crooked side-eye …" she wheezed.

"Gods, you had to … you just had to voice that particular thought aloud, didn't you?" a red-faced Revel said, holding her stomach.

"Me? *Me*? *You* started it!" Leera shook her head, wiping her tears. "Little lizards. I can just imagine the cat hissing—" She made claws of her hands and fake-hissed and Revel pressed a hand to her mouth to suppress her laughter. "Then the entire nobility decrying us as demon spawn and putting up straw effigies of us to burn out front and our little lizard baby sticking out a forked tongue …"

But that didn't seem as funny, and the girls stopped laughing. "All right, that'd be creepy," Leera admitted. "In fact, the more I think about it, the more—" Her face curdled. What if she and Augum *did* have lizard children who grew into dragons?

"Captain. *Captain* …"

Leera stopped herself from imagining pitchforks outside the gates of the Black Castle, home of Arcaner headquarters. "Mmm?"

"I was only jesting. Of *course* you'll have normal children. And they'll be the most celebrated children in the entire kingdom, higher than any lordling prince or princess."

"I don't care about that. I don't want my kids to be celebrated. Gross. Let's just …" She flapped a hand onward. "Get on with it already."

Revel nodded apologetically and the pair continued tromping in the snow.

An hour later they stopped for lunch at the foot of a tall aspen. While crunching on peanuts and salted sticks of celery and the assassin's beef biscuits and bread, Leera inspected the assassin's only other possession—a pouch of coins. Seven castles, six spines, and four crowns. All were shiny new, indicating the man had likely made an exchange at a bank. Which meant he had traveled from afar.

She removed the wave-engraved ring from her finger, splayed a hand over it, and incanted, "*Un vun asperio aurum enchantus.*" The tiny tendrils lit up, but were far too small to examine without a magnifying glass. Still, Leera brought it up to her eyes and, whilst occasionally taking a bite of the assassin's bread, which tasted sumptuously of olive oil and black olives and oregano and rosemary and salt and pepper, examined it as closely as she could.

"So what makes you so sure that ring there simply wasn't the assassin's ring?" Revel asked, sitting beside her and taking turns chewing on her own chunk of his bread and munching on a celery stick. "And he wasn't trying to get it back?"

"He wouldn't even have been born when that ship went down." Leera had almost expected the assassin to have his own ring, but wasn't sure why she had that impression.

"Then it was reactivated when you first slipped it on. Can an Object Track spell even be transferred like that? From mind to mind?"

"An advanced casting using a complicator can get it done. All these castings here—" She pointed at them with the dirty fingernail of an outstretched pinky. "—are well within that arena. Very complicated stuff."

"You know I can't see the tendrils, right?"

"Oh. Right."

"I wish I was allowed to learn the spell ahead."

"Reveal?" Leera leaned close. "You want me to teach it to you?"

"That'd be illegal."

Leera leaned back and continued to examine the ring. "I suppose." She wondered if her shield would dim were she to knowingly break the law. Nothing in the code demanded she follow laws, especially ones crafted by the nobility. Proof of that was that her shield had not dimmed when she had disobeyed the writ ordering her to stay within castle grounds.

Leera took another bite of bread and spoke with her mouth full. "My question is, why would someone go to all that trouble to track down this ring? What is it about this little thing that is worth dying for?"

They stared at the ring in wonder, but no answers were forthcoming. Instead of putting it back on her finger, Leera pocketed it, and Revel went on to ask her questions about the 6th degree, which she would be learning next. Leera answered in expert detail, even casting a couple of spells and discussing their intricacies, promising to go through all four spells of the 6th degree—Mute and Object Invisible and Seal and Elemental Armor—upon their return, as a proper mentor should.

It began to snow when they got underway again, deadening sound and making the sky glitter with tumbling flakes. Leera enjoyed the quiet, the crunch of her boots as they laid fresh prints in the pristine snow, the undulating whiteness of the blanket that covered every branch and rock and fallen log and tree.

"Everyone thinks I'm grumpy but it's a bit of a front I put on," Revel said. "And I just wanted to tell you that I think I'm really lucky to be your apprentice."

"Don't get all mushy on me now," Leera replied, echoing her own mentor Jez, who hated when she and Augum so much as held hands, to this day calling them nasty teenagers—even though they had outgrown their teenage years.

"I just wanted you to know that. Girls—and boys—would kill to be your apprentice. I know they tried to push royals onto you and the royal brats of foreign kingdoms, but you chose me. I never asked, but ... why?"

Leera shrugged. "I guess I saw a little of myself in you. Revel the Rebel and all that."

"So you were a misfit too."

Leera remembered her father handing her the blade she would dub Careena and telling her that he would not care if she wanted to become a blacksmith. All he cared about was that she would be happy. "A little bit," she said with a sly smile. "Now shut up. You're making me ill."

"Yes, Cap," Revel said, but Leera heard a smile in her voice.

On and on the trek went, through forest meadows and over frozen streams and around large boulders, until at long last the two women found themselves staring at the ruins of an ancient curtain wall laced with frozen dead vines. At the forefront was a large and broken archway where there once had stood a portcullis gate, now mostly in rubble.

Leera flared a hand, incanting, "*Un vun asperio aurum enchantus*." A few ancient tendrils lit up on the walls and gate, so faded they were nearly gray.

"Anything?" Revel whispered.

"Just some old alarms and protective enchantments and the like."

"Where? I don't want to trigger them."

"On the wall there and the ground at the archway. And you don't have to worry about that unless you think the dead will rise to protect the place."

"*You* thought the same with the ring and look what happened."

"Point taken. Careful now," Leera whispered, tightening her rucksack rope, which ran diagonally across her chest. Revel did the same, and the pair prowled forth through the archway. Halfway through, after climbing over a series of tight boulders, Leera stopped and whispered, "Hold up a moment. I'm going to disguise another alarm behind us here." She proceeded to jam a long and thin branch into the snow of the portcullis in such a manner that it had to be touched to be removed— even Telekinesis would trigger the alarm. Then she carefully camouflaged it as best she could with snow and rubble before splaying her hands over it and incanting, "*Concutio del alarmo*," setting yet another alarm.

Leera dusted her hands, nodding. "Done. Moving on …"

Beyond the archway were the ruins of various buildings surrounding a huge pile of ancient rubble. Leera paid careful attention to the snow, finding it unbroken except for the occasional rabbit or bird or squirrel tracks—or so she thought. That was more Augum's domain.

"Spooky as heck," Revel whispered. "Can't even hear a single bird."

"There's an old legend that says Anna Atticus Stone was here," Leera said.

"I read this was also the scene of the murder of a female necromancer," Revel replied.

Leera nodded. "Wouldn't surprise me." Horren's Keep had a long and haunted history that went back to Rivican times. The Rivicans, an extinct race that had once enslaved humankind, feeding its warlocks to its gargantuan siege engines, had been defeated by the Arcaner order. In that era, many Arcaners could summon dragons. In the centuries after, the keep garnered a bad reputation that drew the dark-hearted—and the foolhardy.

At the foot of a central wall, they found evidence of an encampment—a group of six rotten tents, only one of which still stood upright. All had been thoroughly snowed over. Leera opened the flap of the one that still stood and found it empty. Revel kicked over the frozen canvas of another. "Picked clean," she reported. "Probably by bandits."

Now and then people mounted expeditions to the keep in search of its rumored ancient treasure. Unfortunately, sometimes all they found were brigands waiting to rob them. Judging by the lack of prints and by the abandoned campsite, it seemed few wandered into the ruins in winter.

"I'm going to memorize this spot in case I ever want to teleport back here," Revel whispered.

"Make it a habit to memorize every place you can," Leera retorted, searching up the wall with a splayed hand, looking for a window frame low enough to climb into. "As you never know when you will need it for a future teleport. You'll be legally allowed to start learning Teleport at the 7th, which is only two terms away."

"I can wait a year I guess."

"Not that you'll want to start 'porting this far, but still." Leera pointed at the lowest window, the glass of which had long been destroyed. "That one there." She flicked her hands, attaching on telekinetically, and tried to haul herself up, only to end up straining until her face went red.

"Gods, how does he do it?" she muttered, having let the Reveal spell snuff from the strain.

"The commander? Isn't his constant practicing of Telekinesis how he got his eyes to flare with lightning?"

"That's *exactly* how he attained The Settling. But I'm not exactly the type to lift barrels about all day. Too lazy and all that."

"But you can get the eye thing through other spells, can't you?"

"You can. It's just few are motivated enough to want to achieve it in the first place. Imagine putting in as much effort as Augum did into Telekinesis—all those countless hours of mental weight-lifting—but with a spell like Darkness or Seal or Blind. You'd have to have several *thousand* castings under your belt. Talk about tedium. And for what? So that your eyes can go all watery with whirlpools and the space around you warps a bit? It's just a—" She rubbed the air over her eyes with an open hand. "—a thing to look at. Eye candy, if you will. Vanity, even. Although I suppose it *does* intimidate opponents," she added, realizing she was insulting her man. "Anyway, give me a boost here, would you?"

Revel clasped her hands together and bent her knees. Leera grabbed hold of the girl's shoulders and stepped onto her hands. Revel winced as she straightened her knees and lifted Leera, who then stepped onto Revel's shoulders.

"Careful of my spectacles," a shaking Revel said through clenched teeth.

Leera stretched to her full height. "Almost ... there ... got it!" Her fingers grabbed hold of the edge and she tried to pull herself up, only to hang there like a fool. She let go with her right hand and telekinetically latched onto the top of the arched window. She heaved and, with great strain, pulled herself over the edge, where she flopped to gasp.

"Gods," she wheezed. "I am way out of practice."

"Take a page from your lover's book and start lifting barrels," Revel's voice filtered in from below.

Leera grabbed hold of a chunk of snow and threw it down.

"Ouch! Careful, almost got my face."

"You're just an aspiring cheek," Leera replied, smilingly slapping her chest. "*I'm* the queen cheek around here. Me."

"Yes, Cap. You're the queen cheek," Revel muttered in resigned tones.

"That's better." Leera flopped back over and lowered her arm. "Grab on."

"How? I can't possibly jump that high."

"You know how."

"Why don't you just haul me up telekinetically, then?"

"Because how else are you going to work that muscle?"

"Ugh."

"And stop whining so much."

Revel muttered something under her breath as she focused on Leera's hand. Then she threw her hand up and Leera felt the girl's tendrils hook on. Revel's face went all red as she huffingly tried to haul herself up, even standing on her tippy toes, but all she accomplished was almost pulling Leera off the ledge, until Revel fell back on her butt, panting.

"You're hopeless," Leera said. "All right, not *entirely* hopeless, but you need to practice. In fact, I'm going to assign you homework. I want you to spend a bit of time every day telekinetically lifting things about.

Start small, like with inkwells and stuff, then work your way up, using rocks or whatever works best, until you can haul yourself up a ledge."

"Sounds … tedious."

"It'll be worth it. Now grab on again. This time I'll do the lifting." When Revel did grab on, Leera added her Telekinesis until the girl slowly lifted off the ground. Their hands soon clasped and Leera hooked her legs on the interior of the window frame, grabbed hold with her other hand, and hauled her over the ledge. There they sat panting, both pushing their spectacles back up their noses.

"Definitely out of practice," Leera muttered, the first to get up and step onto the ruins of an ancient hallway, the opposite wall of which was pockmarked with holes. Leera glanced through one of these holes and, in the pale light that filtered in through the ruins, saw something rather dismaying—a lower central hall that was flooded, or rather entirely frozen over.

"Shoot," she said, a sentiment echoed by her apprentice when she too laid eyes on the ice.

"We'd need an ice warlock to get through that," Revel said.

"Not necessarily," Leera replied, and splayed her hand and recast Reveal. As before, all she found were ancient tendril webs long sunk to permanence, mostly Object Alarms and lighting and heating enchantments, with a few specialized enchantments that likely had something to do with the castle's original defense mechanisms.

They found a large hole in the wall which they climbed through, then jumped down to the ice of the main floor, which was lower than the outside grounds.

"The ice is undisturbed," Leera noted.

"No one's been here since it flooded," Revel said. "Autumn rains?"

"Autumn rains," Leera echoed, wandering the ice. It was about half a foot thick, with dark water below. Ahead was a raised gallery, and submerged just under the ice before it was an old and gouged lectern. She moved on to the ruins of a stone staircase in the corner, one of several strewn about the sprawling room.

"From my research, this particular staircase should go down several floors," Leera said.

"Wait, you want to dive it? Are you serious?"

Leera flipped a hand in a *What's the matter?* manner. "I've been training you in winter diving all season."

"Yeah, but … I mean that was in open water. These are ruins. Anything could be down there. What if we don't find a pocket of air?"

"Then we come back up, simple as that. Worst comes to worst, I can try 'porting us out."

"Have you ever even attempted an underwater Group Teleport before?"

"Er, no, not exactly, but it can't be too different from a normal 'port."

Revel stared at her, mouth hanging open.

Leera waved her concerns aside. "It'll be fine. Thing is, that lower floor is perpetually flooded, so only us water warlocks get to explore it. That cuts down the amount of attempts at treasure finding by the other elements by, what, six-sevenths? Seven-eighths if you factor in necromancers poking about for it. Yep, I think we stand a pretty good chance at finding the treasure ourselves—historically speaking, that is. Being water warlocks and all that."

"Uh-huh. I've never had cause to say this, Cap, but I think that you might be—" Revel pinched at the air. "—*slightly* crazy. Just a wee bit."

Leera patted Revel's upper arm. "Who's crazier, the mentor, or the apprentice who follows her? Now stand back. I'm going to blow a hole in the ice."

Revel looked like she was going to reply, only for Leera to absently wag a finger indicating the discussion was over and it was time to get down to business. Leera then took a calming deep breath before slapping her wrists together, roaring, "*Annihilo!*" A jet of water smashed into the ice, chipping off a chunk and cracking the surface.

"Couple more should do it," Leera muttered, slapping her wrists again and roaring, "*Annihilo!*" This time the 3rd degree First Offensive, cast at 10th degree war-honed strength, blew through the ice—and sent cracks shooting toward them. Leera instinctively shoved Revel away before yanking on the ruins of the staircase above—and just in time, too, for the ice underneath her gave way. Had she fallen into the frigid water without having cast the Endure the Deep spell first, she would have had to warm up around a fire before making the dive as drying one's clothes did not warm one's innards.

Swinging there on a telekinetic tendril, Leera pushed off the wall with a foot, jumped clear of the large ice hole, and slid to a halt beside an anxious Revel. "Nice and deep here," Leera said. "What's going to be fun is casting Unconceal down below. Imagine all the stuff hidden over the eons."

"You really *are* crazy," Revel muttered.

"It's all right if you want to remain up top. You can practice Telekinesis—just keep one eye out. I can set an alarm and you can trigger it in case some bear tries to have you for supper."

Revel glanced between the dark water of the hole and Leera and back again. "You know, why, uh, why don't I set up camp here—" She frantically pointed about, nodding repeatedly. "—yeah, while you, uh, you go for an exploratory dive. And-and-and if there really *is* a need for me down there—I mean, if you think you need me—you can come on up and fetch me and, uh, and I'll dive with you. In the meantime, I'll keep both eyes peeled for anything … unsavory, and save the practicing for someplace safe."

Leera lightly punched Revel's shoulder. "You got it, 'prentie," secretly relieved. This *was* a dangerous dive, and there was no sense in risking Revel's life when the girl was so inexperienced doing these sorts of things.

"All right, while you set camp, I'll set an Area Alarm enchantment in the vicinity and then set you an Object Alarm so you can call on me if something happens." Leera cracked her knuckles as she grinned at the hole. "Then I'll hop in."

TRACKING

AUGUM

For a time, Augum was nothing but a composition of simple thoughts. He saw shapes and colors as a child would — the white trees were triangular and tall, the holes in the ground funny to look at. And he felt cold much like a child too — not understanding what cold was, only that it felt bad. His body shivered and his teeth clattered in response, and that did not feel good.

The most interesting thing of all was that soft white things fell from the sky. They added to all the whiteness, and when he opened his hand to catch them, they vanished on his skin. He stuck out his tongue and felt tiny pangs of cold when those white things fell onto it. He shiveringly giggled, liking the sensation, and stuck out his clumsy tongue again and tried to catch more, until a quiet snuffling sound interrupted his musings.

Was it a cat? A dog? He knew such creatures existed, but he did not know how he knew. And those triangular shapes were trees. Yes, trees, he was sure of it. And the gray puffy things in the sky were clouds. And the white stuff was snow. But there were also holes in that snow — a lot of them, going in every direction, as if someone had come by and repeatedly poked it with a stick.

The snuffling grew louder, closer. The boy stared into the thick falling curtain of snow that made a gentle and continuous *pat* sound all around him. The snuffling frightened him. He did not want to know what was making it.

As he waited, the boy's thoughts slowly clarified to that of a young man's, until he thought he remembered his name. Augum. Augum something. Rock. No, Stone. Augum Stone. Yes, that was it. And he had a duty to perform. Had to do something important, but the fog in his mind was still as thick as the snow.

From within the snowfall, a shape appeared, sniffing at the ground greedily. Augum did not move, not daring to so much as breathe. When the beast came within twenty feet, it raised its head and saw him, and it too froze. It was the size of a deer, and looked like a cross between a dog and mountain cat, with a long snout and rows of teeth and pointed ears and course white fur. For a moment, the only sound was that soft and comforting *pat* of the snow. He wished it would cover him like a mother's blanket. He wished he could disappear.

His thoughts began clarifying rapidly, until he suddenly recognized what he was staring at.

A mirko.

Albeit a mirko with white fur, meaning it was a northern variant. He remembered someone once asking him when he was being silent, "What, mirko got your tongue?" and he remembered why, for mirko were known to rip out the tongue before feasting on the face.

Thinking that made him loose an involuntary whimper—and that was all it took for the beast to lunge forth. Augum instinctively summoned his shield, which under the circumstances was a small and wispy thing of crusted lightning that he could barely keep alight. The beast tore at the shield with its long teeth, and the lightning crust began to crack and break and fall off, vanishing as it did so. He scrambled back on his butt, desperate to keep the shield up, trying to think through the remaining fog as to what he should do.

With his mind rapidly sharpening, the answer became obvious. Lightning. *Lightning!*

He flicked his right wrist, hissing, "*Laitna!*" A tiny bolt of lightning zapped the creature, which yelped and sprang back. Tiny Lightning Bolt, a rather common 3rd degree off-the-books spell for lightning warlocks, was often used in such a manner—as a warning. But he'd been so busy learning more complex and powerful spells that he'd only learned this one last year.

Still sitting on the ground, Augum repeated the gesture, but the mirko lunged over the tiny bolt of lightning and went for his face. He raised his shield and it thudded into it, falling at his feet. He punched its head aside just as it tried to chomp down on his leg with its long teeth, and then he grabbed its fur with his right hand and roared, "*Shyneo!*" His palm lit up with mild lightning, which he infused into the beast. The lightning coursed over the body of the mirko, making it convulse. Augum kicked it away, and the thing stumbled off, its pride wounded.

A gasping Augum grabbed his rucksack, threw it back over his shoulder, and hauled himself to his feet—only to find that the mirko had circled about and was again staring at him from the edge of visibility amidst the curtain of falling snow.

"Persistent, aren't you?" he muttered at it. Its response was to growl menacingly. "Don't you do it. Don't you make me do it …" But it ignored him and began to prowl forth. Augum, knowing it was still too dangerous to teleport in his state, realized the beast would track him until its teeth closed on his flesh. But then he thought of a solution, and drew its outline with a finger, incanting, "*Paralizo carcusa cemente.*"

The beast had been about to lunge again, only to freeze with its rear paws digging into the snow in readiness.

"You're lucky," he said to it, tightening his rucksack strap. "Could have roasted you for supper." He turned and walked off, getting twenty paces when he heard another snuffling sound, and then another. He looked back and saw that two more mirko were sniffing at the frozen one. In the south, mirko were known as solitary hunters. In the north, it appeared they formed loose packs.

Augum cursed under his breath. Wanting to conserve as much stamina in case of the worst, he drew the outline of a small dragon, incanting, "*Summano elementus minimus draco.*" A deer-sized dragon made of pure lightning appeared before him, smaller than his usual casting. It flew in place, keeping itself aloft by flapping crackling blue wings.

He had learned the Birth of the Dragon simul during Arcaner training, and only used it in emergencies, for it was a vicious spell.

"Last warning!" he told the pack, but he might as well have been shouting at the spruces for all the good it did. The mirko spread out and growled and bared their teeth at him. Now thinking quite clearly, but still not well enough to risk a teleport, he resummoned his crest shield, making it thick and black and strong. When the mirko came to within fifteen feet, he pointed forth with two fingers, snapping, "Draco—attack!"

With a snap of its tail, the dragon shot forth, tearing into the first mirko with abandon. The second mirko attacked the dragon, which pulsed with lightning. Flesh and blood and guts flew and the pair of mirko howled and yelped, all while the third one stood frozen, able only to watch.

Seeing the blood made a shadow prowl out from behind Augum's mind. It wanted him to partake in the feast, to touch the blood and paint his face with it before making the praying mantis pose.

To prevent his thoughts from spiraling, Augum turned away. Behind him, the grotesque sounds of a bloodbath continued, until all at once they went silent. He looked back and saw two red stains in the snow, the first one larger than the second. In the middle of that second stain his dragon used its snout to pick at the ripped body of the previously paralyzed mirko, almost as if it were checking for life. Finding none, it attempted to extend its wings and return to the air, but all it managed to do was flap torn remnants. The creature sniffed at those remnants, perhaps puzzled, perhaps not. It was difficult to tell.

Feeling sorry for the summoned beast, Augum used a finger to draw its outline in reverse, whispering, *"Draco null."* The dragon vanished with a *sizzle*, leaving behind a thick silence broken only by the continuous gentle pat of snow.

Augum stared at the two bloodstains and the torn-apart pieces, all that remained of a pack of beasts he wished had left him alone. But such beasts also tormented many a family by snatching a child and ripping it to pieces, and that was when they hunted alone. Who knew what sort of damage they could do in packs.

Except there are few humans in these parts, he thought. He doubted mirko would even try to take on wolven, who would make easy work of them.

Heart heavy, he walked past the field of small holes that were steadily getting filled in by snowfall, creating divots. Something strange had happened here. A spell of unknown origin and working. He walked for a time before realizing he needed to inform Bridget and Leera, and so he summoned the vault, finding two notes, one from his beloved and one from Bridget. He read the one from Leera first.

My love, I am worried about you. Are you safe? Do I need to come up there and look for you? I am on a quest with Revel that might make the future better for both of us. Wish me luck.

There are some oddities happening in Blackhaven, weird moss and stuff, but nothing Bridget can't handle. Please answer as soon as you can.

Love you with all my heart,

—Your feisty girl Leera who misses you ever so much and wants to cuddle you and kiss you and throw you against the wall before throwing you onto our bed. Get back here and warm me up, you fiend.

Augum traced a hand over the words, heart longing to grab Leera and heft her up and spin her about and plant a thousand kisses on her before taking her to bed and after frolicking they would nuzzle and relax.

Yet those fingers stopped at the words *both of us*. What did that mean? Both of us as in Augum and Leera, or both of us as in Leera and Revel? He guessed the latter, for Revel was her apprentice, meaning it was likely a training quest. He turned his attention to Bridget's note.

Dear Brother-in-war, I hope you are safe and that you and Olaf are on your way home. Please tell that big lug that I miss him. As for me, my head is in shambles. Not only am I feeling mentally unwell as I feel constantly beset by the callousness, which has strengthened, but something strange is happening here. A bolt of lightning struck the keep and snuffed arcanery within all of Black Castle. Disturbingly, it also snuffed arcane objects.

Augum felt the hairs on his neck rise upon reading this.

Further, a weird infestation of moss was unleashed into the sewers. If touched, it snuffed one's arcanery.

Alas, that is not the worst of the news. It is as we feared. The royalty and the nobles wish to use us as weapons to expand the kingdom. They say it is a historic opportunity. They have failed us, Aug. I am devastated and don't know how to handle such intrigues. Please return in urgent haste.

Your loving sister-in-war Bridget.

P.S. Be warned that Leera has run off on a quest with her apprentice Revel, and we're supposed to be confined to castle grounds until the investigation into the strange occurrences is complete. The powers that be are worried our arcanery will be snuffed and we'll be captured or killed.

Wanting to respond but having no quill and parchment, he zapped a stick with lightning until it charred, sharpened it against a boulder, charred it again, then used the pointed end to write out a note on the back of each of their notes. He then stuffed them into the vault and made it vanish.

He had to get home, but not before finding his party. And he would start with the last place he knew they would have gone to—Sinew, the town where he met the crimson robe and his unruly brigand companion, Lanfred. Usually he'd split such a long hop into multiple parts, but with his mind feeling sharp and his stamina reservoir near full, it would be a good opportunity to flex the teleport muscle—perhaps even expand it.

He thus focused on a particular alcove he had taken shelter in, recalling the iron-strapped door, how close his head had come to the archway overhead. He imagined the stonework of the building, the snow underfoot, the cobbled street. Then he snapped off, *"Impetus peragro,"* and after a stomach-churning hurl through the black arcane ether that slurped up at his reservoir, reappeared with a *thwomp* in the alcove of a scribe shop—where someone bumped into him.

"Stupid 'lock," a greasy-haired man with an oily beard. "What you is 'portin' inter doorways fer? Huh? And ain't that robe not for 'portin'? That there color is fer 'prentices, ain't it? I reckon you either cast an illegal spell, or you is a charlatan—"

"I have a writ," Augum replied, surprised by the sudden haranguing, wincing against a bright but direct ray of sun that illuminated that part of the town, while the rest was bathed in cloud-shadow.

"Let me see it then." The man thumped a fist against his wolf-hide coat. "I could read words."

"It's not on me at the moment."

"Then I call you a liar and a brigand!"

Augum flared his shield. "I swear on my honor as an Arcaner that I am telling the truth, sir. Behold, it does not dim."

The man glanced between the shield and his face. "What cheap sorcery is this, boy? Swear on your shield? Never 'eard such nonsense!"

"Excuse me," Augum said, and walked past him, snuffing his shield.

"Hey! I was talkin' to ye!"

Augum flapped a dismissive hand at the man over his shoulder, a bad habit he had picked up from Leera. But he had other priorities. The hop had been longer than expected, having sucked a third of his stamina, yet plenty enough remained for small hops to his friends—and a tussle if need be. With no time to waste, he hurried to The Smoked Wing Inn & Tavern, nearly crashing through the door in his haste. All eyes went right to him, and more than a few enlarged with surprise.

Augum glanced from face to greasy face, rage bubbling within him. Many of these lowlifes had been aware of the game but were too cowardly or corrupt to do anything about it, allowing innocent young people to be taken to their bloody deaths.

"Where are they?" he asked, politer than he wanted.

Many laughed outright, others chortled, others still only looked away in shame or pity or cowardness. One particularly large man with an oily bronze face and snowshoes on his back sniggered to his table of card players, who elbowed each other knowingly.

Augum, hardly in a mood for nonsense, flared his ten lightning rings, his lightning eyes, and his shield, revealing the full Arcaner crest. "My name is Augum Arinthian Stone," he declared, brightening all the lightning for effect, turning the tavern blue. "By writ of the Solian king I have been granted permission to wear an apprentice robe. Now I ask again. Where. Is. My. Party?" He wanted to amplify his throat and roar the question until the windows shattered.

The laughter trickled to a halt, with more people lowering their heads and pretending to be busy. No one spoke—except for the big oily-faced man, who said something to his cohorts, all of whom tried to suppress their laughter.

The shadow stepped out from behind Augum's mind and snarled. Augum tilted his head, reached out an arm, made a claw of his hand, and telekinetically grabbed hold of the top of the man's greasy-haired head. That huge man abruptly found himself getting dragged over his card table, flipping it, sending coins and cards and ale sloshing. The man grabbed above his head as he would at an attacker's arm, but there was no hand to grab, only air. He growled and swore and sputtered as he was dragged through the crowd of patrons, who jumped out of their chairs or grabbed their ale and coins in their desperate attempt to avoid him.

"Hey!" the barkeep shouted, running up to his bar and slapping it with an open hand. "What are you doing to my patrons! You put him down, boy!"

Augum gave the barkeep one lightning-eyed look and the man, who was about to slap the counter a second time, backed away instead.

Augum dragged the oily-faced man through the door and outside, where he telekinetically lifted him, warping the space around himself fishbowl-like from the strain, and slammed him against the wall of the tavern between the window and the alcove.

"Where. Is. My. Party?" he growled, one hand raised, the other still keeping his shield lit. The stamina bleed increased from a trickle to a small waterspout.

"Don't know who you're talkin' 'bout, boy."

Augum tilted his head the other way. "You all think because we're Arcaners we have to be nice. But being nice isn't in the code of honor. In fact—" He made a claw of his shield hand and swiped toward the man, hissing, "*Dreadus terrablus*," infusing into the 4th degree Fear spell the imagery of the man's own snowshoes coming undone, and the sinews wrapping their cords around his neck and suffocating him.

The man's unprotected mind, unused to facing arcanery of any sort, wilted like a reed in the wind, and his eyes went wide and his mouth gasped for air and he grabbed at this throat with his ham hands as he struggled to breathe.

Augum reversed the clawing gesture, hissing, "*Dreadus null*," then let him fall to the ground. The man lay there gasping and holding his throat.

"I can do this all day, for my brethren are missing. *They* are now my quest. Do you understand, or shall I—"

Augum's attention was stolen by the man he had almost teleported into in that alcove earlier.

"Hey, boy! Boy!" the man shouted, tottering up on him. "What is you doin' now that—" but he froze upon Augum laying his lightning eyes on him. Now seeing those eyes along with the ten rings and the huge man at his feet, the oily-bearded man turned right around and waddled off as fast as he dared.

Augum returned his attention to the huge man. "Where are they?"

The man sneered. "I don't have to tell you, and you know that. Like you said, you is an Arcaner, and I happen to know all I got to do is bend the knee, and you got to arrest me or let me go. And so I bend the knee, *sir*," he said mockingly. "I bend the knee. Now either take me in or kindly shut the hell up." He ran a hand through his greasy mop of hair and smirked.

Augum could have pressed the point, but in the end, the man was right. He did not *have* to tell Augum anything, and sure, he could suffer for it, but that ran the risk of transgressing the fifth edict—*Thou shall be gallant and fair to those unable to learn the craft.* Would it be gallant or fair to keep questioning and pushing the man? Of course not.

Despite the shadow behind Augum's mind goading him on, craving the man's blood, Augum, reminded by the face of his own shield, merely drew the man's outline, incanting, "*Paralizo carcusa cemente.*" With the man frozen in place, mouth open as if to blurt another taunt, Augum strode back inside, letting the door smash against the wall. With his lightning eyes and arm rings and shield still flared brighter than the day, he pointed at the barkeep—and held the accusing finger up, allowing the place to fall so silent that, when he finally spoke, he was able to whisper, "Where?"

The barkeep straightened behind his bar and folded his arms across his chest. Augum stepped aside and gestured invitingly outside. "Or would you prefer the same treatment?"

The barkeep glanced at the detritus of cards and spilled ale that his servants were cleaning up, swallowed, and walked around his counter. In the mean, Augum tried to solicit someone to meet his gaze so that he could identify his next target, but not one soul dared.

"And how many other kids did you all see get dragged through here?" he roared, grabbing the barkeep by the scruff with his right hand, not allowing him to pass yet. The lightning from his ten arm bands snapped out, crackling menacingly. The man kept flinching, but Augum held him firm.

"How many families are bereft of their sons and daughters, crying by an empty grave! Huh? You loathsome, cowardly dogs." He leaned close to the man's ear, hissing, "You *better* squeal, lest you find yourself without a tavern to run," and he shoved him through the door.

The man stepped outside and saw his beefy patron on the ground, frozen with his mouth open.

"I am running out of patience," Augum said, letting the man appreciate the position of his patron. "Where is my party?"

The barkeep stood beside his patron, folded his arms once more, and put on a sly smile. "I don't have to—"

Augum cut him off with a clawed hand, incanting, "*Dreadus terrablus.*" This time, he infused the fear of the man losing his tavern and having to stoop to cleaning privies for the rest of his life. The barkeep fell to his knees and wailed in distress. Augum let the scene play out in the man's mind for a bit longer before reversing the motion. "*Dreadus null.*"

The barkeep gasped and slapped both hands over his mouth. He looked up at Augum, who opened his hand anew, mouthing, "Where?"

The barkeep slowly pointed with a shaky finger down the street.

"North? North where?"

"The cart trail. They walked the cart trail north after interrogating one of my patrons."

"Were they attacked?"

The man shook his head. "I don't know. *I don't know!*" he repeated when Augum raised his clawed hand threateningly.

"If I ever hear so much as a peep that you turned a blind eye to any Solian citizen—"

"You won't be doing anything, son," a man shouted.

Augum looked over to see three men running up, all dressed in leather armor and furs, shortswords drawn and bucklers at the ready—the constabulary fashion of Ohm. And beyond stood that waddling ale-bellied man who had run off earlier.

"This is not your kingdom," the constable added. "You have no authority here, Arcaner. Begone." He made a motion as if shooing off a dog. "I say, begone!"

"Off with you!" shouted a cohort, making the same motion.

One of the men winked at the barkeep, and Augum realized that the local constabulary was in cahoots. He smiled unkindly. "What makes you think the Arcaner code of honor is restricted by kingdom boundaries? We seek corruption in all its forms." He took a step toward the men, who took a step away from his lightning-infused countenance. "And we are expanding. We will open chapters in the east and west and the south and north. And guess which town I will make a priority to be cleansed of corruption? Hmm?"

"You are nothing but outlaws who—"

"—are sick and tired of the greedy and the corrupt having power over those who cannot defend themselves!" Augum roared, taking another step toward the men, who took another step back. "And we will *not* be cowed," he added, barely conscious of his lightning lashing out, snapping at the snow and toward the men like blue vipers, the shadow of a dragon rising up behind his mind. The crackle got so loud it started to echo off the town's buildings.

That echo pierced his thoughts, and Augum snuffed all of it at once, bathing them in silence. The sun passed behind a cloud, and cold swept through the town—and his soul. He regarded the men with cool eyes, wishing they would attack him so he could quench the thirst of the parched predator. He had been doing too much talking. Only violence satiated the deep longing. At least, for a time …

"And what of your code of honor?" Augum asked. "And how much money did they pay you to keep silent while our young ones were paraded through here to be blooded? Hmm?"

The corrupt constables had the good sense not to escalate the situation, and not only averted their gazes out of guilt, but remained silent.

"Surely there is a part of you that signed up to this duty wanting to make a difference." He glanced over his shoulder, making sure the cowed barkeep and the beefy patron were out of earshot, and stepped closer to the constables. "My party traveled north along the cart trail. I know news travels along that route, and I would be grateful if you shared some."

"Word is they were attacked by the wolven after a few leagues," the leader whispered, eyes flitting to the barkeep. "And we did *not* sign up for this. *They*—" He inclined his head slightly toward the tavern. "—kill any of us who get in their way, constable or not. We who have families to feed and protect cannot always afford the luxury of justice."

"What happened to them after they were attacked? Any casualties?"

"It was a surprise attack, but they ran off to take shelter and lick their wounds. After that, I don't know."

Augum nodded. He glanced back at the barkeep, and realized the constable had taken a huge risk by informing him. "Your silence only buys you time," he said loudly to the three constables, earning himself a small nod of thanks from all of them. "But don't ever let any of this happen again," he added in a whisper, before turning his back and striding northward, leaving the paralyzed man to wait out the incantation, which would take some time — and serve as a visual warning to them all.

Once he got past town, he saw that the road ahead winded down the mountain and then snaked through a great valley between mountains lit by sunbeam slices. The clouds bunched up against those mountains, thick and heavy, with the far north obscured by a thick white curtain of falling snow.

Augum raised a finger and squinted as he counted out rough leagues along the road, choosing the first of three he could see. It was a risk to battle-teleport that far, but he had a clear line of sight and plenty of room from the road itself. As an extra precaution, he envisioned appearing in the center of the road and two feet above the snow. Then he snapped off, "*Impetus peragro.*"

He vanished and reappeared with a *thwomp* in midair — but found himself forty feet above the road, promptly plummeting. With heartbeats to spare, he telekinetically lashed out, grabbed hold of the nearest pine, and swung toward it. At a critical moment, he pulled on the invisible tendril line and raised his butt so that he careened just above the snowy ground. Then he let go, touching down at a high sprint — only to discover that the snow was deep, and he tumbled into it a few feet before coming to a halt upside down.

After some scrambling, he righted himself and spat out a gob of snow. Checking to make sure the vials had not been broken within his rucksack, he slogged through the snow back to the road, which was grooved with cart tracks. Unfortunately, he had appeared in a dip between long valleys, and so could not see ahead, meaning another teleport was out of the question for the time being.

"Not that the first one was very successful," he muttered to himself, feeling lucky to have avoided injury.

He journeyed along that road, sticking to the cart trail, battling with the snow when it got in the way, until he reached the crest of that particular dip. Seeing nothing suspicious in the quarter league ahead, he took extra time focusing on the next road hilltop and again snapped off the incantation. Due to the shorter hop length, he appeared a safe two feet above the road. But just as his boots hit the snow, he lunged aside to avoid a galloping horse that was about to crest the hill road.

"Ho!" the rider called after galloping past, pulling on the reins and making his horse rear up. The man was a snow-skinned warrior dressed in the regalia of the Henawa people—seal-hide coat, fox-fur pants, and moccasins—except everything was white. The two throwing axes, secured to a wolven belt, the stick he carried decorated with bone beads and feathers and shells—all were either naturally bleached or painted white as the snow. Even the horse was white.

He turned about, revealing a wrinkled face that had seen many dawns. His long milk hair was smooth and shiny in the sunlight as it cascaded down his coat. He took one look at Augum and spat an angry phrase in Henawa, pointing his stick at the spot Augum had been standing in only heartbeats prior.

Augum hauled himself up from the snow and raised a finger. "Just a moment," he said, organizing his thoughts. He hoped what little he knew of the Henewa language was enough that casting the complicated 12th degree Tongues spell would allow for conversation.

"*Chunchuha!*" Augum blurted in greeting, priming his mind for the casting. "*Ish ta! Ish ta!*" he added, which he was sure translated to *I'll explain*.

The man kept gesticulating wildly at Augum and the road and his horse whilst angrily going on in his tongue.

Augum opened his hands and pressed them back and forth, saying, "*Ish ta, ish ta,*" urging the man to calm down while he tried to think of as many Henawa words as he could—*Sapinchay* which meant snowskin and *andava* for crazy and *nora* for north and *spudi* for stupid and *weho* for where and *achishi zafu* for honored elder. Once he thought himself prepared, he touched his throat with one hand and pressed three fingers to his temple with the other, incanting, "*Translateo commona linguino Henawa.*"

"... damn fool witch what think you want road appear you cursed ..."

Augum, not very good with the spell yet or the language and so only able to half understand the rider, kept his hands aloft. "Please stop, honored elder," he said, hearing himself say, "*Pleha sot, achishi zafu.*"

The man recoiled as if having drunk something most foul. "Make Henawa ugly with bad words."

"I don't know how to speak Henawa yet, but I'm learning," Augum said, wincing from knowing he was butchering the man's tongue. He tapped his chest. "I'm searching for my companions." He made his fingers walk along the air, unsure of his translation capabilities with the spell. "My companions. My friends. My party."

"*Spudi maniye,*" the man said with a shake of the head, which Augum translated as *Stupid darkskin.* To the snow-skinned Henawa, any skin darker than milk was *maniye.*

"I know, I know, but I just want to find my friends. They were attacked by the wolven somewhere near here."

The word *beyaeeshako,* pronounced *bey-ah-eesh-a-ko* and meaning *wolven,* caught the old man's attention. "*Beyaeeshako?*" he repeated.

Augum nodded furiously. "*Beyaeeshako, beyaeeshako.*" He made the fingers-walking motion again and pointed northward whilst tapping his chest. "My friends were attacked by the *beyaeeshako,*" and he made claws of his hands and fake-growled, mimicking the wolven.

The old Henawa nodded sagely a few times before raising his feathered stick and making a pronouncement-like motion with it whilst declaring, "It witch karma for fool flight."

"Yeah, I'm sorry about that teleport. I didn't see you cresting the hill. Also your horse is white, your clothes are white, and, uh, you know ..." Augum gesticulated at the whole of the man.

The old Henawa nodded in that sage way of his again before pointing with his stick beyond Augum. Then he raised that stick slightly and yanked it to the left. "*Iho kwaha.*"

Even with the help of Tongues, the words remained unfamiliar. Augum flipped his palms questioningly. "*Iho kwaha?*"

The old Henawa frowned before raising two fingers on each side of his head. "*Iho.*"

"Horns," Augum mouthed. "Horns?"

"*Iya, iya,*" the man said with a nod, meaning yes, yes, before pointing at a nearby mountain. "*Kwaha.*"

"Horn mountain," Augum said, and repeated both gestures. "Horn mountain?"

"*Iya, iya. Iho kwaha maniye nuliwi beshba beyaeeshako,*" which Augum heard as "Yes, yes. Horn mountain dark-skinned witches battled wolven."

Augum turned about to see that far ahead there indeed sat two spiky peaks. He turned back about, pressed three fingers over his heart in the Arcaner salute, and said, "*Chesho,*" Henawa for gratitude.

The old Henawa pointed beyond Augum and shook the stick in warning. "*Heho nek.*"

"Hell death," Augum whispered, not quite understanding. "*Chesho, chesho,*" he repeated, and turned to focus on the next distant hilltop he could see. Conscious of the man watching him, he snapped off, "*Impetus peragro,*" and appeared a quarter league away, feet settling nicely into the snow. There he turned and raised an arm in thanks, and saw the distant and now tiny man stare at him before turning about and galloping onward, vanishing beyond the crest of the hill.

"Strange land," Augum muttered, and focused on the next hill. It took another three hops and a meditative rest to replenish stamina before he found himself standing atop another crest and looking down into a valley. The road continued on into the next valley, but before it angled back up on the next hill, there was a dark patch of snow, as if an unusually dark shadow had formed there.

Feeling his heart skip a beat, Augum took a couple of calming breaths before 'porting once again, appearing just before the patch.

But it was no shadow.

It was a frozen pool of blood and guts and fur.

And the torn strips of an amber robe, which happened to be the color of robe Olaf wore.

DENIED

BRIDGET

Dear Sister-in-war,

    I am well, still in north. Also struggling with callousness. Tracked apprentices. They were sold to wolven pack called The Dishonored, who blooded the poor souls. Kidnappers dead. Will hand remains to families upon return.

    Also made contact with honorable wolven pack. Something strange happening here too. Will rejoin my party and return in haste to help address concerns of invading north. Will not be puppets of war.

    I miss and worry about Leera, but also trust her to keep safe.

    Stay strong, dragon sister. We'll figure this all out together.

Your ever-loving brother-in-war Augum.

Bridget felt a pang of sisterly love at reading dragon sister, only to startle upon receiving a knock on her door. "Just a moment!" she called, cramming the note back into the vault, slamming its door, and hissing, "Vaultus null." The door to her room opened just as the Arcaner vault vanished with a quiet whoosh.

Bridget whirled, snapping, "I said just a —" Her face curled with rage upon seeing the old Black Eagle Samira Mahmoute staring at her with expectant eyes. "How dare you impede upon my person!" Bridget snarled, hands curling into fists. "How dare you barge in on me presuming —"

"The Lord High Commander is here and insists upon speaking to you."

Bridget gaped. "What? We have already discussed —"

Mahmoute merely stepped aside, and her bevy of five knights clanked inside the relatively small Black Castle room, followed by another bevy of guards which included another Black Eagle, this time a grumpy middle-aged man. Last came The Sword of the Oak, smiling victoriously, that disgusting mustache of his freshly waxed and extra thin.

"Miss Burns …"

"Captain Burns," Bridget corrected, refusing to step aside to give one of his knights room to maneuver around her, forcing him to squish awkwardly behind the open door.

"I suppose. Now that we understand each other, I wanted to inform you of your first order."

"I beg your pardon?"

"Your first order. You know what orders are—" He raised a mocking eyebrow. "—surely?"

Bridget couldn't help her shoulders from heaving in rage. The shadow from behind her mind was frothing, demanding a duel of honor, for the man's weak blood to be spilled on a polished checkered floor for all to see and inhale its iron tang. Yet he was an Ordinary, a mere soldier, and her code was clear—Thou shall not duel the lower ranks without serious provocation. And orders hardly counted as a provocation.

"Our spies have identified a castle amidst the mountains, long thought to be abandoned, as an outpost of kidnapping brigands." He withdrew a tiny scroll wrapped in twine and offered it. "Once we make a decision, you three will be ordered to turn into dragons and destroy it." He nudged the scroll at her.

Bridget snatched it, ripped off the twine, and opened the scroll.

"The red X," the Lord High Commander said.

Bridget saw a castle named Verhak Rago on the side of a mountain.

"Otherwise known as Vulture's Rock."

"Which is in Ohm …"

"I see you know your borders," he said sarcastically. "Good girl."

Bridget held up the map for all to see before slowly tearing it down the middle. Whilst staring at him, she crumpled the pieces together—and tossed them into his loathsome face. They bounced off and fell to the ground.

The corner of the Lord High Commander's mouth twitched. "You will regret that," he said, taking a step back. "Captain Bridget Burns, I declare that you have committed the crime of insubordination. Therefore, as per the consequences of your own code of honor, you are hereby afflicted with one shield dim."

Bridget's heart almost stopped. She promptly summoned her shield to her arm—and found it still whole. She wanted to laugh in his malicious face, but instead held it before her for all present to see its golden glow.

The Sword of the Oak stared at the shield with an impotent expression that Bridget found thoroughly amusing, yet she dared not so much as smile.

"Damn fool, I thought you said a direct contravention of my command would result in a dim!" he hissed at a fellow knight.

"That was my understanding as well, my lord," a knight in full plate whispered, his face behind the slit visor reddening.

The Lord High Commander was even redder. He raised a quivering finger at Bridget and frothed, "You are hereby confined to these quarters and forbidden to mingle with anyone but your guards!"

"What? You can't do that!"

"I just did."

"What about my dog?"

"I'll have one of your Arcaner brethren see to her." He turned to the same knight. "Bread and water only. Your squad on the door."

The knight stiffened with a sharp salute, snapping, "Sir, yes, sir!"

The Lord High Commander made an Off with you all motion and stormed out, his guard detail clanking along behind rather pathetically, with some remaining behind to watch her door.

Bridget watched them go, amused—and alarmed. But it was Samira Mahmoute who ended up closing the door on them all. The old Tiberran turned about to face Bridget.

"Are you jesting me?" Bridget hissed. "You are going to stand inside here with me? In my own private quarters?"

The woman let her stew in silence before raising a furled-up scroll and floating it to Bridget, who snatched it from the air, snapping, "What's this?"

"This morning's herald. I thought you would appreciate being kept abreast of events in the kingdom."

Bridget unfurled the scroll and saw one headline titled, "Mysterious Happenings in the Black Castle," with little details other than it was being investigated, and a second headline titled, "The Arcaner Order: An Inside Account of the Day to Day." Both were written by Brittany Mires. The former had scant details, while the latter was a rather kind portrayal, avoiding any drama and embarrassments. It did hint that the nobility did not appreciate the order as much as they should, and that Ordinaries had nothing to fear of the order, rather they should support it as a check on the nobility, on the constabulary, and on themselves.

The more Bridget read of the latter piece, the more impressed she became. If Ordinaries gained more trust toward the order, they would send in more tips—and perhaps even support family members aspiring to become warlocks or Arcaners.

Interestingly, there was no mention of what had transpired between her and the king, which Bridget didn't know how to feel about. Part of her wanted the kingdom to know that the nobility were planning on using the trio as battering rams to expand the kingdom, but another part wanted to solve the problem without it getting that far. Still, she had to give Brittany credit—she had done a far better job than anticipated.

Bridget turned the scroll over and read a third headline titled, "Barren Arcaner Leera Jones Continues to Insult," which a disgusted Bridget didn't bother even getting into.

Mahmoute slipped her hands into the pockets of her crimson robe and paced the small room. "One of our duties as Black Eagles is to read up on our history. I came across something rather interesting in the archives. You were once mentored by the esteemed master warlock Anna Atticus Stone, is that not so?"

Bridget tossed the Blackhaven Herald onto her bed, where it refurled with a shloop. "What does that have to do with—" but she was silenced by a mere lift of the old woman's eyebrow, which somehow made Bridget feel guilty for raising her voice at her.

"As I was saying, the esteemed Anna Atticus Stone was once herself mentored by none other than a Black Eagle. A Niterra Bladesong, if I am not mistaken."

Bridget, recalling the name from some obscure reading about local history, folded her arms. "What's your point?"

"My point, my dear captain, is that there is precedence."

"A true mentor advocates for their apprentice, not spies on them."

The old Black Eagle stopped before a window and gazed outside. "The sun is nice when it pierces the clouds. The beams are like brushes—" She made a single stroke of a hand along the air. "—painting joy where they land."

"You do not honestly believe it is in any way ethical to make war for more land, do you?"

Mahmoute turned about to look at Bridget. "It is not my place to question orders. Like you, I follow a strict code of honor—"

"—one that apparently allows for mass slaughter. You are aware of our power as dragons, yet you would deploy us to murder the children of the north."

"I would do no such thing."

"But you would go along with those who would."

"Duty is duty."

"And honor is honor and life is life. Duty trumps neither."

The corner of Mahmoute's mouth rose ever so slightly, as if she understood this all too well. "Are you prepared for the consequences—"

"Yes," Bridget said, stepping forth. "And know this, Black Eagle. I am willing to destroy the ability to summon the dragon within myself—" She snapped her fingers, suddenly feeling more powerful. "—like that. I—" She patted her own chest. "—have that power. And upon facing inevitable corruption, I am duty-bound to use it." She could almost hear the shadow within her squeal in protest. She had never known it to be pathetic before. But all she needed to do was consciously contravene the code of honor and her shield would dim once, which was all it took for her to lose the ability to summon the dragon. And only a sacred pilgrimage could restore that dim.

Mahmoute searched her eyes. "Then you would weaken the kingdom by a third and deprive its people of a great defense, which could in turn lead to a slaughter conducted by the kingdom's enemies."

"I wouldn't be alone renouncing these powers. My brother- and sister-in-war would join me. Our records warn of just such corruption. Our duty is clear."

For the first time, Mahmoute smiled. "Then you indeed have the upper hand," she whispered.

These words surprised Bridget so much that she had to take a seat on her canopy bedstead.

"But you did not hear me say that," the old woman added, smoothing her robe with both hands. "Now how about we do some training."

"What? Now? Here?"

"Have you anything better to do?" When Bridget failed to reply, Mahmoute clapped her hands together with a slap. "Then it is settled." She walked to stand before Bridget, and looked down at her as a mother would upon a daughter, which made Bridget feel simultaneously ill at ease and strangely comforted. "1st to the 10th, and your simuls. Of the 11th, you know Reveal, and of the 12th, Tongues. Of the 17th, Group Teleport. All of these you know or are learning, yes? Disregarding off-the-book spells, of course."

"Er … yes. But how did you—"

"Come, come, child, you three are the most powerful weapons the kingdom can wield. Of course the powers that be will keep abreast of your situation as best as they can. But to be more specific, the Lady High

Inquisitor, with her vast army of spies, has informed me what I need to know."

Bridget rose from the bed. "I am not a child. I am a captain." And a killer and a predator and a queen of the skies who could tear you into shreds without a second thought, a sentiment she did not dare voice aloud.

"I understand. Returning to the topic at hand, I believe you have not had the time yet to learn the rest of the 11th, including the 11th degree elemental spell Enchant Weapon."

"Well we just graduated and have been busy with the order and now the happenings—"

"What about elemental off-the-book spells such as the 11th degree Snaking Vine and the 12th degree Venom Vomit?"

"I know neither. Haven't had the time to—"

"So your choices are clear. If you were to begin one of those here and now in this room, which one would you start?"

An intrigued Bridget slipped both hands into the armpits of her crimson robe. "I would actually much prefer training on Arcane Drain." It was one of the 11th degree spells she had looked forward to learning after graduation, one that could allow her to top up her stamina in battle at the expense of an opponent—a critical maneuver when nearing depletion, especially as a dragon, for the dragon form continually bled off stamina until reversion took place.

"But you could learn that spell with your continually absent and drunken mentor—"

"Don't you dare. Don't. You. Dare. She lost someone she loved in the war and that is how she deals with it. Do not speak about Jez. Are we understood?"

Mahmoute pursed her lips. "What do you know of the spell thus far?"

Bridget allowed her glare to remain for a breath before replying. "I know some of its basic arcaneological requirements of thought and stamina draw. And I know the gesture," and Bridget made a hand-over-hand pulling motion as if tugging on rope. "I've had it cast against me multiple times. Vicious spell."

"When not dodged."

"One can't always be quick."

A knock came at the door.

"Enter!" Bridget called before Mahmoute could say anything.

The door opened and in clanked a fully armored knight rather absurdly carrying a tray with a loaf of bread and a tankard of water. He glanced around, unsure of what to do with it. The blue eyes of a young man nervously peered through the visor slit of his pot helm.

"I'll take it," Bridget said, opening her hands invitingly.

The knight cleared his throat, clanked over, and placed the tray into her hands. "M'lady," he muttered, and clanked off, quietly closing the door behind himself, a simple gesture that told her he was the considerate type.

Bridget set the tray down on a nearby dresser, grabbed the bread, and turned about. "Shall we break bread?" She tore it in half and offered a piece to the old Black Eagle.

"Symbolism has meaning to you," Mahmoute said, stepping forth to accept the bread. "It has meaning for me too." Both women then tore a chunk of it with their teeth and chewed before placing the bread back on the tray. Bridget took a long drink of the cool water and returned to stand in the center of the room, ready for the lesson.

"Arcanatisrossiokadis is a tough spell to master," Mahmoute said, using the ancient name for Arcane Drain, "for not only must your aim be perfect—"

"—particularly while flying."

"Do not interrupt."

"Sorry," Bridget blurted, immediately hating that she had apologized, especially seeing as the stubborn woman had refused to apologize for calling her beloved mentor a drunk. She was still stuck in the mindset of being a pupil at the academy and had a long way to go in learning to be a captain.

"Yes, one must account for an opponent's travel when trying to hook the tendril line, but that shouldn't be too big of a trial for an archer, no?"

Bridget inclined her head in agreement. She had been training in firing her arrows at moving objects since learning the Summon Weapon spell back as a 4th degree learning the 5th—and during a war, no less.

"Once one hits one's target and successfully latches onto their stamina reservoir, a separate process begins that happens in the blink of an eye. One must send a wild surge of one's own arcanery to bust through the opponent's defense."

"Their Mind Armor."

"Correct. The stronger the pulse, the greater the chance of penetration. Once experienced enough in the spell that sort of thing is subconscious, but for you, every step will have to be deliberate. The usual variables and principles will apply—degree relativity, tongue-to-tendril ratios, time spent with Mind Armor and Arcane Drain, experience defending and attacking, so on and so forth. Now, there are three quick gestures involved. The throw, the pulse, and the pull."

The woman stepped beside Bridget and repeated what she had said whilst making the motions—a motion as if throwing a rock, a pulse motion which was a flick of the wrist done at the end of the throw, and finally, once broken in, the hand-over-hand pulling motion.

"Now I want you to cast Reveal and watch the motion work in harmony."

Bridget splayed a hand. "Un vun asperio aurum enchantus." A slew of ancient enchantments, long sunk to permanence, lit up around the room. These included heating and torch runes and core defensive enchantments infused into the structure of the castle itself.

Mahmoute opened the door. "Sir Roberts. To me."

"M'lady," the young blue-eyed knight who had carried the tray in earlier awkwardly clanked inside. His brethren looked on from the hallway, most intrigued as to the goings-on inside. Mahmoute closed the door on them and indicated for the young man to stand by the window.

"Sir Roberts, you are going to act as our training dummy."

"Shall I unsheathe my sword, Black Eagle Mahmoute?"

"That will not be necessary, for the spell will not affect you."

"Why is that, m'lady?"

"Because, unless I am mistaken, you do not have a reservoir of stamina to drain, is that not so?"

"I do not have an arcane bone in my entire body," the young man replied proudly.

Mahmoute went to stand at the opposite end of the small room. "Just relax." She glanced at Bridget. "Mind the gestures," and did a slow-motion version of all three—the throw, the wrist snap, and then the hand-over-hand. She repeated these gestures three times before abruptly doing them in a fluid motion whilst incanting, "Arcan rosso!"

Bridget watched as a tendril vine capped with tiny hooks lashed forth at the young knight's soul. Most interestingly the Black Eagle had snapped her wrist even before the line attached, meaning the pulse, barely visible to the untrained eye, traveled along the line—and hit the knight nearly at the same time as the hooks. It was evidence of how skilled the woman was with the spell.

"The pulse serves as a battering ram," Mahmoute said, still making that hand-over-hand motion even though Bridget could see no energy being pulled from the knight's reservoir. "Note how careful I am with my movements. You can feel the line in your hands—there's a subtle tingling that you must pay attention to. If you miss grabbing hold of the line even once—" She pretended to miss the line, and it instantly vanished. "—you break the connection, and thus the spell. Now come, let me see you go through the motions."

Bridget nodded, stepped beside Mahmoute, and began the long process of perfecting the motions, knowing that the first attempt to actually cast the spell would come later. Sometimes, such spells took months—and even years—to learn. But Bridget, having experienced the spell against her in the war and being of a war-honed keen mind, hoped to perform it much sooner.

TINY GIRL

LEERA

Under the thick ice of Horren's Keep, amidst the swirling silty water, the pale light of Leera's glowing palm lit up an overturned chair. The intricately carved wood was intact, but the upholstery had long rotted away. She imagined a prim and proper young lady once sitting in that very chair, perhaps working an embroidery, reading a book about picking flowers, or waiting for a servant to bring tea.

A half-naked Leera, for she could not possibly swim with Revel's coat, swam onward in her linen undergarments. Since her vision under water was perfect on account of being a water warlock, her spectacles were folded and tucked into a pocket of those undergarments, specially sewn for such use.

As she swam, she checked in on herself that all was well, a habit competent water warlocks practiced regularly when diving. The freshly cast Endure the Deep spell kept the cold at bay and the Breathe Water spell allowed her to breathe water as she would air, which she did calmly, keeping her heart at a steady and low pace.

She was in balance, which also meant her stamina bled at a slow trickle. Done properly, she would have hours under water before either spell failed, at which point she would have to perform an emergency teleport, a very risky proposition in underwater ruins. Nonetheless, Revel promised to keep a fire lit in the ruins above for such a possibility.

She turned over and saw a light follow her above the ice—Revel, watching her every move. Leera waved, turned back over, and swam onward, passing old benches and what remained of tables, all strewn amidst the rubble of a collapsed keep. She got to a staircase, where she knew the real work would begin. Horren's Keep supposedly had a large cellar that went down quite a ways and was said to have many secret rooms. Getting to it, however, was another matter.

The rubble around the staircase was packed tight and was overgrown with moss, meaning this particular obstruction happened years ago — and hadn't been bypassed since. Maybe the last explorer to adventure through had caused it, who knew.

Trying not to think about getting buried alive under water, Leera hooked her feet behind a boulder, reached out, and telekinetically lifted one of the medium-sized stones. It rolled over its neighbor and clunked against another boulder with an underwater *thud*, creating a plume of silt. She repeated this with the other stones, digging farther and farther down, until all at once there came a great rumble and the central hole widened, for the stones below, which had been jammed up against each other, loosened enough to tumble down the stairwell.

After the chaos and the silt subsided, Leera looked up to see the blurry light of Revel standing directly above her. Revel gave a questioning wave, and Leera waved back once, indicating she was all right. She could almost hear Revel praying for her to come back alive. The poor girl had been very anxious watching Leera shrug off her coat, cast Endure the Deep and Breathe Water, and slip into the ice hole. And if something should happen to Leera, it was a long trek home.

Taking a deep but calming watery breath, Leera calmed her heart rate from the exertions and dove into the hole, barely wide enough for her body to slip through.

"Stupid hips," she muttered when they jammed amidst the boulders. But she dared not try to force herself through lest they cave in on her. Instead, she backtracked, turned ninety degrees, and tried again, this time slipping through without a hitch.

She emerged onto a checkered landing in between floors that was covered with rubble. Weaving past the ruins, she swam down two flights, appreciating the exquisite workmanship of the marble banister and how it sparkled in the watery light of her palm.

Although the stairs continued to descend, Leera swam out into the floor below. The ceiling here was high with thick crisscrossing beams, the walls old calcified brick. Some columns had collapsed into loose piles of debris, but most of the structure of the floor remained intact.

She swam into the central space, eyeing a rusty halberd lying on the checkered floor that was covered with silt. Just beyond were the remains of a long supper table flanked by what seemed like a hundred chairs in varying states of decomposition. She heard the echo of a party, a noble man having a gentle conversation with a blushing and dainty woman, the muted clink of cutlery as people feasted in the background.

Her eyes went to a nearby oaken door twice the height of a woman. The heavy thing hung halfway off its rusty hinges, one of many others that lined the hall. She swam up to it and peered inside. Her palm light revealed a room housing a huge pile of casks, most of which had been destroyed. They reminded her of her first adventure into Castle Arinthian, when she and Augum and Bridget had found a secret passage behind a large cask.

That gave her an idea, and she splayed her left hand, focused on communing with the sacred ether, and said, "*Un vun deo,*" the incantation to the wondrous 1st degree Unconceal spell. The spell was a favorite of the young, for it allowed one to sense the intent to conceal. Arcaneologists had long discovered that thought affected and infused itself into the ether, as did language and gestures, together forming the basis of spellcraft. But thought was also traceable and even readable to the trained mind, meaning if someone hid something, that intent could be homed in on.

The spell was thus a favorite of treasure hunters—but it also forced people to be clever with how they hid things. When possible, they hid things behind complicated arcane barriers or vaults that obscured that intent, or hid them far enough away that even the most experienced warlock could not pick up the tendril trail of intent.

Leera, thinking the place thoroughly plundered by now, had been expecting to feel very little, yet the opposite proved true—she felt a tug in almost every direction, mostly downward. There was so much hidden in the castle that her first thought was that it would be impossible to distinguish between the various tendril tugs.

How badly she wanted to cast Reveal! But her right hand was lit with Shine and her left with Unconceal, not to mention she was consciously holding up two other spells already—Breathe Water and Endure the Deep. She was already struggling to maintain them all, prioritizing of course the latter two. And she was only able to keep all four up because they were all low in degree—three 1st degree spells and one 3rd.

Still, Leera wanted to challenge herself, and so while she kept both hands splayed, she incanted, "*Un vun asperio aurum enchantus.*" Her palm light instantly snuffed and she lost the feeling of Unconceal—she had been juggling too much, and piling on an 11th degree spell had caused a collapse. Luckily the core water spells remained intact, for she had compartmentalized that part of her brain to keep a vigilant watch over them. It was a core tenet of water warlock training on how to keep such spells active in the background of one's mind.

Although plunged into pitch darkness, blue tendril webs nonetheless flared all around her—and they were dull, meaning the enchantments were old. The geometries indicated protective arcanery infused into the castle superstructure, long sunk to permanence and dormant. As she glanced about, once again reminded of Castle Arinthian as it had similar old enchantments—as did the Black Castle, for that matter—she absently drifted to the floor—and heard a *click* the moment her feet touched. She looked down and saw that one of her feet had stepped in a tendril patch of brown, which shot an icy bolt of fear down her spine, for brown meant summoning.

As a water warlock, one got attuned to the water around oneself, its taste, whether it warmed or cooled, but especially how it moved against the skin. And Leera felt the water pushing on her back. Instinctively she telekinetically snatched the closest wall and yanked herself aside, the violent motion breaking her concentration for the Reveal spell, snuffing it and once more plunging her into pitch darkness. Something sliced behind her and there came a *clang* as it struck the floor.

"*Shyneo!*" she incanted, lighting her palm and whirling about. There in the doorway stood a skeleton holding a rusted halberd, which it had swung. It raised it and moved toward her, slowed heavily by the water— had the place not been submerged, she very well might have died on the spot.

"Creepy bastard," Leera said, and slapped her wrists together, roaring, "*Annihilo!*" A jet of water shot forth and blasted the skeleton apart. Leera summoned her shield and a bunch of bones *thunked* against it. She nullified her shield in time to see the bones vanish, leaving the halberd to *clunk* to the floor.

"Great. Place is laced with traps." No wonder few got out alive.

She lit Reveal to her left hand and swam forth to study the trap, annoyed she did not have the mental capacity to keep Unconceal alive too. "Got a long way to go, girl," she told herself. But she'd also come a long way too. Gone were the days when a mere skeleton could pose a threat—unless, of course, it had the advantage of surprise.

"And you almost took my head off," she muttered, examining the trap.

The fading of the brown tendril weavings was not quite as pronounced as the walls, indicating the trap was not as old as the castle itself. But that was normal, for such castles had many owners throughout history. Interestingly, the trigger tendrils of this trap were renewing quickly, and that meant it had been cast with high competency. Judging by the speed of the tendril renewal, the trap would reset by the end of the day. A trap that renewed was a feat only a high-degree warlock was capable of casting, but one that renewed this quickly suggested it had been cast by someone very competent as well, perhaps even a master.

Unfortunately for Leera, she was nowhere near competent enough in the skill of arcaneology to determine who had cast these tendril weavings. That sort of skill was acquired over a lifetime of studying tendril geometries, comparing them to others, making detailed notes, and so on.

She left the room and noticed other traps, some barely visible through the silt, telling her she ought to be wary of where she placed her feet.

She swam from room to room, identifying a larder, a pantry, a kitchen, and various storage rooms, all long plundered, not surprising considering their closeness to the surface. Concluding there was nothing significant to gain on this level, she swam back to the staircase and descended to another floor. Although the staircase continued farther, she once again remained to explore. This time it was an underground training yard that sprawled across the entire level, broken only by the occasional brick column, rubble, and countless rusty training equipment—archery targets, rotten fencing, sanded dueling pits, wooden training dummies, and the like.

Thinking it would be a waste of time to explore all of it, she continued down to the next level, only to discover the stairs ended at a precipice. She brightened her palm light, which revealed the floor was missing entirely, having pancaked down onto the floor below.

"Now things get interesting," she said, picking up a rock that allowed her to drift down at a faster pace. Thirty feet below, her feet touched rubble. "And tricky," she added, knowing she could only keep two of the three spells she wanted to cast—Unconceal, Shine, and Reveal—alive. Feeling safe enough, she chose to snuff her light, keep Reveal lit, and recast Unconceal with the incantation, "*Un vun deo.*"

She again felt multiple tugs, so many it was tough to decide which direction to go. The stairway she had used was obliterated and crammed with rubble. Her best bet, she figured, was to find a way down that involved the least amount of work. Reveal showed nothing, so there was no point in keeping it lit. She might as well save the stamina and kill both.

"*Un vun null,*" she thus incanted, able to snuff Unconceal and Reveal at the same time as they shared the same phraseology. There were various ways to kill spells, but using the proper words or phrases was considered the cleanest and most efficient method.

"*Shyneo*," she then incanted, lighting her palm as she swam along the undulating piles of timber trusses, brick, mortar, stone blocks, and various remnants from above—a rusted furnace, a broken washbasin, pieces of a mirror, the door to a wardrobe, a bent tin supper plate, and a loose dresser drawer, among others.

Swimming about revealed nothing to her that would indicate a way down. She swam the perimeter wall, also of brick, and saw nothing interesting—until she spotted the crest of a word peeking out from the rubble. She drifted close, intrigued.

The top of the first and second letters were visible enough. "Starts with a *C* and is followed by an *R*," she said. Even under water, she felt the hairs on the back of her neck rise as she whispered, "Crypt ..."

Typical. Although she should have expected one, it was the last place Leera wanted to explore, and so she swam on, searching for any sign of another doorway. But the rubble was simply too dense, forcing her to return to the spot.

"Fine, *fine*," she muttered, and braced her feet against the largest nearby boulder and began telekinetically hauling rocks and boulders away from the sign. It was a tedious process that sucked precious stamina, which was already bleeding away due to the constant demands of the two active water spells and her Shine spell. Were she better at runecraft, one of her worst subjects at the academy, she would have crafted a torch rune to lend light to the work area. Nonetheless, she eventually found herself staring at a black hole of her own making, just large enough to squeeze through. Since she did not feel water suction pulling downward, she figured the crypt was completely submerged, and possibly a dead end.

She stuck her lit palm into it and peered inside, but the darkness stretched on. She brightened her light, yet only saw floating silt that she had disturbed by moving boulders.

Leera withdrew to check in on her stamina reservoir, feeling it was about half empty. The hole simultaneously called to her and warned her not to enter. But then she was here on a quest on how to nullify a curse that would reverse her being barren. It was thinking of herself and her beloved ten years down the road, the pair smiling whilst holding their newborn babe, that won her over. She swallowed and, with a kick of her feet, dove into the hole.

The silt swirled all about, shrinking visibility to only a few feet. She swam down slowly and carefully, keeping her lit palm forward, feet smoothly kicking at the water. Down into the murky depths she swam, expecting to come upon tombstones—but it was a rotting face that first appeared from within the silty gloom. She screamed out of pure reflex and slammed her wrists together, roaring, "*Annihilo!*" blowing apart the remains of an ancient skeleton.

Fighting the panic that had infused her soul, she desperately turned about, listening and searching for threats. Yet the water was silent. Forcing herself to calm down and hoping not to trigger a trap, she wincingly allowed her feet to touch the ground. When nothing happened, she waited for the silt to calm, drawing comfort from the flat stonework. Soon a sarcophagus revealed itself to her—and its lid was open.

"That's where you came from," she said to a thigh bone, telekinetically flicking it away. It tumbled off into the gloom. Her innards buzzing with childhood fears, she dared to drift closer to the lid of the sarcophagus, where she found an inscription.

Anita Jenemiah Horren
Died howling from black fever in the year 1551

"One thousand seven hundred and ninety-five years ago," Leera whispered after an arithmetical think, marveling at the vast gulf of time between then and now.

She moved on, swimming her way past obelisks and tombs and sarcophagi. A few were open—and some were empty. The rational part of her wanted to believe that the tombs had been robbed and left open, the bodies floating free after the place had flooded. But the little girl in her who had grown up hearing scary tales told around the fire—and the girl who had seen nightmares come to life as a teenager—thought a necromancer had come through stealing and raising bodies.

She kept a vigilant watch, her palm bright, limited only by the swirling silt. But her legs were starting to get tired from all the kicking, so she allowed herself to hop along the ground, figuring the odds were low of someone laying a trap here. Almost immediately, she heard another *click*. She reflexively glanced down but saw nothing, for she hadn't cast Reveal. She quickly dipped aside and hid behind a sealed tomb, allowing her skin to feel the water and her keen senses to tell her what to do.

That's what complacency got you, she thought.

As her stamina trickled away, the swirling hastened. Something was moving within the darkness ahead, perhaps drawn to her light. But no way was she going to snuff her palm and go blind here just so she could cast Reveal.

The swirling got more and more violent, until a huge claw swiped at the silt only three feet away, its long fingers slipping through the silt like a sieve. The arm dragged rotten cloth, and was so large it had to belong to a giant creature—a type Leera had last seen in the war with the Legion.

A wraith, a creature usually composed of multiple bodies.

Heart pounding against her chest, Leera slapped her wrists together, roaring, "*Annihilo!*" The jet of water split the silt and returned a sharp *thwack*, but she had no way of knowing if she had hit the monster, for visibility had dropped to a mere two feet, dangerously less than the beast's reach.

She kicked off, hissing, "*Akseler aqua loa,*" the incantation to the 2nd degree off-the-books Fast Swim, which allowed her to rapidly swim away while expending relatively little stamina. Deep *thuds* followed, as if the beast was knocking over tombs in search of her.

Completely lost amidst the silty darkness, she thought perhaps it was best to take the risk of teleporting through all those layers of rubble. After all, her stamina was depleting quickly. But she also knew she would have to deal with this beast if she wanted to continue the quest.

"Fine, you want a challenge?" she shouted into the gloom. "Here, eat this!" She meticulously drew a shape, incanting, "*Summano elementus minimus draco.*" A water dragon appeared before her, except because it was under water, it was merely an outline, a shimmer amidst the silt. It took to the water as if it were home, floating in place, flapping its wings as gently as a fish moved its fins.

"Where are you, you bonerag?" Leera whispered. "Where are you …"

The *thuds* came closer and closer, until a claw swiped from the gloom, slicing off one of the dragon's wings. The wraith shrieked in the water, a high-pitched sound like a chorus of screaming children.

Leera slammed her wrists together, roaring, "*Annihilo bato!*" sending two jets of the 8th degree Second Offensive at the wraith—and blowing off an arm. At the same time, her dragon tore into the monster's leg. The wraith swiped at the dragon with its remaining claw, slicing off its other wing.

Leera carefully aimed and slapped her wrists together, roaring, "*Annihilo!*" A jet of water shot forth—and slammed into the wraith's huge misshapen skull, exploding it. Instantly the monster sank to the ground, the wingless dragon still mauling it.

A panting Leera snorted a triumphant laugh. "Now *that* was a throwback," she said, referring to the war against the Legion—and their legions of undead.

She checked in with herself. She was down to a third of her stamina pool, and would need to find shelter soon to recuperate. "*Akseler null*," she incanted, snuffing the needless Fast Swim spell.

"Draco—defend me," she ordered, flicking a hand for the poor beast to follow her. Like a dog dropping its favorite bone, it turned about and awkwardly waddled along the silty bottom after her, leaving the wraith to vanish. After swimming two lengths, Leera abruptly turned about and drew the outline in reverse, incanting, "*Summano null*." The wingless dragon vanished. "Sorry, buddy, but I can't have you springing more traps," she said, and swam onward, cursing the silt, until she came upon a wall. From there, she swam alongside it, hoping to come across a doorway or passage—or anything that would lead her inside, and perhaps to a dry spot.

Just as she was about to give up and attempt a dangerous teleport topside, she came across an iron door. The door appeared completely sealed by its own rust, meaning there was a chance the other side was dry. Judging by the hinges, it opened inward too.

With her stamina rapidly running out, nearing the critical threshold that would force her to cast Teleport, she considered all her options, concluding the only way to move the quest forward was to use sheer force against the door. That meant either casting an offensive spell or the 8th degree Strength spell, which would amplify her muscles. She imagined turning the handle and it perhaps breaking off. The alternative was blowing the hinges and then the door. That would take three individual spell castings, whereas forcing the handle would only take one, draining less stamina.

"*Virafortamusala* it is," she muttered, using the ancient name for the Strength spell, something a graduate of the Academy of Arcane Arts was expected to practice on the regular. She flexed every muscle in her entire body, incanting, "*Virtus vis viray*," and felt those muscles strengthen massively. Then she planted a foot against the frame of the door, grabbed the ancient handle with both hands, and pushed it down. The handle squealed like a baby pig. Slowly, she could feel the old mechanism inside grinding.

There came a sudden *crack* from within, the handle swung down, and the door burst open, sucking her inside along with a torrent of gushing water. She tumbled along the ground, pushed by the raging water, but also aware there was air here. With no way to get ahead of the water, she had to simply go with it. It swept her down the corridor, which soon turned right, and pushed her along until she grabbed hold of a doorway. Still holding onto the Strength spell, she was able to haul herself through the torrent and around the doorframe, where she used the Strength spell to shut the iron door against the water.

Safe on the other side, she collapsed against the door, panting. The water sprayed inside from underneath and from around the edges, but judging by the room—what looked like a large servant's quarter, it would take longer to fill than she needed. The corridor she had tumbled along joined the crypt up with this servant's quarter, a bizarre choice of construction that made Leera think it must have been a creepy place to work as a servant. But at least she had a place to rest.

"*Virtus null, bratta null, endura null,*" she said, snuffing Strength, Breathe Water, and Endure the Deep, leaving only her palm lit. Next she reached into her specially sewn pocket, withdrew her spectacles, and placed them on her nose. Already shivering, she hauled herself up and took a look around. The vast room was filled with old bunk beds, tables and benches, and furnaces. She hurried to one of those furnaces, muttering, "Please let it be enchanted." Mercifully, all had a fire rune, which she promptly slapped, incanting, "*Igniato.*" The rusting old furnace burst with flame, and she sighed in relief as she absorbed the comforting warmth.

She ran a hand over her sodden undergarments, incanting, "*Evapa loa aqua,*" and surged the 4th degree off-the-books Evaporate, so that each piece quickly dried with a *thwoom*.

Dry again and basking in the luxury of the flame, she thought back on the journey in the corridor, and how the hallway veered rightward, she estimated she was once again underneath the main structure of the castle. She imagined the door to the crypts had been so rarely used—even in the castle's heyday—that it had rusted over from lack of use. No servant wanted to venture into a crypt. Sometimes not even warlocks, especially the superstitious kind, ventured near.

After getting sufficiently warm, she snuffed her palm, grabbed a bench, and hauled it over. As the water continued to spray into the room through the cracks around the door, she sat cross-legged on the bench and proceeded to meditate. While her stamina recovered at four times the rate, she thought about cuddling with Augum, Sir Pawsalot purring near their heads. She thought about how Augum's face would light up if her quest was successful, and the lineage would one day be able to continue. The more she thought about the countless possible futures that awaited them, the more giddy she became.

By the time she realized she hadn't checked the summonable vault to see if he'd sent a letter, the water had risen to the level of the bench. Having replenished most of her stamina, she stood on top of the bench and looked down at her filthy undergarments. "Not very pretty today, are we?" she muttered, not caring one hoof, and almost wishing she could stroll by that harpy Alanna Haught in exactly what she was wearing, hook an elbow with Augum, and lead him to the nearest bedroom—but not before stealing a glance at the surely fuming Haught woman.

The water lapped onto her toes and was rising quickly now. The door started to squeal and crack, the pressure increasing by the heartbeat. Not wanting to wait until it burst, she concentrated on the nuance of the Endure the Deep spell, incanting, "*Endura o prassa ata o codola.*"

She felt her innards thicken as the cold of the room instantly lessened, but she held off on casting the Breathe Water spell, wanting to explore this area. What she could really use was a map, and she wished she had had the foresight to dig for one in the archives, which were stuffed with maps of old castles.

Then another idea came to her. Not casting Breathe Water allowed her to chronocast two other spells she hadn't been able to incant in tandem earlier—Unconceal and Reveal. With the furnace still providing some light, she flared her left hand, incanting, "*Un vun deo.*" She waited a moment, tuning to the arcane ether, and soon felt a whole jumble of tugs going every which way. She then splayed her right hand, incanting, "*Un vun asperio aurum enchantus,*" and saw the usual castle tendril geometries flare along the walls and floor—and around the various furnaces strewn about the room.

Wading through the knee-deep waters, she followed the strongest pull of the bunch, which took her to a rotting wardrobe. She opened the door and found it empty. Realizing the pull came from beyond, she stepped back, latched on telekinetically, and pulled the heavy wardrobe away from the wall. Then she continued following the pull along the wall behind it until she found a single brick—and embedded directly into that brick was a copper coin, only the serrated edge of which was visible.

Leera gaped at the coin, utterly bewildered. It must have been accidentally embedded into the brick upon the castle's founding. *No, that makes no sense*, she thought, for accidents did not trigger the Unconceal spell, meaning this coin had been purposely hidden.

"Maybe it meant luck in wealth or something," she muttered. People back then were far more superstitious.

As the water rose to her thighs and the still-hot furnace hissed upon those waters touching its hot iron, she moved on to the second-strongest pull, located behind the most distant furnace in the room. There, in the dim light that emanated from the rabidly hissing furnace, she found another coin embedded into the brick. She gaped at it, shaking her head in confusion, before realizing its purpose.

"You clever bastard," Leera whispered. Someone, likely Horren himself, had hidden thousands of coins throughout the castle for the sole purpose of obfuscation. With so many pulls on Unconceal, it would be extremely difficult to untangle them all and find the ones that led to something valuable.

"A genius defense tactic that pretty much defeats Unconceal," she said aloud, turning about and pretending to be telling this revelation to a whole class of students. Except there was no one there, only water that kept rising.

At last, the furnace went out with a steaming *hiss*, plunging her into pitch darkness. Leera heard the door straining and cracking, prompting her to nullify Unconceal and Reveal—and just as she did so, the door burst open, allowing a torrent of water to rage into the room. She barely had time enough to slip her spectacles into her pocket before the water rose to her neck.

She focused on being able to breathe water as she could air, and incanted, "*Bratta fil aqua,*" followed by, "*Shyneo,*" which lit up her palm. She dipped her head below the water and allowed the current to push her around in a whirlpool. When the violence stabilized and the water filled up to the roof, she swam out into the corridor, and allowed the water to push her along. The fact that the water was moving indicated it was still filling out spaces—there had to be a lot of rooms and hallways in this direction.

She passed various rooms, choosing to ignore them as she doubted there would be anything worthy of exploring along a corridor that had already shown a servant's quarter. The water pushed her along, and the corridor turned right again. After a few more rooms, the water joined other water in a winding stairwell. She knew this because the water below was slightly colder and stiller.

She swam down into that colder water, her innards armored against the frigidity, her breathing relatively calm, even though she feared that the deeper she descended, the more difficult the teleport out would be. Already she estimated she was five or six levels below the surface.

Although the stairwell allowed entry to other floors, all of which showed signs of destruction, Leera kept descending, mentally counting the levels as she went, the pressure steadily increasing with each floor. *Seven ... eight ... nine ... ten.* At the tenth floor below ground level, the stairwell ended before a pair of rusted iron doors, one of which stood open and bent in half, as if a giant fist had pounded it.

No doubt done by a treasure explorer of old, she thought, wondering if it had happened before or after the flooding. She swam through the door, and was surprised to see her light shining into darkness, which encompassed the entire area. She felt a yawning depth below her, one that would have sent a novice explorer scurrying back. But to Leera, that depth excited her, and she dove, eager to discover what lay below.

Down, down, down she swam, her light at maximum eye-piercing brightness. At last, with the pressure at such a degree that she would have been crushed without the protection of the Endure the Deep spell, her light revealed a huge pile of rubble. It seemed that the floors above had once again pancaked onto the floors below. Her best estimate, judging by the mighty pressure, was that she was a whopping twenty levels below the surface.

Down here the water was near freezing but at least it was also still and clear, allowing for good visibility. Once her feet touched a boulder, she checked in on herself, making sure all was in balance, before swimming onward to explore. The area was vast and cavernous. The rubble here was mostly composed of bricks, meaning it had come from above, along with everything else—floorboards, broken frames of paintings, practice dummies, shattered vases, countless pieces of furniture, and so on.

With each item, she imagined a life interacting with that object. A woman sitting for a portrait, smiling coyly at her painter. An archer practicing shooting arrows at a target, brow beaded with sweat. A potter turning a wheel, shaping a vase. A cobbler carving out a wooden sandal. And countless workers slaving over floorboards and doorways and ornate friezes.

Halfway through navigating the cavernous walls and finding nothing, she decided to still herself atop a boulder, splay her left hand, and incant, "*Un vun deo.*" Once again, she felt pulls in various directions, but not nearly as many as above. She decided to follow ten of the strongest, and found brick after brick embedded with a coin, finding twenty on this low floor alone. The vast majority of the remaining pulls tugged upward, with only a select few tugging downward. It was those three downward pulls she focused on, and two of those were strong, meaning they were near—and likely also coins embedded into bricks. The third was the weakest, and therefore the deepest. It was that subtle arcane tug that led her to a corner of the cavern.

The rock here was well covered with underwater moss and lichen, meaning it had been under water for some time, perhaps hundreds of years, a good sign that it had remained undisturbed for that long. She looked along the wall, hoping to find another inscription like the one for the crypt, but there was nothing. There was only one thing left to do—dig.

And dig she did, telekinetically lifting one boulder at a time and dumping it aside, steadily creating a hole about the width of a thin well. Even with the aid of war-honed Telekinesis, it was backbreaking labor, and by the time the hole was ten feet deep, her back was killing her.

Sitting at the watery bottom and wary of boulders caving in on her, she checked in on herself, finding her stamina about half depleted. She figured she could maintain digging until she got to two-thirds empty before she would have to reassess, and so she continued on, grabbing one boulder at a time and heaving it up top.

A short ways farther down, she spotted something, only for the rubble around her to rumble menacingly. She had a moment to summon her water shield above her, expand it to a large size, and wedge one edge into the cavern wall before the first boulder smashed into the shield, slamming the shield against her body, which smushed up against the cavern wall. Boulders continued to rain down, squeezing her between her shield and the cavern wall, and causing her to cry out in pain.

Just as quickly as it had begun, the rumbling ceased, leaving behind an overwhelming pressure. Squeezed into this tiny space, Leera could barely breathe. It seemed that the quest had come to an end, and she would have to attempt a dangerous teleport out.

Except that her light glinted against something below her. She shimmied her head against the rock and her shield until she laid eyes on something she could hardly believe, for she was looking at a small golden door with a horizontal slot bisected halfway by a hole. Embossed above was the word *Letters*.

A mailbox. The slot was for folded letters and the bisecting hole was for scrolls. Such things were common in castles, wherein a warlock or herald would routinely scour the boxes, collect all the mail, and have it sent on its way by horse or by warlock courier.

Because the tug of Unconceal angled deep beyond the mailbox, Leera suspected it doubled as a point of entry, and that the mailbox door was actually an ancient door meant for *Tinnimelatonadescoteya*—otherwise known as the Shrink spell. Meaning no one would have been able to get through this miniature door for ages. The knowledge of how to cast Shrink had been lost for centuries, until the trio had helped resurrect it during the Canterran war—a small point of pride for each of them.

There was only one problem—how to cast the Shrink spell and survive this quandary of possibly being buried alive? She thought about the mechanics of the spell and knew that whatever spells she had going would also shrink with her, and that included her shield, meaning the boulders would collapse onto her and crush her to smithereens. Somehow, she had to figure out a way to jam them together, and the only way to do that was to nudge them in place. She wished she could cast the Leyan spell Centarro to solve the puzzle, but the fog-inducing side effects would force her to lose her grip on the water spells that kept her alive.

Unless you solve all of it, including how to open the door and slip through, before the fog wins you over, she thought. What a bold and reckless plan that would be! *You can always teleport out if you think it won't work,* she thought, arguing with herself. *Don't want to waste all this progress, which you may never achieve again. Do it for your future husband and children.*

That did it, and she studied the boulders around her, trying to maintain a steady breathing rhythm throughout. Considering the circumstances, this would be her most dangerous casting of Centarro since the war years ago. She would be gambling everything on a future that held no guarantees.

She felt her heartbeat, heard the high-pitched sound of blood quietly rushing through her ears, felt the way her bones and flesh squished between the cavern wall and her shield, the way the water tasted of old iron and wood and stone and moss, how deathly quiet and still it was down here deep below the surface. With the requisite awareness complete, she took a deep watery breath and incanted, *"Centeratoraye xao xen."*

Immediately her senses sharpened, her focus most profoundly of all. Time seemed to go still, and her heart was like slow rolling waves of thunder that drummed against her chest. She studied the boulders visible around her shield. Unfortunately, it quickly became clear that there was no way to move the boulders, at least not with her powers in Telekinesis and Strength. The moment her shield vanished, she would be crushed to death.

Relax and focus, she told herself, closing her eyes, keeping her breathing balanced with the various pressures on her body. She thought of spell permutations, but none seemed feasible.

Knowing it sometimes helped to let the creative power of Centarro do the legwork, she allowed her mind to wander. She thought of a quaint house, which quickly morphed into a tarred castle, then that castle appeared on top of a snowy mountain, and she saw herself on its terrace, gray starting to creep into her long raven hair, and her husband Augum joined her, smiling with joy—and then her heart leaped when three little children, two girls and a boy, joined them, and each of them had a puzzle which they were trying to piece together and she heard herself say to the littlest girl, "Don't let Mama or Papa solve it for you. You can do it, little one," and the tiny girl squealed and blurted, "I wanna glue it!" and Leera and Augum laughed.

Leera opened her eyes, whispering, "I wanna glue it ..." Seeing the lines and spaces between boulders, it hit her. *Glufusioboundera*, she thought, using the ancient name for the standard 6th degree spell Seal. Gods, what a simple solution too! The spell didn't just work on the spaces between doors, which was the typical use for the spell—as a ward against thieves and invaders—but it worked between any two objects.

She pointed a finger at the nearest line between boulders and incanted, "*Obdura del boundera sen*." She squiggled that finger, making complex but invisible tendril geometries that bound the two surfaces together like glue. She continued drawing along every space between boulders that she could see, right to the edge of the shield, tendril-binding them together.

Then came the Centarric breakthrough, for she realized she could slowly—very slowly—shrink her shield. Such control was only available to the experienced warlock—and Leera was *just* competent enough.

She shrank the edge of the shield and continued binding the seams between rocks. Miraculously, it worked, mostly because the boulders she had already sealed together now wedged against each other, creating a sort of boulder arch of solid rock. By the end of her Seal work, she was able to vanish her shield.

But there was no time to celebrate. Now able to move her arms somewhat freely in the cramped space, she turned her mind to casting the complex Shrink spell. After readying the complex mental details, which included precise pronunciation and mental visualization, made easier by the focus-enhancing effects of Centarro, Leera began with the delicate gesture, for it dictated the ratio of shrinkage. Carefully, she pressed her fingers together, pointed them to the top of her head, and dragged them down along her scrunched body whilst incanting, "*Smolla boda infintessima axteney su*."

Due to the way the spell worked on bones and flesh and organs, the shrinking was incredibly painful, much like thousands of needles stabbing into every bone and muscle. It took all of her focus not to scream. And as she shrank, the water and space around her seemed to expand greatly.

At a crucial point when she was about the size of a mouse, she stopped the movement of her hand, halting the spell. As per the laws of arcanery, size came with a cost paid in relativity. The water felt thicker, her voice when spoken was a mousy—and amusing—squeak, and her palm light, which had been bright prior to shrinking, now barely lit up the boulders. The previously tight space around her now felt cavernous.

While she floated about, she took a brief moment to gather her nerve and forget the awful pain. Luckily, the Shrink enchantment possessed the property of *continuity*, meaning it would last until nullified or disenchanted. That meant Leera did not have to focus on it or worry about it expiring. Ancient records were filled with humorous and tragic stories of people living out their lives as tiny versions of themselves, sometimes because they got injured and could not revert, or because another had cast the spell on them and confined them somewhere, or whatnot.

After calming herself, and mind still sharp and laced with Centarro, she swam up to the golden door. The slot was wide enough to fit most letters and the hole large enough to fit most scrolls.

Leera smiled, for the scroll hole appeared just large enough for her to squeeze through. She swam up to it and looked inside, finding a plain space carved into the cavern itself, a mailbox now the size of a room. She hooked her tiny hands on the fat golden edge and pulled herself inside, only for her stupid hips to again jam against the sides.

"Are you jesting me?" she squeaked, pulling every which way, desperate to get through. She was gambling on finding dry ground on the other side where she could suffer through the side effects of Centarro; otherwise, she would drown. "Are you *jesting* me!" she repeated, face reddening from the strain as she fought with the edge of the hole. But it was no use. "Damn hips!" she squeaked, smacking them. What made Augum whistle appreciatively was now firmly in her way.

Panting, she telekinetically lashed out, snagged the stone wall opposite the mailbox door, and pulled with all her might. She screamed from the strain whilst feeling the flesh on her hips tear alongside a bit of the linen cloth of her undergarments. Finally she felt herself slip through.

Gasping from the effort but acutely conscious of the sands of the hourglass trickling toward fogginess, she splayed a hand and incanted, "*Un vun asperio aurum enchantus.*" The far wall instantly lit up with a blue tendril field the size of a miniature door.

"Gotcha," she squeaked, swimming up to it and studying the tendril web, which was made up of about fifty separate and thin tendril slices. Instantly she recognized what it was she was looking at.

"A kargeyasnara," Leera whispered, the name for a slip-rune sequence puzzle that would only trigger after slotting all the pieces of the runes back into place. Due to their complexity, kargeyasnaras had gone out of fashion centuries ago and were exquisitely difficult to solve, at least without a hint.

"Maybe I came across a hint already," she whispered, studying the tendril geometries closely, Centarric mind singing with creativity. That mind stepped back to take in the whole. This was a mailbox, but also doubled as an entrance into a lord's secret vault or whatnot. Therefore, the rune it formed had to be something personal and memorable not only for that lord, but for his entire lineage. Therefore, there would be something in the records for that lineage to find.

She began to slide the pieces about, which involved simply touching and moving the pieces of runes around, trying to get edges to fit together, all while hundreds of words flashed across Leera's thoughts. Her Centarric mind worked feverishly, and she constantly whispered possibilities. "… Horren … keep … mail slot … mailbox … castle …" Normally, it would be extremely difficult to get an edge to match, but Leera's Centarric brain, a beacon fire of creativity, found one edge that slotted together, and then another, and then another and another, until she had solved ten pieces, forming a fifth of the entirety of the rune word.

While her hand moved quickly to piece together more edges, she tilted her head and tried to guess the rune word—and felt her mind start to slow. Centarro was winding down, meaning she had little time to spare.

The pattern she had slotted together formed what appeared to be an unfinished letter *M*. "But it could be upside down," she said, and turned the runic piece over. Sure enough, the *M* was actually two lowercase *r*'s. "Horren," she whispered, slotting in the rest of the word. Except it kept going. Horren*something*, with a series of letters at the end. "Has to be Horren's ancient name," she whispered, hand slowing down badly, the fog creeping into her vision from the edges, simplifying complexities into inanities.

She had come across the name in her research too. She wanted words to flash across her mind, but it was more like the pages of a book slowly being turned, with only one word a page visible. Then her hand fumbled together another edge, and she saw the letters *c* and *a* together, and it hit her. She quickly slotted the remaining pieces into place and read the word aloud to herself.

"*Horrenocastlo*." Horren's Castle. That was it. Simple.

Once complete, the rune word flashed with white light, activating. The entire wall of runes then swung inward, admitting in water—and sucking a dully thinking Leera right along. She tumbled down a short corridor before her body came up against a series of stairs. She barely managed to climb those stairs and flop onto a landing just above the waterline, which was halted by the ceiling of the passage, the geometry of the hallway acting as an air pocket.

Gasping, and mind devolving to that of a simple child's, Leera nonetheless smiled.

She was in.

GAZING INTO THE SOUL

AUGUM

Following bloody footprints, Augum scrambled up the slope, still haunted by the large patch of frozen blood and guts and fur and a shredded amber robe he had stumbled upon back on the road. A sputtering flame of hope desperately wanted him to believe that the robe did not belong to his party.

The tracks led him to a piney forest, where he found a slew of footprints compacted into a grove splattered with blood—the scene of a second altercation. But what sent his heart thudding to his boots was that he only found one type of footprint that led away from the scene—and they were all wolven.

A suddenly shaky and clammy Augum fell to his knees in the bloody snow. "This is where they died," he whispered. Bridget's betrothed—and Augum's best friend—Olaf Hroljassen. The order's healer, Jengo Okeke. And of course his mentor, Jezebel Terse.

Such a thing was unfathomable. What would he tell Jengo's wife? They had just married, for Unnameables' sake! And how would he even face Bridget?

The more he thought about it, the sicker he felt, until he wanted to keel over and retch—only to spot something of interest.

One pair of human footprints faced north, away from the melee. Augum, a better tracker than most having trained under a diligent mentor in his youth and then taken Survival class at the academy, quickly analyzed them. They stood there on the outside of the fight without more footsteps continuing forth, or even turning back about. And their size and depth indicated they likely belonged to his mentor, Jez. Could it be she had cast Group Teleport mid fight and got the lot of them to safety?

If so, it had likely been a rushed casting, perhaps even to a spot within line of sight—a battle 'port. And Jengo, being a healer, would then have healed them. By gods, they could still be alive!

He shot to his feet, planted himself in those footprints, and looked due north. The peaks of mountains pierced gray clouds that moved along at a glacial pace. Squinting, he could just make out a wide mountain ledge in the distance that would be an ideal hop point. He went through the requisite visualizations and snapped off, "*Impetus peragro*," soon appearing on that exact ledge, but two feet above the snow—and snuggly landing on it.

He glanced around. Sure enough, a mere fifty feet away lay snow disturbed by humans. Hope rose like sunrise, and he ran to the spot. He found more blood there, as well as indentations in the snow as if a body had lain there, likely where healing had taken place. He counted the footprints and expelled a massive sigh of relief upon seeing three distinct pairs—all three party members were alive. And since the footprints remained confined to that small area, he deduced they must have teleported once again. Sure enough, amidst those footprints, he saw that at one point they had all faced inward, meaning they had held hands in a circle.

Identifying which footprints belonged to Jez was key. Jengo was tall and lean, Olaf stubby and large, and Jez was of average size and weight. Judging the three pairs before him, he figured the ones that faced north were hers. He stepped into them and looked along the sight line, wondering what they had been planning. Surely not an attack on the wolven. More likely, they had healed up and continued their search for him.

"Which means Jez would search for the farthest point she could teleport to safely," he said aloud, squinting into the distance. But there were quite a few peaks to choose from along his line of sight. "So which one makes the most sense?"

He checked with the footprints, making sure he was exactly in their place, before pointing forth. His finger landed in the middle of a distant peak. "What height, though?" he asked himself, guessing she would have chosen the same altitude as this location.

The hop would be dangerous, but he needed to find them before the wolven did. And so he again went through the appropriate visualizations before snapping off the incantation to Teleport. This time, he appeared ten feet above the snow, but it was just low enough to avoid injury, for the snow was deep and soft. After climbing out of the hole he had made, he searched about—and spotted another set of prints about a hundred feet down the slope.

Once he got to them, he inspected their configuration and again guessed which ones belonged to Jez. They faced northwest, at a closer peak. He successfully teleport-hopped there, found another group of prints at the same altitude and on a similar ledge, and hopped a fourth time.

He repeated this maneuver no less than six more times, taking breaks to meditate often to replenish his stamina, and backtracking when he could not find footprints.

At dusk, exhausted and ready to camp for the night somewhere even though it was still relatively early hour-wise, he made one last hop toward a northern peak—and received a shriek in the ear upon *thwomping* into existence.

"Gods!" he gasped, stumbling away and raising his arms in attack formation out of trained instinct.

"It's us it's us it's us!" Olaf shouted, arms waving about for him not to fry them with lightning. Whereas Jez's and Jengo's robes peeked out from underneath their furs, he was dressed only in furs.

Augum could hardly believe it, for he was staring at three wonderful friends.

"You're alive, monkey!" Jezebel Terse shouted, and shot to him, lifted him aloft, and whirled him about as if he were her child, which, being an orphan, he sometimes felt like. "We were just discussing how to best move forward in search of you."

Olaf and Jengo promptly joined in, forming a group hug that had Augum wheezing for breath. "Whoa, whoa, whoa, there," he said, trying to pry himself away.

While Olaf and the gangly Jengo let go to beam at him, Jez held him by the shoulders to glance him over. "You're alive," she repeated, breath reeking of wine. "Thank the gods." When viewed from the rear, people sometimes mistook Jez for Leera, for she had shoulder-length raven hair and a similar slouch. But while she also had dark eyes and a mischievous demeanor, she lacked the freckles that were sprinkled across his beloved's face—not to mention Jezebel was taller and around twenty years older than Leera, who sometimes likened her to a fun but crazy aunt.

Olaf and Jengo formally stood together and pressed three fingers over their hearts. "Commander," each said.

Augum mirrored the salute. "Dragoons." He noted that all three of them had puffy eyes; they had not been sleeping well. Whereas the ebony-skinned Jengo had his usual worried look, for he was the worrying type as most healers were, the bulky Olaf wore a gregarious smile, his blond and unruly hair peeking out from under his fur hood, blond eyebrows scraggly.

Jez pressed fists into her waist and cocked her head, wavering in place. "What's the news on the kids? Tell me this wasn't all in vain."

Augum flicked his shoulder, drawing attention to his rucksack. "I'm carrying them."

"Oh." The fists slipped off Jez's waist. "Oh, dear. Ashes?"

"Blood. And their robes. I was thinking of placing the blade before the families."

"That wouldn't be appropriate," Jez replied, hands clasping above her belly. "They weren't in your service. The fools at the academy who should have trained them better ought to be the ones to return the vials."

"I'll think about it." For some reason he had been set on returning the remains to the families, but perhaps she was right. He was merely a courier, and the academy authorities maybe ought to take over.

"And no more of these quests, kiddo," Jez snapped, playfully drumming Augum's cheeks with her hands. "Not without more precautions. To think we got accosted by none other than wolven and then all got lost—" She jabbed a finger into his chest. "I *know* you got lost. Fess up, monkey. How bad did it get? Did you cast *the spell*?" She squinted her eyes and made a show of bobbing her head about as she searched his eyes for signs of guilt. "Did you take flight and wreak havoc?"

He looked away. "No, but I came close."

"Don't sound so morose. You've gotten yourself out of worse binds. Besides, this reunion calls for a celebration," and she threw off her rucksack and fished out a nearly empty bottle of wine. Before Augum could speak, she'd taken a long swig and offered him the bottle.

"Er … no thank you. We still have to teleport."

"Oh, she ain't 'porting anywhere," Jengo muttered, miming raising a bottle several times to his lips behind Jez's back.

"We set up camp in an old cave around the bend," Olaf added, thumbing over his shoulder.

Jez ignored them both. "We were worried *sick* about you, sunshine." She stiffened and pressed a hand over her heart. "Er, I mean, Commander." She burped into her fist. "I keep forgetting you're not fifteen anymore. But you know I love you, right? With all my heart."

Augum sighed as he looked to Jengo. "Let's exchange stories while we pack your camp, then teleport home."

"Never have I heard sweeter words, Three Toes," Olaf replied, playfully smacking Augum on the shoulder. "The north is a chilly place—and I don't just mean the weather. Ain't no place for Endyear, anyway. I say we hit the tavern when we get back. I need some ale and a good roast. The only thing to eat around here is biscuit beef and mirko. And those wolven aren't exactly great hosts."

"Almost carved us Nodian smiles," Jengo added, drawing a finger across his throat while Olaf nodded, mimicking the gesture.

They began to walk, and Jez hooked an arm around Augum's neck, crooning, "I'm *so* glad I don't have to be the sober teleporter anymore." She took a swig of wine, stumbling as she did so, forcing Augum to grab hold of her to keep her up. "Thanks, kiddo. Last bottle, promise. Perfect time to go home. Pain in the butt teleporting back and forth to buy these."

As they talked about their adventures, Augum helped strike camp, noting that the cave the camp resided in had once belonged to a snow bear—or so he judged based on the smattering of bleached mirko bones by the entrance.

"You *what*?" Jez shrieked upon Augum informing her that he had been sold to The Dishonored in arcane manacles. "You weren't supposed to let yourself get disarmed!" she roared, throwing the empty bottle against the wall, where it smashed into pieces that tinkled against the icy floor. "What were you *thinking*?"

"I know, I know, it was a gamble."

"A gamble? *A gamble?* It was *reckless!* You're a commander now. You can't make stupid decisions as if you're still fifteen. It was supposed to be a *trekanasola* and a *proata mentora*, not some sort of … of … is there an old word for *reckless suicide quest*? Anyway, my point stands."

"Jez, take it easy," Olaf muttered. "He came out all right, didn't he?"

Jez ignored him and jabbed two fingers into Augum's chest, hissing, "Understand me, kiddo?"

Augum, surprised at his mentor's ferocity, only nodded. He felt an aching sadness for her, for he had come to discover she had wanted a family with the man she had fallen in love with—a man who had died in the war. They shared that in common. Two souls, two generations apart, unable to carry on their bloodlines. Unable to feel the joy of laughing children. The funny thing was, Jez had always said she hated children.

A weaving Jez looked to the shattered bottle longingly. "We need to get back. Anyone know how to teleport?"

Jengo cleared his throat, voice soft with anguish. "We all know how to teleport, Jez. But only Augum's been granted Group Teleport privileges …" He winced. "Remember?"

Jez blinked at him. "Of *course* I remember. You think I'm stupid?"

"No, I just—"

"Then shut up! Gods, it's like dealing with little brats," she muttered, and went to demolish her tent with her fists.

Augum watched her beat the tent to a pulp, squish it down into a messy blob, and try to jam it into her rucksack. Unable to continue watching her struggle, he offered to help. To his surprise, she let him, slumping back against the frozen wall to stare vacantly through him. As Augum repacked her tent into a neat roll, he continued telling them about his adventures.

"Wait, wait, wait, back up," Jez said, reanimating. "So something snuffed arcanery and unlocked your manacles?"

"Yes," and Augum explained everything he had seen while he slowly squeezed her tent roll into her rucksack.

"Arcaneologically speaking, it shouldn't be possible," Jengo said. "Not without a scion."

"Well, it happened." Augum placed Jez's rucksack beside her and gave her knee a double-tap.

She thanked him with a distant nod.

"I know, I'm just …" Jengo massaged his forehead with the tips of his long fingers. "I guess I don't understand."

"Oh, and Bridget sent word that something similar happened in Blackhaven." All three of them knew about the vault, so he was free to talk about the messages.

Olaf perked up. "She all right?"

"She's fine. Misses you. There's, uh, something else too."

Olaf and Jengo exchanged worried looks.

Augum rubbed his frizzled chin. "I was wrong about the nobility and, in particular, the royals. Because of our support for the throne, I genuinely thought they'd never ask this of us."

"Ask what?" Olaf pressed. "Spit it out, Three Toes."

Augum took a subconscious step back from Jez, unsure if now was the right time to let her in on this news. She looked up at him, lip already curling with anger. "Maybe I'll tell you later—"

"Spit it out, *Three Toes*," Jez mocked. "Or do I have to beat it out of you?"

He knew she was jesting, but it still hurt his feelings to hear her in this state. "They want to use us dragons to expand the kingdom—"

"Gods be damned, I *knew* it!" Jez roared, shooting to her feet and storming about like a whirlwind. "Unnameables *know* I said it, didn't I? *Didn't I!* Where? Where do they want to invade first?"

Augum flipped a hand in an *I don't know manner*.

"So they just want to expand the kingdom, is that what you're telling me? Are you jesting?"

"I hardly know how to jest, you know that."

Olaf thumbed between Augum and the cave entrance. "His sense of humor these days is about as dry as these here bones."

"This isn't supposed to be funny, fatso!" Jez snapped.

"Whoa, whoa, whoa, easy there, Jez," Jengo said, palms raised. "Let's not get ourselves up in a huff and accidentally hurt feelings."

"Piss on your feelings." Jez squeezed her eyes shut as she pinched the bridge of her nose. "I need a drink."

Augum wanted to say, *No, you don't*, but didn't dare stoke her anger further, for she was a cauldron ready to boil over. It hurt that she was hardly a mentor these days. It hurt seeing her in so much pain that she felt the need to drown herself in the bottle. And it hurt that he had to take care of someone twice his age and who he loved like an aunt—sometimes even like a mother.

"Let's finish up. I'll take us home," Augum mumbled. He could command an entire order. Set people straight with a single look. Yet he couldn't do a thing about his anguished mentor. With a sigh, he splayed his hands over the bottle shards.

"Why bother?" Jez snapped.

"Don't want to leave a trace," Augum replied, focusing on seeing the bottle whole again. "*Apreyo*," he incanted, and the shards jumped back together, fusing with a final sealing light. He then tossed the bottle to Olaf, who caught it and stuffed it into his rucksack.

While they each snacked on a chunk of biscuit beef Jengo had handed out, Augum finished telling his tale, and how he had made a connection with the wolven that could be utilized for better relations, perhaps even trade. Then Olaf and Jengo took turns recounting their adventures, how they had attempted to track Augum but lost his trail after he was taken captive in that town. From there, it was a long saga about struggling in the wilds, teleport-hopping about blindly whilst avoiding packs of mirko and wolven and stray bears and tigers and mountain lions, and barely surviving the wolven attack.

"Bastards shredded my robe," Olaf noted with a mouthful, hauling his rucksack over his shoulder. "Lucky I got spares back at home."

"You mentioned you got close to casting *the spell*," Jez said, standing and dusting the snow off her butt with her hands. "*How* close?"

Augum felt the shadow peek out from his mind. "Too close."

"You're casting it too much, then."

"Maybe, but I didn't think I was—"

"No maybes about it. No more sky quests for a while. You're grounded. Literally."

Olaf winced.

"Spit it out, sausage hands."

"You're not his mother, Jez. He's commander of the Arcaner order. I mean this with all due respect, Jez, but you can't tell him what to do."

Jez squared up to the young man, hissing, "I'm his godforsaken mentor. You hear me? *His mentor.*"

"I know you are, but that doesn't mean you can tell him what to do—"

"Damn right it does! Damn *right* it does. I'm also a 17th degree warlock—that's a *grandmage*, kiddos! He's a mere 10th. Sure, he had a few scraps and adventures, but he's still a fresh graduate and only twenty years old, a kid playing man who is largely ignorant to the ways of the world. A mere babe in the arts, all things considering."

"A war-honed 10th degree is hardly a novice," Olaf retorted.

"And the correct term for a 10th degree is *adept*," Jengo threw in.

"Enough," Augum said as Jez ballooned. "We'll talk about it later." In truth he would avoid that as it would mean having to set Jez straight and thus hurt her feelings. He wanted her to feel like she could still command him about and pretend to ground him. He wanted that loving mother figure that she could be to keep him safe from the expectations of his kingdom. But above all, he cherished her ability to brutally and honestly speak her mind to him, something very few others had the temerity to do to a commander and war hero and "dragon."

Jez snarled at Augum. "Link up. You too, beanstalk. Move it, bacon fat."

"I'll be teleporting us though," Augum reminded, taking her hand and Olaf's.

"I *know* that!" Jez replied in a hurt voice that indicated otherwise.

Too drunk to even recall moments prior, Augum thought in dismay.

Jez let go of him to sternly hold up two wiggling fingers before his face.

"A hop and a meditation, I know," Augum said, gently grabbing hold of her hand and lowering it. The 17th degree spell sucked so much stamina that, for a particularly long hop, he could easily find himself down three-quarters of his reservoir. Thus he would have to meditate before performing another hop.

He focused on his first stop, visualizing the conditions and the snow and the terrain, and incanted, "*Impetus peragro grapa lestato exa exaei.*"

The group vanished and reappeared with a *thwomp* on the road, at the top of the valley that looked down upon the first altercation. The sky here was dark, but the snow glittered in the little starlight that shone through the thick cloud banks. A bitter wind rustled the trees, making Augum long for a hot bath with his beloved.

Olaf nodded at the spot. "Surprised us good there."

"Barely got away," Jengo added. "All thanks to this one," and he elbowed Jez, who was staring into the valley with a furrowed brow. "Jez?"

"Mmm?"

"All right there?"

"What are you gawking at, kiddo? Get to meditating so we can keep moving. Sick of everyone's whining. Sick of this quest. Sick of babysitting. Sick of crabapple wine."

Augum exchanged a silent look with Olaf and Jengo, not even needing to urge them to remain silent. They loved Jez almost as much as he did, and it surely hurt them to see her this way.

As the others silently stood watch, with Jez stabbing the snow with a long stick whilst muttering under her breath, Augum sat down, crossed his legs, closed his eyes, emptied his mind, and listened to the snowy conifers sway to a cold wind. He let his thoughts drift without indulging in any particular line of thinking. He did not pursue memories or longings and kept still. Done optimally, meditation renewed stamina at four times the rate. But if one allowed distraction, that rate slowed.

"Done yet, kiddo?" Jez asked.

Augum tried not to sigh. "Halfway there."

"Maybe I should give it a go then—"

"No!" all three boys simultaneously shouted.

"Bunch of party spoilers," Jez muttered.

Some time later, Augum stretched and yawned and got up.

"Finalllly," Jez sang. "Gods, at this rate this will take us a tenday."

The boys ignored the remark and they all linked hands again. After another bout of visualization, Augum next teleported them to the one-road town of Sinew high up in the mountains. Which was a terrible mistake, for Jez immediately broke the circle of hands and tore into The Smoked Wing Inn & Tavern. Augum, Jengo and Olaf simultaneously sighed. By the time they entered after her, the entire tavern had fallen pin-drop silent.

"And I want *that* bottle there, you greasy sack of farts!" Jez hissed at the barkeep, pointing at a huge bottle of Sierran Titan wine. "Pour me a goblet and leave the bottle."

The barkeep took one look at Augum and went pale as parchment. Augum flicked a hand for the barkeep to get on with it. The man grabbed the bottle of Titan wine, popped the cork, and poured Jez a full goblet, leaving the bottle beside the cup. Seeing that Jez wasn't bothering to pay for it, Augum patted his pockets out of habit. Olaf, noticing him do that, unslung his rucksack, withdrew a pouch, counted out the requisite castles and spines, and slid them to the barkeep, who promptly swept them into a belt pouch.

Olaf flipped a hand questioningly at Augum. "Mind if I imbibe?"

Augum, seeing they were going to be there for a short while, surrendered a nod.

"Fire ale," Olaf said to the barkeep, indicating between himself and Jengo. "For the both of us."

"I don't know if I ought to—"

"Oh, shut up," Jez said, eyeballing the lanky young healer.

Jengo cleared his throat. "Er, just one, then."

The barkeep raised a questioning and nervous eyebrow at Augum, who swept a hand, declining one for himself. "Two fires coming up," the barkeep muttered, getting to work.

"Enjoy your drink, then we 'port," Augum said, leaning up against the wall and folding his arms, grateful he didn't have to meditate as it had been a relatively short hop. Eyeing up the place, he recognized some of the same patrons, including the trio of constables and the greasy brigand he had roughed up. He pressed one foot up against the wall and noted how not one would meet his gaze—not an untypical reaction from people who knew who he was or had had an unsavory encounter with him. Very few had the nerve to eyeball a dragon even when in human form.

You're a human first, Augum had to remind himself. *Never forget that.* It wasn't the first time he had had to do it too.

As Jez drank her goblet and demanded the barkeep to refill it for her, Augum felt the shadow slip back into his thoughts. These brigands, even the trappers and hunters, all knew what had been happening with the kidnappings. Any one of them could have said something and prevented two more vials of blood. But the cowards had stayed silent, and now two more families would burst with anguished cries upon receiving the news of their children.

The shadow again called out for vengeance, and the craving to make the praying mantis pose grew so strong that Augum felt a bead of sweat trickle down his forehead and fall past his eyes.

Jengo, who happened to glance back at him, almost dropped his tankard of ale. Augum looked at him and wondered what he'd taste like going down his gullet. He had eaten his prey before, but never whilst in human form, only when his wings were bright and leathery and absorbing the heat of three suns. Always his jaw had been open wide, savoring every morsel ...

Jengo scurried up to him, leaving his drink behind. "Aug ... your *eyes*."

Augum stared at him, wishing the weak fool would make a threatening move so the predator could feed off the violence and escalate the situation to a rabid fight—and then a feast. There was a lot of blood here that could quench his thirst. Then there was the possible destruction. To lift a roof off its moorings and peek inside was a particularly exquisite thrill, much like opening a fresh jar of delectable sweets.

"Are you listening to me, Commander?" Jengo whispered. "Your eyes ... they're *lizard* eyes. The eyes of the dragon." Jengo snapped his fingers before Augum's face, hissing, "*Aug!*"

Augum uncrossed his arms. Suddenly he could hear the blood rushing through his ears and felt the patrons were doing everything they could to avoid looking at him. The entire place had gone still. Olaf's tankard was near his lips, his eyes wide as he gaped at him. Only Jez remained animated, gulping her goblet greedily. Noticing the stillness, she finally lowered her goblet and turned about.

"What's got your tongues all tied up you filthy—what in Sithesian hell!" She braced against the bar with a hand to keep from falling over, the other quickly bringing the goblet to her lips again, only to lower it. "What in Sithesian hell ..." she whispered.

An alarmed Augum turned away, hiding his face in his hood. He urgently began whispering out the entire Sacred Code of the Arcaner. "Thou shall never refuse a challenge from an equal. Thou shall never turn thy back on a foe ..." Thou shall, thou shall, thou shall ...

"Let's get out of here," Olaf said, downing his ale before herding them all outside, all while Augum kept his face hidden within his hood whilst he spat out the code. "... Thou shall guard the honor of the arcane craft. Thou shall seek knowledge that contributes to the craft ..."

"What in the devil planes is going on?" Jez asked, grabbing hold of his shoulders and forcing him to look at her, all while clutching the neck of the Titan wine, which sloshed about near his ear. "What was that? Huh? Illusion arcanery?"

Augum stared at her, mumbling the final edict out before reciting the Arcaner motto, "*Semperis vorto honos.*"

"They're back to normal," Olaf reassured when Augum glanced his way.

"Blab and blab *right* quick," Jez hissed, having to hold onto him lest she trip.

"It's been getting stronger," Augum admitted. He flapped a hand by his temple. "The Callousness of the Predator has been seeping into my thoughts. Sometimes it even speaks to me directly. It constantly wants me to make the pose."

"Gods," Jengo whispered. "You're not ... you're not turning *into* it, are you?"

"No, of course not! Well, maybe. All right, I ... I don't know."

Jez started to shake his shoulders, only to abruptly smother him in a hug. "Oh, monkey," she cooed, patting his back in that motherly-aunt way. "My poor, poor monkey. We'll get you to your girly girl right quick and then she can spoon you up a dollop of honey and make it all better."

Augum lamely patted her back. "I'm fine, Jez."

"You're not fine," she replied, weaving about. "You're *not* fine. No one's fine. We're all drowning. The kingdom is sliding into the deepest parts of hell ..."

"Er ... right."

"When did it start?" Jengo pressed.

Augum continued holding onto Jez, who was silently weeping into his shoulder.

"A while ago."

"Is it the same for the girls?" Olaf pressed. "For my Bridget?"

"I ... I don't know. Maybe."

"It is, isn't it?"

"I loved him so much," Jez whimpered, taking a swig. "I ever tell you we were planning on starting a family?"

"You did, Jez."

"Now both of us can't have a family. All of Sithesia ... we're all going to Hell ..."

Their closest friends knew about Leera, who had once drunkenly told them she was barren, only to regret doing so the day after. But they had done nothing but support her and Augum, and yet somehow that only made Augum—and especially his girl—feel worse. He wished she hadn't said anything at all, but he wasn't sure *why* he wished that. Further, whenever he thought that, he couldn't help but feel shame.

"Keep this between us for now," Augum said, indicating his own eyes whilst glancing between Olaf and Jengo. "That's an order." He needed to understand what was happening to him.

"Yes, Commander," the pair chorused, nodding.

"I'll talk about it with Bridget and Leera." *And get to the bottom of this arcanery snuffing business*, he thought, wanting to think about something else other than the blasted callousness.

Jez withdrew and lifted the bottle to her lips, only to spill some onto her coat. "Oh, I've done it now," she slurred, almost tripping over her own feet just standing there.

Augum gently took the bottle from her hands, and placed one hand into Jengo's, the other into Olaf's. Then he quietly stuck the bottle into the snow behind her while she stared down at her own hands as if wondering how they worked, took a spot between Olaf and Jengo, and visualized the next hop location.

"*Impetus peragro grapa lestato exa exaei.*"

They appeared amidst a copse of tall cedars perched on a flat mountain ledge. Far below and to the north and south, amidst a great valley bathed in brilliant starlight, for the sky here was mostly clear, snaked the Iron Pass, the main passage between his kingdom of Solia and the northern kingdom of Ohm—and beyond. To the south, the torchlit city of Antioc rose like a human-made hill of stone homes surrounded by a mighty wall. The Library of Antioc towered highest in the city, an ancient castle that had been converted into a library centuries ago.

As trained, Augum glanced about the ledge to make sure it had not been disturbed, but the snow here was fresh, even obscuring their old campfire, which they had hidden behind a snowbank.

Jez glanced about too, but not out of wariness of enemies. "Where the hell's the bottle?" she slurred.

"You drank it," Augum lied.

A wavering Jez focused in on him. She stumbled up to him and clumsily made to slap him, but his war-honed reflexes kicked in and he dipped his head back. The momentum made her fall to the snow.

"You hid it before we 'ported, didn't you?" she slurred, clambering to her feet, biting her lower lip and clenching her teeth. "Who gave you the *right*? Huh? You little weasel. You trumped-up little turdling—" She swiped at him, grabbed hold of air when he sidestepped, and squished her hands into fists that she drunkenly shook at him.

Jengo took hold of her arm and dragged her back. "Jez, please. Don't do this."

She whirled on him. "And *you*! Who are *you* to tell *me* what to do? Huh? Jengo *Okeke*," she spat, mocking his awkward last name, mispronouncing it as *okay kay* instead of *oh ke ke*.

"Allow me to cast a calming spell on you at least—"

"Don't you dare. Don't you *dare*! Unlike you snotbags, I am comfortable in my rage. You get me?"

"You're drunk, Auntie Jez," Olaf said.

She whirled on him too, only to find him looking sheepishly down, face slack with sadness.

"We miss our Auntie Jez," Olaf mumbled. "And wish she'd stop being so mean to us."

Jez staggered as if struck. She pressed a shaking arm to her mouth as if to ward off a blow, and kept staggering to the thicket of trees.

Augum sighed and raised a hand, stalling his friends. "I'll get her." He followed Jez, who meandered around the trunks of the massive cedars, finally vanishing behind a trunk as wide as an ox cart. Augum hurried after her, finding her in the midst of slurring an incantation.

"*Impetus—*" but she couldn't finish, for he had slapped a hand over her mouth.

He shook her, roaring, "How could you even *think* to drink and 'port! Huh! How could you do that!"

She stared over his hand with watery eyes. For the first time he noticed that some gray hairs had woven themselves into her unruly hair. Because she looked so much like his beloved, those gray hairs made him think about growing old with Leera. Albeit in an empty, silent home …

"You can't do that," he said, giving her another shake, a gentler one. "You promised you wouldn't do that …"

"I'm perfectly fine to 'port," she mumbled through his hand.

"You're not. Not even close. You 'port and we'll never see you again because you'll end up split in the trunk of a tree or deep underground."

She looked past him, her eyes going vacant.

He removed his hand, whispering, "You're forbidden to lose hope. In fact, I command it."

"You're not my commander," she croaked, still staring off into the distance. "I'm not an Arcaner. I don't have to follow your stupid rules or your dumb commands."

"But you're my mentor. A mentor to a whole bunch of us. A mentor we all look up to." Just as she was about to say something caustic, he gently and playfully slapped her cheek. "Get your act together, Terse. We're tired of your whining." He gambled that this amazing woman would appreciate the one thing she always loved—a bit of cheek. Banter. Witty repartee.

Jez's eyes narrowed before she shoved him hard, making him fall to the snow. "There. Now you're on *your* butt, you ass." But she was smiling.

"Yeah. Yeah, I am." He extended an arm. "Hand up?"

She slapped it away, muttering, "Weasel." But then she changed her mind and drunkenly hauled him up. She pressed the heel of a hand to the side of her head and groaned. "My head is spinning."

"Can I give you some water?"

Her response was to shrug off her rucksack and let it fall to the snow. Augum withdrew a waterskin from it and gave it to Jez, who took a long pull—and to his surprise, kept guzzling. Then she thrust it back at Augum. "Gods I hate you. You know me too well. Why don't you lot leave me alone to bathe in my self-pity? Huh?"

"Because we love you, Auntie Jez," he replied, stuffing the waterskin back into her rucksack.

"And I *hate* being called Auntie Jez."

"You love it."

"I hate it. I hate you and that feral girl of yours and I hate that goodie-goodie Bridget and I hate that beanstalk boy and that fat bumbling oaf and—"

Augum slung the rucksack back over her shoulder, even raising an arm for her to fit the strap diagonally across her chest. "You love us. You love us all and you cannot wait to relax with us at the next Endyear feast.

"Ugh, you're exhausting. Let's just go home already so I can get drunk and forget I even exist."

He wanted to say *You're already two-moon—no, three-moon—drunk.* "Fine, but no more 'porting," he said instead, and stepped aside, allowing her to trundle by. "And when are you going to give me lessons? I've got a whole raft of spells I need to conquer."

"Don't push it, kiddo. I'll get to it when I get to it."

Augum sighed. A lot rested on him advancing. The guilty thought that he needed a sober mentor seeped in, as it had every time she procrastinated with his training.

They reformed a circle of hands and after a focused pause Augum snapped off the incantation to the 17th degree Group Teleport. This time, however, they appeared in their second-to-last destination—on the outer upper terrace of Castle Arinthian.

Augum took a moment to savor being home. Even standing outside the ancient castle, with its old bloodline and echoes of adventure and merriment and black-tar exterior, gave him great comfort.

"One brief stop," Augum said, holding up a finger and shooting to a pair of double doors. He didn't want to give Jez time to hit the kitchens and grab another bottle.

Once inside his room, he ignored everything but his trunk, which he flipped open. He grabbed a certain golden breastplate and a certain ancient shortsword in a scabbard and a small black box, which he flipped open, removing his betrothal ring from within.

He tossed the box back inside, kicked the trunk closed, and returned through the doors, kicking them closed too, all whilst carrying the sword and breastplate under one arm. Once reunited with his colleagues, he slipped on the ring—and expelled a sigh of relief when a strong tug pointed north. His beloved was on her quest just where she had said she was.

"She all right?" Olaf asked.

"I think so. I'll check in with her soon."

"She's a big girl now she can take care of herself," Jez drawled, fidgeting from boredom.

They joined hands and Augum was about to teleport them to their final destination—the training yard of the Black Castle—when he realized he didn't have enough stamina on account of that last hop being so far.

"Uh, I just need a privy break," he said, dumping the breastplate and sword and mouthing to Olaf and Jengo to keep Jez occupied before scooting back inside his room.

"Hurry up then, you weasel, the goblet calls!" Jez called after him.

Augum, having left one of the doors to the terrace slightly open, heard the boys strike up conversation with her. He sat down on his bed, crossed his legs, and meditated, knowing he only needed a short time to get the reservoir full enough for the short hop to the Black Castle.

After a time, there came a scratching at another door, the one that led to the hallway. Knowing what it was, Augum pointed and made the handle turn. The door *clicked* open, and in wandered a chubby tabby. Sir Pawsalot stretched out his front paws, yawned, revealing a magnificent set of teeth, and hopped up on the bed, where he rubbed up against Augum.

Augum scooped him up and plopped him into his lap. "Missed you too, boy," he whispered, and gave his belly a thorough rubbing, moving to behind the ears and then the chin. "You're not scared off, right, boy? I'm not a lizard. I'm me. That's right, you love me and I love you. And don't worry, she'll be back soon, promise. And if not …" He leaned down to kiss the tabby on the forehead, whispering, "Then I'll fetch her."

"Gods help me how long does it take to have a piss these days?" Jez shouted outside. "What, he can't work his robe right? It's freezing out here. Forget this, I'm 'porting to the Hilt—"

"I'm back!" Augum yelled, and let Sir Pawsalot go, figuring he had enough stamina to teleport.

"Bladder of an elephant," Jez muttered when he returned to pick up his breastplate and sword.

"You have enough?" Jengo mouthed, seemingly understanding.

Augum nodded.

Jez drummed fingernails against her gut. "Why do I get the feeling you were stalling?"

"Not stalling at all."

"I'd make you swear on your shield except I know it'd dim. You're a terrible liar, Stone."

Ignoring her, Augum tucked the breastplate and sword under an arm and reached out both hands. "Link up."

They linked up and, after a focused moment, Augum incanted, "*Impetus peragro grapa lestato exa exaei,*" and they vanished and reappeared with a *thwomp* exactly where he intended — in the outer ward of the Black Castle, lit warmly by torchlight.

"Commander!" shrieked a voice.

"He's back! He's back!" shrieked another.

Augum turned to see two women, one sprinting, the other hobbling toward him in the snow — Laudine Cooper and Haylee Tennyson, respectively. Other than a few knights sparring together and some archers shooting at straw targets, the yard was empty.

Laudine practically bowled him over with a hug, making him drop the breastplate and sword. "Er, good to see you, Commander," she said, peeling herself off him whilst smiling that famous dimpled smile of hers. "There's a *lot* that's happened. Happy Endyear! Oh and a *lot* of people had no idea about Leera and *you know what* and are quite shocked."

Augum was going to say he had no idea what she was talking about when Haylee quickly joined in, singing, "Happy Endyear and good to see you back!" and hugged each of them, with Laudine taking her hugs from the others. Whilst Jengo and Olaf were warm to the reception, Jez was cold and distant.

Haylee secretly thumbed at Jez, mouthing to Augum, "She drunk?"

Augum did a quick nod as he telekinetically fetched the breastplate and sword. "I need to change out of this burgundy." He always had a spare crimson robe in Arcaner headquarters, the entrance of which he indicated with an inviting hand. "Fill us in as we walk?"

"I'm going to be sick," Jez blurted, pressing a fist to her mouth.

"Let me take her to a bed," Haylee said. "Jez? Come with me," she said loudly, offering an elbow. "Come, I'll take you to bed."

"I can walk, Wonk Leg," Jez muttered, and got five steps before she tripped over her own feet and tumbled to the snow. "His 'porting is terrible," she complained. Haylee patiently kept her elbow raised, until Jez snatched hold of it and allowed her to lead her away.

"Poor thing," Laudine said as the remaining group got to walking in the opposite direction. "Haven't seen her that drunk since ... well, since she left, I guess."

"Speaking of drunk, shall we hit the tavern?" Olaf asked.

Augum frowned at his good buddy.

"I mean obviously *after* we meet back up with the girls."

"Bridget's confined to quarters," Laudine blurted, halting the boys on the spot.

Augum blinked. "Come again?"

"The Lord High Commander—the new one, The Sword of the Oak—personally ordered her confinement. He's a right bully. You know the sort."

While a quivering Olaf went puce, Augum pointed at the keep and raised a questioning eyebrow.

"Yes, she's in there," Laudine replied. "I'll take you to her room now if you want."

Augum considered it, but then glanced down at his robe. "I need the authority of my robe, so I'll change first."

"We could use a change too," Olaf chimed in as they resumed walking.

"And a bath," Jengo added in a mutter.

"It'll calm me down," Olaf added. "How *dare* they do that to the sweetest, kindest person I know? Well, except when she gets like, you know ... all thorny and stuff after a certain casting. But that's not her," he blurted, nodding fervently. "It's just the predator and all that."

They entered Arcaner headquarters just as a flurry of knights appeared in the yard.

"They're coming to guard you," Laudine warned. "Even sent a warlock courier up north to demand you come back, but I guess he never caught up to you lot," and she kept talking about events as Augum, Olaf and Jengo fetched clean robes and undergarments from a large dresser in the Great Arcaner Hall, then changed behind four-panel folding privacy screens set up for just such occasions. She finished in time for the doors to burst open.

Augum, wishing he could bathe first, nonetheless shed the dirty clothing, donned fresh undergarments and his usual crimson academy robe first, then picked up the golden breastplate, tracing a finger over the etchings. In the area of the heart, a dragon stood before a copse of trees, surrounded above and below by the motto *Defendi au o dominia*—defender of the kingdom. And in the center of the chest was a solitary rose and the words *Isobel, Prima Arcana*—Isobel, the first Arcaner.

He saw his face in the ten-thousand-year-old gold, well worn around all the edges but also polished to a mirror shine. The sheer age of it made him feel like he was its temporary custodian, not its owner. When he met his own eyes, he looked away, fearful he would see lizard pupils. He strapped on the breastplate over his robe and flicked at the scabbarded sword, which shot to his hand. It was an ancient blade that had once belonged to his famous ancestor Atrius Arinthian, who had built Castle Arinthian and had been an Arcaner as well, had served as king, and had even become a Leyan. Made of seamless Dreadnought steel, with a hilt wrapped in fine chain, the blade was infused with ancient arcanery, which included being a key to Castle Arinthian itself. It even had a name—Burden's Edge.

Holding the blade, especially after being away from it for a while, always reminded him of the first time he had laid eyes on it back in his great-grandmother's cave, where it had hung on the wall. And he remembered her passing it on to him. That felt like forever ago, in a time of high adventure and war and anguish …

Once the sword was secured to his golden rope belt underneath the gleaming breastplate, he grabbed the rucksack from the journey, slung it over his shoulder, and emerged from behind the four-panel screen, feeling at home in his commander garb.

"Commander Stone," barked a knight, one of ten. The middle-aged man unfurled a small scroll. "By writ of the king, you are hereby ordered to remain on the grounds of this here castle on account of an unusual threat which is still being investigated. You will be escorted at all times to ensure your safety in the event of spell failure." The knight furled the scroll back up. "The kingdom's dragons must be protected at all costs," he boldly declared.

Augum did not acknowledge the knight and instead held out the rucksack to Laudine. "Would you please hand this to the academy committee as soon as possible? Inside you will find the blood remains of the two recently kidnapped kingdom's apprentices, as well as their robes. You may pass on the story I have told you, and of course that I will submit a full report the moment I have time. Also pass on that I will make myself available to lay the sword at the feet of the parents if that is something the committee finds appropriate."

Laudine accepted the rucksack. "I'll get to it now, Commander," and she strode off, glaring at the knights as she passed, all of whom ignored her.

Jengo and Olaf, who had just emerged from behind their privacy screens, joined him.

"Bridget?" Olaf whispered.

Augum nodded. "Bridget," and he marched forth, still not acknowledging the knights, all of whom stared at him through the slits of their pot helms.

After passing through the doors, Augum found himself the center of the yard's attention—not only curious soldiers and guests and even servants had come out to look at him, but his fellow Arcaners, who surrounded him.

Strangely, he noticed a lot of the women, especially the noble women, whispering behind their hands and looking at him a certain way. But he figured it was because he hadn't been around much of late.

"We'll get to Arcaner business shortly," he told his charges. "Almoner Okeke, would you mind running a few cycles?"

"Er ... I'm not much about combat. More of a healer. All right, completely a healer actually." When Augum only stared at him, Jengo nodded quickly. "I'll do my best, Commander," and he began shepherding the young squires and dragoons back to headquarters.

"They look up to you. You'll be fine!" Olaf called after him as he and Augum continued walking. "You'd think barely surviving Endraga Ra would have inspired a bit more courage in him."

"Some would rather face a jungle of beasts than a crowd of squires."

"Point to you, Three Toes. And I guess I'm one to talk considering I stumble on my own tongue whenever you ask me to lead a cycle."

Augum grunted, conscious of everyone in that yard following him with their eyes. It wasn't long before the first of the Ordinaries mustered up the courage to approach him, a young man of about his age.

"M'lord Stone, will you bless this wretched soul?"

Augum used to refuse such requests, considering them ridiculous and fawning, until Bridget had politely told him that it gave people hope. Realizing she was right, he had consulted the *Codex Arcanera: From Birth to Death, a Life of Honor*, which had a list of blessings, most of which involved calling upon the Unnameables to ward the receiver from evil, or their own failings, or evil spirits, or whatnot. But some had to do with urging the person to listen to their heart. Augum fell in love with one of these in particular.

He pressed a hand to the young man's scalp. "May you have the strength to follow your heart in times dark and dire." The original was in the old tongue, but he had grown tired of translating it over and over, so just spoke the translation.

The young man bowed repeatedly, hands together in prayer. "Thank you, sacred one. Thank you. I shall cherish this day unto my last, and will tell my children how I met *the* Augum Arinthian Stone—"

"I'm honored," Augum mumbled, quickly moving on.

Others soon swarmed in on him. The guests of the castle were nobles who either asked for a blessing or for him to scratch out his autograph on a piece of parchment using a quill they provided, whilst the children of the nobles asked variations of the same question—can you turn into a dragon for us, sir, mister, Lord Stone, Dragon Stone, Great Warrior Arcaner, Hero of the War, Sacred One, and so forth. Titles that held meaning to the masses, cultivated by the heralds and amplified by campfire stories that grew wilder by the year.

"Please!" cried a little girl.

"Not today," Augum said, winking and adding in a whisper, "But keep watch of the skies."

The girl glanced at the dark sky, eyes widening.

"They got bored of Bridget and Leera," Olaf said with a chuckle.

Although Augum gave him a placating half-smile, the truth was more disappointing. Because he was the commander and a man, they flocked to him more. Even though Bridget and Leera deserved equal praise. Even though they had bled and sacrificed just as much. He had tried everything to let them share all the honors, but people wanted their tales of the commander and lead hero. It made him wonder what would happen if he passed on the mantle of commander to, say, Bridget for a time.

He and Olaf and their retinue of ten knights pushed past the throng, entered the keep, and strode up the steps, with the knights clanking along in their full suits. Augum's stomach rumbled at the divine scent of roast turkey and gravy and spices mingling sweetly with pine and cedar garlands. There was nothing like the cozy feeling of seeing everything festooned for the holidays and Endyear candles sitting atop fireplace mantels and window parapets.

On their way up, the pair encountered a certain amber-robed woman standing on a staircase landing between floors, seemingly waiting for Augum alongside her own retinue of ladies-in-waiting. The sight of her made Augum want to groan, for this woman was one of those rising warlock socialites of the court who was constantly trying to gain favor one way or another. Nonetheless, he made sure to be cordial and, as custom demanded, accepted her already outstretched hand after she had curtsied properly.

"Lady Alanna Haught," he said, bowing and placing his lips close to the top of that hand without kissing it. "Happy Endyear."

"And Happy Endyear to you, Commander Stone. We are overjoyed to see you returned safe and sound." She smiled widely, showing her perfect teeth. Today she was particularly unblemished, so much so that her skin looked like alabaster, making her blue eyes stand out vividly amidst that platinum blond hair and glittering jewelry. Her ladies-in-waiting all blushed at his glance and quickly looked away, making a rather obvious show of it.

"Yes, er, it is good to be back," he said, conscious of his entire retinue waiting impatiently on the stairs behind him. "Now if you will excuse me, I must attend to Captain Burns—"

"Please allow us to extend our sincerest condolences to you, Commander," she said as he passed, stopping him in his tracks. "It is a terrible tragedy for you personally, but also for the kingdom—and your noble lineage. I would like to make myself personally available should you ever ..." Lady Haught idly traced a finger by her bejeweled neck. "... need a friend."

Augum looked to Olaf for a clue, but he only shrugged in a *Haven't the faintest* manner. "I am afraid I have just returned from a rather long journey and have no idea what you are referring to, Lady Haught."

"Why, the piece in the *Blackhaven Herald*. Surely you have read it? Oh, dear me, of course you haven't considering the length of your absence. Please forgive me, Commander. It is not my place to speak of such things until you have been properly informed." She curtsied. "Commander Stone," and glided on down the steps, her ladies-in-waiting scurrying after her, still glancing back at him with those spurious but knowing looks.

"What the hell was that about?" Olaf muttered.

"I don't know, but something tells me Bridget will have a clue."

"Think she'll be allowed out for supper?" Olaf asked.

"We'll find out shortly."

ASH

BRIDGET

"You have made great progress, but we still have tendays worth of work ahead of us," Mahmoute said, the fingertips of her hands pressed together. "You truly have a war-honed mind, Captain Burns, for few can turn the theoretical into the practical so quickly. I am honored to aid in further sharpening that keen mind."

A sweaty Bridget was about to incline her head in thanks when there came a knock on the door.

"Bread and water," Mahmoute said with a hint of a smile, and went to the door. But when she opened it, it was not a servant who stood there waiting, but Bridget's betrothed, Olaf, and her brother-in-war and commander, Augum.

Bridget's heart soared—as did she, for laughingly she leapt onto Olaf, allowing him to twirl her about. She showered him with kisses, and he laughed in that boisterous way of his, booming, "Ho, ho, ho, there's my pretty girl! There she is! Gods how I missed you, my love," and he pressed his lips to hers and they shared a meaningful and deep kiss of longing. How overjoyed she was to feel his arms around her again! How she wanted a wedding and children and a home and—

He set her down rather abruptly. "Hello, who's this?" he asked.

Suddenly feeling discarded, instead of answering, Bridget threw her arms around Augum, whispering, "Brother."

"Good to see you, Sister," he said, patting her back.

She let go and cleared her throat, pressing three fingers over the heart. "Commander."

"Captain," Augum replied with a curt bow of the head, returning the three-fingered salute.

Bridget stepped aside to indicate the old Black Eagle. "Along with the knights out in the hall—and I can see you brought your own little retinue—this is my new minder, Black Eagle Samira Mahmoute. She's been training me in Arcane Drain."

The Black Eagle inclined her head at Augum and Olaf. "Commander. Dragoon."

They inclined their heads back.

Bridget gently whapped Olaf's shoulder with the back of a hand, whispering, "Missed you, you big lug."

"And I missed my cinnamon-haired princess," he whispered back. "Wait, why are your hands black and blue?"

"Got a bit of a thumping in sword and buckler training." She'd tell him about her sojourn to Sparrow's Perch later. To avoid social awkwardness, Bridget opened a hand to the side of the room. "Commander, a word?"

"I've received a full report of the goings-on here from Laudine," Augum whispered after they stepped aside. "I'll fill you in on our adventure north when you're ready. But before we talk about anything else, what's this about something in the herald? I was just accosted by Lady Haught, who was rather cryptic. Why do I get the feeling everyone knows something I don't?"

"Oh, uh, well …" Bridget fidgeted, not knowing how to reveal this news to him.

"Just spit it out," he said.

"Er, all right," and she leaned into his ear and whispered how Leera had gotten a bit tipsy one night and divulged certain information about how she was barren to someone who turned out to be a herald.

"Oh," Augum said, face falling. "I see."

"I rather thought you were going to be more upset."

Augum said nothing to this and just stared vacantly through her.

"Lee was mortified," Bridget went on. "So much so that she went on a quest, no doubt to get away from the deep shame of the entire kingdom finding out about a deeply personal matter to her."

"Right …"

"You know I'm here for you if you want to talk about it."

Augum only nodded with that same vacant look which told her he was hurt but did not want to show it. Boys and their pride.

"Anyway, on a change of topic, I want to see the king," Bridget said, making sure to keep her back to the watchful Black Eagle. She wanted to discuss The Callousness of the Predator with Augum and how it was slipping into her psyche but that would have to wait until they were well out of anyone's earshot.

Augum reanimated. "I was thinking the same thing. In fact—" and he began unstrapping Isobel's breastplate.

"What are you doing?"

"It's time they respected you two as much as they respect me." Once unstrapped, he presented the breastplate to her.

"I can't take this. It belongs—"

"—to either of you should I fall in battle. They must know that you would take my place in a heartbeat, and that you are to be respected as much as I am. Besides, this thing doesn't really belong to me. It belongs to the order, and to the eons ahead. I'm only its temporary custodian." He pushed the breastplate, which had a unisex form, at her. "Don it. I will stand behind you as commander."

Bridget stared at the breastplate. "That will be a powerful message, but I am still confined to these quarters by order of the Lord High Commander."

"Is there anything in our code of honor that requires us to follow such men?"

Bridget bit her lip. The code asked for one to swear fealty to *it*, not to any specific individual. Then again, the fifteenth edict stated, " 'Thou shall serve thy lord and king and kingdom with valor and courage and an open heart,' " she declared. "Except we are vassals of the throne, and the Lord High Commander *is* our lord. I must therefore obey his command."

"Ah, but the sixteenth edict states, 'Thou shall root out corruption *in all its forms*, and the sanctity of the truth shall vanquish *any title*.' Would the Lord High Commander's order, rooted in a need for mere control of your person, not be considered a form of corruption? And would the truth therefore not vanquish that title?"

Bridget curled first one lock of her long cinnamon hair around her ear then the other as she thought about it. "He *did* try to dim my shield on my behalf ..."

"Then that speaks volumes of the man, does it not?" Augum replied, and continued to patiently hold Isobel Roseheart's breastplate before her.

After some deep thought on the matter, Bridget decided to accept the breastplate for the message that it would send. Augum was right, people—especially the nobility—needed to know that they were interchangeable as leaders, and that there was no division amongst them. "Now let us beg for council with the king."

Augum nodded and stepped away, allowing her to don the breastplate. Olaf went to stand behind her to help fasten the straps. She felt his face nuzzle into the nape of her neck, which he kissed, whispering, "It suits you, my sweet love."

She smiled back at him, sensing her cheeks redden. Then, noticing the eyes of all those knights upon her person—and especially the silently judging eyes of Mahmoute, she cleared her throat and stepped away from her man.

"We shall seek council from the king," she declared to the old Black Eagle. To her surprise, the woman merely inclined her head. Bridget, feeling as if all of them were waiting upon her, led the entire throng, clanking knights and Mahmoute and Augum and Olaf, out of the room and down the hall.

Olaf and Augum promptly took up positions on either side of her, but just behind to give her authority. She had always felt pride for Augum, for his myriad accomplishments, for believing in the order even when she herself thought it a children's make-believe story. That pride now deepened, for by lending her Isobel's breastplate, he had proven himself above the trappings of command, something few could boast.

The breastplate itself felt heavy, not just from its ancient Dreadnought steelwork, but from the weight of responsibility it represented. She had never truly considered being commander of the order, always figuring that was Augum's destiny, but actually wearing the ancient breastplate made her feel ...

What? Accomplished? she thought. *Ambitious? Determined?* It was hard to articulate, especially considering the conflict between the life she currently lived and the country family life she longed for.

On the way, Bridget nodded at Augum. "Fill me in as we walk?" He caught up to her, and Olaf on her other side, and the pair took turns filling her in on their adventures, with Augum doing more of the talking since he had experienced more mayhem. What he said about the arcane-snuffing occurrence alarmed her, and she explained how two such occurrences had taken place on the Black Castle's grounds, one in the form of lightning and the other as moss.

They marched together as a big group down the stairs, out of the keep, through the yard, and on into the vestibule of the Grand Hall, where the two thrones of the kingdom sat. Four knights guarded the doors, each with a long spear and shield. Upon the group's entrance, the knights angled their spears to block the giant double doors to the throne chamber.

"Captain Bridget Burns and Commander Augum Stone to see the king and queen," Bridget told the guards, not meaning to sound so cold.

One of the knights hesitated, glancing at his cohorts, before stomping the butt of his spear against the marble and turning to his side. The other three straightened their spears allowing him to turn the giant door handle with a ceremonious and rather mechanical twist of the hand. He then stepped through, leaving the three other knights to bar the door with their spears.

Bridget glanced back and saw that Augum also stared coldly at the knights. He had a quietly menacing presence to him, not only as an Arcaner and an Arinthian, but as a dragon. She saw the lives he had taken in his face—the shadows under those hard blue eyes and perpetually furrowed brow that was slowly making permanent creases that only softened when he was with Leera. Yet he was capable of great compassion and thoughtfulness too, giving him depth.

Bridget felt Olaf's hand slip into hers. She squeezed it but let it go, for she had to do this without looking weak to the royalty, or like a woman who needed her man to survive. *I am a dragon*, she thought, and felt the heat of three suns upon her wings. The callous shadow slipped in behind her mind. This time, she allowed it to stay there, lending her courage—and ferocity.

She glanced over at Augum, and he glanced back. They shared a steely-eyed look suitable for war, making her wonder if he was experiencing the callousness as well, before facing forward.

The knight returned, slammed the butt of his spear against the polished floor and boomed, "The king and queen will see the captain and commander now!"

"Oh." Olaf squeezed her midriff, whispering, "Good luck, my sweet love."

She wanted to nod, but the callousness she had allowed into her sanctum scoffed at such a show of weakness, and so she merely strode forth, Augum following. Eyes of the royal retinue, petitioners for the king's attention, rich merchants and loyalists, followed her as she walked. She kept her head rigidly straight until she stopped before the dais, where she inclined that head and pressed three fingers over her Dreadnought-steel heart.

"No curtsy? Has that breastplate made a man of you?" the queen asked in a tone that could cut glass.

"The plate once belonged to the founder of our order, Isobel Roseheart." Realizing she had forgotten an honorific, she quickly threw in, "Your Grace."

"A woman? Indeed?" The queen glanced over at the king bemusedly. "How quaint."

Bridget wanted to sarcastically echo the *indeed* part but thought better of it.

The old boar of a king adjusted his girth in the throne chair. "I am confused. There is a rose on that breastplate. If I am not mistaken, it belongs to your commander. Was it not his reward for resurrecting the Arcaner order? Did he find it too … *womanly* … for his tastes?" His entire retinue chortled.

"Nay, Your Highness," Bridget replied. "It is to show that should one of us fall, another will take their place, and the order will continue forth."

The king drummed the arm of the throne with perfectly manicured fingernails, his myriad rings gleaming in the candlelight. "And what of my nephew? How doth he fare since our last meeting?"

"Squire Carter Southguard is … persistent."

"Persistent? A backhanded compliment if I ever heard one." More chortles.

"He has much to learn."

"And would he don the breastplate if none are left?"

"Of course." The question made her wonder about the king's intentions regarding his nephew.

The king grunted, eyes focusing behind her. "Your return has been overdue, Commander."

Augum stepped forth, inclining his head to each sovereign. "Your Grace. Your Grace."

"Report of your quest."

"I bring ill tidings from the north, Your Highnesses," and Augum detailed how a pack of wolven had been blooding apprentices to distill them into concoctions.

"That is worthy of war," the Lord High Commander interrupted from the rear, reed-thin mustache quivering. The Sword of the Oak stood in the back with the other high councilors.

"I disagree," Augum replied. "The pack is a rogue offshoot known as The Dishonored, outcasts who do not represent wolven kind. I have retrieved the remains of our apprentices and am of the mind that such a thing will not happen again. Alas, I bring graver news still," and he told them of experiencing a similar arcane-nullifying effect to what Bridget had witnessed.

Bridget thought he did so a little quickly, no doubt hoping they would forget about any foolish notions of war with the north.

By the end of it, the king nodded and flicked a dismissive finger. Augum then bowed and stepped back, while the king flicked a second finger and turned his head slightly to the side. This caused the nine high council members to flock in on him to give their counsel.

While they conferred in whispers, Bridget glanced back at Augum, and their eyes met to share anxiety.

Once the council retreated, the king stared at Bridget whilst barking, "Lord High Commander. To me."

The Sword of the Oak presented himself with a double-click of his heels. "Your Grace."

The boar eyes remained on Bridget. "What we did in the war together we did then. This is now. So what is this nonsense I hear that you are still reluctant to do my bidding? I believe I made myself perfectly clear that you are royal subjects sworn to the crown and its military. You are soldiers—nay, *weapons*. And weapons are meant to be unsheathed. The kingdom has only weakened over the centuries. For the first time in an eon, we are in a position to expand our borders. We must let our people—and the generations to follow—prosper."

Bridget cleared her throat, giving herself time to form a rebuttal. "Your Grace, we are indeed weapons, but weapons with a conscience." *What conscience?* the callous shadow laughingly intoned into her mind, making her regret allowing it such a presence.

She cleared her throat again and continued. "Although we are bound to follow *lawful* orders as per the fifteenth edict, the fourth edict is quite clear. 'Thou shall not duel the lower ranks without serious provocation.' Also pertinent is the sixth edict. 'Thou shall never take the life of a weaponless Ordinary.' We cannot make war on those weaker than us simply for the sake of territorial gain. It is against the very spirit of our code of honor—and the order itself."

"Those edicts pertain to individual combat," the Lord High Commander countered. "Not to armies."

"Your Grace," Bridget cut in, ignoring the man she loathed and keeping her gaze on the king, "if you commanded us to make war, and war we did make, we would almost certainly lose our ability to turn into dragons. You would thence find yourself bereft of the very *weapons* that kept the kingdom safe and strong."

"Our shields would dim, Your Grace," Augum chimed in from the rear. "And with that dim would come the loss of the dragon. If war is on the tongue, with personal gain as the intent, then we believe the best thing for the seven kingdoms is for the dragon to die with us."

Boldly said, Bridget thought, nodding along, although she dared not look back so as to maintain some semblance of authority.

The Lord High Commander leaned closer to the king. "This is insubordination of the highest—" but he was cut off by the king raising a hand. "So the three of you are perfectly keen on sitting on your haunches, is that it?" the king asked.

"If a threat presents itself, we will respond accordingly," Bridget replied, quickly adding, "Your Grace."

The king stared at her. "Get out of my sight. Both of you. I need to confer with my *loyal* council members." The emphasis on the word *loyal* sent a shiver down Bridget's spine. It was a dangerous insinuation.

The king flicked an impatient hand and the guards stomped the floor with their spears, the *thud* echoing throughout the hall.

Bridget wanted to ask about being further confined to her room, but instead turned about and strode back toward the double doors. She said nothing to Augum until the pair of giant doors closed behind them, at which point she turned to him.

"I'm not returning to my room. Arcaner supper and alms?"

He smiled. "Supper and alms."

Olaf found her hand again. She looked at him, annoyed at his neediness. No, it wasn't she who was annoyed, but the predator who wanted to dominate all before her. She apologized by softening her eyes, and he wilted, cooing, "There's my sweet love."

They got to walking, the combined retinue of knights clanking in tow, with Mahmoute the Black Eagle keeping closest. *Spying, no doubt*, Bridget thought.

"Where's Jez?" she asked the boys as she unstrapped Isobel's breastplate.

"She's a little tired after, uh," and Olaf raised an imaginary bottle to his lips and made a, "*Glug glug glug*," sound.

Bridget sighed, feeling Mahmoute's judging eyes on the back of her head, for the woman wanted to replace Jez as her mentor.

Olaf flicked the steel of the breastplate with a finger, making a *ting*. "Here, let me help you with that." they stopped in the castle hallway to allow him to help her unstrap the breastplate.

"Thank you for this," Bridget said, handing Augum back the breastplate. He nodded, eyes dropping. "What is it?" she pressed.

Augum glanced uncertainly around at their retinue.

"Give us a moment, please," she said to them. When the knights hesitated, she flipped both palms. "Now, please." They glanced at each other uncertainly before shuffling a ways down the corridor. Mahmoute remained until Bridget, Augum and Olaf stared at her, at which point she pressed her lips together and joined the retinue of knights, well enough out of earshot.

"I left something out of my retelling of events," Augum whispered so softly that Bridget had to strain to hear him. "The predator, it ... it slipped into my eyes."

Bridget gaped. "What? What do you mean?"

Augum looked to Olaf, who blurted, "His eyes turned into a lizard's." He leaned close, murmuring, "Into a dragon's."

Bridget glanced between the two of them, settling her gaze on Olaf. "And are you sure you saw this? It wasn't an illusion?"

Olaf nodded gravely. "Jengo and Jez saw it too."

"Gods ..." Bridget delicately prodded her forehead with her fingertips. "It's been getting to me too. I've been feeling the heat of three suns. It keeps talking to me, wanting me to spread my wings. At one point I made the praying mantis pose and was *this* close to casting *the spell* ..."

"We've got to avoid casting it," Augum whispered.

"I agree," Bridget said. "At least until we learn how to better control the side effects."

As they stood in contemplative silence, Bridget's stomach rumbled.

"I heard that," Olaf said, patting her tummy. "Let's get this belly full," and he winked at Augum, which annoyed Bridget because she knew what it meant—the boys were going to drink. At least, Olaf was. Augum didn't partake much as he had to run the order, but he didn't stop Olaf from getting sloshed either. It was the favored relief for young men—and some of the young women, even in the order. The old book Augum studied religiously was filled with tales of merriment, which he had taken to heart, reviving festivities not thrown in centuries.

Bridget found herself leading the way to the historical Great Arcaner Hall while the boys chatted in the rear about their adventure. Upon arrival, Augum, as commander, sent Olaf, the official standard bearer, on rounding detail, meaning he was to call all available Arcaners and recruits to supper.

Bridget helped by organizing the servants, which the order paid in day wages, the monies coming from the order's coffers.

"How are the books?" Bridget asked when Haylee Tennyson, the order's treasurer, hobbled into the hall.

"Balanced," Haylee replied, watching the throng of servants setting places at the long tables, which were moved in from the side of the vast hall to form a large *U*, with the frontmost table lifted on a dais. "In fact, we're ahead of expectations, what with the tithing and donations that keep coming in. We could probably reduce member tithes to five percent and still have bountiful reserves."

"Let's keep it at ten in case of an emergency," Bridget replied. When not performing Arcaner duties, Arcaners made money for themselves by conducting arcane services for the populace. Ten percent of that work was *proata mentora*, meaning labor without charge and for the benefit of the community. And ten percent of what they *did* earn in their spare hours they tithed to the order.

Haylee nodded, and the two women stood behind their bench seats at the head table, chatting idly about this and that, aware of the retinue's presence. The knights stood in loose groups by the doors, while the old Black Eagle stood near Bridget.

Like a pesky fly, Bridget thought. She couldn't shake the feeling that the woman would report every detail of the trio's activities.

Arcaners streamed into the hall, greeting her and Augum with the three-pronged salute over the heart, with Carter Southguard flashing Bridget a brash grin. She noted how their faces lit up upon seeing their commander had returned, and wondered if she would receive such glowing looks if she were commander. She chided herself for the petty thought. Why would she care about adulation? But then she realized it wasn't about that at all, but about respect, which was essential to a leader.

The tables were set with white cloth trimmed with gold. The plates were a fine porcelain and marked with the full Arcaner crest. That same crest adorned mugs and tankards and forks and spoons and knives, all paid for with communal monies.

The hall soon buzzed with activity, and amongst the attendees were the senior Arcaners—almoner and healer Jengo Okeke, lieutenant and Guardian of the Order Alyssa Fairweather, and Herald Laudine Cooper, who was joined by Herald Brittany Mires, the latter bringing Sabby to Bridget, still on her leash.

"They wanted an Arcaner to take care of her, but I said I'd do it," the girl said with a perfunctory smile.

"I thank you."

The girl milled about for a moment as if she had a question on her mind.

"I thought it was a good piece," Bridget said.

The herald curtsied, face slacking with relief. "Thank you. I hope you do not mind if I stick around for a potential follow-up."

Bridget indicated an empty spot near the end of the high table. "By all means."

While Bridget got reacquainted with Sabby, which involved ear and neck scratches and cuddling and silly cooing, the seniors joined Augum and Bridget and Haylee at the high table, though all still stood behind their benches in wait for the commander's blessing. Even Jez stumbled in, face pale and hair disheveled. Although she was not an Arcaner, she was still a mentor to the trio and thus took her rightful place at the head table, though this time chose a spot at the end of a bench, where she proceeded to tiredly cough into a fist whilst avoiding people's gazes.

But whereas Bridget stood to Augum's left, and Olaf to her left, an empty space remained to Augum's right, which he kept glancing at.

Bridget gently elbowed him in a classic Leera-esque manner, drawing his attention. "Don't worry. She'll be home soon. And if she doesn't come, we'll go and drag her back ourselves."

That drew a faint smile from Augum, who then raised a hand, silencing the rather unruly crowd. "There have been strange occurrences of late that have given us cause for alarm," he boomed. "Rest assured the authorities are investigating as we speak." He went on to tell them a shortened and sanitized version of his adventures to the north, and how he had opened a pathway of communication between Solia and the wolven. He praised the efforts of the order and how they were steadily gaining the trust of the Ordinaries, who needed a source of justice that was impervious to corruption. At the end of his speech, after the applause died down, Augum looked to the rest of the high table. "Any comments from the seniors?"

Jengo's hand shot up as it used to do in class. "I'll be collecting alms for the poor at the end of the meal." The hand turned into a wagging finger. "Don't be stingy, you slovenly fiends!"

The hall burbled with guilty laughter.

"Now let us together recite the Sacred Chivalric Code of the Arcaner," Augum said, and all present recited all seventeen edicts before ending it with the Arcaner motto, "*Semperis vorto honos.*"

Then came the sound of benches scraping against the floor as people took their seats. A line of servants hired by the Arcaner order, liveried in traditional black-and-white garb, walked in holding trays of roasted gravy turkey and potatoes and salt-and-peppered steak and asparagus and leeks and spiced and roasted carrot and buttered bread. In no time, the *clink* and *clatter* of forks and knives scraping porcelain mingled with the burble of amiable conversation.

Bridget spotted Carter Southguard talking animatedly at a girl who was nodding politely but keeping to her plate. When he boomed a laugh at his own jest, she rolled her eyes at her neighbor, a fellow squire.

Still have a thing or two to learn about tact, Squire Southguard, Bridget thought.

While Olaf gulped a tankard of ale, she noticed Augum eating distractedly. "You know what I'm looking forward to in the new year?" she told him. "Learning a new simul."

He nodded as he carved up what remained of his steak. "Same. Can't wait to delve back into that ancient classroom."

"Oh, Cap—Cap! Can you hand this to the commander?"

Bridget leaned back in her chair and looked down the row to see Laudine holding a small sack. "It's his mail."

Bridget flicked a finger and the sack floated over. "Your mail, Aug," she said, plopping it into his lap.

He grimaced, undid the rough string, and fished out a few letters. He opened one and his face curdled. He rifled through the letters and scrolls, before shoving the already opened letter back into the sack and dumping it behind him."

Bridget flipped a questioning hand at him. "What?"

"They're all from women," he muttered, grabbing his fork and stabbing his turkey breast. "You can guess about what."

"No, I—oh. *Oh*. I'm sorry." She returned to her meal, having realized they were letters from women throwing themselves at Augum in hopes he would somehow choose them over Leera. She wanted to quip to him how they ought to have more dignity, but thought it was perhaps better to say nothing at all on the matter.

Sabby, sitting behind Bridget, abruptly perked up and whined. "What is it, girl?" Bridget cooed. "You want some steak too? Hmm? Or do you want to go outside?" Sabby was facing the doors. "I'll take you for a walk after we—"

Suddenly the entire hall shook as a low rumble went through the structure. Everyone instantly ceased eating to look around at each other, with most eyes focusing on the commander. A heartbeat later, all arcane torches snuffed, plunging the hall into semi-darkness. Bridget felt a cold wave through her soul, and instinctively knew what had happened.

Yet it was Augum who first shot to his feet, roaring, "Defensive positions!" The knights, who were already near the entrances, rushed to close and secure the doors. Everyone else took cover behind the mammoth pillars that dotted the hall, with the recruits hiding behind the seniors.

Bridget hunkered behind one of these pillars, where she raised her arm to flare her ten earthen rings—only for nothing to happen. She exchanged a grave look with Augum, who unsheathed Burden's Edge, while she ran for a training bin, shouting, "Weapons here!" She grabbed a short bow and was about to sling the quiver when she found herself staring at blunted arrows. The last time she had felt this vulnerable was during the war with Canterra.

"The armory's below," Mahmoute said, shooting to her side.

Olaf barreled in on Bridget's other side—and his entire robe front was wet and he stank of ale. In the chaos, he had somehow spilled a tankard on himself. *Probably in his rush to guzzle it down*, an infuriated Bridget thought. How was she supposed to depend on him when he prioritized ale in an emergency?

Her gaze returned to the blunted arrows sitting impotently in their quiver. For some reason, she did not know what to do—what could defanged warlocks do with minimal training? Hesitation permeated her being like the sweat dripping from her brow.

Meanwhile, Augum confidently commanded the Arcaners and recruits to grab whatever weapon they could get their hands on, and that included grabbing old pikes and spears and swords hanging along the walls, trophies from past wars. The knights even shared their daggers with some of the warlocks.

"The armory!" Mahmoute said to Augum, who promptly told eight nearby squires to run down and grab the sword and buckler carts from the armory and work together to manually haul them up the stairs. The young Arcaners sprinted through a side hall that eventually led to the kitchen, the location of the stairs.

"Group up, defensive positions," Augum kept repeating. "You, you, you—together. Seniors take point." The Arcaners did as they were told, each captaining a group of recruits and squires and dragoons. Bridget, realizing she did not have anywhere near the commanding resolve of Augum, had grabbed hold of Herald Brittany Mires and her apprentice Carter Southguard when a second rumble shook the hall, quieting everyone. This was followed by a distant *BOOM* that seemed to echo against the buildings of the courtyard.

In the dark and tense hall, everyone glanced at everyone else, as if hoping someone had an answer. But no one said a word.

Olaf suppressed a burp before stepping toward Bridget and protectively slinging both beefy arms around her. Infuriated, she threw him off.

"What'd I do?" he mumbled in hurt tones.

Ignoring him, Bridget raised a finger before a glassy-eyed Carter and a terrified Brittany, urging them to stay where they were, before doing the same to Olaf. Then she slapped the useless quiver aside, threw off her bow, and rushed to the doors.

"Step aside, sir," she commanded the armored knight who stood with his shoulder pressed against the door—and he happened to be the burliest of the lot, a bearded beast of a man with an extra-large pot helm.

"M'lady, I fear there is something out there," he whispered.

"Then let us gander at it so we may act appropriately," she hissed.

"But m'lady, these doors are protected with *magic*. They cannot be broken down."

Bridget gaped at him and his wild eyes full of hope and fear. The word *magic* was one children used. It was for games like Cups and for parlor magicians who yanked objects out of hats and from behind a child's ear. Anyone properly versed in the arts would use the word *arcane* or *arcanery*. He was surrounded by warlocks but ignorant to those arts.

"Sir," she said, placing a hand on his lobstered mail elbow. "My forearm is unlit, therefore the castle's defenses do not function. Do you understand?"

He glanced uncomprehendingly at her forearm.

One of the other knights, a pot-bellied fellow whose gray hair appeared above his visored eyes, whapped him on the helm with the back of his gauntleted hand. "Arm rings, young buck. Arm rings."

"Sir, please step aside so that we may assess—" but Bridget was silenced by a loud and beastly squeal from the yard, one that made bumps rise on her flesh, for it sounded as if it had come from the depths of the darkest jungle. All the knights retreated from the doors, which suddenly appeared threatening.

Only Bridget remained. Now wild-eyed herself, she glanced back at Augum, then at Olaf and Haylee, all of whom had experienced the terrors that were the jungles of Endraga Ra. All three were frozen in place. In fact, not a soul moved.

Breathing rapid shallow breaths, Bridget placed a hand on one of the door handles.

"No, m'lady, no!" hissed the hulking knight. "You'll kill us all!"

With her hand still on the handle, Bridget looked to Mahmoute, who was intently focused on her own forearm, as if demanding it light back up. She glanced to Augum. Her brother-in-war and commander gave a single shake of the head, and she let go of the handle.

"Aye, something is out there," the older of the knights whispered. "Something evil …"

Bridget urged her arm to relight, but it refused to do so. This was the longest one of these nullifying effects had lasted, a fact that froze her very core. Without arcanery, they might as well be straw dummies.

A squeaking clamor came from the hall. People jumped for positions, with the knights raising their blades, only for two carts to appear, pushed by the Arcaner squires Augum had dispatched earlier to the armory.

"Weapons!" one of them whispered, and every single warlock quietly shot to the carts. Bridget ran up to Olaf and flicked a hand at a bow — which of course did not move. Were it any other circumstance, she would have smacked a palm against her face — of *course* she couldn't use Telekinesis! Instead, she reached past her betrothed and grabbed the bow, then a quiver full of steel-tipped arrows which she slung over a shoulder.

She turned around in time to hear a loud *thud* from the pair of doors, as if something was trying to get in. Everyone scrambled to take up positions, with Bridget hiding behind a pillar, nocking an arrow, and drawing a bead on the doors. She could barely breathe and her hands shook so much that she worried she'd strike a friendly.

The doors thudded a second time with such force that the wood cracked and squealed. A fracture in the stonework snaked away from one of the iron hinges. Whatever was on the other side squealed again, the sound beastly and carnivorous, piercing the doors like they were parchment.

Bridget's shoulders rose and fell as she panted as if having sprinted a league. There was an exquisite terror to feeling completely helpless against an unknown force. *So this is what the Ordinaries feel like when facing a warlock*, she thought.

Thud! went the doors again, briefly bending inward as cracks now crept from all four hinges. People braced, expecting a fourth and final hit that would blow the doors open.

Suddenly Bridget felt a spark within her soul. She looked to her forearm and, upon flaring ten earthen arm rings, hissed, "We're back!" She then discarded her bow and nocked arrow, shrugged off the quiver, and made a second drawing motion, this time incanting, "*Summano arma flustrato!*" An earthen bow and already nocked arrow appeared in her hands, the arrow infused with the Confusion enchantment, for she had cast Bluster of the Dragon, an Arcaner simul.

Every warlock did the same, with many additionally summoning their elemental armor and shields. Now it was the warlocks who took charge, with Mahmoute and Augum and Olaf and Alyssa and Bridget shooting to the doors while the knights retreated behind them.

Augum raised three fingers. He dropped one, then a second, and upon dropping the third, pointed his fist at the doors and pumped his arm back and forth. Olaf and Alyssa, having been holding the handles, cranked them and threw open the doors.

In the dark courtyard, amidst the beaten snow just on the other side of the door, was a pile of ash.

"What the …?" Olaf whispered, kneeling and dabbing a finger into the ash. He raised that finger and watched the ash slide off, before looking back, confused as the day he was born.

Bridget crept past him, bow swiveling this way and that as she searched for enemies. Yet the yard was empty of people. She backtracked and, whilst keeping her summoned bow raised, examined the area around the ash.

"Footprints," Augum said, having already taken a knee beside Olaf to examine those very prints. "Giant ones with three wide toes." He shook his head. "These are not familiar to me."

Others pressed in to have a gander, and all shook their heads in the same manner. None had seen such prints before—except for one person.

"They're of a similar type to the ones the investigative committee found in the first strikes," she declared.

A man staggered into view from the archway that connected the inner and outer wards. Everyone with a bow drew a bead on him, whilst the warlocks readied to slap their wrists and blow him to oblivion.

The man was an archer himself, for he wore the livery of the castle guard. He removed his pointed helm as he stumbled forth in the snow, eyes wild and as wide as plums. He came to stand twenty feet before the heavily armored throng, and let the helm slip from his fingers into the snow.

"Somefin took 'em," he gibbered in a thick dockside accent. "Somefin took 'em …"

"Who?" Augum replied. "Who took them?"

The archer raised a single shaking finger as if about to make a point, yet he said nothing.

"Took them where?" Bridget asked.

The man's raised finger pointed still higher, and all eyes looked to the dark sky.

ZYGOTHIKA

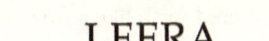

LEERA

It wasn't a startled waking, like one would wake from a nightmare, but rather a long and sordid journey back from an ethereal fog. And so it was that the human first became conscious of simply existing. Then came the thoughts, all jumbled and childlike, and then the feeling of flesh against cold stone, and of her own body trembling, and that she was a girl with a name, a girl lost in pitch darkness …

"Leera," she squeaked, teeth chattering. "That's who I am. Captain Leera Jones … Dragon Leera Matilda Jones …" Yet the voice sounded as if a mouse were talking. Confused, she sat up in the darkness, shivering violently, her undergarments thoroughly soaked through.

"*Shyneo*," she whispered, and her palm lit up with pale watery light that pulsed in time with her slow heartbeat. She saw herself in a corridor, one end of which led to stairs that vanished into standing water. But the proportions were rather strange. She withdrew her spectacles from her specially sewn undergarment pocket and placed them on her nose, hooking one temple at a time around each ear.

With her vision restored, she noticed a giant round thing sitting nearby on a tilt, but with four holes in it. At first she thought it was a shield, albeit one carved out of a horn. Except no horn could possibly be that big unless it belonged to a bull demon or something, and so she drew near — and yelped in surprise, for it was not a shield at all, but —

"A coat button," she squeaked. At last the fog fully lifted and it all came together. Horren's Keep. A Shrink casting. A mailbox slot. A puzzle. She was inside the puzzle, on the way to an ancient treasure room … or something.

"So, yeah, I'm tiny," she said aloud, as if to remind her mind not to freak out. There was something about coming out of a semi-coma in this form that was rather unsettling, making the mind wonder if this was the new norm.

"Heck, no," she said, shaking the odd feeling off. "Now let us focus." The first thing she did was spread her hands over her undergarments, which had been torn from squeezing through the mailbox slot. "*Apreyo*," she said, and watched the fibers reconnect and seal with a white light. "Much better. Got to have *some* dignity."

The hall ahead was dark, the only sound the violent chattering of her teeth that threatened to break. She was so cold that she had clenched her fists, partially obscuring the light from her right hand. But she couldn't unclench it. Instead she tottered forth like a frozen icicle, desperate for a heat source.

Then she stopped. "Idiot," she squeaked at herself. "Just cast Endure the Deep again!" But just as she was about to do that, she spotted something ahead in the corridor—a door, proportional to her tiny size. She shuffled to it, placed a hand on its bronze handle, and turned. It opened inward with a tiny *click*. She thrust her lit fist forth, revealing something she had not been expecting at all—a bedroom, one in proportion to her mouse size.

There was a dresser, a standing cheval mirror, a desk with a chair, and a single canopy bedstead with white linens embroidered on top with a big bear. The furniture had all been crafted with fine mahogany not found in these parts, and all had a thick layer of dust. A single tiny but proportional picture, woven from huge thread and depicting a kitten, hung on the wall above a hearth. And on the bed sat an old plush cat that looked like it had been woven by a giant needle. That one made Leera long for her own cat, Sir Pawsalot.

Unbelievably, she was staring at a *child's* bedroom.

Having forgotten about Endure the Deep and shivering to her very core, she stumbled to the hearth. Mercifully, it had a rune, which she promptly activated by slapping it and incanting, "*Igniato*." The hearth burst with a high fire that began to heat her bones.

"Ahh," she cooed, getting as close to it as she dared, snuffing her hand for the hearth amply lit the small room. Once her front was steaming from the heat, she turned around and heated her backside. She noticed more details about the room—a large and oval carpet, made of thick woolen curls and depicting a pink piglet, rested underneath the furniture. And in the corner of the room was a box of carved wooden toys—a horse, a pig, a cat, a knight, a wagon cart. All were worn from play, and all as dusty as the furniture. She could almost hear the echo of a child's laughter as they played with the toys.

"Horren had children," she blurted, recalling the records but not exactly how many. "He must have shrunk them and allowed them to take safety here." She enjoyed hearing the sound of her squeaky voice. When she had first learned the spell in the recent war, the squeakiness had been a source of great amusement to her, which Bridget had of course labeled "immature." But now it was a source of joy, for it represented a hidden life within a life. Being small felt like being a child on an epic adventure, a feeling she loved.

Leera turned about a few more times, until her skin was hot from the flames. Then she flared her hand, incanting, "*Un vun asperio aurum enchantus*," and was surprised to find the room thick with ancient enchantments long sunk to permanence. She examined the tendril weavings and found layers of complexity. Alarms, protections, the works—all meant to keep whoever had hidden here safe from the outside world. As always when facing ancient alarms, she imagined a skull in a grave getting pinged, and shivered at the thought of the bones stirring.

Satisfied she was safe from harm, she snuffed Reveal and explored the room, lifting the blankets, gently picking up the plush cat, examining the toys and desk. Lastly, she went to the dresser and opened the top drawer, finding neatly folded children's clothes made of cotton and linen and wool. The other drawers yielded much the same.

It gave her an idea, and she splayed a hand in readiness to tune to the arcane ether, whispering, "*Un vun deo*," the incantation to the 1st degree Unconceal spell. At first she felt nothing, but then came the usual tugs from above, strong and clear to her tiny form. The longer she tuned to the ether, the more of those tugs she could feel, until she could feel a weak pull coming from beyond the room and the corridor—and guessing from the direction, likely the mail slot she had already wormed through. She was about to give up on finding new signals when she felt something even gentler, almost like the echo of an old tug, barely discernible among the strong others. It was so weak she had to stand absolutely still and meditate on it, until she felt its pull more distinctly.

This whisp of a pull led her to the desk. Letting the spell die, she felt around the battered old wood, until her fingers felt a groove in the rear. She moved the desk away from the wall, slipped in behind, found the grooves, hooked her nails into them, and opened a small drawer.

There, upon a tiny padded pillow, sat the tiniest chest she had ever seen—about the size of a green pea—at least in relation to her usual size. She picked it up, removed her spectacles to get a closer look, and saw that it was made of gold. She brought it near the fire and carefully opened the lid. Inside was a golden key about the size of a grain of sand. Not even wanting to breathe lest she accidentally blow the chest and its key into the fire, she stared at the tiny contraption in childish wonder.

The implication hit her like a battering ram.

Somewhere in these ruins of an ancient castle was yet another chamber that required a still-lower level of Shrink. A casting that would make her proportionally small to this tiny sand-grain key. A size that would make a fly as big as a whale.

"Gods …" she squeaked. *So damn cute!*

Carefully—ever so carefully—she used a fingernail to flip the lid shut, then she took one of the children's socks, placed the chest inside, wrapped the sock up into a ball, and stuffed it into the sewn-in pocket she used for her spectacles.

Having explored that room thoroughly, she snuffed the hearth, relit her palm, and stepped back out into the corridor. Just down the hall, she found five more children's rooms just like the other one, albeit with varying motifs—one was decorated with cute fish, another with birds, another with squirrels, another with dogs. She found nothing hidden in any of those rooms other than a child's miniature wooden dog figurine, which she placed back on a dresser. The last child's room made her gasp.

"Lucky kid," Leera cooed, for it was a room she would have loved as a child, as everything was carved in the shape of a dragon. The desk had dragon feet, the canopy bedstead was an upside-down dragon, the dresser was a series of dragons sitting atop each other—even the desk chair, with its ball-and-claw feet, was a reclining dragon. The lone picture depicted a dragon in flight and the carpet showed one curled up and sleeping like a cat. She searched the room extra thoroughly but ended up frowning in disappointment when not a single scrap turned up. Not even a hint of something hidden.

But being surrounded by so many dragons also allowed a shadow to open its eyes from behind her soul. It wanted her to make the praying mantis pose and become a tiny dragon. It wanted her to destroy the walls and explore beyond them. To burrow into the depths below to see what they hid from the world above.

"Shut up," Leera snapped, slapping herself on each cheek, retreating out of the room and staring through the doorway into it. "Gods I wish I'd lived here." She closed the door, feeling as if she was closing the door on her own childhood, and moved on, muttering "Who would have thought that Horren, a purported evil necromancer or whatever, loved his kids?"

Another door led to a large family room, for there was a common area with plush cushions before a huge hearth. Above the mantel hung a large painting of a door amidst flames.

"Looks like the door to Hell," Leera muttered, and continued perusing about. She found a miniature set of cards, various old wooden games for families to play together, and a whole bookshelf full of dusty tomes fit for everyone in the family to read. Although they were all in the old tongue, the titles were still quite readable.

She smiled as her fingers traced over the spines. *Jolly Jinxes and Playful Pranks. Uncanny Cantrips for the Canny. Fearful Tales of Youngling Woe. Trials of Teenage Titans. Famous Adventuring Families.* And the whimsical, *When Tiny Tots Pilfer Pudding,* among others. She would have loved to take some back with her, but felt like that would be robbing the ghosts of the young, and so let the books be.

In the back was a mahogany supper table with ten chairs, and to the rear of that table, a whole kitchen, complete with a stone oven and proportional sets of copper pans and spoons and ladles that neatly hung on a lapis-tiled wall.

She searched the place top to bottom but, finding nothing interesting, moved on down the hall, where she found a master bedroom complete with a stunningly beautiful set of golden furniture styled royally. Everything, from the canopy bedstead to the pair of matching dressers to the cheval mirror to the desk to the triple wardrobe was intricately carved with flowers.

"Wow," was all Leera could mumble.

Alas, a thorough search again proved fruitless. But she *did* find a crimson academy robe, complete with the embroidered academy crest, made of velvet and cut in the old style—the sleeves were far too big, as was the hood, and the fringing was cream and ruffled old-lady-like. But she kind of liked it like that.

After arcanely repairing some of the golden threads, which had loosened over time, she donned the robe and stepped before the mirror, singing, "Hello, my lady, aren't you a pwetty, *pwetty* thing!" She stepped back and curtsied. "Sir, I accept this dance, and yes, this is indeed velvet." She scoffed, pressing the fingertips of a hand against her chest. "It certainly is *not* from a curtain, no! Do not insult my seamstress. Now take me to the floor—er, the dance floor, sir."

She drew her hands around her invisible husband, closed her eyes, and gracefully spun in place, dancing with him whilst humming the dreamy, "A Maiden's Love."

"Oh, you find me stunning, do you?" she cooed. "As it so happens, I find you agreeably handsome, sir." She giggled upon his reply like she imagined those prissy highborn women giggled, which was to say, snobbily. "Oh my, sir, those are some naughty, naughty thoughts indeed."

She pretended to rest her head on his shoulders and continued humming the gentle tune. When the song ended, she reached down and made a squeezing motion, pretending to squeeze his butt. Then she hopped back, squealing, "But it was so plump and juicy, sir! One has to sample the peach! *One has to sample the peach!*" Her head bobbed about to the imaginary repartee.

"*Fine*, you can squeeze mine too, then," and she stuck out her butt, only to jump away with a yelp. "Did thou just slap thy lady's behind?" She tut-tutted whilst shaking her head in an exaggerated manner. "Ugh, *so* unchivalrous. No dessert for thee. I said, *no dessert*," only to wilt into his invisible arms, whispering, "All right, maaaaaaybe later—*if you behave.*" She pressed his invisible nose. "And that's a big *if*, you fiend you."

Leera straightened and chuckled at her own antics before sighing longingly at the bed. Gods how she missed Augum. Craved his touch almost more than she could bear.

She looked to the mirror. "Soon, girl. Soon." If he didn't return, she would hunt him down like a bloodhound. She smiled. "Not a bad rhyme." She tilted her head at herself. "Interesting—you simultaneously look fashionable *and* as if you have hopped out of a painting of old. Wonder what the court vultures would say upon laying eyes on this figure." She did a little hip wiggle, imagining the harpies roasting with jealousy when her man paraded her about court.

She only hoped he would take the news well that she had slipped up and revealed the terrible truth that she was barren. She only hoped …

"All right, enough nonsense, young lady," she said in a croaky old voice.

She withdrew the rolled-up sock from her undergarments and stuck it into one of the oversized pockets of the robe. Then she conducted a thorough search, but surprisingly found nothing of interest. She left the room and moved on, soon reaching a dead end filled with storage barrels. She pried the lid of one open and found it full of linen-wrapped parcels. She unfurled one and out rolled a chunk of biscuit beef, an ideal choice for those wanting to hunker down for a while—or travel long distances, for such beef tended to last for decades.

Out of sheer curiosity, she took a nibble, and other than finding it salty and dry as a bone, it tasted fine. She unfurled a bunch more, tucked some into her new yet not-so-new velvet robe, and slowly chewed on the first as she inspected the rest of the barrels. One held winter clothing that had long molded over to the point of decay, one held sugar, another salt, another flour, another an ashy powder that looked like it had once been some type of food, for it stank of moldy rot, and another held dried fish, which stank so rancidly that, upon taking a whiff, Leera slammed the lid shut and stumbled away gasping and coughing.

After gathering herself, she cast Reveal and Unconceal, but found nothing unusual around the barrels or in the wall.

"No miniature door either," she muttered, crinkling her nose. She returned to the children's bedrooms and searched them anew, hand splayed. Then she did the kitchen and finally the family room. Exasperated, she lit the large central hearth, slumped on a cushion in her fine velvet robe, and sat loudly chewing on the beef while her eyes trawled the room, one hand lit with Shine, the other with Unconceal. The books looked interesting, but would take an age to paw through. Except her intuition told her she'd find nothing there either.

Having finished one beef biscuit, she moved on to a second. After tearing off a chunk with her teeth, her eyes settled on the painting above the large hearth. She tilted her head. "Hell," she whispered, tapping her chin with the chunk, mouth chewing like a cow. Her eyes went to the real flames in the hearth below and then back to the painting.

Leera snorted. "Horren, you clever bastard you," and she shot to her feet, snuffed the hearth, and stepped back a few paces. As the hearth still smoked from the leftover heat, she splayed a hand forth and incanted, "*Aquatos.*" A gentle jet of water splashed forth, making the hearth steam and hiss. That arcanely summoned water quickly vanished, but she kept shooting it until she was certain the hearth was cold again. Then she poked around the kitchen until she found what she had been searching for—a straw broom.

She floated it over telekinetically, grabbed the handle, twirled like a dancer, and began to artfully sweep out the dust from around the fake logs whilst humming the spritely tune to "The Heir and the Servant." The logs were decorative and made of stone, meant to make the fire look more real despite it being arcanely enchanted. She flicked a finger and telekinetically had them roll forth until they were clear of the hearth, before she swept the dust out from behind. Then she tossed aside the broom, dusted her hands in a *Job well done* manner, crouched down, and crawled into the hearth.

Recessed into the very back center, down a series of tiny steps, was a tiny door.

"Gotcha," she whispered. What was interesting was that this door did not show a signature Unconceal could pick up. That meant it had been skillfully crafted *without* the intent to conceal—in other words, for all to see. The cleverness came in with the logs, which must have been placed in later, perhaps by a servant with the intention to decorate, meaning the door had been obfuscated without leaving a tendril signature Unconceal could pick up.

"Genius," she declared, withdrawing from the hearth. "Absolute genius."

Leera stood up and took a series of breaths, readying herself mentally for the Shrink casting. Her current mouse size was the smallest she had ever made herself. Shrinking herself down to be proportional to a sand-grain-sized key would be a whole new challenge.

She snuffed Unconceal but kept her palm lit. Mentally prepared, she was about to point to the top of her head to begin the incantation, when she realized something. "Gods, almost forgot," and she withdrew the sock, unwrapped it, withdrew the chest, and placed it near the door. "Wouldn't do much good to accidentally shrink *that* any further, would it?" she muttered.

With the chest in place, she hopped back, refocused, pointed to the top of her head, and incanted, "*Smolla boda infintessima axteney su*," whilst carefully dragging those fingers down. Her body shrank in proportion to that dragging, an agonizing process that made her want to scream from the bone-crunching pain.

When she was about the size of a bumble bee, she stopped—and promptly keeled over, holding herself and trembling, not from cold, but from the horrible memory of the pain of transformation. She loved the effect of the spell, just loathed casting it.

It took some time to shake off the terrible sensations, but she finally clambered back to her feet and dusted herself off. Her Shine spell lit up a small area around her. Everything else was pitch dark. The room now felt like a gargantuan cavern. Dust particles on the ground were huge. Dust from the hearth, previously swept away and ignored, sat about like giant sand dunes. Even clambering over them was a trial. Passing a stone log was like passing a fallen grain silo.

After a trek, she brightened her light, and the outline of the now massive hearth barely became visible. She trod forth, a tiny light in a vast darkness, until her light reflected back in a strange manner. She froze, for a moment thinking she had seen a cluster of eyes. Then something moved ahead in short bursts, something that was definitely coming toward her.

Leera made an unsheathing motion from her hip, hissing, "*Summano arma*," and a watery shortsword appeared in her hand. Then she summoned her shield to her left arm, ready for a battle. Yet her innards trembled with fear, for shrinking oneself also proportionally shrank the power of one's arcanery.

The cluster of eyes soon reappeared rather abruptly over the next dust dune. There they waited, watching her. A hairy arm slowly moved above the dune, followed by another.

Gods, a spider, she thought, swallowing. And it was huge—five times her size at least. Suddenly her sword and shield felt as worthless as a toothpick and a leaf. She looked past the monster and saw the glint of the golden chest sitting by the door.

A complicated spell came to mind no one else had the temerity to learn—Spectral Teleport. But could she cast it now that she was the size of a bumble bee?

She let her shield vanish and readied the sword by holding it behind her at a slashing angle, then focused on the nuance of the spell, which involved visualizing oneself zipping through the arcane ether, appearing for a moment, then quickly vanishing again. Just as the spider shot forth, she snapped out, "*Impetus peragro spectra xae!*"

She vanished and reappeared with a *thwomp* just above the spider in time to slice it along its head with a sickening *shloop*. By the time its hairy arms lashed out at her, she'd vanished with a second *thwomp*, then reappeared along the line of teleportation—which happened to be high above the golden chest. Immediately plummeting, she slowed her fall by telekinetically latching onto the wall and swinging down toward the floor until she connected with the stone at a fast run, the summoned shortsword vanishing from a lack of concentration. After sliding to a halt, she whirled about, watery palm brightly lighting up a desert of dust dunes, blood racing that much quicker after a successful casting.

Something dragged itself forth along the dust. The spider soon appeared, though with a head split open grotesquely. Not wanting to allow it to get any nearer, she drew an outline, incanting, "*Summano elementus minimus draco*." A dragon proportionally the size of a pony— though perhaps the size of an ant in reality—sizzled to life before her. She pointed at the spider, hissing, "Draco—attack!"

Her dragon flicked its watery tail and shot forth. The spider lunged at it, and the pair tussled ferociously. The spider, larger and stronger than the dragon, quickly ripped off both of the dragon's wings, but not before losing three of its eight legs. By the time the spider destroyed the dragon, making it vanish, it was down to two legs, and awkwardly dragged itself toward Leera.

"Don't give up easily, do you, you ugly bastard?" she muttered. She aimed and slapped her wrists together, roaring, "*Annihilo!*" A jet of water drilled right into its multi-eyed face, and it fell into the dust, where it lay still.

Not knowing if it was really dead or simply *playing* dead, Leera slapped her wrists again, shooting a second jet into its face. The way the body nudged back told her the nasty thing was in fact deceased. Yet the cluster of eyes continued to reflect her light.

"Creepy thing." She wiggled her shoulders, shrugging the icky encounter off, and turned her attention to the chest. Now that she was proportional to its size, she could see it was decorated with all sorts of intricate details—books and tomes and scrolls and tablets and artifacts.

She opened the lid and snagged the key, both of which turned out to be surprisingly heavy. Then she walked down the steps and stopped before a stone door fit with a small golden keyhole.

"Wish you two were here with me," she whispered, thinking about Augum and Bridget. How she missed them so! She sighed for the umpteenth time, stuck the key into the hole, and turned. There was a *click* and the door sprang open. She pushed the stone door inward, finding it heavy. Not wanting to get surprised by another spider or something worse, she closed it most of the way behind her, then looked about.

The only thing in the room was a basalt obelisk engraved with golden runes.

"Ah, one of these," she squeaked rather excitedly, for portal pillars reminded her fondly of not only the academy, but adventures long past. And each one was slightly different. The ones at the academy were simple, crafted to be understood quickly, while others were more like puzzles.

"What sort are *you*?" she whispered, pressing a hand to the cold stone. Unlike when she had been a mere fledgling warlock, she quickly recognized the various runic symbols—and the ones that were fake, meant to confuse the undeserving.

The first sequence she recognized as belonging to the 17th degree portal spell, and the second, located below and in tinier symbols, were parts of the incantation to the Shrink spell, which even provided a relative size measure in the word *pebla*—*pebble* in the old tongue, the word engraved underneath a square with a small lump inside it. That word indicated that the portal would be in proportion to her size, a necessity as a full-sized portal would not fit into such a cramped space.

It was also the only word engraved into the pillar, likely because it was an obscure rune. Everything else was a runic symbol—and in the case of the fake ones, slightly different. The correct runes to the basic version of the Portal spell were a simple oval, a square with two upside-down triangles facing each other, a square divided down the middle vertically, and the letter *T* with eyes. The fake ones were variations of those. The Shrink spell had its own sequence of runes, which took some time to identify as they were more obscure. The tricky part would be figuring out the final destination rune, and in this case, there were several.

"A box filled with trees probably means getting tossed outside," Leera said, finger tapping the rune. "A box with tables inside likely means the main supper hall of the castle. A box with vertical bars probably means a prison. A box with rectangular slabs might zip me back to the crypt—let's not go *there* again, eh?" She chuckled, elbowing an imaginary friend and making her sharp eyebrows dance. "A box with a tower inside likely means the highest lookout tower the castle had." She wondered what would happen if she were to teleport somewhere that was ruined, like the tower. Likely she'd appear inside a brick or stone block—or even high up in thin air, as might be the case if she teleported to a long-ruined tower.

"And that would be that," she muttered. " 'Oh, what happened to Leera?' " she squeaked, mimicking a stranger's voice, then she shrugged, voice dropping in imitation of a man's voice. " 'Dis'ppeared. Ain't 'eard of 'er since she went down into 'orren's hellhole. Right shame, it is. She was a good 'un. Dang cute and wit sharp as a blade, if you ask me. Oh, but they did find a leg fused into a brick, aye, that they did.' " She scoffed, voice now mimicking Bridget. "Leera Matilda Jones, will you please focus?" Then she switched back to her own voice and listed off a bunch more runes that she thought represented a larder, a storehouse, a farm, a cellar, a library, an archery range, the inner ward, and the outer ward.

"And then there's this …" Her finger traced the outline of a box within a second box within yet a third box, inside of which was a series of tiny vertical lines sitting on a horizontal line. "Is that what I think it is …?" Her fingers drummed the rune. "Worth giving it a go."

She practiced by pointing at the right sequence of runes as her lips silently moved, working out the details of the spell. Getting any part wrong, or touching the wrong rune once the sequence had begun, could result in a curse being thrown at her, getting teleported outside of the premises—or worse.

When she thought she had it right, she used her lit hand to touch each of the correct runes in the right sequence, whilst incanting, *"Portus ea ire itum smolla porta pebla."* She finished by tapping the rune depicting lines within three boxes. Unlike some pillars, these runes did not light up until she had touched that last one, at which point all the activated ones lit up golden. There was a flash of light as a black oval ripped into existence before her, shooting wind at a fearsome pace.

"Gotcha," she said, voice snatched by the wind.

Still holding the golden key, she realized it would be better to leave it here with the door still ajar, and so she placed it on the floor, where it could easily be found again. Then, with her robe and hair ruffling in that small gale, she took a deep breath and stepped into the black void. After a brief hurtle through the pitch-dark arcane ether, she was spit out onto a stone floor, the portal vanishing behind her with a quiet *whoosh*.

Hand still lit brightly, Leera got up and found herself standing on black marble layered with thick dust. Her light, comparatively weak due to her size—casting strength shrank in proportion, after all—barely reached thirty "tiny" feet ahead. She sensed a cavernous space loomed beyond.

She glanced about and saw that she stood in a recessed slot in a wall, one made specifically for the sole pillar that stood just behind her. With the dust being waist deep, she shoved at the air, squeaking, *"Baka!"* and sent a plume of it flying. The particles were so large and gross looking that she covered her face with her oversized robe sleeve. Once it had settled, she stepped into the space she had created and did it again, repeating this maneuver twice more, until she could step out of the recessed slot in the wall.

Far ahead, through the ocean of dust, she could see that the floor changed from black to white, meaning the floor here was checkered—and that it was a large enough space to get back to regular size.

Even though the mere thought of inducing the bone-crunching pain of expansion made her shiver, she nonetheless mentally prepared herself to nullify Shrink. After a series of deep, girding breaths, she pressed the fingers of one hand together, pointed them down by her knees, and incanted, *"Smolla null,"* then drew them back up herself. And while she did so, her body blew up—as did the pain. Every bone and muscle and organ stretched and exploded. She heard her innards cracking and groaning, and it was all she could do to remain focused.

Once she felt the telltale inner plumpness of her organs and limbs reaching their regular size, she collapsed onto her knees, wanting to retch from the sheer memory of that harrowing pain. "Gods I hate that part of the spell," she croaked, palm light barely at candle strength. But it was good to be back to normal size.

After recovering her wits, she got up, dusted herself off, brightened her palm—and gasped.

For she stood in a giant castle-style cube of a room approximately four stories high, one filled with balconies. Each balcony held something different, from what appeared to be specimens in jars, to half-sculpted statues and marble busts, to a collection of taxidermy animals, to who knew what—she could only see so far from the base floor, which seemed mostly composed of library shelving filled with books.

But it was what was in the center of that bottom floor, directly ahead, that gave Leera pause, for it was the same living room she had already visited while mouse-sized, minus the walls. Everything else was the same as the miniature version—the cushions before the hearth and mantel, the painting that hung above that mantel that now hung in space. The shelves of toys and various family books. The supper table and chairs. Even the kitchen. She didn't know what to make of it.

Not knowing what to expect, Leera switched focus, splayed the fingers of her left hand, and incanted, "*Un vun asperio aurum enchantus.*" The entire place lit up with dense and complex tendril geometries long sunk to permanence and faded from time. Judging by their elegant beauty, all were master castings. Interestingly, the most complex geometries resided in the center with the living area.

Intrigued, Leera approached, stopping before a particular floor enchantment so complex she stooped down to examine it further. She traced the lines with a finger, identifying the geometries as she went. "There's the trigger," she murmured, talking to herself to stave off the silence. "If I'm not mistaken, these intricate blue tendrils are of the illusory family tree of enchantments. And these brown tendril edges here seem to point to variables of … can it be summoning? Yes, but not the threatening sort."

She recognized she'd seen such geometries before, and a smile slipped into the corner of her lips. She stood up. "It's going to be a pleasure to meet you," she whispered, and took a step forth onto the pattern. The tendril enchantments lit up and exploded forth into a complex miasma of tangled weavings that formed figural shapes. Realizing she didn't need to see the geometries, she lowered her hand, incanting, "*Un vun null,*" snuffing Reveal.

There came the sound of a child's laughter as a little girl skipped by Leera, who gasped a second time, for bathed in the pale watery light of her palm stood an entire family. Or rather, they milled about performing various tasks. The mustachioed father, middle-aged and happy, doted on his wife, while their six children of various ages, from the little girl all the way to sulky teenagers, sat around the living room, some reading books, some playing games together.

"Ooh, my sweet, my sweet," sang the father, slowly dancing around his wife.

"Ooh, my sweet, my sweet," echoed the wife, smiling lovingly at her husband.

All were ghostly and all wore varying colors of robe, even the little girl, though perhaps to get her used to wearing a warlock robe rather than her being able to cast arcanery. Her robe was blue, meaning at least a 3rd degree, surely well beyond her capabilities. None saw Leera, nor seemed to be aware of anything beyond the living room.

For some reason Leera couldn't fathom, as the scene played itself out before her, of a family merely enjoying the simple pleasures of life, tears began rolling down her cheeks, dripping off her chin.

She sat down, crossed her legs, and watched them live their moments. The father seemed to show only love and kindness to his wife and his children, yet when he glanced away, there was a strikingly cold look to his dark eyes, and his face, when at rest, twisted into a cruel grimace. Yet both helped each other set the table for supper, flicking at copper forks and spoons, which telekinetically shot from an invisible wall and settled into place beside plain porcelain plates. And in the center of that table sat a fat Endyear candle on a bed of holly.

"Faaaaather," whined the little girl, dumping herself into a chair by the table where the family was assembling. "Beseech you, canst I not go out to play?" she asked in a refined Solian tongue of old, speaking close enough to the Endyear candle for it to waver about.

"Pray don't blow out the candle, sweetie," the mother chided, pointing at her chair so that it scraped backward a bit on the floor. " 'Shouldst the candle dieth after Endyear, all would be clear …' " the woman said, and Leera, knowing the old proverb well, mouthed along to the rest of the words. " 'Shouldst it dieth prior, the house would know naught but ire.' "

"I wouldst nay *ever* condemn the house, Ma. So, Father? Mayest I go? By your leave, of course?"

"Thou mayest frolic after supper, ye little devil, ye," the father sang back, readying a ceramic bowl of steaming potatoes. "Only keep eyes on the rabble. Some take to scheming all too naturally."

The little girl rolled her eyes and sighed. "Yes, Papa, knowest I this."

"Tomorrow be Merrygive," a teenage son noted, casually shuffling a deck of cards.

"Butter cookies for the old giveth by the young," the mother sang, floating a large bowl of soup to the table. "But this year, the lot of you will aid your ma in the baking."

This elicited a groan from the younglings.

And on it went, the repartee, the idle conversations and the guessing games and laughter and the readying for a rich feast, all mingling with the sound of two people in love humming various tunes, now and then touching in that loving way …

Leera's eyes unfocused. She imagined Augum humming to her as they set places for their children in Castle Arinthian. Or perhaps in some far-off hillside home where no one knew them, or expected anything of them.

It was that resolve to one day have a family of her own with her beloved man that made her shoot to her feet—and just in time to witness the family take their places at the table and join hands. When the last of those hands joined, the family smiled … and dissipated into nothingness. The lamps and hearth and Endyear candle, previously lit in the scene, faded to darkness, leaving an afterglow amidst the echo of that little girl's laughter.

The loneliness hit so profoundly that Leera staggered as if struck, clutching—and mangling—the robe over her heart, which had likely once belonged to that very woman she had just seen.

She looked around. The knowledge here was priceless. But it was also the tomb of a family. She knew that, just didn't know where the family was buried.

Then she noticed the floor beneath the carpet, for it seemed to cover golden rectangular lines. She stepped forth into the silent and dead living room and used her foot to peel back the edge of the carpet, revealing an inscription. And the more she peeled back, the more she found.

Teptus Abadeyus Horren, husband, father, warlock, researcher
Lorassa Juna Horren, wife, mother, warlock, researcher
Sired Millicent, Bevera, Yasheeka, Togus, Giyus, Hakora, Minelda, Bob

She snorted at Bob. "All those interesting names, and then they call one Bob. And eight kids—busy bees indeed! I wouldn't want more than one, maybe two. But then again, you had servants, didn't you?"

There were more names underneath as the bloodline continued, but she didn't bother uncovering them all, and curled the carpet back. Her quest was clear. As rich a bounty as she had stumbled across, she'd come for one piece of knowledge only. Now she just had to find it.

Her eyes fell to the bookshelves that lined the walls of the large room. In between, in the middle of each of the four walls, was a staircase that rose to the three higher floors and balconies. By one of these staircases, a black slab jutted out of the floor. Curious as to what it was, she strode up to it and saw it was etched with various golden ovals, each paired with a rune. The runes were squares, and within each square was a simple motif—a tower, a knife and fork, a barrel, and so on, all the way to a copse of trees. As with the portal pillar, each represented a different room in the castle above. She noted the one with the trees, for it would almost certainly lead to the outdoors.

Scanning the bookshelves was interesting from an arcaneological perspective but fruitless for her quest, for it would take forever to understand the titles, all of which were in the tedious old tongue, a task she had no patience for.

She craned her neck to examine the balconies. "What if …?" Inspired, she ran up the closest winding staircase, and was soon standing in a corridor that surrounded the floor, giving access to the various balconies. She went to the first balcony and saw that it was full of shelves filled with jars of geological specimens—rocks, clay, earth, dirt, dust, and so on. Each was meticulously catalogued in the old tongue, sometimes in squiggly script, sometimes in neat and loopy script. The former she thought belonged to the husband and the latter to the wife.

"What a team they must have made," Leera whispered, tracing a little heart that had replaced the dot of the letter *i*.

She moved on, hurrying out of sheer excitement and curiosity, ignoring the deep thirst gnawing at her dry lips—she had neglected to bring a skin of water, and the salted biscuit beef had dried out her stomach, lending a small sense of urgency.

She peeked in on balcony after balcony, not knowing what she was looking for, until she hit the second of the three floors—and her eyes fell upon a slew of jars sitting on shelves filled with the fetuses of animals—and humans. The sight would have previously terrorized her, but in the context of the other balconies, which had been filled with proper research, she felt a deep benevolence from these jars, for they represented the gathering of knowledge.

She stepped onto the balcony, eyes poring over the various other objects sitting on various tables and stands—books, scrolls, even tablets of old. She was most drawn to a central lectern, which had a huge book on display, half open, a crimson silk bookmark slicing its middle.

Her fingers trawled the handwritten wording, fine and articulate, but in the old tongue, which she translated under her breath. " '*Baby 17 ... lizard ... hair of possum ... deceased. Baby 18 ... lizard ... eggshell ... deceased.*' " Line after line of such cataloguing, each with a different physical variable.

"You were experimenting with birth," Leera whispered. "Using ritualistic ingredients as variables ..." The thought that perhaps the Horrens had been experimenting with death intruded rudely into her mind, but she refused to let it spoil her quest.

She flipped the huge pages back, hand skimming along the words, until she came to a certain chapter titled *Kusus*—Curses in the old tongue. The entire chapter was filled with a wide repertoire of warlock curses, line after line of them, all alphabetically organized, with a bibliographical reference that seemed to correlate with the main floor library. These days, such knowledge would be locked up in highly restricted archives.

But it was a certain word that her finger and eyes desperately searched for—and when they stopped on it, her heart skipped a beat.

Zygothika—Ei Rivika necromantos kusu tos murtos o utera. " '*Zygothika—* A Rivican necromantic curse that kills the womb,' " she whispered in translation, already worrying that the phrase *kills the womb* sounded so permanent.

She had done enough research about ancient curses to at least be familiar with the name of the curse. Alas, the curse was so old that the name was all that remained in the available records she had gotten a hold of—until now, for at the end of the line was a bibliographical reference— *Kusu.Za.1.*

Heart pumping, Leera raced back down the staircase to the main floor, then pawed at the bookshelves until she found the section titled *Kusu*—for curses. "*Zee a, zee a, zee a,*" she kept repeating, until she found a thin black spine labeled at the base with the neat script, *Kusu. Za.1.*

Having been searching for such a book for years, she reverently knelt before the shelf, slipped the book out of its slot, and placed it on her lap. The binding was a strange black leather of a skin she did not recognize, with a simple crimson word sliced into the flesh of the book as if carved by a knife.

" 'Zygothika,' " she whispered, fingers tracing the spiky word. Those fingers slipped under the cover and attempted to open the book—except it remained shut. "What the—" She tried again, to no avail, almost like it was glued. A sinking feeling settled into her stomach, and she splayed a hand over the book, incanting, "*Un vun asperio aurum enchantus.*" Sure enough, a dense tendril web appeared, indicating the book was tightly sealed with key-lock arcanery she did not recognize. The sheer complexity told her it would be quite the challenge to decipher.

"Could be a particularly complicated kargeyasnara," she muttered, "which has of course long sunk to permanence." She slapped the book with her palm. "Blasted thing! So close yet so far ..."

Suddenly an alarm blared in her head—the one she had placed at the archway gate to Horren's Keep! Another assassin, no doubt, one clever enough to have skipped right to where her trail had led. And this one would find Revel first—and surely murder her.

"Not if I can help it," Leera said, shooting to her feet. Not wanting to risk teleporting through rock—after all, she had no idea where this room really was—she instead ran to the black slab of stone etched with golden ovals. Without hesitating, she pressed her lit palm against the one with the copse of trees, only to realize she did not know the activation word. Seeing none on the front of the slab, she glanced behind—and saw a single golden word, *Lorassa*.

"The name of his wife," Leera whispered, refocusing on the oval. She pressed her hand to it again and said, "*Lorassa.*" A portal flared to life, shooting wind from within its dense blackness. Leera stepped through, emerging in a dark snowy forest that *thwoomed* and swayed and cracked from a cold and blustery wind.

She spotted what looked like the rear of the ruins of Horren's Keep, and set off at a run, feet crunching through unbroken snow. She climbed through a hole in the ruined curtain wall that looked like it had been punched through by a giant, and quickly found herself back in the main hall.

"Revel!" Leera called in a hissing whisper, shooting down the stairs, hands in attack formation. "Revel!"

"That you, Cap?" the girl replied too loudly, emerging from around a corner. "Writhing worms of the devil, you're all right!" she blurted, abruptly hugging her. "Was starting to worry you'd drowned. What the hell are you wearing, though?" Revel asked, eyeing Leera's ancient frill-edged robe. "And what's that evil-looking book about?"

"Never mind all this right now—someone tripped the archway alarm," Leera replied, unhooking Revel—it was weird to receive a hug from her apprentice. Now she knew what Jez felt like when Leera tried to show her too much affection. "Let's grab what we can and 'port out of here. We don't have long until the assassin figures out how to get inside. Go, go, go!"

Whilst keeping alert to their surroundings, the pair worked quickly to tear down their tents and stuff everything into their rucksacks, with Leera guzzling on a waterskin along the way.

Leera finished stuffing that waterskin into her rucksack on top of her tent when she heard a groaning noise from up in a hallway. She snuffed her palm and grabbed hold of Revel, Group Teleport on her lips. "Intruder in the hallway," she whispered in the darkness, lit only by patches of pale starlight that filtered in through the windows. Whoever it was had been clumsy—or in a rush to get to them. Either way, they were too slow. But Leera also wanted to see if she could capture the person and interrogate them. After all, she didn't want to have to dodge assassins for the rest of her days. Her stamina reservoir was full and reflexes keyed.

"We're taking the high ground," Leera whispered, prowling to the closest staircase, one hand clutching Revel's arm in case she had to teleport them out of there.

Just as she was about to peek out from the top of the stairs, two people careened around the corner—and slammed directly into them. Leera summoned her shield and was about to slap her wrists together—

"Lee, Lee, Lee, it's us!" an all too familiar voice shouted.

"*Shyneo!*" Leera snapped, flaring her palm. Her heart soared, for she found herself staring at her beloved Augum and her best friend Bridget. She almost burst into tears, but instead of crying, she threw her arms around their necks and squeezed them close.

THE TRIO REUNITED

AUGUM

Augum could barely breathe from the stranglehold of love Leera had on him. Bridget was the first to squirm away, only because Leera wanted him all to herself. She proceeded to shower his face with kisses whilst cooing, "Oh my sweet love found his beloved girl using his betrothal ring …"

"I did, yes," he replied, showering her with kisses back. He thumbed over his shoulder. "I recognized your tendril artistry on the stick and thought I'd give you a head's up by triggering it."

"Shoot, I guess I'm not as good at hiding things as I thought," Leera muttered. "Anyway oh my gosh I missed you you'll never *belieeeeeve* what I've been through and the stuff I've found I mean Horren is a genius how he confounded people trying to use Unconceal by hiding coins in bricks all over the place and oh I shrank myself down to the size of a mouse and then a bumblebee and I battled a spider and almost froze to death and there's a shipwreck ring and I uncovered Horren's long-hidden lair and he had a family and children that he loved and they sometimes took shelter in a miniature home underground which led to a still more secret lair which I'm going to tell the arcaneologists about so they can catalogue the place and its treasures but anyway that's where I found a certain book—"

"Lee, Lee, Lee, slow down," Augum had to say, trying to gently get her to stop mauling him—only to find himself drawn into a deeper kiss, which quickly devolved into a full-on make out. Next thing he knew they were all over each other.

"Ugh, you two," Bridget muttered, turning her back whilst Revel gaped, eyes wide with shock, until Bridget grabbed her arm and turned her about too, adding, "Let's give them a moment, shall we?"

"I've got a *lot* to tell you as well," Augum whispered, running one hand through her raven hair and the other holding onto her waist. Being taller, he looked down at her face. He enjoyed the smattering of freckles, that mischievous smile, those dark and voluminous eyes which reflected back love and loyalty and caring and deep friendship and understanding …

"I bet you do," Leera cooed.

"Did you get my letter?"

"What letter?"

"The one I stuck in the vault."

"Oh, uh, I've been meaning to check it but got caught up mucking about and trying not to drown. What'd you say, anyway?"

"Only that I love and miss you and that the kingdom is sliding into oblivion."

"Aww, love you and missed you too." She squeezed him, then stamped her foot, testing the ground. "Not in oblivion yet. How'd you get here so fast, anyway?"

"I've been to Horren's Keep for an Arcane Army Combat class excursion to study one of the battles here," Augum replied. "But before we get into things, um, I found out about the herald piece …"

"Oh. That." Her grip loosened, but he kept his firm. "Sorry about that," she mumbled, looking away. "I done goofed."

"I heard the tale. And I forgive you."

"You … you do?"

He waved the matter aside. "Let them gossip and conspire and twist themselves into knots making a thing out of it. *We* is what's important. Us." He'd had a long think on it and resolved to support his girl no matter what.

She melted in his arms and kissed him, whispering, "Maybe."

"What's that mean?"

She smiled coyly. "You'll see. Let's just say I didn't make this trek for nothing. But I'll get to all that."

"Fine, but in the mean, spill the ale about your adventures, missy. And hello, Revel."

"Hi, Commander," Revel blurted awkwardly.

They quickly traded tales, and only when they had unpeeled themselves from each other did Leera pinch Bridget to tell her side, until they were practically talking over each other to make themselves heard in their excitement. Augum told of his experience up north, with the wolven and the arcane snuffing effect, whilst Bridget told of her travails with the royal court and how they wanted to use the trio as weapons to conquer more land and about the latest strange snuffing circumstances and how she and Augum weren't supposed to be away from the castle but had snuck out to fetch Leera themselves anyway. Leera's tale was the longest, and she told of her escapades into the lake and the ring and the assassin and her adventures into Horren's Keep.

"Wait, wait, wait, back up a moment there, missy," an alarmed Augum said, scrubbing the air with a hand. "What's this about an assassin?"

"Oh, it's nothing, just some fool sending another fool to get this back—" and she withdrew the shipwreck ring and presented it with both hands like a trophy. "I suspect the ring leads to more treasure or something."

"Let me see that," Bridget snapped, and snatched it from Leera, readying to flare her hand over it.

"Don't bother. I've already inspected it," Leera said. "We need a proper arcaneologist to have a gander, as it's old arcanery. Can't see the tendrils anyway, at least without an Ohmish glass. I have one in my room back in our castle, which you can borrow if you ever need it for—"

"Never mind all that." Bridget raised her straight eyebrow at Leera. "And you thought it was wise to simply ..." She looked to Augum with that *Can you believe this girl?* look. "... put this ring on?"

Leera thought about it and crinkled her nose. "Well, when you put it like *that*, obviously it wasn't my brightest moment. I wore it more like a trophy, so I guess I didn't think too deep into it. I mean, how was I supposed to know that a ring I found at the bottom of the lake—" She thumbed over her shoulder. "—that went down like fifty years ago would still activate? That wreck was *deep*, and I found a whole bunch of old coins with it and I'm proud of how I survived it and—"

"The assassin," Augum interjected, eyes darting about in search of threats. "Why did someone come after you?"

"I'm telling you, I think there's more treasure about, and the ring can point to it or something."

"Is that why you're dressed like you're from another era?" Bridget pressed.

"Oh, this getup? Neat, eh? I found it in the ruins along with this!" Leera made a show of withdrawing a book from her rucksack and ceremoniously presenting it to them, low-throatedly singing, "Lookie, lookie, lookie at mah cookie!"

Augum took the book and tried to open it, but the pages seemed stuck solid. "Is it glued or something? And what does *Zygothika* mean anyway? And why is the binding so ... demonic looking?"

"It's the answer!"

"To what?"

"What's even the question?" Bridget muttered.

Leera grabbed his shoulder with a hand, drew near to his ear, and whispered, "It's *the answer* to our future family together." She drew back to proudly grin at him.

Utterly confused, he blinked.

She whapped his arm, repeating, "To our future *family*." She rubbed her tummy. "Get it ...?"

He stared at her, looked to the book, back at her, then to her tummy. "No ..."

"Yes."

"No ..."

She pressed her fists to her waist. "What do you mean, no? *Yes!*"

He swayed as if she'd punched him in the gut. All this time he had been working on himself, preparing his mind for the fact that he was the last Arinthian, the last heir to a two-thousand-year-old dynasty, and now the love of his life was telling him it might be possible to reverse the curse she had sustained in the war, which meant they could one day have a family together ...

"Let me see that," Bridget snapped, yanking the book from Leera's clutches. "*Un vun asperio aurum enchantus*," she incanted, splaying a hand over the book. "Just as I thought. It's necromantic."

"Of *course* it's necromantic!" Leera protested. She stabbed the book with a finger. "*That's* the curse Tyranecron inflicted on me! Don't you get it? Inside that book, probably somewhere in the back, there's going to be a solution to undo it!" She nodded encouragingly whilst glancing between Augum and Bridget with wild optimism in her eyes.

Bridget wilted. "Oh, sister ..."

"What do you mean *oh sister*?" Leera practically shouted whilst Revel meekly stepped back, giving them space. "Don't you *oh sister* me! This is it! This is how our kids will play together because we—" She indicated back and forth between herself and Augum. "—are going to have kids now! I mean, not *right away* of course but in like a few years or a decade or so but still ..."

As Bridget gaped and Revel fiddled with the strap of her rucksack as if wishing she was anywhere else, Leera placed two hands on Augum's shoulders, which suddenly felt as heavy as lead. "I get it. You're in shock.

But know this, my love. Your lineage will not die with me. We're going to have a family together. Isn't that exciting?" Whilst gripping his shoulder she looked to Bridget. "And your kids will no longer be alone. I mean they weren't going to be alone anyway. It's just now they'll have more friends to grow up with and play with and go to the academy with ..."

A dazed Augum smiled when she looked back at him with those eyes that desperately sought encouragement. She smiled back, only for the smile to waver. "What's the matter?"

"Nothing. Like you said, I'm just in shock. It's, uh, it's a lot to—" He twirled a hand by his head. "—you know, to take in." He drew her close, nuzzling his nose into her hair and whispering, "I've got hope." Yet he couldn't help but wonder if she was going on an impossible quest all because of that stupid herald piece, which must have wounded her deeply.

"Me too," she said. "I know it will work. I just have to solve the puzzle on how to open the book and then get to reading and researching and undoing." She nodded repeatedly. "Lots and *lots* of undoing. For sure. Yeah."

"It's necromantic," Bridget repeated.

Leera snatched the book back from her. "Yes, I *know* that, thank you very much for repeating it, Miss Highhorse Know-it-all Teacher's Pet Valedictorian. And why are your hands black and blue? You shouldn't be bedding Ollie so roughly." While she huffingly stuffed the book back into her rucksack, a red-faced Bridget placed an anxious gaze on Augum, which he interpreted as, *She's a fool to think it's that simple.* He agreed, but didn't want to snuff the precious flame of hope.

Revel withdrew a skin of water and offered it to him, meekly saying, "Commander?"

Augum numbly took the skin, uncorked it, and took a long pull. He stuck the cork back in and handed it back to her, mumbling his thanks. Then he glanced around for a spot to sit, mumbling something about needing a moment. Finding none, he stumped to the stairway and sat down on the top step. Even contemplating the *possibility* of successfully nullifying the curse allowed for a whole new future to unroll before his mind like a richly woven carpet. The castle, the order, the training, the history ... all of it had a purpose. He could pass it on! *He could pass it on ...*

He imagined teaching his children about all the wonderful things in life. The knowledge he and Leera—by then his wife—would have accumulated. The lessons passed down from his many mentors and teachers. He imagined their children playing together with Bridget's children and Jengo's future children and all the other kids and maybe even going to the academy and watching them adventure on their own. The first time one of them moved a pebble, their first arm ring after achieving their 1st degree …

Leera sat beside him, beaming at him. "*Now* you get it," she whispered, watching him.

"We ought to get married already," he blurted.

Leera laughed. "Yes, we ought to. We really ought to. But such weddings need a lot of planning, and you and I aren't exactly the wedding planner types."

He looked at her. Her unruly raven hair, the smudge of watery dirt on her cheek, speckled with those constellation freckles, the audacious and wild hope in her eyes … Every time he thought she could not look more beautiful, she proved him wrong. How he longed for alone time with her!

She seemed to sense this, for she leaned in close to rub her nose against his a few times, whispering, "Later, my love. Later …"

"We need to get back," Bridget blurted. "Before things escalate. I mean with the city. The snuffing and all that. You know what I mean. I didn't get a chance to delve into it, yet, Lee, but the city sustained a major attack."

Leera got up. "What, did the moss grow limbs? I'm jesting, don't look at me like that. What attack?"

A still-dazed Augum stood as well. "A slew of commoners and even some warlocks were kidnapped," he said. "Snatched from the sky."

Bridget nodded along. "Based on the descriptions given, we believe they were kidnapped by …" She looked to Augum.

Leera flipped both hands. "By who? Spit it out already."

"Gargoyles," Augum finally said.

Leera glanced between them as if thinking they'd lost their minds. She looked to Revel, who stared with the same slack look, before saying, "Come again?"

"Summoned ones," Bridget threw in.

"Everyone's working on the problem," Augum explained. "No one knows who is actually responsible, especially because of the new arcanery-snuffing ability they used to get it done. But, yeah, the citizens described them as …"

"—gargoyles," Leera said lamely. "As in those found in children's tales. The things on drainage spouts. The emblem of the Antioc library."

Augum and Bridget nodded along.

Leera seemed unimpressed. "Uh-huh."

"The entire city is up in arms," Bridget continued. "So we need to get you back immediately."

"And I don't want you wearing that shipwreck ring either," Augum threw in.

"Gargoyles. Really."

"Yes, gargoyles, and we know how silly that sounds," Augum said. "Still, no wearing that ring, missy."

"Fine, I won't. Sheesh."

After Leera and Revel threw on their rucksacks, Augum offered his hand to his beloved, which she took. He then raised his other to Bridget. Revel quickly inserted herself between the women, nervously mumbling, "Don't forget me too …"

Augum focused on the grounds of the Black Castle and incanted, "*Impetus peragro grapa lestato exa exaei.*"

The moment they appeared amidst the training yard in the outer ward, a soldier placed a long trumpet to his lips and blew three high-pitched notes before shouting, "The trio doth return! The trio doth return! The trio doth return!"

"Did he really have to announce that three times?" Leera muttered.

A whole company of knights, archers and soldiers led by a lieutenant, apparently waiting for that very call, emerged from the archway between the inner and outer wards, jogging up to surround them. Just as Augum thought they were going to be arrested, the soldiers turned their backs on them to face outward in search of threats. Some knights stepped aside to let the new Lord High Commander through.

"How *dare* you disobey my orders!" The Sword of the Oak roared, chiseled face cherry red, spittle shooting forth and flecking his mustache.

"My betrothed takes precedence above all," Augum replied. "There was no time for dilly-dallying."

"We needed to make sure a fellow dragon was safe," Bridget added rather diplomatically. "Which required us dragons in attendance."

"Nonsense. *Nonsense!* The city is under attack!"

"*Was* under attack," Bridget corrected.

"And it could be attacked again at any moment!"

"We set up alarms for our brethren to trigger in case that happened," Augum replied, annoyed with this trumped-up meddler. He was starting to see why the man annoyed Bridget so much.

"We returned as quick as time allowed," Bridget added.

"Who the hell is this muskrat-looking goon to badger *us*?" Leera asked, ignoring the man.

"You *little* upstart! How *dare* you! You know exactly who I am!"

"This is the new Lord High Commander, Lee," Bridget whispered.

Leera shrugged. "That's nice."

The Sword of the Oak stepped up to Leera. "You *will* obey my commands."

Leera was unfazed. "Uh-huh."

"And you will obey them promptly and unquestioningly."

"Sure."

"Do not dare question my authority—"

"Wouldn't dream of it."

Augum had to step in beside Leera. "Er, she's had a long quest."

The Lord High Commander thrust a finger into Augum's face. "Keep your subordinates in line, *Commander*."

Augum had to restrain a suddenly ballooning Leera, whispering at her, "Now's not the time, my love. Now is not the time ..." He kept his face averted from the Lord High Commander lest he reveal how enraged he was at this man overstepping his authority. How dare he try to control them! How *dare* he!

The soldiers made way for Black Eagle Mahmoute, who stepped in beside Bridget. "You are all commanded to remain under guard in case of an attack."

"That's obvious," Leera muttered, only to receive shushing eyes from Bridget. She folded her arms. "Ugh, now I'm annoyed."

"Let's focus on the attack," Augum said, turning back to the Lord High Commander, trying not to get distracted by his overly waxed mustache. "What news?"

But the man scowled, turned his back on them, and marched off. Augum watched him go, knowing he would have to deal with the man sooner or later. But there were more important matters to attend to for the moment, and so he turned to Mahmoute. "What news, Black Eagle Mahmoute?"

"I am not your herald, Commander," the woman replied. "I am your guardian."

Augum tossed his hands, muttering, "Can't get a straight answer from anyone anymore." He rubbed his brow, nodded to himself, grabbed Leera's hand, and marched to the Great Arcaner Hall. Prior to departing to fetch Leera, he had sent a quiet command to have every Arcaner return to the hall for further instruction. The city had been attacked by an unknown force, and the order needed to regroup under its commander.

The entire retinue of knights and archers and soldiers followed, their armor clanking and leather padding squealing, weapons at the ready and glinting in the castle torchlight.

"Commander, Commander!" squeaked the voice of Herald Brittany Mires, who was jumping up and down on the other side of the column of soldiers that kept her from coming near. "Can I get a quote for the morning's herald? What think you of the attack?"

Augum stopped, and the entire procession clanked to a halt with him. He turned his head to the herald. "Tell the city we are on high alert and will get to the bottom of this." Then he resumed his stride.

"I know it's late at night, but how many were taken? Commander? How many?"

Augum, not knowing the answer to that, ignored the question and continued on.

Another woman, Guardian Alyssa Fairweather, soon tried to get past the retinue. This time Augum made them step aside to allow her in, and promptly asked her for a report.

"Whole city's on lockdown and curfew," Alyssa reported. "The gates are closed, and they've brought out ballistae from the armory, set every soldier and constable on high alert, and positioned archers and army warlocks on major rooftops. The royalty, high council, and important nobles have all been swept underground."

"Any word on who was responsible for the attack?" Bridget asked.

"The constables and arcaneologists and pretty much everyone we know is on that very task."

"And?" Leera pressed.

"Nothing. Not a peep from anyone. No evidence other than the ash and people saying they saw beasts in the sky that looked like ..." She grimaced, as if not wanting to believe what was going to come out of her mouth.

Leera raised a sharp eyebrow. "Gargoyles?"

Alyssa flicked a hand at her in acknowledgment before continuing. "Whoever summoned them was stealthy, both physically and arcanely speaking."

Augum exchanged a look with the girls. Whoever was responsible was crafty and dangerous.

A tumult from the gates caught his attention, and he halted again. "What's that noise?"

"It's the commoners," Alyssa said. "They're at the gates trying to get answers and take shelter with the three of you."

"They think dragons can protect them," Leera muttered.

"As a precaution, the guards have raised the drawbridges."

"Perhaps it would be prudent to conduct a flyby," Mahmoute said. "One dragon would raise the morale of the people."

"I thought you stayed out of offering your opinion," Augum said.

"I am not a herald, but a guardian. There *is* a difference, Commander."

Augum looked at Leera. He hadn't told her yet about the lizard-eye thing. "No, no flyby, at least not tonight. It's too dark, anyway, and might actually spook the city." Nor did he want to risk aggravating The Callousness of the Predator unless absolutely necessary. He looked to Alyssa. "Get Laudine to perform a herald-style corner shout at the bridge throng."

"What do you want her to announce?"

"That Arcaners stand with the citizens of the city and will do everything in their power to protect them."

"You got it, Commander," and Alyssa peeled away from the group.

They soon stepped into the Great Arcaner Hall, which was already filled with Arcaner recruits and squires and dragoons and servants. All went quiet upon his entrance. They had to make room for the retinue of knights, who awkwardly squeezed in amidst the gathering. Their lieutenant quietly ordered them to take up positions by the doors.

Augum squeezed Leera's hand before letting it go to stand at the front of the hall, where he proceeded to stick his hands under his armpits in that commander fashion they knew him for. "I know you're all tired as it's been a long day. Here's the situation. The city was attacked by an unknown force. The reports are that multiple people have been snatched from the skies by—" He readjusted his weight to his other foot as his eyes swept the many faces before him. "—summoned gargoyles and taken who knows where. So this is what we're going to do. I want three day-to-night rotations protecting the city, eight hours a shift. Squads of five— one dragoon, two squires, and two recruits. Captains will organize squads with the seniors, taking any extra bodies for their own squads." This being their first real crisis, he thought it prudent to establish a firm command structure within the order and get the girls involved as much as possible in that structure.

"The point of this is to show the city that we're here for them. Meaning engage as you see fit, but don't take needless risks. I'd prefer you to run and fight another day instead of getting your guts slapped against the walls."

This caused a burble of nervous laughter from the throng.

"We know little about this enemy, so until we do, be wary. Once the first shift starts, I want everyone else to get a good night's sleep, but keep an ear out for city bells in case of a second attack." He raised a finger. "At *all* times, I want you close to available shelters in case your arms get snuffed. And arm yourself with real weapons and shields in case of a snuff. Everyone clear on their instructions?"

"Sir, yes, sir!" strong voices shouted back.

"Good. Now let's get you sorted into squads."

* * *

Later that already late evening, a sweaty Augum slipped into an oval iron-banded wooden tub heated underneath by a low arcane flame. The steaming water, scented with lemon and salt, felt hot and soothing against his skin.

"Mmm," he droned as he slid in up to his neck. The light lemon and salt made the myriad tiny cuts he had sustained in his travels sting a little, but he knew that sting would dissipate. His thoughts were still in bed — and with Leera, for the coupling had thoroughly quenched the longing that had built up since his quest had begun.

Sitting on a stone ledge under a stained-glass window, a single candle wavered in a cold draft on a bed of holly. As with most Black Castle windows that faced the courtyard, the *V*-shaped ledge was around five feet deep on account of the thick walls, the window designed to open and double as an archer slot. Several stories below, knights and soldiers milled about nervously in the snowy yard, chattering in low voices, their armor glinting in the torchlight.

The door creaked open, and a naked Leera stepped inside, humming the tune to the romantic "Lover's Lure." She paced up to the tub, tested the water with her toes, and slipped inside opposite him. She slid down to her neck, closed her eyes, and continued humming blissfully. Under the water, their legs intertwined as they had in bed. For a time, they sat contentedly absorbing the warmth.

Augum watched her hands play with the water, making small dancing columns which she idly twirled into miniature tornadoes that then splashed against the side of the tub, dissipating. Water warlocks could telekinetically manipulate water, but Leera was particularly adept at it, able to do such things with her eyes closed.

"Want me to wash your hair?" he eventually offered.

"Oh, yes, *puleeeease*."

She turned about, dipped her head below the waters, rose back up, and melted against him. He dipped a hand into a shallow basin filled with Tiberran rosemary-scented soap, lathered it onto her hair, and began massaging her scalp. "So, uh, theoretically —"

"Theoretically," she echoed, certainly knowing where he was going with this particular conversation.

" — were we to have kids in a few years —"

"Maybe even ten or so."

"Right. Whenever we decide, er … how many kids would you want?"

She shrugged. "I don't know. One. Two. A dozen."

He laughed.

"Don't stop," she purred, and he continued gently washing her hair.

"Got to get all that old water stench out," he whispered into her ear.

"It was quite the adventure, mister. Wish you could swim."

"I can swim!" he said, offended.

She snorted. "Like an elephant."

"I resent that. I'm a decent swimmer."

Her head wobbled about. "I can teach you to be a *great* swimmer."

"I'm not much of a fan of those dark and spooky depths. I'd probably end up drowning. Now rinse off, missy."

She reached back with both arms, hooked them behind his neck, and slid down into the water before him. He massaged the soap out of her hair. She remained below for far too long a time for his comfort before finally pulling on his neck to drag herself above the water again.

"Show off," he muttered.

"My turn," she said, twirling a finger. "Back to me, mister."

He turned around and felt her press herself against his back. Her arms slid around him and she squeezed him close.

"You're supposed to be lathering."

"I'm getting there," she cooed into his ear.

He smiled. Thoughts of bedding her again fought with his exhaustion.

She dipped a hand into the soap and began lathering up his hair.

"Anyway, I much prefer the skies than the depths," he said. "Which one calls to you more? Water or sky?"

She stopped lathering. "I don't know …" she whispered in a distant voice. He tapped her hand and she continued, muttering, "You are a filthy beast, sir."

"It was a long adventure."

"No more risks like that. No more getting captured for the sake of people's remains."

"I didn't expect their kidnappings to end in being blooded by wolven."

She said nothing. After a relaxing scalp massage, she tapped his head. "Down you go."

Echoing her, he reached back, hooked his arms behind her neck, and slid down into the water in front of her. She lovingly worked the lather out of his hair. When he tried to see how long he could go without needing a breath, she squeezed his nose to help, which made him snort and jump up out of the water.

She flicked water at him. "You're splashing everywhere."

He wiped his eyes and leaned back against her. She drew him up, leaned against the back of the tub, embraced him with both arms, and they melted into each other. For a time, he enjoyed his love's company and the scented warmth of the bath. While she idly massaged his chest with her thumbs, he idly traced patterns into her peach fuzz arms, their legs once more intertwined, his thoughts drifting like the mist that rose from the heat. The candle wavered, making shadows about the marble bathing room, the only sound the gentle hiss of arcane flames burbling below the tub.

"There's something I fear about having children," he whispered.

"Changing nappies?"

He wanted to chortle but his fears kept the levity at bay. "No. Something … something happened. In a tavern up north."

She nudged him. "You going to tell me or dawdle about like a fool?"

"It's to do with my eyes. Er … Olaf and Jez saw …"

"Saw what? Gods, how people dance about instead of just getting to the point …"

"They saw them turn into …" He switched to a whisper. "Dragon eyes."

He felt Leera freeze. He unspooled her arms, sat up, and turned about to face her in the tub. "I … I wanted to tell you that The Callousness of the Predator has been getting stronger in me."

She lay limply, the life drained from her face, eyes low.

"Do you hear me, my love?"

She cleared her throat, nodded, sat up, and grabbed hold of his hands under water, interlacing their fingers. "It's been getting stronger for me too," she whispered.

"And for Bridget. We can't cast it for a while. Despite all the training—and I realize we still have a long way to go in that training—it's been getting stronger. I love the skies, but I don't want to *become* the beast we've awakened within ourselves."

She nodded along, eyes still distant. "I don't want our kids to … you know …"

He smirked. "I *highly* doubt they'll be little lizards."

She splashed his face. "Eww, don't jest about things like that. Eww, eww, eww."

"Sorry."

She leaned her head against his shoulder, draped her arms around him, and nuzzled close. "Apology accepted."

They rested against each other, but the hot water and the exhaustion from the adventure and frolicking in bed finally caught up to Augum, and he yawned. A moment later, Leera caught the yawn, sat up, stretched like a cat, and raised a sharp eyebrow at him. "Bed?"

He nodded. "Bed." Tomorrow would be a big day.

ON HIGH ALERT

BRIDGET

With wings stretched wide and heated from three blistering suns high above, the earthen queen of the skies soared over a range of pillars that towered above the jungle. Prey was bountiful down below, for the jungle teemed with life ripe for the mauling.

But she wanted a savory feast. Something full of juicy, sweet fat. At last, she spotted it with her dragon vision—a lone and rotund herbivore, its long neck feasting on the highest—and thus freshest—leaves in the canopy. Usually these giant beasts used the high trees as cover, but this one had let its rump carelessly stray onto a small glade, allowing itself to be seen.

Keeping herself between the suns and the beast so she was invisible to it, she tucked in her wings and dove. The wind whistled sharply as her speed increased, the jungle nearing rapidly. The wave of Fear that came naturally to all dragons soon splashed across that jungle. Beasts scattered in sheer terror, not knowing why they felt so afraid. She feasted on their terror, for it confirmed her reign.

That terror finally reached the leaf-eater. In the last moments, she could see her own shadow reflected in its large and stupid and watery eyes. While it instantly knew it had made a fatal mistake, *she* knew she would have quite the feast. It tried to dip back into the jungle, but the speed of the dive was too great, the leaf-eater's lumbering far too slow. The trees crashed asunder from her wind-screaming ram and her black claws extended and her maw opened and—

Bridget startled awake to a pale shaft of light coming in through the stained-glass window. She was lying on her stomach, the silken covers halfway up her bare back. A high-pitched whine sounded from nearby as Sabby stirred. She felt the bed depress beside her before feeling a long slobbery tongue drag across her face.

"Love you too, girl," Bridget croaked, fending off the love by petting and scratching and ruffling Sabby. Mollified, Sabby went to rather obnoxiously slurp from her water dish, while Bridget wiped the slime off with her sheet, stretched, yawned, and turned toward Olaf—only to find him lying on his side staring at her, head propped up on his fist.

"Morning and Happy fifth day of Endyear, honey blossom," Olaf whispered, curling a lock of her hair away from her face and around her ear.

"Morning and Happy Endyear," she mumbled self-consciously. Feeling puffy-faced, she hid half her face behind her arm and peeked out with a single eye.

"Looked like you were having quite the dream. Hope it was a good one."

"I think it was," she said, voice muffled by her arm, trying to recall what she had been dreaming. All she knew was that she was suddenly quite ravenous, so it must have been a dream about a banquet or something. "You're awake early."

"Was just admiring my future wife."

She smiled, but she could tell something was on his mind. "Castle for your thoughts?"

"I was just thinking that …" He lay back, fingers fiddling above his belly. "… that maybe we should actually, uh, you know, we should wait on having a family."

She shot up in bed so abruptly she startled Sabby. "What? What do you mean?"

"Please, don't be upset. I mean with how the kingdom needs you three to focus and defend it and you have so many responsibilities running the order—which we still haven't really established as a stable entity or whatever and there's plenty of time of course as we're still young so—"

"Where's all this coming from?" she interrupted. She sat back against the ornate headboard, drew the duvet up to cover her chest, grabbed a pillow, and pressed it to her stomach like a soft shield.

Olaf sat up as well, dragging the duvet up his naked chest.

"Stop fiddling about and talk to me."

He swallowed. "I just … I'm scared what our children will, you know …"

"No, I *don't* know." *Spit it out*, she wanted to snap, feeling irrationally angry for some reason.

"Er …" He twirled a hand in a forward motion as if to jog his thoughts along. "What with Augum suddenly, you know …" The hand flicked to indicate his own eyes.

Bridget narrowed hers. "Are you talking about when he made lizard eyes?"

Olaf swallowed.

"So if I'm reading you correctly, you think The Callousness of the Predator will turn me into a horrible mother to our future children, that it? Say it."

"I-I-I just think we should slow down and wait until we know it's safe to, you know …"

She couldn't help the tears from welling. A mixture of shame and anger rolled through her innards. Suddenly she felt tainted and strange and inhuman. And it was that latter feeling that brought forth a certain shadow, a vulture that had been perching behind her thoughts, waiting for the wounded human to die so it could finally feast on its wretched carcass.

The shadow rose within her and spread its mighty wings, craving the heat of three suns. *You are the queen of the skies*, it told her, *and of the jungles and of all the lands. And this worm … this insignificant larva … will only slow you down. None of them—including this loaf of a man who pretends to love you when convenient—know the raw power you can muster with a single pose. The destruction you could wreak …*

She did not flinch upon hearing these words. Instead, she wanted to rail at her so-called betrothed. To roar how *dare* he insinuate she was anything less than human, or that their children would suffer under her care. She wanted to take the pillow and shove it in his face and ram it down his throat until he choked on his words …

Instead, in the coldest tone she could muster, she only said, "I see."

He looked at her—and recoiled as if bitten. "Gods …" he whispered, chin trembling as he drew the cover up to his chin.

"What's the matter?" she spat as Sabby growled from the foot of the bed. "Your honey blossom not so sweet anymore? Huh?"

"Unnameables … your eyes …"

Bridget tossed the pillow at his face. He flinched, letting it bounce off. She rose up like a viper from the swamps of rage. "Finally coming to understand what you're marrying, are you? Guess what—so am I! A weakling. A pushover. A drunk. Useless baggage—that's what you are!" She shoved his chest with a hand, repeating, "*That's what you are!*"

"You don't mean that," he gibbered.

" 'You don't mean that,' " she mocked. "You ever listen to yourself? You sound like a weasel. A *weasel!* No idea what I ever saw in you." *Slay this fool*, her thoughts spat at her. "Do you know what would happen if you and I met in the jungle right now? I'd toss you into my gullet without a second thought—"

"You're talking as if you cast the spell. Did you turn into the dragon last night?"

"You dumb fat oaf, of course I didn't—" She froze. But she'd dreamed it. Now she remembered. And the man before her had the same look that stupid lumbering beast had …

"You did, didn't you?" Olaf whispered. "And you don't even remember …"

Bridget looked away and shook her head. "I didn't cast the spell. But I … I dreamt it." She felt the shadow recede, taking with it the rage and leaving behind a void of stinging regret. She looked back at him, wanting to apologize, when there came a sharp triple knock on the door.

"Captain Burns," said a man's voice. "Your presence is urgently required in a meeting of kingdom ambassadors. It seems the capitals of other kingdoms were also attacked."

"I'll be right there," Bridget replied. She extended a hand to Olaf but he turned away.

"Go," he said hollowly. "We can speak later." There was no mistaking the hurt in his voice.

"The matter is rather urgent, Captain," said the voice from the other side.

"Yes, yes, dressing now!" Not wanting to rush an apology, she threw on her crimson robe, checked a cheval mirror that her hair was somewhat presentable, and placed her hand on the door handle. "Ollie, I—"

"Just go," he said, sitting on the edge of the bed, back to her, shoulders slumped.

Her heart hurt seeing him like that. It hurt that she had done this to him so many times after a casting, yet this time felt different because it *hadn't* been after a casting. She hadn't turned into a dragon. She'd been herself—or some variant thereof. And that terrified her. Now with this lizard-eyes thing … what if she really *was* turning into a dragon?

That thought hardened her soft heart. She threw open the door and was met with a slew of eyes staring through slitted pot helms. There must have been twenty guards outside her door alone. Without another glance back, she slammed the door closed behind herself and followed the messenger. The knights clanked along, evenly surrounding her on all sides, those wary eyes on the alert for threats. Everyone they passed took notice, and she felt like the most guarded person in all of Solia—like a queen. And every time someone looked away from her iron gaze, she felt her reign strengthen.

Leaf-eaters, she thought. *All of them.*

It wasn't long before she found herself standing in the throne room, which was packed with emissaries and ambassadors and nobles and guards and Black Eagles and high councilors and who knew how many lackeys. Yet despite the power in the room, predominantly male, many eyes went to her.

She strode through them like a warrior, chin held high, face impassive—though her mind was split. One half was still in that room longing for her betrothed and wanting to fight for the idea of a family, and the other was gnawing on a fatty feast in a humid jungle buzzing with the colorful sounds of countless birds and beasts and insects. She had recalled the dream on the way, having pieced it together from the labyrinth of her mind, and now was satisfying her lust for blood by feasting on the remains of that dumb herbivore, the watery eyes of which popped on her tongue like fish eggs.

What hope had her so-called future husband against such carnivorous pleasures of the flesh?

Her spirits rose slightly at the sight of Augum and Leera, who walked in together, hand in hand. Yet a twinge of jealousy reared its ugly head, for although the pair suffered the same affliction as her, if they turned into lizardly beasts, they would at least have each other. For herself, she felt a terrible loneliness only the jungle could quench. Only there could she find a true and equal mate. Perhaps her destiny was not a family in some claustrophobic stone home minding chickens and geese and a drunkard husband and unruly brats, but one of eggs in a nest and a strong mate by her side while they ruled over a dense jungle lit by three baking suns …

Stop it! she told herself, halting and pressing five fingers into her forehead, squeezing her eyes shut. *Lest the dragon reappear behind your eyes again …* Gods, what would happen if the king saw those eyes? Resolving to be more careful, she got underway, acknowledged Augum and Leera with a nod, and received smiling nods from both of them, which annoyed her. They were throwing it in her face that she was alone and they had each other. That she was a solitary hunter while they were a pack of two. And now that lascivious raven-haired wench threatened to undo the curse the gods had saddled her with and make a nest for herself when she ought to remain as barren as a—

"Shut up!" she roared, grabbing her head and tearing at her scalp. "Shut up!" she punched the side of her head—only to freeze, for every single eye in there was staring at her.

Leera and Augum shot to her side, each whispering a variant of the same question.

"I'm *fine!*" she said loudly for all to hear. "I'm fine. Just suffering the side effects of a spell I was practicing," she lied. "It's over now. I'm fine," she repeated, smoothing her robe. "Please begin. And my apologies." She made a show of curtsying properly, for the king and queen had rushed onto the podium even before the harker's announcement. Everyone else followed suit, and a hush fell over the hall.

As the royals seated themselves on their golden thrones, a late trumpet sounded. "All hail the king and queen of Solia! May the Unnameables bless a long and healthy reign that will last a thousand years beyond and—"

"The hell was that?" Leera hissed out of the side of her mouth as the harker droned on.

"Nothing. I'm fine," Bridget hissed back.

"Certainly didn't *sound* like nothing—"

"Just drop it, will you?"

Leera went silent, though gave her a suspicious side-eye that only annoyed Bridget further. She had to make an effort to focus on the meeting, which delved right into it.

"… attacks were coordinated on all kingdom capitals," the harker loudly stated. "Reports are coming in that a handful have been snatched from each capital. Other than the summoned gargoyles, no enemy has been spotted or named as being responsible."

"The Sierran delegation urgently requests a flyby of your dragons to instill the fear of the gods into these mysterious interlopers," the Sierran ambassador said, his fingertips pressed together before a golden robe embroidered with palm trees. He was a tall man with night-black skin who spoke in a voice that carried well. Like the other ambassadors, he was surrounded by a retinue of advisors.

"A flyby over *each* capital!" the Tiberran ambassador called, a short woman in a wrapped garment, a silken pink cloth draped over one shoulder.

The ambassadors to the rest of the seven kingdoms each chimed in with similar sentiments. But their argument quickly devolved into who should receive the flyby first, with those with the strongest ties to Solia demanding pride of first flight.

"And all three dragons should fly in unison," the Nodian ambassador shouted, a warrior chief woman with two curved blades hanging from her hips.

The hall rumbled in agreement.

Although the boar of a Solian king seemed to enjoy this tussle to gain his good graces, he raised a finger, silencing his raucous audience. "There shall be no flights over the other kingdoms," he declared, then raised his entire hand when the arguments started anew. "We will not risk our new weapons until we know what we are dealing with."

Bridget exchanged a furious look with Augum and Leera. The three of them loathed being reduced to mere weapons. She was about to step forth to raise a complaint when Augum stalled her with a shake of the head, mouthing, "*Not the time, sister.*" Bridget hesitated, but realizing she was letting the predator take the reins of her anger, nodded. She thanked the gods her brother-in-war had a level head on his shoulders. Last thing they needed was a quarrel before the ambassadors, which would only enrage the royalty—all because she couldn't control herself. That lack of control sent a shiver through her very being.

The king turned to an old man with a shaved pate and a thin line tattooed down the center that represented the dividing line between the past and the future, with the line itself representing the fragile and fleeting moment. "Ambassador Lakbah, my spies tell me your people have something to do with these raids."

The old monk glanced about uncertainly. "Your Royal Highness," he began in perfect Solian, "I assure you my people have nothing—"

"Yet you allowed those mongrel wolf kin to blood our children," the powder-faced queen interrupted in that reedy voice of hers that oozed judgment.

"We cannot be held responsible for the acts of a breakaway pack of dishonorable wolven—"

"Then you will not mind if we take their lands," the king slyly threw in, "since you do not seem to care who controls them."

"B-b-but that is ... we are a peaceful people ... of course we could not possibly entertain ... I mean such a thing would be tantamount to ..." The monk gulped as he looked to the other ambassadors for strength. "... to *war*, Your Highness."

Bridget's blood was boiling. She knew the game the royalty was playing, which was to take advantage of the situation for one's personal gain, something she wanted no part of. Except as a captain, she had to not only hold her tongue, but show no emotion. Royals played dangerous games, and if the three of them stepped out of line, those royals would not be above taking captives to enforce loyalty, or worse actions. Sure, the three of them could turn into dragons, but they still had friends, still had to sleep and eat and drink and live in places made of stone. And they still had a freshly resurrected order to run and protect, one that could easily find itself branded as an outlaw order, as had happened many times in history.

People are relying on you, she thought. *Don't foul this up.*

They are also unworthy leaf-eaters who should be kneeling before your might, the part of her mind that had feasted on the herbivore hissed. That part made her take a shuddering breath and calmly think about the Sacred Chivalric Code of the Arcaner, which seemed to help.

The lot argued on at length. For a time the king listened, but then he raised a hand, silencing the hall. "I have heard enough. My mind is not altered. There shall be no flybys. Our three weapons will remain in the city until ordered otherwise. I want hourly reports from all investigators and commanders. Vassals, may your oaths of loyalty keep you safe and strong," he added, boar eyes sweeping over the trio in particular. He stood, and the queen stood alongside and the hall stiffened as the pair strode out with their entourage. Once he was gone, the hall erupted into a burble of anxious chatting.

Augum and Leera turned to Bridget to speak, but she beat them to it, whispering, "I don't want to talk about it here."

"Our hall, then," Augum said, but just as he turned to walk off, the Sierran ambassador, who had been angling for them in the crowd, grabbed Bridget's arm.

"Forgive me, Dragon," the man said, quickly letting go and sheepishly looking between all three of them. "But you must understand that we are defenseless against this new threat. A few of our people were snatched from the skies, and it is thus *in* the skies that this threat ought to be faced. All I am asking for is a single flyby, even by one of you—"

"The king has given his orders," a voice interrupted.

They turned to see the Lord High Commander catching up to the trio with his retinue of guards. "And you will never again speak to our weapons without royal consent. To do otherwise will present immediate grounds for expulsion from the kingdom."

The ambassador hesitated before bowing lightly and melding back into the crowd.

The Sword of the Oak placed his cold gaze on the trio, one at a time. "To ensure you lot do not fly off on another rogue quest, your writ of Group Teleport has been revoked."

"That's *so* petty," Leera remarked, only to be stayed by a gentle hand from Augum.

"We obey kingdom law," Augum said, and turned to walk away, practically dragging Leera with him.

Bridget glared at the Lord High Commander, who sneered back at her with that thin mustache that curled up obnoxiously, before she followed Augum and Leera.

Since the Great Arcaner Hall was near the Grand Hall, it wasn't long until the trio were clustered together. Their retinue of knights—once again joined by Black Eagle Mahmoute—stood in groups by the various entrances, with Mahmoute watching them from across the room. Meanwhile, servants who served the order meekly prepared the tables for that morning's communal breakfast.

Augum idly covered his mouth to prevent lip-reading. "What do you two think?" he whispered.

Leera did the same. "I think they're all swine and are angling for expansion. This whole thing could be a ploy for more land."

"I don't think the attacks are a ploy," Bridget countered, "as they'd have only occurred here. But I do think there's more going on than we know about."

"So what was all that about earlier, anyway?" Leera pressed.

Bridget sighed. "I suffered the callousness after ..."

Leera raised an eyebrow. "After what?"

Bridget leaned in close, murmuring, "After having a dream."

The pair gaped at her.

"You're jesting, right?" Leera said.

"Wish I was. Ollie's been worried ..." She couldn't even say it. Couldn't bring up what he had mentioned about waiting to have children on account of his fears about her temperament. "And it happened to me too," she added in a murmur, indicating her eyes. "This very morning after the dream and I, uh, got irrationally angry with him."

"The training did say it would take a long time to master control over the side effects," Augum said. "Years ... decades ..."

"And we've only had the time to get through half of that training," Leera threw in. "I mean, sure, we meditate a little here and there, but something tells me it needs to be more of an involved effort. And I say that as someone who *hates* involved effort."

"Then we have to recommit to it," Bridget said. "Which means continuing—and finishing—the ancient lessons."

Leera groaned. "But they're boring as all heck. Besides, we don't have time to spend a tenday straight staring at grass in some meadow from bygone times just to … to feel more present!"

Augum calmed her with a pat on the hand.

"Sorry," Leera muttered. "Just frustrated."

"Hey, y'all, can I butt in?" Guardian Fairweather asked, stepping near and offering a three-fingered salute over the heart, which the trio returned. "There's a sack full of tips from the city," she said, thumbing over her shoulder. "Everyone and their uncle and their dog thinks they've seen something suspicious or know someone suspicious or think the devil himself is stalking their house."

"Get Haylee and Jengo and a team of squires to sift through it," Augum replied. "See if anything solid comes up."

Alyssa nodded. "On it," and she strode off.

Laudine came up to them next, exchanging salutes. "I think some of those letters are because of my criers. I sent out a bunch of squires to do some street corner shouting yesterday—just as you told me to, mind—crying out how we support the people, but it seems I may have overdone it a bit. Oh, and the crowd of worshippers at the gates is *slightly* bigger today."

"That's all we need, more dragon worshippers," Leera muttered.

Bridget sighed. Yes, being worshipped as a dragon was tedious, but she also understood why people did it. To them, the trio were straight out of a mythological tale of old. In their eyes, they were living gods. And worshipping something real was better than being enslaved to superstition or worshipping false prophets.

She felt the shadow of wings darken her soul. *Go and bask in the worship. They recognize you as a queen. Revel in your power, revel in—*

"Shut up," Bridget hissed, then made a show of coughing to hide what she had just said.

"Er, your orders, Aug—er, Commander?" a confused Laudine pressed.

"Go and help the others sort the mail, if you don't mind," Augum said, eyeing Bridget with suspicion.

Laudine flashed a dimpled smile and pressed three fingers over her heart. "Aye, aye, sir," and ran after Alyssa.

"I'm fine," Bridget snapped before Augum or Leera even opened their mouths.

"Uh-huh," Leera only muttered.

Arcaners began to trickle into the hall in readiness for breakfast, including Olaf, holding Sabby's leash—and pointedly ignoring Bridget.

The shadow within her laughed and wanted to shout that he was a weak man-boy who hardly deserved her attention, but the human side wanted to run to him and apologize. She did neither, and as a bunch of Arcaners came up to Augum to ask what was going on, Bridget rubbed her face. She wished she could spend time learning how to better stave off the predator, yet there was hardly time, for she felt like another attack on the kingdom was imminent. Perhaps one even more devastating. And if that happened, they needed a way to deal with it.

"Hey, Cap."

Bridget turned to see the heir to the Solian throne and her apprentice Carter Southguard staring at her. "I, uh, would like your blessing to take the dragoon trial."

"Absolutely not," she blurted. "You're not ready. Not even close."

"With all due respect, Captain, I *feel* that I am ready."

She stepped up to him, hating she had to look up at him. "You are *not* and you *will* die."

Carter searched her eyes. "Just like that, huh?"

"Just like that. You haven't even finished the courses yet. You simply haven't put in the hours, Squire."

"The city needs me. And I'm certain that given time I too can attain the rank of dragon and help you on your quests in defending—"

"Excise that nonsense right out of your head," Bridget snapped, sounding harsher than she had meant to. "You are rushing the process, and if you keep insisting on doing so, I will have no choice but to drop you as my apprentice and inform the king that his nephew has a death wish."

He scowled. "You are holding me back. Why? Because you're afraid of my king uncle?"

Bridget tried not to let the fury show on her face. "No, because I genuinely believe you are not ready to take the trial."

"In other words, you don't believe in me, your own apprentice."

"You are simply not ready, Squire. What part of that are you having a hard time understanding? You attempt the trial now, you will die. Ask yourself this—why rush it? Why not wait until you've put in the hours and your mentor gives you the nod?"

He thought about this. "So you're saying I *can* pass the trial."

Bridget stepped away from him. "Of *course* you can. But not yet. Not even close. You need a lot more training, especially up here." She tapped his temple, making him flinch.

"You're not holding me back on account of my king uncle?"

Bridget scoffed. "No." She could have said some other choice things here, but luckily still had the temperament to hold her tongue.

He bit his lip in thought but eventually surrendered a nod.

She expelled a sigh of relief. "Good. Dismissed."

"Cap." He saluted, turned on his heel, kicked back a bench to make room, and took a seat.

"Royals are all the same," Leera said. "Spoiled rotten. Mine is a dour little thing, at least, which can be fun."

Bridget stole a glance at Olaf and saw that he kept his back turned to her as he chatted with a fellow Arcaner. Sabby was sitting on her haunches beside him, staring at Bridget with her long tongue hanging out of her mouth. Bridget turned away, resisting the urge to go to them both. Her mood rose upon spotting Jez, who made a beeline right to them.

"Hey, kiddos," the woman sang, flapping at her heart with a lame attempt at a salute.

"You're not an Arcaner. You don't have to salute us," Leera said. "And you reek of wine," she added under her breath.

"Yeah, been a long night. Anyway, I heard about the revocation of your Group Teleport privileges. If anyone needs a group hitch—" She opened her hands invitingly. "—you're welcome to come to me."

"We won't be circumventing the order," Augum said loudly, but he flared his eyes meaningfully at all of them in a manner Bridget interpreted as, *Unless there's an emergency.*

Leera patted her tummy. "I'm starved. Let's eat."

They sat down for breakfast in the usual places at the head of the table, with Olaf coldly taking his place beside Bridget, who resolved to focus on more pressing issues. After wishing each other happy fifth day of Endyear and reciting the code of honor and washing their hands in lemon water provided by the servants, they dove into sunny-side-up eggs and bacon and freshly baked bread and spiced carrot soup, all served with aromatic Tiberran tea and Canterran orange juice. The meal was tense, with the soldiers looking on hungrily and Mahmoute standing close and to the rear of the trio.

Leera, who sat on one side of Augum, leaned forth to whisper to Bridget, "She's like a vulture back there. What'd you do to deserve her?"

Bridget, juggling multiple problem about in her brain at once, most notably how to face the threat of their arcanery snuffing, was not in the mood for conversation. She thus flipped a hand in a *What can you do?* manner and poked away at her eggs as she continued to ponder possible solutions. Yet she was acutely conscious of Olaf sitting beside her loudly shoveling food into his mouth and looking everywhere but at her, amiably talking to people further down the table as if nothing at all was wrong. Sabby, meanwhile, stuck her snout into Leera's lap and whined. Bridget consoled her with a distracted petting.

The other squires and dragoons chatted in low voices, trading gossip and rumors. One was that a single kingdom had discovered new knowledge—or more likely uncovered ancient knowledge—on how to snuff arcanery and was using it to distract from some hidden aim. Another theory was that warlocks as a whole had awakened an ancient race that now wanted its revenge on the continent. Another was that the wolven had something to do with it. Another said that the threat was actually coming from overseas, from the unknown lands beyond. Another one said that some fool of a warlock had opened a gate into Hell itself. One particularly absurd theory postulated that a whole new race had teleported in from another plane in readiness to enslave all of Sithesia.

But the teleport part had Bridget thinking, and then it hit her. She leaned over to Augum and Leera and whispered, "We need to teleport off just as it hits, then teleport back once the snuffing spell has passed through. That's the only way around the effect." She shrugged. "Unless we uncover a way to shield ourselves from it."

Augum nodded as he dabbed at his lip with a cloth. "Now you're thinking like a commander. Tactically, it could work. Brilliant, Bridge. Well done."

Still troubled by how she'd been reacting to The Callousness of the Predator, and letting it get to her, Bridget did not so much as smile, nor did she take pride in the compliment. She barely even gave a nod.

"It'd mean we'd have to pick teleportation spots outside the radius of effect," Leera chimed in. "Somewhere outside the city. From what I've heard, the last casting this mysterious enemy performed reached a radius that remained within the city—and stayed mostly above ground. It didn't penetrate too deep."

Some time after they resumed thoughtfully poking away at their meal, an ebony hand slid in beside Bridget, leaving behind a folded parchment. She looked up to see Jengo.

"You ought to have a peek at that one, Cap," he whispered, and walked back to his place at the end of the high table, where a bunch of them sorted through piles of mail as they ate.

Bridget, feeling Mahmoute's eyes on the back of her head, surreptitiously slipped the parchment before her and opened it up.

Captain Burns,
Meet me in the larder.
C.D.

"C.D.," she mouthed, tucking the note into a pocket. Whose initials were those? A scroll unfurled in her mind's eye filled with names, which she methodically ran through, until finally arriving at Constable Depassier.

Bridget took a drink of water, dabbed her lips with a cloth, and excused herself to present company, saying she needed to visit the lavatory. She kept her gaze averted from Olaf—who did not so much as look up. Simultaneously wanting to scream at him and at herself, she whirled away and strode off.

As she marched, the shadow within her imagined grabbing Olaf by the scruff and violently shaking him whilst roaring, "You think I want *you* as the father to *my* children! Answer me, you loaf of a—"

Bridget halted upon turning a corner to press one hand against a cool marble wall and the other against her heart. And oh how that heart pained!

"I'm turning into a monster," she mumbled, feeling tears coming on.

That was when she saw a shadow slink across the floor from around the corner, and knew she was being followed. She got herself together and moved on, and upon stepping into the buttery, which was next door to the larder, she waited for her shadow. But her tail beat her to it, speaking the moment she appeared.

"Who are you going to see, Captain?" Mahmoute asked.

Bridget opened her mouth to say something indignant like, "Why are you following me?" but thought better of it. The woman had been tasked as a spy. Was there any sense in antagonizing her? What if there was a smarter way to interact? What if she could earn the woman's trust somehow?

"I'm going to see someone who knows something," Bridget whispered. "Something pertinent to what is going on." Now came the gamble. She raised her chin slightly, eyes locked with Mahmoute. "I will return shortly."

The old Black Eagle studied her. "My loyalties lie with the crown, Captain."

"And my loyalties lie with the kingdom, Black Eagle."

The woman raised a single eyebrow before her gaze flicked to Bridget's left arm. "Let us hope that remains the case," and she turned about and let her be.

Bridget glanced down at her arm and realized the woman had been implying that her loyalty belonged to the order over the kingdom. But upon further reflection, the old Black Eagle might have been implying that Bridget's loyalties could fall prey to The Callousness of the Predator.

No, she thought, walking on toward the larder. *She does not know about that … does she?* The trio had kept that secret as close to their chests as possible. After every casting of the mighty Spirit of the Dragon simul, upon reverting back to human form, they had teleported to pre-designated places that allowed them to suffer the side effects under the supervision of a trusted ally, or sometimes alone.

"Constable Depassier," Bridget whispered, stepping into the dark larder, the torches of which had been snuffed.

"I am glad you came, Captain," Depassier said from the shadows. His sour-bellied outline was barely visible alongside a slew of stacked barrels.

Bridget stepped closer and splayed a hand. "I hope you do not mind …"

"I would expect no less."

"*Un vun asperio aurum enchantus*," Bridget whispered. Whereas various ancient and faded tendrils lit up on the castle walls, infused into the structure itself, the man remained dark.

"I am no doppelganger," he said, referring to the 19th degree standard spell of the same name that was sometimes used for spying.

Bridget snuffed her palm. "Forgive me, Constable."

"No forgiveness necessary, Captain. I well understand the demands of security, especially with you." He stepped closer, rubbing his wide nose between his thumb and index finger, face appearing in what torchlight rebounded from the kitchen, which hummed with activity. "I wanted to let you know that my investigation has thus far been fruitless."

"Fruitless? What do you mean?"

"We have only been able to observe the effects, but not the causes. The offenders responsible for those effects have yet to be identified … or even seen."

"The footprints—"

"—were likely left behind by summoned gargoyles. But the question of *who* summoned those gargoyles, who attacked the keep with that mysterious lightning and planted that moss that invaded the sewers, has not been answered."

"So you have … nothing?"

"Nothing."

"Then why all this secrecy? Why meet in the dark?"

"Because in the absence of evidence, we must look to the actions themselves. The first attack was on the kingdom's symbolic point of power—the keep, where the royals reside. This drew out our initial defenses, which I suspect was observed and noted. The second attack struck the sewers, which perhaps was a trial to see how that sort of arcanery spread and how easily it could be found. And the third was a mass summoning of gargoyles that kidnapped some citizens, taking them who knows where. Each is an escalation."

"Escalating to what?" When the man let silence speak on his behalf, Bridget gasped. "An invasion …"

"That is my conclusion as well. But what that invasion will look like is anyone's guess. Will there be more kidnappings, or something else entirely?"

"Why are you telling me specifically this news?"

" '*Defendi au o dominia*,' " he said, quoting the engraving on their golden breastplates. "Whether you wanted the responsibility or not, you three have become the kingdom's champions and its defenders. By being the only three in all the seven kingdoms of the continent to summon dragons, you have also become all of Sithesia's champions. Regardless of who is in charge, you must be kept abreast."

"Are you saying …" but her throat went dry upon the implication.

"That something dark is coming for all of us—and by *us*, I mean for all the kingdoms. I fear the worst, Captain. You must warn your cohorts. You must be on the alert. And you must serve us all, not just this kingdom … but the kingdoms beyond."

Bridget swallowed. Suddenly the weight on her shoulders felt like a mountain. The dream of having a rural family life faded, hurting her heart. This was not what she wanted.

"Thank you, Constable. I will confer with my colleagues. Please keep me abreast of any new developments."

He saluted in the military fashion. "That I will, Captain."

Bridget returned his salute with the Arcaner one and strode off.

"Captain …"

Bridget turned at the doorway.

"May the Unnameables watch over you three."

"May they watch over us all," she replied, and left, innards throbbing with anxiety … and anguish.

RING AND REVELATION

LEERA

"It's a kargeyasnara all right," Jezebel Terse said from across a library table, hand splayed above the Zygothika book as she studied the tendril geometries of its locking mechanism. "An old one at that."

Leera, sitting opposite and still sweaty from that morning's intense group yard training, used her fist to prop up her head, skewing her spectacles. "Ugh, I *hate* slip-rune sequence puzzles …"

Jez grimaced. "And probably the most complicated one I've ever seen."

"Oh, lovely."

With her right hand splayed with Reveal, Jez lifted a finger from her left hand and the book floated before her face so she could study it closer. "I've seen these tendril patterns before," she said after a time, and floated the book back to the table. She grabbed a goblet of wine she had carried in from outside, and looked darkly at Leera.

"I know it's necromancy," Leera said.

"Actually, I think I've read about how to solve this sort of kargeyasnara." Jez took a sip of wine, and kept sipping until it was practically a gulp. She put the goblet down and smacked her lips. "The Nodians sure know how to age grapes." Then she shot to her feet, kicking the chair back so roughly it tilted over and fell with a clatter, drawing annoyed eyes from the noble Ordinaries who were there to read. None dared to say a word, for the last time Leera was confronted, she had left in a booming huff that had caused one old lady to pee herself from fright. In fact, Leera was still supposed to be banned from stepping inside the library, but no one had the nerve to enforce that ban. That included the curmudgeonly librarian who, upon spotting Jez and Leera trounce into the place, had skittered off to the farthest corner of the library to organize an unsorted pile of books, a job usually reserved for young apprentices.

"Where are you going?" Leera asked.

"To fetch the book that discusses this very problem."

"You're not going to drink 'n' 'port again, are you?"

"No."

"Liar."

"That was only my first cup of the day."

"Liar."

"All right, my second, but still. I don't 'port after four. Er, usually. Stop playing mother. That's my role as your mentor."

Leera's lip curled as she wanted to say something sarcastic like, "Maybe you should try doing more mentoring and less drinking," but she hadn't the nerve. Instead, she said, "You believe any of what Bridget shared from the constable?"

Jez glanced about, but the few other patrons in the library were deeply absorbed in their reading and far enough away for her to shrug. "I don't know. I just don't know ..."

For a moment they both silently contemplated the ramifications. Entire kingdoms were mobilizing their forces, training them throughout the night and day for the possibility of invasion. Everyone was taking it seriously and an ominous tension hung in the air. At last Jez reanimated, pointing both index fingers at Leera. "Be back shortly," she sang, flicking a hand and telekinetically raising the chair back up. "Don't make any trouble."

"I don't make trouble," Leera muttered, slumping back in her chair and folding her arms, but Jez was already gone, taking her goblet with her and leaving behind a stuffy silence. A shaft of sunlight pierced a stained-glass window, making the floating dust particles glitter. The place smelled of candle wax and aged oak and old musty books.

"I'd need a hundred lifetimes to get through them all," Leera mumbled. Already bored with waiting, she reached into a pocket and withdrew the shipwreck ring. As her thoughts drifted, she took turns between idly playing with her betrothal ring and the shipwreck ring in her palm. If all of Sithesia was indeed under threat, then what the constable had said to Bridget implied that the other kingdoms would try to woo the trio into defending them. They had already been warned by the Lord High Commander not to speak to strangers. Even now, Leera's personal guard detail stood outside the library. Jez, under the guise of wanting to train her apprentice, had snapped at them that they were far too loud and had kicked them out.

Leera happened to glance at her hand and realized she had accidentally slipped the shipwreck ring onto her ring finger. She immediately took it off, mumbling, "Oops." It wasn't the first time she'd done it either since returning to the castle, probably because she kept daydreaming about getting married and having kids and bringing them up and watching Augum play with them and Bridget's kids play with them and everyone living happily ever after.

Her eyes nonetheless flitted to the closed library doors. The other patrons had their heads down, absorbed in their books. Hopefully that one assassin was all there was to it, and the brief time the ring had been spending on her finger wouldn't be enough to get a solid lock on her position. Interestingly, the particular tracking arcanery involved only worked when the ring was worn—or so Jez had told her after studying the ring. Leera had been meaning to see an arcaneologist about it, but everything else was getting in the way.

Time passed as slowly as the sunbeam, and Leera found herself trying to keep from dozing off. She fetched a random book from a shelf and tried to occupy herself with that, but *Dinner Habits of the Nobility* was hardly a topic of interest, and so she shoved it away and resumed playing with the shipwreck ring, making it spin on its side and watching it slow down, until it made a whirring sound as it wound to a halt. This of course drew more annoyed looks, but no one said a word.

"Pasty-faced cowards," Leera muttered, telekinetically shooting the ring back and forth on the table between her hands before boring of the game and tucking it into a pocket of her robe.

The doors opened and in walked the silhouette of a refined woman, the bright rear sunlight casting her front in shadow. Leera admired the stunning gown—until she recognized the face as belonging to her nemesis, Alanna Haught.

The woman who wanted to steal her betrothed from her glanced around, spotted Leera, and began striding toward her. For some reason, she was without her usual retinue of drooling servants.

Leera, eager to confront the woman, shot to her feet—only to wince, for her face had crossed the path of the sunbeam. She stepped away from it, and saw that Alanna had stopped to stare open-mouthed in shock. This surprised and confused Leera, who flipped her hands in a *What's your problem?* manner.

But instead of saying anything, Alanna turned about on her heel and strode right out of there.

"Wait, where are you going?" Leera called after her, laughing. "What's the matter? Don't want to admit you lost? That he loves *me* and would never entertain a vapid social vulture like yourself?" But the door closed, and the woman was gone. Too bad too as Leera had wanted to rub it in how she was going to overcome the ancient curse and raise a family with Augum. She had really been looking forward to seeing the look of confusion and defeat on Alanna's stupid powdered face.

"Except now I'm the one who's confused," she muttered, dumping herself back into the chair. That very morning, on the back of the *Blackhaven Herald*, there was a gossip column about some random noble opining that on account of Leera Jones's barrenness, Alanna Haught would be a far more suitable match for Augum and that the ancient lineage deserved to be carried on. It was of course written by the same herald who had taken advantage of Leera's drunken pity party. Normally Leera would have flown into a rage upon reading such a thing, but on that day she had secretly smiled to herself, for she was supremely confident that she would solve the problem.

The door of the library opened again and Leera stood up, hoping it was Alanna returning for the verbal thrashing she so richly deserved. But it was Jez, carrying a fresh bottle of wine in one hand and a book in the other.

"Don't look so bored to see me," Jez muttered, tossing the book onto the table with a *slap* that echoed throughout the place. "Why are you wearing that silly old robe, anyway? You look like you stepped off a stage play about olden times."

Leera, playing with the frilly cuff of the velvet robe, shrugged. "I like the repulsed look the powder-faced flash me every time their overly painted eyeballs see me in it."

"It looks sweaty."

"It's surprisingly not. In fact I find it cozy warm and perfect for winter."

Jez snorted as she kicked back her chair with a loud squeak, dumped herself into it, tipped the bottle to her lips and took a pull. One of the older women at a distant table loudly tut-tutted. Jez raised the bottle toward the woman. "Want some? No? Then keep it down. Some of us are trying to study here." At this, all but one of the patrons got up and left in a huff.

"Sheesh, Jez," Leera said, spinning the book about and reading the title. " '*The Known Chronicles of the Indefatigable Anna Atticus Stone.*' " The cover depicted an artist's painting of Mrs. Stone as an old woman surrounded by lightning, holding a scion in one hand and her staff in the other, the three spokes of the Academy of Arcane Arts looming behind her.

"Published before the wars," Jez said. "Cobbled together from interviews Mrs. Stone gave to various academics which were supposed to have been kept secret, but you know how these sorts of heralds work—" She rubbed her fingers together, miming a coin, implying bribery. "So it's an unofficial biography." Jez reached out, opened the book, and riffled the pages, stopping three-quarters of the way through. "That part there," she said, tapping the page.

Leera read it aloud. " ' "I was quite flummoxed by the kargeyasnara," the archmage was quoted as telling the old archivist. "I believed I had solved all of its components. The pieces should, in theory, thus slide into place. Yet it failed to move." The old archivist remembers the venerable woman raising a finger at this moment and saying, "What I had failed to account for was that it was a necromantic spell, and thus an added dimension needed to be factored in. As it turned out, the solving of the kargeyasnara required nothing short of true and potent *malice*." ' " Leera looked up.

"Interesting, eh?" Jez said. "Just for fun, read on."

" ' "Once solved, I thence learned this terrible spell, which I shall not name, to unlock a certain door in a *hall* of certain doors. Once this particular door was opened, granting me access to what at the time my cohort and I believed was none other than the mythical plane of Hell, where my daughter was being held, I felt a supreme rush of terror." ' "

"It goes on to chronicle her adventure in a Hellian plane," Jez explained. "The chronicling herald gives a skeptical account, of course, and tries to refute the entire story, saying it was preposterous and so on. The short of it is that Mrs. Stone used a necromantic spell to get into a plane she thought was Hell, apparently so she could save her daughter."

Leera tilted her head. "And what did Mrs. Stone find?"

Jez set the wine on the table, folded her arms, and leaned in close. "This is where it gets interesting. Mrs. Stone claims she found a library of ancient forbidden knowledge. She wanted it chronicled for posterity in case it was ever needed. She protected this hall of doors or whatever with powerful arcanery, but left behind records that detail her expedition. And before you ask, no, those records are not available as they're locked up in the deep vaults of the kingdom's archives."

Jez flicked a hand and snatched the book back.

"Wait, I want to read that—"

"You can't. I wasn't even supposed to take it out."

"You ... you *stole* it?"

"Just borrowed it. It's locked up for all sorts of reasons, but I've got friends at the Library of Antioc, so I was able to, you know—" She winked as she stood.

"Jez, really, I can't believe you sometimes. And you promised you wouldn't teleport—"

"I made no such promise. I'm only two or three goblets in. See, this is why I didn't want to become an Arcaner. My shield would have dimmed fifty times over by now."

"Some example you set."

"You love me."

"I do, but, I mean …"

"What?" Jez lifted the bottle.

Leera snatched it out of her hand. "No drinking and 'porting."

Jez made a clumsy effort to snatch it back, but Leera simply moved the bottle out of the way, and Jez lost her balance and fell onto the table.

"I illustrate my point," Leera said as the last patron gawked at them from a distant table.

Jez straightened and smoothed out her turquoise robe, stained with myriad small blotches of wine. "I'm completely fine."

"You're going to end up teleporting underground and we'll never hear from you again." Leera had to look away lest Jez see the tears that had welled.

"Oh, monkey, I promise I'll be extra careful, all right? *All right?*"

Leera shrugged in a *You're going to do whatever it is you're going to do anyway* manner.

Jez sighed. "Be back in a bit," and she strode off.

Leera watched her go, heart heavy. If the stubborn woman would only busy herself with mentorship or maybe help run the order or let herself find a new decent man—or even a hobby—she could get herself right. She needed to focus on herself, stop living in the past and what could have been, and take her mind off the bottle …

Leera sighed, pressed the bottle to her lips, and took a swig, finding it mildly tasty. She was about to do it again when she realized it was barely after lunch, and instead shoved the bottle away, annoyed with herself. "Don't be *that* sort of warlock," she muttered. Too many got bored with the tedious training and academics required of the arts, taking cheap pleasure from the bottle instead.

She sat there for a time, contemplating leaving to catch up with Augum and Bridget, but wanted to finish her time with Jez and work on the kargeyasnara together. Quality time with their mentor was precious these days, especially because the more drunk Jez got, the more belligerent she became, and so they always had a limited amount of time, usually around midday, before things spiraled.

She splayed her hand, recast Reveal, and returned to studying the kargeyasnara that kept the Zygothika book locked, trying to figure out how malice would factor into solving the pieces. After getting nowhere for a while, she angrily shoved the book away and snuffed Reveal.

The door to the library opened. Leera looked up expecting to see Jez, but instead once again saw Alanna.

"Well, well, well," Leera said, folding her arms, itching for a fight. She flicked a finger and the chair opposite dragged itself free of the table. "Why don't you pull up a chair."

Alanna glanced around in a calculating manner, surveying the place and the lone remaining patron, who looked up to glance at her—only to immediately look back down. She raised a supple hand and made a smooth motion akin to petting a cat, whispering, "*Senna dormo coma torpos*," and the man's head slumped onto his book as he began to gently snore.

This caught Leera completely off guard. Why would Alanna cast the 8th degree Sleep against a mere Ordinary? "Casting spells against innocent Ordinaries is an arrestable offense," she said. "I ought to summon the constables just to watch you get dragged out crying like a little girl, but I am curious what you have to say to me." Of course, someone as well connected as Alanna Haught would easily bribe her way out of the situation, but still.

Alanna looked toward the distant sound of books being sorted in a corner of the library as if gauging if the librarian could overhear her before walking over to Leera's table. Even though Leera had won Augum's heart, Alanna's classic beauty made her innards roil with jealousy. Her pale slenderness and her perfect posture and her perfect skin and her tall height made Leera feel like an ogre in comparison.

Alanna looked from the bottle of wine, to the book, and then to Leera's left hand.

"Wish the betrothal ring was on *your* finger, don't you?" Leera hissed, playing with the ivy ring that connected her to Augum in more ways than one. "I got news for you, missy. It ain't going to happen."

Alanna locked gazes with her, her face strangely emotionless. She placed a hand on the chair, drew it beneath her, and sat down, not bothering to smooth her dress like a proper lady would.

"You had a lackey plant that stupid story in the herald this morning about you being more suitable for Augum, didn't you?" Leera pressed. "Pathetic."

Alanna placed her hands together in a formal manner, her back rigid. She leaned closer and whispered, "Dragon Jones, you have something of great import on your person."

Leera, who had been expecting something else entirely and already had a caustic reply ready on her tongue, hesitated. "Er ... what?"

Alanna looked over at the lone patron she had put to sleep, then again toward the sound of books being sorted, before gazing back at Leera with a focus unbecoming of the young woman. "I am not Alanna Haught," she whispered.

Leera felt the hairs on her arms rise. She was staring at either a doppelganger or someone who had cast Metamorphosis. *Likely the latter*, she thought. Either way, it was advanced arcanery.

"I am what is known to my kind as a *retriever*." She raised a staying hand, anticipating Leera's response. "But you no longer need to fear us."

"You wanted me killed—"

"The retriever tasked on you did not know who you are."

"But you recognized me."

"That I did."

"Why choose Alanna Haught?"

"She was an excellent vessel to copy as she walked freely about, was tied in name to you as per the heralds, and was hardly ever questioned."

"Metamorphosis?"

The woman gave a single nod.

15th *degree, standard,* Leera's academy-trained mind reflexively thought. A notoriously tricky ritual spell to get right, one governed heavily by codes of ethics that, if violated, could result in arrest or even arcastration—the complete stripping of one's rings.

Realizing why the woman had initially looked to Leera's hand, and without taking her gaze off the stranger, Leera reached into a pocket and withdrew the ring. "Explain to me why you wanted me murdered for this."

The woman kept her hands placidly together. "The knowledge I am about to impart is forbidden to all but kings and queens and their high councils and ambassadors. You and your commander and your fellow captain have been deemed critical."

"Critical to what?"

"The defense of the seven kingdoms. Of all of Sithesia."

Leera gaped like a fool, and closed her mouth with effort.

"The ring you found activates when worn. It allows for certain privileges unavailable to those outside our order."

"And which order is that?"

"We are the Order of the Defense of the Coasts. Our motto is *Defendis au o kostas.*"

"Defenders of the coasts," Leera translated in a whisper.

"We are sworn to deep secrecy for a reason." The metamorphosized woman looked to her left, as if seeing through the walls. "Sithesia is not the only continent on this plane. Other lands reside far, far away. Wild lands filled with terrible beasts. But also lands filled with peoples unknown to the humans of this continent. Dangerous peoples. Peoples that would terrify the humans of Sithesia and utterly subvert their beliefs. Between these continents are turbulent waters filled with great serpents and violent arcane storms that prevent teleportation."

"I don't believe you. Is this … is this a prank of some sort? A jest?"

The woman looked to Leera once more. "I am afraid it is neither, Dragon Jones." She looked to Leera's hand. "The ring you hold is one used by our order to not only communicate with each other, but to part the waters, so to speak, for the ring partially protects a ship against the monsters and the storms." She raised a finger. "But only partially. Passage is still near impossible. In fact, there has not been a single successful passage across the ocean in my lifetime."

"If—*if*—this is all true, why are you telling me all of this?"

"I was tasked with retrieving the ring, but upon seeing that it was you, one of three capable of turning into a dragon, I turned around and communicated with my order. A command was issued after yesterday's attack against all the capitals. A committee was being formed to liaise with the three of you, but since time is of the essence and I was close anyhow, the committee tasked me to reach out to you alone."

"I still don't understand …"

The woman looked eastward again. "We believe a people beyond the oceans have found a way to break through the serpents and storms."

"For what purpose?"

The mysterious woman placed her gaze on Leera. "We do not know. We do not even know which people it is."

"What kind of peoples are out there?"

"A great many of a great many kind. What we do know is that they war with each other. That over there—" She nodded eastward. "—humans are slaves. That arcanery is wielded differently. Over there, necromancy is still a primary element. Beasts speak in their beastly tongues and have kingdoms of their own. Powerful kingdoms. Warring kingdoms."

Leera shook her head. "No, I don't believe it, any of it. It's too fantastical …"

"Those who had never seen someone move a pebble without touching it would say the same. To those who had never met a wolven, talking wolves are but children's tales. Yet they exist just north of us. And of course, you yourself are but a walking myth. I hear they have parades on your behalf. Celebrate you as walking gods. Ask blessings of you. And yet how human you are in person. A mere child who—"

"A woman grown, actually," Leera countered. "Four years past my childhood."

"My point is that such revelations are a shock even to kings and queens. Take the time you need, then explain this to Dragon Stone and Dragon Burns—" The fake Alanna Haught raised a finger in warning. "—but not one soul more. Wear the ring, and when the time comes, we will reach out to you, for we have seen signs. Like tsunami markers leftover from ancient times, so portents of old speak to us once more. Something is coming, Dragon Jones. Something this continent has not seen in a long, long time—perhaps ever. Something beyond the oceans." She stood up. "And you, as dragons, will be called upon to defend us all."

The woman turned and walked off.

Leera reached out to ask a thousand more questions, but not one slipped past her lips. She was in too great a shock.

Once the doors closed, the lone remaining patron of the library stirred, waking groggily from his nap. He stretched, yawned, and smacked his gums.

Leera thought she was dreaming.

A SECRET ROOM

AUGUM

Upon Leera delivering him the news about a secret order that protected the coasts, Augum swallowed, throat dry.

"You're right," he whispered. "I *don't* believe it and I *do* think you're crazy …" He was already dealing with so much—the running of the order whilst navigating the constraints on their movements, the worries the royalty wanted to use them to expand the kingdom, and of course all these strange occurrences—that he wasn't sure he could believe something this big was next.

He glanced through the stained-glass window and watched as a shaft of sunlight vanished, replaced by darkness. The entire northern sky over the last hour had darkened ominously. Another blizzard seemed to be moving in.

What a relentless winter, he thought.

The trio sat on stools around a small and high round table, one of several in a dingy Black Castle common room that usually served as a meeting spot for servants, where they got together to have drinks and be merry. It being the early afternoon, everyone was busy and the space was empty. A low fire crackled in a large stone hearth. On the mantel sat a fluttering Endyear candle on a bed of holly, and hanging on the stone above were a series of freshly cut pine boughs and garlands. Combined with the cedar logs in the fire, the place smelled gently of forest and tradition.

Augum, figuring it would be difficult for someone to listen in here as they were in the very center of the room, thought it a perfect spot to meet. Leera had insisted on the meeting, delivering the news in a whisper and with a hand over her mouth, her back turned to the assigned knights, which stood guard at the entrance. Mahmoute leaned against the doorframe, routinely glancing between the hall and the trio. For a time after Leera had caught them up on everything, Bridget and Augum sat with their mouths hanging open.

At last, Bridget placed her hand before her mouth and whispered, "Why haven't these foreign invaders targeted the three of us yet?"

Leera shrugged. "Your guess is as good as mine."

Augum thought about it. "It's possible they don't know who we are."

Leera scoffed. "Come on. Posters of us hang on every second block."

"In this city maybe, but not the other kingdoms, whose posters mostly show us in dragon form. They rarely show our faces. For all the invaders know, they're posters about theatrical plays. And you said it yourself, that other assassin—"

"—retriever—"

"—whatever. Anyway, *he* didn't know who you are. So it's possible these invaders might not know who we are because we haven't turned into dragons in a while. We haven't revealed ourselves to their own eyes."

"Aug's right," Bridget whispered. "These potential invaders might have started their prodding *after*. But it's also possible they know that the kingdom can summon dragons but don't know enough about our language and culture to discern who amongst us can do it. Also, if that mysterious retriever is right and we're dealing with invaders we have never experienced or laid eyes upon, then it's possible that these foreigners might have never come into contact with us either. Maybe all they want is resources and land and, as Constable Depassier told me, are simply prodding all the kingdoms for weaknesses."

Augum dumped his elbows on the table and rubbed his face, his forehead, and his eyes. While he did so, he considered the situation. The coastal defenses had reached out for a reason—they had seen portents of old and were expecting an invasion. But an invasion usually required a staging ground. A landing area.

He ran his hands through his hair before leaning close, a hand before his mouth. "Can you reach out to the order of coastal defense?"

Leera smoothed out the frilly cuff of her robe. "They didn't teach me how. I have no idea how to use the ring, and the arcanery is complex and foreign to me."

Augum couldn't help having a hard time believing all of this. The coastal defense order. The foreign invaders. It was too elaborate, too secret and strange. Coming from a long history of intrigue, his inclination was to believe in a shadowy conspiracy, likely something about trying to lure the three of them into starting a war with a foreign kingdom and taking their land.

Leera propped up her head on her fist and glared at him. "I know that look."

"What look?"

"*That* look, right there. That look of pure skepticism. What, you think I got hoodwinked? That someone dug into my mind?"

"I thought no such thing—"

"Because I'll have you know my Mind Armor is an iron fortress—"

"Stop it, both of you," Bridget whispered, placing a hand on each of them. "This is hardly the time to bicker."

"Excuse me," said a voice amidst the knights. "Move, would you?"

The trio turned to see Jez trying to get past the guards.

"I said *scootch*, you rusting bucket of—"

"Let her pass," Augum snapped, annoyed with them for doing this to everyone the knights should have recognized by now.

"Wait," Mahmoute said, sticking an arm before Jez whilst splaying a hand and casting Reveal.

"I'm not a doppelganger," Jez muttered, folding her arms.

Augum shared a look with Leera. Did they know about the metamorphosized woman who had taken the form of Alanna earlier?

"Standard precautions, Terse," Mahmoute said coldly, waving her by.

"Thank you so much," Jez replied, giving a sarcastic curtsy—and having to grab hold of a nearby knight for balance lest she fall over.

"You prove why Captain Burns needs me as her mentor," Mahmoute said.

Jez whirled on her. "You *dare*—"

"I dare and you, woman, are drunk. Again."

Jez ballooned, only to end up sputtering angrily, seemingly unable to make a counterargument. She balled her fists, raised her chin, and stormed past the guard detail to the trio. "Hey if you don't want me as your mentor that's fine I totally understand—"

"It's not like that, Jez," Bridget said, placing a calming hand on her arm. "Mahmoute stepping in was purely out of convenience seeing as you were gone and—"

Jez slapped Bridget's hand away. "Spare me," she said, voice cracking, her feelings obviously hurt. "Anyway, shut your gobs. I didn't come to talk about any of that." She glanced over her shoulder again before leaning close, only to burp into her fist, mumbling, "Excuse me."

Augum and the girls grimaced from the strong wine breath.

"The Ohmish ambassador requests an urgent and private audience with you," she whispered.

"All three of us?" Augum asked.

"No, just you, kiddo. But since ambassadors have been forbidden to speak with you lot, he is unsure how to do it."

Augum thought about it before whispering, "Do you know any secret rooms we could meet in?"

"A few," and Jez closed her eyes and winced, as if it pained her to consider the options, all while wavering in place—despite holding onto the table.

The trio exchanged a worried look. It was painful watching their longtime mentor struggle like this. The reality was that the freshly graduated trio *did* need mentoring if they wanted to earn their 11th degree. Augum knew that meant that if Jez kept up on this course, they might have to replace her, a possibility he was hardly ready to face—or much wanted to, considering how beloved Jez was to them.

Jez opened her eyes. "I know just the spot," and she leaned into Augum's ear and whispered where to find it. "Meet him there at the fourth bell. Have the girls run a distraction or something. You know what I mean, just figure it out."

Augum nodded.

She nodded back and idly reached out to grab a bottle that wasn't there. She snorted. "Knew I forgot something." She punched Bridget and Leera on the upper arms and strode off.

"Ouch," both girls said, rubbing their arms.

"I'm worried about her," Bridget said.

"Join the club," Leera muttered. "She's been drinkin' 'n' 'porting like an idiot."

"We'll have to deal with her another time," Augum said, leaning close and murmuring, "In the mean, let's put our heads together to come up with a distraction so I can meet the ambassador."

An hour later the trio led a hastily gathered Arcaner sparring session in the castle yard, composed of those who were not on patrol or catching up on sleep. By then, the sky overhead was bursting with black clouds and the winds shrieked, the flags and standards of the castle madly flapping about.

When the city bells began to gong four times, indicating the fourth hour of the afternoon, Leera raised an arm, the signal for Augum to prepare. She placed the fingers of her other hand into her mouth and loosed a shrill whistle. "Eyes on me, people!" she boomed in an arcanely amplified voice.

As the throng of Arcaner squires and dragoons stopped their cycling of spells to focus on Leera, Augum edged to a prearranged spot in the yard that was directly opposite the doors of the Great Arcaner Hall. Although most of the knights watched Leera, a few—including Mahmoute—kept stealing glances at him.

"Those of you who know how to cast Summon Minor Wall get ready! The rest of you take notes and don't be afraid to ask questions! I want them in long strips east to west." Leera moved her arms left and right, indicating the length of the yard. "Since I want to focus on precision, Bridget and I will demonstrate the first casting." She looked to Bridget, mouthing, "*Ready?*"

Upon receiving a nod, the girls performed the complicated gestures required of the spell, which began with a palm forward and in the up position, establishing a connection to the arcane ether. They quickly transitioned to a flat palm to stabilize the connection before moving the palm down to initiate arcane draw. Next the palm curled into a fist which grabbed hold of the arcane tendrils. The fist then opened back to a palm and sliced across in a line, drawing the base of the wall line. Finally, the palm slammed against the other palm, albeit in a perpendicular manner, forming a *T*. This all happened whilst chorusing, "*Summano valla minimus girata barricada!*"

Two ten-foot walls flanked Augum with a double *whoosh*, one of shimmering water and the other of crackling earth, creating a passage directly to the Great Arcaner Hall. Except there was one problem—two of the knights had also been trapped within that passage. With their backs turned to him, Augum had to think quickly, and he ran a hand over his body, incanting, "*Armari obscura chameleano traversa.*"

By the time the knights looked in his direction, Augum's entire body was camouflaged with his surroundings. He waited until they glanced at each other before hurrying as quickly as the spell allowed—after all, Chameleon cast with the travel extension made a shimmering effect when one moved, and if one moved too quickly, the spell could easily fail, rendering one visible.

Mahmoute protested that their vision of the yard was being obstructed, but Leera, voice amplified, barreled right over her, shouting, "Now the rest of you—go!" Every Arcaner in the yard able to do so chorused, "*Summano valla minimus girata barricada!*" There was a multitude of *whooshes* as more walls sprang up, with at least one casting fizzling out in a puff, and Augum couldn't help but think that that particular Arcaner needed more training.

Now at the doors to the Great Arcaner Hall, Augum waited until the knights were once again looking away before he padded inside, gently closing the doors behind him. Still chameleonic, he hurried south—right past a pair of young male servants, one of whom whispered, "Did a gust of wind just open one of the doors?"

"Maybe a ghost slipped in," the other jested.

Augum, his form shimmering only barely in the dim torchlight, next slipped into a short hallway that led past a castle tower, then on into a southwestern solar and magisterial library. The voluminous room was split by three massive square columns, its walls covered floor to ceiling with bookshelves holding various tomes that all had to do with running the kingdom—mostly tomes of law, but also tomes of accounting, tomes of procedures and ceremonies, tomes of manor and castle management, tomes of population, and so on and so forth. A stairway led to the sprawling underground, but Augum kept moving, searching the eastern shelf for a certain book.

He found the section titled, *Defunct Kingdom Law*, and after a brief search, tracked down the thin spine of a book titled, *Magisterial Boundaries of the Surrounding Woodland in the Years After The Founding*. Checking that he was alone, he grabbed the spine and pulled the top. It swiveled out, the bottom of which was hinged into a mechanism. There was a gentle *click* and the entire section swung inward. He slipped into a pitch-dark room and quietly closed the door behind himself.

"Is anyone there?" asked a voice.

Augum raised his palm and whispered, "*Shyneo.*" It burst with blue lightning that lit up a long rectangular room filled with dusty weapons and shields—and the face of a monk whose bald head was bisected by a thin tattooed line.

"I see only a floating light and a shimmer," the monk said.

"Forgive me," Augum replied, and ran a hand down his body, incanting, "*Chameleano null,*" making his body visible.

The monk placed three fingers over his heart. "I believe this is the appropriate salute, is it not?"

Augum returned the salute. "It is." Then he bowed. "It is an honor to receive you, sir."

"And I you, young warrior." The monk bowed back. "Since we have not been properly introduced, I am Ambassador Lakbah, and I represent the kingdom of Ohm. And of course, I know who you are, Dragon."

Augum gave a second bow, indicating he respected the monk's seniority, another Ohmish tradition used by the higher castes of the kingdom. "It is an honor, Ambassador Lakbah." He always had questions for monks, existential questions. But this was hardly the time.

The monk glanced about. "I was not expecting an armory."

"It's one of many hidden away in case of a sudden attack," Augum explained.

"Then it is good the weapons are dusty."

"The castle has not been penetrated in many an age."

"Is it safe for us to speak here?"

"My colleague informed me that it is. I also checked my person for tracking pebbles and enchantments of that sort. I am clean."

The monk nodded, reached into a pocket, and withdrew a wax candle in the shape of a branch. "May I?"

Augum, curious what he was on about, nodded. "Of course."

The monk found a small dusty table carved into an octagon out of mahogany, carried it to the center of the long room, and placed the candle on top. Then he stepped back and opened a hand at it. "An old custom of parlay."

"But we are not enemies."

"No, but your king would like otherwise."

A flush of shame pricked Augum's cheeks. "So you know …"

"For some time now." Ambassador Lakbah's hand, which remained aloft, nudged forward. "Please."

Augum stepped up to the candle and, with his lit palm, stretched out a lightning-infused finger. The crackling in that finger got more intense, the lightning snapping out until the wick caught light. Augum then snuffed his palm and stepped back so that they faced each other over the lone candlelight which wavered about in a draft.

"A storm is coming," the monk said, voice echoing softly in the musty room. "And I speak not of the one gathering outside at this very moment. Your king longs to betray our people in the hopes of expanding his kingdom and making a name for himself in the ages to come."

"A long time ago, your great-grandmother, the legendary Anna Atticus Stone, had an opportunity. For a brief time, she had in her possession two scions on account of defeating a legendary opponent in a legendary duel. Your great-grandmother could have kept both scions for herself. She could have given the other to a kingdom in exchange for their favor. She could have even sold it for a vast fortune. Instead, she gifted it to us, so that each kingdom had one apiece. That lone gift became the basis of a strong pact between us, ensuring peace. Solia is, after all, our southern neighbor."

"Mrs. Stone is a great woman."

"Is …? Forgive me, Commander, but I was led to believe she passed into the Great Beyond."

"She lives still." Augum's eyes trawled toward the ceiling. "She meditates amongst the dunes of the low-rise kingdom."

"She is in the plane of the knowledge-keepers then."

"In Ley, yes, slowly building a bridge to our plane." *Though that could take generations*, he thought.

The monk considered this. "Some would call such talk blasphemy. Others delusion." He inclined his head respectfully. "I am grateful you entrust me not to think either."

Augum inclined his head in turn, but said nothing. Ambassadors were supposed to be crafty and cunning and diplomatic, which oft meant compromising one's morals for one's kingdom. He had yet to trust one, monk or no.

"She is a great woman indeed," the monk continued, "and from all accounts, you are a great young man. I hope you take after her example."

Augum knew his meaning. Not wanting to verbalize even a hint of treason, he gave a single and subtle nod.

"Now let me deliver the message I have been tasked with passing on. On this very evening, a small pack of wolven await your arrival."

Augum was about to reply that he did not understand, only to realize who the ambassador was referring to—it had to be the leaders he had saved, a selection of The Honored.

"They wish to build a new pact together, just as your great-grandmother helped build a pact between our great nations.

"What is their aim?"

"They have something to show you. Something they say at least one of the three defenders of Sithesia will need to see with their own eyes."

"Have you seen this … thing?"

"I asked, but the wolven said it is too dangerous for me to see it."

"How long would it take?"

"I was instructed to tell you to provision well in case of the worst."

"I cannot leave my betrothed and my sister-in-war."

"From what I understand, what you will lay your eyes on, they will also want to see for themselves."

"What if it's a trap?"

"You do not know me, Dragon Stone, but let me say this. I know these wolven. You have gotten to know them too. Unlike The Dishonored, they are honor-bound. What they told me, in the manner they told me it, I know they speak the truth. Their concern is not just for their kingdom, but for all kingdoms." The monk leaned forth so that his lower face was lit directly by the candlelight. "What they will show you will reveal their worst nightmare."

Augum searched the man's wrinkled face, bisected by that tattooed line that represented the moment. Then it hit him. "They found the incursion point ..." Where the invasion would land.

"That I do not know, young warrior. But whatever it is, it has them all scared. And wolven are never scared." He reached into a pocket and withdrew a small scroll tied with a silken ribbon. He held it forth. "This is a map. Meet them at the *X* at the tenth hour of this very eve."

Augum accepted the map. "The three of us have been approached by a secretive organization I believe you are aware of—the Order of the Defense of the Coasts. What can you tell me about them?"

"They are an ancient and highly secretive order primarily composed of water warlocks—for obvious reasons. They task kings and queens of each kingdom to give them a steady supply of warlocks to replace their number. These men and women are sometimes condemned criminals who are given a second chance at a new life."

The monk raised his chin. "I am glad you have been approached. This is no time for deep secrecy, and whether kings and queens like it or not, the three of you are Sithesia's most potent weapons."

"I hate being called that," Augum spat, a shadow rising behind his mind.

The monk briefly inclined his head. "I apologize. I know it must be demeaning."

"It is." Augum let the candle waver between them as he waited for the predator to slink back into the shadows. Then he sighed. "I have questions. Not for you as an ambassador, but as a monk. Since there is no time to ask these questions, perhaps you can pass on a single wisdom from your people to lend comfort to a troubled mind."

"I can see the trouble in the reflection of your war-hardened gaze, young warrior. I can feel it billowing off your soul as potently as the cold. Mmm, a wisdom ..." The monk let his brows crease as he focused on the candle in thought. "If the past is an echo of hardship and the future a whisper of promise, what then is the present?"

"I was not expecting a riddle," Augum blurted stupidly.

"Learning," the monk answered before Augum could. "The answer is learning." He extended a long and weathered finger, raised it to the top of his scalp, and pressed it against the thin tattooed line. "May the Unnameables bless thee on thy journey with good fortune," he began, slowly moving that finger downward along the line, "thy body with strong health, thy mind with profound wisdom, and thy heart with courage." He removed the finger after dragging it to his neck, where the line disappeared beneath his robe. "Just as your great-grandmother performed a deed for all the kingdoms, so now you are asked to do the same. Not for your kingdom or for your order ... but for all of us."

As the candle fluttered weakly between them, Augum surrendered a grave nod in acknowledgment.

REASONS TO QUIVER

BRIDGET

"I know you're upset," Bridget whispered to Olaf, hugging him tightly. "But we need to do this. We'll leave alarms behind in case of an emergency that requires us. The usual spot. In the mean, take care of Sabby for me, would you? You know she likes long walks around the yard."

"I will." Olaf squeezed her back, but not as strongly as he usually did. "How long will it take, anyway?"

Bridget, knowing he was still hurt from their last conversation, let go, then gripped his hands, noting how he did not meet her gaze. Refraining from sighing, she glanced to the windowsill, before which a lone candle sat on a table. Outside, gust after violent gust rattled that window, making the candle flutter and shadows dance. "I don't know …"

"You sure the quest needs all three of you?"

"We've thought about it in great detail. It needs all three of us in case one of us has to cast the dragon. The other two can then keep an eye out and cast it in turn if need be. They can throw guards and Black Eagles at us by the bushelful, but we're each other's best guardians."

"The royals are going to be right enraged with you lot."

"That's why we're not taking anyone else with us who they can make an example out of. I'm already terrified that they'll question you."

"Of course they'll question me. Make me swear on my shield. And I'll tell them the truth that I don't know where you went. But I'll also say it's a vital quest for the kingdom's sake—for the sake of all kingdoms, actually." His eyes briefly met hers. "Except … what if it's a trap?"

"We'll be on our guard."

He let his hands slip away from hers, turned about, and grabbed a wool blanket with the crest of the Academy of Arcane Arts, which he then began folding for Bridget. "I regret not having the courage to finish the dragon quest when we were in Endraga Ra."

Bridget patted Sabby, who lay on the bed, tired from a long day of running about the yard. "You did your best."

"It wasn't good enough. I can't protect you." He dropped his head, mumbling, "I feel like a failure …"

"Oh, Ollie …" She wrapped her arms around him from the rear. "You're not a failure. You're a dragoon who survived Endraga Ra. And one day, we will build a family together. Do you understand? A family. Me and you."

She felt him swallow.

Hurt by his silence, she let go, still recalling their argument, which they had not discussed since, as there hadn't been time. The whole kingdom was mobilizing to face an unknown threat, and she had been training squires and dragoons, barely having enough time to eat.

He feared her terrorizing their children as a predator-infused mother, and she feared losing him. He felt he wasn't good enough for her, that he couldn't protect her, while she had to once again run away on a vital quest. Every time she had to leave to turn into the dragon for a quest over the last few years, it had put a strain on their relationship. Now that gulf was wider than ever.

"Tell me you still love me," she whispered, voice shaking.

To her horror, he only stood there. The window rattled and the candle threatened to snuff.

A shadow slipped out from behind the curtain of her mind, and the hurt morphed into rage. *He's dead weight*, she thought. *Leave the fat sack of self-pity. Become the queen of the skies you are destined to be.*

Sabby stirred, looked up at Bridget in fear. Bridget snatched the blanket from Olaf's hands and jammed it into her rucksack. "Get out," she hissed coldly.

"Bridge, I—"

She turned her back on him. "I said get the hell out."

A gentle hand fell onto her shoulder. The human part of her wanted desperately to grab that hand. Instead, she shrugged it off. "You heard me."

There was the sound of a leash being attached to a collar. "Come on, girl." The door quietly opened, and the chatter of knights standing somewhere out in the hallway died down. For a moment it remained open, as if Olaf lingered in the doorway. Then came the sound of the door softly closing. She turned, hoping he had stayed, but there was no one there. He was gone.

A rush of sorrow and regret splashed across Bridget's soul, and she dropped her head. "Where the hell did you go now that I need you, you bastard?" she snapped. The words had not been aimed at her betrothed, but at The Callousness of the Predator, which she felt had abandoned her when she needed its strength to deal with the raw emotions of hurt and betrayal and rejection.

She padded up to the nightstand and removed her betrothal ring, which both of them wore. Like Augum and Leera's rings, they were bound together so that each could track the other. But she could not allow any of those royal goons to find her, and placed her ring on the nightstand beside the bed. She had forgotten to tell him, meaning he would read it as a rejection of their betrothal. She wanted to write a note to explain, but that shadowy part returned to inform her that that would be weak, and that he deserved to squirm for not believing in them, for not believing in her …

"Damn you," she snapped. "Damn us …" She unslung her rucksack and dumped it onto the bed. It had to remain hidden, meaning she had to cast the notoriously unstable 6th degree spell *Visinobiectamasat*—Object Invisible in common parlance. The spell's knowledge base had so deteriorated over time that these days it was mostly taught for the academy exam.

She focused on the rucksack and its contents and aligned how they would become balanced between the ether and this plane of existence. Within that balance rested the art—and the trick—of invisibility. After a deep breath, she splayed her hands over the rucksack and whispered, "*Obiectum visinabla balan.*" It vanished with a quiet *whoosh*.

She carefully picked it up, testing the invisibility. When it remained unseen, she fumbled about until she found the strap and slowly slung it over her shoulder, praying that it wouldn't suddenly become visible while she walked with her guard detail. Then she went to the candle, only to catch a glint from her betrothal ring, which sat on the nightstand as if abandoned.

She stared at it, listening to the howl of the wind outside, the high-pitched shriek it made as it forced its way through ancient cracks. The window rattled violently as if a robber were trying to get in, and the candle snuffed of its own accord, bathing Bridget in darkness, the room now lit only by the reflection of wavering torchlight that lit up the ceiling from the yard below.

"And damn me," she whispered. With the glint of the ring gone, she turned her back on it and opened the door. Her guard detail, composed of ten knights and Samira Mahmoute, was milling about outside. The guards, who had been chatting idly with each other, ignored the Black Eagle, while the old woman stood as if she had been waiting for Bridget's emergence.

Bridget hesitated only a moment before she strode past.

"Trouble in dreamland?" one of the guards jested.

Bridget halted in her steps. The shadow silently rose above her mind and spread its wings. She turned her head to look at the helmed culprit — and was met by a chorus of gasps. A bunch of the knights retreated whilst signing skyward, mumbling for the gods to protect their souls.

"The gods cannot protect you from the wrath of the jungle," she said in a menacing voice. "In fact, the gods condemn you to fall prey to the strong. In the jungles of Endraga Ra, there is only one law — the weak shall feel their flesh torn from their bones by the strong." Her serpent eyes flitted from one knight to another, all of whom either dropped their gazes or seemingly could not look away. "Leaf-eaters like you can only hide. Should you stray within sight of a predator …" She raised and flexed her forearm, summoning ten writhing rings of ivy.

The knights retreated until their backs were against the castle walls. One whispered, "Merciful Unnameables please protect us from this evil …"

Bridget's lizard eyes looked to Mahmoute, whose face, for the first time ever, creased with genuine concern. Bridget snorted at her, seeing her as nothing compared to her winged might. She looked back at the group of knights and pointed at them with her ivy-ringed arm. "Stay," she commanded, as if talking to Sabby.

After staring them down, she moved on, and was glad she did not hear their oafish clanking. Their armor and weapons were useless in a fight anyhow.

Unless your arcanery is snuffed, you fool, the rational part of her mind squeaked.

"Shut up. I didn't ask for your opinion," Bridget snapped back. She walked quickly down the stairs, her steps light and nimble. But just as she reached the front doors of the keep, which was guarded by no less than ten soldiers, a voice rang out from behind.

"And where would one of our gallant dragon captains be slithering off to at this time of night?"

Bridget, fearing that the lizard eyes of the dragon remained, did not dare turn around. "For a leisurely evening stroll, Lord High Commander," she replied.

"Sarcasm does not suit you, young lady," the man said, each footstep clanking as he descended the stairs, only for them to cease after a bit. "And why is only one of your detail following you? Mahmoute. Explain yourself."

The Black Eagle, who had evidently been following Bridget, remained silent. Bridget, still with her back turned, imagined her at the top of the stairs and the Lord High Commander halfway down.

"Answer me, Black Eagle."

"I believe she goes to the Great Arcaner Hall to perform training with her cohorts, Lord High Commander."

"And why is her retinue not following?"

A moment of hesitation. "They have been ordered to remain at their posts to her room."

"*She* is their post! She is! Do you understand, you stupid Tiberran witch?"

Another silence. "Yes, Lord High Commander."

"You stay with her. I will fetch them. And you, Captain—you are ordered not to leave castle grounds under any circumstance." He clanked off.

Bridget turned to see Mahmoute padding down the stairs.

"You know, don't you?" Bridget whispered upon their meeting, somehow sensing the dragon eyes had abandoned her.

Mahmoute nodded past Bridget's shoulder. Bridget glanced back to see that her rucksack had once more become visible, meaning the enchantment had failed in that short walk, revealing her poor skill with the spell. Luckily the Lord High Commander had been too fixated on being obeyed to put two and two together.

"Is it that important?" Mahmoute whispered back. "The quest?"

Bridget nodded. "It is. And this time, it is not for just one kingdom, but for all kingdoms …"

Mahmoute searched her face. "Your castle teleport privileges have also been revoked. You know what that means."

"I do." Revocation of the trio's privileges, which bypassed the powerful and ancient arcaneological protections that prevented teleportation in and out of castle grounds, meant that none of them could teleport out or in if they tried.

"Then we best hurry along."

Bridget, shocked that Mahmoute wanted to help them, nonetheless turned and strode quickly through the front doors, ignoring the guards. The outdoors met her with a fierce gale that threw frost and snow sideways at her face, making it quite the effort to travail the snowy grounds.

Bridget considered asking the woman why she was helping them and if she still relayed everything like a good spy would. But she did not want to antagonize one of the few voices that seemed to understand her in that moment. Maybe because she craved a stable mentor who was actually around a lot, but she was starting to trust the Black Eagle, at least a little bit. At least for now …

"The knights will tell the tale of your eyes," Mahmoute said over the wind. "Word will spread."

"It was bound to happen." Bridget's thoughts turned to Olaf and his look of fear upon seeing them. Then she imagined a child looking upon her, and her heart broke. What if they let the people down? What if the people turned against them? Then what? Would they no longer look upon them as human? And then another thought strayed into her mind. Did *she* even still see herself as human?

Mercifully, Mahmoute spoke no more on the subject, and they soon took shelter in the Great Arcaner Hall, where Augum and Leera were already waiting, each having apparently shrugged off their details. Both wore their rucksacks and stiffened upon Mahmoute's entry.

"There's no time to explain, but she understands," Bridget said, striding up to them. "Have you enchanted the pebbles?"

Augum and Leera nodded. Bridget then ran up to a high ledge, stood on her tippy toes and, after spotting three pebbles sitting side-by-side, grabbed the one on the right. She held it in the palm of her left hand and spread the fingers of her right hand over it. "*Concutio del alarmo*," she incanted, infusing the pebble with the 3rd degree Object Alarm enchantment that would ring an alarm in her head should anyone other than her touch it. Then she placed it back onto the shelf and looked to Mahmoute whilst thumbing over her shoulder.

"The middle one rings an alarm in Commander Stone's head, the left one in Captain Jones's, and the right one to me."

"I will only touch them in case of an emergency."

"Thank you for understanding," Bridget said, then turned to Augum and Leera. "They've yanked our castle teleport privileges."

Augum and Leera cursed at the same time.

"But not mine," Mahmoute said, extending both her hands to them. When they hesitated, she half-turned her head toward the doorway, adding, "Your guard detail will be here shortly. You do not have much time."

The trio joined hands with her.

"What will they do to you?" Bridget asked.

"I am not an Arcaner, so my shield cannot dim, giving me away. Thus I can lie to them and tell them you gave me the slip. I will tell them you may be searching for a way out of the castle. This will give you time."

"And should they later question us and demand we swear on our shields?"

Mahmoute stared at Bridget in silence before asking, "Where do you wish to go?"

"Anywhere in the city will do. We'll hop from there," Augum replied.

"So be it. *Impetus peragro grapa lestato exa exaei*," Mahmoute incanted, and Bridget felt her body get yanked away. After a heartbeat of tumbling through the arcane ether, they appeared in a snowy brick alley somewhere in Blackhaven. Loose boards stuck out of snowdrifts, which the wind whipped up into miniature tornadoes.

"Why are you helping us?" Leera asked when they broke hands.

"Because I believe your sister-in-war that the quest you are about to undertake is a quest for us all. My oath to the royalty is sacred, but what good is that oath with no royalty or kingdom to protect? Now I must return. May the Unnameables watch over you."

They passed on their humblest thanks, but Mahmoute interrupted them midway by snapping out the incantation to Teleport and vanishing with a *thwomp*.

"At least *someone's* on our side from that lot," Leera muttered. "You considering her as a mentor?"

"How'd you guess?" Bridget asked.

Leera shrugged. "Intuition."

"Onward to Castle Arinthian to quickly collect provisions," Augum declared. "Then we hop on to the mark on the map. Individual 'ports to save stamina."

The trio each snapped off "*Impetus peragro*," teleporting themselves to the windy and dark terrace of Castle Arinthian.

"Be as quick as you can," Bridget said over the wind, and they split up, each shooting to their room. Upon entering hers, Bridget felt a pang of loneliness, for not only was Sabby not there to greet her, but neither was Olaf. And since her ring finger was barren … would the man even want her after what he had heard her say? What he had seen in her eyes? What man would want a family with a woman who could potentially terrorize him and his children? What man wanted a wife who constantly outshone him? Who was more powerful, the larger breadwinner by far, and so on?

She strode to her trunk, repeatedly and violently kicked the lid until it popped open, and yanked out a golden breastplate with the words *Defendi au o dominia* inscribed underneath a dragon that stood before a copse of trees. She threw it onto her bed, then pointed and telekinetically sent flying after it a fur coat and fur mitts, her fur-lined winter boots, and lastly a wooden bow and a quiver of steel-tipped arrows just in case their arcanery was snuffed.

Even looking at the bow made her second-guess the quest. Prudence dictated they take an Ordinary guard detail, yet there was no time to scrounge one up that had the requisite loyalty to them — or competency, for that matter, as fighting alongside warlocks was its own artform. Sure, there were a few guards posted in Castle Arinthian, but they would not be prepared for such a quest, not to mention they had families the trio had gotten to know. In the case of an attack, they would have to rely on the strength of their wolven allies.

"Hope you trust them, Aug," she muttered, leaving the things on her bed for the time being, and strode out of her room and on down through the bowels of the castle, for she was in charge of gathering additional provisions. The few servants and denizens were already asleep, and no one was expecting them, so the castle was empty and quiet. The only sound was that of the windows rattling in the fierce wind, and the occasional whistle of a gust pushing through ancient cracks.

Finally she skidded to a halt in the large kitchen in the rear of the main floor of the castle, and began rifling through the cabinets and stores. She scrounged biscuit beef, journey bread, and whatever other provisions she could scrounge. All of these she threw into a basket she had pilfered before racing back up the stairs.

Halfway to her room, just as she careened around a landing in between floors, there came a sudden *whoosh* — and the arcane torches snuffed, plunging the castle into pitch darkness. That *whoosh* passed through her soul, and she instantly knew it had robbed her of her arcanery.

Suddenly feeling totally vulnerable, Bridget pressed herself against the cold stone wall of the landing, shoulders heaving as she panted as quietly as she could, the basket clutched to her chest before her. Was something outside the castle, or had this effect reached them from afar? Her frantic heart told her it was the former. An unknown entity or entities lurked nearby, wanting something. An entity that could see through the powerful and ancient Invisibility enchantments that usually protected the castle. And the snuffing would also mean that the castle would be visible to the kingdom. Just as panic began to infuse into her being, she realized that the storm outside would prevent anyone else from seeing the castle sitting atop Mount Barrow.

Needing to get to her friends, she wanted to move, but her feet were like lead weights. She was wholly unaccustomed to being this defenseless. In fact, she felt naked without her arcanery, which in turn made her feel like a scared little girl. She hadn't even thought to bring the bow and quiver downstairs. A single sword blow could end her existence. Heck, a mere swipe of a knife was all it would take …

"Just move," she hissed, and finally forced herself to pad up the stairs, using the cold marble balustrade as guidance, jumping at every rattle of the windows and shriek of a gust. The drafts felt icy on her skin, the darkness impenetrable. At any moment she thought she would bump into something that would tear her flesh apart and feast on her bones. She hoped that thinking such thoughts would bring The Callousness of the Predator to the fore, as it could aid her resolve, but it was entirely absent, which also felt a bit like a release.

As she stepped onto the Prince and Princess floor, the location of their rooms, a small patch of pale starlight that peeked in through the storm clouds helped guide her the rest of the way. After slipping into her room, the first thing she did was dump the basket onto the bed, sling the quiver, grab the bow, withdraw an arrow, and nock it. Then she crept up to a row of windows that overlooked the terrace, conscious that the pair of doors that did the same were unlocked. She nudged the curtain aside with the tip of the arrow and peeked outside.

All she saw were swirls of snow pushed around by a fierce wind that seemed to make the entire castle shriek and howl and groan.

The door to the hall opened with a creak and Bridget whirled about, ready to shoot.

"Bridge, you there?" Leera whispered. "It's us."

"By the window," she replied, and saw the faint outline of two silhouettes slink into the room. She also caught the glint of shortswords—Leera had to be wielding Careena and Augum Burden's Edge. And both had already strapped on their golden breastplates, while Bridget was acutely conscious of hers lying on the bed.

"See anything?" Augum whispered.

"Nothing," Bridget replied. She kept swiveling the tip of her arrow between the doorway that led to the hall, the double doors that led to the terrace, and the curtains, which kept swaying in drafts.

Augum nudged a curtain aside, only to spring away. "Something's out there," he whispered, and they scuttled away from the windows, until their backs were pressed against the far wall.

As those windows whistled from fierce gusts that pummeled the outside of the castle, Bridget found herself holding her breath. She stood in behind Augum and Leera, both of whom held their swords forth—and it did not escape her notice that those swords trembled.

Suddenly the doors rattled from a loud *BANG*, and the trio jumped in fright. Bridget almost loosed the arrow, the tip of which shook from the fear that had gripped her soul like a vice. *BANG* went the doors again, jumping on their hinges. Bridget thought for sure that the next hit would blow those doors open.

But no third hit came. Instead, torchlight flooded in from the hall.

Bridget felt a warmth return to her soul. She tried to summon her arm rings—and felt an immense wave of relief upon seeing ten earthen rings spring to life around her forearm.

Augum and Leera promptly did the same, with Augum additionally drawing a shape in midair whilst incanting, "*Summano elementus minimus draco.*" A lightning dragon crackled to life before them, lighting the room in blue. "Draco—keep guard," he commanded, and the dragon stood in place, ready for its next command.

Bridget tossed her bow aside, shrugged off the quiver, and made the motion to draw upon a bow, incanting, "*Summano arma.*" An earthen bow and an already drawn arrow appeared in her hands, along with a quiver full of earthen arrows on her back.

Augum raised his arm and the handle of one of the doors jiggled from his Telekinesis.

"Careful, love," Leera whispered, pointing Careena at the door, for the sword had been enchanted to allow it to be used as a conduit of the First Offensive spell, a gift from Augum and her mentors for her seventeenth birthday.

Bridget stepped aside to get clear aim away from the lightning dragon that stood between them and the doors.

There came a *click* from the handle, and the strong draft going through the castle on account of the open hallway door forced the door to pop open outward. Lit by the small dragon's blue lightning, the swirling outdoor wind also pushed in a pile of ash that had lain in a heap on the snowy terrace.

"It ran out of time," Bridget declared, not daring to lower her bow in case it was a trap.

"Let's clear the terrace then check the castle," Augum said.

They moved forth, with Augum commanding the dragon to stay ahead of them. All they found were the same footprints outside—four sets, each on one side of the terrace, and each looking like it had been investigating a way to get inside.

"They can snuff the castle's arcanery to bypass its protections, but seem to have a problem with doors," Leera noted. "As summoned beasts, they might be too stupid to figure them out."

After clearing the terrace, they checked the rest of the castle, but found no intrusions, and no sign that anyone had even woken up. The few guards on post at the top of the tower and at the vestibule by the entrance reported nothing either, only that the torches had randomly gone out before flaring back a short time later.

"No alarms from the city," Bridget said once they returned to her room, referring to the pebbles they had left behind. "It might have been an isolated attack."

"Hardly much of an attack," Leera muttered. "More like a probing."

"Then again, the alarms could have been snuffed, so be ready for a sudden ring in your head," Bridget added. "And we should note that whoever summoned those things had the power to see the castle." Castle Arinthian's Invisibility was so powerful that it was theorized it would take a master warlock to see through it.

"Unless they used their arcane snuffing ability first," Augum countered. "Which would render the castle visible."

Bridget nodded along. "Maybe they use that ability in random locations, wondering what might turn up."

Leera opened her hands. "Poof! Oh, look, a castle atop a mountain! Hmm, let's probe it." She snapped her fingers. "Drat, the doors didn't open. Guess we should just give up." She flipped her hand at Bridget. "Doesn't make sense, does it?"

"No, it doesn't."

"In any case, they must be aware of us three now," Leera whispered, eyes darting about. "Whoever *they* is ..."

"Or they stumbled across the castle by blind luck and became curious," Bridget replied. "Or maybe they did not find it interesting enough to break into. After all, it's not like we have guards out there. We simply don't have enough information."

Augum glanced between her and Leera. "Until we do, or until we get an alarm from the city, I say we continue the quest."

Bridget looked to Leera and both women agreed with a nod.

After distributing their provisions, helping Bridget strap on her golden breastplate, and donning their winter coats and mitts and boots, the trio stepped out onto the terrace.

Bridget, Ordinary bow and quiver slung over her shoulder, was the first to extend her mitted hands. "Let's remember that at the slightest inclination that this mysterious enemy is going to snuff our arcanery, we need to teleport away. And I mean right quick."

"Agreed," Augum replied, linking hands. "I'm going to 'port us a quarter league off from the focal. *Impetus peragro grapa lestato exa exaei.*"

They appeared on a windy and desolate road surrounded by starlit snowy flatlands. To the north rose the majestic Northern Peaks. To the south, the city of Antioc, with its castle-like library. And far to the southwest, barely visible in the darkness, hung the heavy clouds of a winter storm.

Augum checked his shield—and all three expelled a sigh of relief when it remained undimmed. It seemed casting Group Teleport after having the privilege revoked and directly countermanding orders was still ethical to the Arcaner spirit. Bridget thought it was likely because those orders and the revocation were themselves unethical.

Without a word, the trio began the trek north to the meeting ground. Augum took the lead as he knew the way, with Bridget falling in beside Leera.

"I miss flying," Leera said from within her hood, her breath steaming in the frigid air. "I mean, look at that awesome view."

Bridget looked ahead at the moon- and starlit mountains, at the way the snow sparkled in the cool light. She recalled diving through the ranges, the rocks silently flitting past her long snout, her wings cushioning the air, and feeling every contour of the mountain as she dove. And the more she thought about it, the more she longed for it too, and the less she felt guilty about what had happened with Olaf and the knights.

"My guards saw my lizard eyes," Bridget said.

To her surprise, Leera only shrugged as she said, "Bound to happen."

"Word will spread," Bridget went on. "Like wildfire. Aug? What do you think?"

"What do I think? I think the kingdom has more pressing problems at the moment."

Bridget nodded, for it was a good point. "I had a fight with Ollie," she then blurted.

Leera glanced over to raise an eyebrow in an *Oh really, what about?* fashion.

"He, uh … he saw them—" Bridget flipped a hand at her eyes. "—as well. And now he thinks I'll, uh, I'll terrorize, you know …"

Leera snorted. "Terrorize your kids?" Then she slapped a hand over her mouth. "I'm sorry. That wasn't funny." She cleared her throat. "Give him time. He'll see how ridiculous that is. I'm certain we'll have the side effect long figured out by then."

"I also have this sneaking suspicion that he thinks our children will be half, you know …"

"Of *course* you're not going to have lizard children! You're human. I think. Wait, let me check—" and Leera moved in and grabbed Bridget's jaw with her clunky mitt and moved it from side to side as she inspected her face with a pretend studious expression.

"Stop that," Bridget had to say, slapping the mitt away.

Leera shrugged. "Looks *mooooostly* human, but you *do* have a big forehead."

"I do *not* have a … a—" Bridget yanked off her mitt to prod her forehead. "—a big forehead!"

"Huge. Massive. Could land a pelican on that thing."

"You're abominable."

"You love me."

"Ugh."

Leera elbowed her, whispering, "For the record, you don't have a big forehead."

"Thank you," Bridget said, donning her mitt and bobbing her head about proudly.

"But your kids might have one."

"Come here—" and Bridget started chasing Leera about like they were twelve again.

Meanwhile, Augum turned around and walked backward, grinningly shaking his head at their antics.

Leera, being the slippery eel that she was, evaded Bridget's grabs, forcing Bridget to telekinetically yank on her, then tackle her into a bank of pristine snowdrifts.

"Oof!" went both girls.

Bridget grabbed a handful of snow. "You must be *hangry*. Eat this—" and she squished the snow into Leera's face and mushed it about.

"Arrrgh!" Leera shouted, voice garbled through the snow. She grabbed onto Bridget and rolled her over, then pinned her arms to her sides and her legs underneath her—Leera had always been a better wrestler.

"Since we're playing bully, *I* think you're thirsty," a snow-faced Leera said, and she started to form a gob of spit at her lips.

"Don't you dare! *Don't you dare!*" Bridget squealed, moving her head from side to side in her attempt to dodge the gob of spit. "Aug! Auuuug! Get your weasel of a woman off me!"

"All right, all right, that's enough," Augum said, corralling Leera off Bridget.

"Aww, but I formed up a good one there," Leera cooed. "She's practically half dog anyway so to her spit is, like, natural and stuff. Ugh, Bridgey-poo, you *know* I wouldn't have actually done it, stop acting so affronted."

Bridget scowled as she hauled herself up and brushed the snow off. "That is utterly disgusting. You're so immature, Lee. Really now."

"Got it out of yourselves?" Augum asked. "Can we move on? We've got a rather pressing engagement."

Bridget nodded. Then the moment Leera nodded, Bridget shoved at the air, roaring, "*Baka!*" But it had been a feint with the intent of scaring Leera—which worked, for Leera wildly flailed her arms about and fell back on her butt. This was such an amusing sight that even Augum seemed to be stifling laughter.

"Ass," Leera muttered, hauling herself up, but she was smiling.

"Truce?" Bridget asked, extending a mitt.

Leera eyed the mitt with suspicion but grabbed it anyway. "Truce."

Bridget nodded as they shook and the pair continued walking onward. Usually Leera didn't let anyone get away with anything, so Bridget suspected this was more of a sisterly act on her behalf. Leera had been her best friend since childhood, and she had this uncanny way of knowing how Bridget felt without the pair exchanging a single word. Despite being rowdy and mischievous, Leera was also fiercely loyal and kind and quietly compassionate—in her own way. She was as close to a sister as a person could be, and Bridget cherished her dearly.

Bridget allowed Augum to walk up ahead enough so that the wind would swallow her words before they got to him. "He might leave me," she said.

Leera scoffed. "Don't be ridiculous."

"I've pushed him away enough. Been mean enough. And I can tell that being around me makes him feel like less of a man. He cannot protect me like Augum can protect you. I outrank him as a captain, I'm far more famous than him, and he constantly says I'm smarter than him too. At our worst fights, he says I should leave him for someone closer to my level. I asked him what he means by that but he just stays pouty silent."

"Then he's being a child. Why don't I have Aug talk to him?"

"No," Bridget blurted. "I mean, well, not yet. I don't want to make him feel worse."

"Him and Aug are best friends. Ollie respects him more than anyone in Sithesia. If he's going to listen to anyone, it's Aug."

Bridget considered this. "I'll think about it."

"You do that." Leera punched Bridget's shoulder. "You two will work it out. You always do."

Bridget did not reply.

THE SEAHORSES

LEERA

As the trio crept up a steep and snowy slope, Leera kept her eyes on the alert. "I know you've met these wolven and all that, Aug, but this could still be a trap."

Augum, who huffingly clambered ahead, said nothing, which annoyed her. The least he could do was acknowledge her point.

Leera smacked her gums in irritation and glanced back. The slope stretched down into the valley where they had left the road behind. Looming beyond, lit silver by a bright moon, the bulky storm clouds that had beset Blackhaven had now overcome Antioc, and neared rapidly. Unless they teleported off, the storm was bound to catch up to them.

"Ready to 'port just in case!" Bridget shouted over the wind from behind her. "Focal—Antioc Library."

"Focal—Antioc Library!" Leera echoed, which meant they would teleport to the bridge at the Antioc Library in an emergency.

"Focal—Antioc Library!" Augum finally echoed over his shoulder from up ahead.

Leera prepared Teleport on her lips. She hadn't met a wolven in a long time, not since the war with the Legion. She wondered if they were all like that lone wolven had been—callous and cunning and opportunistic and transactional.

Raptos, that was his name, she thought. After that encounter, she did not trust wolven, no matter how honorable they called themselves.

Augum halted. "Look—they've made themselves visible to us."

Leera glanced up the slope to see a small group of white wolves standing on hind legs—wolven had gathered on the target ledge the map had pointed to. She flared the fingers of a hand, incanting, "*Un vun asperio aurum enchantus.*" The wolven did not light up with tendrils, indicating no arcaneological guile—at least from that distance.

"Just a reminder that the wolven can cast arcanery like we can, but in a different form. Also, the gray one is the chief and his name is Chief Golan, the calm one's name is Tafus, and the angry one's name is Rogor."

"Names suitable for rocks," Leera muttered, knowing she'd have a hard time remembering such names. She kept Reveal lit and Teleport on her lips even as they clambered over the lip of that ledge. She supposed it was a good sign that the wolven had stepped back to give them breathing room. They were nine to twelve feet tall. She had forgotten how large wolven were. And strong looking. There were four in all, and only one had ears, which if she recalled correctly meant a female. Of the three males, one looked mean, one placid, and one old and gray, exactly as Augum had described them.

Leera couldn't remember much else about wolven, this despite studying them in the academy. She tended to discard information she deemed not immediately necessary.

"All three of you have come," the gray chief said in surprisingly good common.

Augum opened a hand toward Leera. "Captain Leera Jones." The hand swiveled the other way. "Captain Bridget Burns."

The gray looked between Leera and Bridget. "Your mate and your sister, is that not so?"

"Betrothed," Leera blurted. "Future wife. And-and-and we're going to make cubs together!" She cringed. Gods strike her down, why had she opened her stupid mouth to say that?

Augum and Bridget glanced at her with mild surprise.

The gray was nonplussed. "We have brought our shaman," he said, indicating over his shoulder. "She will teleport us to the location."

The lone female wolven, dressed in sealskin and beaded bone necklaces and shell armlets and with four horns protruding from some sort of skull hat, stepped forth. "We travel to The Northern Salt," she said, answering their unasked question. "Let me bless you for the journey."

"Er, no need," Augum said.

"It is my custom."

Seeing Augum and Bridget hesitate gave Leera courage, and she took a step forth. "Is it an arcane blessing or the spiritual sort?"

The shaman growled something at her.

"That didn't sound friendly," Leera muttered, backing up a step.

"Your female insults our people," the gray said to Augum. "Control her."

Augum scratched the back of his neck. "Er … she is rather free-spirited, if you know what I mean."

The wolven all stared at him.

I'm not going to take chances with these long snouts, Leera thought. "Fine, bless us, but don't mind me checking that everything is swell. *Un vun asperio aurum enchantus,*" she said loudly, despite the spell being already lit. Then she nodded at the shaman. "Go on, then."

The shaman snarled at her. She raised a paw and held it before Augum, growling out some words in wolven. Leera noted that no tendrils sprang from the female's paw. The wolven then blessed Bridget before rather reluctantly—and only by the barked urging of the gray—blessing Leera.

"Thank you for the blessing," Augum said, which Leera knew was the diplomatic thing to say.

The shaman extended her arms to Augum and Bridget. "Let us link paws."

Leera wanted to blurt, "Wait, you actually *know* that sort of arcanery?" but realized that would be an even greater insult, and so she focused on the coming teleport—whilst trying to avoid thinking about a trap. If Augum trusted these beasts, then so would she. Besides, there was too much at stake for the kingdoms to be completely devoid of trust.

Once everyone linked hands and paws, the shaman uttered a series of musical growls. The moment the last syllable died, Leera felt herself get yanked into the arcane ether. A few rolling heartbeats later, with a *thwomp*, she found herself tossed onto solid ice.

Leera jumped to her feet, hands in the attack position, but there was nothing to attack, for they stood on the side of a snowy mountain. But what she did see, far on the other side of a valley, was a castle sitting snugly halfway up a mountain. A few windows were lit with a warm glow, and the walls were studded with torches that flickered in the wind.

"I don't recognize it," Augum said.

"That is the Ohmish castle known as *Verhak Rago,*" the calm one, whose name Leera had already forgotten, said. "Which translates to Vulture's Rock."

Bridget gasped, only to clear her throat.

"What, swallow a bug?" Leera asked.

"Nothing," Bridget blurted, flaring meaningful eyes at her and mouthing, "I'll tell you later." She turned to the chief. "Forgive me, but what do the Ohmish use the castle for?"

"It is a castle for Ohmish brigands and thieves and the combined scum of you lowlander lot," the angry one, Rogor or Rorog or Rooroo or whatever, growled. Leera knew she would have the hardest time with his name.

"Our Dishonored sometimes trade with them," the chief continued. "It is a constant source of trouble for both Ohm and The Honored."

"The Honored being you lot, right?" Leera asked. "The good wolven among you?"

"You prove yourself to be like most lowlander scum," the angry one snarled. "And were we to be anywhere else—" but he was cut off by a growl from his chief and fell silent.

"Sawry, Rooroo," Leera muttered.

The angry one only lifted a lip of his snout at her, revealing a row of pointed teeth, but said nothing.

"What interest would the castle have?" Bridget pressed. "That is, from a strategic perspective? Only asking because, uh, it seems to be in the middle of nowhere."

It was the calm one who replied. "Much war was made from that stronghold in ancient times, with various factions using it as a staging ground for raids. But in the prolonged years of peace, the castle fell into disrepair ... and disrepute."

"I see. Thank you."

"Since the castle has no bearing on our quest," the chief said, "and is something you will forget about anyway when you see what it is we have to show you, let us move on."

Without another word, and with Augum shooting Bridget the same questioning look as to why she had asked about the castle, they linked up hands and paws and allowed the female shaman to teleport them to the next location, which turned out to be the side of another mountain. But this time an ocean stretched before them—and glimmering in the distance, islands. Yet the land was subtly bathed in an eerie green, for high above in the sky, amidst a brilliant field of stars, there hung monstrous and slowly wavering curtains of strange green light.

The shaman looked skyward and uttered something in wolven.

"What did she say?" Augum asked.

"The gods defend us with their walls," the thoughtful-looking one translated.

Leera snorted.

"Your lowlander female mocks the gods," the angry one said to Augum.

Leera replied as if he'd spoken to her. "It's not that. It's just that our people believe the green curtain protects all the kingdoms from terrifying evils beyond."

"Nothing less than lowlander blasphemy," the angry one retorted.

"I'm not saying I believe that either," Leera said. "My point is there are multiple interpretations of such celestial events and each one merits consideration. Our ancestors thought fire came from the gods but we now know that flint and steel can spark—"

"Lee," Bridget said, placing a staying hand on her arm. "Perhaps this isn't the best time."

"Oh. Right."

"Yes, something of greater import awaits," the gray said, extending his paws. "Now for the third jump."

Augum exchanged looks with the girls before settling his gaze on the gray. "How many hops will this take?"

"Seven teleportations will take us far to the north along the east coast," the shaman replied. "Beyond the maps of your kingdoms, to where the sun does not rise in the snow months."

The trio exchanged looks once more, for it would be the farthest they had ever traveled in Sithesia. They nonetheless clasped hands a third time and the shaman once more sang out the incantation in wolven.

This happened four more times, each hop going farther and farther north and east, to lands colder and colder, bypassing frosty mountains and slowly tumbling glaciers and plains of snow and oceans of ice, speaking little to each other, with the shaman taking breaks in between to renew her wolven stamina, until they stood in a shallow valley between rolling hills of snowdrift resembling frozen ocean waves. The sky was clear but cluttered with stars and a majestic moon that made every granule of snow glitter. Far, far to the south and high up in the sky hung the green curtains.

Leera noted that the snow here, which was waist-deep but had a layer of icy crust, had been trampled prior to one or two snowfalls. "Are these your footprints?" she asked the gray.

"They are," he replied. "We came at the call of a scout. Our scouting territory is vast."

"Not even the Henawa travel this far," the calm one noted, and the four wolven turned and began walking up the nearest slope. The trio dutifully followed, their breath frosting in the frigid air. A bitterly cold wind made them all bundle up, but the wolven, long used to the snow, seemed untroubled.

The gray stopped twenty feet from the top of the hill. "Behold, for what you witness, you witness on behalf of all the kingdoms, those even you do not recognize. Now let us hunker," and he dropped to all fours and prowled ahead like a hunter, his cohorts following his lead.

"Now *that's* a little ominous," Leera muttered. She looked to Augum and Bridget. "Chameleon with the travel extension?"

After they nodded, the trio ran a hand down their bodies, incanting, "*Armari obscura chameleano traversa.*" With their bodies nearly see-through, they prowled after the wolven.

Leera, eager to see what lay ahead, moved a little quicker and was the first to get her eyes over the hill. What she saw made her gasp and freeze in place. For deep in the east, amidst a flat horizon, and floating on a black ocean, was the massive silhouette of the largest—and strangest—ship she had ever seen.

Leera squinted from behind her spectacles. "Gods, that thing must have like a dozen masts. And look how spiky they all are. Demonic looking, even. But I don't see any sails, at least not in this darkness. They must be furled."

"Where is it from?" Augum asked.

"That we do not know," the calm one replied.

"We should have brought a spyglass," Bridget muttered.

"Shoot, I left one back in the castle," Augum said.

"We sent scouts and a shaman to investigate down to that shore there," the gray said, pointing eastward to where the ice of land met the dark ocean. "None returned."

"It could be the ones summoning gargoyles," Augum said, and his shimmering silhouette glanced at Leera and Bridget. "Their staging ground for an invasion."

"We have tablets going back to ancient times," the calm one said. "If the old stories are true, then they could be the first ship of many."

The ominous thought plunged everyone into contemplative silence.

"Your wolven went by land, is that right?" Leera eventually asked.

"Yes," the chief replied.

"They burrowed under the snow," the calm one added.

"Why don't I try going around and swimming in—"

"No," Augum blurted. "I mean, it's way too dangerous. If it's the same attackers, they could easily render your arcanery null and you'd drown."

"I'd teleport away before that happened."

"We don't always see it coming," Bridget countered. "I agree with Aug. It's way too dangerous."

"So is walking in. So is battle-'porting closer. Whatever those things are, I *highly* doubt they'll be searching the waters." She looked to the gray one. "Who *are* they, anyway?"

The old wolven glanced at his cohorts. "We do not know. But we have seen small silhouettes take to the skies from afar."

"More of their summoned gargoyles?" Bridget said to Augum.

He wobbled his shimmering head about in a *Perhaps, perhaps not* manner.

Leera wanted to argue further about making her way around the strange ship when a distant echo stalled her. "What's that?" she whispered, glancing about.

"What's what?" Bridget asked.

Another echo came, this one louder. "That echo. There it is again."

The gray looked to the other wolven. "Our hearing is superior to humans and we hear nothing."

The echo strengthened and became words. "... *do not* ..." it said.

"Do not," she repeated. "Do not what ...?"

A chameleonic Augum grabbed hold of her hand. "You all right?" whispering, "*Is it the predator?*"

She raised a shimmering finger, only to realize it was hardly visible, and so she whispered, "Hush, trying to listen." Luckily, the echo came again.

"... do not ... approach ..."

"Don't approach!" she blurted. Then she realized it had to be coastal defense reaching out to her—except coastal defense was a high secret, so the wolven were not allowed to know about it.

"Meet me ... in the deep ..." the voice echoed. It was female and slightly croaky, giving Leera the impression the speaker was old. "... the ring ... will guide you ... focus on its path ... like Unconceal ... come now ..."

"We'll be right back," Leera told the wolven, and tugged on Augum and Bridget's shimmering coats before backtracking away from the hilltop.

"What's going on?" a shimmering Bridget asked after they had walked a little ways back down the valley.

"I have to go," Leera whispered, keeping her back to the wolven. "I was contacted by you-know-who. As much as I want to camp here and watch that strange ship, they said to come right now."

Augum's shimmering body moved. "*Chameleano null,*" he incanted, making himself visible. Bridget and Leera promptly did the same. He checked up the slope where the wolven remained in place before leaning close to mouth, *"Coastal defense?"*

Leera nodded. Then she hooked arms around Bridget and Augum's necks and brought them close enough so their foreheads touched. "A voice instructed me to follow the pull of the ring."

"We're coming with you," Augum blurted. "And that's non-negotiable."

Leera smiled at him and nodded. She loved their company, so for her that wasn't a problem.

"How far?" Bridget asked, nodding at Leera's mitted hand.

Leera focused on the ring, marrying the principles required to feel a tendril tug in the arcane ether. "Not sure, but the tug is firm and to the south and a little to the east. Meaning likely on the coast."

"What about the wolven?" Bridget asked, looking to Augum.

"I'll talk to them and say we have a secondary quest we have to attend to and ask them to keep monitoring the ship from afar. I'll set an alarm for them to trigger in case something happens." After the girls agreed, he strode back up the slope to speak with the wolven.

"Why does everything feel like a trap?" Bridget asked while they waited.

Leera watched Augum tear a piece of journey bread he had retrieved from within his rucksack, stick it into the snow, and set an alarm on it. "Because we're so used to being paranoid about everything, that's why. Sometimes we just have to have a little trust."

Augum soon clambered back down the slope. "As a gesture of friendship, the chief offered for the shaman to 'port us along the coast. She's been part of scouting parties so she knows the terrain, though I don't think she looked too happy about it."

Leera approved of this with a nod. "At least that'll save us a trek."

"She'll drop us off then return to stick close to her colleagues," Augum added. "And in case of the worst, we've memorized enough stops along the way to make it back here."

After the wolven held a brief discussion up top in their growling tongue, the shaman joined the trio. Saying nothing, she extended her paws, and they formed a circle. Knowing how aloof wolven could be, Leera wasn't surprised when the others did not say goodbye—or even acknowledge their departure.

After an incantation and a *thwomp*, they appeared on a stony beach caked with frozen boulders. The waves crashed hard against the shore, which was also battered by a fierce easterly wind that sent a shiver into Leera's bones. She checked the ring and felt that the pull was significantly closer, and that a hop half that distance ought to do it, which she verbalized to the wolven in language that would not give away details.

They next appeared near the edge of a cliff littered with clusters of stubby cedars. The wind here was even stronger, howling as it scraped against the cliff. The sound of crashing surf echoed from down below. Leera checked with the ring and felt the pull was nearby—and almost directly east, into the ocean, which did not entirely surprise her. But she would not say that part aloud just yet.

"This is it," she declared.

"Thank you for your kindness," Augum told the shaman.

"In return you must protect us all," the shaman replied.

"Hardly much of a bargain," Leera muttered, making fun of the wolven tendency to turn everything into a transaction. At least, that had been her experience with Raptos.

The shaman ignored her and growled off an incantation, vanishing with a *thwomp*.

Bridget glanced about. "Place sure is desolate …"

Augum squeezed Leera's hand. "Where to from here?"

Leera felt a guilty pang in her chest. "I'm afraid this is as far as you two go."

"What? Why?"

Leera's reply was to look to the ocean.

Augum's hand slipped out of hers. "Oh …"

She grabbed it back and held it against her chest. "We must trust that these are allies—"

"—who at one time tried to have you killed," Augum interrupted.

"I'm no fool. I'll be on the alert." She took off her mitt and slid a hand onto his cheek, drawing him near. Bridget tactfully turned her back to allow them a longing and tender kiss. "I'll be back soon, my love," Leera whispered, and set an alarm on a stick in case of an emergency, which she embedded into the snow.

"We'll make camp here and wait," Augum said.

She nodded. "Good. By the way, what was up with that castle back there, Bridge?"

"Remember when I told you two about that possible future order that would start a war for land?"

They nodded.

"It would begin there. That's the castle our royals would want us to level as dragons."

Before Augum could reply, Leera punched Bridget on the upper arm. "Well then I'm glad you tore up that plan in their stupid faces. Ignore those warmongers, they're fools. Now come gimme a hug," and she hugged and said her goodbyes to Bridget before stripping her coat, mitts, boots, and even her robe, leaving her in her undergarments.

"Wait, you do this *every* time?" Bridget asked, taking the bundle of clothes from her. "In this weather?"

"It's hard to swim with a sail on your back," Leera replied, shrugging. "It's just easier this way." She tossed Augum her rucksack.

"You be careful," he said, and they hugged again.

"I will." She playfully shoved him off, threw him a sly smirk, and paced up to the wind-scoured cliff edge to peer down into the dark ocean, the waves of which reflected the moonlight. She judged a forty-foot drop, dangerous but survivable. After a focused breath, she incanted, "*Bratta fil aqua,*" which triggered the 1st degree off-the-books water element spell Breathe Water. Then she incanted "*Endura o prassa ata o codola,*" casting the 3rd degree off-the-books Endure the Deep, and felt her lungs expand and her inners harden to pressure and cold. Lastly, she removed her spectacles and clutched them protectively in her hand. After kissing her hand and blowing it back at Augum, receiving one back along with a wave from Bridget, she stepped off the cliff.

The fall was rapid, sending her hair flying behind her. After a heart-jamming plummet, she pierced the icy surface of the violent waters like a dagger. She immediately flared her arms and legs—and just in time, too, for a foot pressed into the top of a slimy boulder. It was shallower than it had appeared from above.

"*Shyneo,*" she incanted, flaring her hand with a bright light that illuminated a quickly moving shore of rocks and sharp barnacles. Needing to get away as quickly as possible, she focused on the nuance of the 9th degree off-the-books elemental spell Speed of the Dolphin, pointed both hands at her feet, and incanted, "*Kwiko au o dolfa fusio fota talla,*" all while steadily drawing the hands together, until she felt her feet fuse and expand to make a large flipper. Then, just as the violent wind-pushed surf threatened to slam her into the boulder wall at the base of the cliff, she kicked off and swam into the nether dark.

The floor rapidly dropped off below her, but she continued to follow the pull of the ring. The ocean water was salty and cold and bitter and tasted of seaweed. As she steadily descended, she tucked her spectacles into that specially crafted pocket in her undergarments, then checked in on herself. Her stamina levels were high, and it wasn't too difficult holding four spells up considering three were low-degree and the fourth, Speed of the Dolphin, hardly required much concentration to keep up at all.

She also routinely checked her surroundings. This being the ocean, it was a whole other realm, and unlike the lake, there were actual carnivorous beasts she would have to watch for. It was during one of these sweeps of the head, as she looked to her right, that there appeared a gaping cat-sized jaw filled with rows of teeth—and it was swimming right for her.

Out of sheer reflex, Leera flicked her dolphin tail and zipped aside, barely missing the teeth. She felt the pull of the water as the beast—a mammoth eel by the look of its long body—swam past. It quickly curled back around, a serpent ready to swallow her whole. She only had a heartbeat to slap her wrists and roar, "*Annihilo bato!*" Two sharp jets of water drilled a pair of watermelon-sized holes in its flesh, making it recoil.

Yet the attack only seemed to enrage the animal, which thrashed about in pain so violently that its tail smashed her across the chest, sending her reeling in the water—and temporarily knocking the water breath out of her. She double-kicked with her tail and furiously swam toward the pull of the ring, checking behind her throughout.

The eel regained its senses, opened its massive jaws, and dove after her. Still water-winded, she waited until it was within three feet before she pointed backward, telekinetically latched onto its lower jaw, and made it go upward. The force pushed her down and the creature up, its long body slithering by like a snake, the side with the two holes spewing internals into the ocean, which she knew would quickly attract other predators.

The eel turned about and went for another pass. But it had made two fatal mistakes—giving her time to catch her breath, and giving her time to aim. Leera slapped her wrists together, roaring, "*Annihilo bato!*" and sent two more jets of water right at its face. One jet blew through an eye, and the other through the forehead—and thus the brain.

The creature instantly went still, its momentum gliding it right at Leera, who again had to telekinetically shove the thing aside lest its teeth accidentally impale her fragile flesh. It slithered by as silent as the grave, its long body slowly angling into a dive, until all that was left was its long tail before it vanished into the dark depths below.

Counting her blessings, Leera glanced about. Other than some white-tipped sharks pursuing the body, no other beast had presented itself. She shook the fear from the encounter off, gave a double-kick of her dolphin tail, and swam onward.

Down she steadily dove into the cold salty depths, her head on a constant swivel, her pale light lighting ocean particles and crustaceans and jellies and small fish that either darted away or swam near to investigate before also darting away. She swam fast, eager to get there, to leave these unknown waters, wondering what she would find.

At long last, the pull took her to a sandy ocean floor pockmarked with coral- and seaweed-infested boulders. Crabs and lobsters and starfish crawled amidst these in search of prey or shelter. She swam along the sandy bottom, keeping alert, when her light revealed a large black rock in the shape of a small hill. And in the center of that hill was a hole ten feet in diameter.

Ever cautious, Leera splayed her left hand and incanted, "*Un vun asperio aurum enchantus.*" The hole lit up with blue protective tendrils, ones she did not recognize. But what struck her was that they had long sunk to permanence, meaning they were ancient. The order of coastal defense was far older than she had thought.

She swam up close to them and saw that the tendrils were of the barrier sort that likely kept monsters out. She raised her aqua-ringed hand and pressed it forth through the web. When nothing happened, she swam through, figuring the ring acted as a gate key.

The hole turned out to be a tunnel of rock that culminated in a pool lit by torchlight. She swam up to that pool and cagily raised her head above its surface.

There on a wide ledge and flanked by a pair of ensconced torches stood an old woman dressed in a simple green linen robe.

"Greetings, fellow Solian," the woman croaked. "Or should I say … Dragon?" She was rather plump, with skin so pale it might as well be alabaster, black hair that stood out starkly against that skin, and a face grooved with deep wrinkles. Almost like an old version of Leera's apprentice, Revel.

Leera swam forth to the stone edge and pulled herself out of the water, awkwardly flopping onto her side on account of her dolphin tail. "*Endura null, bratta null,*" she incanted, snuffing Endure the Deep and Breathe Water, before also snuffing her palm light. "Leera is fine."

"And my name is Mrs. Silanna Seahorse, of the northeastern coastal guard."

Leera blinked. "Mrs. … *Seahorse?*"

"Yes. We coastal guardians like to take on water-themed names as a sort of swimming jest. Get it? Not a *running* jest, but a *swimming* jest." She beamed. "Oh, this is simply marvelous—*marvelous!* I have not had a visitor in almost a decade—other than fellow members of the order, of course."

Leera pointed both hands at her fused tail and spread them apart, incanting, "*Kwiko null.*" The flipper melted away, leaving behind her two naked feet.

Mrs. Seahorse reached out a hand, which Leera took, allowing her to haul her to her feet. Leera then withdrew her spectacles and placed them on her nose, not minding in the least that they were speckled with water droplets.

"Your hair," she blurted, getting her first good look at the woman. "It's seaweed!"

"Quite fashionable, isn't it?" The old woman gave a clumsy twirl whilst primping her hair with both hands. "I rather think I'd be quite the attraction at a ball."

"You, uh, would certainly make an impression." Leera wondered if the woman was aware of how strongly she smelled of fish. Somehow, she doubted it. She noted that, much like the assassin, she too had waves tattooed on an arm.

Mrs. Seahorse glanced Leera over. "I see the fashions have changed a little since I last visited the city."

Leera self-consciously covered herself up with her hands, mumbling, "I just find swimming easier without the robe, which tends to act like a sail, if you know what I mean."

"I *do* know, but I find modesty to be a grand virtue. Why should we make those poor fish suffer the sight of our ghastly bodies?"

Leera blinked a few times, not knowing what to say to that.

"Please, young dragon miss, join me in my home."

"Er, my friends wait for me above and there's a great threat to the north—"

"Yes, yes, we shall get to all that. But first, allow me my courtesies as I so rarely receive visitors."

"Er … all right."

The woman stared at Leera expectantly. When Leera only stared in confusion, Mrs. Seahorse cleared her throat. "Sorry, do you mind?" She flared her eyes down at Leera's body.

Leera glanced down to see she was dripping all over the stone floor. "Oh! My apologies." She opened a hand and ran it over her sodden undergarments, incanting, "*Evapa loa aqua.*" She made sure to surge the spell, at the cost of a chunk of stamina, so that the water immediately evaporated.

Mrs. Seahorse gave an approving nod, then turned and clumsily hop-skipped forth, giggling like a young girl. Leera wondered if she had spent too much time under water over the years.

Skipping merrily, with Leera secretly mimicking one of those skips to her own amusement, Mrs. Seahorse led her through a rocky hallway which opened into a living room that stole Leera's breath away, for it was an underwater cave with windows. And visible through those windows, lit by torchlight from within, was a vibrant coral reef brimming with sea creatures—sea anemones and crabs and lobsters and eels and all manner of fish. There were blue and green and orange and yellow and red corals and various weeds that slowly waved about in the current.

And the living room itself was interesting, for all the furniture was made of dried driftwood—a long couch and two armchairs and a coffee table and even the dressers and bookshelves, which overflowed with books and scrolls and tablets. The carpet was a type of seaweed and patterned to look like floating islands amidst a blue ocean.

"It's beautiful," Leera whispered. "It reminds me of a cave I visited a long time ago that once belonged to Anna Atticus Stone."

"Is that so!" Mrs. Seahorse cooed in a gossipy tone. "This was forever ago, but she was my teacher at one point. A brilliant, *brilliant* woman." Her face soured. "If not a little grumpy sometimes."

"Tell me about it," Leera muttered, all too well remembering Mrs. Stone's harsh lessons and pointed frown. But she also remembered how much quiet love the woman had for her and Augum and Bridget, and wondered if she'd ever have another mentor like that again.

"I was quite the rambunctious pupil and oft found myself in detention. Dear me, where are my manners?" The old woman skittered over to the couch and plumped up its cushions by viciously punching them with a fist, sending small plumes of dust that made Leera suppress coughs. "Please, do have a seat." She abruptly straightened, all the wrinkles of her face twisting into such overt happiness that Leera thought the woman might pull a muscle. "Tea?" she sang in a drawn-out squeak.

"Tea would be lovely, thank you," Leera said, taking a seat in the center of the couch, still trying to suppress the occasional cough with the back of her forearm.

Mrs. Seahorse pointed at a blanket on a bench and floated it over. It unfurled before her, revealing an old academy crest, the wool full of holes. She cleared her throat in that same manner again and, whilst looking away, covered Leera's body with it, using pinching fingers as if Leera were diseased.

"Er … thanks," Leera mumbled, cheeks red from the shame of having to be covered up.

The woman shuffled over to a kitchen neatly organized with highly polished copper ladles and pans, the rocky walls tiled with an assortment of colorful shells. She placed a charred copper kettle into a hearth and stoked the flames.

"So what is it like to become a dragon?" Mrs. Seahorse asked. "Is it actually a dragon or a form of it? Do you get to fly, or do you command a dragon to fly on your behalf? Or is it all an elaborate and effective illusion? Oh, I have so many questions."

"We turn into dragons. It's a spell."

"Really? How exciting! I've read a little about dragons in the archives, but that was all supposed to be folk tales and mythology and such. I didn't actually believe such a thing could be done."

"Yes, it's, uh, a rather interesting experience," Leera mumbled, glancing about in wonder at the home. She could imagine using a cave such as this to relax from the bustle and attention of the city. Except building one would be quite the challenge, for an earth warlock would have to be hired and be enchanted with the ability to breathe underwater and deal with pressure and then there was the telekinetic hauling of materials and supplies and the countless—

"I've heard all about you three through the order's ring network," Mrs. Seahorse said, slicing through Leera's thoughts. "We're as secret as an order gets but gods help me are we a gossipy bunch. No surprise seeing as we're all we each have. We're from all the seven kingdoms but we're also all water warlocks, so we have a lot in common. Some of us even went to the same classes."

"How do you become an order member?" Leera asked. "And who's in charge?"

"Unless you've been told who's in charge, I'm not allowed to tell you. And you become a member by invitation only. Then it's for life."

"How many of you are there?"

"A lot. We've got patrol zones and there's one of us every so many leagues up and down the coasts."

"Do you have families?"

"Some do, yes, but the kids and spouses are all sworn to secrecy. Under penalty of death, of course."

"Of course …" Leera wondered what she had gotten herself into. "What are you protecting the kingdoms from?"

Mrs. Seahorse glanced over her shoulder to look at Leera as if she were daft. "Why, pirates and monsters, my dear. Pirates and monsters. And land-crawlin' hoodlums, but—" She stabbed the air with a finger. "—*but*, legally speaking, they turn into pirates the moment they step on a ship and try to rob someone." She returned to fussing about. "The pirates try to steal anything that floats, while the monsters mostly try to capsize kingdom trade ships, but sometimes one crawls onto land and goes on a wee killing spree." She withdrew the kettle from the fire and fiddled with it at the counter whilst humming a friendly tune. She soon returned, holding a tray with a teapot and two cups and saucers—all of it, tray included, made of seashells. She floated a teacup before Leera, who grabbed it, then floated the teapot, which tipped itself over to pour out a greenish hot liquid. The old woman then straightened to beam expectantly at Leera.

Leera blew on the steaming teacup before taking a sip. A salty and slightly fishy tang exploded onto her tongue. "Wow, this is ... most interesting. I don't think I've tasted anything like it before."

"It's red seaweed tea," Mrs. Seahorse said, primping her seaweed hair. "Lovely, isn't it?"

And certainly tastes like it, Leera thought. But she said, "Er ... quite lovely, yes." It reminded her of her late mother's rancid concoctions.

Mrs. Seahorse nodded proudly, telekinetically poured herself a cup, and sat down directly beside Leera—despite the couch being flanked by two empty armchairs.

"Now then," she said and took a slurping sip. "About these gargoyles."

"Oh, you've seen the summoned beasts as well?" Leera asked, shoving over to the farthest spot on the couch.

"Summoned? My word, girl, they're not just summoned. They *are*."

"Are ... what?"

"Gargoyles."

"The summoned are, yes."

"Do they not teach reasoning and rhetoric in the academy anymore? I just told you, you silly girl, they are not just the summoned. They *are*."

Leera rubbed her forehead, wondering if the woman had cast a subtle Confusion spell on her or something. "Are you saying the things summoning the gargoyles ... are also gargoyles?"

"There we go! Not so difficult now, was it?"

Leera didn't want to argue all the ways the woman could have explained that better. "Gargoyles, like the statues they have at the Library of Antioc? Like the drainage spouts? Gargoyles ... like from the stories of old?"

"No, not like statues. The real thing. From yonder," and she flicked a hand at the wall whilst giving a whistle that quickly increased in pitch.

Leera looked to the wall. "You mean like from beyond the oceans?"

"Oh, yes. Yes, yes, yes. Well beyond. Far, *far* beyond. You know, one of the most frustrating things about being a coastal guardian is that when you try to tell land-crawlers that there might just be something beyond this continent, they look at you like you swallowed stinkroot or committed blasphemy. Mind, we're not supposed to talk about such things, but one sometimes cannot help oneself. The world is much, *much* bigger than people think."

Leera took a slurping sip of her tea as she listened, surprised she was starting to enjoy that salty fishy tang.

"But people cannot fathom such things no more than they can fathom dragons—until they see them with their own eyes. Even then, they sometimes go stark raving mad, don't they?"

"Er … I guess. So, uh, what do these invader gargoyles want?"

The woman shrugged. "How should I know?"

"Since you're that certain they're gargoyles, you must know more about them." Leera doubted the woman even had that part right.

"I know they're gargoyles because I swam up to them and—" She pronged two fingers at her eyes and flicked those fingers up whilst making a *pop* sound with her mouth. "—looked up."

"You're saying it *is* safe to swim up to them …"

"Er, *safe* is a relative term here, but, if you're subtle about it, sure, why not."

"Right. So, uh, why did you summon me?"

"I wanted to meet you, of course. Everyone does. And to invite you to become one of us. We all think you'd make a fine coastal guardian, especially because you can turn into a dragon. In fact, I bet you could probably capture a pirate ship on your own instead of working with a whole team. The efficiency of it … we could upend the corruption dynamics of the coast. Think of the trade implications, kingdom inter-dynamics, the opportunities for land-crawlers and travel. And then some of the larger monsters that take ten of us to vanquish …" She nodded, whistling appreciatively. "You *can* swim as a dragon, right?"

"Er, of course, but—"

"Well, then, I mean, isn't it just the most perfect match? Of course, you'd have to give up your old life entirely and turn your back on your friends and home kingdom, but the rewards speak for themselves, don't they? We'd even help build you a cave here where you can seduce a flipper—that's a derogatory word only we are allowed to call each other, by the way, don't use that until you become one of us unless you want to be stuck in seaweed prison." She pressed a hand to her chest and clucked a chortle. "That was a jest, my dear, a jest." She took a loud, slurping sip of her tea. "Yes indeed, we think you'd make a fine guardie. That's what we call ourselves—guardies."

Leera gaped, wondering if the woman was crazy.

"And to warn you not to venture too close."

"Er ... sorry?"

"That's the other reason we called on you. To warn you not to venture too close to the gargoyles, as they have this incredible and annoying ability to snuff arcanery completely."

"We noticed—"

"I mean, just this morning, Barnacle Bill found himself choking underwater when one of those beasts nullified his ability to breathe underwater. Poor chap nearly drowned. So as long as you stay clear of them you shouldn't have any trouble."

Leera set her teacup down. "Excuse me, but we believe they're about to invade all of Sithesia."

The woman snorted her tea. "Invade. Utter nonsense. Gargoyles are an inquisitive lot."

"How do you know that?"

"Because ... well ... I mean ..." The woman grimaced as she angled her head this way and that. "They're portrayed as being quite bookish, aren't they? At the libraries and the like. Surely that's for a reason. They're almost certainly exploring. I'm certain we have a lot to learn from each other. I just wish they'd be open to dialogue."

Leera's eyebrows threatened to crawl above her forehead. "Dialogue ...?"

"Yes, dialogue, as all civilized peoples are wont to do."

"But *are* they civilized? These ... creatures? They attacked us—multiple times."

The woman flapped a hand dismissively. "That could have been anybody, really."

"They were gargoyles. Summoned gargoyles. That nipped people right off the streets. Then turned to ash."

"Maybe that's someone else under the guise of gargoyles. Maybe that's someone who wants to smear their character because they're afraid of how different they are."

"Don't listen to her!" barked a gravelly voice from the corridor.

Leera jumped to her feet, hands in attack position, the blanket sliding off. An old man dressed in a similar green linen robe hobbled into view, and the woman yelped and telekinetically yanked on the blanket to hang before Leera.

The grizzled old man ignored this completely as he waved his arms about. "Don't listen to that old loon all she does is ramble about inanities the fact is we're all going to die and probably sooner than later and you lot need to go on up there and destroy that ship before everything goes to hell—"

"Stumpy, sweetie, really, you're being obscene."

It did not escape Leera's notice that one of the man's feet was missing altogether, so he hobbled on a fleshy but calloused stump.

"We all agree on this but you, Sil," the man barked back. He was plumper than his wife, had a wild nest of gray hair that surrounded a bald patch, and his skin was even paler than hers and riddled with blotches. "And you should have left it to the others for a proper introduction. Gods know what nonsense you've been telling this girl."

Leera subconsciously grabbed the blanket and held it close. "Er … what's going on?"

"This is my silly husband Larry, who everyone calls Stumpy."

The man reached out a hand and hobbled over, nearly tripping in his haste. "Larry Seahorse, Order of the Coastal Guard, at your service, young dragon." After vigorously shaking Leera's hand—and having her fear he would rip her arm off—he abruptly let go to point at his foot. "To forestall your silent question, I lost it a long time ago to a dastardly serpent. A vicious and long thing with rows of teeth."

"Might have bumped into it on the way here," Leera muttered.

The man either hadn't heard or pretended not to. "I tried to get the foot back so I could take it to a healer and have them cast the 12th degree Reunite Severed Limb spell but I nearly passed out chasing the blasted thing—not to mention I had a league-long tail of sharks following me—and had to teleport my way back for Mrs. Seahorse to bind me up before I bled out." He whistled in the same manner as his wife. "That was a close one, it was."

"He was quite the mess," his wife said, shaking her head. "Quite the mess indeed. Tea, sweetie?"

"Later, my little shell bean—" He raised two gnarled fingers before Leera's face, his green eyes wild with intensity. "We're. All. Going. To. Die."

"Why, of course we are, dear," his wife cooed. "Nobody lives forever. Give us a kissie, kissie, kissie," and they pecked each other on the lips.

"No, my little wiggle wump, I mean we are going to die soon and I am talking about gargoyles and gargoyles are smart—no, brilliant—and they are here to eat us all—everybody. I'm telling you, we're fish paste."

He leaned close to Leera, who had to lean away to avoid his rotten fish breath. "Fish. Paste. That's the end goal here. That's why they've come."

"Have you been talking to the Urchins again, honeybunny?"

"No, of course not!" He pressed a hand to the side of his mouth, hiding it from his wife as he whispered, "Mr. and Mrs. Urchin and their foul spawn are complete loons."

"This is all a little much," Leera mumbled, using the blanket as a shield and taking another step away from the man's foul breath, which seemed to permeate the room now.

"Wouldn't she make a perfect guardie, darling?"

"There won't *be* a coastal guard after those things are done with us! Fish paste! *Fish paste!*" Mr. Seahorse pressed a fist to the side of his mouth as he furrowed his shaggy eyebrows. "Although perhaps the better wording would be gargoyle paste. Or human paste? What do you think?" He raised shaggy eyebrows at Leera and waggled them. "Hmm?"

"Er …"

"I like fish paste. It's what I know." He stumped away. "Tea, my little sea cucumber?"

"Coming right up, my hobbled sea squirrel."

Mr. Seahorse wiped his brow with a cloth, then ran that cloth over his hair before hanging it back up on the wall alongside the copper implements. He whirled about. "So they sent you north to turn into a dragon and destroy them. Is that right?"

"Er …"

"Except they don't realize you can't turn into a dragon."

"Stumpy! Don't be rude, honey."

"What? We all know it's true, salt muffin. It's a scare tactic. They use these three poor young warlocks as patsies, giving people heroes to worship while they summon illusory dragons and have them fly about to scare the commoners into going to the chapel more and making sure all the dirt-trodders pay their tithes and taxes and bake their bread and smile and nod their graces and be good little tadpoles that stay in their little ponds."

"But the girl insists she can turn into a dragon."

"Really?" Mr. Seahorse folded his hairy arms across his barrel chest. "All right then. Go on, girl. Prove it. Turn into a dragon."

"Uh … I mean … that's not something we can just do—"

"See? *See?* I told you, my pepper blossom, it's all for show. They have a whole range of excuses and are trained to toss them at people like salt from a salt pouch. You know how silly those land-thumpers are and their silly superstitions. The excuses are crafted to play right into their fears and their gullibility."

He wagged a finger at Leera, grinning victoriously. "She can't turn into a dragon because the entire masquerade would crumble like fish pie left on a beach. They train them with a litany of excuses to employ at such requests." He grabbed his bulging stomach and whined, exaggerating each phrase worse than the last. "I don't feel well. My tummy hurts. It's that time of the moon. There's not enough room. That's not something we can just do." He scoffed. "Don't worry, lass, it's the same with us guardies whenever a knuckle-dragging landie asks us about the order. Order? What order? There ain't no order. Those water warlocks you see wrestling serpents are on training exercises sent by the academies. That ship that got saved? It was a miracle ordained by The Fates or The Unnameables or whatever fancy comes to—"

"Sorry, but can we discuss the gargoyles?" Leera interrupted, losing patience.

"Gargoyles! Right! We are doomed to suffer being cranked out as fish paste. Pasted into paste. *Is* it ground into paste, lovebug? How do you make paste?"

"I grind it, sugar plum."

"Grind. Right."

Leera, seeing she was getting nowhere and would hardly be able to trust what they said about these so-called gargoyles anyway, raised the finger wearing the nautical ring. "Can you teach me about this ring?"

At this, both husband and wife animated and started talking at the same time.

"It's a darling of an artifact—" the wife cooed.

"Quite ancient—" the husband vociferated, trying to barrel over his wife's words, making her screech louder in turn.

"—passed down generation after generation—"

"—highly, *highly* coveted—"

"—all sorts of interesting powers—"

"Please, I can't understand you!" Leera had to shout, making the pair abruptly halt and gape as if wounded. "Forgive me, but one at a time. Please." She looked to the wife and nodded encouragingly while smiling as kindly as she could. The last thing she wanted to do was offend these weirdos and have them turn *her* into fish paste or stick her in a seaweed prison or something.

"You ever heard of speaking orbs?" Mrs. Seahorse began.

"Yes, back in the war we used them to communicate together—"

"This is the same thing. You've got to say the name."

"And every name is bound into the arcanery of the ring for all time," Mr. Seahorse added.

"Meaning you can speak to the dead if you wanted to, to those who wore the rings prior—"

"But of course they won't reply."

Mrs. Seahorse smilingly nodded. "Or you can start conversations with a bunch of people."

"But you're new, so you're not allowed to do that until we deem you worthy," Mr. Seahorse threw in.

"It's how we share recipes and gossip. Just last tenday I learned how to squish out the most delectable poison-clam chowder!"

"It really is quite good," Mr. Seahorse said, a hand pressed to the side of his mouth. "As long as you scrape off the top, that is. Otherwise it's a trip to Pukeville, if you know what I mean." He drew a hand to his mouth and shot it outward, exploding open the hand, then repeated the motion from his bottom, making Leera recoil.

"In the mean, you can say—" Mrs. Seahorse lifted the ring to her lips. "—contact—it's Jones, isn't it? Yes, of course it is," she said before Leera could reply. "Contact Leera Jones. Hello, young lady."

Leera jumped out of reflex, for those very words sounded off in her head at the exact same moment.

"Oh, look at that, she's already been coded into the arcanery," Mr. Seahorse said. "Or was it tuned? I forget. Anyway, looks like you're well on your way, young lady. Welcome aboard. Get it? Aboard?"

"We do love our sea puns," Mrs. Seahorse said, taking a slurping sip of her tea, which Leera heard in her head, making her wince from the strange and ugly sound of it.

"Love, *love* sea puns."

"And to stop communication, simply say, 'cease contact' into the ring, like I just did. Now you try it."

Leera raised the ring to her lips. "Contact Silanna Seahorse. Er, hello."

"There you go! Perfect. Don't forget to cut contact."

"Cease contact."

"Excellent! Now let us work on guidance."

"Yes, she absolutely needs to learn that one too," Mr. Seahorse chimed in.

"Guiding means you can guide someone to your location," Mrs. Seahorse explained.

"Like Mrs. Seahorse guided you to her."

"It's how we find each other out in the vast ocean."

"And it's a vast, vast ocean."

"Much, *much* larger than anyone thinks."

"Like here to the moon."

"Not that far, dear. Don't be ridiculous. He likes to exaggerate."

"I like to exaggerate."

The pair nodded, grinning like fools.

Leera glanced between them. "So about this guidance power …"

"Right, look at us babbling on. Silly us," Mrs. Seahorse said.

"Silly, silly us," Mr. Seahorse added with a shake of the head.

"You can either guide someone to your location or guide yourself to them."

"To guide a specific ring-wearer to you, use an inverse thought pattern of Object Track whilst incanting into the ring, '*Guidosio Larry Seahorse tei mi.*' Although the ring does most of the heavy lifting arcanely speaking, it's still important to give it a bit of help. "

"Guide Larry Seahorse to me," Leera translated in a murmur, "whilst inverting Object Track. Got it." She'd learned inversion techniques at the academy, so didn't anticipate a problem.

The man thumbed his chest. "And that creates a pull for me—" He turned the thumb around. "—toward you. Now give it a go."

Leera reached out her free hand and formed her thoughts inversely to the usual demands of Object Track, as if she were pushing that object onto the ether instead of trying to locate it, all while incanting into the ring, "*Guidosio Larry Seahorse tei mi.*" She felt a brief tickle in her innards before it fizzled.

"There you are!" Mr. Seahorse sang, throwing his hands toward Leera. "The moment your target—meaning me—places eyes on you, the spell concludes. That's why you probably felt a fizzle. But I most certainly felt a pull directly to you. Excellent adoption, young lady. She's quite astute," he said to his wife, head bobbing up and down. "Much quicker on the uptake than everyone else."

"She really is," Mrs. Seahorse replied, head bobbing in the same manner before she took over. "It's even easier to guide yourself to a specific ring-wearer. Simply incant '*Locata Silanna Seahorse*' into the ring like I did there, all while using the usual principles of Object Track. Now you try."

Leera reached out her free hand and used her ring hand to incant into the ring, "*Locata Silanna Seahorse.*"

"Did you feel a pull toward me?"

"Er, yes, I did actu—"

"Of course you did, you clever thing! That's how you found us in the first place! Here we are!" Mrs. Seahorse twiddled her fingers at Leera, singing, "Fun, isn't it?"

"So much fun," Leera said flatly. Still, she was impressed. The arcanery was slightly more advanced than the standard Object Track spell everyone used.

"Can I get these rings for my friends—"

Mr. Seahorse shook his head. "Absolutely not—"

Mrs. Seahorse did the same. "Will never happen—"

"Only water warlocks permitted by the order get one."

"Anyone else gets hunted down like a seal and slaughtered."

Husband and wife nodded in tandem.

"Oh. I see." Leera looked longingly at the doorway, wanting to find an excuse to get back to Augum and Bridget.

"The ring has some other features," Mr. Seahorse added, "but you won't find out about those until you're an elder member."

"Just don't lose it," Mrs. Seahorse blurted. "The ring, that is. They're invaluable to us."

"But can't you track them down again?"

Husband and wife shook their heads. "The arcanery doesn't work that way," Mr. Seahorse said. "It's annoying, we know, and that aspect of the ring is rather antiquated. Sometimes we get around the limitation by casting our own Object Track spell on it—"

"—when we remember to do so," Mrs. Seahorse interjected.

"The problem is the spell lapses relatively quickly and it gets tedious to cast it again and again and again and next thing you know you find yourself not bothering to do it at all. Anyway, the default is that the ring has to get worn to activate, and then we send a retriever out after it. You drop it down into some ocean depth and, well …" Mr. Seahorse made a hand-washing motion before flipping those hands open.

"Meaning I'm trackable as long as I'm wearing it."

"Of course, dear," Mrs. Seahorse said, head bobbing up and down.

"Once it tunes to you, we can find you and you can find us using names," Mr. Seahorse added. "Which of course only works if we *know* your name."

Mrs. Seahorse wrung her hands. "Yes, the order is deeply apologetic for trying to, uh, you know …"

"Kill me?"

The couple went red as they squirmed in place.

"I still don't understand why the order needs to be so secretive."

"Because we are watchmen, constables, soldiers, spies and, sometimes, saboteurs," the husband replied. "For the kingdoms, that is."

"There are many clever monsters and beasts and entities out there that would love to know our locations and how we function and all our lovely little secrets," the wife added.

"Not to mention we have to always stay one step ahead of the pirates, who sometimes get a little crafty and try to track us down and—" Mr. Seahorse drew a finger across his throat. "—carve us a Nodian smile, to use your landie parlance."

"You'll understand once you confiscate your first pirate ship."

"If you ever capture one of your own, you get to keep the anchor as a trophy." Mr. Seahorse pointed into a corner of the room, at what appeared to be a hat and coat rack covered in soiled clothes, but was actually a rusting anchor. "I was able to commandeer her on my own as she was mostly empty of men on account of being full of mirko poop, which at the time was considered a delicacy in some Sierran dish. Of course, that dish went out of fashion when people started dying from the ol' double-ended vomit." He scratched his bald spot. "Or maybe it was a Canterran dish. I can't recall."

"It's amazing what landies try to get away with," his wife threw in.

The pair nodded as if their necks were made of bouncy rubber.

"Right. Guess that makes sense," Leera muttered. "Anyway, I should probably get back to my friends. Is there, uh, anything else you think I should know?"

"Oh, there's a million and one things you should know," Mrs. Seahorse said. "About the order, about the oceans."

"Right. Anything specific before I go?"

The husband's face darkened along with his voice. "There are beasts beyond the oceans. Frightful beasts in frightful lands. But they have rarely been able to cross the oceans, which themselves are full of terrors, including monstrous storms that subvert arcanery, preventing teleportation." He raised a finger. "The ring you carry gives some—*some*—protection against those monsters and those storms."

Leera glanced down at the ring, wondering why in Sithesia they would mention that. Did they expect her to try to cross the oceans or something? The idea seemed preposterous. But just as she was about to press the point, Mr. Seahorse raised his chin, face proud.

" '*Monstrosi del o duva, monstrosi infenatti. Defenda, defenda, defenda.*' "

"Monsters in the deep, monsters beyond," Mrs. Seahorse translated. "Defend, defend, defend."

"Use the ring wisely, Dragon Leera Jones," Mr. Seahorse continued. "Protect the coasts. Protect Sithesia. For I fear that something dark this way comes." He looked to the windows, where a school of fish swam by. "That ship is ill tidings."

"My betrothed says it's a staging ground for an invasion."

"Is that the one named Augum? You have permission from the order to speak about us amongst each other. And you tell your Augum that Larry Seahorse agrees. That is why you must destroy the ship before the infection spreads. Before they destroy us all."

"But see if maybe you can parlay with them and keep things nice and civil," Mrs. Seahorse chimed in, beaming. "Maybe we could learn some new recipes from each other. Oh and although you'll be considered a partial agent, please do think about joining the order full-time."

"I'll, uh, certainly give it lots of consideration," Leera replied as she drifted toward the exit, thinking she'd rather have double-ended vomit than give up her life to live amongst such loons. "Er, thank you for everything."

"Oh, you're most welcome, love," Mrs. Seahorse sang. "It was quite the treat for us too." She flicked at the teapot, which lifted into the air. "Another cup?"

"No, I really ought to go, thank you." Leera wiggled the finger with the nautical ring about. "But I'll, uh, be in touch."

"Lovely," Mrs. Seahorse replied, and husband and wife saw Leera to the pond, with Mrs. Seahorse insisting Leera keep the blanket on her shoulder until she cast her water spells and slipped into the water.

"Please let me know if anyone in the order spots more of those ships," Leera said, arms wading about in the salty waters of the pool.

"We will, dear," Mrs. Seahorse replied, smiling broadly.

After saying their goodbyes, Leera thanked them again for their hospitality and dipped her head below the water, intending on swimming closer to the surface before teleporting the rest of the way back.

WINGS

AUGUM

Augum spread his hands and stuck them down near the firepit, which he and Bridget had recessed into the snow to make it hard to spot from a distance. He savored the heat of the low fire, its fresh cedar scent, the occasional sharp *crack* as a branch popped.

He and Bridget sat with their backs to the bitter wind, the cliff thirty feet behind, surf crashing rhythmically below. Stubby cedars surrounded them like young but tired sentinels, their thin trunks bent away from the wind. Two A-shaped tents ruffled close by, one for Bridget and one for Augum and Leera. Inside lay their rucksacks, Leera's shortsword Careena and her robe, Bridget's Ordinary bow and quiver, and the trio's golden breastplates, which were too cold and bulky to continually wear. High above, the cloudless black sky sparkled with unfathomable numbers of brilliant stars and a bright moon that would soon dip below the horizon.

"And can you imagine what other things they've been scheming about behind our backs?" Bridget continued, for they'd been having a conversation about the royals wanting to use them as weapons to expand the kingdom. "Or what they planned on doing with that stronghold if we *did* capture it for them?"

"I try not to think about it," Augum replied. "Thing is, they must be aware that our shields would dim if we behaved like that, nullifying the ability to turn into a dragon. And then where would the kingdom be? Weaker than ever, that's where it'd be."

"Maybe they're hoping to find some sort of loophole."

"Maybe." He sighed, tired of talking about it.

"When are you going to take on an apprentice again, anyway?" Bridget asked, chin propped up on a hand, elbow on a thigh. "It's unseemly for the leader of the order not to have one. You should have two—maybe even three—little sheep bleating at your door, begging for advice on that volatile element of yours."

Augum chortled. "Nice to see you make a jest for a change."

"What's that supposed to mean?"

"You're so serious all the time."

"Olaf say that?"

"No."

"Liar. Spill the oats."

"I'm not about to roll my best buddy into the fire." Ollie had mentioned it a few times, usually when near cross-eyed from the drink.

"I'm not asking you to betray him. I'm just asking if he's confiding in you."

"Isn't that what good friends do? Confide in each other?"

"Of course. It's just ..."

"I know your worries. I have them too."

"Except both of you come from an equal footing. Ollie thinks himself inferior for not achieving dragon rank. He says he can't protect me. And now he worries I'll be an evil mother to our future children because of ..." She swallowed, seemingly unable to say it. "I truly hope Leera finds a way to break that curse," she said instead.

When Augum did not reply, Bridget drew her legs up, curled her arms around her knees, and softly asked, "How does that make you feel?"

"It makes me feel feelings is what it does." Augum shook his head. "All this time I thought I was the end of the lineage. Two thousand years of history would end with me. And now ... now there's this faint hope. I-I-I didn't even think she really *wanted* children, you know?"

"She does," Bridget blurted. "Desperately. But not now. In like a decade. Can you wait that long? Assuming of course she breaks this curse ..."

Augum snorted. "I was planning on us dying together old and spent and having only each other—and of course our friends—" He nodded at Bridget, who smiled bittersweetly. "—as company. For me, having children at any time with her would be an unexpected gift ... even a miracle."

"Have you told her that?"

"Er ... haven't, uh, had much time to—"

"Nonsense, Aug. Nonsense."

"Fine, I haven't had the courage yet to face these things, all right? Happy now?"

Bridget laid her head sideways on her knees and watched him with a small smile.

"Stop gawking."

"You love her."

"You're annoying me."

"You love her so much."

He wanted to hiss, *Obviously*, but instead chose to ignore her as he grabbed a stick to poke the fire with. He didn't quite know why he was annoyed with her at the moment.

Bridget propped her chin on top of her knees and stared into the flames. "My dream is that our kids will play together. I want three boys and three girls."

Augum fiddled with the logs in the fire, causing sparks to roll skyward in waves. "Want me to talk to Ollie?"

"No," Bridget blurted. "Well ... maybe. No. I don't know."

"Does he know you want six kids?"

"Er ... no," she mumbled in a small voice.

He flipped his hand questioningly at her.

"Fine, I'm a hypocrite." She wobbled her head in a Leera-esque fashion, sarcastically snapping, "Happy now?"

He stabbed the fire more aggressively, making it plume a shower of sparks. "No ..."

A protracted silence passed between them before Bridget spoke again. "You didn't answer my original question about taking on an apprentice again."

"Well, the last two didn't exactly pan out, did they?" One had lightning-surged, blowing himself up trying to impress Augum, and the other died taking the dragoon trial. He still remembered showing up at the lone mother's door—for the father had perished in the war against Canterra—and seeing her collapse with a knowing shriek the moment she laid eyes on him. It had been a mess.

"Tragedies of fate, and everyone is sorry you had to go through that." She flicked at a log that had rolled too close to her foot, plonking it back onto the fire. "At least you weren't saddled with an heir to the throne. Every time I see the king he asks how his precious nephew fares. I can't help but get the impression that the old boar is hoping to somehow take command of the order through the boy, or prodding him to try for dragon rank. Kid looks up to you. You should have a word with him and set him straight as he doesn't quite listen to me."

"Then he's a fool."

"He wants to take the dragoon trial — *before* doing all the work."

"Then he's a double fool. He'd get killed. Instantly."

"That's what I told him. The entitlement is …" She rubbed her face. "Ugh."

"I'll talk to him next time we have a moment's peace, remind him that he is expected to obey and respect you."

"He's a womanizing brat who doesn't respect women. You should take him on as your apprentice."

"What, so he never learns to respect women?"

Bridget blinked. "See, that's why you're the commander and I merely stick my hands in my armpits like a cheap imposter."

Augum snorted. "You'll get there." He kept idly prodding the fire, enjoying seeing little bursts of sparks erupt forth. He had used Burden's Edge to chop down already dead trees, breaking them up further by stomping on them or using his mitted hands. Bridget had scavenged the rest nearby — there was a lot of tinder buried under the snow, which he had dried out by frying it with lightning. There was something calming about building a fire in the wilds and warming the soul with one's efforts.

"I can take watch until she returns," Augum offered. "You go ahead and catch some shuteye."

Bridget shrugged. "I'll stay up with you."

He glanced at the black ocean. "Still not used to her diving."

"Water warlocks are a special breed."

"Maybe she'll bring us a fresh salmon or pike."

"Speaking of —" Bridget tromped over to her tent, withdrew her rucksack, and fished out a loaf of journey bread. Seeing the bread made Augum's stomach rumble, and he retrieved his rucksack as well. Soon they had an array of foods set on a blanket before the fire.

"You did good provisioning," Augum said, using a knife to spread butter onto journey bread.

"I just threw in whatever I could get my hands on. Reminds me of the old days."

"Our adventuring youth," he said with a hint of sarcasm as he pinched salt and pepper from a small pouch and sprinkled it over buttered bread. He raised it before his face like a trophy and took a savory bite, toning, "Mmm."

Bridget, meanwhile, peeled back a banana. "I love warlock markets."

Augum had to agree as he bit into a sweet apple. As castellan of Castle Arinthian, he had hired a warlock procurer to teleport fresh ingredients in from the Blackhaven warlock markets on a daily basis, ensuring the highest quality foods for the denizens of the castle, which these days mostly consisted of staff—soldiers and servants and sometimes their families. Even thinking about some of those sumptuous meals made Augum long for the castle's comforts. Blackhaven in comparison was an unfriendly and cold place where one had to watch one's back, whereas Castle Arinthian was filled only with allies and friends.

As they ate in silence, with the cold wind whistling through the trees and making the tents flap, and the low fire merrily crackling away, he amused himself with remembrances of prior adventures in that castle, only for Bridget to cut them short.

"I'm scared, Aug," Bridget whispered, holding a chunk of journey bread with both hands.

Augum quieted his loud chewing.

"I'm scared we're losing who we are. That the dragon is taking over. I'm scared of losing Ollie, of the life I dreamed of one day living. Of having a farm and a gaggle of geese and a flock of children. I'm scared that when I *do* have children, I'll accidentally let the predator inside me near them. I can't even fathom what would happen, and if something did, I'd never forgive myself—ever."

She curled strands of her long cinnamon hair around one ear and then the other. "And now I'm scared for the kingdoms. They expect us to protect them, but they have no idea that we can't turn into dragons whenever we please, and that even when we do, it hurts us to do so. They think that we can simply—" She snapped her fingers. "—and poof, off we go to save the day. And we can't tell them otherwise because we want our enemies to think that we *can* cast the spell without repercussions. They don't know that the ancient training is inadequate because of all the gaps in knowledge and how much time that training takes to complete. And even when we *do* finish that training, we're going to have to keep retaking it as it's going to take decades for those lessons to sink in. They haven't the faintest idea. The *faintest* idea …"

Augum's nodded along as his eyes unfocused into the flames.

"I've been avoiding thinking about the repercussions of this arcanery-snuffing ability the enemy—whoever they are—is using against us." She looked at him. "What if they can force reversion?"

Augum imagined diving as the dragon, only to find his form reverting, and then tumbling through the air as an arcanely snuffed human—albeit one blighted by the side effects of pure callousness. "I hadn't considered that." Thinking about the dragon piqued the interest of the dark watcher behind the curtain, forcing Augum to take a calming breath lest it devour the precious empathy he had been protecting like freshly sparked kindling in a gale.

"If that happens, we're dead," Bridget said, munching on a mouthful of journey bread while holding a hand over her mouth. "At least it'd be relatively quick, I guess. And excuse me for talking while eating."

Augum couldn't care less about politeness at the moment, for he felt a wave of anger wash over him even thinking about being forced to revert. Such an enemy would feel his wrath one way or another, a wrath precious few had survived.

"Then we have to make certain it *doesn't* happen," he said. He looked to the north, now dark as the moon had set, and imagined swooping down on that mysterious ship and ripping it apart plank by plank. Whatever—or whoever—dared to think they could stage an invasion would be in for a rude surprise.

But thinking of the ship also made him consider the strange happenings—and not just the arcanery snuffing, but the snatching of people right off the streets. He thought of the wolven paying for kidnapped apprentices and blooding them, but that had been a completely different style, and concluded that the wolven likely had nothing to do with what had been happening to the kingdom. Although that did lead him to another idea.

"What if it's a slave ship?" he asked.

Bridget straightened her legs toward the fire and stretched. "Certainly possible. Our people must have a use to the enemy for them to go to all that trouble; otherwise they'd have killed them. My question is, why summon gargoyles? Warlocks don't summon gargoyles. They summon—"

"—elementals, right," he said. Generally that was true. Though summoners—warlocks who specialized in summoning beasts—were known to summon all sorts of creatures. But they were nearly as rare a breed of warlock as telepaths.

They discussed the mystery at length, which only led to more questions. When Bridget yawned twice in a row, Augum insisted she go to sleep, and after helping with the cleanup of the food, she grudgingly hauled herself up and plodded into the tent. He could hear her plop onto her blanket and almost immediately go quiet, meaning she had conked out.

"Poor thing," he muttered, and glanced back toward the cliff. "Come on, girl, where are you …?"

The constant sound of the wind and the gentle crackle of the flames and his general exhaustion made it a challenge to keep his eyelids from closing. He checked the pull of his betrothal ring for the umpteenth time and still felt Leera east of his position. He yawned, stretched, and yawned again. He rubbed his face, poked the fire, and even cycled through a few basic spells, the quiet ones that wouldn't wake Bridget up. And it was during this cycling, just as he finished practice-casting the 4th degree Deafness on a tree, that a distinct alarm blared in his head—the one he had set on a pebble in the Great Arcaner Hall.

"Alarm!" Augum shouted, and there came an immediate commotion from inside the tent as Bridget scrambled out.

"I didn't get it!" she reported.

He grabbed hold of the twig Leera had enchanted with Object Alarm then twirled a finger about. "Doesn't matter. Close camp," and they set to packing everything away as quickly as they could, until each was wearing their golden breastplate and had a rucksack slung over their back, with Bridget shouldering her bow and quiver and Augum additionally holding Careena and Leera's rucksack and garments.

He turned toward the black ocean, whispering, "Come on, come on, come on …" Where *was* she? He checked in with the ring. She was still east of there. Was the pull getting stronger though?

"Why only yours and not mine?" Bridget asked.

He shook his head. It could be anything. There could have been a scramble and no time to grab the other pebbles. A fellow Arcaner might have required only him for Arcaner duties. It could have even been a servant's accidental touch …

"Come on, come on, come on …"

"We need to go, Aug."

"I'm not leaving without her."

"Maybe I should go then, while you wait …"

Suddenly there came a *thwomp* as Leera appeared between them and the fire. Dripping head to foot, she nullified some water spells before blurting, "What happened? Everything all right?"

"Augum received an alarm from the city," Bridget said.

Leera ran a hand over her undergarments, incanting, "*Evapa loa aqua.*" Once they were dry, she donned her spectacles, threw on her boots, snagged her robe, which Augum had offered to her, and drew it over her head. He then helped her strap on her golden breastplate and don her coat and mitts, finally wrapping his arms around her torso and giving her a loving squeeze whilst whispering, "Glad you're back."

"And I got a heck of a story to tell you two," she said. "But later. We got some hops to make."

Augum extended his hands to the girls in readiness for a Group Teleport—only to freeze, for a *second* alarm blared in his head.

"Second alarm," he reported, making ominous eye contact with the girls. "This one from up north."

"The wolven saw something," Bridget said.

"Or they're under attack," Leera added.

The girls looked to him as captains waiting for their commander to make the fateful decision.

"Our first duty is to our kingdom," he declared.

They grabbed hands and Augum thought of the closest spot to the west they had teleported along on the wolven journey. Then he incanted, *"Impetus peragro grapa lestato exa exaei,"* appearing on the side of a mountain. They kept this up, hopping from one spot to another, taking turns and meditating as needed, until they stood on the ledge where they had first met the wolven earlier that night.

With the blizzard still raging in full force here, Leera kept hold of their hands as she mentally prepared to take her turn for the next hop, which would take them to the Black Castle. She then incanted, *"Impetus peragro grapa lestato exa exaei."*

Except nothing happened.

"I must be exhausted or something," she said. "You try, Aug."

He took over, but the same thing happened.

"They revoked it!" Bridget blurted. "Remember? They revoked our teleport privileges to get in and out of the Black Castle!"

"I'll take us to the foot of the main drawbridge," he said, and mentally changed the destination before once again snapping off the incantation. This time he felt the familiar yank, and was soon spit out onto a stone ledge—with a precipice before it. On the distant other side, barely visible in the whiteout, was the raised drawbridge that led to the Black Castle.

Although the city was being pummeled by a fierce blizzard, there could still be heard the muted sounds of people screaming—as well as the gonging of every bell in the city.

The first thing Augum did was grab both girls by the arm to get their attention. "We stick together at all times. If one of us senses an arcanery null coming, we shout, ''Port, 'port, 'port!' and teleport off to Castle Arinthian's terrace. So keep the mental image of the castle in your head at all times." He then pressed a hand to his throat, incanting, *"Amplifico,"* and felt it expand. "Hello!" he shouted at the drawbridge. "It's Commander Augum Stone! I'm with Captain Burns and Captain Jones! Can you let us in!"

But there was no response.

"What in Sithesian hell is going on?" Leera said.

"I don't see any guards atop the walls," Bridget added.

Augum pressed a hand on the pommel of Burden's Edge. "Let's try the west entrance."

The trio followed the moat westward, into a blistering wind that pushed snow into their faces. Now and then, a distant scream sounded from somewhere within the blizzard, too indistinct to locate. Augum couldn't be sure, but he also thought he heard the telltale sound of teleportation, often right after a scream. Were people being snatched off the streets again?

They were halfway around the castle—with still not a soul in sight—when there came a particularly close shriek from the top of a nearby building.

Augum skidded to a halt in the snow, glanced up and, through the blizzard, spotted an unusually large silhouette standing on a rooftop terrace. He pointed at it. "Battle 'porting there!"

"We're following," Leera said.

Augum envisioned himself standing on that very terrace and snapped, "*Impetus peragro!*" His body shot forth with a *thwomp*, instantly followed by another *thwomp* as he blinked back into existence, this time in the center of the terrace, which was filled with thick wooden tables and benches—and the body of a green-robed warlock lying in the middle, an older woman judging by the long gray hair splayed around her.

Crouching over her, as if having been feasting on her soul, was a fifteen-foot muscled gray creature with enormous wings that had gathered some snow in the blizzard. It stood up and turned about—and in one of its clawed hands it held some sort of object that looked like a small black pyramid.

Augum, battle reflexes keyed up, didn't think, only acted. He yanked, hissing, "*Disablo!*" and the miniature pyramid shot out of its grasp, spinning away. And while it spun in midair, Augum realized that the creature before him was a beast straight out of mythology class. A creature with a short snout and pointed ears and a long tail. A creature that adorned the crest of the Library of Antioc and its castle-like exterior.

A gargoyle.

Most interestingly, a slew of fiery runes, like molten engravings on rock, decorated its body. He couldn't recall ever seeing runes on a creature's skin before, living or summoned.

The monster straightened, loosed a growl, and reached for the tumbling pyramid, but Augum was quicker and telekinetically yanked it to his hand, and the gargoyle's giant hand swiped through empty air.

As there came two consecutive *thwomps* nearby from Bridget and Leera appearing, the gargoyle extended a black-clawed finger of its left hand and touched one of the runes on its body. A gigantic fiery blade exploded to life in its right fist.

"Gods ..." Augum said, and the trio slapped their wrists together, roaring, "*Annihilo bato!*" At the same time, the gargoyle touched another fiery rune, and with a *whoosh*, its body instantly blackened—just before dual bolts of lightning, twin vines, and twin jets of water smashed into its body.

Leaving behind nothing but char marks.

Bridget quickly nocked a steel-tipped arrow into her Ordinary bow and let it fly, but the arrow plonked off with a metallic *ting*, and she dropped the useless bow and let the quiver fall from her shoulder.

"It's immune!" Augum shouted, ducking a monstrous sweep of the fiery blade that *whooshed* over the trio's heads. "Physicals!" he added, and he drew a shape in midair as he straightened, hissing, "*Summano elementus minimus draco!*"

A dragon about the size of a pony and made of pure lightning crackled into existence between himself and the gargoyle. "Draco—attack!" Augum shouted, pointing. With a whip of its tail, the dragon shot forth.

"*Summano elementus minimus draco!*" the girls chorused, summoning earth and water elemental dragons, and also commanding theirs to attack.

The gargoyle swiped at the lightning dragon with its burning blade, but the dragon was quicker and dipped underneath it, chomping its maw on the gargoyle's thigh. But it was difficult to tell if the bite had penetrated. In a frenzied heartbeat the earth and water dragons lunged at the gargoyle, with the former latching onto its left forearm, which the gargoyle had raised defensively, and the latter onto its free leg.

The gargoyle's return swing sliced neatly through the water dragon, making a loud *hiss* whilst it split the dragon into two pieces that promptly vanished—and snuffing the portion of the fiery blade that had cleaved through the dragon.

"Splash it, splash it, splash it!" Augum shouted.

Leera stepped forth and threw an arm out, incanting, "*Aquatos!*" A jet of water splashed forth at the blade, snuffing it with another *hiss*.

Bridget simultaneously made a bow-drawing motion, incanting, "*Summano arma flustrato!*" An earthen bow, already nocked with an arrow, appeared in her hands, the next ten arrows infused with Confusion as per the dictates of the Bluster of the Dragon simul she had cast. There came a *twang* as she let the nocked arrow fly. It zipped forth and caromed off the gargoyle's face, its tip diverted, before vanishing harmlessly back into the ether.

Seeing no indication that Confusion had taken root, Augum realized he needed to see tendrils, and quickly incanted, "*Un vun asperio aurum enchantus.*" The earth and lightning dragons lit up with arcanery—but not the gargoyle. "It's dark!" he alerted, meaning entirely physical. *Like a golem*, he thought. Although crafted by ancient arcanery, golems were also impervious to it—and immensely strong and tough, using their physical might to destroy opponents. Luckily they were incredibly rare, and only served as guardians.

The gargoyle raised the forearm clamped by the earth dragon, angled its large blade toward it, and pierced its earthen flesh. The dragon squealed as the gargoyle ripped its sword up and down, until the dragon was torn apart, quickly vanishing.

"Cursed thing's turned itself into stone!" Leera shouted. "Physicals only!" and she telekinetically snagged a heavy bench made of half-sawn logs and hauled it into the air behind the gargoyle, who had turned its attention on the remaining lightning dragon still trying to mow down on its thigh.

"Give her a hand!" Bridget shouted, and raised an arm.

The three worked together to lift the massive bench above the gargoyle's head. They then yanked downward, with Augum introducing such telekinetic force that the space around him warped fishbowl-like. The gargoyle, which had just torn the lightning dragon asunder with its blade, looked up in time to see the bench smash into its head, crumpling the beast underneath the half-sawn logs.

When Augum saw that the blackened skin had returned to gray, he sprinted forth and unsheathed Burden's Edge, shouting, "*Summano arma grau!*" The shortsword burst with lightning and lengthened into a longsword, its next ten strikes infused with the Slam spell as per the dictates of the Roar of the Dragon simul. The sheer violence of the motions involved made him lose focus on Reveal, causing it to fail, but he didn't care.

The gargoyle, pinned and dazed by the heavy bench, reached out—not at one of its runic engravings, as he had expected, but at the tiny pyramid in Augum's hand. He felt it rip from his clutches—but that didn't stop him from thrusting the sword forth. There came a massive *crack* of thunder as the blade jammed into the gargoyle's mouth—the *crack* a result of the Roar of the Dragon simul triggering. The pyramid smacked into the gargoyle's hand, only to tumble onto the snow, for the hand had fallen to the terrace, lifeless. Blood as red as a human's dribbled from the face, staining the snow.

A panting Leera ran up beside him, one hand holding Careena. "Is it dead?"

Augum nodded. "I think so."

Bridget ran past both of them, hurdled the bench, and skidded to a halt before the body of the face-down woman. She crouched before her, reached down under the hood to press a hand to her neck, then looked up with a grave face. A single shake of her head indicated the woman was gone.

One less warlock in an already warlock-starved kingdom, Augum thought morosely, wondering who the poor woman was.

He returned his attention to the beast and nudged the gargoyle's heavy arm with a foot, but it did not move. He grabbed hold of Burden's Edge and, whilst the girls looked away, yanked the blade free. The head rolled aside, the body unmoving. He crouched, placed a hand on the beast's forehead, and whispered, "May your soul find the peace together we could not reach." Then he wiped the sword in the snow, sheathed it, and pointed at the black pyramid. It shot to his hand, ice-cold from the snow.

"What is that thing?" Leera whispered, keeping her hooded face away from the snow-filled wind, which was attacking them from the side.

"No idea …"

The trio seemed to have the same thought, for all of them flared a hand, incanting, "*Un vun asperio aurum enchantus.*" Augum saw the pyramid light up with dense tendril geometries, all in varying shades of blue.

"The underlying geometries are similar to what I'm familiar with," Bridget noted. "But the patterns are completely different. At a cursory glance, I don't recognize a single enchantment."

Augum switched focus to the Disenchant spell, incanting, "*Exotus mia enchantus duo dai ideum exat.*"

Bridget grabbed his arm, almost shrieking, "What are you doing?"

"Just trying something. Trust me, all right?" After she hesitantly let go, he lifted a finger and attempted to move a peripheral tendril. It refused to budge. "See that?"

"It's sunk to permanence," Leera whispered. "Whatever it is, it's old. Maybe even ancient."

Augum switched back to Reveal, then turned the pyramid about in his palm, inspecting it closer. He noted how each side was laced with different tendril geometries, dense and unfathomably foreign.

Augum tapped one side of the pyramid. "This tendril pattern here looks a bit like it belongs to an Object Track enchantment, doesn't it?"

"Except the tendrils are different," Bridget replied. "Organized in a whole other way. Wait, I recognize the geometric sequence there," she noted, pointing at the bottom. "See that looping configuration? The first and third order leading edges on the tendrils?"

Leera raised her spectacles above her eyes and leaned in close. "Those sort of look like Arcane Drain geometries."

They exchanged dark looks before their eyes went to the fallen woman. The trio moved around the gargoyle and the bench and met near the body. Bridget crouched and turned her body over — and sprang back with a gasp, for staring at them was a ghastly face that looked like it had been left out in the sun for a year.

Augum crouched in her place to examine the face closer, noting how even the eyes had been dried out like a fish's, and the skin was waxy and gray. "It sucked her dry." He looked up, keeping his face averted from the snowy wind. "Water *and* blood."

"And I'm willing to bet her arcane essence as well," Leera added. "Meaning all her stamina." She nodded at the pyramid in Augum's grasp. "All sucked into that thing."

Bridget looked back at the gargoyle. "Or maybe the gargoyle used the object as a means to siphon the woman's ... er ... innards or whatnot."

"But why?" Leera asked, searching their faces. When no one had a response, she flipped a hand at the object. "If one of those sides *is* laced with a tracking enchantment, we should expect a visit."

Bridget went to pick up the steel-tipped arrow and showed off its blunted end, which had been bent away from the strike. "So much for training with Ordinary weapons." Yet she still reshouldered the quiver and bow, saying how she might as well keep them for now.

A distant scream pierced the blizzard, followed by a *thwomp*.

"Where's that coming from?" Bridget asked.

Another one came from a completely different direction, and from farther off.

"They turn to stone as a defense mechanism against our arcanery," Leera noted. "So I say we turn into dragons and pulverize them. Rip them limb from limb with our bare paws."

Augum was about to agree when he realized something. "Wait. What *didn't* the gargoyle do?" He looked between the girls.

"It didn't snuff our arcanery," Bridget whispered.

Their eyes once again fell upon the pyramidal object.

"That has to be one of its powers," Leera said. "The question is, does every gargoyle have one?"

"Let's keep our rings up," Bridget said. "To make sure we're still arcanic."

"Agreed," Leera said, and they each flared their ten arm rings. "So what say you two? Time to cast Spirit of the Dragon?"

Augum thought about it and shook his head. "We cannot risk having our arcanery snuffed in midair, causing reversion—at least until we know how to defeat them. But that doesn't mean we shouldn't try taking them on just as we did here—" He nodded at the vanquished gargoyle. "—physically. And we do that by sticking together. Let's push forth to the castle, and if anything happens, we meet—"

He was interrupted by a great *whoosh* that rumbled through the city.

They whirled toward the enormous sound, which seemed to come from the castle. Augum felt something coming, and was about to raise the alarm when Bridget beat him to it, shouting, "'Port, 'port, 'port!" Then she snapped, "*Impetus peragro!*" and vanished with a *thwomp*.

Augum and Leera, behind by only heartbeats, followed suit, shouting, "*Impetus peragro!*"

But halfway through incanting, a cold *whoosh* overtook them, and they found themselves stranded.

With their arms snuffed, all they could do was glance at each other.

A CITY UNDER SIEGE

BRIDGET

With a *thwomp*, Bridget appeared on the snowy terrace of Castle Arinthian, just as they had planned. Tense, she waited for Augum and Leera, counting each heartbeat as it thumped against her chest. Here at least the blizzard had passed, and the sky was clearing.

Although she'd gone way too long without sleep, her mind was frantic and alert—and scared. She loathed war, but she could handle roughly knowing what to expect in standard battles. It was the unknown that terrified her. And gargoyles, myths come to life, were one heck of an unknown. All she wanted to do was get her hands on a bunch of old books on the subject and pore through them in search of clues. But there was no time for such luxuries.

"Come on, come on, where are you two?" she asked the wind. Realizing they could have teleported to the other side, she raced around the terrace, for it surrounded the entire castle, and skidded to a halt at the northwest corner. The castle, sitting atop Mount Barrow, allowed for a perfect view of a city embroiled in a thick blizzard haze, within which colorful flashes went off repeatedly, with lightning being the most frequent cause.

Except the lightning was not blue, but black—or rather, black*ish*, for it still lit up with white light, yet there were distinct black veins darker than the night. And the blizzard itself had a strange tint to it, a little too blue. Something told her that warlock arms were snuffing throughout the city. Back in the war against the Legion, seven artifacts known as scions had been able to snuff arcanery—but that had been in a small area. The idea that a whole city could be snuffed made the hair on the nape of her neck rise.

She heard a pair of doors open behind her and spun about, expecting to see Augum and Leera—and instead saw a group of people rushing forth, servants and soldiers, all denizens of the castle.

"What's happening?" one asked.

Bridget turned back to face the distant city. "We're under attack."

"By who?"

"Get back inside. All of you. Now!" she roared when they hesitated. "And keep the doors shut behind you!" she yelled after them, knowing she was scaring them.

She ran around the castle terrace but the other towns, distant specks of torchlight, seemed to have been left alone—for the time being. Even Antioc was a tiny distant glittering pool of torchlight sparkling in the vast night.

Bridget returned to the northwest corner, desperately worried about Augum and Leera. She had to meet up with them, but where? Whereas Augum and Leera could find each other with their betrothal rings, Bridget had nothing, and in the chaos, she had forgotten to enchant something on their person with Object Track. Yet she also wondered if the snuffing would have temporarily turned off the Object Track enchantments—or perhaps even disenchanted them completely.

She waited on the terrace, hoping they'd show up. Every passing heartbeat that they failed to arrive strengthened her fear that the snuffing had overtaken them prior to teleportation. If that was the case, she could only pray they were in hiding.

With them failing to arrive, and seeing Blackhaven under that fearsome barrage, she decided to return to the city. Not wanting to step into an arcane snuff trap, she chose the place she figured would likely be the safest—the Academy of Arcane Arts. Maybe she could meet up with some senior warlocks and together stage a counterattack or something.

She visualized the Steps of the Crescent Moon and incanted, "*Impetus peragro.*" After a brief hurtle through the dark arcane ether, she was spit out before a wide swath of crescent-shaped steps buried under snow.

At the top of those stairs, amidst the swirling blizzard, stood the imposing twenty-foot statue of none other than Anna Atticus Stone, the trio's former mentor. Mrs. Stone stood staring into the horizon with an iron but snow-encrusted face, a visage that greeted all newcomers to the academy. Her famously long braided ponytail hung loosely down her back. A hand clutched a staff topped with an orb that represented the scion she had carried nearly her entire life.

"If only you were here to guide us, Mrs. Stone," Bridget whispered.

Hearing the occasional *crack* of thunder echo through the city, Bridget raced up the steps and on toward the academy. The grounds were empty—not surprising considering it was the middle of Endyear. The academy was composed of three giant buildings, each shooting out from the central courtyard like a black and seamless loaf of bread. At the entrance of each was supposed to be a giant portal.

Except, for the first time in her life, Bridget found herself staring at a blank wall.

The entrance portals had been snuffed.

"Or snuffed on purpose from within," she said. She raised her arm and drew an immediate sigh of relief when ten rings of earth successfully appeared around her forearm. She snuffed them, for even keeping rings up drew a tiny amount of stamina which she did not want to expend at the moment, and ran onward to the other wings, both of which were also dark. A quiet horror crept into her soul upon seeing that all three wings of the academy were inaccessible. But she had to admit the design of such structures was genius—there was no way in, meaning that if someone *did* snuff arcanery, they would also snuff the ability to get inside the academy.

Bridget glanced about and for the first time noticed different sets of footprints amidst the human ones—the gargoyles had been here too. The question was, had they gotten inside? The stone walls seemed untouched, but who knew if they had found another way in, perhaps prior to the portals getting extinguished. The thought sent a chill down her spine.

She ran about in search of someone—anyone—but found only footprints. Not a soul was in sight. At least there weren't any signs of bloodshed either.

The echo of a scream reached her ears. Bridget whirled about to face that direction, chest heaving, but only found herself gazing at the blankness of the blizzard. She had to get a grip—the city was under attack. In that very moment, people were getting snatched—and some were getting bled dry. She was wasting precious time.

Bridget closed her eyes to think where Augum and Leera would likely go, and realized it would have to be the western drawbridge of the Black Castle. But that was also where the tinted blizzard had struck. *Unless the snuffing spell or whatever has passed,* she thought. Then she thought of Olaf—and felt a guilty pang for not having thought of him sooner. Was he all right? Was he thinking of her? A nasty, sarcastic side of her thought, *If anything, he's thinking about how he can't protect you,* which only added a flush of shame to her cheeks. *Focus, would you!*

"I'm taking the risk," she declared to the swirling whiteness. It was a time to take risks, and she flared her arm rings. For her own peace of mind, she needed to be visually aware of her arcanery working.

Bridget thought of the layout of the western drawbridge and incanted, "*Impetus peragro.*" She appeared in the snow at the very foot of the drawbridge—and felt her heart drop upon seeing that it had been raised. She looked about, but in the limited visibility of the blizzard, once again saw no one. She checked her forearm. Her rings were still active. No snuff had occurred.

"Captain Burns requesting entry!" she shouted at the drawbridge, hands cupping her mouth. But the howling winds swallowed her voice. She thought to cast Amplify, but figured it'd only be a waste of precious stamina. Her utter exhaustion did not help. She craved a hot meal and a warm bed, the latter more so than the former. And in that bed she imagined Olaf waiting for her, like a dutiful future husband. Yet she knew he would loathe her thinking that. Loathe feeling emasculated more than he already felt.

A scream pierced the blizzard, followed by another. They were close and to the south, where she had left Augum and Leera.

Heart pounding, Bridget imagined standing in the exact spot she had teleported away from prior to the *whoosh* overtaking them, then incanted, "*Impetus peragro!*" She appeared on the terrace and found herself staring at the fallen gargoyle, still pinned under a heavy bench, the husk of that unfortunate woman still lying nearby. But there was no sign of Augum and Leera, other than their footprints, which led to a trap door that lay open in the snow. They'd gotten away.

She hopped down onto the ladder and descended into darkness. "*Shyneo,*" she whispered, lighting her palm up with ivy and adjusting the green light to a dim candle glow that barely lit up the corridor.

"Aug …? Lee …?" she whispered. "It's Bridge." It was a multi-level stone dwelling with numerous rooms, all furnished with luxuries unavailable to the commoner—gilded sofas and armchairs and paintings and vases and statues and marble busts and silverware sitting behind glass cabinetry. Other than the howl of the wind outside and the rattle of windows, the place was tomb silent.

"Momma?" squeaked a mousy voice.

Bridget, who had been in the corridor at the time, turned to see a little girl holding a rumpled bear in her arms. She stood before a window, in a pool of wavering torchlight that bled in from outside, shadows of snowflakes flying past.

"You're not Mommy," the girl squeaked.

"No, but I'm here to—" Bridget froze, for a shadow came before the torchlight, bathing the girl in darkness. The child turned around—and screamed. Bridget shot forth as the window shattered and two giant clawed hands snatched the girl. Without slowing her sprint, she smashed into the window frame and reached out in time to hear a *thwomp* that instantly cut the scream off. Her hand opened and closed, clasping at nothing, as she found herself gaping at a nearby balcony. There on the balustrade was an indentation in the snow that showed something had perched on it. The girl was gone.

The horror of an entire city being snatched overcame her, and she slid out of the frame and fell to her knees. She imagined that little girl getting her bear torn from her grasp, then her soul getting sucked out and her face drying into a husk.

Bridget slapped a hand over her mouth, wanting to retch. To escape. To fight, tooth and claw.

The shadow reared up within her. It wanted vengeance. Destruction on a scale unfathomed since the war. And she—one of only three—was capable of delivering that destruction. Oh how these beasts would pay! She would tear their wings off like they were flies.

"No!" she blurted, rising, remembering how dangerous that would be to do alone. "Not yet. Not yet …" She would find Augum and Leera first. Then they would mount an attack. Somehow. Some way. Together they would be strong. Together they would solve the problem.

Bridget found the staircase and ran downstairs, until she was outside. There she lost the footprints amidst countless others—she was not a tracker like Augum was, and to her they all looked alike, a jumble of panicked humanity trying to find shelter.

The girl's scream haunted her. She could still hear it. Still see the window breaking inward, the quick snatching …

That was when she realized she had had an opportunity in that moment that she had missed in her panic—she could have cast Reveal and conducted a Teleport sniff, which entailed examining the swirling leftover tendrils, which happened after every teleportation, and deducing the direction and even the distance of travel.

"But you *know* the final destination already …" she whispered, seeing the distant outline of a dark ship in her mind's eye.

Another scream sounded from nearby, this one in an alley. Bridget shot forth so quickly she slipped in the snow and had to take a moment to get her footing before she set to a sprint. She soon skidded in that alley—and found herself facing the back of another gargoyle, who was bent over an old man, a commoner by the look of his plain woolen winter garb. This gargoyle had tears in its wings, and she watched those tears stitch back together seamlessly, as if someone had cast Repair on them.

Bridget could have done any number of things. Performed any combination of maneuvers or spells. Instead, she blurted, "Hey!"

The gargoyle, a sixteen-footer with enormous wings, rose, and turned. And this one did not hold a pyramid, but it did have a number of runes emblazoned on its skin, though perhaps half as many as the last one.

Monster and human stared off, one more than three times the size of the other. Facing such a thing, a part of Bridget felt like that little girl. But a stronger part of her, the part that allowed a certain shadow to open the curtain of her mind, had her tilting her head to the side, wanting to tear this creature apart.

The gargoyle raised a black-clawed finger. Bridget allowed this, sensing where it was going. That finger then pressed one of the runes, and a giant cleaver made of pure ice appeared in its fist. It looked to her in taunting wait.

Bridget took the hint and, after shrugging off her Ordinary bow and quiver, slowly made a bow-drawing motion, incanting, "*Summano arma flustrato.*" An earthen bow, already nocked with an earthen arrow enchanted with the Confusion spell, appeared in her hands. She aimed directly between its eyes and waited. The very moment it raised its foot to move forth, she let the arrow fly with a *twang*.

Perhaps the beast had not anticipated the speed, or perhaps it had never encountered a bow and arrow before—whatever the reason, it did not have the reflexes to flinch. Instead, it tried to raise its sword, as if hoping to block the arrow. But that arrow was too quick, and it struck right between the eyes, piercing the gray flesh. The plodding giant fell forward, crashing into the snowy ground with a rumble. The summoned arrow vanished, and a pool of blood began to form under its gargoyle snout.

Bridget gaped at it. A sixteen-footer felled by a single arrow. Now that was something.

Bridget was about to go to the man when there came a quiet *whoosh* behind her—a certain and unmistakable rustle she, as someone who could turn into a dragon, knew belonged to multiple sets of wings. But this time she ran her free hand over her body, incanting, "*Armari obscura chameleano traversa*"—Chameleon with the travel extension. With her entire body and clothing and her summoned bow blending in with the snowy alley, she pressed herself against the brick wall.

From there, Bridget watched gliding shadows—wings and all—flit by, disappearing around the corner. She reached back into her quiver, withdrew a Confusion-enchanted arrow, nocked it, drew the earthen bowstring back, aimed at the alley entrance, and waited.

The shadows soon spilled into the alley, and there appeared two looming gargoyles—ten-footers, the smallest she'd seen yet. Like a pair of spies, each looked into the alley from one side, glanced at the other, and stepped in. Neither held a miniature pyramid, and each had only a handful of runes emblazoned on its flesh, telling Bridget they were novices.

They walked past, oblivious to the bow and quiver she had dropped and the fresh footprints she had left, even marring them in their haste to get to their fallen comrade, who they bent over to inspect. One growled at the other, indicating the old man. The other growled back, and they seemed to argue a bit before the first one grabbed the fallen gargoyle, growled out a phrase whilst touching a rune, and vanished with the body.

They take their fallen with them, Bridget thought. *Interesting*. Despite the beast's inhumanity, she was disappointed she hadn't had a chance to dispense the Final Valediction.

The remaining gargoyle drew up to its full height and glanced around the alley in a suspicious manner. Bridget pointed the arrow at its head, waiting to see what it would do. It finally spotted the bow and quiver and footprints, and its gaze followed the latter right to where Bridget stood.

The gargoyle stared for a moment before suddenly reaching for a rune. *Twang!* went another arrow. But this gargoyle seemed ready and flinched. The arrow that had been shooting toward its head instead pierced a wing. The head nonetheless snapped sideways, telling Bridget her Confusion casting had impacted the mind anyway. It staggered in the same direction as if punched, giving Bridget time to draw a third arrow—and rendering herself visible from the quick motion.

Twang! went the bow, and this time the arrow stuck into its chest with a *thwack*. The gargoyle gasped and staggered backward. It looked down and grabbed the arrow, only for the arrow to vanish in its grip.

Bridget nocked a fourth arrow and let it loose. It struck near the heart, beside the other hole. The gargoyle tried to grab this one too, but in its confusion it fumbled about, and the arrow disappeared anyway. Bridget kept drawing and firing. *Twang* and *thwack* went arrow after arrow, until the ten-foot beast fell to its knees, its chest dotted with small bloody waterfalls. There it remained, swaying, eyes roving about in complete bewilderment, before it fell forward, dead.

Bridget stood with a tenth arrow nocked, shoulders rising and falling as she plumed clouds of breath. She had just killed two gargoyles. One had challenged her, underestimating her. The other had not been quick enough. They were defeatable.

She lowered her bow but kept it in hand, and came up to the beast. "May your soul find the peace together we could not reach," she whispered, not wanting to bend down and touch its forehead, as tradition demanded. Backing off, she went to the old man. When she turned him over, she had to look away, for he too had been sucked dry of water and blood. As before, the question was, why?

Then she remembered the torn wings. The gargoyle had sustained injuries and had been healing itself—the dehydration and bleeding was some form of regeneration!

"I need to warn the others," she whispered. She considered teleporting back to Castle Arinthian's terrace to see if Augum and Leera had teleported there, but more and more screams pierced the blizzard. The problem was they were difficult to locate, as the blizzard dispersed and muffled sound.

Still holding her nocked bow with both hands, and this time choosing to leave the useless Ordinary bow and quiver behind as it only slowed her reaction time, she left the alley—and came to an immediate halt. A ten-foot-high cluster of writhing vines was creeping forth on the street. The oncoming wall stood stark green against the pristine white of the blizzard. Like constrictor snakes, some of those vines held onto objects—chairs, tables, barrels, carts—she even glimpsed what she thought was a human leg, all of it slowly tumbling in its embrace.

As the vine wall crawled along the street, its offshoots broke windows and smashed down doors, creeping into homes like burglars. With wide eyes, she witnessed it drag out a man who had apparently been hiding inside. He screamed, was promptly muffled by a vine, then smuggled into the wall's writhing density.

Bridget's first instinct was to run. Not only would this creeping thing choke her out, or tear her apart, but it might snuff her arcanery with a single touch.

Except she wanted to try something first, and incanted, "*Summano null*," making the bow, arrow, and quiver vanish. Then she drew the full complex gestural complement required of the 7th degree Summon Minor Wall spell, whilst incanting, "*Summano valla minimus girata barricada*."

A tall wall of stationary vine and branches and earth *whooshed* into existence before her, blockading the street. Then she waited. She was about to say something like, "Got you, you vicious thing," when a tentacle-like vine poked over the wall. Then another, and another, until the entire vine cluster had climbed over.

"Gods ..." she whispered, watching her entire wall get consumed. When the vines hit the street and writhed at her, she thought to try another spell—Summon Minor Event, 10th degree, elemental. After aligning her thoughts, she pointed before the path of the ever-advancing wall, incanting *"Summano fissera erta multato!"*

Three fissures ruptured from her position and shot forth, the ground cracking and groaning as it split apart. The fissures reached underneath the wall and continued onward. Parts of the wall buckled downward, but the entirety of the writhing structure kept it together, and the wall soon rolled over the fissures.

"Shoot," Bridget said. Out of ideas and not wanting to waste any more precious stamina—higher-degree spells sucked exponentially more stamina than lower-degree ones—she ran back toward the Black Castle's western drawbridge, hoping Augum and Leera would be there now and they could find a way back inside the castle. She prayed that Olaf and Jez and Haylee and Jengo and all their other wonderful friends—not to mention those who had joined the order, including the recruits—had found shelter.

She got to the drawbridge and skidded to a halt, for two gargoyles crawled along its surface, their claws digging into the planks—and these gargoyles lacked wings. They were twelve-footers and overly muscular. Bridget made a drawing a bowstring motion, incanting, *"Summano arma flustrato,"* and let the bowstring go. *Twang* went the arrow, thwacking into the planks just above one of the gargoyle's heads.

Both looked her way and detached, falling toward the moat, the waters of which were kept slightly heated by arcane flames to avoid freezing. Bridget retrieved another arrow from her quiver and in one fluid motion nocked it and fired at the surface of the moat. The arrow caught one of the gargoyles square in the chest before it slapped into the water with a splash.

Whilst keeping hold of her bow, Bridget used her right hand to draw a figure in the air, incanting, *"Summano elementus minimus draco."* An earthen dragon crunched into existence before her, its wings flapping to stay aloft. Then she reached back, grabbed another earthen arrow, nocked it, and drew back the earthen bowstring. The moment one of the gargoyles popped its gray head above the moat, she let the arrow fly. But this time the gargoyle ducked, and the arrow smacked against the other side of the moat wall.

Bridget pointed. "Draco—attack!" Her summoned dragon flicked its tail and shot forth with a powerful flap of its wings.

The gargoyle popped up again, but this time it strategically placed itself so that the coming dragon was between it and Bridget. Bridget nonetheless nocked an arrow again and side-stepped. The second gargoyle she had struck earlier popped its head up, struggling to climb the moat wall. Bridget, knowing her arrow's Confusion enchantment had taken root, drew back, aimed, and fired.

The first gargoyle growled a warning at its comrade, but it was too late, and her arrow pierced the already stricken gargoyle in the forehead with a sickly *thwoot*. The monster's head snapped back and the creature fell into the moat, surely dead.

The first gargoyle jumped onto the landing and tackled her dragon head-on. Bridget sprinted forth in aid. As the dragon and gargoyle tussled, each viciously snapping and clawing at the other, Bridget extended a hand and tried to telekinetically grab the gargoyle, hoping to slow or even restrain it. But doing it one-handed only resulted in the gargoyle easily flicking off the arcane hold, and so she tossed aside her summoned bow and shrugged off the summoned quiver, causing both to vanish, then used both hands to grab a telekinetic hold of one of the gargoyle's arms, the hand of which the beast had been using to choke the dragon—albeit at the cost of allowing the dragon to viciously tear at its chest with both front paws.

Bridget strained with all her telekinetic might and managed to get the gargoyle to let go of the dragon's neck, which resulted in the dragon snapping its jaws around the gargoyle's neck. Squirts of blood shot forth, and the dragon began furiously writhing about, even spinning in place like an alligator, until the gargoyle went limp. Yet the dragon continued its mauling.

"Draco—to me!" Bridget said. The dragon let go and shot to Bridget's side, where it sat back on its haunches like a dutiful dog, its tail wagging back and forth. That wagging made Bridget's heart constrict, for it reminded her of Sabby, and then of Olaf. At least the pair would likely be together …

Her summoned dragon turned its head to look past her. She glanced back—and saw figures emerging from the blizzard. More wingless gargoyles were trekking forth, except their backs were turned to her, for they were dragging people—whole lines of humans, all chained together and struggling and begging and crying. There were ten gargoyles, each dragging a human chain line of no less than ten people—one hundred captured souls in all.

Then she realized that the first two wingless gargoyles had been trying to lower the drawbridge.

Seeing those wretches flash-boiled her blood. Realizing she had to do something drastic, she raised her right leg and her two arms above her head in the praying mantis pose, preparing to cast the mythical Spirit of the Dragon simul that would turn her into the queen of the skies. She formed the complex array of thoughts that layered the spell correctly and began the incantation.

"*Xae carna draca—*" only to hear a monstrous *crack* of lightning that flashed a blackish light. She immediately halted the spell and thought of Castle Arinthian's terrace, incanting, "*Impetus per—*" Here a *whoosh* sliced through her soul like a cold knife. "*—agro!*" she finished, and went nowhere. With her dragon forcefully banished back into the ether, she raised her forearm and saw that her rings had been snuffed.

She was as defenseless as a newborn babe.

One of the wingless gargoyles glanced over its shoulder, spotted her, and barked a warning, causing the others to halt their dragging. But instead of rushing her, all ten howled toward the sky.

Bridget, not wanting to find out why or to whom they were calling, yelped and sprinted southward along the moat as fast as her feet would carry her, the howling chasing her like a group of banshees. The moment she could no longer see the chain gangs, she veered westward into the city, heart pounding. She jumped into an alley, turned into another one—and crashed into a shaggy-haired man dressed in thick woolen pants and a long-sleeved shirt, sending both of them to the ground.

"Gods, sir, are you all right?" she asked, picking herself up. "Are you hurt? Are you—" Her voice died when the man, who was facing away, began growling. "Sir …?"

While he sat on all fours like a dog, the man's head slowly turned, revealing a manic face with froth coming from his mouth.

Bridget slowly backed away, whispering, "What in the dark Fates …"

The man rose, a broken piece of glass in one hand, blood dripping from the fingers. He kept growling.

Bridget's gaze flitted to her forearm, but finding it still dark, she glanced around—and spotted a nearby open door to the back of what appeared to be a restaurant, at least judging by the spilled vegetables and cookware lying about in the doorway.

The moment she slowly began backing toward it, the man barked and shot at her. She yelped and skittered into the kitchen, trying to slam the door in his face—only to have it jam against a pot with a metallic *thud*. The rabid man plowed into the door, sending her flying backward into the dark space. The door flew open and the shard-wielding man launched himself at her, growling like a rabid dog. Desperate to survive, she kicked out and connected a foot into his abdomen, sending him stumbling back.

A yelping Bridget then scrabbled about with her hands until one closed over a small cast-iron frying pan—which she immediately swung upon the man's second lunge. There was a *gong* as the pan connected with the glass shard, sending it skittering across the slimy floor. Remembering her sword and buckler lesson, she swung that pan the other way and smacked the side of his head, which in turn slammed into a cabinet.

The man grunted as he dropped to all fours again, swaying in place and drooling onto one of her boots. She scrambled away from underneath, grabbed a cabinet, and hauled herself to her feet, shoulders heaving as she fought to catch her breath, both hands white-knuckling the frying pan.

The man's growling deepened as the white froth bubbled from his mouth. He looked up at her with reddened animalistic eyes, the growl strengthening.

"You stay back, sir," Bridget said, retreating until her back pressed against a wall. She glanced about in the dim torchlight that flooded in from the alley, until she spotted the broken handle of a mop—and a long fish knife, which happened to be near the man. The man stood—and his gaze followed hers, until he saw the same knife. Both immediately lunged forth. But Bridget slipped in her haste and, realizing she would be too late, instead grabbed the broken mop handle.

The shaggy-haired man grabbed the long knife and shot forth, growling and barking like a rabid animal.

Bridget, desperately trying to remember her sword and buckler training, swung the pan sideways to meet his wild slice. There was a metallic *ting* as the knife met the iron. Yet with her back against the wall and sensing that his next slice would gut her alive, she roared and impaled him with the broken end of the mop handle.

The man gasped as he tumbled into her, his chin resting on her shoulder beside her ear, where she heard him wheezing between gurgling growls.

"I'm sorry," she whispered as he slid to the floor before her, his growls and gasps steadily subsiding until they went silent altogether. In the flickering torchlight, she could see his eyes remained open but sightless.

Bridget slapped a hand to her mouth and burst with a cry, the pan falling to the ground with a clatter. She fell to her knees and just sat there crying and crying and crying, both hands now clutched firmly over her mouth as she rocked back and forth, until a distant and primal gargoyle roar of attack brought her to her senses.

She placed a shaking hand to the man's forehead, whispering, "May your soul find the peace together we could not reach."

Then she stood staring down at the strangely enraged man, suspecting that the gargoyles had done something to him, enchanting him with that rage. Perhaps he had not been useful to them. *Either that, or the poor man had gone insane upon seeing a gargoyle*, she thought.

Another primal gargoyle war cry sounded, this one closer than the last. Not wanting to hide with this man whose life she had taken with her bare hands, a heavy-hearted Bridget went to the door, peeked out, and, seeing that the alley was clear, ran off, until she found an open window, which she crawled through, closing it behind herself.

There, amidst a snowed-in brick building that looked like it was being used to forge iron farming implements, she waited in the darkness, chest heaving, repeatedly checking her forearm, willing her rings to return … and still hearing the last growling gasps of that strange rabid man.

DESPERATE ALLEY

LEERA

The shortsword Careena wavered before Leera, her nerves jangling the blade about. She could not recall ever having to rely on a mere blade to survive. Without her arcanery, she felt naked and exposed and fragile.

So this is what Ordinaries feel like on the day to day, she thought, feeling compassion for them more than ever.

At least she had Augum, who stood beside her holding Burden's Edge before him with a steady hand. The pair were inside a windowless brick building filled with hay, their shortswords pointed at the door they had slammed shut behind them during their frantic escape. Thin slices of torchlight filtered in through the rough planks of the door and underneath and around its edges. Beyond was the sound of snowy dragging and the clank of chains and the whimpering and crying of humans in utter despair.

After being caught in the first arcane snuffing, they had wound their way back to the western drawbridge. Except every time they thought their arcanery would return, they would either stumble into another snuff or get overtaken by one. The second was a writhing vine that had snagged their feet, forcing them to hack and slash their way out. The third was a frosty plume that had billowed into the alley they had taken shelter in. And the latest was a nearby lightning strike. The city was suffering a full-on barrage.

Leera forced the tip of her trembling blade to settle down. *Remember your training,* she thought. *Remember your training.* But that training was entirely reliant on being able to cast spells. Very little of it had involved using Ordinary weapons. Sure, she'd hacked and slashed at training dummies here and there, even parried and jabbed a real soldier using wooden swords, but how in Sithesia was that supposed to do much when facing a fifteen-foot mountain of muscle? And not human muscle, either, but gargoyle muscle, which had potent monster strength.

The dragging soon subsided, leaving behind a fierce wind that rattled the wooden door on its hinges. Augum went up to the door and pressed his ear against it. "They're capturing our people."

Leera lowered her sword. "Poor souls. What do those fiends want with them?"

"I think Bridget was right—they want them for the purposes of slavery. I'm just glad she got away in time."

Leera was about to say that she worried the gargoyles wanted humans for something worse, but did not want to voice it aloud lest it become true. "Gods, I feel so vulnerable," she whispered instead.

"Imagine how they feel."

"I get terrified even thinking such thoughts. It's like we're back in the jungles of Endraga Ra, fighting for our lives against beasts far stronger and deadlier than us." Leera nodded at his rucksack, inside of which was that miniature pyramidal artifact they had captured from one of the gargoyles. "We need to figure out how to use that thing against them. After we get our arcanery back, that is. I say we hide in here until we can flare our rings again."

"Agreed." Augum withdrew from the door, grabbed her by the hand, and pressed himself against her. "I'm just so glad that ... that you're here with me." He kissed her.

"Me too," she whispered between kissing him back. Violence and mortal peril sometimes brought such passions out of them, and the next thing they knew they were dragging each other toward a hay bale.

But this time Leera stopped him. "As much as I want to, you know it's too dangerous."

"I do." His eyes glinted in the darkness with longing for her, but he kept nodding. "I do."

"We're fiends," she muttered, nibbling at his lips, wanting to give in to temptation and risk and longing—and wanting him to as well.

Now it was Augum who pulled back in the darkness, though not without a playful squeeze of her butt. He dumped himself onto a hay bale, jabbed the tip of Burden's Edge into the soft earth near it, and ran his hands through his hair. Leera plopped down beside him, jabbed Careena into the earth beside Burden's Edge, and playfully yanked his hood back.

"There, now you can get at that greasy mop better," she whispered.

"Even in the darkness I can see that cheeky grin," he replied, raising his hood, muttering something about it being too cold. He sighed. "The people expect us to protect them. Yet here we are, as useless as dull knives. How I long to spread my wings—"

"—and bring destruction upon the usurpers," she finished for him.

"That almost sounded like it belonged in some play."

"I have my moments." She leaned up against him, laying her head on his shoulder.

"You certainly do," Augum whispered, and laid his head on hers.

"You ought to have a word with Ollie," Leera whispered.

"About Bridget? What am I supposed to say?"

"That she loves him. That she needs him. That she's embroiled in a terrible internal battle and fears losing herself *and* him and that she needs his support more than ever."

"How am I supposed to articulate all that?"

Leera shrugged. "You're good with words. You'll figure something out."

For a time they sat there waiting, now and then checking their arms. Even though they were practically defenseless, danger did not make them as afraid as those who rarely experienced it. They could ponder and reflect and consult and think, whereas those unused to constantly facing mortality oft froze up or panicked.

Suddenly the doorframe lit up with multiple silent flashes of blue and black lightning, followed quickly by a monstrous *crack* of thunder that reverberated throughout the building. They jumped to their feet just as a cold *whoosh* ripped through their souls.

"Shoot," Leera said, grabbing Careena. "Cursed beasts are doing it to keep us from mounting a defense."

"A clever tactic," Augum muttered, slumping back onto the hay bale.

Leera paced back and forth in the dark, swinging her blade about in an attempt to get used to its clunky weight and speed relative to a summoned blade. "I don't understand something. How can they snuff all arcanery but continue to be able to perform it unscathed?"

"They've got to have some sort of mitigation strategy. Maybe a self-snuff or something before re-ignition."

"Maybe they briefly turn to stone."

"Certainly possible, but laborious."

Leera stabbed at a pretend gargoyle and stopped pacing, Careena held before her. "What if they have something on them that they use?"

"Like the pyramid thingy?"

Leera lowered the blade and turned to look at Augum. "Or something else. Something that either automatically triggers or is manually triggered by the gargoyle."

Augum sighed. "We should have inspected the fallen gargoyle closer."

"We still can. Let's go back. It's only a couple of blocks away."

They peered at each other in the darkness before Augum snatched Burden's Edge and the pair hurried to the door. He pressed a hand into Leera's chest, meaning for her to wait, but she grabbed it and pressed it to her cheek. "Did I tell you I love you yet today?" she whispered.

"Only about a hundred times," he whispered.

"Then let's make it a hundred and one. I love you."

"And I love *you*." He kissed her, and she kissed him back. Then she playfully shoved him forth. "Just be sure to keep us out of sight, *Commander*."

"Yes, *Captain*." He smiled back at her, a slit of torchlight illuminating a sliver of his smiling face.

She crinkled her nose. "I'm going to piss my robe if we run into something."

The smile burst into a silent laugh before he composed himself. "Eloquent, Miss Jones. Very eloquent."

"You're marrying a saddler's daughter."

"And you're marrying a farm boy."

"A match made by The Fates." In the light of the crack he was looking through, she saw his cheek puff with a smile.

"Ready?" he whispered. "Here. We. Go—!"

He opened the door and they stepped out into the windy blizzard. The alley was full of drag marks—and streaks of blood. They glanced at each other ominously before darting into a perpendicular nearby alley, then snuck along the old brick walls. From there they navigated alley after alley, peeking out when able, crossing streets scattered with random things like spilled baskets and carts and clothing and shoes and splatters of blood, until they reached another street.

"It's that block there," Augum whispered, nodding ahead. "On three. One … two … three!"

They darted across the street, swords swinging as they ran. Just as they entered the alley, a bolt of lightning slapped into the brick right above their heads, near instantly followed by a mammoth *crack* of thunder.

"Gods!" Leera yelped, and slipped in her haste to duck. She tumbled forth, and was helped back to her feet by Augum.

The alley was a long one, but they still ran for it, with Augum pushing her from the rear and shouting, "Go, go, go!"

The alley lit up as a second bolt of lightning followed them, this one grazing by Augum's shoulder.

He's keeping himself between me and the gargoyle because he's immune, Leera thought. Augum had been born with what was known as an ancestral gift—immunity to lightning, perhaps on account that he shared the same birthday as that of his famous ancestor Atrius Arinthian, the founder of the Arinthian line. They had discovered the immunity during the war, when the Lord of the Legion himself had struck Augum with a bolt of 20th degree lightning, yet he had come out without a scratch—other than his robe being torn and burnt, that was. So whenever they faced a lightning warlock in the wild—which was rare, as very few had the temerity to challenge them after the last war—Augum took point.

They were almost at the end of the alley. Leera turned right, where the entrance to another alley lay. But that exposed her. There was a flash of light. Simultaneously, she felt Augum shove her from the back. Then came a *hiss* and a *crack*—and a yelp of pain from Augum, along with the sickening sound of him slamming into the brick end of the alley.

Leera finished tumbling and scrambled to her feet, crying out, "Aug! Aug!" He lay in a crumpled heap at the base of the wall, amidst a pile of snowdrift. She was about to run to him when she realized she needed to be careful as she was arcanely defenseless. Instead, she poked her head out—and spotted the torchlit outline of a winged gargoyle flying forth, a ten-footer, small by their sort. It noticed her and slapped its wrists together whilst growling a guttural word. She didn't even have time to think how interesting it was that it used the same gesture as a human warlock, for a bolt of lightning surged forth, forcing her to duck back into the perpendicular alley. The bolt smashed into the brick beside her, exploding it inward and leaving behind a smoking hole.

Leera gaped at the hole, realizing she could squeeze through it and escape. But no way would she leave Augum behind. The kingdom could burn in Hell for all she cared. If the love of her life was getting captured, she would get captured too. And if he was to be sucked dry and bled of water and blood, then she would die right alongside him. There was no life without Augum. There was no moving forward.

She took a tight hold of Careena and positioned herself against the wall of the corner, each thundering heartbeat feeling like an hour. Were she able to cast arcanery, she would have pointed the blade around the corner and fired off a few First Offensives, for the blade had been specially enchanted to allow such a thing—a heck of a birthday present she had received after turning seventeen. But being snuffed, she had to hold tight.

The backlit shadow of the gargoyle appeared, its wings flapping as it soared forth. How she longed to become the dragon and tear the beast's wings off with her claws. How she longed for vengeance on everyone's behalf.

The shadow grew larger and larger, until she could hear the leathery flap of its wings. Whilst gripping Careena's hilt tightly with both hands, and with her wide eyes staring at Augum's seemingly lifeless body gathering snow, and with her chest heaving with frantic breaths, she waited until the very last moment. Then, as the gargoyle turned the corner, she jumped forth with a battle roar and sliced the air.

The gargoyle screamed a shrill and animalistic scream, for its right arm was sent twirling, spraying blood in a circular pattern. Leera roared again and returned with a second slice, this one amputating its leg.

The gargoyle fell to the snowy ground, but still reached for Leera. She felt a strong telekinetic pull yank her toward its screaming maw. But years of battle instincts took over, and she *just* managed to angle Careena between herself and the gargoyle, using her forward momentum to pierce its chest with the tip. The gargoyle flailed and smashed its remaining arm into the side of her head so hard she saw white as she was sent crunching into the wall, where she crumpled in a loose heap of limbs and blood.

Leera moaned and groggily tried to understand what had happened. She saw her hands and, after seeing her own blood drip onto them from her head, realized they were empty. The first thing she did was grab a brick. Then she looked to the gargoyle and saw it grab Careena's hilt and yank it from its chest with a growling howl, causing a spray of blood to shoot forth.

The beast looked at her, and never had she seen such malice from a creature. Its lizard eyes smoked with rage, and its snouted face contorted with pure fury. Yet its body was a fountain of blood, and it was weakening by the heartbeat. Still, it used what strength it had to launch Careena like a spear at Leera, who was only five feet away.

Although her arcanery had been snuffed, she still had her reflexes, and she raised the brick before herself like a miniature shield. There was a metallic *ting* as the tip smacked into the brick, cleaving it in two—and nicking her palm. Shards of brick fell to the snow alongside the blade.

Without missing a beat Leera grabbed the blade from the ground and scrambled forth, her feet slipping in the icy snow as she rabidly struggled to stab the beast dead. The gargoyle, weakened to the point of molasses-like movement, nonetheless pressed a rune on its flesh—just as her blade sliced at its throat.

There came a stony *ting* as the blade bounced off—infuriatingly, the gargoyle had turned to stone. Yet it still bled and was as weak as a kitten, barely able to move. Wanting to take no chances, Leera picked up another brick, raised it over her head, and smashed its face. The brick fell apart, but she grabbed another and did it again, and again, and again, roaring like a girl possessed, until the gargoyle's flesh turned gray, and it lay in a pool of its own blood.

A panting Leera fell back onto the snow, staring uncomprehendingly at the fallen beast. "May your soul find the peace together we could not reach," she wheezed. She did not know if gargoyles even had souls, but figured they at least deserved to be honored as combatants. If anything, the Final Valediction eased the guilt of slaughter.

She scrambled after Augum and turned him over, whispering, "Love? Love, are you all right?"

Her heart leapt upon seeing small plumes of frosty mist regularly escaping his mouth, yet he remained unconscious. She dragged him farther into the perpendicular alley, keeping him out of sight of the street. There she swept him into her lap and repeatedly smoothed his umber hair away from his sweaty face, ignoring her ringing skull and the warm stickiness oozing down the side of her head and into the neck of her robe. "I got you, my love. I got you. You're safe. You're safe …" She kissed his forehead and nuzzled him close, feeling strangely alone.

"Wake up, my love. Wake up …"

Ten watery rings abruptly flared to life around her forearm. "Where the hell were you when I needed you!" she hissed at them, adding in a mutter, "Cursed Fates …" She swallowed, blurting, "I didn't mean that. I didn't mean that!" She wasn't the superstitious sort, but the last thing she wanted to do was taunt The Fates right now.

As Leera waited for Augum to wake up, she spotted the hilt of Burden's Edge sticking out of the snow. She flicked a finger at it and telekinetically dragged it to her hand, then awkwardly slipped it back into its sheath at Augum's belt.

She patted his slowly rising chest, whispering, "It's back by your side, my love. Snug as a bug under a rug."

There came a groan from Augum as he stirred awake in her lap, eyelids opening snail slow.

"Hey," she whispered, soothingly rubbing his cheek with the back of her hand. "You're back …"

Augum only groaned, eyes roving about as if he were drunk.

"You took a hard knock, but I got the bastard for you. Just take your time and—" She froze, for the shadow of a waving tail caught her eye in the nearby alley that led to the street. That shadow enlarged to the figure of a gargoyle, and was quickly joined by another shadow, and then a third and a fourth—and none of them had wings. These shadows crept forth as if expecting to be attacked.

A fifth shadow appeared, this one peeking from behind the curtains of her mind. It stared at her with the expectation of vengeance. *Thou shall never turn thy back on a foe,* she thought. *Show them what you're made of, that some of you are not to be trifled with, and that you can exact a terrible vengeance.*

Even as the rational side of her frantically screamed that she ought to cast Group Teleport and whisk Augum to safety, Leera found herself gently laying him aside. "Shut up, you scared little girl," she whispered at that rational side. "You are an Arcaner warrior. Act like it."

But it's a needless risk! the rational part argued.

"The Sacred Chivalric Code of the Arcaner is not optional," she spat back. The truth was, she wanted vengeance not only on behalf of her betrothed, but on behalf of her people, the city, and the kingdom.

Leera thus got to her feet, sheathed Careena to free her hands for spell casting, and stepped around the corner to face four wingless gargoyles. All halted their creeping and rose to their full height of about ten feet, but not one had runes on their gray skin. Standing twenty feet away, they silently stared at her as if wondering what she would do.

Then one seemed to swallow and back track, then the second, then the third, leaving only one to glare defiantly at her, its tail weaving behind it like a cobra. Its cohorts retreated to the entrance of the alley and waited there. The lone ten-footer flexed all of its muscles—and they were mighty muscles indeed, gray and veiny and tight and potent. The muscles of a beast groomed and built for battle. But taking into account that these gargoyles were wingless and possessed no runes, she figured they were of a lower caste amongst their kind.

"What do you want?" Leera asked. "Why are you here?"

The gargoyle raised its chin and growled out a phrase.

Leera considered casting the 12th degree Tongues, but realized the spell required a basic understanding of the target language to even stand a chance at working. "You are not wanted here," she instead spat, making a dismissive *Off with you* motion with her hands. "Git! Shoo! Leave my kingdom …" She raised her own chin in turn. "… or die."

The gargoyle snarled, its tail lashing about as if urging it to gather the courage to attack her.

One of its cohorts barked a word in their tongue, and the lone gargoyle snarled again, seemingly in defiance. It raised a hand and slowly crushed its clawed fingers into a fist.

"I am not afraid of you," Leera spat, taking several steps forth and smacking her golden breastplate with a fist, her ten watery rings on full display. "Come on! *Come on!* I dare you!"

The gargoyle backtracked a few paces, feigned turning away — then whipped its tail and leapt at her.

Even with its quick spring, it was still ten feet away, giving Leera plenty enough time to slap her wrists together and roar, "*Annihilo bato!*" Two potent jets of water shot forth with a dual *hiss*. The gargoyle artfully snapped its tail in response, changing its momentum in midair. One jet missed cleanly, slamming into a brick wall, and the other, which aimed at its torso, instead blew through that tail, slicing it clean off. It fell to the ground like a dead tentacle.

The gargoyle growled in pain, landed on its feet, and lunged in a manner that was obviously more awkward on account of it having lost its tail, which gargoyles apparently used for balance. Five feet off now, Leera took no chance and slapped her wrists a second time, roaring, "*Annihilo bato!*" The gargoyle tried rolling aside, but without its tail, it was too slow, and this time both jets of water drilled into its flesh, one into the right shoulder, nearly severing the arm, and the other into the chest.

It grunted and fell to the snow. Leera glanced past it to see its brethren snort and walk off, as if in disdain.

The gargoyle tried to get up, but its right arm refused to work. It picked it up and jangled it about, the flesh still loosely attached to the shoulder. It moaned pitifully, as if not understanding what was happening, and looked up at her with eyes that were now watery.

"Is that self-pity?" she asked the creature. "Do you feel remorse at getting caught out for your arrogance?" The shadow within her stepped so close she could feel its cold darkness as much as she could feel the heat of three suns burning upon her wings. "And you expect … what? What do you expect now other than death?"

There came a moaning and familiar grunt behind her. Not wanting to take her eyes off the monster, she backtracked, then chanced a glance backward — and saw Augum clambering to his feet.

"I got this, my love," she said. "You stay there."

Augum winced and stumbled back against the brick wall, where he rested, one hand pressed to his scalp, the other on the pommel of his blade.

Leera turned her cold attention back to the gargoyle, who flipped over onto its back to face the blizzard heavens. It opened its maw and shrieked. It took Leera a moment to realize it was not a scream of terror or pain, but a cry for assistance. She was about to slap her wrists together to end the beast's life when Augum blurted, "Thou shall be gallant and fair to those unable to learn the craft. Thou shall never take the life of a weaponless Ordinary. Thou shall always accept a bent knee. Thou shall guard the honor of the arcane craft."

She glared at the gargoyle, now gasping for its life. "These are monsters, Aug …"

"But we aren't. We aren't …"

Leera lowered her hands, knowing he was right. She watched as the gargoyle's breathing slowed, but did not wait for its final breath. Instead she went to Augum, who was struggling to stay standing—the knock to the head must have been extra hard.

"I think I got a concussion," he mumbled. "And not for the first time." He did a double-take upon spotting her head. "You're injured …"

"Just a scratch." Her head hurt, sure, but the wound would soon congeal and scab over. She draped his arm around her shoulder. "We best get you to a healer."

"First we need to inspect the very first gargoyle we vanquished, remember?" He pointed up at a nearby roof. "I think it's that roof there."

But where he pointed, a gargoyle touched down on top of that roof, this one winged. And then a second one touched down beside it, and this one held something black in its hand. The body of the first lit up with a slew of icy runes, and the body of the second with molten runes of fire. Both looked down upon Augum and Leera.

"Damn," Leera said, focusing on the terrace of Castle Arinthian. "*Impetus peragro—*" she began incanting, witnessing the gargoyle with the pyramidal stone growl something into it. "*—grapa lestato—*" Simultaneously, the other gargoyle touched a rune on its body with a clawed finger, which remained there. "*—exa exaei.*" Before she vanished with Augum, she witnessed a bubble of snuffing fire rapidly expand outward. It overcame the icy gargoyle—but she caught a glimpse of its runes—*and they remained icy*.

With that visual engraved into her memory, she and Augum appeared with a *thwomp* on the northwest terrace of Castle Arinthian.

"They have to press a special rune on their bodies to prevent the snuffing!" she blurted, staring at the distant city consumed in a blizzard haze that kept lighting up with colorful and rapid flashes of snuffing arcanery. She wondered if it was possible to take advantage of that knowledge down the line, when they were ready to mount a counter attack. Yet with the fearsome barrage of snuffing the city was experiencing, she couldn't imagine mounting any sort of attack anytime soon. Based on that last experience, even going back right now felt like suicide as it would certainly lead to an immediate snuffing.

Augum wincingly pressed a limp wrist to the side of his head. "I don't feel too good …"

Leera snapped out of it. "I know, my love. Hang in there." She helped him hobble through the closest pair of doors, which led to her room—out of habit, she always teleported outside her own doors. She closed the door behind her, plunging them into cool and quiet darkness, within which a questioning *meow* greeted her.

"Hi, Bumblebutt," Leera cooed, laying Augum down on her bed. Sir Pawsalot hopped up onto the bed beside her and rubbed against her arm. She scratched his chin, whispering, "I missed you too, sweetums. Don't worry. You're safe." She hurried to a silken ribbon hanging from the wall and pulled it. The other end would ring a bell down in the servant's quarters. Then she plopped down beside Augum and stroked his cheek. To the melting of her heart, Sir Pawsalot curled around Augum's head, as if knowing it needed nurturing.

"You're such a sweetie," Leera cooed, rubbing behind each of Sir Pawsalot's ears. "We love you so much, you little cutie."

"My brain feels like it's going to explode," Augum mumbled, wincing.

"Shh, don't talk, my love. Just relax." She worried about him. Such strong knocks to the head could lead to brain swelling or even bleeding, which could kill out of the blue. Or at least that was what Jengo always warned about.

Leera looked to the doors, which rattled from the strong gusts. In the whistling and windy and quiet darkness, she wondered if there was anyone left in the castle. She could not bear the thought that they might be alone, the others all kidnapped.

But now that the blood in her veins calmed from that frantic fight, a terrible exhaustion descended, and she realized she badly needed sleep.

Then came a soft knock on her door, and a cagey question, "My lady, is that you?"

"Yes, come in, Gertie!" Leera quietly called, recognizing the voice and polite tone. The door opened with a creak and her newly hired servant, the blond-haired Gertrude Dolores Hooper, stepped inside, gently closing the door behind herself. Now wearing the gold, blue and burgundy livery of Castle Arinthian that reflected its crest, Gertrude artfully curtsied and bowed her head in a proper manner. "My lady returns in the dead of a frightful night," she whispered.

"My betrothed is hurt."

"Your betrothed?" Gertrude stepped closer and gasped. "Commander Stone."

"*Shyneo*," Leera said, lighting up her palm with dim watery light, revealing a sleeping Augum beside her, Sir Pawsalot purring whilst curled around his head. "He took a hard knock to the head and I am afraid for his wellbeing. I don't suppose there is a healer present in the castle at the moment?"

"I am afraid there is not, my lady. I believe the highest rank is a man named Clayborne, who is the master's servant." She nodded at Augum.

It annoyed Leera that Gertrude had called Augum master. Then she realized she would likely refer to her as mistress too. She said nothing as now was hardly the time to nitpick at trivialities. Besides, by the look of deep purple circles under Gertrude's eyes, the poor girl hadn't slept much either on account of all the chaos.

"Shall I fetch him, my lady?"

"No, let him sleep." Leera did not want to tell the girl that another Ordinary would be useless to her at the moment.

"Gods, my lady is injured as well!"

"It's just a scratch, I'm fine."

"My lady is bleeding. Please allow me to—"

"It's *fine*."

"Yes, my lady," Gertrude mumbled, face tight with worry.

Augum mumbled something from beside Leera.

"What, my love?"

"I said … I'm fine. Just a slight …" He winced. "… headache."

"Liar."

"Kingdom cannot spare … healers right now. They're … too busy."

Leera ignored him and looked to Gertrude. "What about the kitchens? Anyone up early?"

"I believe it is indeed that early hour for the kitchen staff to have begun their day." She grimaced as if trying to remember a name. "The head chef is a … a Priya Okeke, yes."

Jengo's wife, Leera thought, heart sinking on behalf of the young woman. She would want to know about her husband, and Leera would have no news for her. "Can you see if she can make something to ease Augum's head pain? Tell her he took a hard knock to the head."

"Right away, my lady." Gertrude curtsied with a bow of her head then went to the door, only to turn around.

"My lady, forgive me, but may I ask what is happening out there?"

"The kingdom has been attacked."

"Attacked by who?"

Leera's eyes unfocused as she saw silhouettes. "Monsters ..."

"What ... what sort of monsters?"

"Gargoyles, Gertie. Gargoyles. Yes, that sounds ridiculous. No, it's not a jest. But I wish it was, Gertie. I truly wish it was ..."

"Gods ..." Gertrude lingered a moment, no doubt full of questions. Mercifully she did not ask any, and departed, once again softly closing the door behind herself.

Leera snuffed her palm and delicately prodded her head wound. As she suspected, the blood had already congealed into a lump. She gently lay back with Augum and wondered about Bridget, only to realize she already had a way to communicate with her. She got back up with a groan, summoned her shield, and incanted, "*Summano vaultus arcanus.*" The vault appeared with a *whoosh*.

She felt an immediate flush of relief upon seeing Bridget's door was still lit, indicating she was at least alive. She opened the farthest door on the left, which belonged to her, but only found the note Augum had written while up north, which detailed things he'd already told her. Since the girls flanked Augum's central door, they oft used a wooden stick to push a note into the other end, for they could not open each other's doors.

Leera thus schlepped to her desk, rummaged for quill, ink, and parchment, then scribbled out a quick note telling Bridget where they were. Then she looked around for a wooden stick. Finding none, she ripped off a wooden support bar attached to the back of her desk, stabbed the note into the end of it, and pushed it deep into the vault, hoping that by withdrawing the stick the action would leave the note in Bridget's vault. It worked in theory but sometimes in practice the notes got left in Augum's side.

With the task done and too exhausted to bother with arcanely repairing her desk—or setting an alarm on her doors—Leera dumped the support bar onto her desk, closed and nullified the vault, then plopped down on the bed beside Augum—only to get right back up again to struggle out of the cursed breastplate, which was about as comfortable to lie down in as a barrel.

After fighting with the stupid strapping and also removing the sheathed Careena from her belt, she finally plopped back onto the bed, too exhausted to even wash her grimy face—gods and how she needed a bath!

Like Sir Pawsalot, she curled up against Augum, draped an arm over his chest, and listened to his rhythmic breathing. But soon the whistle of the wind and Sir Pawsalot's purring had her drifting into the lands of dreams, and she forgot that she was supposed to wait for someone from the kitchens.

CASTELLAN DUTIES

AUGUM

Augum awoke in darkness to someone nudging him.

"Commander Stone," a young woman's voice whispered amidst the sound of windows rattling from a whistling wind. "My lord Stone ... it's Priya."

Augum blearily opened his eyes to see a portable brass-based candle sitting on a bedside table and fluttering in a cold draft. It dimly lit Priya's sienna face, the piercings in her lips, nose, and ears glinting. She was dressed in the gold, blue and burgundy livery of the castle but with a cerulean cloth draped around her shoulder to honor her Tiberran roots.

"I brought you something," she whispered, holding a steaming porcelain cup sitting in a saucer, both of which were decorated with the House Arinthian crest that the trio had together crafted to represent the castle—a shield split by three bands in blue, gold, and burgundy, with two lions flanking a sheaf of wheat above three pine trees.

Augum focused on the crest, taking solace from its depictions. The lions were a traditional symbol of the Arinthian lineage. The sheaf of wheat represented the cash crop of the castle. Although Augum had teleported the castle in the last war and made it invisible, the castle's original spot was amidst the town of Arinthia, located about one hundred and fifty leagues to the northeast. And the three pine trees represented three separate things—the trio's friendship, servitude to the kingdom, and Ravenwood, the forest that surrounded Arinthia. The pine was also the traditional emblem of their kingdom of Solia.

" 'Adversi alua probata,' " he whispered, reading the motto underneath their crest.

"Against all odds," Priya whispered in translation, patiently holding the teacup.

Those words strengthened his resolve to overcome the malaise his body was feeling, the weariness in his bones and the headache beating on his brain.

Hearing someone snoozing beside him and feeling the weight of an arm draped across his chest, he looked over to see a tangle of raven hair cascading across Leera's face, her head freshly bandaged. Her sheathed sword and breastplate lay unstrapped on the floor. Both of them stank of sweat.

"I brought you Ohmish lotus tea, which ought to help your head," Priya said, drawing back his attention and holding the cup forth. "I also took the liberty of wrapping Captain Jones's head. She's a heavy sleeper."

"Yes, she is." Augum, still in his golden breastplate, which felt horribly uncomfortable in bed, awkwardly slid up to a sitting position, only to receive an annoyed *meow* from Sir Pawsalot, who had been curled up around his head.

"Sorry, little fella," he mumbled, moving Sir Pawsalot over to lie behind Leera's head, where he curled up, flashing Augum a mild look of annoyance. The furball nonetheless slowly blinked a few times before shutting his eyes and returning to a peaceful snooze.

Augum delicately moved Leera's arm but kept it draped across his lap, comforted by her touch. "Gods, I feel like someone smashed my head in with a battering ram," he mumbled, pressing a palm to the side of his head with one hand whilst accepting the tea with the other. "Thank you, Priya. For everything."

"It was no bother. May I assist my lord in removing the breastplate?"

"No, there might be an attack here. But thank you." He checked that his blade still hung from his waist. Any moment, their arcanery could be snuffed, which meant they would need all the physical protection they could muster.

"On Miss Hooper's initiative, we have taken the liberty of posting two guards outside your room. All you need do is call."

"Miss … Hooper?"

"My lady Jones's new servant."

"Oh. Right." Still, he was confused. Had he met her?

"I've also taken the liberty of bringing you an Endyear candle." Priya nodded at the hearth, on the mantel of which sat a fat candle on a bed of holly. She took a seat on the bed beside him. "My lord …"

"Augum," he blurted, wincing from the pain of talking. "You are Jengo's wife. You need not defer to me." He said it even though servants would always obey protocol, not to mention they expected it of each other. She thus said nothing to this, only watched him take a sip of tea, which tasted bitter on the tongue despite a slice of lemon and a dab of honey mixed in. Yet even after the first sip, the headache subsided a little.

"Thank you for this," he whispered, resting his arm over Leera's and idly rubbing it with his thumb.

"I will stay until you finish your tea to make sure it eases your pain." Priya's hands writhed in her lap. "Commander, forgive me, but have you news of my husband? The other servants have heard awful rumors and there have been sightings in the sky and strange sounds from outside and the capital is blinking rapidly with all sorts of strange lights—"

Augum halted her worries by patting her writhing hands. "Rest assured that Jengo is very capable of keeping himself safe. Healers in general have a knack for it."

"But have you any news? By eye or word of mouth?"

Augum withdrew his hand. "I admit I know little at the moment. We got snuffed and beat up, forcing us to flee and take shelter. The city is in chaos. The Black Castle raised its drawbridges. We ... we mounted no counterattack because every single time we got somewhere we ended up snuffed."

"But surely you can teleport back inside ..."

Augum shook his head. "The newly appointed Lord High Commander revoked our teleportation permissions from the castle's arcaneological foundations."

"Why would he do such a foolish thing?"

"To punish us. To keep us from leaving on quests."

"Then he is a fool. A great fool."

"On that we can certainly agree."

"Can you stop it all? Perhaps by ..." She dropped her voice to a murmur. "... turning into the dragon?"

Augum took a longer sip of tea and thought about it. "The problem is we have no way to prevent the snuffing of our arcanery. Until we can somehow survive a snuff, we'd be wasting ourselves as ..." He grimaced at the word he was about to use. "... as weapons."

"I see. My lord, I fear for my Jengo. I fear for the city. For the kingdom."

He stared into his cup. He wanted to say that he did too, but knew that she wanted to draw courage from him, and so he said, "We'll do what we can. Just have to regroup." He'd learned that sometimes it was more important to regain one's bearings before rushing back into a fray.

Mentally and physically exhausted, Augum sipped his tea, and for a time they sat together in windy and rattling silence, the Endyear candle fluttering about in a draft, a snoozing Leera and Sir Pawsalot lending peace to the moment. Upon finishing the tea, he placed the empty cup on the side table and thanked Priya again, mentioning how it had helped his head a little bit. Priya, who had been staring at the red velvet curtains that swayed in drafts, animated back to life and stood up from the bed.

"You ought to sleep, Commander," she whispered, picking up the empty teacup and the wavering brass-based candle.

"How does everyone fare?" he whispered. "In the castle, that is."

"They are tense and afraid. The first footman would like to speak to you, but I told him to wait until I saw you. I think you ought to sleep first."

"Please send him in." He hadn't seen Charles Poorman, his most trusted servant, in some time, and despite everything, he would like to hear a report on the castle's workings. Charles always had his ear close to the ground in such matters, and Augum felt like he badly needed a dose of normalcy to calm his worries. Besides, as castellan he needed to make sure the castle and its denizens were safe.

Priya curtsied and went to the door, where she hesitated.

"Speak your mind, Priya. Please."

"Is Captain Burns all right? She did not return with you."

Augum's heart skipped a beat. He needed to check the vault in case Bridget had messaged. "I'm not sure. On second thought, please wait to send Charles in. I'll call on him."

"He'll be in the hall, Commander." Priya curtsied and quietly opened the door.

Augum caught a glimpse of two guards and the stubby form of Charles Poorman, all of whom glanced toward the dark room prior to the door closing.

Augum gently unspooled Leera's arm from his lap, only for her to moan, squeeze him tighter, and cuddle up to him. He smiled. She was always such an adorable deep sleeper. He squeezed her close then tried to trick her by spooling her arm around Sir Pawsalot, but Leera moaned sleepily again, a touch more annoyed this time, and dragged her arm back onto Augum's lap.

"Fine, fine, fine," Augum whispered, patting Leera's arm. He would summon the vault in bed. First he summoned his shield, then he whispered, "*Summano vaultus arcanus*," and the triple-doored vault appeared above the bed with a quiet *whoosh*, bathing the room in ghostly light. Sir Pawsalot abruptly raised his head at this rude interruption.

Seeing it was only the vault, which he had seen many times before—he was quite used to their arcanery, after all—the tabby stood up, stretched his front paws out, yawned, and resettled around Leera's head, this time curling the other way to avert his face from the unnatural light invading the room.

Reassured by Bridget's still-lit crest, Augum reached up, opened his door, searched for a note—and found one. He snatched it telekinetically—for it was just out of arm's reach—and opened it up. Then he promptly realized it was a note from Leera to Bridget, telling her where they were. Grimacing, he stuffed the note into Bridget's side of the vault, shut the door, and swiped at the air, snapping, "*Vaultus null*." The vault vanished with another *whoosh*.

Not wanting to unspool himself from Leera, Augum proceeded to telekinetically raise one of Leera's shoes and use it to knock against the door. That knock was soon returned along with a muted voice. "My lord, it is your devoted servant Charles Poorman wishing to have a word."

"Come in!" Augum whisper-called.

The door creaked open and in stepped the stubby Charles Poorman, holding a brass-based candle he'd likely received from Priya. Augum used the torchlight from the hallway to press a finger to his lips to remind Charles to speak softly.

"My lord," Charles whispered, delicately closing the door and tottering over to Augum's bedside, his close-set eyes carefully examining the scene. He was in his mid-twenties but looked much older, mostly on account of his large square nose and shelf chin and his perfectly parted wavy hair. Although an Ordinary, he constantly learned as much about the arcane arts as he could and took great pride in his position as first footman and Augum's personal servant.

"Charles," Augum said. "Good of you to come."

Charles bowed deeply. "My heart gladdens upon seeing that thou art well, my lord, and wish thee a Happy Endyear." There had been a time when Charles's formalities annoyed Augum for how old it made him feel. Since then, he'd learned to appreciate the man's professionalism, his dedication to his work, and his unquestionable loyalty.

"As well as can be under the circumstances, and Happy Endyear to you. What news of the castle?"

"All stationed guards on emergency duty. No one is permitted to leave the castle—not that anyone is available to teleport people in and out anyway."

Augum nodded along. Most of the guards were Ordinaries, with only a few possessing minor arcane abilities. The ancient castle was innately arcanely strong, sat atop a mountain, and was invisible, meaning it usually needed very little protection. There was a rotating squad of Arcaners and warlocks—usually the trio and Jez, among a precious few others—who ferried guards and servants back and forth between Arinthia and the castle so that they could see their families.

"Any word from my Arcaner brethren?" he pressed. "From Captain Burns?"

"Nay, my lord. No visitors other than you and Captain Jones."

"What of supplies?"

"The warlock provisioner stopped coming on account of being called to duty, but your efforts as castellan have ensured that the castle is amply provisioned. We could survive a siege."

"Morale?"

"Low, my lord. Everyone fears an attack. All sorts of wild rumors are flying about. Is it true that these gargoyle beasts can snuff arcanery whenever they please?"

"That seems to be the case."

"Then I fear it is my duty to advise the castellan that he ought to consider teleporting this castle to an entirely new location."

Augum nodded. "I appreciate the advice, but for now I will keep the castle where it is." It had been a big ordeal to move the castle, which had included a permanent sacrifice of a Dreadnought item from the castle's vault, among other things. "But that may change if the beasts penetrate the interior," Augum added. "Were any internal arcaneological functions affected?"

"All arcane activity ceased during that one brief period, my lord, but immediately relit after the snuffing event passed. The torches, the ovens, the hearths—everything seems to be in good working order. No permanent damage to report."

"And the arcaneological protections?"

"The guards report the castle's defenses seem to remain intact and active, including the powerful invisibility enchantment."

"Good. Good …"

"Forgive me, my lord, but has the army been mobilized?"

"I would imagine so, Charles. I would imagine so."

"Very good, my lord." The stubby servant adjusted his grip on the brass candle. "Is there anything I can be of service with, my lord?"

"Actually, yes. Can you hop up into our library and bring me every book on gargoyle mythology you can?" Bridget had taken it upon herself to clean and stock the castle's empty library with books in her spare time.

It was a perpetual work in progress, one that would take years to complete.

"Right away, my lord. Shall I send for breakfast?"

Augum rubbed his tired eyes. "When the sun rises. The city ... how does it look?"

"Like it is in the midst of a strobing storm of strange lights."

Then it would be useless to teleport back so soon, Augum thought. It was hard not to envision the raw terror the people of the city had to be feeling. He could still hear the echo of those sudden screams that were sometimes abruptly silenced from a teleport. He tried not to think about his colleagues and acquaintances and the innocent, all the families getting ripped from their beds ...

Realizing he was taking up the man's time, Augum nodded. "Thank you, Charles."

Charles bowed. "My lord," and quietly departed.

Augum used the dim light of the Endyear candle to locate his rucksack, which he floated over, withdrawing the black pyramidal cube. He then spread the fingers of his lit hand, incanting, "*Un vun asperio aurum enchantus.*" Dense and complex blue tendril geometries appeared on every one of its five sides. The side that concerned Augum the most was the one that appeared to have tendril tracings of Object Track, or some form of it.

He turned it over, wondering which one of the sides was responsible for snuffing and which one for draining. He couldn't believe there existed knowledge outside of scions to snuff arcanery, and that it had been brought from overseas—or who knew where, perhaps another plane—and used against them in such an impactful manner.

"Devastating," he whispered, turning the pyramid over in his hands. The arcanery was remarkable in its foreignness, the weavings unlike any he had ever seen. He had a hard time fathoming how they had been structured, and an even harder time picturing a fifteen-foot gargoyle using its huge claws to cast such intricate tiny webbings. That led him to thinking about what lands the gargoyles came from and what those lands looked like, what sort of homes they lived in, what kind of society they kept. He thought of the wolven and how they sent their cubs into separate elemental packs, and wondered if the gargoyles acted similarly. He wondered how they warred and who they warred with, then imagined a swarm of a thousand gargoyles descending on a city.

"Devastating ..." he whispered again. He wondered if perhaps he ought to teleport the pyramidal artifact away from the castle, just in case the gargoyles could track it down. But there was also the possibility that the artifact was tuned to that one gargoyle, which the trio had vanquished, and so the artifact was not traceable.

"But you ought not to take that chance, Commander," he said to himself, realizing that bringing it to the castle had been a risk he ought not to have taken. He'd just been too injured and too exhausted to think things through.

Resolved to take the necessary precaution, he slowly slipped Leera's arm off his lap. Then he got off the bed and went to the doors, opened one, and stepped outside. The terrace was windy and dark, with a subtle blush on the distant cloudy horizon, heralding a winter dawn that was still hours away. Immediately he went to the stone crenelations that edged the entire terrace and looked to the capital.

"Gods," he whispered, for the city was a flashing mess of otherworldly lights. He couldn't imagine a single warlock getting a spell off amidst that pulsing carnage. It was one thing to go up against a human force, which was somewhat predictable, quite another to face a beastly race with a whole new way of performing—and snuffing—arcanery. And the cold fact that the enemy naturally wielded the snuffing power of the scion was something that made his heart quicken with fear.

How in Sithesia were they going to survive such an onslaught? And if it spread, the entire continent could fall …

Augum had to force himself to turn away from the visual of the city, lest his anxieties destroy all hope.

He went to Leera's doors and spread his hands over each doorknob, incanting, "*Concutio del alarmo*," setting an alarm on each. Then he turned his attention to thinking of a spot where he could hide the artifact. Only one came to mind right off the get-go, and it was a lone gnarled oak tree in the middle of The Tallows where he and his friends sometimes retreated to for quiet reading and relaxation time.

"*Impetus peragro*," he incanted, and appeared beneath its branches. All around the dark Tallows stretched, its tall yellow grass poking through a knee-high layer of snow, unbroken except for occasional tiny bird tracks.

Augum lit up his palm with a dim lightning glow, dug into the snow at the base of the tree, stuck the artifact there, cast another Object Alarm on it, then covered it with a branch—and cast an alarm on that branch. He carefully buried both under the snow. Just as he was about to teleport back, an alarm rang in his head—Leera's doors had been touched!

"*Impetus peragro!*" he snapped, and appeared with a *thwomp* right behind a crimson-robed woman, who spun about with a yelp.

"Gods how you startled me, Augum Arinthian Stone!" Bridget said, hands pressed to her chest. Then she abruptly flung herself at him, pulling him into a tight hug and burst into tears.

"It's all right, you're safe now," he said, fearing what she had been through.

"I killed a man," she blurted. "I killed a man with my bare hands I mean with a mop handle but he was rabid and I don't know if it's because he went insane from seeing something or if the gargoyles cursed him and he went after me when I was snuffed and he was growling like a beast and it was all I could do to stop him from gutting me like a fish oh gods it was horrible so horrible—"

"Shh, it's all right," Augum whispered, patting her back. "It's all right. You're safe now. You're in the castle. And you did what you had to do, Bridge. You survived."

"—and I don't know where Ollie is and I'm ashamed of my own thoughts and I don't know what's happening and I'm just so *so* exhausted I can barely think straight—"

"Shh, shh, it's all right. You're safe now. You're safe ..."

She kept tight hold of him for a while, blubbering on like that, until suddenly pulling away and repeatedly smoothing her robe and wiping her tears, declaring, "I'm sorry, I'm sorry. I need to get it together. I'm a captain now. I'm a captain who still has her shield and code of honor ..."

"It's all right, Bridge. And you need not apologize to me. You hear me?"

She looked at him and nodded several times. "Right. Right. I'm fine. I'm fine now ..." Yet her gaze went to the city. "They're keeping up a steady barrage of that snuffing. The moment my arm happened to relight, I immediately 'ported out, and just barely at that as I heard another thunderclap sound off nearby. It's hell over there, Aug. Hell ..."

"I know. I know ..."

"Thanks for listening. I just needed to ..." She tossed her hands forth. "... let that out. Gods that was harrowing."

"I'm sorry you went through that but I'm glad you're alive."

"Me too. Me too ..."

"Ollie's all right too, don't worry about him," he added.

"I know," she said, though the worry in her tone suggested otherwise.

They stood in silence, with Bridget curling her frizzy long hair around her ears, until she reanimated, blurting, "I got Leera's message, that's why I came here. The army was finally mobilized, but I'm not sure how effective they will be as they're not well organized—no surprise considering who their Lord High Commander is. Where's Lee?"

Augum nodded at the doors. "Getting some badly needed shuteye."

"I seriously need some of that. Haven't slept a wink yet. My thoughts are mush. We need to regroup before we launch an assault. But I need to rest. Just a little while at least."

"Agreed, and it's not like we can do anything anyway until those snuffs calm down in frequency. Come on. Let's get you warm." He opened one of the doors and ushered her inside. Leera stirred in bed but did not wake. It was a perpetual worry for him that someone could sneak up on her.

Bridget went to the dead hearth and slapped the rune beside it, incanting, "*Igniato.*" It burst with fire, and she held her hands before it.

There came a knock at the door. Not wanting to wake his girl, Augum opened it. He was greeted by Charles, who was holding a small stack of books.

"Everything I could find on the subject of gargoyles, my lord," Charles reported in a whisper, tottering into the room. The pair of guards outside the room each nodded at Augum, who nodded back. Both were in their late teens and had dark rings under their eyes. There was a monstrous class divide between Ordinaries and warlocks, one he felt most acutely with common soldiers his age. They had to do grunt work and oft lived menial, boring lives, while he got to experience the full breadth of adventure, arcanery, and its consequences. Why had The Fates blessed him but not them? Ordinaries asked the same questions, yet everyone worked together to defend the kingdom, doing their jobs, for after all the moaning and groaning, what could be done about it?

On the other hand, Ordinaries were also free of the responsibilities and expectations that warlocks had. They could live their lives mostly as they chose and did not have to suffer grueling training and constant threats of death.

"How many do we have on shift?" Augum whispered to one of them.

"Five, m'lord," the first of the pair whispered. "One at the main doors, two here, one in the watchtower, one on patrol."

Usually there were two on patrol and two on the main doors, which meant these two got pulled from those ranks. "How many on standby?"

"Ten on standby, all asleep."

"When does your watch end?"

"At the strike of the eighth morning bell."

In that very moment, five gentle and soothing gongs sounded in the halls of the castle, muted as it was night hours.

"Three more hours," Augum said under his breath. "And when does the whole detail get changed?" Usually, the entire guard detail was rotated out every tenday, with the soldiers getting posts in Arinthia.

"Four days, m'lord. We're alert enough. It's just that we've lost some sleep the night before due to ongoing events."

"Of course. Please let me know if you need anything."

"A word to our families," the other blurted, sheepishly withdrawing a large bundle of letters, some of which were sealed with wax. "That we're all right."

"We haven't had an escort in some days. Ms. Terse has been absent."

Augum accepted the bundle. "Hopefully we will hear word from her soon. In the mean, I'll take care of this personally for you." Although he delegated much of the day-to-day responsibilities of running the castle to his steward Hanad Haroun, as castellan, he still carried all final responsibility, which meant picking up the slack in times of trial. Sometimes he mixed Arcaner squires into the guard detail to give them a break, but it was Endyear and he wanted his Arcaners training hard whilst also having time with their families, for guard detail could be exquisitely boring. It was also expensive, hence why he hired Ordinary soldiers as they were the cheapest, knights and warlocks being far too pricey. Such was the reality of castle finances, as his steward had so delicately put it.

After exchanging a few more cordial pleasantries, Augum thanked the soldiers for their service and slipped back into the room. There he found Bridget by the fire, already absorbed in the books.

"You should catch some shuteye too," he whispered.

"I will. Promise," she mumbled, flipping pages, rubbing each eye with the palm of her hand in an effort to keep them open.

Charles bowed before Augum. "My lord. Can I be of further service?"

"You can catch some sleep."

"I'm fine, my lord. I'd rather stay on call."

Augum nodded his thanks and Charles excused himself to stand outside in the hall. As he left, he let in Leera's new servant, a young woman with blond hair. She carried a large silver tray with a porcelain plate of sunny-side-up eggs and bacon and sausages and jam-smeared bread and a teapot and already poured teacup of fragrant steaming tea.

"You must be Miss Gertrude Hooper," Augum whispered to her. "Leera told me about you. I must thank you for taking care of my beloved. She is my everything." His eyes lingered on the tray. "And you read my mind. That looks divine." His gurgling stomach agreed.

She smiled and curtsied. "Happy to be of service, my lord."

"My girl can be ravenous. Prepare for her hunger when she wakes." He made claws of his hands and swiped at the air.

The girl pressed a hand over her mouth as she chortled. "I will be sure to do so, my lord."

Nodding, he turned to Bridget, putting a hand on her shoulder. "I'm going to make a brief hop to Arinthia to check on them and pass on letters and news. I just wanted you to know that I—" He checked over his shoulder, waiting until Gertrude had excused herself from the room before continuing. "—buried the artifact under that tree we like to study under."

"Smart thinking," Bridget replied without looking up, a finger quickly trawling page after page as she searched for clues about gargoyles. "Mind if I stay? Charles told me your plan with these books and I want to stay busy lest I crash."

"But you *do* need sleep."

"I can manage for now. The kingdom's under attack and there's not a moment to lose."

Augum patted her shoulder. "I'm sure Ollie's fine."

She looked up, eyes suddenly watery. "We parted on such bad terms. I … I at least should have told him I love him …"

Augum smiled down at Bridget. "He knows, Bridge. He knows."

She sighed and returned to the page. "They heal, you know. The gargoyles. At least some of them have the power to suck a person dry of their blood and water and use that to heal themselves."

Augum rubbed his cheeks and then the scruff under his chin. "I'm not entirely surprised," he finally said. "But it is good to know. By the way, Leera mentioned something about seeing a gargoyle use a rune to prevent itself from getting snuffed."

"Now that *is* interesting …" The flames of the hearth gently crackled as they pondered the significance of that tidbit. "Don't be gone long and don't forget to enchant an alarm on something."

"Right." He enchanted an empty inkwell and placed it near Bridget. "I'll come back as soon as I can."

"Aug?"

"Mmm?"

"Snag a guard detail once you get there."

He gave a non-committal shrug and looked to Leera, happy to see Sir Pawsalot still curled around her tangled head of hair.

"I mean it, Aug. Don't take unnecessary risks. I don't want what happened to me to happen to you. We're going to have to work together with Ordinaries to survive."

Augum surrendered a nod. "If they can spare some, I'll take one," and he slipped outside before she could argue with him some more—she was always a bit of a worry wart, which sometimes grated on his nerves. He was just glad to be performing a normal errand for a change, even a brief one, as it would help clear his head, all while helping out his subordinates.

After focusing on the small town of Arinthia, he incanted, "*Impetus peragro*," and vanished with a *thwomp*. He appeared in a flat area of empty snow that had been the ancient and long-standing home of Castle Arinthian. The only thing remaining was the fountain out front, which depicted two warlocks frozen in a perpetual duel.

The Ravenwood, with its towering pines and spruces and firs and cedars, surrounded the grounds. Arinthia itself was built upon the ancient ruins of a town that had used the castle as shelter in prior eras, supplying it with troops and servants and keeping its stocks full.

It was snowing and windy and cloudy, yet the far eastern sky already began to blush with the slowly coming dawn, which came later in winter. Augum, letter bundle tucked under an arm and too tired to jog in the knee-high snow, pushed onward, soon reaching the guardhouse. Only a handful of the windows of the quaint stone-and-wood buildings of Arinthia were lit with candlelight.

Various buildings loomed in the snowy darkness—communal oven, surgeon, armorer, bowyer, carpenter, stone worker, tinkerer, and blacksmith. A large iron lantern hung underneath a sign that read "The Swinging Lantern Inn & Tavern." Hidden in the snowfall beyond sat others he enjoyed visiting now and then as castellan—Ben the Ropemaker, Tabitha's General Goods, The Good Medicine Shop, Lordrick's Leathers, Clayton the Cloth Merchant, and Hubert's Hay, Feed and Flour, which always donated a portion of each purchase to the poor every time he paid them a visit. And many others, some having sprung up only in the last year or so. He knew many names and faces, for they had bled together in the wars. He felt he owed them his best as castellan and as a hero of the kingdom.

But he had also been quite busy with running the Arcaner order, and so did not come around nearly as oft as he had used to. That and every time he did come, he was swarmed by the town's residents, especially the children, making every visit a somewhat tedious affair.

Just as he made his way to the barracks, two patrolling guards, both archers, spotted him—and promptly ran over.

"M'lord!" each said, repeatedly bowing before him, each passing on Endyear wishes. Both were in their mid-twenties.

"How good of you to come in these trying times!" the shorter of the pair said, a scruffy fellow with stained and crooked teeth. "We have heard some dark and surely tall tales."

"Is it true a calamity has befallen our brethren in the city of Blackhaven?" the taller asked.

"I am afraid it is," Augum replied. "The kingdom is under attack."

"By who?" the shorter asked.

Augum considered how to respond.

"Why does our lord hesitate?" the taller pressed.

"Winged monsters known as gargoyles," Augum finally said, figuring it was best to be blunt.

The soldiers glanced at each other.

"M'lord has quite the sense of humor," the shorter one said, and he brushed snow off his shoulders as he laughed, only for that laugh to die upon seeing the look on Augum's face. "M'lord is not jesting."

"I wish it *were* a jest," Augum said.

"Gods …"

"Fates have mercy on us all," said the other.

"Have you had any sightings?" Augum asked.

Both shook their heads.

"Is everyone accounted for in town? No disappearances?"

"None to report, sir," the taller one replied. "Except that a mail-carryin' 'lock from Antioc came through late last night and reported nothing had happened there."

"Then they hit the capital and nothing else really," Augum muttered to himself, rubbing his scruff. "Still, best be on your guard. What about anything peculiar? See anything like that?"

Both shook their heads again, only for the shorter to raise a finger. "Although, there *has* been a wee bit of a weed infestation in the barley fields, m'lord."

"That's right. It crept into one of the barns overnight and took it over," the taller added. "It's a slow mover, so the boys have been hacking away at it."

"Still, ain't nothin' like I ever seen," the shorter chimed in.

"Don't let any warlocks touch it," Augum said.

"There hardly ain't any about anyway," the shorter said. "Other than the passer-through, haven't seen any in days, come to think of it."

Augum, about to continue on to the barracks, changed his mind. "I'm going to have a gander at this infestation. I want you both to pass on to the barracks and to the families that the guard detail up at the castle is all right and alert. And make sure these are given to the families."

"Very good, m'lord," the taller one said, accepting the bundle of letters. "Was just about to inquire about them."

He pointed westward. "Barley field, you said?"

"The Chaddertons have been up all night snipping away at it," the shorter one replied.

Augum nodded and slogged onward, but then he saw Bridget's disapproving face swim before his mind and turned about. "Can I trouble one of you to come along?"

"I'll do it," the shorter one blurted.

"Damn," the taller one muttered.

The shorter one elbowed him. "Too slow, my good fellow."

While the shorter one caught up to Augum, the taller one bowed and walked off toward the barracks, bundle of letters under his arm.

"What's your name?" Augum asked as they stepped over the ancient ruins of what used to form the outer curtain wall of Castle Arinthian.

The shorter fellow slung his longbow with a shrug of the shoulder. "Hendricks, m'lord."

"And how long have you been on detail?"

"Three years now, m'lord. Was slavin' up in the mines during the Canterran siege. Those curs." His countenance darkened with memory, only for him to liven up. "I must say, m'lord, that this is a great honor for me."

Augum grunted, already regretting taking the soldier along. This sort of sentiment happened every single time he went into public.

"The reason I signed up here was because I wanted to work for someone who can stare death in the face and not blink. Someone who can guard the kingdom for real. Hope you don't mind me sayin' so, m'lord, but you ain't the sort who fancies himself fine with a blade, nor is you a mere jousting champion or famed archer. You is a hero—a *true* hero. And such a person comes but once in a generation or two."

"I'm but one of three," Augum replied. "Captain Burns and Captain Jones are due the same honor."

"Er … sure they are, but they is …"

"They is what, soldier?" Augum asked in a tired tone, already dreading the answer.

"Well, they is *women*, m'lord," Hendricks whispered.

Augum tried not to roll his eyes.

"And the gods saw fit to make women …" Hendricks shrugged. "You know …"

"I don't, actually." Augum, far too exhausted to discuss this tired old narrative, just wanting him to stop.

"Er … weak, m'lord. Women is meant for the home. For rearin' wee babes and tendin' to the house and servin' their husbands and—"

Augum stopped to face the man. "Do you see what I'm wearing?"

"The finest golden breastplate I have ever laid eyes upon, m'lord."

"It was crafted for the Founder of the Arcaner order—"

"And that order is composed of some of the bravest men of Solia."

"This breastplate was crafted around ten thousand years ago for the founder, whose name was Isobel Roseheart."

The young man blinked uncomprehendingly.

"She was a woman," Augum had to explain.

"Oh. I see. I guess there *are* exceptions, m'lord."

Augum gaped at him. "Archer."

The guard stiffened with a salute. "Sir, yes, sir!"

"Speak no more on the subject."

The young man reddened, mumbling, "Yes, sir. As you please, sir."

"Just …" Augum sighed and flapped a hand onward. "… lead me to the Chaddertons."

"Sir, yes, sir. This way, sir."

"And stop it with the constant sirs."

"Sir, yes—er, as you wish, m'lord."

As they trekked through frozen fields that grew potatoes and cabbage and peas and leeks in the summer, with Augum keeping a vigilant eye out, Hendricks seemed to struggle with a thought, made evident by the way his face squirmed.

"M'lord, why do you think the gods have blessed you lot whilst keeping us Ordinaries, well … ordinary? And don't say it's 'cause we don't try hard enough. I done near broke my brain tryin' to move a pebble when I was supposed to have come to the age o' the blossoming."

"Sometimes it's persistence, Hendricks. Some of you learn arcanery when you're eighty years old. But in truth, I'm afraid I don't have a full answer. Why are some of us born with bigger ears than others, or different colored eyes? Why are some of us better with subjects like arithmetic while others struggle with its basics?" Augum shrugged. "I'm not smart enough to understand such things." He raised a finger at the archer. "But it was a good question."

Hendricks's face split with a gigantic smile. "I reckon that do be the greatest compliment I ever received," he mumbled, nodding to himself. "Yes, sir, it do be. I'll be tellin' me wee ones how's I once impressed the lord dragon in the flesh." He glanced Augum from foot to head. "Er, that's all story, ain't it? The dragon stuff? Illusions cast by you warlocks, ain't that right? You don't *really* turn into a dragon, do you, sir?"

Augum stopped to look at the archer. He felt the shadow slip out from his mind and into his eyes. The archer yelped and sprang back.

"I reckon you is tryin' to frighten me, sir—and I is frightened, yes I am. Is m'lord angry with me?"

Augum had to look away lest the thoughts of carnage overtake him. How easily the longing for blood came. How he craved to spread his wings and let loose. But it was not for this man to experience. There was a new enemy who deserved that wrath ...

"I apologize," Augum said, continuing forth. "That was not for you to see."

"'S all right, m'lord. I don't understand your witch—er, warlock ways any more than I did when I was a wee boy." Yet the archer kept his distance after that, saying little else other than how "stiff of a winter mornin'" it was, for a chill breeze had blown through.

As the blush of dawn steadily lightened the clouds in the far east, they stepped over a rotting fence of gray hardwood.

"Right on ahead there, m'lord."

They walked onto a barren field that seasonally yielded barley. Ahead, amidst streaming curtains of falling snow, loomed the outline of a home and, beside it, a gray barn. It was the latter that drew their attention, for it was encased in yellow moss. Every window and door and plank was covered in it. Men and women stood on ladders all around the structure, snipping and hacking away at the moss with pincers and knives and sickles.

"They call it mustard moss on account of its color," Hendricks said. He cupped his mouth with his hands and shouted, "Ho! Our lord doth cometh!"

The men and women climbed down their ladders and assembled in attention, every single one curtsying or bowing and wishing, "Happy Endyear, m'lord."

"Happy Endyear to you as well, but please don't stop on my account," Augum said as he neared. But just as they reluctantly returned to their labors, the moss began moving as one giant sheet. It slowly sloughed off the building and crept along the snow—toward Augum. The farmers yelped and retreated away from it, signing skyward and muttering curses and prayers of protection.

"What in the sick hells," Hendricks whispered, pulling his bow off his shoulder and reaching for his quiver.

"That won't do you any good," Augum said, daring to step a little closer to get a better look. Yet the closer he stepped, the faster the moss moved, almost at a walking pace, forcing him to backtrack.

"By gods, it's after *you*, m'lord."

Augum watched the way the tiny yellow tentacles writhed forth. He took a few steps to the left and then to the right. Each time, the sheet of moss followed. "*Shyneo*," he incanted, lighting up his palm. The moss reacted by flaring, every tentacle on its forward lip rising like attacking spearmen of a vanguard army.

"Not me," Augum whispered. "It wants my arcanery."

"What do we do, m'lord?" one of the farmers called out.

"Stand back," Augum said. "I say stand back!" When they did so, and with the moss writhing along the snow toward him, forcing him to ever retreat, he made a sweeping-along-the-ground motion, incanting, "*Laitna fiuria potam*." A lightning river cascaded forth from his fingertips. It ripped into the moss, causing it to *sizzle* and *crackle*, burning whole swaths through it and splitting the moss into three wide columns that soon merged back into one sheet—albeit a smaller one.

Augum kept stepping back and repeating the spell, burning the moss into cinder and ash, until all that remained was a tiny patch.

"Does anyone have a stoppered jar?" he asked the farmers.

"I do, m'lord!" an aproned woman shouted, and ran into her farmhouse.

As Augum waited, he walked about in a circle, watching as the moss followed him and thinking how peculiar it was. The woman soon returned with a large empty pickling jar and even offered to scoop the moss up for him. Not wanting to touch it, Augum agreed, and the woman squatted down and used her bare hand to easily scoop up the remaining bit of moss into the jar. Then she stoppered it with a wide cork lid and beamingly handed it over to Augum.

"Guess we Ordinaries have our blessings too," Hendricks said, watching as the moss probed the interior of the jar like a snail, always angling toward Augum. "'Cause that moss don't care two bits for us Ordinary folks. Seems to only want you 'locks."

"Seems so," Augum mumbled, inspecting the jar. "Seems so ..."

MYSTERY OF THE SHARD

BRIDGET

" 'These travelers of the seas, who barely survived the crossing of the oceans, would find themselves marooned in lands of sheer terror,' " a bleary-eyed Bridget whispered, a finger trawling across a crinkled page from an old book. " 'There they would fight tooth and nail against beasts of folklore, who were themselves merely defending their kingdoms as hawks defend their nests. It was thus the sailors of the seas who brought back those fanciful tales that wrought so many a book of adventurous pleasure, during a time when the knowledge of how to cross said oceans was still a treasure passed down from one salt-blooded captain to the next. Mclidian the Mariner penned the famous poem: Lions and tigers and minotaurs and wyverns and lizards and krakens and gargoyles and goblins. In lands beyond such beasts rove, battling kingdoms in trials of woe …' "

Bridget looked to the nearby hearth, with its gently fluttering Endyear candle above on the mantel, and imagined lands teeming with such strange beasts, battling each other from their respective kingdoms or territories. Were the mythologies perhaps not allegorical tales as thought, but true representations that had been twisted over time into mythological proportions? After all, it had been as such with dragons, so why not with other continents? Was Sithesia but one of who knew how many others? But then what of those who believed Sithesia to be the center of the universe? How would they react to such discoveries? And the same question could be asked in respect to other planes—Ley and Endraga Ra, for example, which in conversation was treated the same as a folk tale.

"Don't get ahead of yourself, as these gargoyles could have come from another plane," Bridget muttered, turning the page to a chapter about the dangers of the oceans. Although her tired eyes followed the words along the page, her exhausted mind absorbed nothing, and instead wandered. She thought of flying across the oceans. Settling on islands like tired seagulls on passing fishing boats before taking the next hop. But that involved all sorts of dangers, including not being able to get back or getting stranded out in the open ocean. She thought of sitting inside the hold of a rocking ship, the last place an earth warlock wanted to be, exhausted and sick from the long journey. And just how long would such a voyage take? Months? Years? Decades? How big was the world or the plane or whatever it was they lived in?

It was trying to fathom these great questions no one had answers for that led her on a fantasy expedition, this one filled with friends, including Olaf, who in her mind took to the oceans with a bright smile, always pointing ahead and shouting, "Ho! Onward we go!" And their dog Sabby would jump at their sides with that big tongue hanging out of her husky snout and their children—she saw three—five—no, eight!—children around them, four girls and four boys and they would be jumping up and down excitedly crying out, "Mama! Mama! Look you there! We see laaaaaaaaaaaand! Laaaaaaaand hooooooooo!" And her handsome husband Olaf Burns would turn to her and plant a loving kiss on her lips before placing his hands on her shoulders and saying, "You did it. You built a bridge to the other side. To the lands beyond. You found a new continent." And she would say, "We built a bridge! We built a bridge!"

"Bridge," a voice said, echoing the sentiment. Suddenly her ship rocked in an ocean gale. "Bridge … wake up."

Bridget startled awake, the tempest of the ocean replaced by the crackle of a nearby hearth. By trying to rouse her, someone had rocked the ship of her dreams.

"Ollie?" she croaked, raising her face, only to find the page stuck to her cheek—she must have fallen asleep on the book.

"No word from Ollie yet, I'm afraid. Sorry to wake you as I know you need the rest, but I thought you would want to see this." Someone planted a jar filled with yellow moss before her.

Bridget blearily looked up to see Augum standing over her. "I just had the strangest, most vivid dream," she said, rubbing her sore and puffy eyes. "We traveled across the oceans in a ship and Olaf was there and so were my future children and he had taken my last name of Burns and he was happy that we built a bridge over the seas …"

"Sounds like quite the adventure."

"Adventure? It was more than an adventure …" But that made no sense, and she couldn't articulate what she had felt. Something about family and belonging and togetherness. She looked to the jar. "What's this, anyway?"

"A souvenir from a farm in Arinthia. Watch this." He reached down and turned the jar around.

"What am I looking at? Gargoyle moss?"

"Just watch."

She looked on as the moss crawled back toward the closest side of the jar. "What in Sithesia …?"

"Strange, isn't it? It didn't bother with the Ordinaries, but boy did it want to seek me out. I think it was drawn to my arcanery."

Bridget picked up the jar and revolved it in her hands, and was amazed that the moss, regardless of which way the jar was turned, always moved toward her or Augum—whoever was closest.

"Found anything good in those books?"

Bridget distractedly flipped back a page in the book and pushed it at Augum, who sat cross-legged beside her. Meanwhile Leera snoozed away in the bed, her breathing rhythmic and quiet.

" 'Lions and tigers and minotaurs and wyverns and lizards and krakens and gargoyles and goblins. In lands beyond such beasts thus roved, battling kingdoms in trials of woe.' " Augum flipped the book over to read the cover title. "*Ruminations on the Origins of Sithesian Mythologies*. Huh. You suggesting there're other kingdoms out there like the territories of the wolven? In lands beyond the oceans?"

"I don't know what I'm suggesting." She ran a hand through her long cinnamon hair, dug her fingernails into her scalp, and rubbed. "I hope he's all right."

"They're all trained to take shelter when needed. We'll get to them soon enough anyhow after we regroup." Augum's face softened. "I shouldn't have woken you. I'm sorry."

"No, it's fine. I only needed a nap," Bridget absently replied, for staring at the moss gave her an idea. She put down the jar and stood up, glancing around.

"Whatcha looking for?"

Her eyes settled on a fur cube lodged under Leera's clothes, which Leera had purchased at the academy arcane shop some time ago. Upon command, the cube arcanely turned into a coat, which could then be turned back into a cube for easy transport. She flicked a finger and the cube wrenched itself free from Leera's garments and shot to her hand.

"Clever," Augum said, catching on. "I'll open it for you." He settled before the jar and readied the lid. Upon receiving a nod from her, he unstopped the lid long enough for her to drop the cube inside. The pair then watched as the moss descended upon the cube, covering it completely. For a while, nothing happened except for the moss seemingly pulsing up and down, almost like it was breathing. Then it began to change colors, the coloring moving across its body in miniature waves that went faster and faster, until it reached a crescendo. Suddenly the moss burst with a multicolored flame, quickly fusing down into ashes, without damaging the cube. Amidst those ashes, something gleamed within.

Bridget and Augum glanced at each other before Bridget opened the jar, reached inside, and withdrew a tiny crystal shard. Like an opal, it seemed to change color depending on how it caught the light. She held it in her palm, flared a hand over it, incanted, "*Un vun asperio aurum enchantus,*" and found herself staring at a compacted blue-tendril essence of basic arcanery.

Augum, meanwhile, fetched the cube and incanted, "*Expandio cota.*" But nothing happened. "It sucked it dry," he declared.

Bridget examined the cube. "Not necessarily. The tendrils are gray but have not been disenchanted. Such arcane contraptions and artifacts sometimes recharge their arcanery from the arcane ether. I suggest we monitor it."

Augum in turn cast Reveal and the pair watched the cube and the tiny shard carefully. Sure enough, in time, bit by bit, the gray tendril geometries of the cube began to regain their blue color.

"At the current rate of regeneration, I estimate that the cube should be fully functional by tomorrow," Bridget noted. "Although the moss did indeed suck it dry, that drainage was not for nothing—" She held up the tiny shard. "Assuming the gargoyles started the moss, the question then is, what purpose do these shards serve?"

Neither one of them had a satisfactory answer to that, leaving them to ruminate over the tiny shard in silence. Bridget, still studying its tendril geometries, noticed that they were not just basic, but seemed to serve no function. There were no tendril tracings of, for example, an Object Track casting, or an Arcane Drain spell. The geometries simply indicated that the object was dense with arcanery.

Augum yawned for the third time in a row. "If you're not going to sleep, then I am. But one of us should be awake at all times."

Without looking away from the tiny shard, Bridget waved a hand toward the bed. "Go join your girl."

"I think I will." He patted her shoulder and began unstrapping his golden breastplate. "Don't let me sleep for more than a few hours. I want us to form a plan of defense and return to the city and get back in the fight."

Transfixed by the slowly regenerating cube tendrils and the tendrils of the shard, she only grunted in agreement. After washing his face in a ceramic basin, Augum slipped into bed with Leera, cuddling with her before promptly falling asleep, their arms draped over each other, Sir Pawsalot curled up behind their heads.

Bridget glanced over at them and felt her heart fill with envy. Here those two rascals were as cool and calm with each other as ever, knowing they might not be able to have children, yet she struggled with … with what, exactly?

"Stop being such a brat," she muttered, turning away and resolving to do something constructive. She returned her attention to the shard. Was it her sleep-deprived state, or did she spot a depth to the geometries? She rubbed her eyes and refocused. Yes, sublayers seemed to be hidden beneath the top layer of first-order geometries. Although she had good eyesight, these were far too small to see with the naked eye.

While the curtains continued to steadily lighten with dawn, she got up and quietly rummaged around the mess of Leera's room. "You live like a pig, girl," she muttered, kicking aside Leera's crumpled undergarments and mismatched socks. At last she found what she had been looking for beside a miniature chest—a bronze magnifying glass. Before moving on, she nudged the lid of the chest open—and found herself staring at a pile of coins.

For some reason her sleep-addled mind thought it was a fresh haul, perhaps found through illicit means, before realizing Leera had told her about it already. This was the shipwreck bounty she had been talking about before the gargoyles happened.

Bridget snorted and kicked closed the chest, then returned to the shard. She hovered the magnifying glass over the shard and examined the tendril geometries. "Yes, there's depth here, all right," she muttered, nodding to herself. Everything about this arcanery was foreign, from the tapestry-like weavings to the jagged leading order tendril edges.

"Don't recognize the fractaline patterns," she muttered. She had learned about fractaline patterns in the academy, which were patterns that never repeated yet stayed similar no matter the size. Tree branches, mountains, rivers, they all had similar patterns within themselves that never perfectly repeated. So too it was with the depths of tendril geometries.

The tendrils were bright blue, indicating freshness. They did not move nor did they change, indicating stability. She searched for a clue as to that underlying layer's function, but it remained elusive.

Ven del dubu, kel o sprutu, Bridget thought. " 'When in doubt, check the sprout,' " she translated aloud, quoting an academy proverb she had learned in Advanced Arcaneology class. It meant when one was unsure about what a tendril did, one could check the result. But how to trigger this arcanery?

"What if it functions like a key-lock mechanism?" she muttered. "Like a kargeyasnara?" She tried to imagine what sort of tendril geometries would fit into the jagged edges to make the shard function, but that quickly proved futile, for it was like trying to mentally concoct a piece of tree bark that perfectly slotted into a piece of bark from another tree.

Maybe she could identify the family of geometries and narrow it down from there. But to do that, she either needed an artifact enchanted with similar arcanery — or a series of comparison charts. Luckily she still had a book on the latter in her room, acquired from 10th degree Advanced Arcaneology class at the academy.

Bridget set down the magnifying glass, placed the opalescent shard into the glass jar, and rubbed her face. "Ugh, could use something to wake me up first." And some food. Her stomach was a cavern.

She got up, stretched her weary bones, and pulled on the ribbon. When Leera's servant Gertrude Hooper showed up, Bridget politely asked for the same breakfast she had served Augum earlier, as well as something strong to wake her up.

"We have all the teas of the seven kingdoms, Captain Burns," Gertrude whispered at the door.

"How about coffee?"

"I believe we have Tiberran, Canterran, and Nodian coffee."

"A large cup of Nodian coffee, please. With milk and honey." *That should wake me up.*

"Right away, Captain Burns." Gertrude curtsied and departed.

Bridget, meanwhile, was about to go to her room only to double back and cast an Object Alarm enchantment on each exterior handle of the double doors. The wind remained strong, the clouds still gray and heavy, threatening another snowfall. Out of curiosity, she took the terrace route to her room in order to get a look at Blackhaven, but it was obscured by blizzard clouds. The frequency of colorful flashes within had slowed a touch, but were still too dangerous to teleport into.

"Please be safe," she whispered. "All of you. Hunker and weather the storm as best as you can."

Frustrated from feeling so impotent, she whirled about and opened one of the double doors to her room, home of no less than five bookshelves. Her fingers soon danced over the spines of numerous books, many of which were for various academy classes—*Advanced Arcanery for the Element of Earth, 10th degree, 77th Edition. Sword & Sorcery, 10th degree, 225th Edition. Sithesian Languages and their Ancient Origins. Solian Legends, Myths, and Lost Histories. Great Duels of the Last Hundred Years,* and countless books on arcaneology and history and mythology, among odd others.

At last she found what she was for looking—*An Annotated Treatise on Arcaneological Families of Tendril Geometries and their Subgroups, 114th Edition.* It was a thick leather-bound book that took both hands to withdraw off the shelf and carry.

Classically the book was the precursor to studying the 11th degree spell Reveal and delving deep into arcaneology, but for Bridget, who had learned Reveal well ahead in a time of war, it had been an enlightenment. Besides wanting to become a teacher, there were two other professions she would seriously consider—librarian and arcaneologist, the latter mostly thanks to this book.

With the thousand-page tome pressed to her chest, Bridget returned to Leera's room through the hallway this time, receiving a greeting from Charles Poorman and the two guards, one of whom quietly opened the door for her, whispering, "Captain."

"Please hold it," Gertrude Hooper whispered from the stairs, hurrying up with a silver platter laden with a true bounty—sunny side up eggs beside strips of golden bacon and two shining sausages, toasted bread with a small bowl of jam, three types of cheese, quarter-cut strawberries, a fig, an apple, orange juice, and steaming Nodian coffee. "The kitchen threw some extras in, my lady," the woman said.

The guards salivated over the tray.

"Have them served next," Bridget said to Gertrude. "And be sure you eat as well."

"Yes, Captain."

"Just something small will do," one of the guards sheepishly said.

Gertrude placed the tray by the hearth and excused herself, with Bridget's compliments and thanks. Bridget then dumped the heavy book by the jar and licked her lips over the eggs and bacon in particular.

Bridget carved up one of the eggs and placed it, yolk intact, onto a piece of toast. Then she bit down and enjoyed the yolk exploding onto her tongue. After a divine sip of strong Nodian coffee that sent her blood racing with alertness, she nibbled at everything in turn, taking her time, relishing the various flavors that temporarily made her forget the kingdom's troubles.

Once well into the meal, she turned a finger in the air, and the book she had brought rotated on the floor to face her. She flicked the finger and the cover flipped open, and she kept flicking until the pages turned to the index. She munched on the apple as her eyes trawled the page, stopping at the index titled *Arcaneological families of alarms, page 160*.

She flipped to that page and found herself staring at various fractaline tendril geometries in chart form. She absently reached for the opalescent shard, readying to cast Reveal, when she noticed the shard, which she had dumped in the center of the jar, was now at an edge, with a drag trail through the ash that had been left from the moss burning up. Had she knocked the jar accidentally, causing the shard to move? But then wouldn't the ash have moved with the shard as per the principle of momentum?

Out of curiosity, she unstopped the jar, reached inside, and moved the shard back to the middle of the jar. The moment she let go, the shard moved back toward the edge. Except this time it wasn't toward her, but toward the door that led to the hallway.

Bridget swallowed the apple chunk she had been chewing, put the apple down, and raised the jar before her eyes. She turned it about and watched as the shard dragged itself through the ash and pressed up against the glass in the same direction.

She got up and walked toward that direction, stepping through the hall door, where the guards promptly jumped to attention with a salute, trying to hide the jam-slathered bread they had been eating behind their hands, while Charles asked if he could be of service.

"Not at the moment, but thank you," Bridget absently mumbled, carrying the jar onward into her room and then stepping through her doors and out onto the terrace. There she found herself pressed against the corner of the crenelated terrace wall that faced Blackhaven.

How strange, Bridget thought. *Strange and interesting and scary.*

Needing to study the tendril geometries of the shard closer, she returned to Leera's room and sat down beside the book. She flared her hand, recast Reveal, reached inside the jar, fished out the shard, and picked up the magnifying glass. Then she compared the tendril geometries with those depicted in the chapter about arcaneological families of alarms. The hand-drawn charts were a series of patterned lines, sometimes appearing like waves, at other times like jagged lines, sometimes like tangled noodles, or even like piles of needles. It really depended on the enchantment string involved.

"A poor match, but not far off," she mumbled, turning back to the index. She next tried the Offensive family, but that was an even worse match. She flipped around from arcaneological family to family. Not one was an exact fractaline match of the patterns she was seeing under the magnifying glass. The closest was still the Object Track families, followed by Unconceal and Telekinesis.

"Perhaps it's a fusion of the three," she muttered to herself. "A spell unknown to us Sithesians." That had to be it. A new family of enchantments would make sense considering the creatures they were dealing with.

Having witnessed the shard being pulled toward the city, all three roughly fit. "But pulled toward what?" she whispered, and looked toward the doors, trying to envision something beyond. She remembered seeing the writhing vines in the city and the prior sewer infestation. Assuming all would have devoured arcanery from susceptible sources — she doubted it could devour arcanery that was sunk to permanence — then other shards would have been created around the city. And then those shards in turn would have likely felt a pull toward that something. But … what? What could be pulling these shards toward itself? Or were these shards seeking home?

Bridget held up the shard before her eyes, feeling its tiny tug. One thing was for certain. The trio had to go wherever these shards were trying to get to.

FORTESCUE

LEERA

The purr of a cat stirred Leera awake. She stretched, yawned, and smacked her gums. Sir Pawsalot, who had been curled around her head, took that as his cue to do the same—a long noodle stretch, a tooth-revealing yawn, and a smack of his gums, adding a long lick of his own nose with his sandpaper tongue.

She reached up, drew him onto her chest, and used both hands to simultaneously rub his chin and his rump. The purring amplified as Sir Pawsalot closed his eyes and raised his rump and leaned into the rubbing that Leera deftly delivered. Once both feline and woman were satisfied, Leera leaned over to kiss a still-sleeping Augum on the cheek, pushed Sir Pawsalot into the crook of Augum's arm, and sat up.

Pale light shone between the slits of the red velvet curtains that swayed in cold drafts. Part of Leera wanted to worry about the kingdom, but she resolved to give her brain a chance to wake up from its stupor first.

Her vision trawled her messy room. An Endyear candle burned on a mantel above a low-burning hearth fire—and before that hearth lay a snoozing Bridget, curled up like Sabby. Seeing Bridget gladdened her heart. She only wished Sabby was cuddling with the poor girl too.

Beside Bridget sat a tray of mostly finished breakfast foods, including a half-full cup of dark liquid which, judging by the faint leftover smell, was coffee. There was also an empty stoppered jar with what looked like ashes in it.

Leera slid off the bed and ran a hand through her hair—only for it to get stuck in a bandage. She gently removed this bandage, noting how the wound had been cleaned and was barely a small crust—it had been one of those sharp small cuts that bled a lot but left little evidence.

"Thanks, Gertie," she whispered, assuming it must have been her new lady-in-waiting. "Knew it was a good choice to snag you, girl."

Desperately wanting to brush her tangled hair, she got up with a mild groan, lumbered over to her vanity, and glanced at herself in the pale light. She had circles under her eyes, her hair appeared as if she had been struck by lightning, and her freckled skin was dry and as pale as the light.

"Never has a creature so hideous stalked these swamps," she muttered, pawing around for a boar bristle brush. But finding anything in that mess turned out to be quite the chore, and after figuring she ought to finally let Gertrude clean her room—she had explicitly told her to leave the mess alone so she could find stuff—she gave up and shuffled over to the tray by Bridget. There she picked up the mug and downed the cold coffee in one long swig, scratching her butt with her free hand.

"Nodian," she muttered, licking her lips and tipping back the mug, trying to scavenge another drop or two. "Good even cold." She put the mug down and noticed the book Bridget had been studying, which lay open to reveal a slew of charts of arcaneological tendril pattern groupings. She stepped on the page, flicked a finger, and telekinetically flipped the cover over.

" '*An Annotated Treatise on Arcaneological Families of Tendril Geometries and their Subgroups, 114th Edition.*' " Leera snorted. "Bookworm," and she flipped the cover back, her foot having served as a bookmark.

Then she noticed the magnifying glass. "Now what could you have been using that for, Bridgey-poo?"

Thinking nothing much of it, Leera traipsed over to a washbasin. She splashed her face, dried it off with a towel she then tossed aside, made another fruitless attempt at finding that boar bristle brush, gave up, and went to her wardrobe. There she fished out a clean crimson robe and a set of clean undergarments, taking her time changing. Once robed, she went to the hallway door—only to hear voices on the other side. Two soldiers were quietly chatting with two servants—Gertrude Hooper and Charles Poorman—seemingly about castle gossip, who was dating who, who had insulted who, and so on, none of which held Leera's interest. The servants were no doubt trying to get their minds off the terrible happenings.

"But will we ever get back to normal times again?" she heard Hooper whisper.

"Good question," Leera muttered. Not in the mood for people yet, she chose instead to walk out onto the terrace—and was blinded by a shaft of sunlight. Scowling at it like a long-dead mummy, she used her foot to nudge the door closed, guessing the outer handles were alarmed—she didn't want to wake Augum or Bridget—and pressed forward into the wind.

But the sun, streaming in through a small break in the gray bank of clouds, soon disappeared again, leaving in its wake a most bitter chill. Leera raised her hood to protect herself and made her way around the terrace, examining the countryside. No fires, which was good, she supposed. Antioc seemed fine. As for Blackhaven, it was still ensnared in a thick blizzard that flickered with colorful silent flashes, although it seemed to her that the rate of that flashing had slowed.

"We need to get back there," she muttered, realizing they had left the city too long. But now they would be refreshed and ready to go. She didn't know how they would overcome the arcane snuffing effect, but she knew they had to try.

She took a hallway route back through the castle.

"My lady!" Gertrude blurted upon spotting her, hands pressed to her chest as if she'd gotten caught flirting with one of the guards.

"Gertie, can I trouble you to get the kitchen to whip up a second breakfast for all of us?"

"Er ... the kitchen has moved on to lunch detail, my lady, and I believe the commander and Captain Burns have already eaten."

"Lunch for all of us anyway, we're going to need the energy. The three of us are about to return to the city. And more of that Nodian scourge, please."

"The coffee, my lady?"

Instead of saying yes, Leera pointed at Gertrude with her index fingers and flicked a nod.

"Right away, my lady."

"Oh, and Gertie, thanks for—" and Leera knocked on the side of her head while making a clicking sound with her tongue.

"Er, sorry, my lady?"

"For the healing wrap."

"That wasn't me, my lady. It was Priya. But I will be sure to pass your gratitude on to her."

"Ah, thank you."

Gertrude hesitated as she opened the door for Leera. "Are you ... are you going to become dragons?"

Leera paused in the doorway. "I don't know. I don't know *what* we're going to do ..." She strode in, Gertrude closing the door behind her. The first thing Leera did was ready all three of their rucksacks, setting them side by side on the end of the bed. Next she secured Careena's sheath to her hemp rope belt, sliding Careena inside and giving the pommel a reassuring double-tap. Lastly, she strapped on the golden Dreadnought breastplate, pressing a loving hand onto the dragon-motif crest.

" '*Defendi au o dominia*,' " she whispered, quoting the motto. The three of them would be the last line of defense. If they fell, so would the kingdom. They had to get this right. Enough hiding.

Once ready, she went around the bed and sat down beside Augum. But instead of waking him, she watched him sleep. Sir Pawsalot still snoozed in the crook of one arm, while the other rested over his eyes. He had grown a bit of a scruff, but she didn't mind it at all—rather thought it made him look more handsome. She leaned down and nibbled on his lips, whispering, "Wake up, love." She longed for more—wished they had time and privacy for more—but the hourglass trickled onward. They had dawdled enough as it was.

Augum finally stirred, wrapping an arm around her neck and drawing her cheek to his lips. "Mmm," he toned, giving her a kiss. "Just a bit more sleep …"

"Lunch is on its way, and so is coffee. Then we have to go." She rubbed a hand on his face, trying to irritate him into wakefulness, cooing, "Get up, sleepy bum. Geeet uuuuuup." Augum tried defending against the hand, but she easily dodged his clumsiness and kept badgering him, smearing her hands on his nose and cheeks and mouth.

"Gross," he muttered.

"Bridget's leftovers are next if you don't start strapping up."

He moaned, rubbed his eyes, ran a hand through his scruffy brown hair, and sat up with a groan. Sir Pawsalot, annoyed, sauntered off to resettle on Augum's warm pillow.

"Come on. I'll help you with the breastplate," she said, fetching it.

"Can I eat first?" He blearily glanced about in search of the food.

"It's on its way." She nudged Isobel Roseheart's ten-thousand-year-old golden breastplate at him. "Come on, mister. We got gargs to slaughter."

"Gargs?"

She shrugged. "Gargies. Gargoyles."

He snorted. "You just think of that?"

"Yes."

He accepted the breastplate. "Derogatory. I like it."

She sat down beside him and slid the breastplate onto him, then resisted the girlish urge to tickle him as she strapped him up. But she did give his butt a squeeze, whispering, "Miss you."

"I'm right here."

"That's not what I meant."

He flashed her a sly grin. "Cheeky girl."

"You two at it again?" Bridget croaked from near the hearth. She groaned and curled back the other way.

"We will be if you don't get up," Leera said, and threw a pillow at her, which hit Bridget in the back. Bridget groaned, grabbed the pillow, and pressed it to her head. "Just one more hour."

"You had enough sleep, princess. Get strapped and grab a bow and quiver. Lunch is on its way up, then we got a kingdom to save." Leera dragged over Bridget's golden breastplate and unceremoniously dumped it on top of the pillow. When Bridget still did not move, Leera began to repeatedly prod her back with her toe. "Get uuuup, Bridgey-pooooo … geeeet uuuuuup …"

"Gods I hate you sometimes," Bridget muttered, stirring herself into a sitting position, face creased with sleep lines.

"You love me." Leera sat down behind her best friend, adjusted her hair for her, then strapped the breastplate onto her while Bridget sat dazedly staring into the fire. A single bell gonged throughout the castle.

"Is it afternoon or night?" Bridget croaked.

"Seeing as there's light coming in through the curtains, what do you think?"

"Smartass," Bridget muttered, whapping Leera's hand away when she tried to fix her hair a second time.

"By the way, have you seen my hairbrush anywhere?" Leera asked.

"No. Might help if you cleaned up your pigsty now and then."

Leera wrapped her hands around Bridget's waist, cooing, "Don't be so grumpy, Bridgey-poo …"

Bridget threw her hands off her. "Stop annoying me."

"Just trying to get you up. Are you up?"

"I'm up. I'm up. Leave me alone already."

Lunch soon arrived—three steaming trays held by three servants, one set before each of them. They dug in, with Bridget informing Augum and Leera about her discovery with the shard.

"Any theories on where the shard wants to go?" Leera pressed, mouth filled with a roasted pork loin—the kitchens kept a hog and a goose and several chickens in the cellar for slaughter, but only a few, and only prior to slaughter, all purchased from Arinthia.

Bridget stabbed a small potato with a fork. "We can deduce the gargoyles need the arcanery. We can also deduce they've been using the moss to root out hiding warlocks. Who knows, maybe that's how they found this castle." The skewered potato halted before her lips. "But then no one's reported moss in or around the castle, so who knows." She placed the potato in her mouth and chewed with a disconcerted grimace.

Augum crunched on a stalk of buttered and salted asparagus. "The real question is, what do the gargoyles need the arcanery for?"

They discussed various theories as they ate, caught each other up on what each had learned individually, then began planning their approach and how they would react once they encountered the gargoyles.

"We call them gargs now," Leera said, correcting Bridget. "Or gargies if you prefer. They don't deserve our respect."

"I don't think it's wise to underestimate them," Bridget countered.

Leera flipped her hands, glancing between Augum and Bridget. "Who's underestimating them? No one's underestimating anyone here. We're just insulting them. There's a difference."

Bridget rolled her eyes but did not argue further. Satisfied she had made her point, Leera nodded, picked up her last asparagus, and nibbled on its buttery end. She wagged it at the jar. "Just don't lose it." Then she wagged the asparagus at Augum. "What about the pyramid thing we captured? Did that move toward the city too?"

Augum slapped his forehead. "Gods, I completely forgot about that." He shot to his feet. "I didn't get an alarm, so it wasn't tracked down."

"You hid it?" Leera asked. "Smart."

"Yeah, by that tree we sit under in the summer."

"The one in The Tallows?"

"That's the one. I'll fetch it now."

"No," Leera blurted. "From here on we stick together. Let's fetch it together then hop to the city."

They agreed and quickly finished up, then did some last-moment tightening of their breastplates, securing of any swords and tightening of belts, before throwing their rucksacks over their shoulders. Bridget grabbed a bow and quiver from one of the guards and, for the first time ever, a sheathed dagger.

"I hope never to use it, but just in case ..." a pale Bridget informed them, swallowing, as if remembering something harrowing.

"Should we snag stuff from the vault?" Leera asked Augum. The castle had a sealed vault with a selection of potent arcanely enchanted equipment that they had used in the Legion war.

He shook his head. "Not unless we absolutely need to. I don't want any of it falling to enemy hands in case of a snuff and a capture."

Before they left, Leera placed both hands on Gertrude's shoulders. "I charge you with a sacred quest, Gertie."

Gertrude swallowed. "Er … all right, my lady, but I hope it's not anything dangerous …"

"That depends on if you can avoid getting buried."

"Buried, my lady …? Er … what sort of quest is this?"

"I charge thee …"

"Charge me …?"

"With …"

"With …?"

Leera threw open her arms at her room. "Cleaning this hovel."

Gertrude blurted out a laugh before smacking a hand over her mouth. "I will have it done, my lady," she said, sighing in immense relief.

They said their goodbyes, each giving Sir Pawsalot a scratch or cuddle, and after Augum imparted some last-moment instructions about castle care to Charles Poorman, the trio went to the terrace and in order to save stamina teleported individually to their favorite tree in the middle of The Tallows.

Upon appearing, each spread their hands into attack positions. But seeing nothing there, Augum pushed his way through the snow to the lone oak tree and dug about. It took a moment, but he soon fished out a small black pyramid.

"I guess that thing doesn't work the same way as the shards," Bridget noted. She unslung her rucksack and withdrew the jar, rotating it in her hands. They watched as the shard kept moving within, always aiming at Blackhaven. "Interesting," she said, and stuffed it back into her rucksack.

"Wait, what if we could get it to work?" Leera asked, nodding at the pyramid.

"We tried that, remember?" Bridget countered. "We can't even recognize the tendril geometries."

"Yeah, but we haven't taken it to a proper arcaneologist. An expert."

"If there's time," Augum said. "We need to save the city first. We need to save our people."

"But what if tracking down where the shards go will only result in us getting our arcanery snuffed? What if that pyramid thingy could somehow prevent that from happening? Shouldn't we at least *try* first?"

Augum exchanged looks with Bridget.

"She has a point," Bridget said.

"Yes, she—meaning me—certainly has a point," Leera cheekily countered.

Bridget ignored her and the three of them glanced past the looming Mount Barrow, toward the city of Blackhaven still in the thrall of a blizzard. Every heartbeat or so, the giant plume lit up with a flash, most often with blackish lightning, creating veins that made it look like a necrotic brain.

"We all got pinned down in there," Bridget said, "forcing us to hide. All it would take is a little bad luck and we'd find ourselves enslaved ... or worse."

"Then the kingdoms would have *no* hope," Leera added.

Bridget wagged a finger at Leera. "Last night you said something about the gargoyles having to press a rune on their bodies to prevent being snuffed."

"I did indeed," and Leera proceeded to detail exactly what she had witnessed.

At the end of her retelling, Augum rubbed his scruffy chin. "So they counteract the snuffing of arcanery ... using arcanery?"

"Using runecraft," Leera corrected. "Which technically *is* arcanery, I know, but the mechanics are different." She shrugged. "Then again, maybe it's all the same in how they use it. But it's not like I'm the expert or anything—Runes was like my worst subject. Anyway, the point is, if *they* can learn this snuff-prevention runecraft or arcanery or whatever, then so can we."

Augum sighed. "Maybe. Maybe ..."

"Regardless, we should still take this artifact to a competent arcaneologist," Bridget threw in.

Augum hefted the pyramid in his hand. "I guess we're all thinking of the same person and shop, aren't we?"

The girls nodded.

"Fortescue," Leera said, raising an arm toward Augum and Bridget. "Everyone remember where it is, right? Good. Meet you there. Oh, and flare up so that we know if we're snuffed," and she flared her ten watery arm rings. Then she took a concentrative breath, visualizing the target destination as vividly as possible, before incanting, "*Impetus peragro.*"

One by one, the arm-lit trio appeared in a dingy and snow-filled alley, tighter than most on account of its age. The snows of the blizzard swirled in the high winds, ruffling their robes and making them shield their faces with their arms.

Not two heartbeats in, the air lit up brightly. *Crack* went a bolt of lightning so close they didn't have time to think before the *whoosh* blew through them, instantly snuffing their arm rings.

"Damn," Augum said, unsheathing Burden's Edge.

Leera followed suit by unsheathing Careena and stepping before a small and battered oak door set into old stonework—albeit a door without a handle. Etched in the stone above were the words *The Recalcitrant Scholar*.

"Been a while," she said, raising a fist and rapping on the door with her knuckles, muttering, "Hope the old coot's still alive."

"She's very old so knock louder," Bridget said while on the lookout with Augum.

Leera thumped the door with the side of her fist. "Come on, come on, come on," she sang, dancing from foot to foot. "Let us in before a garg appears."

"Maybe she's been kidnapped," Augum said.

"Don't say that," Leera blurted. "I don't even want to entertain such a—"

The door was flung open, revealing an old woman hunched over a cane, trembling to stay upright. Cloudy eyes hiding behind thick spectacles squinted at Leera.

"Who are you and what do you want?" Pierra Fortescue barked. The old arcaneologist had mottled ebony skin and chin whiskers and wore a headscarf and a dirty turquoise robe stretched by a protuberant belly. A string of mud-colored pearls clung to a leathery neck, from which also hung a gold chain leading to a gigantic magnifying glass.

"You're alive," Leera blurted, cheeks immediately prickling from the shame of saying something so stupid.

"Not for long, no doubt. Are you human? I have been snuffed and thus cannot tell. But I suppose you would not answer me if you were, or perhaps whisk me off. I therefore conclude that you must be human. And warlocks to boot. Or used to be." She fiddled with the giant magnifying glass and brought it to her eyes, magnifying one of those eyes to saucer proportions. "I recognize you," she said, giant eye blinking. "You're the dragons who rove the skies, the ones I helped in the war with—"

"Mrs. Fortescue, please, can we enter?" Leera pressed.

"We must speak urgently," Augum added, holding up the pyramid. "We've captured an artifact from the invaders."

"Now look what we have here," Mrs. Fortescue cooed, taking the pyramid with grubby hands.

Even through the blizzard, the entire sky seemed to light up with light.

"Ooh, that was a big one," Mrs. Fortescue said. She raised three fingers, dropping one at a time. "Three ... two ... one." They heard the *crack* and felt the *whoosh* rip through the area. "And far. Notice how it comes with the sound and not the light? Interesting, is it not?"

"Mrs. Fortescue, *please* ..." Bridget said.

"Yes, yes, just close the door behind you," and the old woman shuffled inside.

The trio piled in and quickly slammed the door behind them, plunging them into near darkness, for only a single candle lit up a distant desk strewn with parchments and ornate leather-bound books. Looming in that darkness stood towering cubbyholes overflowing with more books and scrolls and tablets, with still more sitting in teetering piles throughout the place. There was a heavy smell of minerals and myrrh and stale parchment. Unlit iron candelabras draped in cobwebs hung from a high ceiling.

"How did you know it was safe to open the door?" Leera asked, sheathing Careena while Augum sheathed Burden's Edge.

Without looking, Mrs. Fortescue used her cane to point at a pinprick of light near the side of the door. "Peephole. I didn't see wings, but I did see the blur of red clothing, so I took a risk calculating they were crimson robes." She nodded, inspecting the pyramid as she shuffled onward. "I was proven right."

"You saw them?" Augum pressed. "The gargoyles?"

Mrs. Fortescue grunted and with a tired groan plopped down on a chair behind her desk. She placed the pyramid beside an assortment of exotic bird-feather quills and drew the fat candle near. Then she fumbled for her magnifying glass, but was having such a hard time with it that Bridget rushed over to fetch it and hold it over the pyramid.

"Thank you, dear," Mrs. Fortescue said.

"Happy Endyear, Mrs. Fortescue," Bridget replied.

"Bah."

Leera glanced about but did not see any sign of an Endyear candle — or of any decorations.

"Now then, we have here a smooth stone of unknown origin. Tiny gold flecks. Perfect and sharply cut edges." Mrs. Fortescue's head bobbed up and down. "Mmm, we would have to time it."

"Time it …?" Leera asked. "Time what?"

Mrs. Fortescue raised a finger and held it aloft until there came another *crack* and another *whoosh*. "That."

"There's a ship to the distant north," Augum blurted. "A gigantic landing ship with many sails."

"There might be more up and down the coast," Leera added. "But we have not had confirmation yet." She would have heard something from Mr. and Mrs. Seahorse.

"We haven't been able to get back into the Black Castle," Augum went on. "Let alone get in contact with the ambassadors to the other kingdoms. They've been kidnapping people left and right. Draining others, sometimes their blood and water."

Leera shook her head sadly. "We don't know much at all."

Mrs. Fortescue grunted to all their points whilst studying the pyramid. "What *do* you know?"

"We know that there is a summoned moss that is attracted to arcanery, which the moss then uses to create some sort of shard," Bridget said, unslinging her rucksack whilst trying to hold the magnifying glass, only to end up handing the bag to Leera as Mrs. Fortescue whapped Bridget's hand to get her to keep the magnifying glass still. Leera fished out the jar with the opalescent shard and placed it on the desk beside the pyramid.

After Bridget explained a bit more about how the shard was created, Leera flicked the jar with a finger, making a glass *ting* sound. "It moves toward something." She rotated the jar and Mrs. Fortescue watched the shard move to always face the same direction.

"Like lodestone," Mrs. Fortescue muttered. "But what of the ash?"

"The soot is what remains of the moss," Bridget added. "The moss sucked out the arcanery, burning itself in the process and reducing down to that tiny shard there, which seems to want to go somewhere."

"Mmm," Mrs. Fortescue toned, using the magnifier to study the shard through the glass. "Mmm."

"Do you think they know of our existence?" Augum asked. "Us as dragons, that is?"

"If they did, would you still be around to ask the question?" Mrs. Fortescue said without looking up. "Perhaps they await your first casting of the Spirit of the Dragon simul, which would reveal to them who you are. Perhaps they feel themselves superior to you and have no fear of you. Perhaps they do not believe you exist, having arrived after you last turned into them. Perhaps they care not at all about your existence one way or another."

"What do they want from us?" Leera asked.

"Since the dawn of civilization—no, since the epoch of the club and rock and the awakening of fire, what did all superior beings want with inferior ones?"

The trio exchanged ominous looks. No one wanted to voice the answer to that question.

"Does the tree deserve to be cut down for firewood? Does the chicken deserve to be slaughtered for its meat? Do humans deserve annihilation and absorption?" Mrs. Fortescue looked up, cloudy eyes glancing past them to stare beyond the walls. "Three dragons?" She snorted. "We'd need hundreds …"

Leera pressed her hands on the old woman's desk and leaned forth. "What are you saying, Mrs. Fortescue? That we can't beat them? What do you know about gargoyles? What are you not telling us?"

"Omnio incipus equa liberatus corsisi mei." Mrs. Fortescue nodded at the trio expectantly, to which they chorused, " 'All begin equal but only the curious thrive,' " quoting the famed motto of the Library of Antioc. Mrs. Fortescue leaned back, allowing Bridget to place the magnifying glass on the desk before the woman and join Augum and Leera. "Curiosity oft begets answers, though sometimes such answers prefer the darkness to the light."

She folded her wrinkled hands on top of her belly and expelled a wheezing breath. "Some of us have had the privilege of seeing through the clutter of history, which is filled with countless allegories and parables and myths and legends. Some such tales were blown out of proportion from their original happenings, while others were made up to convey a point. To tell a story. And some have to be fitted together like puzzle pieces. In fact, we have accounts from the sea wanderers themselves—" She looked to the cubbyholes, raised a finger, and wiggled it about, only to grimace and drop the finger when nothing happened. "Force of habit. Third cubby from the top. Use the ladder, please. I don't want you scaling my shelves like monkeys and ruining precious work."

"Yes, Mrs. Fortescue," Augum said, stepping over to draw an old iron ladder forth, prop it up against the cubbies, and climb it to reach the third cubby from the high ceiling. "Is this it, Mrs. Fortescue? *Terrible Tales of the High Seas?*"

Mrs. Fortescue's reply was a mere grunt.

Augum brought down an old and shabby book. Upon stepping off the ladder, he let the book slam onto the floor with a *thud*. "Sorry," he muttered as Leera suppressed a snort behind a fist at his forgetful attempt at Telekinesis. He picked it up and rushed it to Mrs. Fortescue, mumbling, "Same force of habit."

She grunted again, opened the book to a certain chapter, and read an excerpt aloud. " 'It was with great violence that these beasts of the ocean attacked us, nearly tearing our ship asunder as they had our sister ships in times past. But The Fates kept our bow straight and the vicious winds, whipped up by our talented air warlock, kept us slicing through the waves. The bow, fitted with a sword, cleaved ocean beasts in two when they attempted to ram into the ship. Some had to be harpooned to be eaten, others blasted apart by our best warlocks.

" 'And then there were the storms. One could not fathom the deafening winds that threatened to break the mast and capsize the vessel. Waves so tall the entire ship seemed like a cup bobbing between swells. Lightning unlike any lightning humans had ever seen. And these tempests could hardly be calmed and sometimes caused unusual happenings. Once a rain of fish came down upon our decks. On another day, a rain of black oil. A freshly oiled sister ship suffered a bolt of lightning and instantly went up like tinder, and sailors screamed even as they jumped into the violent sea to douse their burning bodies. Their flames snuffed, and they were quickly torn apart by the predators lurking beneath the waves, their screams quenched suddenly when their heads were yanked below water.

" 'But these monsters and storms were nothing against what we faced on the other side. Whole kingdoms of beasts who fought each other. It was only by the grace of the Unnameables that three of us made it back, and only because our mighty warlock teleported us the final leg when our poor ship at last succumbed to the largest serpent these old salt eyes had ever seen.' "

Mrs. Fortescue closed the book. "You ask me what I know. I know that the lands beyond are not for humans. That humans there are prey for predators. Over there, our best existence is as slaves."

"This language we understand," Leera cut in, feeling the strange need to defend their honor as humans—and feeling a shadow rear up behind her thoughts. "For we are predators of the skies. We can destroy and annihilate, as we did in the last war."

Mrs. Fortescue looked at her and her eyes swept downward. Leera looked down to discover she was holding a clenched fist. She relaxed her hand and dropped it, clearing her throat. "Forgive me, Mrs. Fortescue."

"I know what you are," the old woman whispered. "But you ought to take heed and not turn into that which you defend against. Quoting Theodorus Winkfield, 'Ask thyself, are thou a beast or art thou a soul?' " She looked to the pyramid. "To have a soul is to be human."

Leera wanted to reveal to this venerable old woman that they already struggled with this. She wanted to tell her about The Callousness of the Predator and how it threatened their very souls. But it was dangerous to reveal that secret, lest it fall into the wrong hands.

"Do gargoyles have souls?" she asked instead.

"Does a lion have a soul, or do we simply project pride unto his mane? Yet even the lion can feel pain upon sustaining a wound, or sorrow upon seeing its cub perish."

"So far we have seen two kinds of gargoyles," Bridget said. "Soldier types who cannot fly and cannot cast arcanery, and ones who *can* fly *and* cast arcanery, usually using runes emblazoned on their very bodies."

"Runes on their bodies. That is an arcanery unfamiliar to us humans."

Suddenly, ten rings of water, lightning, and earth flared around the trio's respective forearms, indicating they all had access to their arcanery once again.

"Quickly now," Mrs. Fortescue said, waving Bridget back over whilst turning her attention to the pyramid and flaring a hand over it. "*Un vun asperio aurum enchantus*," she incanted. Bridget grabbed the woman's magnifying glass and held it above the pyramid.

"Interesting," Mrs. Fortescue said. "Interesting." She turned the pyramid about in her hands, continually repeating the same word. After having examined all five sides, she put it down and impatiently indicated the jar.

Leera realized the gesture was meant for her, and so she unstopped the jar, withdrew the opalescent shard, and held it before the giant magnifying glass.

"Interesting …"

"Forgive me for opining, venerable one," Bridget whispered, keeping the magnifying glass steady, "but I tried comparing the sublayer to known arcaneological families. The best I came up with is a combination of three families—Object Track, Unconceal, and Telekinesis."

"I would say you are within the correct arena, my dear. The general arcaneological framework of this shard is simple. It is indeed a reduction—that is, a compression of arcanery, turning it into a vessel. But that sublayer is a seeking enchantment enchanted to bring this item to a pre-determined destination. It's remarkably complex arcanery—"

The doorframe lit up with several rapid flashes of bright light, immediately followed by a monstrous and equal number of cracks of thunder that shook the building, bringing with them a *whoosh* that once again snuffed their arcanery.

Mrs. Fortescue grunted and dumped the shard back into the jar. It bounced a couple of times at the bottom before settling—and sliding to one edge. She tilted her head at it. "Interesting. Its own enchantment did not snuff. It is immune to the snuffing effect." She tapped the jar with a chipped fingernail. "Their incantations factored for this very thing. This is premeditated and highly advanced arcanery."

"Where does it want to go and why?" Leera asked.

She pushed the jar toward her. "That I do not know, Champion. But think about what a vessel of potent arcanery could mean. What would be the purpose of such a construct?"

Leera thought it a rhetorical question and so did not reply. Judging by their silence, Augum and Bridget evidently thought the same.

As Bridget took her rucksack back from Leera and stuffed the jar into it, Mrs. Fortescue returned her attention to the pyramid, steepling her hands before it and pressing those hands against her nose. The trio quieted, letting her concentrate. Outside, the wind gusted, rattling the door and making whistling noises through the old beams of the shop.

"From what I was able to gather in my limited time observing this artifact, which I shall dub a *pentastone* as it has five sides, I can conclude that each side is responsible for a different effect. The first side is a complex Object Track enchantment, which renders this artifact dangerous."

"We concluded that too," Augum said. "But we have not been tracked."

"That you know of. The second side I recognize from having studied an artifact I believe you three are familiar with—a scion. I had the fortune to study one when I was a budding arcaneologist, and I recognize some of the snuffing signatures."

"We witnessed the gargoyle use it for that exact purpose," Augum said.

"The third side is of the arcaneological healing family, but no more can I tell you on that as I did not have the time to look further into it, and the tendril geometries are quite foreign to me. The tendril patterns of the fourth side are even less familiar to me, and I would hesitate to even guess at its function. The bottom, however—" She turned the pentastone over to reveal the bottom. "The bottom derives from the necromantic family of arcaneology. I believe it can be triggered to drain arcanery, for I recognize the Arcane Drain tendril pattern methodology."

The trio exchanged more ominous looks.

"Of all its visible functions, it is the sublayer that interests me most, for like the shard, it reveals to me that the pentastone also acts as a vessel of arcane stamina, but one significantly more potent than that shard." She leaned back and sighed. "I am afraid that is all I can tell you about this artifact."

Leera fidgeted with her hands. "So ... so there's no function to block the snuffing?"

"None that I could discern as such."

"I watched one of the gargoyles press a rune on its body to prevent a snuff," Leera added. "We were really hoping we could use this artifact to do the same."

Mrs. Fortescue hummed. "Perhaps you can learn how to cast such a preventative power yourselves, or perhaps track down another artifact to accomplish the feat. Unfortunately, I fear that such knowledge resides not on this continent."

"You think it's overseas, in the land of the gargoyle," Leera said.

The old woman gave a single nod before raising a knobby, arthritic finger. "In our history, there have only been seven artifacts known to have the power to snuff arcanery."

"The scions," Leera whispered, thinking of those ancient crystal orbs.

"And so we have not had enough experience with the arcane snuffing effect to mount a defense against it. The gargoyles, however, seem to have that experience and knowledge. You must therefore look to them. For the sake of us all, I hope you glean or steal or earn that knowledge. However you can do it, it must be done. For as long as they can snuff our arcanery, we are nearly defenseless."

Her words left them standing in cold silence.

"You've been very helpful, Mrs. Fortescue. Thank you," Augum finally said, taking the pentastone and placing it in his rucksack.

"Follow where the shard takes you. Study the gargoyles from a distance. When able, teleport away before the snuff hits you. And this ship you told me about … would that be where they take our kidnapped people to?"

"We don't know," Leera said. "It's certainly big enough, so it's possible."

"Mmm." She raised her whiskered chin. "If my suspicions are correct, that ship, and perhaps more like it, will be used to transport slaves back to their land." She shook her head sadly. "Eons of denunciations. Now, through their suffering, Ordinaries will learn the true value of us warlocks." She looked to each of them. "Assuming, of course, that you can save them. That you can save us all. I am not one for such blessings, but may the Unnameables lend you speed in your quest, and may The Fates light your path in the dark days to come."

"Please, leave this place," Leera begged. "The moment your arcanery returns, take flight."

"And go where? I am an old woman. My hands and knees and bones ache. I can barely eat or stand or sleep. What existence would I carve out there without my books and scrolls and servants? I am tired. Here at least I have provisions. If they come, they come."

The trio, not knowing what to say, bowed out of respect to the old woman. As they went to the door, Mrs. Fortescue, leaning heavily on her cane for support, shakily stood up. "I am Pierra Avis Fortescue, of the clan Fortescue, of the Sierran desert of the south. Remember me while I am still here, for the end of our world is nigh."

"We will remember you, Mrs. Fortescue," Augum whispered. "But our world lives still …"

"So don't give up on us just yet," Leera said, raising her hood in preparation for the blizzard. "The gargs have yet to see the dragon flex its wings." She winked, sniffing and trying to keep the tears from falling, before opening the door, checking that the coast was clear, and being the first to step through.

THE SPIRIT OF THE DRAGON

AUGUM

With his hood up, Augum used his left arm to protect his face from the onslaught of the blizzard, the cold hilt of Burden's Edge clasped tightly in his right hand. The narrow alleys made the gusts that much fiercer, swirling snow about and piling it up in dune-like drifts. The fresh snowfall turned the trek into a slog.

He kept checking over his shoulder to make sure the girls were still there. Now and then Bridget would say things like, "Take a right. Now a left. Keep going down this alley." They were following the shard's lead. Like a ship's swiveling lodestone, it always pointed in one direction.

The screams of the city had subsided overnight. Now and then, one still pierced the blizzard like a knife. It made Augum fear for everyone they knew and everyone in Sithesia. He admired how stoic Bridget was, for she had to be terrified for her beloved Olaf. He could only hope that his best friend was hunkering in the bowels of the Black Castle along with the others.

Augum wasn't the praying type, but he kept thinking things like, *Unnameables keep them safe*, and *Fates let them be*. He tried not to think of his friends and their terrified faces, of the countless innocents getting torn from their beds, or of the question surely on everyone's mind: *Where are our dragons? Why have they not come to defend us?*

Trying to figure out how to engage the enemy is where we are, Augum thought. Warring against another human kingdom was generally predictable. Warring against beasts from myth with the ability to snuff arcanery was something else entirely. And all it would take was one mistake, one slip up, and it would be over …

The trio battled the winds, meandering through alley after alley, avoiding the cobbled streets when possible, with no idea if wherever the shard was taking them would appear around a corner or was still leagues away. Due to the regular occurrence of snuffing strikes, they were without their arcanery most of the time. At one point, while fully able to cast arcanery, they heard the rhythmic marching of troops from a nearby street.

"That's got to be the army mobilizing," Augum said to the girls. "Let's go and talk with the commander and—"

"No," Leera blurted. "They'll want our help but we can't get mixed up in a fight right now."

"I agree with Lee," Bridget said. "We need to focus."

Augum looked longingly down the alley that led to the street of marching soldiers. The pull of duty and honor was strong. Then the callous shadow peeked out from behind its curtain to remind him that greater glories awaited, and he nodded and continued forth.

Sometime later in the Rose Quarter, as they wound their way around an old boarded-up stone tower surrounded by a copse of oaks and maples, Bridget blurted, "Wait! Look." She held forth the jar, and they saw that the shard had started to climb a little ways up the interior of the glass surface.

Not knowing what this meant, they only exchanged a look before continuing on.

"Mrs. Stone supposedly once lived here for a time," Bridget noted as they passed the stubby, boarded-up tower.

"She supposedly lived everywhere and did everything," Leera muttered.

A block later, they found themselves standing at high walls that surrounded the courthouse and prison.

Augum glanced at the jar and saw that the shard was halfway up its surface, angling skyward. Whatever it was it wanted to reach was close.

"What's that noise?" Leera asked. "Anyone else hear that?"

They stood still to listen. Sure enough, amidst the winds, Augum began to pick out a constant rumble, like two millstones grinding together.

"What is that?" Leera asked.

No one had an answer, and so they pressed forth, this time walking around the walls of the courthouse and prison. And as they did so, the shard moved within the glass to always point toward those walls—whatever the shard wanted was within the compound.

Suddenly Augum heard the flap of wings, and hissed, "Duck!" They pressed themselves against the wall and hunkered as twenty gargoyles flew overhead and into the compound.

Augum realized it would be foolish to try to get through the main entrance, which would surely be watched and guarded. He glanced about and found exactly what he was looking for—a five-story building, tall enough to see into the compound.

After explaining his plan to the girls, they set off toward the building, which was a multi-residence construct with a steeply pitched roof, balustraded balconies and, ironically, gargoyle motif rain spouts. One of the pair of gilded front doors, usually guarded by a footman as it was a residence for the nobility, was hanging askew, and there was glass and wine all over the floor.

Except it wasn't wine, as Augum discovered after stepping in it and finding it sticky.

"Someone's party was rudely interrupted," Leera muttered.

Just as they were going to step inside the lobby of the building, there came a growling from nearby. Instinctively they hunkered in the doorway of the broken door, searching for the source of the noise.

"Back where we came from," Bridget whispered.

Augum, noticing how her breathing changed, placed a hand on her shoulder. He was about to tell her that this time they had their arcanery when a bluish curtain of snow swept through, and he felt the telltale *whoosh* that heralded a snuffing.

"Shoot," Leera said, and she and Augum unsheathed their swords.

A suddenly pale Bridget scrambled to stuff the jar into her rucksack, unsling her bow, and shakily notch an arrow.

Augum refocused on the direction they had come from, until the silhouettes of three animals emerged, their forms hazy in the snowfall.

"Just wild dogs, let's go," Leera said.

Bridget grabbed Leera as she turned away. "Those aren't dogs."

Sure enough, the three animals turned out to be people on all fours—a middle-aged man and woman, the latter with an apron, and a young man. They were sniffing at the trio's footprints half a block away, and approaching fast.

Bridget gasped, the bow trembling in her hands. "It's a family. Unnameables, it's a family …"

"They'd gone insane," Leera said.

Augum studied the pitiful people carefully. Their movements were quick and instinctual, eyes darting about, noses sniffing this way and that. Froth gathered at the corner of their mouths, as if they had gone rabid.

He shook his head. "That is not insanity. I think it's … I think it's some form of necromancy."

Bridget repeatedly shook her head, bow trembling so violently it dislodged the nocked arrow. "We can't kill them, we can't kill them, we can't kill them …"

"You two go inside, I'll get them to chase me a bit, then lose them and meet you back here."

Leera immediately grabbed his arm, firmly saying, "*No*. We don't split up. Besides, the snow is too thick for running."

Realizing she was right, yet the rabid people were now only a quarter block away, Augum knew they only had two options—hide or fight. But something about that sniffing told him the cursed family would hunt them down, and perhaps draw the gargoyles to them. He glanced at the askew door, and an idea came to him.

"Quick, inside and barricade the doors," he blurted, and they propped up the broken door and shoved everything in the lobby against it—two long gilded settees, four armchairs, and a smattering of gilded tables.

Just as Augum finished piling up a decorative wine barrel, there came a snuffling set of growls—and a slam against the doors, which kept rattling thereafter as the unfortunate creatures scrabbled at it like wild dogs.

The trio backed away.

"It's holding," Augum said. "Let's get a move on," and they turned about to search for a way up.

"What's on the ceiling?" Leera asked as they padded down the lobby.

Augum looked up to see sets of scrape marks, usually in pairs. They went along the halls and even into the rooms. He shook his head in an *I don't know* fashion. He was about to ask Bridget what she thought when he noticed her standing still, staring back at the entrance, shoulders heaving as she white-knuckled her bow.

"Hey," he whispered. "We can't help them now."

She swallowed, nodded, and reluctantly shouldered her bow and tucked the arrow back into the quiver. "I think you're right about necromancy," she said, withdrawing the jar. "Which might mean gargoyles can use necromancy as a primary element."

"If that's the case, then something tells me we haven't seen anything yet," Leera replied, and after exchanging ominous looks, they continued on.

The building was luxurious enough that it had an arcanely enchanted iron elevator mechanism—which they avoided, for they did not want to get stuck between floors. They instead took the nearby marble stairs, and, with the growling and snuffling fading behind them, wound their way toward the top floor, where the scrape marks continued and the rumbling noise became much more pronounced. After passing the third floor, a second harmonic joined the first, a higher-pitch hum much like a hive of bees. Augum realized why that was.

"We're above the courthouse wall," he whispered.

They finally reached the fifth floor, stepped onto a lush crimson carpet—and promptly found the detritus of a whole supper—overturned bowls of soup and plates of chicken and potatoes and scattered flatware and shards of fine porcelain and etched glass. Tables and chairs lay about in pieces and every single door was ajar.

"The whole floor was caught having a party," Leera whispered, picking up a piece of chicken only to toss it aside. "It's ice cold." She peeked into a room only to whisk her head back and sigh.

Augum looked inside and saw a body—or rather a dried-out husk depleted of its blood and water.

One room in particular was brighter than the others, and so they skulked toward it. From within, a wispy curtain with a rose pattern fluttered out into the hallway like a ghost trying to escape. But as they neared, it wasn't roses Augum had spotted, but blood.

Mistook it like I mistook the wine, he thought, pressing against the hallway wall before peeking inside. The room was filled with rubble— and a giant hole in the wall, large enough for gargoyles to step through. The ceiling scrape marks began from that hole, telling Augum they were the result of the tips of gargoyle wings dragging along the ceiling. Part of one wall was studded with three crossbow bolts, indicating some of the residents had guards, likely to protect themselves from kidnappers or assassins—the rich had their problems with the corrupt underworld.

There were splatters of blood near the large hole, telling Augum that one of the gargoyles might have sustained a hit. And that explained the husk of a body, which must have been used to heal the wounded monster.

Augum led the girls into the room and they flanked the gaping hole in the wall, with Augum on one side and the girls on the other. The blizzard was thick and it was difficult to see anything through it, but all they needed was a temporary lull between gusts to snag a peek.

Bridget held up the jar and they all saw that the shard was now pressed against the middle of the glass side. Whatever it wanted to reach was directly ahead. As was his habit of late, Augum checked his forearm, dismayed to see it dark. The feeling of near total vulnerability was awful and humbling, yet it had to be how Ordinaries felt all the time. At least it made him take extra care. He was quieter and more watchful and extremely careful with how much of his body he showed through that hole, for who knew what gargoyle vision was like. And at least it gave them all a reprieve from the shadow that stalked their thoughts.

They kept watch for some time, until at last there came a lull in the winds, and the snowfall thinned enough for them to glimpse something thin and tall and opalescent standing amidst the court and prison grounds, like a pole, but with edges. Now and then a gargoyle could be seen flying around it, appearing and then disappearing into the blizzard.

"I swear that looked like an obelisk," Leera noted.

Bridget raised the jar. "Whatever it is, it's made of the same stuff as the shard."

Through another break, Augum saw that the grounds were filled with gargoyles, a whole army of them. Most were wingless, yet even one would be a menace to a warlock stripped of arcanery.

Steadily the snowfall petered out to a patter, but not the chill winds, which remained in gusting force. The better visibility allowed them to see that the pole was indeed a giant opalescent obelisk, and it was constantly bombarded by small objects that at first glance appeared to be birds.

"It's attracting other shards," Bridget noted.

Leera nodded down. "Look at the grounds."

The gargoyles were parading slaves about—men, women and children. Amongst them were nobles and commoners and soldiers and knights and archers and even warlocks, all roped or chained together. Interestingly, every single one had a shovel and was being led to or, once exhausted, dragged away from a giant hole in the court grounds.

"They're digging," Leera whispered. "But to what?"

Augum looked at the iron-gated entrance of the compound and saw that they opened toward the Black Castle, which was just across the way. He envisioned the underground and instantly realized what they were doing.

"The Royal Armory," he blurted. "Gods, they're trying to get into the armory …"

Guarded by powerful arcanery and thick walls, the Royal Armory was located underneath the city, with a tunnel leading from the Black Castle. It held the kingdom's greatest secrets and treasures, including ancient weapons and armors and all sort of invaluable artifacts. But it was also heavily guarded—and blocked off by enormous ancient doors made of solid Dreadnought steel that, once closed, would require monstrous force to break through should the enchantments be rendered null.

"They're digging around the doors," Augum said. "Trying another way into the vaults."

Bridget shook her head. "It won't work as Dreadnought steel surrounds the entire complex. There's no battering ram large enough to smash through it. They'd need something like ..." Her words stumbled to a halt as she stared at the grounds.

Augum looked to the compound and saw that a group of winged gargoyles had encircled the base of the obelisk and appeared to be performing some sort of ritual, for their arms were moving in a synchronized fashion. Then one of them, a winged gargoyle of average size, stepped forth and hugged the opalescent obelisk, which began to glow brightly. The rumble and the buzzing hum increased.

The obelisk's glow got so bright they had to turn away. There was a monstrous *thwoom* noise, and when they looked back, the obelisk was gone—as was the gargoyle that had hugged the obelisk. In its place stood a monstrous gargoyle two barns wide.

"Gods ..." Leera said.

"It's some form of spell like Incarnate," Bridget added, referring to the 17th degree elemental spell that temporarily turned a warlock into a giant version of themselves.

"Except I'm not sure this one is temporary," Augum muttered.

The giant gargoyle's skin was slightly translucent, as if it had taken on the opalescent property of the obelisk, and there were a series of runes on its chest. Its wings unfolded like a butterfly's. It flexed them a few times before folding them up on its back. The now relatively small gargoyles at its feet broke their circle, and the huge gargoyle lumbered through—toward the slaves, all of whom screamed and tried to run away, only to get snagged and tangled up in their chains and ropes.

Their overseeing gargoyles began to whip them, herding them like cattle, though mercifully away from the hole they had started digging. The giant gargoyle stepped on a wretched man, instantly killing him and causing the slaves to scream anew. Oblivious to their concerns, it took their place in the hole and began digging with its giant claws.

"Will it be strong enough to punch through the steel of the vault?" Leera asked, looking at Augum.

"I don't know, but I'm not going to wait around to find out." He looked to the girls. "It's time to spread some wings and launch an attack. Let's put our heads together and form a plan."

And plan they did, working quickly to toss ideas around and discard the impractical and overly dangerous ones, like attacking the giant gargoyle within the vicinity of any snuffing abilities. They also realized the best course of action was to only let one of them turn into a dragon; that way the other two could swoop in to help should things go awry. And if one dragon could defeat the best the gargoyles had to offer, the beasts might flee the kingdom altogether. They even chose a remote location they had all visited together—a farm which happened to have hosted Jengo's wedding, one that had given the group privacy to celebrate without outsiders interfering.

"Then it's settled," Augum said. "Soon as we get our arcanery back again, we'll teleport off and I'll cast the sacred simul, while you two keep alert and ready to support."

No sooner had he finished talking than their arm rings flared to life. "Now!" he said, and they each incanted, "*Impetus peragro!*"

With a triple *thwomp*, the trio appeared amidst a barren snowy field with undulating crop rows. A farmhouse overgrown with dead ivy sat in the distance beside a decrepit wooden grain silo, the entire area surrounded by snowy pines and spruces and cedars. Large snowflakes gently tumbled from the heavens, the wind now and then moving them about in wavy curtains.

Augum recalled seeing torches surrounding a big bell tent in that very spot, a joyous celebration, a grand feast, and a party that went well into the night. He still heard the echoes of laughter and merriment, and couldn't help from longing for the same for himself and Leera—and even Bridget and Olaf.

Bridget raised her chin. "Put the fear of the gods into them, Aug."

Leera drew him into a tight hug, pressing his head to her shoulder, whispering, "Draw the bastard here and kick its tailed ass. We'll take shelter by the farmhouse, where we'll be watching and ready." She kissed him, and he kissed her back. Then she unspooled from him to lightly punch his upper arm. "Good luck up there, and be careful. Love you."

"Love you too," Augum whispered. He nodded his thanks to the girls, turned his back, and stepped well away from them to face the city. Surrounded by nothing but white and the gentle patter of snow falling on his shoulders, he drew back his hood and tightened the strap of the rucksack.

This was it. He would finally cast the ancient simul that would turn him into the mightiest predator of them all.

The callous shadow loomed behind his mind, and even though it was cloudy here, he could feel the heat of three suns all the way from the impossibly distant plane of Endraga Ra beat down on his skin. As the wind whistled past his ears, he felt the shadow lick its chops, eager for him to get on with it and satisfy that built-up thirst. And yet he had to keep it on a leash, for duty called.

But first, the ritual …

Augum took several breaths that centered his focus whilst recalling the lessons of Endraga Ra. Of a special time spent learning the sacred spell and its myriad complexities. *Spread your wings, step into the mind of a bird, a hawk on the hunt. See the ground far below. Feel the wind upon your wings, the flex of your tail, the sharpness of your claws and teeth, the muscles in your arms and legs.* Although the spell could be cast faster, he took his time, wanting a perfect casting.

Finally, with his thoughts aligned just so, he raised a leg and both arms in the praying mantis pose, which demanded nuance and precision. He held that pose for one last meditative breath, seeing himself as a dragon loafing amidst the jungles of Endraga Ra, enjoying a moment of peace before the kill. Then he incanted, *"Xae carna draca arcan doma legenda rava!"*

He felt his skin burst and bulk up, quickly swallowing up his robe and rucksack and sword, all of which would be trapped inside him. His arms and legs extended and grew claws, while giant wings and a long tail sprouted from his back. His innards buzzed as his arcanery amplified mightily, a bonus of becoming a dragon, along with the natural Fear aura that he emanated like an invisible wave—which he quickly turned off so as not to soak the girls in terror.

He flexed his forearm, enjoying seeing all ten lightning rings briefly flare to life before letting them go. Then he did the same with his eyes, flaring them with lightning. He opened and stretched out his wings to their full length, then rattled them toward the south, imagining his enemies pissing themselves from the terror, as had happened plenty of times before.

Having gathered himself, he slapped the ground with his dragon tail, enjoying feeling the earth rumble beneath him, before springing off his powerful hind legs and launching into the air. His wings bit into the air and began flapping, raising him ever higher.

When he had first started casting the Spirit of the Dragon simul, he had been one and a half barns wide, extended wingtip to wingtip. Now, having better learned and grown with the spell, he was two barns wide, the same size as the summoned gargoyle. It was the same with the girls. He only hoped they would not need to turn into their forms.

With the wind whistling over his wings, Augum felt freedom surge through his soul. This was what he had been born to do. He, the lord of the skies, would teach these invaders a lesson they would never forget — that his kingdom was not defenseless. That Solians could fight back. And these beasts would pay dearly for thinking otherwise.

He stayed just below the clouds, the city looming ahead, nearing rapidly. *Now tactics*, he thought, and spread the claws of his left hand, incanting, "*Un vun asperio aurum enchantus.*" Reveal should allow him to see nullification bubbles coming, giving him a chance to evade them, though something that would be difficult to do in the claustrophobic and blind streets of the city.

War and dueling tactics, learned in class and in training and in prior battles, paraded before his mind. Principles like arcane perpendicularity and arcanic relativity and arcaneological dilation and geometric lensing and tongue-to-tendril ratios, spell permutations and combos and simuls and tricks — all presented themselves before him like called-upon soldiers, each verbalizing their capability. Already he could see the beginning of the battle. Already he could hear the roar of the city.

As he swooped in low, flying over the Black Castle to have a look at it, a few cheers went up from soldiers manning ballistae and archers standing in ranks alongside knights on horseback — but no sign of any warlocks. Still, news would quickly spread — their dragons were back and mounting an onslaught!

Through the falling snow, Augum set his sights on the courthouse and prison — and on the giant gargoyle digging like a dog on those grounds, half its body already obscured by dirt.

Augum touched his throat, incanting, "*Amplifico*," and felt it expand mightily. He opened his black-toothed maw and loosed a roar the city hadn't heard since the last war, a roar that shook every window and caromed through every alley, a predatorial roar of warning. Then he raised his wings, using them as a brake, and flared them to their largest width.

Like a giant hive of bees, the tiny gargoyles in the prison and courthouse grounds looked up — and pointed. A few triggered their pentastones, for Augum saw tendril bubbles expand — and die out rather quickly. These were weak castings that could not reach him.

Then came a rapid flash as a thick bolt of lightning crashed so close he felt its heat on his scales. Down below, it blew apart a chapel's steeple, releasing a rapidly expanding snuff bubble that rushed toward him like an arcane bomb.

But Augum was ready for this, and visualized himself flying above the enemy. *"Impetus peragro,"* he growled, and appeared two hundred feet above where the enemy dug—and glimpsed that tendril bomb fly through the spot he had been hovering in.

Knowing he only had moments, he dove and loosed his natural dragon-amplified Fear aura, which splashed across every creature below, human and gargoyle alike, all of whom screamed as one. The former shrieked as men and women and children, and the latter squealed in their demonic-sounding tongue. And while the enemy screamed, they did not cast nor did they defend. Only the large summoned gargoyle seemed unfazed. Like a big and stupid dog, it looked up from its digging to see what all the fuss was about.

Meanwhile, a diving Augum swooped low over a line of wingless gargoyles, raking a black claw through their flesh, skewering three, eviscerating five, and decapitating two. Limbs and heads flew and tumbled amidst the chorus of screams. The cacophonic noise and sheer violence of it all made the predator within him salivate.

The lord of war cometh, Augum thought, remembering an ancient proverb he had read in the Arcaner codex, *and bringeth with him the mightiest of furies …*

He rose skyward, shaking off the gargoyles he had skewered, which had piled up on his claws like meat on the prongs of a fork. As the dead beasts slammed into the empty snowed-over streets of Blackhaven, he dove toward a street filled with gargoyles waiting to get into the prison grounds. His mighty Fear aura splashed ahead of him, paralyzing most in place with that potent terror weak prey felt before an apex predator. As if he were a farmer scything wheat, his claws went through them like a hot knife through butter—all he wanted was to stick their flesh between giant slices of bread and chomp down on a gargoyle sandwich.

Amidst the slicing sound of flesh clogging his claws and smacking against brick and stone, he loosed another roar of carnage. As he did so, a couple of unfortunate gargoyles fell into his roaring maw, which he promptly chomped down upon. To his dismay, they tasted like lizard—dry and thin and chewy, and were so disappointing in flavor that he spat them out.

Having lost his forward momentum from bowling through the enemy throng, he flapped his great wings and raised himself skyward, shaking their remains from his claws, watching gargoyle pieces fall and splat the ground below and smash into the sides of buildings with explosive bursts of brick and stone. He took the wave of dragon Fear with him, along with the satisfaction from hearing a shrill gargoyle scream in its wake, for the enemy finally got to witness what had been dormant — a beast that would lend no quarter, unafraid to rip them apart with its long teeth and claws.

As he rose still higher toward the low cloud ceiling, he looked over his muscled shoulder to see that some of the winged gargoyles had recovered quickly from the Fear wave, and used their pentastones to cast bubbles of elemental snuff that expanded outward. Luckily those snuff bubbles were not fast enough to catch up to his flying, and petered out soon enough.

He veered about just below the clouds, and spotted the summoned gargoyle take to the air with a mighty flap of its wings. What annoyed him though was that the beast was joined by other winged gargoyles, forming a swarm. In terms of size, it was like a vulture being surrounded by sparrows — except some of these sparrows had the power to force Augum to revert, which wouldn't do at all.

Wanting to mow another line of carnage through the enemy but realizing there was not enough time, Augum instead veered around to fly northward, goading the gargoyles to follow. Sure enough, the normal-sized ones quickly fell behind the large one. The trick was to isolate the large one. But how to do that? As he pondered the problem, he snuffed Reveal, wanting to conserve stamina.

He decided that time spent in the air would do the trick, and he overflew Bridget and Leera's position. He thought he saw them hunkering behind the barn, tiny figures amidst a curtain of white. He hoped they caught on to his plan and remained hidden.

Onward he flew, a coniferous white forest spreading below. The white-capped Anchor Lake sloshed to the west and the windswept Northern Peaks loomed to the far north like the teeth of a sleeping giant. He slowly turned eastward, always checking that the gargoyles followed. The large one was a slow flyer, forcing him to slow his pace to match, keeping the monster a thousand feet to the rear. As for its small-winged kin, they fell farther and farther behind, so that by the time he had made a wide U-turn, they were but specks, like a flock of seagulls desperate to keep up.

Back south he flew, then gently turned to the southwest, aiming to be above the barn at the critical moment. Judging by the distance of the gargoyles, he hoped to have time enough to take the big brute on.

He checked in with his soul, figuring he still had at least four-fifths of his stamina reserves. One drawback of being in dragon form was that the spell continually siphoned stamina until reversion took place. He could revert sooner, but doing so would still sap every bit of stamina he had not spent. Total drainage was one of the unforgiving costs of the spell—along with the side effect known as The Callousness of the Predator, which had already been bleeding into his day-to-day life for a while now.

But the girls would help him deal with the callous shadow. For now, he needed to confront the giant gargoyle and see if he could take it on as a dragon. He glided lower and lower, until his clawed feet grazed the top of the snow and, like a duck landing on water, touched down three hundred feet from the barn where the girls had taken shelter. He folded in his wings and turned about on all fours, ready for a fight.

The giant gargoyle was on its way, its wings extended as it glided toward him. He thought of various spell combinations that would work best, along with offensives and mind spells. The trick was to end it as quickly as possible, before the normal-sized gargoyles caught up and snuffed him. Either way, whether he got into trouble or he vanquished the beast, he and the girls were to teleport away to a predetermined location, where he could safely revert and hand himself over to their care.

The giant gargoyle soared closer and closer, its claws extended and ready for evisceration. He thought it would land, but it kept coming. Augum raised himself up on his hind legs, using his tail as support, and ran a paw over his body, incanting, "*Armari elementus totalus.*" Lightning crackled to life around his body, quickly solidifying to a thin crust that would serve as armor—strengthened by his golden Dreadnought breastplate, buried deep inside his body. Sure, the summoned armor crust would impede his movement a little, but he wanted to be as safe as possible.

He next spread the claws of his left hand, incanting, "*Un vun asperio aurum enchantus,*" which would allow him to see tendril geometries—a necessity if the gargoyle was capable of snuffing. If so, he would have to be quick to teleport off in time; otherwise, he was dead.

When the giant gargoyle got within striking range, Augum slapped his scaled wrists together, roaring, "*Annihilo bato!*" Two tree-trunk-sized bolts of lightning, amplified mightily by his dragon form, ripped toward the summoned invader. The giant beast was surprisingly quick to react, and artfully used its wings to dip below the strikes, which crackled over its head.

While it dipped, it growled and touched a rune on its body, and a gigantic blade of fire appeared in its clawed hand. Augum took up the challenge and made an unsheathing motion from his hip, roaring, "*Summano arma grau!*" A giant blade of pure lightning appeared in his clawed fist. The next ten strikes of that blade would unleash the Slam spell, as per the Roar of the Dragon simul.

The invading beast swooped by and sliced at him. Augum raised his sword in perpendicular and the two blades met with a *crack* of thunder and an explosion of sparks that rained onto the snow, sizzling like grease. The strike had been so forceful that it knocked their blades backward. Alas, the gargoyle hardly flinched from the sound of Augum's thunder.

The beast flew past and growled something whilst pressing a separate rune on its chest, summoning a fiery round shield to its left arm. It touched down fifty feet away and bashed the shield with its sword whilst roaring a battle cry that washed over the land and surrounding forest.

Augum reared up on his hind legs, flared his lightning eyes and arm rings, and rattled his wings as he loosed a mighty roar of his own, showing the beast that he was hardly intimidated. But he also glanced over his shoulder, already seeing the flock of gargoyles flying toward them from a league away or so.

Needing to be efficient, he turned his attention back to the giant gargoyle in time to witness it charge. He made a claw of his left hand and incanted, *"Dreadus terrablus!"* Reveal allowed him to see the writhing tendrils shoot at the giant, but the beast touched the side of a triangular rune divided into three sections whilst growling a word, turning its flesh into stone, and the tendrils broke against its bulk as if meeting a battering ram—the blasted thing had become immune to such arcanery!

Realizing this would likely be a mostly physical confrontation, Augum summoned a giant lightning shield to his left forearm and readied his thunder-amplified blade. The granite gargoyle swung first. Augum stepped aside and swung upward. The gargoyle dipped its body sideways and thrust inward. Augum, standing sideways to the attacker, blocked with his shield and elbowed the beast on its chin. The gargoyle grunted, and Augum used the moment to bring his sword down, aiming for its neck. Cleverly, it swung its shield above its head, and there came a *crack* of thunder as the lightning smashed into the hissing fire of the shield.

On account of their titanic size, each step and strike sent a rumble through the ground, making the nearby snow dance. Unfortunately, the violent motions also made Augum lose his concentration with the Reveal spell, fizzling it.

Augum kneed the gargoyle in the chest, causing its body to jump up, exposing its face to an elbow bash that gave a sweet *crunch*. The gargoyle stumbled backward and Augum pressed with a series of swings and slashes and thrusts. Sparks rained explosively alongside cracks of thunder as each strike was blocked with the fiery blade or the shield — the giant was surprisingly adept at sword and shield play. Annoyed, Augum shoved at the air, roaring, *"Baka!"* and sent the gargoyle tumbling. Realizing that would only prolong the duel, he cursed at himself and, with a whip of the tail to gain momentum, shot forth.

The gargoyle clambered to its feet and pressed a second side of the triple-divided rune, growling something. Its limbs instantly began moving quickly, as if the rune had doubled its agility — but its flesh returned to normal too.

Augum, suspecting the gargoyle was now susceptible to his arcanery once more, thought to test his theory by wiggling a hand and incanting, *"Flustrato!"* The gargoyle twirled aside, easily dodging. Augum's jiggling arm followed. *"Flustrato! Flustrato! Flustrato!"* The artful twirls continued, making a mockery of his attacks. As big as it was, the gargoyle's quickening allowed it great dexterity, making trying to hit from a distance a waste of time.

Augum thus jumped into the air and unfolded his wings halfway to allow for a slight glidepath. He reared back with his blade and swung it in a large arc that would connect at the apex — only to swivel the blade low at the last moment, aiming to cut the beast's legs out from under it.

The freshly quickened gargoyle easily swung its fiery shield downward, and there was a hissing *thunk* and a mighty *crack* of thunder as the lightning blade connected with the fire. The gargoyle whirled about with its blade, allowing for Augum to slide past. The fiery blade then smashed square into his neck. With a *hiss*, the elemental armor rumbled as cracks ripped down the length of the armor — one more strike and it would shatter. Were it not for his golden breastplate, he was sure the armor would have blown apart.

Augum stumbled back in surprise at being struck, and the quickened beast used his hesitation to growl whilst slipping a hand past a rune — then shooting that hand forth. Augum felt something connect with his soul, and before he knew what was happening, the gargoyle quickly began throwing one arm over the other, as if pulling on a rope. A cold surge shot from his soul to the gargoyle.

"No!" Augum roared, realizing the beast had cast its version of the 11th degree Arcane Drain. He spun about, using his blade to sever the invisible tendril connection. By the time he whirled back around, the quickened gargoyle was bolting forth at him, its fiery blade swinging about in an attempt to decapitate him.

Augum barely raised his lightning sword in time to meet the fiery blade. Another *crack* of thunder emanated from his sword that only made the gargoyle blink. Their blades danced in a display of fire and lightning that showered sparks and loosed cracks of thunder, until all ten had been depleted. Still those blades sang their deadly song. Thrust, parry, counter-thrust, block, swing—then the beast jumped over a particularly clumsy swing and smashed its fiery blade into his chest. As Augum stumbled backward, the already cracked lightning armor splintered and vanished. It had protected him from two strikes. Now protected only by his natural dragon scales, the next hit could easily be lethal.

Suddenly there came a *thwomp* directly to his left. Spying the edge of a wingtip, Augum's war-honed reflexes kicked in and he sliced his giant lightning blade in a vicious arc—and eviscerated a normal-sized gargoyle in half. The two parts spun as they fell to the snow, each spraying a fountain of blood, the head emitting a sickly gurgle. The predator within salivated at the sight.

Augum stole a quick glance back and saw the rest of the flock was half a league off—and closing fast. He was running out of time.

Refocusing, he growled and jumped back into the fray. With the dance of death resumed, Augum, tired of testing mere might and agility, chose to switch tactics and began telekinetically flicking with his left hand, bouncing the fiery blade inward or away, until at last one of his thrusts connected, searing a hole into the gargoyle's side. The beast recoiled, roaring in pain.

"*Flustrato!*" Augum snapped, but the gargoyle sensed the attack and whirled inward, surprising him again with its speed. He barely had time to raise his sword to meet the strike. *Clang!* Another shower of sparks. With their blades locked, fire hissing against the crackle of lightning, the gargoyle pushed forth. Augum the dragon strained against its might, and for a moment they were at an even keel, eye to eye, titan to titan.

Then Augum flexed every muscle in his body, roaring, "*Virtus vis viray!*" The Strength spell made every muscle that much more potent, and he easily threw the gargoyle backward. Yet even as the beast sailed through the air, it pressed the other side of that same triple-divided rune and growled a word. Its feet slammed into the ground with a rumble, and it opened its arms and its maw and roared another battle cry, its muscles bulging with veins.

Seeing that its limbs moved at their normal speed, Augum guessed that it too had cast a Strength spell, using that same rune, which he deduced must have three powers—stone, strength, and agility, only one of which could be triggered at a time.

That also left it exposed, and Augum switched tactics again, nullifying his sword and shield in favor of greater arm speed. He began a barrage of arcane attacks, arms a blur. "*Flustrato! Flustrato! Dreadus terrablus! Effectus xadius!*" — Two Confusion castings followed by a Fear and a Slow casting. The gargoyle dodged the first spell, but the latter three seemed to hit, for its head snapped back three times.

As it stumbled backward, Augum used the time to draw a shape in the air, roaring, "*Summano elementus minimus draco!*" A wagon-sized dragon made of pure lightning appeared before him. He pointed a claw, growling, "Draco — attack the wings and torso!"

With a flick of its lightning tail, his summoned dragon shot forth. The gargoyle, trying to come to its senses, raised its fiery blade. In turn, Augum yanked at the air, roaring, "*Disablo!*" and the blade vanished — just as the summoned dragon slammed into the gargoyle. Like a rabid dog, it began tearing at the beast's flesh with its lightning maw, spraying blood onto the pristine snow. With the gargoyle half dazed and frightened, the dragon quickly managed to gnaw off one of its wings, which flopped aside, squirting blood.

Augum took a quick moment to glance skyward and saw that the coming gargoyles were now a quarter league off. He had to finish this fight — and finish it now.

Just as he was about to launch a final attack, there came a simultaneous double *thwomp* — two gargoyles had appeared, one on each flank. Training and dueling instinct immediately kicked in, and he pointed at the right-most gargoyle, a mere twenty feet away, latched on telekinetically, and yanked so hard that the space around him warped. He ducked as the flailing gargoyle sailed past — and watched it slam into the other gargoyle at such a speed both emitted the pulping *crack* of multiple bones shattering. They rolled off into the snow, squealing in pain.

Augum followed that roll by slamming his wrists together, roaring, "*Annihilo!*" and took barbarous satisfaction from watching his tree-sized lightning bolt explode the pair in a shower of blood and guts.

As the giant gargoyle wrestled with his summoned dragon, and was now quickly gaining the upper hand, Augum hunkered down and pushed off with his powerful hind legs, launching himself back into the air, wings unfolding. He made an unsheathing motion, incanting, "*Summano arma!*" and a huge lightning longsword appeared in his fist. On the declining arc, he brought that sword down, aiming for the giant gargoyle's head.

Just before connection, as it was being mangled raw, the gargoyle somehow reached the right rune—and turned to stone. The longsword smashed into the creature—and caromed right off, as useless as a stick against rock. As Augum landed astride the beast's chest, which was damaged from the lightning dragon's tearing, the giant gargoyle grabbed Augum's summoned dragon by the head and smashed a fist into it, exploding it into lightning shards. The dragon fell apart and vanished.

Augum gave the gargoyle no time to react. He let go of his sword, letting it vanish back into the ether, and slammed a clawed fist through the spot his summoned dragon had been in. That fist connected with the stone gargoyle's head, which smacked back against the ground with a *crack* as his wrist bent in an awkward fashion, sending a jolt of pain up his lizard arm.

Knowing he'd broken his wrist, Augum jumped back into the air—just out of reach of the scrambling gargoyle, which tried to latch onto him. Augum gave it its wish, telekinetically hooked on with both good and broken hand, and yanked. The gargoyle lurched into the air, spraying the snow with more blood. Augum winced from the pain of the grinding wrist bones. But he needed both arms, and hauled the flailing one-winged beast skyward, his wings straining.

The giant gargoyle growled and smacked a rune, resummoning its fiery blade. Augum attempted to dive behind it, but the gargoyle cleverly raised its blade over and behind its head and slashed his belly as he careened by. Even as he gasped in pain, he threw an arm around its neck and squeezed. The pair tumbled downward, with Augum using his wings to quicken the pace of the fall.

I'm going to destroy you, he thought, imagining himself in the jungles of Endraga Ra. *And now you end.* At the last moment, he turned their bodies so that the gargoyle faced downward, and threw it forth—then shoved at it, roaring, "*Baka!*"

The giant gargoyle accelerated to breakneck speed—and smashed into the ground so violently that an explosion of earth and snow shot upward. Augum then landed on the back of its head with both of his heels and heard a distinct *crunch* as the stone head gave way underneath him.

The gargoyle went still.

After taking a moment to savor the victory, Augum rolled aside and keeled over to grab his belly, which bled profusely. He glanced up to see the normal-sized gargoyles were less than five hundred feet away. Then he looked at the giant and saw it turn back into flesh before shrinking to become the original gargoyle that had hugged the obelisk. To be absolutely certain it was dead, Augum raised a clawed foot and brought his heel down on its back, and heard multiple crunches as he ground the beast underfoot.

"May your soul find the peace together we could not reach," he growled, the predator within him reveling in the experience of pulping a worthy foe. He stared at the remains, finding it fascinating that it had taken draining a whole city's worth of arcanery to create this one giant gargoyle—and it had been a formidable opponent indeed, as evidenced by his throbbing stomach and wrist. Had it not been for his training, his experience, and his golden Dreadnought breastplate and its amplification of his Summon Elemental Armor spell, he would have surely succumbed to its fearsome attacks.

He groaned as he stood and turned to face the farm, where he saw two figures standing in wait. Bridget and Leera would not risk coming to him, what with the gargoyles so close. He would go to them and they would teleport together.

A viciousness rudely barged in upon his thoughts. He envisioned appearing in their midst, grabbing the wenches, and tossing them into his gullet. He could almost hear their gurgling screams as he crunched on their bones. Could they sense this, staring at him across this distance? That he looked upon them as prey? That his dragon snout was salivating at the thought of pulverizing their flesh?

How he wished he could remain in form forever and dominate this weak land! How unfortunate that the Spirit of the Dragon continually bled stamina, eventually forcing reversion …

Dizzy and weak from the injuries, he checked in on his stamina reservoir—and found it near empty. Had he been an oil lamp, only fumes would remain, no doubt on account of that blasted Arcane Drain spell.

With the gargoyles a hundred feet away and about to enter standard combat spell range, and with his vision darkening, he imagined standing behind Bridget and Leera, and incanted, "*Impetus peragro*," yanking his body into the ether. After a heartbeat, and with a deep *thwomp*, he shot out onto the snow, tumbling like a dragon ragdoll—and feeling his flesh return to being human. As it did, the full potency of The Callousness of the Predator enveloped what remained of his consciousness.

He found it fascinating how his blood sprayed outward as he cartwheeled, and relished the looks of horror on the faces of the girls. At last his body jammed sideways in the snow, rucksack and Burden's Edge still attached to his back and belt respectively, chest encased in a golden breastplate.

Bridget and Leera raced to him.

"Come to watch me die?" he croaked when they arrived, amused at their urgency. Why the hurry? Why would anyone hurry to do anything? His calmness brought consciousness back to the fore. Or perhaps it had been the cartwheeling, which had pushed blood back into his head through centrifugal force.

"You know, I can be quite smart," he said as the girls each grabbed an arm. Beyond, a whole swarm of gargoyles flapped toward them. "Better hurry if you want to live 'cause they're right on my heels," he reported as Bridget began the Group Teleport incantation. He cared not if he or they lived or died. Sure, to live would be slightly more interesting, but death would afford peace from this tiresome existence.

He was about to voice that thought aloud when Bridget's spell fired and he felt his body get yanked once more. This time, the violence of it also snuffed consciousness.

ALL TOO QUICK

BRIDGET

The trio appeared amidst the familiar burnt-out tree homes of Sparrow's Perch, the spot Bridget had chosen. The snow here was fresh, the cloud cover thick, and the trees swayed in a cold and bitter westerly.

"Lay him on his side! I'll strip the breastplate and you work on a bandage!" Bridget called, and she and Leera worked to lower an unconscious Augum to the snow. While Bridget scrambled at the straps of the breastplate, Leera incanted, *"Virtus vis viray!"* Arcanely strengthened, she tore Augum's robe sleeve off then tore it into two. The moment Bridget unpeeled the breastplate off Augum, Leera used both strips to wrap his wounded torso. While she did this, Bridget raised Augum's legs onto her knees.

"He'll be fine," she declared more confidently than she felt. "He'll be fine."

Leera said nothing except, *"Virtus null,"* nullifying the Strength spell. She tied the torso bandage off and laid Augum on his back.

Bridget watched her cradle him close and whisper something she could not hear. She wanted to say that they were lucky to know someone so brave. That he was a strong soul and a good leader. She wanted to say these things for Leera, to ease her worries, but instead found herself worrying about Olaf … and about their kingdom.

Meanwhile, Augum stirred awake in Leera's arms.

"Damn," he croaked.

"What is it, my love?" Leera asked, pressing a gentle hand to his chest.

"I'm still alive."

Leera snorted at this.

"Let go of my legs. And you—get your hand off me."

"My love, you're suffering from the side effects—"

"I said, get your grubby paws off me."

While Leera sighed and withdrew her hand from his chest, Bridget reluctantly placed Augum's legs onto the snow.

Augum turned his head. "Hey, look—more dead people."

Bridget looked in the same direction and saw that he was referring to the grave markers which honored Bridget's and Leera's parents, and a whole village of people that his father had slain in the Legion War.

Augum's lips twisted with a cruel grin. "My precious *papa* put them there."

Bridget made eye contact with Leera. "I'm sorry. I shouldn't have taken us here."

Leera waved the matter aside, but she glanced over to the grave markers nonetheless.

"Staring at them won't bring them back," Augum remarked.

"Oh, hush. You don't mean that," Bridget said. She should have chosen someplace neutral.

"Yes, I do. You know I do."

"The predator means it, sure, but not the Augum we both know."

This made the smile turn into a frown. "You're a lousy, useless wench who doesn't deserve her man. He might be ugly and fat as a ham but he's still a better friend than you are. Certainly funnier, too. And he's right— you *would* mistreat your children. You know it and I know it. Probably end up mangling them, in fact. Or worse."

Bridget's heart rammed against her chest.

Now it was Leera who turned to look at Bridget. "We trained each other to ignore this stuff. Let it go."

Bridget couldn't stop her chin from trembling or the tears from welling. The problem was she felt the words were true. She *didn't* deserve Olaf. He *was* funnier than her. And if she didn't find a way to suppress the predator, she *would* mistreat her children ... or worse.

"Pathetic. Yes, cry. Cry like a little girl. You baby. You weakling. I can't believe you think yourself worthy of being a queen of the skies. Both of you wenches didn't have the guts to summon it and help me. You left me out there to fend for myself—"

"Because that was the damn plan!" Leera roared, snarling. She shoved Augum and stood up to hover over him. "You don't think I have it in me?"

The anger Augum and Leera expressed snapped Bridget out of her pity party. "Lee! Lee—stop it!" she hissed, pawing at her robe, only to have Leera smack her hand away.

Augum curled his lip. "You don't have anything in that stupid empty head of yours, let alone courage. Gods, would you look at that ugly donkey face. And that hoof nose. Disgusting."

Leera began breathing rapid, shallow breaths. "Oh, yeah?"

"Yeah."

"Lee!"

Leera reared her fist back. "*Yeah?*"

"Yeah! Do it, you donkey wench! Do it!"

"Lee—no—!" Bridget shouted, jumping to her feet and scrambling for Leera's arm. But it was too late. Down came the fist to smack Augum in the face. His nose exploded with a sickening *crunch*, and blood poured down over his lips and chin. He groaned in pain, pressing a hand over his nose to staunch the flow.

"Now what have you got to say, huh?" Leera shouted while Bridget frantically tried to grab her arms, but Leera had always been a better wrestler and grappler, and easily shook off Bridget's clumsy attempts. "Now what've you got to say! Oh, did you break your wrist? Here, let me help you make it better—" and she telekinetically yanked his floppy wrist forth, which was purple and swollen—and grabbed it and pulled it backward, causing Augum to howl in pain.

"Now who's whining like a little girl?" Leera hissed, laughing and throwing the hand back at Augum's wrecked face.

"Lee—look at me!" Bridget had to telekinetically yank on her and whirl her about—and that was when she saw that Leera's eyes were those of a lizard—those of the *dragon*.

Leera snarled at Bridget. "You *dare* yank on me?"

"Lee! Your eyes! Get a grip! *Get a grip!*" Bridget knew she had to get Leera to calm down before she did something that would irrevocably damage her and Augum's relationship. It was bad enough that she and Olaf were on shaky ground, but allowing these two to tear apart what they had worked so hard to build up would be devastating not only for them, but for their friends—and even for the entire kingdom, whose future hopes rested on the strength of their love.

"Don't do something you'll deeply regret," Bridget whispered. "You hear me, Lee? Don't do it."

Leera blinked. She looked down at her coiled fist, which had surely been about to meet Bridget's face. She looked back up at Bridget, who saw that the lizard eyes were gone, replaced by Leera's once more.

"Please," Bridget whispered, and watched Leera look to Augum's exploded face, go ashen, and drop to her knees beside him.

"That all you got, you witch?" Augum snarled, holding his nose and wincing. He fumbled for Burden's Edge with his free hand, but got nowhere with a broken wrist, and gave up. Instead, he spat a gob of blood right into Leera's face. All she did was close her eyes, as if feeling she deserved it.

"Your looks are improving already," he croaked, voice weakening again. "Now if only you weren't … weren't so … so stupid …" Augum's eyes rolled into the back of his lolling head as he lost consciousness, falling into Leera's waiting arms.

"He's losing too much blood," Bridget said, noticing how the snow beneath him was slowly staining crimson. "We need to get him to a healer."

"There's no sense in using Group Teleport until we know where to go," Leera replied, sniffling while she cuddled her beloved close, holding one hand to his face to stem the flow of blood from his nose. "Why don't you hop around and see if you can find someone?"

"Good idea." Bridget hesitated, not wanting to leave her friends. "You be kind to each other. Lee? Be kind to each other."

"Gods, don't you think I know that!" Leera roared without looking up, only to press a hand against the air. "I'm sorry. I'm sorry. I let it slip in. Fates forgive me, I let it slip in and take over and … now look what I've done."

"Nothing you can't fix. Talk it out. If anybody can do it, you two can. And it's not your fault. We just have to figure out a way through the predator. That's all." Bridget squeezed Leera's shoulder.

Leera pressed a clammy hand over Bridget's and squeezed back. "I know," she whispered. "I know …" She looked up. "Good luck, Sister-in-war."

"You too, Sister-in-war." Bridget stepped away. The last thing she saw and heard before snapping off the incantation to Teleport was Leera holding Augum's nose with one hand to staunch the blood flow whilst stroking his hair with the other and whispering how terribly sorry she was.

Heart hurting from the ordeal, Bridget first appeared before the Steps of the Crescent Moon of the academy. She rushed up to the courtyard, only to find the grounds empty and the portals to the three wings inactive. It was still in lockdown—either that, or snuffed by force.

Seeing the empty courtyard and hearing nothing but eerie silence unsettled her. She glanced about, recalling skipping along these very grounds when she had been a mere aspirant, eyes hopeful and a satchel overflowing with books and lesson scrolls, blissfully unaware that in a matter of quints the Legion would take it over and throw the kingdom into chaos. That had been six years ago, yet felt like multiple lifetimes.

"I won't let this happen again," she whispered. "You hear me! I won't let this happen again!" she roared, voice echoing off the gigantic loaf-like buildings that made up the three wings of the academy.

She ran back to the steps and next teleported to Mercy of the Unnameables, the largest of the city's infirmaries, but found herself standing before a partially ruined building—the gargoyles must have destroyed it to prevent healing from taking place. Here too rang an eerie silence, as if the whole city was empty.

"Unnameables help my poor Solia," she whispered. She would call on The Fates too if it would help. Whatever it took.

Alarmed, she visualized the southern drawbridge to the Black Castle, and incanted, *"Impetus peragro,"* appearing just before its base. To her surprise, the drawbridge had been lowered. Being the only one around, she raced forth into the castle, shouting, "Hello? Hello! Is anyone there!" But all that came back was an echo.

She halted in the empty courtyard, the snow of which was filled with footprints—both human and gargoyle. Discarded weapons lay strewn about, everything from swords and axes and spears to bows and quivers.

Then she spotted the doors. Almost every single one was either torn off its hinges, open, or destroyed.

"No ..." she whispered, running to the Great Arcaner Hall. "No—!" She slid in through the doorway and found the place a mess—tables and chairs lay overturned, dishware smashed. Splatters of blood were everywhere, along with drag marks in that blood that led outside. Bridget followed them, hands as clammy as Leera's and mouth dry. Something was wrong. Terribly wrong. The drag marks abruptly ended in the snow.

"Teleportation," she mumbled, seeing a pair of running footprints end in the same manner. The gargoyles had snatched people left and right, at times directly from the air it seemed. All of it was sudden and rushed, as if they were in a hurry ...

"Hello!" she called out again, turning in place. "Is anyone there! Please, someone shout out!" All that came back was the echo of her own voice. Realizing that many must have taken shelter below, she turned about to run back into the Great Arcaner Hall—only to stumble into a mist that had been silently sweeping over the whole castle behind her back.

It's on account of the cold mixing with the lake water, she told herself, which created a mist that then drifted over the city now and then.

Yet she felt goosebumps rise on her arms. Immediately she thought of Sparrow's Perch and standing beside Augum and Leera. "*Impetus peragro!*" she shouted, voice frantic.

But nothing happened.

Gods. She'd felt it too, just hadn't wanted to admit she hadn't reacted in time. "Why didn't I teleport out instead of hesitating?" she whispered, backing away, unsure of which direction was which. She unslung her bow and fumbled about the quiver for an arrow, finally manage to nock one.

But not wanting to make any more noise in the snow, and surrounded by ethereal blankness, she decided to crouch and wait it out, like a little girl hiding under blankets and hoping the imaginary monster in her closet would leave her alone.

"This is only a nightmare. This isn't really happening," she whispered, trying to relight her arm rings. But her arm remained dark, and the mist killed sound to such a degree that she could hear the pounding of her drum heart, as if it wanted to alert of a grave danger.

A quiet sound made her freeze. She held her breath as she stared into the mist. She didn't know why, but she couldn't help but whisper, "Ollie ...? Is that you?" She imagined him running forth with that goofy grin and grabbing her and twirling her about and planting kisses on her neck while she giggled like a girl with a school crush and she imagined him telling her that he believed in her and they would make beautiful children and would love and nurture them and they would build a house in the country and she would run a small school and they would have a flock of geese and a dog and—

There was a *whoosh.* Bridget's hopes rose and she urged her arm rings to light.

Instead, there came a *crunch* as a shadow landed in the snow ahead—the *whoosh* been the sound of wings in flight. A still-crouching Bridget slowly looked up to see a large and dark shape not unlike a dragon, one mirroring her soul. Like a rattlesnake intimidating its opponent, the gargoyle spread its wings. She almost expected them to vibrate, just as she had done as a dragon. And it was giant, a fifteen-footer.

"No, no, no ..." she said, shooting to her feet and sprinting the other way, discarding the bow which she knew would be useless against such a monster. "No, no, no, no, no—"

She heard the rustle and swoop of wings, then felt great arms slap around her. Her body rose skyward, giving her a fleeting moment to think some final thoughts.

I'm sorry, Ollie. I'm sorry, everyone. I'm sorry ...

Then she heard the all too familiar sound of a *thwomp* and felt a heart-wrenching yank.

It was all too quick and all too sudden.

A queen of the skies had become prey.

IN DESPERATE DARKNESS

LEERA

"All this raw power at my disposal yet I feel as vulnerable as ever," Leera mumbled, stroking Augum's pale cheek as he lay in her lap, one arm bare as she had used his sleeve to create a bandage. She pressed that bare arm under hers to keep it warm.

Around them, the snow-laden conifers rustled in a bitter wind, and the western sky was pink with a sunset hidden behind clouds. The early winter night would soon descend.

Leera began shivering. "What the heck's taking her so long, eh?" She unslung her rucksack, withdrew a waterskin, and took a guzzling pull. She then placed it to Augum's lips and trickled some in.

Augum choked and coughed, but then greedily sipped at the waterskin like a cub. His eyes fluttered open. "You again," he croaked, nose slightly crooked and stuffed up with blood.

"Me again."

"I look at your face and I want to slap you."

"I look at yours and I want to kiss you."

He sneered, albeit weakly. "You think I want to have children with you?"

"I *know* you do."

"I don't, actually. I only want dragon spawn, which you can't provide. You will fail in your quest to undo the curse, and I will find a mate in my true home—the jungles of Endraga Ra. As for you?" He scoffed, which caused him to cough. "You will be … you will be barren forever."

The shadow threw open the curtains behind her mind, but she shut them immediately, choosing to turn away.

"That's right. Look away, you coward. Gods, you stink. When's the last time you took a bath, you pig? Wretched, ugly girl. You don't deserve me. You understand? *You don't deserve me.*"

"I don't know how long I can do this for …" Leera whispered to herself. It was too painful to hear such naked words.

"Nobody's asking you to do anything. Why don't you piss off and leave me be. Go play in the mud or slice your own throat or something, no one cares."

"We both know it is the callous predator who speaks, not you."

"I am the lord of the skies. I am a dragon. I *am* Augum Arinthian Stone." His eyes looked her face over with utter disdain. "Who are *you*? A sniveling, stinky, ugly girl. You are nothing. *Nothing* …" he whispered, head lolling once again.

"You need to stay conscious until Bridge returns," she said, nudging him. "Keep insulting me if you must."

Those eyes rolled back into focus. He opened his mouth to continue his barrage, only to suffer a coughing spasm that spat blood onto his lips. She wiped it with her sleeve and held his head, continuing to stroke his greasy umber hair. The shadow within her wanted to retaliate, at the very least to call him out on stinking like a filthy pig himself. That shadow also wanted her to dump him onto the snow, stand up, and turn her back on him forever. Maybe boot him in the face prior to turning her back. How *dare* he presume himself above her station! *How dare he!*

But all she had to do was remember any soft moments with him—a tender cuddle, an evening bedding, a bath, even reading a book in silence together—and the anger melted like snow in spring.

She squeezed him close, whispering, "You're the love of my life. I will *always* love you …"

He groaned, turning his cheek away, apparently lacking the strength to reply—or too disgusted by the love.

Amidst the wind, there came the *crack* of a twig. Her head shot toward the noise, which had come from behind the ruins of a tree home. Alarmed, she slipped the waterskin back into her rucksack and tightened the strap.

Augum looked toward the home. "I belong … in the jungle," he wheezed. "This is misery. I … I welcome death."

"Shh, my love," Leera whispered, gently lowering him to the snow and beginning the process of strapping his breastplate back on. "Something's over there."

"Hey, watch the wound you idiot. Anyway, when death comes … I hope … I hope it's quick for me … and … and prolonged for you …"

His words pierced her heart, as they usually did when he was the predator—and as hers did to him when their roles were reversed. But someone always needed to keep watch, for the affected were also vulnerable as they were unable to cast arcanery until the side effect passed. Such was the price of turning into a dragon.

After loosely strapping the breastplate back onto him, Leera rose to her feet, hands balling into fists. *Come on, Bridge, where are you?* she thought. *Come on, come on, come on …*

A small, triangular shape crept into view from behind the tree home. This was followed by a snout and a face—the face of a gargoyle.

As if hoping not to be spotted—which was ridiculous considering she was wearing a crimson robe that stood out like blood against the snow— Leera stood frozen.

Then, mysteriously, the gargoyle's face slipped back behind the home, as if it too hoped it hadn't been seen.

Leera wanted to grab Augum and teleport the pair of them off. But then how would they ever find Bridget? In their foolish haste, they had completely forgotten to enchant each other with Object Track enchantments!

Without taking her eyes off the tree home, Leera nudged Augum with her foot, whispering, "Play dead."

A wheezing Augum only stared up at her, his eyelids half closed, broken wrist bent at an awkward angle, the makeshift bandage peeking out from under his breastplate soaked through. She paced to the right, trying to keep her steps from crunching in the snow. Slowly the muscled form of a gargoyle came into view—it was cavorting—no, whispering with another gargoyle. Neither had wings. Both were ten-footers and looked back at her as if surprised she had the gall to peek back at them. It was a surreal moment for Leera to find herself staring at two gargoyles openly conspiring to attack her.

Then she realized they were soldiers. Neither had the power of the winged ones. And neither carried a pentastone.

She raised her hands, and the gargoyles stiffened as if hoping she would ignore them. Just as she was about to slap her wrists together to blast them to bits, they sprinted off. Knowing she couldn't let them get away lest they call for reinforcements, Leera tore after them.

As they dipped around the trees, Leera skidded to a halt and timed it, slamming her wrists together at a crucial moment and roaring, "*Annihilo bato!*" Two potent jets of water shot forth like spears. A sprinting gargoyle ran behind a tree. When it emerged on the other side, its head exploded from a jet of water. The body tumbled forth, skidding in the snow, while the head misted red.

The second gargoyle was luckier, for the jet smashed into a tree, felling it. But it wasn't so lucky to avoid that tree, which fell directly across its path. The beast slammed into the trunk and loosed a long and high-pitched whine that would travel far. Leera ran up to it and, just as it loosed a second, louder whine, she slapped her wrists again. "*Annihilo!*" vaporing its head on the spot.

She glanced around the woods and saw two pairs of tracks leading toward the tree home from the west. Seeing nothing else, she ran back to Augum—only to halt the moment she emerged around the tree home, for a barely conscious Augum was being lifted by a winged fifteen-foot gargoyle emblazoned with runes—and holding a pentastone.

The gargoyle looked up at her and flared its gray nostrils. Fates be damned, the clever thing had used a couple goons as a lure!

Heart threatening to punch a hole in her chest, Leera unsheathed Careena and pointed it at the gargoyle, incanting, "*Summano arma dreadus terrablus!*" Careena was enveloped with a watery sheen, infused with ten castings of the Fear spell. She then raised two fingers of her left hand and flicked them forth twice, taunting the gargoyle to accept a straight-up fight.

"Take the bait, you ugly brute," she whispered, voice trembling with the fear that all the monster needed to do was touch a rune and teleport off with Augum. Something told her if that happened, she would never see him again.

The gargoyle, standing thirty feet away, tilted its big head and studied her, its pointed ears roving about in search of other threats.

Leera opened her arms, summoned a watery shield to her left arm, and thumped her chest, snarling and baring her teeth. "Come on! I challenge you! I challenge you, you coward!"

The gargoyle bared its teeth back and growled.

Leera knew she would only have a moment, and readied a certain spell upon her lips. As far as she knew, she was the only one in all of Solia to have learned the complicated spell.

The fifteen-footer dumped Augum and raised the pentastone. Never had Leera spoken an incantation as quickly, spitting, "*Impetus peragro spectra xae!*" And as she incanted, she began the arc of a sword swing. With a *thwomp*, she shot forth through the ether, blinking back into existence right beside the gargoyle's left arm, the one clutching the pentastone. She finished the arc of the swing, chopping off the arm at the elbow. Right as the gargoyle's other arm swatted at her with its vicious claws, she vanished with another *thwomp*, and appeared thirty feet away along the teleport path.

She whirled about and saw the gargoyle look down at its arm and scream—the Fear spell tied to her sword strike must have taken root. Not wanting to give it another chance to pick up the pentastone, Leera remembered that Careena had been specially enchanted to channel the First Offensive, and so pointed the blade and roared, "*Annihilo!*" A jet of water shot forth, blowing through the gargoyle's thick thigh.

The gargoyle's stricken leg gave way and it fell to one knee.

"*Annihilo!*" Leera shouted again. Another jet punched a pumpkin-sized hole through a wing. She marched forth, sword pointed as she shouted, "*Annihilo! Annihilo! Annihilo!*" Each shot cooly drew upon her stamina.

The gargoyle summoned a shield, and there came three successive *thwaps* as the jets drilled into the shield, which in turn smacked against the gargoyle's snout. She could still see its head snapping back, no doubt from the Fear castings which slipped forth into it by sheer momentum.

Whilst screaming its peculiar shrill scream, it reached for the pentastone, still clutched in the claws of its severed arm. Leera, sprinting forth, pointed with her other hand and yanked, and the arm flicked toward her. The pentastone shot out of reach of the screaming gargoyle, who instead touched a rune—and gasped, for a shortsword had pierced its other thigh.

Augum, while playing dead, had surreptitiously unsheathed Burden's Edge—and taken an opportune moment to stab the beast.

The stab allowed for a sprinting Leera to close the gap and lunge, swinging Careena over her head with all her might. The blade hissed through the air before slicing off the gargoyle's wrist. Yet the beast was quick, moving at twice its former speed—it had triggered some sort of speed or agility rune. It tried to touch another rune with its bloody arm stub, but Leera used her left hand to snatch that arm telekinetically, holding it long enough for her to chop the arm off with Careena.

The now armless fifteen-footer shrieked in pain.

Leera spun, taking Careena on a wild arc. It neatly sliced through the air—and lopped off the gargoyle's head, which fell back and stuck into the snow with a *thump*. The headless and armless body stood motionless for a moment before falling forward with a second *thump*.

Leera dropped Careena and shot to Augum. Placing her knee on Burden's Edge—one never knew when dealing with the predator—she gently lifted his head up.

He was barely breathing, eyes only slits, face pale as death. "We can't wait for Bridget anymore," she declared. "Something must have happened. I'm taking you into town myself. We'll use the vault to communicate with her."

Augum did not have the strength to reply. She put him down to quickly wipe both blades before sheathing them, then grabbed the pentastone, which took some force to uncurl the claws, and jammed it into her rucksack. Finally she took hold of Augum and envisioned herself at the first place she could think of that she thought had the highest chance of having a healer—the Academy of Arcane Arts. She only hoped it was reopened.

"*Impetus peragro grapa lestato exa exaei,*" she incanted, and together they appeared at the foot of the Steps of the Crescent Moon.

As always, the first thing Leera did was look up at the tall statue of an old Anna Atticus Stone, who stared into the horizon with her steely eyes, lending her courage.

But there was no time to reminisce, and she tried hauling Augum up. Except he was too heavy for her, forcing her to flex all her muscles and incant, "*Virtus vis viray.*" Strengthened by the 8th degree Strength spell, she easily hauled him up, throwing his arm around her shoulders, and walked him a few paces before he moaned in pain and collapsed, clutching weakly at his breastplate, the bandage beneath soaked through.

She raised a finger. "Wait here then. I'll only be a moment," and she raced up the steps. Her heart sank upon spotting the three large loaf-like spokes of a wheel that composed the three wings of the academy—the ends of which were blank. No portal appeared, meaning the academy was either still shut down or gargoyles had snuffed the portals.

She raced back down and replied to his querying look, "Academy's closed. Next stop, the Black Castle." After a concentrative breath during which she visualized the destination, she spat out the incantation to Group Teleport—except nothing happened.

At first she thought she'd been snuffed and hadn't noticed, only for her ten watery arm rings to light upon command.

"Shoot, I'm depleted," she said, realizing in all the chaos and worrying about Augum that she hadn't checked in with her stamina reservoir, which had been drained by the fighting—and especially the 17th degree Group Teleport spell.

"I'm sorry, my love, but I need to meditate." She ran back with him to the statue of Mrs. Stone and took shelter under its shadow. There she crossed her legs, hauled Augum onto her lap, snuffed Strength, and calmed her breathing.

But meditation proved particularly difficult in light of everything, especially hearing the shallow breathing of her betrothed. It thus took far longer to regain the necessary bulk of stamina that would take them to the Black Castle than she would have liked. In the meantime, she noticed something interesting—silence. The snuffing barrage had ceased against the city. There were no shrieks or shouts or sounds of battle anywhere, only the whistle of the blizzard.

At last, judging she had enough stamina for the spell and some in case they got into trouble, she recast the spell, and the pair appeared at the foot of the southern drawbridge. This time her heart leapt, for the bridge was down. The castle was open.

Unable to carry Augum on her own, she recast Strength, laced an arm underneath his legs, another under his back, and heaved him up. Then she awkwardly ran forth.

"Hello?" she called out once she had reached the mammoth gate, the torches of which still burned brightly. "Anyone here? Gods, what happened to all the guards?" she muttered to Augum, who failed to respond—he had fallen unconscious, which sent an anxious flutter of worry through her soul.

She stepped into the main torchlit courtyard but found it eerily silent and empty, other than the blizzard swirling flakes about brushing against various dropped weapons. The snow was heavily trodden as well, but that could have been from the training. Then she noticed that most of the doors, even to the prison tower, were open. Those gaping doors made her feel like she was the last conscious person in the entire kingdom.

Sensing that something was very wrong, she hesitated to call out again. Instead, she waddled toward the open doors of the Great Arcaner Hall—only for her steps to trickle to a halt when a strange mist began to billow out from the hall.

"Thaaaat's not good," she sang, and was about to turn away when a high shadow of wings, backlit by fluttering torchlight, caught her eye. Acting on pure instinct, she dropped Augum onto the snow, spun about, and slapped her wrists together, roaring, "*Annihilo!*"

A jet of water shot forth—and caught the wing of a gargoyle, blasting it right off the beast. It spiraled toward the ground shrieking like a banshee, before slamming into a mostly empty hay cart, obliterating it in a plume of planks and hay. The gargoyle groaned and began to reorient itself.

Not wanting to leave Augum, Leera unsheathed Careena, carefully aimed the blade flat, and incanted. "*Annihilo!*" A jet exploded from her arm, channeled down the blade, crossed the distance to the cart, and smashed into the gargoyle's head, exploding it on the spot. The beast fell back with a *thud*.

"Gotcha," Leera said, sheathing Careena—the blade was easier to aim with than slapping one's wrists. She hauled Augum back up, mumbling, "Thanks for having her enchanted for me. She's a peach." Yet the humor did not lighten her heart.

Seeing that the mist was still present in the Arcaner headquarters, she waddled to the Grand Hall, sitting perpendicular to the Arcane Hall. Once near, she flicked a finger and telekinetically nudged the half-open door just enough to fit Augum's dangling legs through.

Inside, the Grand Hall had been ransacked, the benches and chairs overturned, parchments strewn everywhere. At the head, both thrones sat on their sides, having been shoved off the platform. Keeping alert and constantly checking over her shoulder, a Strength-amplified Leera waddled forth, the sheathed Careena slapping into her hip with each step.

"The hell happened here?" she whispered to Augum despite him still being unconscious. Yet it made her feel better to not feel so alone, so she kept at it. "I don't like the look of this, my love. Not at all."

She moved in through the side entrance which led to the Great Arcaner Hall, but found it blocked with mist. Instead she chose the back entrance behind the thrones, which she once again found open. This led to a slype—a covered entrance that connected the inner ward with the kitchen and pantry and Arcaner hall. Luckily, the mist seemed to mostly hang about in the Arcaner hall, which meant the stairs in the kitchen should be clear.

Leera raced forth, hoping the others had taken shelter underground, as per protocol. Perhaps even in the great vault of the Royal Armory itself, which was nearly impossible to penetrate as it was protected by ancient arcane protections and thick Dreadnought steel—precisely why the gargoyles had summoned a monster version of a gargoyle to try to bash through.

"And you managed to thwart that quest, my love," Leera whispered to Augum.

After checking that the coast was clear, she slipped through the kitchens and hurried down the stairs, which opened out to the sprawling servant's quarter, where most of the castle's servants stayed. But it too was silent and empty.

She took a few heartbeats to listen to the silence, trying to discern any enemy noises, before hurrying down an eastward passage, which she knew led to the underground arena and the Hall of Ceremony, as well as the regular army barracks and their armory. She got thirty feet before finding herself staring at a patchwork infestation of purple moss that began moving molasses-slow toward her.

"Oh, no you don't," she hissed, and hopped over the patches, careful not to touch them. With Augum dangling like a ragdoll in her arms, she hopped her way to a four-way fork in the passage and chose the northern route, which brought her into the Hall of Ceremony, a huge and empty room reserved for special ceremonies and royal suppers.

Then she heard a distant and rhythmic thudding.

Leera could have hugged the walls, but not wanting to take any more time moving than necessary, she made a beeline to the eastern hall, which led to the castle smithy—and stairs that would eventually lead to the Royal Armory. It was one of a series of entrances hidden throughout the city.

It was to the latter that she ran, taking an eastern passage that forked off into a sub-passage, which in turn led her to a room with a descending spiral staircase, lit by torches. Here the thudding became clearer, and gave her the impression of a battering ram banging against steel.

"Bastards are still trying to get into the armory," she whispered, clutching Augum close to her chest. With her arcanery steadily draining away on account of holding up the Strength spell, she realized she would have to make a choice. She could go down there and face the gargoyles that were trying to break in, which meant risking being snuffed, which would in turn lead to their death or capture.

She chose the other option, which was to turn around and search for someone—anyone—to come to their aid. At this point, she would settle for classic Ordinary healing if it meant saving Augum's life.

She hurried back through the Hall of Ceremony, hop-scotched her way through the patches of moss, and went on through the arena, a huge chamber with a high ceiling, bleachers, and a long oval sandy pit oft used for tournaments, but mostly training. Beyond lay the cellars and the castle Trainers, which were her last hope as they were located in a giant underground chamber with plenty enough room to hide.

The doors were closed. "A good sign, I suppose," she whispered, grabbing a handle and opening the door. She was met with darkness. That was unusual for Trainers, which were composed of arcane obstacles meant to train warlocks in the degrees. But the place was so large it would take forever to find someone, and so she thought to take a risk.

After closing the door behind her, she whispered, *"Shyneo,"* lighting her palm with pale watery light. That light revealed a series of dusty mushroom-like platforms hovering over a central ravine that snaked on into the darkness. Long-dead ivy hung from the rotting planks. Various other obstacles and dusty training equipment sat along the cavern walls.

Knowing Trainers, Leera suspected that the complexity only grew the further one ventured into the cavern. Alas, these were ancient Trainers that had grown out of favor on account of them being too brutal and old. Most warlocks preferred the Trainers in the academy, the ones in the Antioc Library, or even the ones in Castle Arinthian, which went all the way up to the 20th degree, while the others only went up to the 10th.

"Hello?" she whispered. "Anyone there? It's Captain Jones." She repeated herself, albeit louder. Receiving no response, she mustered up her courage, touched her throat, and incanted, "*Amplifico*. Hello!" she shouted, voice amplified to a boom. "Is there anyone here? It's Captain Jones! I have Commander Stone with me and he urgently needs healing!"

Her voice echoed throughout the vast chamber, returning in waves before dying out altogether. With the silence came the death of hope. They were alone. Everyone else was either dead, taken hostage, or hiding in the armory.

Exhausted and not knowing what to do next, Leera let her light die as she slipped to the floor, clutching onto Augum as if he was all she had left in the world. In a sense, it felt like that.

"*Amplifico null, virtus null,*" she blubbered, nullifying the Amplify and Strength spells in order to conserve her precious arcane stamina. Holding Augum tightly, she fumbled about for ideas on what to do. She could return to Castle Arinthian, where there were still people, or venture to the other cities, which as far as she knew had yet to be attacked. Or she could—

A sound drew her attention, and she flared a hand, whispering, "*Shyneo.*" This time, she lit her palm up brightly, until she spotted movement behind a wooden obstacle in the shape of a horse. She shot to her feet and stepped forth, keeping Augum just behind her.

"Hello?" she called out, battle instincts raging and fear coursing through her veins, for in that moment a stark realization had come to her—she couldn't teleport away even if she wanted to, as her teleport privileges had been revoked from the castle's protective core arcane architecture. If something happened here, she would be forced to stand her ground—and with little stamina to use.

"Who's there?"

A timid but familiar voice called out, "Captain Jones? Is that really you?" A blond-haired head poked out from behind the figure of a heavily dented and charred suit of armor sitting on a stand, one of many.

"Hayles?" Leera blurted. "That you, Haylee Tennyson?"

"Yes, it's me!" Dragoon Haylee Tennyson, the order's treasurer, stepped forth, one hand splayed and the other clutching a cane which she used for support as she had a wonky leg. "Before you come any closer, I need to verify it's really you. What did I do on your graduation that you got mad at me for?"

"You used a glue rune to stick my shoes to the side of the stage so that I had to go up there barefoot. And I'm *still* made at you for that."

"Gods, it really *is* you," and Haylee hobbled forth, until the pair embraced.

"I'm not really mad anymore," Leera mumbled, patting Haylee on the back.

"I know. Aug!" she blurted upon spotting his crumpled form lying on the ground behind Leera.

"He's hurt. Who else is with you? Tell me there's a healer …"

"A whole bunch of us, mostly servants and a few Arcaners. But yes, we have—"

"Lee!" a voice cut in.

Leera looked past Haylee—and never had her heart soared as highly as when she placed eyes on none other than Jengo Okeke, a healer.

Augum would be saved.

ICEBERGS

AUGUM

Augum was groggy to wake. Wherever he was, it was pitch dark and quiet, and there were the sounds of people snoozing nearby. The air smelled like a musty stone cavern, with wet drips plopping into puddles.

He sat up with a groan and rubbed his eyes, then ran a hand through his greasy hair. The last thing he remembered was flopping about in Leera's arms, barely conscious. Recalling that he'd been injured, he checked himself over and realized someone had healed him.

Then he remembered the awful things he had said to Leera, and as happened every time with The Callousness of the Predator, an acidic guilt burned his innards. He cringed so hard that he drew his legs in, buried his face into his knees, and expelled a deep sigh.

"Gods, you are one horrible person," he whispered, loathing himself. "How could you do that to her even as the predator?"

Yet the answer was all too apparent. Because the predator didn't care in the least.

After beating himself up for a time, he thought of his poor kingdom, his friends, and Bridget, and realized self-pity was the last thing he should be entertaining. He thus unspooled and whispered, "*Shyneo*," lighting his palm with a dim candle strength. It revealed that he was on a patch of long dried-out grass surrounded by a grove of dead aspens. Once, this place had seen arcane light, which allowed for such growth. But the arcane mechanism had long been shut off or had simply stopped working.

A group of people slept amidst the aspens—servants, soldiers, knights, and warlocks. Some he recognized, others he didn't. Jengo slept with one arm curled around a tree trunk as if embracing his beloved

Priya. Sitting up nearby, watching Augum with a hurt look, was the love of his life, Leera. She looked away when he met her glassy eyes.

He scooted over to her, placed his arms around her, and pressed her to him. She let him do it, albeit limply.

"I didn't mean a single word," he whispered. "Not one."

"I know," she whispered back. "But they still stung. Every single one."

He rubbed her upper arm with his lit hand whilst running his other hand gently through her hair. "We must train harder then, so we can ignore each other better. We must be stronger."

She sat in silence for a bit. "Do you really think me that ugly? That I have a hoof nose?"

"Gods, no. Gods, no. There is not one part of me that thinks that. You are the most beautiful girl I've ever laid eyes on, with the cutest button nose. Period. *Period*. You know the predator uses what it thinks in the moment will hurt the most."

"Well it struck true, that's for sure."

"I'm sorry. Truly. Nothing is sweeter than entwining myself with you and appreciating your beauty and how cute you are and how much I love you. Nothing. Look at me." He raised her chin so that her dark, voluminous eyes met his. "*Nothing*."

Those eyes watered and she looked away. "Your hand is filthy. You're ruining my perfectly groomed hair."

He chortled. "We both stink."

"Especially you," then she added under her breath, "like a pig."

"I'm a filthy hog. But I'm *your* filthy hog."

Usually she'd continue the witty repartee, but she remained quiet.

"You're tired," he whispered. "Why don't you catch some sleep."

"Bridget's gone. No idea where she is. I checked our summonable you-know-what. She didn't leave a note. The others report that the kidnappings escalated heavily last night. No sign of Olaf or Jez or the others, so hopefully they found shelter somewhere. But you know what we did while all that was happening? We slept. We slept while they took our people. So, *no*, I'm not going to sleep, thank you very much. In fact, I'm going to go over there and kick the living snot out of those gargs." She stood up, reaching out a hand. "And you're going to help me."

He took it, allowing her to haul him up. "Go where?"

"They're trying to break into the Royal Armory, where apparently everyone else took shelter. Or at least those who could get away."

Jengo, still curled up around the tree trunk, was startled awake.

"All right there, buddy?" Augum whispered, drawing an arm around Leera's waist and squishing her to him. Again, she allowed it, but without enthusiasm, which told him he'd been particularly cruel this time as the predator. Should he be given the chance, he vowed to redouble his efforts with the training.

Jengo sat up to gape at him blankly. "Augum," he blurted a little too loudly, causing Augum and Leera to shush him. "Sorry," he whispered. "Bad dream."

"Priya's safe," Augum said. *At least last we checked*, he thought.

Jengo pressed both hands against his chest and expelled a massive sigh of relief. "Glad to hear it." He used the heel of a palm to rub his eyes. "How's your abdomen, anyway?"

"Everything's working as it should. Thank you so much—" Augum flopped his hand back and forth. "—and for the wrist too." He didn't mention the broken nose, not wanting to remind Leera of what had happened.

"Just doing my duty, Commander."

"Then let me ask another of you, Almoner Okeke. Lee and I are going on a short quest. Can you bolster us?" As a rare Arcaner healer, Jengo had the power to grant boosts, which they had used in the war—and now and then when facing particularly tough brigands for which turning into the dragon was not suitable.

Jengo hauled himself to his feet, dusting off his robe. "Of course." He pressed a hand to the rose engraved into Augum's golden breastplate while nine rings of white light appeared around his forearm. "*Summano semperis vorto honos,*" he incanted, casting the Ally of the Dragon simul that bolstered competence in the arcane arts by two degrees in strength. Then he incanted, "*Summano stamino au draca persona,*" casting the Stamina of the Dragon simul, which fattened up their stamina reserves by an estimated sixty percent. But Jengo *still* wasn't done, incanting, "*Summano minad au draca persona.*" Mind of the Dragon was his latest learning, which strengthened Mind Armor enough to sustain one extra attack of a mind spell.

Each of these boosts grew more potent as he grew more learned, but were also heavily subjected to the arcaneological principle of diminishing returns, being less and less effective with each forward progression.

"Do you want me to come along?" Jengo asked after boosting Leera and receiving their gratitude.

"Better not," Leera said, nodding to the sleeping others. "Just in case …"

"Right."

Leera pushed away from Augum to unsling and rummage in her rucksack. "By the way, I captured us a second one of these," and she withdrew a second pentastone.

"Are those what they've been using to snuff us?" Jengo asked.

"Among other things," and Leera tossed it over to him. "Have a study if you like." She elbowed Augum. "No more wasting time. I've already cast an alarm enchantment for him." She pointed at a twig. "That one there."

"Got it, Cap," Jengo replied, only to toss the pentastone back. "I don't know Reveal yet. It's illegal for me."

"We'll have to remedy that," Augum replied. "Seeing as it's now wartime and all." Wartime made it legal for warlocks to learn spells more than two degrees ahead. *If there's anyone left to train Jengo*, he thought rather darkly.

Jengo pressed three fingers over his heart. "Good luck, Captain, Commander."

Augum and Leera returned the salute and departed, Augum lighting the way with his dimly lit palm. He slipped his other hand into hers, but she held on weakly. They walked a meandering dirt path along the ravine, passing various ancient training obstacles, some rotten, others rusted through, others still overgrown with dead moss or ivy.

"We fought wars," Augum said along the way, breaking the silence. "Traveled to places few have been to. Saw things nobody has ever—*ever*—seen. Yet I ... I never thought I'd see our kingdom overwhelmed by a beastly race. If anything, I thought it'd fall to human hands." He took a shaky breath. "I don't know why, but I have a bad feeling in my stomach. And you're the only person I can say that to."

She swallowed, glanced over, looked away, and squeezed his hand. "I'm afraid as well. We don't know much about these beasts or where they came from. It feels like ... like we humans are the prey. And with this stupid predator thing shadowing our every thought more and more, it feels like all the three of us have been doing is ..." She made a claw of her free hand. "... barely holding on." The hand dropped. "And because of the predator, I feel like that cursed jungle has followed us home. I don't know. I don't know what I mean by that."

Augum nodded along and squeezed back. "I know exactly what you mean."

"Gods I'm worried about Bridge. About everyone."

"Me too. Me too ..."

Having nothing more to add—for what else was there to say, only action mattered now—they walked in silence until they reached the entrance to the Trainer, at which point they each cast Reveal and Chameleon, the latter with the travel extension. Augum then snuffed his hand and they exited the Trainer and crossed the hall to enter the arena. All was quiet, though they soon heard a distant and rhythmic thudding.

"There they go again," Leera whispered.

When they exited the arena, they came upon a patchwork of moss that began writhing toward them. Leera was about to hop around it when Augum stalled her. "Let me try something first that worked before," and had her step behind him. Then he made a brushing-along-the-ground motion with his arms, incanting, *"Laitna fiuria potam."* A river of lightning poured forth, frying the moss on the spot. It burned like a miniature brushfire, turning into ash. Because it was all connected in a rough patchwork, not one bit of it survived.

"Prone to lightning and fire. Good to know," Leera said as they moved on into the Hall of Ceremony. Augum recalled having numerous suppers there with the royals and the high nobility. Now it was as silent as a tomb.

The thudding steadily got louder as they approached the spiral staircase. Reveal showed no additional arcanery—no traps or the like. But they were on high alert as they descended, keeping to a slow pace to maintain the Chameleon spell.

The final turn of the spiral staircase had them peeking out onto a huge room with a pair of giant steel doors at the other end. Numerous ovals were etched into the wall, which, if triggered, would summon portals to strategic points in the kingdom. But that was not what got their attention, rather a giant battering ram—one of the kingdom's own, in fact—had been summoned into the room. It was bashing the central divide between the two steel doors, and was manned by six wingless gargoyles and one winged gargoyle.

"The winged one has a pentastone," Augum whispered.

"I'll take it out."

He glanced over at her shimmering form. "How?"

"Spectral Teleport."

"Brilliant." He had seen her deploy the spell out in the field—and it was something to behold.

Together they concocted a surprise attack, with each summoning their sword—and holding it behind the curvature of the stairs to minimize the light. But just as the pair was about to enact their plan, which included Augum teleporting right after Leera, Augum snatched her hand.

"Wait," he hissed. "We've been revoked, remember?"

He heard her slap her own forehead. "Gods, again I forgot."

"Change of plans. We sneak up on it, then attack the remainder."

"Agreed."

"Snuff first, unsheathe, then we move out," he whispered, giving her hand a loving squeeze.

They snuffed their swords, unsheathed Burden's Edge and Careena respectively, and prowled forth as chameleonic shimmers. The walk to the gargoyles was less than a hundred feet, but felt like a thousand, mainly on account of them walking extra slowly so as not to accidentally fizzle the Chameleon spell.

Augum saw Leera's shimmering form move slightly ahead of him but did not try to overtake. Instead, he got to watch as Leera suddenly appeared mid-motion through the arc of a vicious swing. There was a sickening *sloop* as the arm holding the pentastone flopped to the ground. The gargoyle shrieked in pain and looked down at its own arm. As it tried to fathom what had happened, Augum swung his blade in a high arc. With one clean slice, he lopped off its head.

The other gargoyles, having seen the latter event, roared—and charged.

Leera dropped Careena, which clattered to the ground, and slapped her wrists together, roaring, "*Annihilo bato!*" Two jets of water tore through two of the charging enemies, felling them on the spot—she had chosen the imprecision of a double strike over the precision of a single one with Careena, something Augum thought was a smart move.

Augum also let go of Burden's Edge and slapped his wrists together, incanting the same spell. Two prongs of lightning felled two more. Just as Leera was about to strike the remaining two down, Augum, seeing that the remaining gargoyles did not have any runes on their bodies, threw up a staying hand. "Take them prisoner!" he shouted, and Leera had to angle her wrists ceiling-ward at the last moment, where her two jets landed.

The two remaining gargoyles ran at them with their claws out, one at Leera and one at Augum. Augum promptly drew the outline of his attacker's figure, incanting, "*Paralizo carcusa cemente!*" It froze in midstride, rolling along the ground like a training dummy. He looked back to see that Leera had done the same with hers.

"Rope. We need rope," Augum said, and soon found it on the battering ram, which had halted after being abandoned. He unspooled a bunch and threw some to Leera, and the pair worked together to tie their two prisoners up.

"Not fun to be captured, is it?" Leera asked, kicking one in the ribs. "Is it!" They were ten-footers and muscled, but she did not seem afraid of them. Augum, on the other hand, was wary of them both, and made sure to keep them face down, for even their beastly gaze gave him the creeps.

Having unleashed some of her frustrations by giving the gargoyles a few choice kicks, Leera strode up to the giant doors. She unsheathed Careena and used the tip to tap out a human-like pattern against one of the steel doors, trying to communicate that it was safe to open up. But with no answer forthcoming, she soon gave up.

Augum, meanwhile, walked from gargoyle body to gargoyle body, whispering, "May your soul find the peace together we could not reach."

Afterward, they decided to lift the captured gargoyles up telekinetically and carry them to the Trainer, where they could be secured further with more rope and repeatedly kept in arcane paralysis. They moved quickly, listening to the corridors often. But no other sounds were heard, and they soon dropped the pair of captives off with Jengo, who woke some of the others to help keep watch.

"What are you going to do now?" Jengo asked as the pair of gargoyles were being tied up further behind them, using some old rope scavenged from the abandoned training equipment.

"Search and destroy," Augum said without hesitation. Leera looked at him with mild surprise, to which he shrugged. "No more hiding now that the barrage has passed," he added. "All we have to do is take out the ones holding a pentastone and we can manage it."

She nodded. "Agreed."

Not wanting to waste another precious moment, Augum set an alarm for Jengo to join the one Leera had enchanted. After leaving instructions with the remaining lot to stay put for now, the pair quickly moved off, promising to return as soon as they could.

They moved swiftly through the underground of the castle, searching for enemies, emboldened by their recent successes. Although Augum knew that all it would take was one slip-up, he figured they stood a good chance as long as they maintained vigilant alertness.

Encountering nothing, they moved on to the keep, and then the inner and outer wards, all of which had been deserted. By then the blizzard had passed, leaving behind quickly moving cloud banks, a bitter wind, and buildups of snowdrift. Exasperated, they ran across the western drawbridge and on into the city.

"Where is everyone?" Augum asked as they searched street after empty street.

"Are they hiding, or what?" Leera countered. "Like a ghost town …"

The shops, the alleys, the homes, the apartments—all were empty, silent except for the whistle of the wind.

"Eerie," Augum remarked, then pressed a hand to his throat.

"What are you doing?"

"Going on a hunch. But just in case, ready to 'port back to the drawbridge." When she nodded, he incanted "*Amplifico*. Hello!" he shouted, voice booming through the snow-laden streets, returning with multiple echoes. "Is there anybody here?"

There was no response.

Leera swallowed. "They didn't … they didn't really snatch the whole *city*, did they?"

Augum did not want to voice his suspicions aloud and simply continued shouting as they walked the empty streets. After the third block, at last someone emerged from within the partial ruins of a bread shop—a balding old man using two walking sticks to prop himself up, for he was missing a leg.

"They took those who didn't go underground!" he wheezed, hobbling forth as fast as he dared. "They took 'em all! Rest went rabid and got skewered or died or whatnot."

Augum and Leera met him halfway as he kept slipping on the snowy cobbles.

"They took 'em all. But I saws 'em fly, I did." He lifted a stick and pointed north. "That-a-way. They was carryin' whole bulgin' sacks o' people and teleportin' off. Saw it with me own eyes, I did."

Augum and Leera exchanged one look and blurted, "The ship."

"Now we know why it's so large," he said.

"You two look mighty familiar," the old man said.

"We need to hop it back there," Leera said, ignoring him.

The man pointed a cane at them. "If you really can turn into dragons, you ought to do that and go on and bring our people back. Undo all this, I says."

"We won't let them get away with it, sir," Augum said. "First stop, wolven meeting point. You know the one."

She nodded. "I do."

Together they chorused, "*Impetus peragro*," and zipped off, leaving the man gaping.

They appeared on a snowy ledge north of Antioc. It was a long hop, so they took a bit of time to meditate and renew their stamina. But not wanting to wait too long, they soon hopped off again, appearing amidst another blizzard in the mountainous north. On and on they went, passing the green sky curtains that were said to keep great evils from beyond at bay, taking recuperative rests as necessary, until they stood under a brilliant field of stars in an empty spot where the wolven had kept watch.

"The blasted furballs abandoned their posts," Leera hissed.

"We don't know that, but also we didn't answer their alarm right away," Augum said as he scrambled up the nearby hill, Leera trailing. When he got up to the top, he froze, stomach dropping to his feet. Leera soon joined him.

"Fates help us," she whispered.

Ahead, amidst an empty black ocean, floated nothing but a smattering of icebergs.

Not wanting to give up, Augum pointed at the farthest iceberg. "That one there with the high flat peak."

"Battle 'Port?"

He nodded, envisioned standing atop that icy ledge, the sound of the lapping waves and the wind, the hard crust of ice underneath his feet. Leera had evidently done the same, for both simultaneously incanted, "*Impetus peragro*," and vanished and reappeared with dual *thwomps* atop that very ledge.

The iceberg was fifty feet in height and perhaps three hundred feet in length. The only sound was the lapping of those waves and the whistle of a bitter, cold wind. A black and empty ocean loomed ahead, the horizon barely visible in the starlight—a horizon as flat as a table, one that mirrored a vast and starry sky. Not a single light like one would see on a ship glimmered in any direction. Not so much as a speck.

For a time, Augum and Leera merely stood there, mouths agape, chests heaving from exhaustion and panic. Both seemed to come to the same conclusion, yet neither wanted to voice aloud the implication of what they were staring at. To Augum, never had a body of water looked that terrifying. Never had he felt so hollow, so defeated.

It was Leera who broke the silence.

"Bridget's on that ship," she whispered. "Our friends are on that ship. Who knows *how* many Solians are on that blasted ..." She raised a fist, lip quivering.

Augum felt her rage and his own panic and blurted, "Let's take to the air for a better vantage point—"

"Yes, yes! If we can spot the mast, we can fly after them—"

"Rip the enemy apart and bring everybody home."

"Agreed, agreed! Wait ... what about the snuffing?"

Augum thought about it and doubts started creeping in. "We'd have to be careful. Once we spot the ship, we cast Reveal—and keep it up. The snuffs appear as incoming tendril bubbles, which can be dodged in the air. Just avoid casting things like Spectral Teleport."

"But how would we be able to get close?"

"Maybe we could sneak on board under cover of darkness or something."

Leera raised an eyebrow. "In dragon form?"

"I know, I know, the more I think about it, the crazier it sounds. But we still have to try."

"Agreed, we can't give up on them. They're relying on us."

"And if we don't find the ship and get low on stamina, we 'port back. But we stay apart. I'll 'port back to the abandoned camp, and you 'port back here. Then once the side effects wear off, you can teleport to the camp to meet me. Agreed?" He figured as a water warlock it was safer for her to be on the iceberg.

She nodded, eyes already steeled on the horizon.

"But I don't plan on returning without them," he added, though how they would accomplish that, with such a massive ship, he had no idea. He'd worry about that later.

They stepped apart to give each other space and a moment to focus on the spell's mental requirements. Then they raised their arms and one leg, making the praying mantis pose, and incanted, "*Xae carna draca arcan doma legenda rava!*"

Quickly their bodies expanded, swallowing up their robes. Wings sprouted from their backs, and their hands enlarged and grew claws. Their faces elongated into snouts, growing rows of lethal and long teeth.

Now mighty beasts of an ancient era, they lowered their haunches and launched into the air, the sheer force of it rocking the giant iceberg in the water. Their wings flapped, slicing the air, pulling them higher and higher, until the icebergs were specks and all that was ahead was a mirror slice of the black and starry heavens and the glittering ocean below.

They flew on into the night, two mighty beasts hungry for war. Flew until a bank of thick black clouds began to swallow that very horizon. Flew higher than they'd ever flown, looking down upon tiny tufts of dark clouds, upon a black ocean marbled with waves. Throughout their search, they said little, their heads swiveling this way and that in a desperate search of that ship.

At last, when the muscles of their wings burned from the frantic effort and a full moon threatened to vanish behind those clouds, which would plunge them into darkness, and their stamina reserves, which bled at a constant rate even though they had cast no other arcanery, had nearly run dry, Augum stopped flapping, transitioning to a glide.

"We need to go back," he said amidst a mounting headwind. "Lee, do you hear me? We need to go back!"

"No, they're out there!" Leera growled over her shoulder, continuing her flapping, slowly leaving him behind.

"We're almost out of stams! We barely have enough to get back with as it is!"

"No!"

"Lee—think about it. What good will it do for us to revert out here and plunge into the ocean? They must have turned the ship invisible or something. I just ... I didn't think about it but we should have cast Reveal. I don't know why I didn't—"

"Because you're a terrible leader!" Leera's wings dipped as she abruptly turned. "You shouldn't have let us sit on our butts at the castle because you thought us tired! You coward, you! This is your fault! You're the commander!" She swooped by him, snapping her jaws in his face. "Damn fool!"

Augum felt the shadow rise within. "You *dare*. I'm your commander! I did my best to—"

"Meet me back on the iceberg," she snapped, and incanted, "*Impetus peragro!*"

Blood raging, Augum envisioned standing atop the iceberg. "*Impetus peragro!*" There was a mighty *thwomp* as he appeared atop that iceberg—and he didn't even have time to blink before he saw a clawed fist hook about and smash his snout. He grunted as he tumbled backward down the iceberg, which rocked like a skiff. He slammed against a bottom ledge in time to see the silhouette of wings unfurl against a starry sky. Leera launched herself off, claws glinting in the darkness.

Blood raging with anger and resentment and betrayal, Augum saw his enemy coming down upon him and knew she wanted to rip his throat out. Knew that this was life or death. He was lord of the jungle and of the skies. No one—*no one*, least of all this trumped-up wench who thought she deserved his company—would triumph over his might.

He slammed his wrists together, roaring, "*Annihilo!*" sending a massive bolt of lightning forth. But she was quick on the uptake, summoning a huge watery shield which absorbed the lightning blast with a *sizzle*. As it did so, she extended her right arm, shining with ten watery rings, and hissed, "*Flustrato!*"

Instead of rolling aside, he let the tendrils slam against the mighty castle of his armored mind. He bellowed a laugh as he sprang to his feet, hissing, "You're *nothing* against my—"

She tucked in her wings after one last forward flap, turning herself into a giant dart, and crashed into him with her shoulder.

They slammed against the iceberg, and a giant crack snaked outward from beneath him. There they tussled, roaring and hissing and spitting and biting at each other.

Then his enemy gasped—and began shrinking. He jumped up to boom a triumphant laugh into the night sky, his wings spread like the conqueror he was. When he looked back, he saw a girl lying on the ice, her body rolling along with the iceberg.

"Look how tiny you are," he growled, enjoying casting his mighty shadow over her miniscule form. "*I* am the victor. *I* am the mighty one. You are a worm. And now you end. Here and now, you end."

"You don't have the guts!" she shouted, though she scrambled back on her elbows.

"That's where you're wrong, wench. You think I'm a coward? Then you seeing otherwise will be most fitting." He raised his fists skyward — and brought them down to squash her miserable bug life.

But the little wench had jammed her foot against the crack and sprang backward. His fists slammed into the crack, cleaving the iceberg in two. It took him a moment to balance himself on his swaying half. Meanwhile, Leera grabbed onto her tiny island and bobbed just out of reach.

A looming Augum laughed. "Look at you. Pathetic." He spread his hands apart, readying to slam his wrists together. "Ready for obliteration?"

Her eyes narrowed. "Do it," she hissed, shoulders heaving.

Augum slammed his wrists together, roaring, "*Annihilo!*"

By the time his wrists connected, they had begun transforming. He had felt it coming, of course, but had hoped to complete his quest of vanquishing this mangy usurper before it was too late. Alas, nothing but a fizzle sounded, and he shrank quickly.

She laughed uproariously. Even made a show of it by falling to the ground, clutching her belly, and laughing to the sky.

Outraged and sublimely callous, Augum slapped his wrists together at her, roaring, "*Annihilo!*" Nothing happened, though he collected some measure of satisfaction watching her instinctively yelp and roll aside — and almost fall into the frigid waters.

Now it was he who clutched his stomach to laugh, even pointing at her with his other hand.

"You sound so fake," she said, panting. "You're a loser. A fake loser."

"Shut up," he snapped, annoyed with how she always had a retort. He would never admit that she was wittier than him.

As their icebergs drifted apart, she paced to and fro, watching him like a prowling shark. "If you aren't the coward I called you, then dive into the water and come at me. Do it. Come at me."

"So I can freeze to death?" He began pacing in the same manner, eyeing her, loathing her. "I'm not as stupid as you are, wench. You're the water warlock. *You* come at *me*. You can dry yourself after the effects wear off anyway."

She looked to the waters as if considering doing just that.

"You know you want to. Come at me so we can scrap. I'll even let you haul yourself up first." He stepped back. "See? You got room. Come at me, wench." Yet the predator imagined kicking her in the face as soon as she appeared above the ice—if she even got that far through the frigid waters.

Her eyes, which were already narrow, narrowed further, hunter-like. "You are an idiot to think I'd lower myself below you like that. I'd be too cold to fight, and you know it. I'm smarter than you. Sharper, funnier, wittier. I'm a queen of the skies and you're nothing but a groveler and a terrible leader who let the capital of his kingdom get kidnapped. A pathetic *loser*."

Augum paced up to the edge to glare at her, shoulders heaving. She matched him by stepping up to her edge to glare back at him, defiant and proud. By now they were more than twenty feet apart, and drifting farther by the heartbeat.

For a time, they continued to throw barbs and petty insults, each trying to wound the other, until the icebergs were fifty feet apart. Their voices carried well in the cold wind, and so they continued lobbing those insults and taunts, until both seemed to tire at the same time.

Once they were a hundred feet apart, a softness bled into Augum's soul, and the world, which had seemed dark and gray and hard and nothing but a jungle for him to stalk and prey upon the weak, started to gain some color, the jungle replaced by the cold harshness of the deep north. The wind whistled as it picked up, the clouds on the horizon rapidly nearing.

A storm approached. How appropriate.

Amidst that cold and black vastness, the tiniest spark of humanity flared within his dead firepit soul. Like surf coming from afar, a wave of guilt washed in. Although Augum was back, what had transpired remained, thorns embedded into the shield of his heart.

Hurt, he fell back onto the ice, feeling lost. They'd let The Callousness of the Predator bleed into their conscious selves in a way that had never happened before. Tears dribbled from the corners of each eye, quickly freezing against his skin in that bitter wind.

There came a *thwomp*, and a shadow appeared above him. He closed his eyes, ready for her to end him, and so he remained prostrate, his back getting colder and colder against the ice. Part of him wanted her to end him, for she was right. He had failed as a commander. He had failed to keep their kingdom safe.

Instead of killing him with a First Offensive, he heard her kneel beside him, gently spool one arm underneath him and the other around his neck, and hug him.

"I'm sorry," she whimpered, body making small convulsions as she shed tears of sorrow and regret. "I'm sorry …"

"Me too," he whispered, holding onto her tightly, caressing her raven hair.

"Gods, I love you."

"I love you too. More than anything. More than life itself."

"Me too. Me too …"

He kissed her cheek and cuddled her close, and for a time they nuzzled and forgave each other as best they could, whispering soothing words of love, until they sat staring out into the void, Augum holding his beloved before himself.

"We have multiple challenges ahead," Augum said as the wind kept steadily building up, a precursor to the coming storm that loomed on the horizon as a black mass that obscured the stars. "The predator has breached the walls of normality. We need to get control of it."

"Which means continuing the ancient lessons," Leera replied, thumbs caressing his forearms as he held onto her.

"We'll need to warn everyone to prepare for a potential full-scale invasion," Augum added. "And we'll need to find out where that ship came from and where it's going."

"And somehow follow it," Leera threw in.

"Which means we'll need to find a ship worthy of the task."

"And we need to figure out how to work those pentastones."

"And gather provisions and a potent group of adventurers to come along with us on that ship."

Leera nodded. "It's going to be tough."

"Very tough." Augum kissed the top of her head. "I love you, and I still want to marry you. More than ever."

She looked up at him with those dark and voluminous eyes. "And I you. More than ever. We'll get through this. We'll find them, bring them back, and get through this." Her hand intertwined with his. "Together."

"Together," he repeated, and nuzzled her close, so that they were cheek to cheek.

As distant lightning began to flicker, lighting up a towering black mountain of roiling clouds, Augum and Leera sat holding each other, two lone souls in a vast northern emptiness. Danger waited for them beyond that horizon. A danger they would have to face on two fronts— as warlock dragons saving their kingdoms, and as fragile humans battling their own souls.

Although the destination was unknown, the quest ahead was clear.

PERSONAL THOUGHTS
FROM THE AUTHOR

So what did you think of *Whispers of Wrath*? Did you have as much fun reading it as I had writing it? I'm going to dive right into writing book two, which you can expect in December of 2025.

In the meantime, I invite you to leave an honest review on *Whisper of Wrath's* Amazon page. Also, I mostly rely on word of mouth, so if you enjoy my work, please consider sharing something on social media (you're the reason I have a career). You're also welcome to email me with your thoughts of the book (email below).

I challenged myself with *Whispers of Wrath* in a whole new way. Having learned a single point of view writing from Augum's perspective in *The Arinthian Line* and *Fury of a Rising Dragon* series', and then Anna Atticus Stone's perspective in *Chronicles of Anna Atticus Stone*, I wanted to try tackling doing three perspectives in one book. It felt like a natural progression for me, and I thoroughly enjoyed exploring the world through the eyes of Bridget and Leera in addition to Augum. I have some ideas of how I can utilize this multiple POV skill set in future series'.

Speaking of *The Arinthian Line* series, I'm actually writing this note on the 10th anniversary of publishing *Arcane*, which thrust Augum, Bridget and Leera on their first grand adventure together as a bunch of hopeful, rambunctious, and brave fourteen-year-olds. Who would have thought that, twelve books later, I'm still enjoying their tale this much? I'm ten years older and hopefully a little wiser, but no less awed by the world I get to step into on a near daily basis for months of the year (there's a *lot* of lore to keep track of now, though).

Each of these books takes a whole year to write and edit, so it's difficult to express my gratitude to you for your support, for all those wonderful emails and comments that show me how much the work affects you. I've been a full-time author since 2015. *2015!* That's *nine* years of my life, in a dream profession. Wow. Just … wow.

Although last year our beloved tabby Buddha passed away, my wife and I have a new companion now, Miso. He's a spritely black house panther who loves to cuddle, purr up a storm, zoom around the house, and ride on our shoulders whilst gently nibbling and licking our ears.

Thank you for reading *Whispers of Wrath*, and I look forward to continuing the *Arcane Legacy* series with book 2, coming December 2025.

Oh and this year I added stuff to the end of the book: a glossary of spells, simuls, general terms, and other goodies, so keep reading!

All my best to you and those you love,

—Sever

P.S. A gentle reminder that honest reviews play a vital part in readers discovering new books. Please consider leaving one on Amazon for *Whispers of Wrath*, or any of my works you have read (bonus points for leaving one on Goodreads too).

P.P.S. To receive email notice of my new releases, as well as news relevant to my work, subscribe to my newsletter at **severbronny.com/contact**. I don't email often, so you don't have to worry about mailbox clutter.

November 2024

ADVANCE READER TEAM

Want a chance to read my next book before its retail release? Consider joining my Advance Reader Team at severbronny.com/team (spots are limited, as is the application window).

EMAIL THE AUTHOR

Want to tell me what you thought of the book, ask a question, report an error, or just say hello? Email me at sever@severbronny.com

FOLLOW ME ON AMAZON

Hit the "Follow" button on my author profile ensuring you will get an email from Amazon whenever I release a new book or put up a pre-order.

CONNECT VIA SOCIAL MEDIA

Home:	severbronny.com
Facebook:	facebook.com/authorseverbronny
Reddit:	reddit.com/r/severbronny
Instagram:	@severbronny
Fan-run Discord:	Link can be found at severbronny.com/discussion
X:	@severbronny
Bluesky:	@severbronny

Visit severbronny.com for world lore, a glossary of spells, simuls, general terms, an author FAQ, and much more. And via severbronny.com/discussion you can visit the fan-run Discord to chat with fellow readers, duel in the arena, chat about lore and world theories, even role-play within the world.

ALSO BY SEVER BRONNY:

THE ARINTHIAN LINE

Pursued by a murderous tyrant, fourteen-year-old warlocks Augum, Bridget and Leera train under the legendary Anna Atticus Stone—while exploring the secrets of an ancient abandoned castle. The saga that began it all.

Arcane
Riven
Valor
Clash
Legend

FURY OF A RISING DRAGON

When a kingdom threatens invasion, sixteen-year-olds Augum, Bridget and Leera attempt to resurrect an ancient and forbidden order of warlock-knights, hoping to summon dragons to their aid.

Burden's Edge
Honor's Price
Mercy's Trial
Champion's Wrath

CHRONICLES OF ANNA ATTICUS STONE

Young warlock prodigy Anna Atticus Stone is tormented by her vile sister as she tries to get into the mysterious Academy of Arcane Arts. But her sister has other plans.

Prodigy of Thunder
The Arcane Artist
Flames of Stone

All available from Amazon

Arcane (The Arinthian Line, book 1) blurb:

Nominated for the Epic Fantasy Fanatics Readers Choice Award

Orphan and former farm slave Augum dreams of becoming a warlock. But that would take courage and aptitude, both of which he lacks. Doesn't help that his mentor is a cranky recluse who sends him on strange errands.

When a vicious tyrant ravages the kingdom in a quest for seven mythic artifacts, Augum discovers his mentor possesses one. They flee to a mysterious castle with other aspiring warlocks, including two quirky girls. Adventure ensues as the aspirants explore the castle's secrets and learn spellcraft.

But not everything is as it seems, and when a sudden betrayal plunges the group into a terrifying ordeal, survival will hinge on Augum's daring, his aptitude in the arcane arts . . . and on friendships forged in fire.

An enduring bestseller, Arcane is the beginning of an epic coming-of-age fantasy saga beloved by fans the world over.

Audiobooks narrated by Grammy and Hugo winner Stefan Rudnicki Suitable for ages 10 to retiree

THE SACRED CHIVALRIC CODE OF THE ARCANER

Thou shall never refuse a challenge from an equal.

Thou shall never turn thy back on a foe.

Thou shall always show thy stripes before thine enemy.

Thou shall not duel the lower ranks without serious provocation.

Thou shall be gallant and fair to those unable to learn the craft.

Thou shall never take the life of a weaponless Ordinary.

Thou shall always accept a bent knee.

Thou shall give succor to widows and orphans and beggars.

Thou shall refuse pecuniary reward for doing thy duty.

Thou shall fight for the welfare of all.

Thou shall guard the honor of the arcane craft.

Thou shall seek knowledge that contributes to the craft.

Thou shall preserve and honor the Hallowed Trust.

Thou shall never break thy word.

Thou shall serve thy lord and king and kingdom with valor and courage and an open heart.

But thou shall also root out corruption in all its forms, and the sanctity of the truth shall vanquish any title.

Thou shall swear fealty to this code of honor, for it is the war ye are locked in from this moment on.

SPELL GLOSSARY

- <u>Note</u>: Spells which have not yet been published in detail will not have their trigger phrases listed. Triggers with blank underlines indicate scenario-specific input needed by caster.
- (OTB): Off-the-books
- Highlighted rows are elemental spells
- For brevity, most extensions and off-the-books elemental spells are omitted from this glossary. See fan-run Discord for a more complete list: severbronny.com/discussion

DEG	NAME	TRIGGER
1st	Telekinesis	(non-verbal)
	Repair	*Apreyo*
	Unconceal	*Un vun deo*
	Shine	*Shyneo*
2nd	Shield	(non-verbal)
	Push	*Baka*
	Disarm	*Disablo*
	Slam	*Grau*
3rd	Mind Armor	(non-verbal)
	Object Alarm	*Concutio del alarmo*
	Object Track	*Vestigio itemo discovaro*
	The First Offensive	*Annihilo*
(OTB)	Centarro	*Centeratoraye xao xen*
4th	Fear	*Dreadus terrablus*
	Deafness	*Voidus aurus*
	Confusion	*Flustrato*
	Summon Minor Elemental	*Summano elementus minimus*
5th	Amplify	*Amplifico*
	Darkness	*Voidus vis*
	Paralyze	*Paralizo carcusa cemente*
	Summon Weapon	*Summano arma*
6th	Mute	*Voidus lingua*
	Object Invisible	*Obiectum visinabla balan*
	Seal	*Obdura del boundera sen*
	Elemental Armor	*Armari elementus totalus*
7th	Slow	*Effectus xadius*
	Blind	*Voidus occa*

	Minor Illusion	*Illusea _____*
	Summon Minor Wall	*Summano valla minimus girata barricada*
8th	**Sleep**	*Senna dormo coma torpos*
	Chameleon	*Armari obscura chameleano*
	Strength	*Virtus vis viray*
	The Second Offensive	*Annihilo bato*
9th	**Teleport**	*Impetus peragro*
	Shrink	*Smolla boda infintessima axtenay su*
	Frenzy	*Enta frenza harka natar*
	Craft Trap	*Infusio gato captum* + other spell incantation
10th	**Area Alarm**	*Concutio del arregando alarmo*
	Sphere of Protection	*Sfaera au praentergo buboa*
	Disenchant	*Exotus mia enchantus duo dai ideum exat*
	Summon Minor Event	*Summano _____*
11th	**Reveal**	*Un vun asperio aurum enchantus*
	Greater Repair	*Apreyo enchantus delicato obiectum roa*
	Arcane Drain	*Arcan rosso*
	Enchant Weapon	
12th	**Decoy**	*Impostra persona _____*
	Compel Truth	*Kompella o minad veta honesta*
	Tongues	*Translateo commona linguino ___*
	Summon Major Wall	*Summano valla marjorus girata barricada*
13th	**Create Simple Object**	*Obiectum minfassa _____*
	Complex Enchantment	
	Memory Wipe	*Erassa memora au o minad*
	The Third Offensive	*Annihilo ito*
14th	**Paralyze Group**	*Paralizo carcusa cemente____*
	Bewitch	*Hoodvinka _____*
	Major Illusion	
	Summon Major Elemental	*Summano elementus marjorus*
15th	**Invisibility**	*Arcan persona visinabla balan*
	Sanctuary	
	Metamorphosis	*Persona morpha mat agateo kipat*

	Summon Midling Event	
16th	Convey Degree	*(Ritual)*
	Memorial Ceremony	*(Ritual in song)*
	Modify Memory	
	Summon Army	
17th	Portal	*Portus ea ire itum*
	Teleport Group	*Impetus peragro grapa lestato exa exaei*
	Immunity	
	Incarnate	
18th	Area Conceal	
	Area Spell Void	
	Create Scroll	*Infusio skrul _____*
	The Fourth Offensive	*Annihilo dio*
19th	Doppelganger	
	Combat Portal	*Portus da / ata ei portus da*
	Possession	
	Summon Champion Elemental	*Summano elementus kampiona*
20th	Arcastrate	
	Slow Time	*Muerto tempus ideus deo didaeiee*
	Indestructible Object	
	Summon Major Event	

20th degree mastery and beyond:

Yet to be published (some spells already explored, others hinted at). See fan-run Discord server for theories and observations: severbronny.com/discussion

ARCANER SIMULS

Birth of the Dragon
Summano elementus minimus draco
Spells involved: Summon Minor Elemental
Degree: 5th
Effect: Summons a small dragon in place of a standard elemental. Dragon has slightly greater ferocity and strength.

Roar of the Dragon
Summano arma grau
Spells involved: Slam + Summon Weapon
Degree: 6th
Effect: Primes summoned weapon with X hits of Slam, where X is warlock's degree

Awe of the Dragon
Summano arma dreadus terrablus
Spells involved: Fear + Summon Weapon
Degree: 6th
Effect: Primes summoned weapon with X hits of Fear, where X is warlock's degree

Bluster of the Dragon
Summano arma flustrato
Spells involved: Confusion + Summon Weapon
Degree: 6th
Effect: Primes summoned weapon with X hits of Confusion, where X is warlock's degree

Mirror of the Dragon
Mimicus
Spells involved: Shield + Reflect
Degree: 7th

Effect: Turns summoned shield into an arcane mirror, reflecting incoming spell back at the attacker

Mind of the Dragon
Summano minad au draca persona
Spells involved: Shield + Mind Armor
Degree: 7th
Effect: Strengthens subject's Mind Armor to withstand one additional strike from a mind spell

Spirit of the Dragon
Xae carna draca arcan doma legenda rava
Spells involved: Unknown
Degree: 15th
Effect: Turns caster into a dragon

DEGREE AND ROBE COLOR	TITLE
1st - 2nd degree: Burgundy	Apprentice
3rd - 4th: Royal blue	Apprentice
5th - 6th: Emerald	Initiate
7th - 8th: Amber	Initiate
9th - 12th: Crimson	Adept
13th - 16th: Purple	Mage
17th - 19th: Turquoise	Grandmage
20th: White	Archmage
20th Mastery: Opalescent	Master

GENERAL GLOSSARY

Arcastration: The total stripping of the ability to cast arcanery via the Acastrate spell.

Chronocast: Casting one spell after another in quick succession (common).

Cycle: Practicing every spell one knows, back-to-back.

Er priem: Performing a service without pay or benefit; community service.

Feat of Legend: A legendary casting.

Hallowed Trust: An old tradition wherein a warlock will cease to battle an opponent to give him or her their degree via the Convey Degree spell. A day of peace and celebration is declared, and the enemies are expected to share a toast and a cup of wine or ale, before returning to combat the next morning.

Learning "wild": Learning by intuition. Highly dangerous. Warlocks are taught early on in the academy to stop indulging in their wild tendencies lest it kill them. Lightning warlocks are most prone to dying this way.

Magic: Fake arcanery. Parlor tricks, card tricks, and the like. Used as a derogatory term against warlocks to cheapen their craft.

Permanence: A perfectly cast enchantment stands the chance to sink to permanence after 100-300 years, depending on the skill of the caster. Youngest known warlock to cast a spell that sunk to permanence was Atrius Arinthian.

Proata mentora: Performing tutelage to less experienced warlocks; can also be community service. Warlocks are expected to do Proata mentora for 10% of their time, although healers are expected to do it for 20% of their time.

Quint: Used in the Academy of Arcane Arts to denote a five-day "week" consisting of four classes and one Study Day. The Sithesian calendar is exactly 30 days long, and thus 360 days are in a year.

Simulcast: Casting an elemental and a standard spell at the same time (rare).

Sun-tuned / moon-tuned: Artifact may only be used once per day / once per moon cycle.

The Settling: When a warlock works hard enough and advances well beyond the standard competencies of their degree, their eyes may flare with their element. Happens naturally.

The seven kingdoms of Sithesia: Solia, Canterra, Nodia, Tiberra, Ohm, Abrandia, Sierra

The Sleeving: When all twenty arm rings fuse into one band, indicating the warlock has achieved mastery. Happens naturally.

ACKNOWLEDGEMENTS

My work could not have been possible without the love and support of many people. And that starts with my beloved wife, Tansy, who believed in me and my work every single step of the way. You had a choice, Tanz, and you chose the path of support. You helped me build something that will outlive both of us. Love you so much, babe.

The editorial team:
Tansy Bronny (sound-boarding, developmental editing, proofreading, all books)
Elizabeth Darkley, Arrowhead Editing (line edit books 1, 2, 4 *FoaRD*, book 1, 2, 3 *CoAAS*, *Arcane Legacy* book 1)
Drew Mildon (beta reading, all books)

The audiobook team:
The Arinthian Line narrator Stefan Rudnicki + team, courtesy of Skyboat
Fury of a Rising Dragon narrator Gary Furlong + team, courtesy of Tantor
Chronicles of Anna Atticus Stone narrator Moira Quirk + team, courtesy of Podium
Arcane Legacy: To be announced

The cover design team:
Sever Bronny (*The Arinthian Line*)
Deranged Doctor Designs + team (*Fury of a Rising Dragon, Chronicles of Anna Atticus Stone, Arcane Legacy*)

Additional special thanks:
Thank you to my friends and family, much love to each of you. Thank you to the Advance Reader Team (you know who you are)! Thank you to all those who participate in discussions on my website and in the fan-run Discord server, especially Atticus Monroe for all his contributions since its inception. And thank you to the thousands of you that have written me over the years. I cherish your letters.

Last but certainly not least, thank you to every single reader out there. It is because of you that I've been able to be a full-time author since 2015, a career I am grateful for every single day.

ABOUT THE AUTHOR

Sever Bronny has been a full-time author since 2015, having published the bestselling coming-of-age series *The Arinthian Line (Arcane, Riven, Valor, Clash, Legend)*, the follow-up series, *Fury of a Rising Dragon (Burden's Edge, Honor's Price, Mercy's Trial, Champion's Wrath)* and *Chronicles of Anna Atticus Stone (Prodigy of Thunder, The Arcane Artist, Flames of Stone)*. He is now working through his fourth saga, *Arcane Legacy (Whispers of Wrath, remaining titles to be announced)*. He has also released three albums with his industrial-rock music project Tribal Machine, including the full-length concept album *The Orwellian Night*. One of his songs can be heard in the feature-length film *The Gene Generation*. He lives in British Columbia, Canada, with beloved wife, Tansy, and house panther Miso. Connect with him at his website **severbronny.com**, subscribe to his newsletter to keep up on events, and duel as warlocks and discuss fan theories in his fan-run Discord server.

www.ingramcontent.com/pod-product-compliance
Lightning Source LLC
Chambersburg PA
CBHW030919020726
47498CB00001B/36